APOCRYPHA

A NOVEL

LISA MOWAT

APOCRYPHA

Special thanks to Sarah Everding for making my manuscript a book, my family and friends for their advice and consent, the editorial and support staff at CreateSpace for lighting the way, and above all, the enduring patience of my husband.

Library of Congress Control Number: 2010900085

For Michael

℞ This is the sole record of my being. The events that follow occurred beyond the state of grace, within and without substance. I recognize the very nature of this record defies merit and in that it is unlikely to be found, let alone understood, by any who might benefit from it, my purpose is questionable. I can only declare the most selfish of reasons: that as an entity without equal in measure or intent, I must know myself, if only to convince myself that I exist at all.

I am Maihael. Unmatched by all save one. Salvation of all, save one. Yet of all my brethren my memory is incomplete, stolen by the one who haunts me still. Though my spirit remains ageless, my sentience is new, my mind weak. I am bound by the will of others, by prophecy and expectation beyond my making or control. How am I believed when I do not believe myself?

With this record, I hope to find what I have lost.

I am lost.

[Spharic. Introduction translated from *Kor Dai Maihael*. Mund Dai 800 BC]

MARCH 15

19__

Dear Mom and Dad,

Thanks for the journal. It was a very thoughtful birthday present in spite of the fact I do not now, nor do I ever plan to make a regular habit of keeping one. However, I understand your motivation. In spite of my candor,

19__ which I think is significant for a sixteen year old, you wonder as parents if you're really "getting through to me". You worry that I'm keeping secrets from you. That I'm having sex, doing drugs and skipping school.

What you should be worried about is having a daughter dull enough to write any of it down in a journal where

19__ her parents could find it.

Alas, I will not be recording anything within these pages. If you ever do find yourself wondering if I am engaged in any of the above mentioned activities, you need only weigh the odds.

The good news is I won't lie to you. I won't fill these pages

19__ with feel good fiction intended to mislead you. I won't fill these pages at all. But I will keep this journal. I will keep it where you can find it and where I will see it every day; I will treasure it and peruse every empty page. After all, they are not empty. They are full of what has been forgotten. Lost records of my

19__ lost years.

Because that is what I am.

Lost.

[Introduction from private journal
of Sophie Davids. March 15, 1989]

DISSIPATION

2003 The reality of love is annoying car trips.
After three years, it is an unspoken rule: when we visit my relatives, I drive. Doubtless, this rule would apply to my husband if we visited his relatives, but since he doesn't have any, my drive to ride ratio sucks. My one reward is getting to drive his BMW—in this case, like it's the 24 at Le Mans. My personal best between Tacoma and Bellingham is just under an hour and forty minutes. Today, I won't beat my record. It's raining and I–5 is slow.

My hand searches the radio. Every song I find is about love. There is nothing to listen to. No one to talk to. Nowhere to go.

There is too much time.

Looking over at him, his shoulders are back. His head rests to the side with his mouth slightly open so I can imagine snoring when he doesn't. He is at rest.

My eternal passenger.

Beautiful.

So is this car. So is our house. So is my life.

All I want to know is when it will end.

After three years, no one can tell.

I don't know why I worry. I'm afraid of where we are headed and I never used to be. That used to be him. I still don't know what he was afraid of in the beginning, only it seemed to be everywhere—a fear so overwhelming, it was in everything he said and did, following him everywhere he went. Then one day it stopped. At some point after we married, he stopped pretending he was fine. I don't know why any more than I know what wakes him in the car after he has been comatose for ninety minutes.

It isn't the radio or the sound of my voice. None of my theories proved out, and I tested them. It isn't the speed of the car. It isn't the time on the road or the length of the journey. He only wakes the moment we leave the highway at our destination. I tried to trick him, getting off at a rest stop once, even getting out of the car. He was still asleep when I got back.

Once again, we arrive. At the flip of a blinker and the application of brakes, his mouth closes. Slowly, his head comes up. Aside from opening his eyes and sitting up a smidge more, he says and does nothing else. No snort or yawn or rubbing of eyes. Small things I wonder if I miss. He looks over at me and smiles.

His best defense.

Ignoring it, I focus on the vanity plate of the car ahead. He turns off the radio, waiting for me to say something, but I drive in silence. Finally, he caves.

"How was traffic?"

"A Hostess truck flipped. There were Twinkies everywhere."

"You're lying."

"I'll never tell."

"You promise you'll wake me if it ever happens?"

"As if it were possible."

"Sorry." He twitches. "I'll drive back."

"What's Psalm 46?"

He looks out the windshield at the car in front of us.

"It's a prophecy."

"About what?"

"Deliverance."

He sees me smirk and blinks. "Not the movie."

"Bummer."

"No dueling banjos, but there is a river. Do you want me to sing it for you?"

"Sing it?"

"All prophecies are sung."

His attitude is matter-of-fact, but the memory of hearing him sing the first time makes me look at him incredulously.

"You're kidding."

"Sotto voce."

"Not in the car."

"I can put the windows down."

"It's raining."

Nodding absently, he impatiently watches the pedestrians in the crosswalk. His energy is barely contained, food foremost on his mind.

"Do you know what you're going to tell Maeve about staying with the cousins?"

"I was hoping you'd slept on it for me." I say dryly.

"Is it really so annoying that I sleep in the car?"

"You sleep everywhere."

"I get tired."

"I thought you were getting better?"

"That was before I started sleeping in a bed every night."

"Sleeping in a bed every night makes you tired?"

He looks at me sideways. "Not just the sleeping."

"This is some sort of payback?"

With a shrug, he crosses his legs. "We all have to make sacrifices."

"Wow. Glad to know you're taking one for the team."

"You know I don't feel that way."

Gripping the wheel, I say nothing.

I feel his hand on my lap. "Our anniversary is this month."

"So is Easter with the cousins."

"We don't have to go. We can make plans. Go away somewhere."

"Where?"

"Anywhere."

My brows go up. "Anywhere?"

"Within reason."

"That won't get us out of staying with Kate and Duane."

"Why do you feel so obligated to go?"

"If you had family, you'd know."

"This *is* my family."

"Then you can tell Maeve we don't want to spend Easter with her pregnant daughter and son-in-law at their new cabin on Hood Canal because we want to run away for our anniversary instead."

"Why can't you?"

"Coming from me it'd be like saying we'd rather spend the weekend fornicating at an undisclosed location."

"Vulgar and disrespectful."

"Yours truly."

He looks away. "It would be better coming from you."

"Chicken."

I feel him shoot me a look. "Because I don't want to offend Maeve?"

"You just don't want to spend a weekend alone with me."

"I spend all my weekends alone with you."

Batting my eyes, I smile. "We all have to make sacrifices."

"Then we go." His voice is quiet.

I squint for a parking spot. "Why didn't I think of that?"

He doesn't say anything else, only stares out the window. We're in the middle of Fairhaven, surrounded by turn-of-the-century buildings infested with boutiques and coffee shops. I pull the car into a parking space. The café is only a block away. Getting out of the car, I rub a kink in my neck and head down the sidewalk.

His voice follows me. "Do you think Maeve got a cake?"

"There's Twinkie under the tires."

"It's your birthday." He mutters. "You should have a cake."

"You want cake. I don't need cake. I need a drink."

"A cake." He repeats.

"A drink."

"With your name on it?"

"Martini."

"Sophie … please."

"It's my birthday. You can eat cake on yours."

He steps past me to open the café door. "Please, eat first."

Inside, a waitress passes with a cocktail in each hand. Only the tragedy of spilling them stops me from wrestling her to the ground. His hands grip my shoulders and steer me toward a familiar face.

"Hello, sweets!"

Sitting in a quiet corner, Maeve sets down a glass of wine and gets to her feet. Tall and swaying, she rises from the table in a navy cashmere wrap and loose slacks. Her tanned face is framed by auburn ringlets haphazardly wound into something resembling a French twist.

"Sophie!" Tossing her shawl over her shoulder, she embraces me and plants a kiss on my cheek. "Happy birthday, sweetheart."

She turns to my husband. "Give me a kiss, darling."

As he kisses her cheek, she winks at me over his shoulder. Feeling a headache coming on, I try to smile, taking a chair with my back to the window.

Resuming her seat, Maeve reaches over to pat the back of my hand. "I'm so sorry it rained on you! How was your drive?"

"Dry."

As I speak, I catch the eye of a passing waiter. "Please, I'm dying. Sapphire martini, two olives?"

He displays perfect teeth and dimples. With a nod, he looks at the rest of us expectantly.

"The same." Auntie beams.

My husband watches me as he speaks. "Water for me, thank you."

I plant a plate of bread in front of his disapproval. "The cake comes after the meal."

Our waiter introduces himself as Scott and disappears to answer our prayers with diligence and speed. My aunt pays scant attention to the courtesy, watching me with anticipation. I know what she wants to ask, though she'll try not to be obvious.

"How are your parents? Still happy they chose to live in Hawaii?"

"They love it. Dad's teaching part-time at the college, and Mom has a garden planted, with plans for a koi pond."

"I would love a koi pond!" Auntie squints. "I wonder if I have enough space for one. My neighbor, Sue, put one in." She raises her brows. "She has a husband for the hard labor."

Visits with Maeve usually turn to the vivisection of relationships between men and women; I'm only surprised at the record time in which the subject has come up. The martinis haven't even been made yet.

Her finger traces the stem of her wine glass.

"I always envied your parents' marriage. They've always been so steady with one another. I often wonder why I never found that myself …" Her voice trails as she watches our waiter flirt at the next table.

Stealing a piece of bread from my husband, I start to butter it. "It would have helped if the last two didn't die, don't you think?"

Maeve drains her glass.

"Mmm-hmm ... but even if Ted and Andy hadn't passed, I'd have chalked up two divorces, anyway. Dark thinking, I know, but I don't think I could be happy with one person forever."

"A tall order for anyone." I tear at my bread, trying to decipher the specials scrawled on a chalk board. "I couldn't do it."

"Sophia!" My aunt drops both hands to the table. "Please tell me you aren't getting divorced. It's only been three years! I was relying on you to be the one who broke the curse."

Dropping my bread onto a plate, I take a sip of water before answering.

"We aren't getting divorced. I mean, I don't think I could be with someone *forever*. In my case, it's just till I die." I shrug. "As far as our wedding vows went, that's all I committed to."

Letting my eyes drift up from my water glass, I catch my husband's gaze and notice he's stopped eating. I shrug.

What?

Maeve ponders.

"Wedding vows ... never used them, I always eloped. Course some people take vows very seriously. Duane wrote theirs; it took him a year." She rolls her eyes. "He had them printed on vellum and sent to everyone who got an invitation."

"Yes." I smile. "We got ours."

Auntie grins. "Pray tell, what did you do with it?"

"I've saved it for my scrapbooking project."

"Really? I never saw you as a scrapbooker. Is this a new hobby?"

"Just something to fill the gap between a useful life and blowing my brains out."

Maeve sniffs as I ignore the despair growing next to me. Auntie's attention strays when Scott arrives with our drinks.

My hands reach for the frosted grail before me. "Thank God."

Maeve winks at Scott as he sets her drink before her. "Excellent. Thank you."

He flashes his dimples. "Would you like me to go over the fresh sheet?"

Auntie takes a sip from her glass and leans forward. "Please, do."

I nurse my head with gin while Scott recites specials with the combined efficacy of a flight steward and a troubadour. My aunt interrupts at appropriate times with nodding approval. My husband observes them with the discretion of a field biologist, his gloom forgotten. Auntie concludes with an order of starters and another round of martinis.

"We should make a toast to you both on your upcoming anniversary." She winks at me. "Still satisfied with your man?"

As I appraise him, my man looks back at me. I note the rumpled shirt collar peeking from a charcoal cardigan gilt with dog hair. A tangle of amber waves stray into soulless blue eyes, staring from an immaculate face. Who wouldn't be?

Picking up my martini, I take another drink. "He's keeping me happy."

He sighs. "Trying."

"Marriage ..." I sit back. "You wanted to know what it was like."

She laughs at him. "My dear, if you wanted to know, all you had to do was ask. Four times engaged and three times married, the Lord of the Rings hasn't got me beat. But it's kismet you found Sophie. She deserves you."

My eyes widen. "God, help me."

"You deserve me." He raises his water glass. "Remember that."

"Kate and Duane seem to be happy." Maeve casually stirs her drink. "You know I had my reservations about Duane, but he's not all bad, and if he's what she wants, she should have him."

I reach for my unfinished piece of bread. "How are they?"

She pauses over her martini before reciting a list of their recent accomplishments. There is Duane's promotion at his insurance brokerage, Kate's budding practice as a therapist, the new cabin on Hood Canal, and of course, the baby. Duane wants to be a father, and Kate wants a father. I can accept it. All of it. I just don't want to spend Easter weekend with it.

"Of course, Kate really wants to have a grown-ups weekend with you. At eight months, there won't be many more opportunities to entertain child free."

Maeve pauses for a response, preferably confirmation we have accepted Kate's invitation for Easter weekend.

"I'm still waiting to see if I can get Monday off, but as soon as I know ..." I pop an olive in my mouth.

The thought of Duane replicating himself disturbs me. It suddenly doesn't seem fair my husband can't, not that he really needs to, but the birth of Duane's child should trigger the end of days at least. My husband nudges me under the table. I glance at him, expecting admonishment for thinking ill of Duane's unholy seed, but he looks relieved.

We're saved.

His thought lingers in my mind as Scott appears with a platter of food.

The conversation shifts to eating, to travel, to books. The cousins do not come up again. Auntie Maeve is politely unfazed by the volume of food my husband eats. Due to high divorce rates, my family is consistently good at ignoring spousal idiosyncrasy. As Maeve watches one man eat enough food for three people, she is only amused. I never admit it is a fraction of what he can eat, and she never asks.

Sophie started classes today. Her mood is not positive. In spite of her desire to help others, her distaste for the legal profession is clouding her ability to think objectively about the necessity of obtaining her degree. She has also grown preoccupied with emotional needs. With the onset of child-bearing age, her instinct to seek a mate distracts her.

In this regard, her relationship with Anthony does not seem satisfactory. He is loyal and trustworthy but displays a possessiveness that discourages her growth as a person. He does not support her pursuit of education or display interest in her personal and professional goals. He is particularly fearful of other males sharing in her life. This has made open contact with her difficult.

A change in gender could be the solution, but the cost I cannot predict. Sophie is most attuned to developing relationships with males at this time and might not facilitate a friendship with a woman. However, to take advantage of her gender preference as I am would be confusing for her and misleading on my part. She deserves the same quality of lifemate in this life as in previous lives, certainly better than the last one.

Anthony's presence would be ideal were it not for his extreme vigilance toward males in general. Even if Sophie accepts me, he will not. How to sustain my connection to her without intruding into their relationship I am unsure. I cannot believe that simply because Sophie is a woman, I will no longer share her company.

I have tried to make myself known to her at the coffee shop she frequents. I know she has noted me and remembers me. Speaking with her is difficult. She is rarely alone. When alone, she is at study and I should not disturb her, or she is talking to Anthony on her phone. The school campus is closed and my presence would not go undetected without causing alarm. The rest of her time is spent in her car or the apartment she shares with Anthony.

She exercises regularly at Wright Park, but she is most fearful of being watched by men there. It is a fear I cannot account for and may be associated with events I am unaware of. To allay this fear, I have stayed away from the park.

I have stayed away from her.

For twenty-three years I have protected her from my influence to the best of my ability. But I do not think I can go much longer.

I miss Daniel.

[Spharic. Entry translated from *Kor Dai Maihael*. Mund Dai Sep 9, 1999.]

1999 One year left. That was what I kept telling myself. Not that summer was over and I was getting out of bed at the butt crack of dawn to sit through three hours of American Jurisprudence. Not that I would rather eat the law books in my bag than read them.

Not that I would rather be dead than a lawyer.

Nearing Grounds for Coffee, I made out an empty spot through the rain pouring down my windshield and passed by. Parking downtown was iffy, and normally I would have jumped on it, but this was Biblical rain and I was in a shitty enough mood without getting soaked to boot. Rolling the dice, I hoped for something closer. My prayers were answered when a black BMW began to back out in front of me. It was parked almost in front of the door.

Slipping into the spot, I pulled my hood over my head, squinting against the spatter that soaked the inside of my car door the moment I opened it. Dashing for the coffee house, I slid inside. It was crowded with the morning rush, humid with damp clothes and dripping umbrellas, but the smell of brewing beans made it all wonderful.

The line to order was short. It was the pick-up line that was long, twisting back on itself until it looked little more than a mob of furtive eyes and pricked ears. Squeezing myself at the end of it, I decided what was really needed were two pick-up lines: one for the straight latte crowd and one for the whip and sprinkle set. It was coffee after all. Not dessert.

"Good morning."

A voice startled me and I turned to see a man standing next to my shoulder. Looking up, I recognized him as a regular at Grounds. Tall, attractive, very blue eyes that looked like contacts. No name. He smiled; his eyes didn't.

"Hi." I wasn't sure if I was smiling or not. "Am I in your way?"

"No, I already ordered."

Nodding, I turned away, still feeling the eyes on me.

My cell rang. Reaching inside my raincoat, I pulled it out and glanced at the number. Anthony.

I flipped it open. "Hey, what's up?"

"I got a break. You in school?"

"Not yet. I'm at Grounds. Wanna come?"

"Perfect. I'll be there in five."

Closing my phone, I slipped it back in my coat and peeked over the crowd into the lounge. The odds of finding a place to sit were diminishing.

"Excuse me."

The man behind me touched my shoulder as he passed into the lounge. The back of his trench still dripped with rain. I wondered where he was going if he was waiting for his order.

The restroom?

With a sigh, I focused on the pick-up counter. My coffee couldn't come soon enough. After gnawing on my lip for five sluggish minutes, I finally made it to the lounge with latte in hand, my eyes scanning the room for any available seating.

Not surprisingly, the armchairs by the fire were taken, as were the sofas, the high boys, and the tables by the windows, one of which was annoyingly occupied by a single individual reading a paper.

"Nuts."

I was about to return to the front door to wait for Anthony when the lone person at the table waved at me. As the paper lowered, I saw who it was. Taking a sip of my latte, I smiled and went to him. He folded his paper expectantly.

"How much for a seat?"

"Feel free." He replied smoothly.

Reaching a long arm across the table, he removed his trench from the back of the empty chair across from him. As I sat down, he draped his coat on the back of his own. He wore no jacket, only a pale blue button-down shirt. It was loose at his neck, no tie.

I indicated the pick-up line. "I thought you ordered something."

"I did."

There was only a sugar dispenser on the table.

"Where is it?"

"Before you arrived. I finished and left, and then came back."

"You forgot something?"

"Waiting for someone."

I looked around the room. "Did they show?"

His eyes finally seemed to express something. "We'll see."

A smile pulled at my mouth. "Business or pleasure?"

"Necessity."

With a snicker, I lifted my cup to my lips.

His brows rose. "What is it?"

"You're good."

He said nothing, only made a small smile while I added sugar to my coffee. I said nothing as I stirred with my swizzle.

"What do you do?" He finally asked.

I tasted my coffee, then added more sugar. "Torture myself."

"How?"

"By going to law school and meeting mysterious strangers in coffee shops."

"Then why do it?"

"Necessity."

I grinned at him as his smile grew, hinting at perfect teeth and vague dimples. His eyes looked past me and his face went blank.

"There you are!"

Anthony crossed the lounge to us, shedding his police slicker, a rush of air preceding him. When I looked back at my companion, he was on his feet.

"Where are you going?"

"I'm late." He pulled on his trench. "It was nice meeting you."

With barely a smile, he passed Anthony for the door.

Anthony watched him leave and looked back at me. "Who was that?"

Slumping back in my chair, I shrugged. "Must not like cops."

Anthony took off his hat, dropping it on the paper the stranger left behind, the patent brim soaking the print. I followed his gaze as he stared tensely through the window. Stretching up in my seat, I watched the man in the trench cross the street before quickly walking up the sidewalk.

"You know him?" Anthony asked.

Watching the man disappear, I shook my head absently. "Nope."

"I'm gonna grab a cup."

Tossing his slicker onto the chair across from me, Anthony left me alone.

It wasn't long. The first wave of customers had dropped off, there was no line, and Anthony was strictly a drip man. Pushing the newspaper aside, he set a plate with a giant scone on it on the table. As he sat down, he handed me a fork. I could see questions in his eyes, but he didn't want to annoy me. His instincts were good. I was in no mood for questions.

Both of us cut into the scone. We ate in silence before I realized he was waiting for me to lead.

I swallowed. "How's work?"

"Uh, uh." He warned me off the topic with a shake of his head.

"Good scone." I tried again with a smirk.

"Uh, huh." He nodded with a laugh.

I washed my scone down with some coffee. "When will you be home?"

He looked at his watch. "The rest of my day is paperwork. I'll be home by lunch."

"Okay. I'll be home by lunch, too."

He eyed me. "Don't you have class this afternoon?"

I made a face. "We'll see how I feel after lunch."

"You're ditching classes already? It's only been a week."

"Don't push me. It's a miracle I show up."

"Sophie, you know how I feel about lawyers, but they do work. If they're good, it's all they do. It's a big commitment."

"It's a good degree to have if I want to earn more."

"You don't want the money. You hate it. You quit your AG internship to volunteer at the YWCA instead."

"You're the devil."

He put up his hands. "An advocate. Nothing more."

"So after two years, I march into the registrar's office and throw my books in their face?"

"I'd suggest withdrawing without assaulting anybody. That's a degree you don't want."

"Good point." I took another sip of coffee. "Wouldn't look good on my resume if I applied at the women's shelter."

"Tell ya what." Anthony put down his fork. "I'm back to a regular shift tomorrow. I'll take you out to dinner when you finish your classes today. *All of your classes.*" He pointed his fork at me as I rolled my eyes. "We don't talk about work;

we don't talk about school; we sleep on it. Tomorrow, do whatever you want."

"Whatever I want?"

"Whatever you want." He nodded. "Start fresh. Do it right."

"Tomorrow." My head dropped back on my shoulders as I repeated the words. "Whatever I want."

"What do you say?"

Sitting up, I looked him in the eye. "I'm in."

I promised Anthony I wouldn't ditch class. When lunch rolled around, I called him at home to say I was staying on campus to study instead. He acted impressed. I told him to can it. He told me to think about where I wanted to go for dinner. I told him someplace close. I didn't want to drive anywhere. I was tired.

I needed coffee.

Problem was, the coffee at the law school sucked. A glaring oversight given the cycle of alcohol and No-Doz needed to fuel the legal mind. The closest coffee house that wasn't a Starbucks was Grounds for Coffee four blocks away. Weighing my options, I peeked out the windows of the law library and noticed it stopped raining. Even lugging a thousand pages of *Overview of the American Judiciary*, for a good cup of coffee, I could do four blocks.

When I got to Grounds, it was as busy as it was that morning, this time with the lunch crowd. After noshing through a bag of popcorn in the back of class, I wasn't hungry. With a gut full of organic packing peanuts, a latte was all I needed to assure my complete failure as a nutritionist, if not a law student. Sidestepping the lineup for food, it wasn't long before I found myself, latte in hand, exactly where I was four hours earlier.

The lounge was still crowded. Again, all the armchairs around the fireplace were taken, as were the sofas and stools. There was a free table, but I didn't want to take it as I was by myself and not eating.

I was about to leave when a woman reading by the fireplace reached for her purse and stood up to collect her coffee mug. Glancing around the room, I floated as close to her chair as I could without looking flagrantly predatory. Another woman entered the lounge and saw what was happening. As she approached, I smiled, sending her the other way.

As soon as the reader abandoned her position, I dropped into the chair, delighted to finally have one of the best seats in the house. It seemed fair consolation for having the worst reading material. However, read it I would, even if I decided to end my legal career the next day. That would be then; this was now.

Setting my latte on the side table next to me, I ignored the alternative newspaper someone sadistically left behind and diligently pried open my *History of the American Judiciary*.

I skimmed the forward.

I skimmed the essay on British Common Law.

I skipped the chapter on John Marshall altogether.

"How much do you remember when you read so quickly?"

I lifted my face to a familiar sight. Behind a newspaper, a pair of eyes glittered. Without seeing his face, I heard enough.

"How long have you been sitting there?"

The paper shrugged. "I came here for lunch."

"You come here a lot."

"No more than you."

Slowly, I rested my book on my lap. "I remember enough."

He lowered his paper. "Have you eaten?"

I shook my head. "Forgot."

He smiled. It made my chest hurt. I didn't smile back.

His smile faded. "You need to stay healthy if you're going to torture yourself."

"I've decided to quit." The words came from nowhere.

His smile evaporated altogether. "Quit?"

"Torturing myself."

"You're leaving school?"

I think I nodded.

"But I thought …" He seemed to stop himself. "I thought …"

It was odd to hear him falter, like hearing a CD skip.

"Thought what?"

"After two years?"

"How do you know that?"

His face reset. "I've seen you here … with your books."

It was plausible. I knew I'd seen him at Grounds before. Many times.

But I couldn't remember seeing him two years ago.

"I'm sorry." He abruptly broke my thoughts. "It isn't any of my business."

Sitting back, he lifted the paper. For a moment I stared at it. My eyes wandered across the print to his hands. His fingers were trim, long and bare.

"What is your business, anyway?" I asked the paper.

"Antiques and restoration." The paper answered.

My brows rose. "That explains the hours."

The paper came down. "The hours?"

"How you can while away the day in a coffee house."

"I'm not here all day."

"No." I smirked, "You had someplace pretty important to get to this morning."

"I'm sorry. That was rude of me."

"Afraid of cops?"

"No."

"You blew out of here like you had an outstanding warrant."

"I didn't want to intrude."

"Intrude? It was your table."

It was for you.

"What?"

He blinked. "I didn't say anything."

He was right; he hadn't.

"Sorry, I thought you did."

Feeling confused, I turned to my coffee.

"I'm keeping you from your studies."

I glanced over my cup as I took a sip. "Don't stop on my account."

With a small smile, he raised the paper. Needless to say, I was disappointed. Sighing, I looked down at his shoes. Black leather mocs.

"Nice shoes, by the way."

"Thank you." The paper said.

For a moment I watched the fire, then turned to stare out the windows, then back at his shoes. Eventually, I noticed the open book on my lap.

And snapped it shut.

"This is ridiculous. Anthony's right; I hate it."

The paper came down.

I looked the stranger in the eyes. "Why do I do it?"

"I don't know you well enough to answer that."

"Bullshit."

"Excuse me?"

"Who really knows anybody? I'm as likely to get a straight answer from you as my own mother."

"You don't know me."

"You don't know my mother."

"Might I suggest you give yourself some time to think this over?"

"Two years wasn't enough?"

"It's possible you haven't been thinking but acting on rote. Out of habit."

"Maybe that's my problem. I've lost the habit. I'm just not a student anymore."

He seemed to stare through me. "It's my fault. You were doing fine until I interrupted you. I only noticed you seemed to be skipping pages."

"I was."

His eyes refocused on mine. "That can't be a very effective study method."

I smirked. "Are you serious?"

He dropped his gaze. Apparently he was.

With a cough, I cleared my throat. "You're right; it isn't."

He kept his eyes down. "You're very fortunate to have the opportunity to receive an education. It shouldn't be squandered on a whim."

It was a sentence with all the wrong words in it. Or all the right ones.

"Squandered?" As my voice pitched, he looked at me. "On a *whim*? I've got over a hundred thousand opportunities I'll be paying off for the rest of my life. You can call me a quitter if you want, but I'm not whimsical."

Standing up, I dropped the book at his feet. "That cost me twenty opportunities, used and I skipped the chapter on John Marshall. Tell me if it was worth it."

Leaving my book and my latte behind, I walked out.

The feminization of beasts, demons, and vengeful spirits is a prime example of fact spawning ruthless fiction.

It is recurrent in the Prophetic Line that the union of a singular with any biological life form is more than twice as likely to produce female offspring than not. Females are inherently stronger in the womb and make healthier infants than males. Such favorable odds are crucial to the survival of a seeing Child maturing past attainment. Naturally, such Children have been seen, heard and feared by humans who have had contact with them in the past. These encounters have led to the evolution of myths emphasizing the most obvious trait the majority of these Children shared, specifically their gender. The fact these Children were most often seen as girls or women coincided conveniently with the turn in universal human identity from the feminine to the masculine.

A comprehensive study of the harpy is worth while as a prime example of the universal she-beast myth all human cultures share. As the halves of a hybrid Child will display both human and singular characteristics, namely both a material and immaterial form, so the harpy is a creature half human and half beast. Most often the beastly half is bird-like, artistically represented by wings and talons, the original symbolism of wings as a figurative representation of the spirit to be later misinterpreted as literal transfiguration. Where men with wings evolved into angels, women with wings became predatory monsters. This willful vilification spread to feminine avatars predating the harpy myth, Medusa and Hecate among them.

That universal human identity should have swung so far to the masculine saddens me, though I have come to accept gender fixation as core to the human condition. My own experience indicates what lies at the root of this fixation is a struggle for influence. Between both genders, the majority of humans are fearful of the empowered feminine. The masculine is threatened because the universe Itself seems to favor the feminine, thus our own preference as singulars to spawn female offspring when capable of procreating. As it is only through a human female that a hybrid Child can enter the material world she is somehow held to account. Perhaps it is easier to subjugate the female, to despise and condemn her, than guard her against my own kind.

Of course, humans do not know me as a singular. As Michael, I am portrayed as a male harpy, an angel both empowered and benevolent. I am perceived as sexually impotent and thus not a threat to the human masculine. A female, however, is never perceived by human males as impotent. A woman's sexuality is not a matter of performance, but intrinsic to her being. If it is a matter of the ends justifying the means, the human masculine must go far to keep the feminine disempowered. To render Samson impotent, Delilah cut off his hair. To render Medusa impotent, Perseus cut off her head.

[Spharic. Notation translated from *Thae Harpyia*. Bef. 12th c.]

(Embossed manuscript cover, *Thae Harpyia]*

2003 I don't know why I tell my mother the things I do.
Generally, I exercise pretty good judgment. No recaps of late nights, no bedroom stories, no men. Just about everything beyond those boundaries is fair game. Most of the time, it's good. She listens, points out things I've missed, shares her insights. I've learned her moods, learned to anticipate her opinions. So why I tell her what's on my mind when I know she'll tell me what I don't want to hear is beyond me.

"Sophia, be nice. This is family. She's your cousin, and it's only one weekend."

My mother is Chinese. When she says, "This is family," the debate is over.

"It'll be a three-day weekend, Ma. With Duane, a fetus, and three cats."

"She's having a baby; she needs you. Someday you'll have a baby and then you'll understand."

Almost forgot. Babies. I retreat from the minefield of grandkids.

"It's all right, Mom. I already called Kate and told her we're going."

"Then why do you bother me?"

"I just needed to confirm there was no way out of this one."

"Oh!"

Long distance doesn't hide the satisfaction I hear in her voice.

"How is Dad?"

"Oh, he has really bad sunburn. And lots of freckles, just like you! I remember when you were little and you'd play outside all day. You would come in with freckles on your nose. Freckles on freckles! They were jumping on your nose!"

The freckles are from my father's side, but she repeats her alibi on the off chance someday I'll feel the need to hold one of them accountable.

"Well, I'll talk to Dad next time I call. I'll try again when he's home."

"Okay. How is Michael?"

"He's fine."

"Are you feeding him enough?"

"I don't think that's possible."

"You're being nice to him?"

"When he deserves it."

"Sophia, he is good to you, and you can be so mean. You don't want to be like your aunt, always so hard on men."

My mother operates under the suspicion my aunt is somehow responsible for the deaths of her last two husbands.

"Don't worry; I love Mike too much to divorce him, and nothing can kill him so we're safe."

"Be good, Sophie."

When I hang up, my neck feels a twinge.

Travel is not one of my favorite pastimes. It's not the moving; it's the packing. If I could get whatever I needed wherever I went, it wouldn't be a problem. Toothbrush in pocket, done. However, unlike my mother who has perfect eyesight, my father borders on legally blind, all but assuring I would endure lifelong slavery to contacts, cleaning solution, and Visine. The worst case scenario is losing a lens, so I always pack extras. Since I like boys who make passes, I haven't worn glasses in years.

Staying with people adds another dimension to trips, even more so when you add pets. Michael and I have a dog, a Shepherd Malamute mix named Lodi. Lodi lives outside in a dog house that he painstakingly carpets with fur. He is flatulent, drools, and is a habitual gooser, but at 125 pounds, I figure he can call his own shots.

Needless to say, we understand our dog isn't for everyone. Even though Lodi loves Hood Canal, he will stay at a dog ranch. We respect the cousins don't appreciate slobbery gas giants, nor would their cats Tic, Tac, and Toe—I kid you not. Unfortunately, Tic, Tac, and Toe will be joining us. Although I love most animals, I am indifferent when it comes to cats and downright hostile when they are anti-social. One of the cousins' cats, I think its Toe, is all right. But I'm positive that Tic and Tac are harpies disguised as cats.

I shared this theory with Michael to his amusement. He told me he hasn't seen a harpy in ages, but he's sure these are just cats. I asked how he could be sure if it's been ages since he last saw a harpy. He said if he really suspected they were harpies, he would feel obliged to kill them. I told him if they destroy another article of my clothing, I will feel the same obligation. He pointed out that cats are believed to ward away harpies, which makes perfect sense to me. If anything can keep a harpy away, Tic and Tac can do the job.

Needless to say, I am deciding what cat-proof items of clothing to take with me when I hear Lodi barking in our drive. It's not Michael; Lodi wouldn't bark if it were. The sound of tires on gravel spurs me downstairs and out the front door. There is a white Accord parked outside and I recognize Marta behind the wheel. Lodi is inspecting her through the passenger window. His tail is still, signing his indecision about granting her security clearance. I am undecided about her unannounced visit.

Marta owns a little boutique a few streets from our house called Dragonfly. She is obsessed with the orient to an extreme, and ever since I visited her spa with my mother, she has made befriending me a hobby. My mother's directive to be nice has me call Lodi away from her car.

"Hello!" She shouts from her car window. "Sorry to drop in like this, but I have some new teas I thought you should try."

As I approach, she reaches over to the passenger seat and retrieves a parcel. When she emerges, she is bundled in a red silk jacket and wine-colored cords. Her bobbed hair is dyed an unnatural jet black and pinned back by a pair of glasses, somehow reminding me of someone I have met before.

"I tried to remember where you told me you lived. Your description of your drive is very good. I knew I found the place when I saw your cedars. You told me they were large, but good Lord! That's some old-growth timber!"

"They have to be." I point to the ravine behind our house. "If they weren't here, this house probably wouldn't be here, either."

"What a lovely place. Those roses are huge! Is that a slate roof?"

"Yeah, Michael salvaged it from a demolition."

"That's right. I remember, you told me he reclaims things."

"Recycle, reuse, renew. Would you like to come in?"

Lodi is giving Marta a thorough sniffing over and has zeroed in on the parcel. Deciding to spare her a goosing, I quickly usher her inside.

"Thank you for having me. I hope I'm not here at a bad time. You weren't in the middle of anything?"

"No, not at all." The distraction from packing doesn't hurt my feelings.

Marta hands me the parcel and takes off her coat. Underneath she displays a jade necklace over a turtleneck printed with a pattern of Chinese characters. Her eyes are already running around the small foyer and into the sitting room that makes up most of the first floor of our house.

I wave the parcel at her. "Would you like some?"

"Why not?" She follows me down the hall to the kitchen. "There are three varieties there. What makes these special is they were all mixed by a Chinese herbalist in Vancouver. I think there are labels saying which is which."

Pulling the wrapper from the box, I open the lid. Inside I find three smaller bags of loose tea. One has a foil wrap that looks like silver leaf. They are all unmarked.

"That one there is special. Isn't there a label?"

Sniffing it, my eyes begin to burn with tears. "Oh yeah, that's special all right."

It reeks like a blend of scotch broom and cat hair.

"Too strong?" Marta looks slightly panicked.

"Maybe it just needs water."

I start a kettle on the stove and then set porcelain on the kitchen table.

Taking a seat, Marta picks up a cup and holds it to the light.

"Wedgwood. Lovely."

"Glad you appreciate them. To me, a cup is pretty much a cup." I sit down across the table from her.

"They belong to your husband?" She has moved to examining the saucers.

"My stuff is in one room upstairs; everything else here is his, including the house."

"How long have you been married?"

"Three years."

"Well, I'm sure that in time you'll get a chance to add some of your own things."

"I don't need much."

Marta sits back in her chair, looking around her with the expression of a tourist on a bus. Now that I observe her, I figure her to be around forty.

"It's a different sort of house, isn't it? Not Victorian … but it has an oriental feel."

"It's arts and crafts. The builder was a Greene and Greene fan."

"That's what I thought!" Her voice is exuberant. "Just like a Greene and Greene house."

"I wouldn't go that far—more like a doll house version."

"Still, it's picture perfect."

I laugh. "If you say so. I just keep the place from being buried in dog hair and overgrown with weeds. The yard was pretty bad before I moved in."

"How long have you lived here?

"About four years now."

"So you lived here before you were married?"

"Mike and I have been friends for a long time."

"Really?" Her voice goes up and octave.

Yes, I think, *really.*

Glancing at the clock on the wall, I see I need to start dinner in half an hour and the water can't boil fast enough.

"How's Dragonfly doing?" Changing the subject, my voice is all interest.

Marta claps her hands together and rubs them. "Business couldn't be better, but I have a lot of loyal customers. My clients are like family so our relationships weather thick and thin. They know I want them to stay healthy above everything else."

She leans forward. "You know I take what I do very seriously. Living is about wellness, and wellness is everything around us, isn't it? I tell them it's more than getting treatments or taking herbs; it's about surrounding oneself with the right energy, the right intentions, and that includes the right people. Don't you agree?"

"Amen to that." Easter weekend with the cousins looms again.

She continues as though my presence is compulsory, which it pretty much is at this point.

"You know most of my clients are very busy professionals. They've spent all their lives focused on one goal, but now most of them don't even know what it was. They don't enjoy their work, the kids are gone, or out of touch—and their marriages, well a lot of them are hanging on by a thread when I meet them. Bad to be without a compass."

I'm wondering what to say to this when she starts again.

"Now your mother, is she from China?"

"Yes."

"Then she raised you to value your spiritual health, didn't she?

I open my mouth.

"The rest of the world is way ahead of us on that." Marta says to the china cupboard. "You know, my mother was part Colombian? She raised me to recognize that every living thing has a soul as well as a body. Just because you see a healthy body doesn't mean there's a healthy soul inside. But in the modern world, everything is science and technology ... no one cares about their souls anymore. A lot of people in this world are dying from the inside out and they don't know it."

"So you save souls for a living." I get up to find a tea ball.

She laughs. "In a manner of speaking, yes! I can't claim to succeed, but I try."

"There's never been a shortage of clients in that profession."

"I don't like to think of it as a profession—more a calling. I inherited my mother's intuition where spiritual healing is concerned. She could read a person's aura like a book. I don't think I'm that good, but I can definitely get an overall sense of a person's aura. Yours, if you don't mind my saying, is very strong. Both you and your mother are old souls. You're very open, but your mother's a tough cookie. I wouldn't mess with her!"

"I don't know about her aura." I answer without breaking my tea ball search. "But she is a rolling stone, I'll give you that."

Sifting the kitchen drawers, I remember Mom saying she thought Marta was a crackpot. And Mom says I'm mean.

"Do your parents live hereabouts?"

"They used to; now they live in Hawaii." *Where did I put the tea ball?*

"How nice. How did they choose Hawaii?"

"My father's parents are there." *Is it with the coffee filters?*

"Is your father Hawaiian?"

"No, he looks like Sunny Jim." *Tea ball …*

"Well, you're a beautiful hybrid. They did a wonderful job."

"Thanks." My voice goes flat. "I'll let them know." *Did she call me a hybrid?*

Marta flushes. "I didn't mean that to sound like it did. I'm sorry. Like I said, my mother was part Colombian and my father was Irish, but I wasn't mixed so well. It's a terrible thing to feel like two people."

I return to the table with my tea ball. "Don't worry about it."

"Isn't it strange who we end up marrying? Sometimes I wonder how my parents found each other, how they were able to get past each other's differences. And yet they were meant for each other."

"Sounds like my parents."

Opening the tea ball, I consider the satchels of tea on the table between us. I decide against the cat hair in favor of what smells like an infused jasmine. Marta is no help.

"Do you believe in reincarnation?"

"Oh, yeah." I raise my brows.

"Were you raised to believe in it? I mean, because of your mother's influence?"

"Mom never told me what to believe in; it's just something I always felt. Now I have a name for it."

"See! That's that intuition I was telling you about."

"And your intuition told you I was out of tea?"

Marta gives a nervous laugh and pushes back in her chair again.

"As a healer, it's my habit to make house calls. I delivered some remedies to Mrs. Farrell … I don't know if you've met her; she lives up the street from you. Anyway, she's consulted me in the past, and she hasn't been feeling well all winter. Since she's your closest neighbor, I couldn't resist stopping by. That's my excuse!"

"I'm sorry to hear that. I've only met her once, but she seems nice. We don't see much of our neighbors. I grew up five streets away from here and always thought this house was haunted. It's good to know that she hasn't gone unnoticed."

"She did seem to be curious about you and your husband. You know, the way elderly ladies can be some times."

Since Marta isn't elderly, I assume she doesn't see a resemblance.

With a knowing smile, I rise from the table to check on the water. "I'll have to give her some satisfaction then."

"Oh, I don't mean to make you think she's a gossip or anything…"

"Of course not. Maybe I'll invite her to tea, now that I have some."

The tea kettle isn't boiling up to Mother's standards, but I feel under the circumstances she'll forgive me. With my back to Marta, I pour a dash of steaming water into the porcelain pot to warm it before dropping in the tea ball. When I look over my shoulder, I see Marta sniffing at the cat hair tea.

"Care for a biscuit?"

She startles. "Oh, if you have any that would be wonderful."

I cross to the pantry and open the door where my husband's weekly supply of cookies and candy are stored. There is one package of chocolate-dipped short bread left. Snatching it, I go to the counter, grabbing a plate out of the dish rack on my way. Quickly tearing the lid from the box, I plate the cookies and grab the tea pot before returning to the table.

"I'm sure I'm not the first to say so, but your husband has collected some beautiful things here." Marta has left her chair and is inspecting the Wedgwood in the china cabinet next to the pantry. Josiah Wedgwood gave them to Mike as a gift, but that conversation topic presents some challenges.

"Do you mind if I look around?" She asks as I pour.

"Go ahead; that's what saucers are for." I drop a cookie onto the edge of her saucer as I hand her a cup of tea.

"Oh, thank you." She takes her tea and wanders out to the dining room and then into the sitting room.

Standing in the doorway with my tea, I watch her pause to look at the botanical prints on the wall. As she passes the fireplace she spots the photos on the mantel.

"These are lovely old photos. Your husband's family?"

"Actually, those are from my family."

"This must be your wedding picture." Marta picks it up, dropping her glasses to her nose to squint through them.

"Yes, we got married in Hawaii."

"You make a beautiful couple. He's very handsome." She frowns. "Does he have any of his family photos here?"

The fib comes easily. "He keeps an album in his study."

Marta looks at me with raised eyebrows. "Study?"

"Through there."

Marta follows my gaze to the far end of the sitting room. The heavy paneled doors look ominously shut. She doesn't ask to look in and I don't invite her to. Crossing the room, I sink into an armchair with my tea, ready to close shop. The grandfather clock in the foyer chimes four.

"There are some very old things here." She finally announces.

"If you're up for a challenge, try finding something new."

She finally sits across from me on the sofa, absently chewing on her cookie. "You have a lovely view of the gully." Her eyes stare past my shoulder out the window.

"Michael likes trees." My conversational skills have checked out for the day.

"Did he grow up here?"

"His father gave him the house."

"That explains it!" Marta nearly drops her teacup. "When I checked on Mrs. Farrell, she told me she first met you walking your dog, and well—I think I should tell you—it might be her age, but I think she has your husband confused with his father. She told me your husband lived here for fifty years and she was shocked he married at his age, especially to such a young girl. When I saw your wedding photo, well, I knew something wasn't making sense."

"Wow, that would be a January–December romance." I feel my skin tingle. "Well, I suppose that's funny … and understandable. I think Michael looks like his father, so your theory is probably right."

Marta opens her mouth, but I cut her off at the pass.

"Well, I have a dinner to get going. It was nice of you—"

"Of course!" Marta pops the rest of her cookie in her mouth before jumping to her feet like she sat on a bee. "I'm so sorry! Here I am just dropping in on you, and now I've put a wrench in your schedule. I do hope I haven't made dinner late."

She sets her teacup on the coffee table and heads for the door as I follow her.

"Thanks so much for the tea and cookies." She turns and shakes my hand.

"It was easy." I pull her coat from the coat rack and help her get into it. "You had the tea, I had the cookies."

When I open the door, I notice Lodi sitting by her car. He gets to his feet as she nears him and I give him a hard look to stay put, but Marta promptly hops into her car to avoid another security check. Haphazardly navigating the turnabout, she tosses me a wave over her shoulder. As she disappears from view, I drop to sit on the stoop and let out my breath.

Hey So So,

Hope you've been enjoying the lovely sun. I know last week was rotten for jogging. Not that you were out much. Lucky you, you've been busy studying for finals so you only had time to get one run in. I hope you aren't going to regret missing the exercise. You've got quite the candy habit. Remember when we used to go to Rankos and have a Sugar Bowl? I don't think I ever beat you. Not once. A couple times you got pretty sick. No more Red Vines. I haven't been to Rankos since, not that I'm missing much, candy is the least of my problems right? Hey, hey, what's with the car? You finally ditched the Chevy and got an orange cream-sicle? Don't get me wrong, it's a Saab, it's a step up, like twenty from what you were driving, but what's with the color? And the roof liner? Can you even see where you're going in that thing? If you want, I know a guy who can paint and detail it at cost. When he isn't huffing paint, he gets it on pretty good. Anyway he owes me. I figure it's never a bad policy to spot a buddy with skills. Let me know if you're interested. I'll know where to reach you.

Gray Jay

[Police evidence. Letter from Gregory Jacobs to Sophie Davids. #202 of 730 for 1994]

1999 "He knew what year you were?"

My jaws clenched. I should have kept my mouth shut.

"He guessed. He remembered seeing me at Grounds over the last couple years."

"He's been watching you for two years?"

"Relax, Tony, it's not like I'm Princess Di or anything. I'm sure he'll find someone else who appreciates his zeal for higher education. He's good-looking enough."

Our waitress delivered a martini and a scotch.

"Sounds like Ted Bundy. Your instinct said the guy was creepy. You should be listening to that."

I washed down a bite of crostini with iced Sapphire. "Not psycho killer creepy."

"And you can tell the difference? They teach you profiling in law school?"

"Yeah, psycho killers generally don't stress about study technique. He was more ... spooky." I begin to wind pasta on my fork.

"Did he follow you back to school?"

"I don't think so." I take a mouthful of linguini.

"Ever see him on campus?"

Chewing, I pause. "Nope."

"How can you be sure?"

"Trust me." I swallow. "I would have noticed."

"Do you have any reason to go back?"

I shook my head. "Cleaned out my locker and ditched my books at the book store before you picked me up. No loose ends. I will never darken their door again."

"You should probably get your coffee someplace else for a while."

Sipping my martini, I smirked. "You really think he's stalking me?"

"I don't think he was worried about your educational opportunities as much as his opportunity to predict when and where you'd be."

I thought about that morning. He claimed he'd been there, left, and returned again to wait for someone only to fly out the door at the sight of Anthony. I remembered the look on his face, the way his expression changed the moment Tony came in the room. When I saw him again at lunch, he apologized for leaving but gave no excuse about where he went.

He didn't want to intrude.

I go back to eating linguini. "At first I thought he was trying to hit on me, but I don't think that was it."

"What else? He just wanted to make friends?"

"No." I swallowed. "I think he thought we already were."

Anthony reclined in his seat with his scotch. "Psycho."

"Yeah, but he was ..."

"What?"

Letting out a breath, I paused to load my fork. "I don't know. Earnest."

"An earnest psycho." Taking a drink, Tony narrowed his green eyes. "You promise me you'll tell me if you see this guy again?"

My mouth was full of pasta. "And then what, you'll whack him?"

"I'm not kidding around here, Sophie. And you aren't going back to that coffee shop."

"If you whack him, can I watch?" I snickered as Tony tried to keep a straight face.

"Why do you make it so hard for a guy to show he cares about you?"

"Why do guys have to try so hard to show it? Whatever happened to flowers and drugstore candy?"

He sneered. "I'd pay money to see you eat drugstore candy."

We were both candy snobs and started dating after running into each other a dozen separate times at the local See's Candy store. I liked nuts and he liked chews.

Leaning over the table, I smiled. "That's the only thing you have to pay to see."

A light went on in his eyes. "Check, please!"

It wasn't late as we left the restaurant, but it was fall and already dark when we began to walk back to our apartment. Strolling through Wright Park, we took a detour and found a view of Commencement Bay. The rain had cleared and the mountain was out with a moon heavy above it.

In spite of the romantic moment, Anthony was distracted.

I probably shouldn't have told him about the stranger. He was the only one of us alarmed by it. It was a fluke. Interesting dinner conversation, nothing more. All I wanted to think about was celebrating my freedom with a good man. His trade not having a very high opinion of the court system in general, Tony was quietly thrilled I quit. He wanted me to do what made me happy. No pressure, no expectations. I was in love with life again.

Planning my future could wait. It wasn't going anywhere, anyway.

The next morning, I slept in. When I got up, Tony had already left for work. He had set the kitchen table with an empty cereal bowl, a spoon on a napkin, and a juice glass. There was a box of Lucky Charms, a carafe of his fresh-squeezed orange juice, a bottle of Absolut with a ribbon on it.

And there was a note.

What would I do now?

Whatever I wanted.

Despite Tony's mandate, I still heard the voice:

Get a job. Pay your loans. Tell your parents you quit school.

Tell Anthony you don't love him.
This was a strange thought, because I did love him.
You like him.
No, I loved him.
Are you in love with him?
I started to look for the milk for my cereal.
The milk is sour.
Opening the refrigerator, I grabbed the milk. The date was still good. I opened the carton to sniff it, then hesitated.
Why?
People sniffed milk all the time.
The rational part of my brain kicked in. Of course the milk was good; Tony had cereal that morning.
He had coffee and a bagel.
I stood motionless in the kitchen.
My brain started again, trying to remember how he took his coffee.
Black.
Voice or no voice, I wasn't sniffing the milk.
I looked in the carton. There wasn't much left anyway. Why take a chance?
Pouring the milk down the sink, I watched strands of curdles beach around the drain. Returning to the table, I opened the bottle of Absolut, poured a shot into the juice glass, and topped it off with OJ. I drained the glass.
"I'm going for a jog in the park." I spoke aloud. "Me and no one else, got it?"
I waited. There was nothing.
"Got it?" I demanded.
Got it.
"Shit!"
Slamming the glass on the table, I ran into the bedroom. My body started to shake as I pulled on yoga pants, a sweatshirt, and my running shoes. The feeling of being watched was making my skin crawl. In minutes, I was on the street. Wright Park was only three blocks away. There was no need to warm up. I was already sweating.
It was nothing, I told myself.
With each step, I felt lighter.
I reached the park.
Nothing.
All I heard was the sound of feet on gravel and wind in the trees.
I heard my breath.
I was breathing again.
I was alone again.
Alone.

It wasn't exactly divine intervention, more an awakening. As for the voice in my head, I decided it was the result of my failure to choose cereal over vodka. It wasn't hard to accept. At least it was a better theory than the alternative. From that moment on, I dedicated myself to the mission of starting a new life as an adult and not a student. I was starting over and I would do it right.

By the first week of November, I checked all of the to-dos off of my list:

I told my parents I quit school.

I got a job as a grant writer.

I told Anthony I loved him.

I hadn't set foot in Grounds for Coffee.

Life as an adult was commencing tolerably enough.

With the help of a fellow volunteer at the YWCA, I found a job at St. Joseph's Hospital in the grant writing department of their nonprofit foundation. Their annual fund drive was about to drop and would be wrapped by a New Year's Eve ball. At the turn of the millennium, they would unveil the final amount raised in an orgy of wining, dining, and marathon schmoozing. The bigger the number, the happier the administrators, the happier life for the tribe. Their optimism that a computer-fueled apocalypse wouldn't end the world at midnight gave me hope.

A planning committee organized the event. Each department volunteered a staff member to sit on the committee. Being the resident newbie, I was the grant writing department's virgin, which meant letting them down was unavoidable. Evelyn Whittier, a.k.a. Evil Lyn, was the chair of the committee. Short and shaped like a tree ornament, she wore a beehive to perfection and spoke with the charm of an automated teller. She was also the director of the annual fund drive with a reputation for managing her staff like psychiatric outpatients. Every year, she chaired the New Year's committee and staff did whatever they could to avoid it.

In spite of what I'd heard, I held out hope there was an upside to her beyond the hairdo. As soon as the prospective members of the planning committee were confirmed, she sent out a directive e-mail. The strategic planning session would be on Monday, at 0700, in the conference room at Grounds for Coffee.

I wondered if I should tell Anthony.

Anthony didn't want me to go to Grounds until enough time had passed. Though it hadn't come up, I sensed we weren't there yet. The one thing in my favor was that the conference room had a separate entrance on another street. I could go in without entering the coffee shop. If the stranger was there, he didn't have to know I was.

Maybe enough time had passed. It had been over a month and I hadn't seen his shadow since I'd walked out of Grounds the day I left school. I didn't know what I would do if I did see him. Part of me even wondered if I would still recognize him. I knew his face but couldn't seem to remember it.

Monday morning, I tried to put the stranger's face together in my mind. Something vague, generic, with slightly more personality than a mannequin. A plaster saint. With blue glass eyes. Impossible. The rational part of my brain posited he didn't exist.

Data analysis complete.

As always, I was punctual. I arrived at Grounds for Coffee ten minutes early and used the conference room entrance. Other committee members were already there. Some were claiming their seats, others were on their way into the shop to get coffee. A platter loaded with muffins and bagels anchored the boardroom table.

Amy Duncan from finance came in behind me. "Jeez! It's freezing out there."

"Yeah, so what's with the hose and heels, fashion plate?"

She grinned as I checked out her knee-length burgundy dress and ostrich stilettos. By fall, I dressed exclusively in pants and flats, but Amy was as girlie as you could get and proud of it.

"It's wool. It keeps me warm enough."

"I bet. That outfit come with a matching space heater?"

She giggled. "No, but that's what coffee's for, right?"

"Hey." I glanced around the confined meeting space. "I'm kind of squeezed back here. Would you mind getting my coffee for me?" I gave her a twenty. "Get two. It's on me this morning."

"Sure thing! What do you want?"

"Keep it simple. I'll have whatever you're having. I'll save a seat for you."

"Back in a jiff." She beamed.

Sitting back in my chair, I caught the eye of a man sitting across from me and we smiled at each other. I recognized him as Dan Fogel, the HR department's front man. Tall and questionably thin, he seemed well liked around the office. Continuing around the table, I tried to place faces with names. By the time Amy got back with our coffee, I knew them all.

The one I still didn't know I didn't expect to see at the meeting anyway.

As meetings went, it was painlessly predictable. Evelyn Whittier spent forty-five minutes sharing her vision of what the thank you event would be that year. She had Amy draft the to-do list on a flip chart, outlining how the rest of us would make it happen. All the while, I tried to calculate how many meetings like this I would sit through per year, multiplied by the number of years it would take to pay off my tuition. I couldn't come up with a hard number, somewhere between forever and eternity. At least I already had someone to kill all that time with.

A kid with spiky green hair knocked on the door and poked his head in.

"Excuse me, is there a Sophia Davids here?"

My first instinct was to act like I didn't know her. Everyone in the room looked at me.

"Yes."

"There's a call for you. Phone's at the front counter."

"Thanks." My skin felt cold.

Excusing myself, I went into the coffee shop. As I passed through the lounge, I tried not to look at anyone directly. Staring straight ahead, I focused on the lobby where the front counter was.

I wasn't going to look at the armchair.

As I passed, my eyes disobeyed. I caught my breath as I saw a man with a paper.

The paper lowered just enough. It wasn't him. Breathing again, I ran to the front of the shop and flanked the line of people waiting for their orders. I spotted spiky green hair. Spiky saw me and waved me over, handing me a receiver.

"Hello?"

It was Anthony's voice.

"Is everything okay?"

"Yeah, what's wrong?"

"I called your cell; you didn't pick up, so I called the receptionist and got your assistant. She said you were at Grounds and I've been freaking out ever since."

"Shit, I don't know how that happened. My cell hasn't rung the whole time."

I started to dig through my purse and found my cell phone.

Dead as a fish.

"I think my cell is toast. I thought I charged it-"

"Why didn't you tell me you were going there?"

"I'm in a conference room with a dozen people. I didn't think it required a police escort."

"Sophie, we agreed you'd get your coffee somewhere else."

Anthony had the professional law enforcement edge to his voice.

"I didn't come here for coffee; I'm working. Relax, the meeting just wrapped. I'm headed for the door as soon as you hang up."

"I'm calling your office in fifteen. If you aren't there, I'm coming to find you."

"Don't you think you're overreacting?"

"Sophie, how long did Gregory stalk you?"

Gray Jay. Seeing his face, I let out a sigh. I'd done the math.

"Five years—but he was harmless."

"Yeah, because he killed himself instead of you. It's barely a month since you saw this guy and that doesn't mean he hasn't seen you."

"Are you trying to scare the shit out of me?"

"Sophie, I've seen this before. Some people just send out a vibe. All I'm saying is you have a history and I'm not taking any chances. Will you please call me as soon as you get to your desk?"

"Relax, I'm on my way."

Leaving the receiver on the counter, I made a beeline for the conference room. The meeting was breaking up as I blew through to leave by the back exit. Amy tried to catch my eye, but I ducked out onto the street. My car was half a block away, a silver Jetta. Hopping in, I tried not to hit anyone as I backed out. I told myself there was no rush—the hospital was downtown. With light traffic, it wouldn't take longer than ten minutes to get back.

Four blocks from Grounds, my engine died.

No check engine light, no loud noise, just silence and a dark instrument panel. The only time I had a car die like that was when the alternator went out on my Impala in college. My Jetta was a year old. The car was still coasting a good 20 mph when I spotted a tow zone and slid into it. At least no one could claim I'd parked there for anything other than the designated purpose.

Not that I cared.

All I was thinking about was getting to a phone so Tony wouldn't put out an APB on me. Up the street, I spotted a phone kiosk. Old school, but I had quarters; this could work. Quickly reaching the kiosk, I was about to pick up the receiver when I saw the keypad on the phone was missing.

"I'm afraid that phone is out of service."

The voice was calm, perfectly modulated. For a moment, I imagined the phone company really had been implanting chips in people's brains. Standing at the curb, I saw him leaning against a black BMW.

"I'm cursed." I was surprised that my voice was normal.

"I would like to help you if you'll let me."

"You can get me out of trouble as easily as you can get me in. I'm not interested."

"I know it's asking a lot for you to trust me, but if I'd meant to harm you, that would have happened by now."

"Thanks, I feel safer already."

"I only want to speak with you alone."

"If you're trying to keep me from leaving school, you're a month too late."

"I know."

"If you're going to tell me to dump Anthony, you should know I don't take relationship advice from stalkers."

To this he had no reply. His expression was impassive but knowing.

I threw my purse on the ground.

"I knew it! God! I thought I was going crazy. It was you, wasn't it? You're the—the voice—*the thing with the milk!* Christ, you're in my head. You're worse than a stalker!"

"Can I give you a ride?"

"Give me a ride? No! I want off the ride! Thank you!"

"In less than ten minutes, Anthony will be calling your desk."

I made a short laugh. "You're good."

"That wasn't me."

"And my cell phone? My car? Coincidence?"

"I didn't want you to call him if you saw me. It hasn't been easy to approach you. All I ask is you hear me out. After, you can do whatever you want."

"You're the second guy to tell me that."

"I'm the first to mean it."

This pissed me off until I realized the stranger wasn't the only man I'd been hiding from all morning. Sensing a way out, I wanted to take him at his word.

"How long is this hearing out going to take?"

"Longer than you have to get back to your desk in time."

My arms crossed. "I've pretty much written off making that deadline."

He approached, stooping to pick up my purse. When he offered it, our eyes met.

"I'll get you there in time."

The words echoed in my head.

Snatching my purse from his hand, I watched him return to his car and casually open the passenger door. Waiting on the sidewalk, his gaze rested on me, bluer than any sea. He was the devil. Had to be. But where do you run? I'd seen all the movies. You couldn't kill the devil. I didn't even believe in God. I was screwed.

Taking a breath, I walked up to his car and dropped into the front seat. The door barely seemed to close than we were moving through traffic. His eyes never left the road. Mine traced his profile for browsing mug shots later. It would be easy to spot. It was perfect.

And perfectly unbelievable.

But I had to believe this was real. We had come to some unspoken agreement. I would hear him out and he wouldn't bother me again.

Unless, I agreed to bear his children and burn for an eternity in hell.

It was my best guess at what he wanted, and it appeared it would have to do. He said nothing in the car. I expected he would ask to meet somewhere at least, but he seemed to have made up his mind and further input from me was unnecessary. He parked in front of the hospital and walked around to open my door. I was already out of the car.

Slamming the door shut, I stared him down.

"What do I tell him?"

"That's up to you. You can tell him everything, something, or nothing."

"That's it?" I glared at him. "All this cat and mouse to ask me to meet with you?"

"I wanted to do it in person."

"Next time use a Post-It and shove it up your ass."

I stormed into the building.

You're welcome.

"If my car gets towed, you're paying for it!" I yelled over my shoulder.

Intent unknown. Memory forgotten. Thought wasted.
The end is beyond sight. Metatron will not see it.
Lost is the way. Lost it will stay. Lost are they.

[Spharic. First triptych of the last prophetic line
translated from *Ho Pro Fanai*. d. 0]

2003 "What exit are we supposed to take?"

"Hmm?" I don't look up from my book.

"What exit are we supposed to take?" His voice repeats like a recording of itself.

"I don't remember."

"Kate e-mailed you directions."

I look over at Mike as he stares at the road.

"So?" I go back to reading. "I didn't bring them."

"What if we get lost?"

"You don't get lost; that's a metaphysical impossibility."

"What if something unexpected happened?"

"What's wrong? Something in your third eye?"

"I'm not infallible."

"Well, then …" Briefly, I glance up. "We're getting a divorce when we get back."

"You've been very quiet."

"Be a lot quieter if I was sleeping."

"I thought talking made you feel better."

Closing my book, I shift in my seat so I can look at him.

"Okay."

"You're unhappy about staying with the cousins this weekend."

"Check."

"You're also unhappy about what Marta told you about Mrs. Farrell."

"Check."

"But it isn't really about either the cousins or Mrs. Farrell."

I say nothing.

He looks me full in the face. "Am I right?"

"Don't stop; you're good."

He looks back at the road. "You don't want to feel better."

There is resignation in his voice. Resentment.

I take a breath. "Then there's nothing left to say."

Shifting back in my seat, I open my book and try to find where I left off.

"No, please, say something."

"Like what?" I pretend to read. "I wish you were a person and not a pooka?"

"You regret marrying me?"

"That's a rhetorical question coming from you."

A hand squeezes my heart.

What can I do?

His thought is gentle in my mind.

I stop reading. "There's nothing to do, Michael. That's love. It has ups, it has downs. I'm down. I'll forget about it … probably as soon as Duane opens his mouth."

Returning to my book, I feel my hand reach for his lap.

His hand grasps it in an instant.

He doesn't let go until we are parked in the cousins' drive.

The "cabin" is a cedar-shingled two-story with low eaves, gray stain, and distressed French doors. The front yard appears recently landscaped with bunched sea grasses and driftwood carefully arranged to look natural. A red Hummer is parked in front of a detached garage.

Duane is the first out to greet us. His wiry frame is kinetic energy layered in Polartec, topped with straw-colored hair. Typically, his first instinct is to greet Michael. Man-to-man relations are a priority in Duane's social hierarchy of needs, though I admit, his attempts to impress Mike hold a unique entertainment value.

Mike doesn't wait for Duane to come to his side of the car. He is already getting our bags from the trunk, so his hands are full when Duane tries to high-five him. The high-five is Duane's favorite way to greet a man he considers a buddy.

"Hey, Mike! Let me help you with those." Duane volunteers.

Mike is already heading for the house, the luggage of no consequence.

"Thanks, I got it. Nice place."

"Sophia!" Duane takes hold of my shoulders to plant a kiss on each cheek.

"Hey, Duane, thanks for inviting us. It's been a while since we've seen you guys."

"Kate's really been looking forward to catching up with you."

"How is she?" I start up the faux cobbles to their front door.

"Big as a barn." He laughs from behind me.

"Every girl's dream." I mumble under my breath.

Kate waits at the bottom of a flight of stairs, one hand on the banister and one on her belly. Dressed in black chenille, she is a younger version of Maeve and an older version of me. With the same hair and eyes, we were mistaken for sisters growing up. I asked Kate if it bothered her in-laws that she had a slightly Asian appearance. She said Duane's dad told him everyone knew Asian was the "other white meat."

"If you'll excuse me, ladies, I'm going to check on the chowder." Duane gives a wink and disappears down a hall that I guess leads to the kitchen.

"He's really happy with his chowder recipe. It's a favorite with his tailgating buddies."

Not able to approach her head on, I reach around Kate's shoulders and give her a squeeze from the side. She is clearly very expectant and very happy.

I grin. "You've changed."

"I'll say, and from what I've been hearing, I'll never be the same again."

"When's the drop date?"

"April twentieth, give or take a week." She crosses her fingers.

"Sounds worse than waiting for the cable guy."

She squeezes my arm with a squeal. "But this is way bigger than cable!"

She looks like she is about to tip over; I grab her arm.

"Whoa, you okay?"

She takes a few breaths to steady herself. "I'm just excited; it's been really hard for me to unwind." She perks up before I say anything. "I'm so glad you could make it.

It was Duane's idea to get in a little quiet time before the next eighteen years."

"Well." I glance around. "If you're looking for a quiet time, Mike's your guy."

Kate points upstairs. "He already went up. I hope he didn't get lost."

She starts climbing and I brace myself to catch her.

When she looks back at me, I shrug casually. "I tell him to get lost all the time—hasn't worked yet."

My cousin gasps a laugh. "I don't know why he puts up with you, Sophie."

"He thrives on abuse."

At the top of the stairs, I see Michael emerge from a room at the end of the hall. Generally unnervingly sedate, he seems unusually tense.

Kate calls to him. "Oh good, you went to the right one. The other guest room has a bad heater." She glares over her shoulder at me. "Just one of many things that didn't get done right."

As I pass my husband in the hall, I nod at the stairs. "Duane's in the kitchen."

I pick up the conversation with my cousin. "You should be a pro at dealing with contractors by now."

Kate rolls her eyes. "Not exactly how I like to spend my time, thank you."

"Maybe you guys need to stop building houses."

"Oh this *is* the last one, believe me. Especially with a bun in the oven."

Reaching the end of the hall, Kate points through the door of our guest room. "This is the room I would have put you in, anyway. Its got the view."

The room has a flat screen over a gas fireplace at one end and a king bed with a sea grass headboard at the other. To the right of the bed is a small walk-in closet. To the left is the bath. Most of the exterior wall is lined with double-hung windows overlooking Hood Canal. Toe, the only nice cat belonging to Kate, sniffs our bags on the bed.

"It's beautiful, Kate!" I go to the windows. "I don't think I'd go back to Bellevue if I had a place like this."

"That's my confession." She sighs. "I'd love to sell our place in Newport and just live here, but Duane will never leave his job, especially after his promotion. It's all he's wanted for such a long time."

"I see." Is the most diplomatic response I come up with.

When I look past Kate, I spot Michael standing in the hall like a statue.

Go talk to Duane.

He doesn't budge.

Chicken.

Kate continues, "And of course, there are the grandparents. Duane's family wants us to stay close, but I'm trying not to think that far ahead."

"Have you discussed this with him?" I glance back at Michael, but he is gone.

She smiles a knowing smile. "When I married Duane, I knew the Nelson family was part of the deal." With a shrug, she tosses up her hands. "Time to pay up."

I smile sympathetically.

The subject changes when Kate turns my attention to the finishes and décor of the bedroom. She shows me the master bedroom and the study before we return downstairs. We tour the great room, the AV room, the dining room, all following a Cape Cod theme à la Pottery Barn. Kate and Duane love antiques, but without any time to collect the real thing, they buy replicas of what they want. The end result is a look that is superficially pleasing and oddly artificial at the same time. The few antiques they do have, Michael gave them. Of course, my husband is older than his antiques and looks like he came from Pottery Barn, so I keep my opinions to myself.

The tour ends in the kitchen, where Duane's chowder simmers on the stove next to fresh corn bread.

"Where are the guys?" Kate looks out the dinette window. "Oh, found 'em. Looks like they're in the garage."

"Shocking."

"God, what is it with men and the internal combustion engine?" Kate rolls her eyes at me.

"Didn't you know?" I pat her on the shoulder. "It's the closest they can come to making a baby."

"Lucky thing they don't have to carry it around in them for nine months."

"Actually, when you think of it, cars and babies are a lot alike."

She nods thoughtfully. "They're expensive, noisy, smelly ..."

"But." I add. "You drive your car crazy instead of the other way around."

We decide to supervise our men and head for the garage through a utility door in the kitchen. Crossing the yard to the garage, I see Duane has the hood on the Hummer raised. So is his voice.

"I think the lousy mileage is worth it! I can go off-road anywhere I want in this. That's where gas beats the competition. A guy at the office bought some cutting-edge hybrid, but it's totally gutless. We'll never stop using gas because there isn't anything else out there that's better."

I listen for Michael's response.

"There are more efficient renewable fuel alternatives. The motivation to develop them has been discouraged while fossil fuels have offered short-term benefits to consumers at great profit to the petroleum industry. While humans choose expediency over sustainability, the damage to the environment could become irreversible."

The calm of his voice only sounds more alien when contrasted with Duane's complete lack of critical thinking skills.

"You really believe that? So what if the temperature goes up a couple degrees? Come on, if there were such great alternatives, you can't tell me someone wouldn't have jumped on it by now. America is built on the entrepreneurial spirit. I'll buy that the gas companies haven't been out to help the competition, but I don't believe for the last hundred years there's been a conspiracy to make the world dependent on oil. Oil won because it works and there's plenty of it. You can't run the world on wind mills and solar panels."

Mike doesn't give up.

"Oil and coal have had an inherent advantage in that the knowledge necessary to obtain and convert them is comparatively low. Only recently has the technology for renewable power developed to allow sustainable sources to be converted into practical and reliable sources of power. As human power consumption grows exponentially, it is short-sighted to write off experimental technology for failing to keep pace."

I wait for Duane to get personal. His arguments usually turn accusatory when confronted with facts.

"We still have plenty of oil. It's the alternative fuel people who are trying to manipulate the market with environmental disaster stories. If they weren't scaring people like you with global warming, who would spend the money to go all electric? You couldn't give me the power I need for this baby with electric alone. You drive a BMW. How many horses does that thing have?"

I interrupt. "Three sixty."

Duane drops the hood and sees us.

"Hey! You guys ready to eat?"

Kate folds her arms around her belly expectantly. "Your the cook tonight. You tell us."

"Although ... " I chime in. "He does have a point about your BMW, Mike."

My husband only takes a breath and glares at the sky over my head.

Winking at Mike, Duane rubs his hands. "Follow me, ladies and gentleman."

The rest of the evening is relatively painless. After introducing us to his famous chowder, Duane spends most of the evening giving us the play-by-play of how he finally scored his promotion. I can't help observing Kate's expression during the course of Duane's narration after what she said upstairs.

We don't linger after dinner. With the excuse of being tired from our drive, we retire early, but it's really so Michael can break into his stash of cookies. Although generally quiet, he is ominously so after three bowls of chowder and two servings of Kate's cobbler. Of our four pieces of luggage, only two contain clothes; the other two are full of food, mostly cookies and boxes of petit fours. In spite of these reserves, the weekend will be hard on him.

As I ready for bed, Michael is opening a bag of Orange Pim's.

"That wasn't bad." Wrapping my bathrobe around me, I stretch out on the bed.

He says nothing.

Sitting at the foot of the bed in his pajamas, he keeps his back to me, eating cookies while a woman sells griddles on QVC. He watches her make pancakes with all the apparent concentration of a kid watching cartoons on a Saturday morning.

"Duane's chowder was good."

He remains silent.

Rolling over, I nudge him with my foot.

Still no response.

"You're not a chicken."

Finishing a cookie, Mike reaches in the bag for another. Pulling one out, he offers it to me without taking his eyes off the TV. Sitting up in bed, I accept. As I bite into it, I consider the advantages of portable electric grills.

Sophie has agreed to meet me. Unfortunately, my plans to approach her at the coffee shop went amiss and I was forced to stop her on the street. It would have been less frightening to approach her in a familiar setting. I thought disabling her cell phone would have prevented any interference from Anthony, but his instincts were better than I realized. As a result, I was forced to intervene more assertively than I had wished, and now I'm afraid she is angry with me again.

I angered her the last time I spoke with her at the coffee shop, though I am still unsure why. She does not seem to display her temper as quickly with others. Her thoughts of me today were difficult. She is curious and I think she likes me. Still, she thought me the devil and shared some unpleasant images I would rather not be associated with. I fear these thoughts are spurred by some memory. If Daniel was angry with me, he would be perfectly justified. If Sophie ever remembers, she might never forgive me.

Perhaps I should have given more thought as to where we would meet, but given her reaction to me the last time, I was far from sure she would accept. The conservatory is undergoing repairs and will be a pleasant place to sit in the morning. Daniel liked gardens. I assume Sophie must as well.

Still, I am afraid.

I have pondered what to tell her. There is so much and so little. I must be as honest as I can. I have always tried. Sophie values the truth and I want to speak it, but I fear the truth I will offer isn't what she will care to know. I fear she will want to know everything about what I am and nothing about who I am. The mere fact of my existence will overwhelm her and my need for her friendship will seem pathetic by comparison. She will laugh at me.

But she has said yes. She has acknowledged me.

Right now, I cannot hope for more.

[Spharic. Entry translated from *Kor Dai Maihael*. Mund Dai. Nov 1999]

1999 "It was impossible to tell Anthony nothing of what happened after I left Grounds for Coffee. It was impossible to tell him everything. So I settled on something.

My car broke down, a co-worker drove by and I hitched a ride to the office, the car was probably being towed as we spoke. That was my story. Anthony said he would drive by the tow zone and see if my car was still there. If it was, he'd flag it so it wouldn't get towed; if it wasn't, he'd take care of it. He knew people.

Twenty minutes later, Anthony called to tell me my car was still there. Not only that, but he'd used his set of keys to get in and start it. It was running fine, but the check engine light was on. I told him I'd take it into my mechanic the next day. A car problem was also a great excuse to play hooky tomorrow. If I was lucky, I'd hear from the stranger and get our interview over with sooner rather than later.

I was feeling lucky.

In the morning, I woke well before I normally would. Any other day off I would have been tempted to sleep in, but that night I couldn't sleep.

Anthony left for his shift in early morning darkness. I heard him lock the door and listened to his footsteps fade down the stairs. If he'd known about my encounter, he would have put me under twenty-four-hour surveillance by now. If the stranger had been a normal stalker, I would have gladly accepted it. Who knew there was such a thing as a normal stalker, anyway?

But there is. Normal stalkers actually have to follow you to know what you're up to. Normal stalkers actually have to be in your presence to make themselves heard. Normally, stalkers are human.

I would have to take care of this myself. It seemed if I didn't hear the stranger out, he might not go away. Then again, maybe he would. Maybe I could simply order him out of my life. If I was forceful enough. Demanding enough. Cruel enough.

The rest of the morning, I searched for a routine. My Fruit Loops and juice were waiting for me, but no milk advisory went off in my head as I went to the refrigerator. No voice told me if Anthony had grabbed a bagel that morning or not. Leaving my purse behind in the apartment, I pocketed my keys in my sweats and pulled on my fleece cap. I'd called my mechanic the day before and arranged to leave my car. His garage was only eight blocks from our apartment. I planned to walk back by way of Wright Park and get in a short jog.

It was right after I dropped off my car that I heard it.

I'll see you at the conservatory.

I looked at my watch. Five after eight. Was the conservatory even open this early?

No.

There was no way I was meeting him alone at the conservatory.

I'm not going to hurt you.

I pulled my hat down over my ears as I strolled down the sidewalk. I tried to pretend I wasn't hearing it—that on a bright, beautiful fall morning, I wasn't scared to death.

Please, don't be frightened of me.
My pace quickened.
I would never hurt you, Sophie.
It knew what I was thinking. It knew where I was. It knew my name.
I was going insane.
I thought about checking myself into a hospital. Telling them I was hearing voices. God, I wasn't even thirty yet and I'd spend the rest of my life on medication. Maybe all the shit I'd done in school was finally catching up with me.
You're not going insane.
Like I'd take his word for it.
There's nothing wrong with you. It's me. I shouldn't be talking to you, I shouldn't …
A squirrel darted in front of me and froze, making me stop short at a curb. The voice had stopped. The squirrel and I stared at each other.
One of us had to say something.
"What are you?"
The squirrel looked at me like I was nuts.
I thought … I was a friend, but I'm not. I'm a stranger to you, less than that … worse. I was wrong to approach you the way I did. I'm sorry.
He was sorry?
I am. Please forgive me. I'm not very good at meeting people.
"Meeting people?"
The squirrel faced me, sniffing the air.
I like you.
The hair on the back of my neck stood up.
I'm sorry. I shouldn't have said that.
I was feeling Gray again. Feeling a dread that never left.
If you don't want to see me, I understand. I'll leave you alone. Please, Sophie. Don't feel this way. This isn't what I wanted. I'll leave and I won't bother you again.
Tears stung my eyes, but they were angry. "What do you want?"
There was no answer. The squirrel turned away. In the pit of my stomach, I felt panic.
To be friends.
"Friends?" I choked.
You don't believe me.
I did. I remembered sitting by the fire with him at Grounds. How he made me feel.
Did you like me?
I did. I wondered why we couldn't have met for coffee instead.
I've been trying to meet you for coffee for two years.
"But you never said anything!" My hands went in the air, sending the squirrel behind a telephone pole. "You can stall my car but you couldn't buy me a latte?"
Others have tried.
He was right. I'd never told a guy to drop dead, but it would have been redundant. When I looked up from the sidewalk, the trees bordering Wright Park were across the street. The conservatory waited on the other side.

We don't have to meet.

"I said I would." I wiped my eyes.

I pushed you. It was wrong. You didn't want to and you don't have to.

"Well, I'm almost there." As I stepped from the curb, the squirrel ran ahead of me, disappearing under a parked car.

Sophie, please don't come to the conservatory. I'm—Sophie! Stop!

It sounded like an overreaction.

When the UPS truck sped past, missing me by inches, I realized my body had taken the directive seriously. Catching a breath of exhaust, I backed up onto the curb and leaned against a lamp post.

Sophie? Are you all right?

"Jesus …" Every inch of me tingled with adrenalin. "Thanks."

My name is Michael.

"Michael, right." My morning OJ suddenly felt like it needed a chaser. "You sure we couldn't just meet in a bar?"

We shouldn't meet at all.

"I have to meet you." Checking both ways, I crossed the street into the park and started for the conservatory. "That was the deal, remember?"

Deal?

"I hear you out, and you stop stalking me."

I told you, you don't have to. I'll leave you alone, I promise.

Sniffing, I rubbed my nose. "I thought you wanted to be friends?"

There was silence.

"Michael?"

I do.

"Then we do this right."

Right?

"Start over."

Pretend we never met?

"I think we're past that." I glanced around me. "How about some ground rules?"

If you wish.

"Great. What the hell are you?"

Is that important?

"I can't be friends with someone I don't trust, and before that can happen, I'll need to know what I'm friends with."

I told you, my name is Michael.

"That's who you are, not what."

Isn't that more important than what I am?

"What you are says a lot about who you are."

For a moment, there was only the sound of gravel under my feet. I wasn't going to ask again. This was a deal breaker, and he knew it. My steps slowed as I looked up at the leaves beginning to turn. My head was silent. My thoughts still.

What do you think I am?

"A name's not much to go on."

What if I told you my name was what I was.

I felt myself smirk. "What's a Michael?"

There has only ever been one.

"What do you mean? Half the guys I know are named Michael. You sound like that guy on *Highlander.*"

I mean I am the first. I was Michael before the dawn of living memory and will be when all is past.

Nodding, I took a breath. "Okay. *The* Michael." I stopped in my tracks. "Whoa, like the angel?"

Does it make you feel better?

I blinked. "Kinda."

Because I'm not the devil?

"That's a plus."

And because I won't want to have sex with you?

"Um." I try not to go there. "It lowers the stakes."

The stakes are always high for me.

My feet began to move again. "Why?"

You could still send me away.

"Why does it sound so bad when you say it? Like I'm tossing you in a pit?"

That is what it feels like to be alone.

"The risk of getting tossed would be lower if you weren't stalking me."

I'll stop.

"Thank you."

Sophie?

"Yes?"

What's the difference between stalking you and seeing you?

"Well, normally a guy would call ahead to let me know he wanted to see me."

Isn't that what I did?

"On a phone. Uninvited telepathy definitely falls under stalking."

I'm sorry. From now on I'll call.

"And only after asking for my number."

I already know your number.

"Stalking." I pitched my voice.

Sorry. May I have your number?

"You already have it."

May I use it?

"You may."

Should I call Anthony, too?

My lips slipped between my teeth. "Let's wait on that."

Shouldn't he know we're seeing each other?

Feeling my thoughts were an open book, I tried to move the conversation along.

"We're just getting to know each other; let's take it one step at a time."

He doesn't like me.

"Is that why you tried to tell me I didn't love him?"

You don't love him.

I stopped walking again. "What?!"

A passing jogger looked over his shoulder at me.

I'm sorry. That is none of my business.

"Damn straight." I mumbled as I began to march down the gravel path. "Why would you say something like that? How would you know?"

You're right. I don't.

As I crossed the bridge over the duck pond, his words ate at me.

"You don't even have any friends. What do you know about love?"

Your friendship is all I have ever known. I know nothing about love.

"See, you still sound like a stalker." I shook my head. "When you make it sound like we've been friends and we don't even know each other, that's creepy."

I'm sorry. I'll stop.

"Anthony's a good man."

He is.

"A little overprotective, but he's a cop, right?"

Of course.

"You're going to stay away from him, right?"

Of course.

"You promise?"

I promise.

"No telepathy, no tricks."

I never play tricks on people.

"That's why my car's in the shop right now."

That wasn't—that was wrong of me. I was trying to speak with you and I didn't know how. I angered you when we last met at the coffee shop. I angered you when I spoke to your thoughts. You never came back for coffee and I didn't want to go to your apartment. Anthony was always watching and if I called you on the phone—

"Post-Its." I cut him off.

I didn't know about Post-Its.

"Now you do."

Anthony doesn't make it easy for a man to get close to you.

"Fair enough; then again, you're not a man, are you?"

I don't have wings.

"So, you're not really an angel?"

Angels don't have them either.

"So, you are?"

If I want to be, I shouldn't meet with you anywhere, let alone a conservatory.

"It sounds like we're both taking a risk."

Everything has its price.

"Then why risk paying it? Why are you here?"

The conservatory was clearly in sight, hugging the crest of a hill overlooking the park. As I climbed to it, I realized I was feeling unusually out of breath. I realized I could see his face in my mind and was curious to see it again.

I realized I was waiting for no one to answer me.

"Michael?"

There was no answer.

By the time I reached the conservatory doors, I was running.

They were shut. A sign in the glass said they were closed for renovations. My eyes focused on my reflection, panting at me on sweating panes. Without looking at the door handle, I felt my hand reach for it and pull. It opened.

For a moment I stood there, feeling the warm draft of damp air on my face. If he had wanted to hurt me, he could have let the UPS truck do the job.

I stepped inside, the humidity of the place suffocating me instantly.

"Michael?"

In the foyer of the conservatory, two wings stretched away on either side of me. One led to a gallery and gift shop, one into a jungle that wasn't. I went into the jungle. Following a narrow path, my eyes didn't know what to look for as I wandered blind turns. Spiny trees, bound in vines and clinging orchids, blotted out the sunlight overhead. A serpentine koi pond rippled at my feet. The fish swam from my approach, leading the way. Rounding a curtain of ti leaves, I came to the waterfall I'd been hearing since I entered the garden. A bench faced it, empty save for a book: my used copy of *Overview of the American Judiciary*. As I neared, I saw a note on the cover. I picked up the book with both hands.

It was written on a Post-It.

My fingers ran across the paper.

It was real. He was real. I wasn't crazy.

Checking myself into Western State Mental Hospital wasn't the answer.

Tucking the book under my arm, I ran from the conservatory on a mission.

But I had to go back to the apartment first.

I'd left my library card in my purse by the door.

The downtown library was blissfully empty on a weekday afternoon. Commandeering a table in the back of the reference section, I began to load it with any book I could find relating to spiritual, religious, mythological, and/or paranormal subject matter. It was a lot of books. As I read, I tried to narrow my selection process to those volumes that looked well researched, including non-Western beliefs and female authors when I could find them.

I decided to start with what I had to go on, which pretty much began and ended with his name. Of all my questions, it was the only thing he was firm on. The problem was I couldn't find anything firmer than that in any of the books I pulled. It was possible the problem was with me. I wasn't religious or even superstitious. My parents hadn't raised me in a particular church, and outside of required courses in comparative theology, my understanding, let alone interest, in things spiritual was fleeting. Thus, between theology and myth, superstition and legend, they all seemed equally incredible to me. This was the opposite of what I was trying to find: credible evidence of what Michael really was.

Scientifically, the results weren't much better. Disappointing, but not surprising. Though I embraced the realm of scientific discovery as essential to our evolution as a species for good or ill, I didn't lie awake at night wondering if there was intelligent life in the universe. Beyond the occasional sci-fi flick, I didn't worry about alien invasions, UFOs, government conspiracies, or Roswell. Somewhere along the way, science and I had both decided the expenditure of thought on alien life beyond what was immediately tangible strayed too close to the nutty bin. As a result, theorizing about intelligent life other than our own seemed to be left to, well, the nuts. There was no shortage of those books in the library. And I wasn't in the fiction section.

Five hours later, I was finished scouring the stacks and returned to my table empty-handed. My stomach was equally empty. I was about to abandon my research for the nearest deli, when something caught my eye. A Post-It note on a book.

I thought you would find this informative.

Looking around, I saw no one on the floor, nor had I heard anyone while I was there. I'd have to remember to amend our definition of stalking the next time we spoke. Turning my attention to the book, I removed the Post-It from the cover, *Conceptions of Contemporary Faith* by Virginia Carpio, 1978. I raised my brows and wondered how I'd missed seeing it. At least I had something worth checking out. Adding it to the pile of books that made the cut, I went to the check-out desk.

A short, cherubic man grinned at me as I handed him my card.

"You'll get your exercise today." He eyed the hefty collections of mythology and religious archeology I strained to slide over to him.

"I'm dating my professor. He likes to talk about this stuff over dinner."

He wasn't fooled.

"Good one. If you'd said, 'Just doing a little light reading,' I would have been disappointed."

I feigned injury. "You don't think I could bag a professor?"

He made a face as he scanned my books. "As a public servant, I am not at liberty to discuss it."

"You're no fun." My brow arched. "I thought behind the Dewey Decimal System, librarians were a bunch of social anarchists." I began to bag my books.

"I'm no snitch." He smiled at me and then frowned as he picked up the book Michael had left. "Where did you find this?"

I shrugged. "On a table."

"It isn't one of ours. Someone must have left it behind."

"No one was around where I found it."

With a grin, he slid it back to me with a wink. "I'm no snitch."

~

[*Archangel Michael Casting the Enemies of God from Heaven*. Guido Reni.
Plate from *Conceptions of Contemporary Faith*. V. Carpio. d. 1978]

...The origin of angels is rooted in spiritual beliefs predating the written word. Not surprisingly, our earliest interpretations are significantly different from how we identify them today. Pre-Christian cultures first gave name to them as ambiguous spirits, without wings, gender or association to any particular deity. All early humans appear to have shared this belief at some time. The universal traits of such spirits being they were not of human origin, superior to humans in ability and intellect, but inferior to gods. Indifferent to the plight of mankind, they were both feared and worshipped, seen as both potentially dangerous or helpful depending on their inclinations.

Given these early beliefs predate most written records, there remains controversy over the evolution of individual angels, whether they were named before the gods they were later associated with or in some cases even became the gods themselves. It is well known gods of Egypt, India, and the Greco-Roman world were capable of appearing in the guise of animals and people. Whether these accounts were originally recorded as intercession by the gods themselves or by an angelic emissary remains unresolved.

Christianity shares in this confusion. Some interpretations of the Old Testament describe Moses receipt of the Ten Commandments as taken from God himself, while others claim an angel delivered the word of God. The angel is sometimes identified as Michael, but often remains unnamed. The angels that wrestle Jacob, stay the hand of Abraham, and warn Lot, remain unidentified. In these instances. it could be surmised their names were expunged in an effort to emphasize their function as an extension of God over being an emissary. Stripped of names, the individuality and eventually the free will of angels recedes. That Christianity classifies angels as subservient to God, but capable of exercising free will ultimately becomes an attempt to reconcile later monotheistic belief with a historical record of inscrutable angelic deeds.

Michael is a prime example of the evolution of angel from roaming spirit, to advocate of men, to messenger of God, to saint. Of all the angels in western belief, Michael is easily the most prevalent. Early records from Babylon to Phoenicia, Egypt to Israel, Greece and Rome all evidence a spirit named Mael, Mahal, Maihael, Mikal, and many other variants of the same name. In spite of this prevalence, there is disagreement as to his intent and purpose, which only the exercise of free will might excuse.

Early accounts of Michael depict a sometimes male, sometimes female, spirit that was a guide to the lost and a healer of the sick. Most famous for casting Satan out of Heaven, this story is neither recorded in the Old Testament nor Apocryphal texts, but is strictly Catholic in origin. Old Testament records of Michael's accomplishments show an occasional, if not inconsistent, advocate of men. These inconsistencies continue into modern times, where he both is a defender of Israel and patron saint of Germany.

Currently accepted by the Catholic Church as the principal archangel of the lowest order of angels, he has been called upon as a warrior and pacifist healer, a protector of the innocent and destroyer at the end of days. This confusion of roles reinforces a persistent ambiguity surrounding the angel myth. Perhaps it is this very ambiguity that gives Michael a humanity which has helped to popularize him. As the patron saint of firefighters and policemen, he exemplifies the thin line between justifying uncertain means to accomplish unpredictable ends.

[Excerpt from *Conceptions of Contemporary Faith*. V. Carpio. d. 1978]

2003 The next morning, I awake to the sight of three empty cookie bags on the bedside table. Michael is already gone, out on a run with Duane, who is a pathological marathoner. I spot two ransacked bakery boxes next to our luggage. Petit fours, breakfast of champions.

The night before, Duane shared his plan of getting up before dawn to go for a run, but I lied about a sore knee. My husband, always prepared to run interference, dutifully volunteered to join Duane in my stead. Duane and Michael had gone running before—whenever there was a family gathering it was their opportunity to do some male bonding. This left me alone with Kate for some bonding of our own.

I find her in the kitchen, taking stock of the food for our Easter dinner. A giant ham is dressed and sitting in a heavy Creuset on the stove.

"Jesus, that's the biggest ham I've ever seen."

"It's Biblical; just don't say Jesus in front of Duane! You know how he is about that, especially on Easter." Kate laughs to soften the admonishment.

"Thanks, I always forget." Not really. "That does bring to mind my surprise that you guys chose this weekend to get away. I thought Duane's family would be churchin' it up today."

"Clark and Maxine flew to Arizona to spend the weekend with Ken and the grandkids. Ken bought the tickets ..." She gives me a look with a raised brow.

"Oh." I raise my brows back at her.

"Apparently, Ken's working on the side now and has some investment property he's interested in. Duane thinks it's more than coincidental this is the year his brother suddenly wanted to spend quality time with Mom and Dad."

"I'm sure his dad is aware of that, too."

"That's what I told Duane, but he's still hot about it. Anyway, he wanted to stay away from Kirkland this weekend to try to forget about it. It would have kept coming up at the church potluck, anyway; they all know his parents and where they went this weekend. Those people know everything about you once you join the flock."

"Well, I hope Duane doesn't feel deprived of the Spirit of the Lord this weekend on our account." I go to the refrigerator and look for some juice.

Kate starts to laugh. "On the contrary, he's on his mission right now. He thinks Michael is ripe for conversion."

"No!" I nearly drop the carton of OJ.

"You had to see it coming!" Kate joins me at the refrigerator to pull out breakfast ingredients. "Duane thinks Mike has all of the qualities of ideal manhood except he isn't spiritual enough."

I laugh out loud as Kate takes a glass from the cupboard and pours my juice.

"I'm sorry." I pull myself together. "This is so perfect, I can't even tell you."

"What's so funny? I mean, aside from Duane driving Mike nuts this weekend."

"You might be surprised." I take a swig of my juice. "Mike's more spiritual than he looks."

"Really? Was he raised in a church?"

"Not really." I scratch my ear. "Let's just say he knows the topic."

"Did he study religion in college?" Kate paused. "Come to think of it, after all this time, I don't know your husband's alma mater. Where'd he go to school?"

"U. W."

"So did Duane. What year?"

"You know, I'm not sure off the top of my head. I'll have to ask him."

"What did he study?"

"Standard liberal arts. Comparative theology is kind of a hobby for him is all. Mike has some strong opinions he keeps to himself."

"Oh dear."

"Don't worry." I grin. "It'll make for an interesting car ride home."

Duane and Mike return while Kate and I are getting brunch ready. They pass through the kitchen by way of the utility door. Duane looks exhausted while Michael looks like someone who ran around the block a couple times.

"I swear I could smell that bacon a mile away. It was the only thing that got me back!" Duane pulls off his hat and pecks Kate on the cheek. "Morning, sweet pea."

"Do I get one of those?" I look at my own husband expectantly.

As he leaves the kitchen, he leans over and plants a kiss. "I'm going to clean up; be down in a minute."

"You didn't call me sweet pea."

"Sweet pea." He calls back over his shoulder.

Watching him disappear down the hall, I see him skip up the stairs to our room four at a time. In spite of his vigor, I am worried. Over brunch, I watch Michael eat six poached eggs when normally he would eat a dozen.

"You can have more eggs if you want." Kate encourages him. "I know what it's like to be hungry all the time. I bought enough food for ten of us this weekend."

What would ten people eat in four days? I wonder if it would be enough for Mike. Probably. If the rest of us weren't here ...

"If I ran like Mike does I could eat enough for ten people." Duane is finished at four eggs. "I can't believe you don't compete."

We look at Michael, who hasn't looked up from his plate since he sat down.

"Michael isn't a very competitive person." I answer for him.

"Where did you guys run?" Kate reaches for the toast.

"To tell the truth I kinda got lost, but Mike seemed to know where we were."

We look at Michael again. Finishing his food, he answers. "We did a loop."

Duane shrugs back at Kate and me. "We did a loop."

"Did you have any revelations on your loop?" I ask as Kate big-eyes me.

Mike and Duane look at each other, and Duane laughs. "Just the usual guy stuff."

Kate shoots me a look. "Apparently, not something us girls need to know about."

"That's what guys always say." I smile sweetly at Mike. "But we always get it out of them sooner or later."

"Really?" He grins.

Rising from the table, I pick up my empty plate and walk around to collect his. "Mealtime's over."

After helping the cousins round up the remains of brunch, I slip upstairs.

Michael surprises me the moment I walk in our room. His approach is never something I get used to. It is wonderful, like being washed over by a flood of warm light. I hold his arms away to get a look at him. He must be tired, but his face looks almost normal. Still flush from his morning run, he looks as though he has blood in his veins. His skin is more than warm, almost hot. But the eyes never look human, even less so when he is aroused. Now, they burn like blue coals.

He reaches to stroke the side of my face. He whispers in my head. The rest of the world seems to melt away. I'm about to destroy his clothes, but—

A part of me worries.

What is it?

"Are you sure you're up for this?" I feel his hands in my hair.

Don't worry about me.

"What if something happens?" I smell the sweet scent of his breath.

A metaphysical impossibility.

"You said you weren't infallible." I taste the electricity on his lips.

It's our anniversary.

"You'll be exhausted." I see the irises of his eyes are blind with light.

I'm not a chicken.

"What if they hear us?"

He picks me up and carries me to the bed. Saying nothing, he unzips my sweater and starts to kiss my neck. My ears fill with the rush of his blood.

They're watching a movie.

I begin to relax. Running my fingers through his hair, I pull him to me, kiss him deeply, inhaling his breath, which, in denial of the heat of his skin, is bitter cold.

My rational mind is annoyed by this reckless abandon.

"Which movie?" it whispers between kisses.

I hear him chuckle as the tip of his nose traces a line between my breasts.

Harvey.

We spend most of the afternoon in our room. Not that there is an encore session. That is beyond his capacity. He is tired to the point of physical weakness and will sleep until dinner when he will rejoin us to slay the Biblical ham.

Leaving my husband to recover from recent events, I wander downstairs to see if I can help with dinner. The house is filled with the smell of ham and Kate's famous hot cross buns. I find my cousin emptying a bag of carrots in the sink.

"Let me peel those."

"Awesome! That is the least pleasant thing to prepare for dinner tonight. I always cut myself."

"Then by all means, allow me to take the cutting." I put out my hand as she hands me a peeler.

Silently, I go to work.

"So …" Kate fishes nonchalantly. "Did you get it out of him?"

"He's still suffering for his insolence." I smile at her grin. "How was *Harvey*?"

She laughs as she turns out a hot tin of buns. "I didn't think we had the volume that high! I love that movie. When I was a kid, I never understood why you couldn't see Harvey. Now I wonder why he looks like a rabbit. I mean, if he can do all the things he does in the movie, why can't he just look like a person instead of an invisible, six-foot-tall rabbit."

"Good point. Maybe he's invisible because he can't make himself seen to more than one person?"

"But why a rabbit?"

"Maybe he thinks he isn't as frightening as a rabbit? He's much more endearing as a rabbit, anyway."

"I don't think I'd want a six-foot rabbit hanging around all the time."

How a six-foot rabbit could be worse than Duane is debatable. I'd take the rabbit.

"Of course." Kate continues slowly. "You would have the perks of a pooka."

I smile. "One can only imagine what those would be."

We snicker as Kate slides an apple pie in the oven.

"Hey there, ladies!" Duane steps into the kitchen from the side door with an armful of wood. "It smells amazing in here."

"I thought you had a gas fireplace." I ask.

"Heavens no! Not for downstairs!" Kate interjects. "Duane had to have the real thing for the cabin."

"That's part of what having a cabin is all about!" Duane plays indignant as he heads for the great room. "Men get soft when they forget the basics, like chopping their own wood and building a fire."

"With fat wood from Lands' End and a Bic lighter." Kate mumbles.

"I've got a pile of these carrots going, Kate. Where do you want 'em?"

"Oh, I've got a pot for those." She bends over and pulls open a pot drawer. After some rummaging, she lifts out a pot but drops it.

"*Ah!*"

She leans against the counter with a gasp and holds her stomach.

"Kate!" I rush to hold her up. "What's going on? Duane!"

"It's nothing." She squeaks. "Just a little shot across the bow."

Duane flies into the kitchen and scrutinizes his wife with a taut expression on his face.

"What happened?"

"She was picking up a pot and she just about collapsed. Is she okay? Should we get to a hospital?"

Kate grabs my hand. "No, you guys! I'm fine. See, everything's fine. It was just a false alarm. Just get me to that chair."

Duane catches my expression as we help her across the kitchen to the dinette.

"The doctors told us to keep an eye out. Maeve had preeclampsia when she had Kate. The specialist told us it was slight, but there was a possibility she might go into labor early, but not this early. They said she didn't need to be near a hospital till the last two weeks."

"You realize the nearest hospital is probably in Bremerton." My accusation is clear.

"Oh!" Kate is crushing my hand. "I think I'm wet."

"Shit." I glare at what looks like rust-tinged water trickling down the chair leg. My glare shifts to Duane. "I think the kid's coming anyway. Call 911."

"I can drive her."

"The hell you can! You'll both get killed. You can't fly through traffic all the way to Bremerton with her in the back seat."

"I can't wait for an ambulance to get here! I could be halfway to the hospital by then!"

I grab Duane by his jacket. "The only reason I'm asking is because I don't know your address. Call 911 or I will!"

Duane pulls his cell out of a pocket and dials.

Getting on my knees, I look in Kate's eyes. "You want to lie down?"

She nods with her lips pursed.

"Okay. We'll keep you here. I'll get some pillows for you. Don't try to walk anywhere. Try to keep breathing; don't hold your breath." I have no idea what I'm telling her, but it sounds reasonable.

Running into the great room, I grab a couple cushions from a sofa and run back to the kitchen. I drop the cushions in front of Kate and glance at Duane. He is still on the phone as I get my arms around Kate and slowly lower her onto the floor.

Michael, I need some help here.

Kate begins to shriek as I grab some kitchen shears and start to cut away her sweats.

Jesus.

At least I didn't say it out loud.

Michael, wake up!

I shout to Duane. "Get us some towels and a blanket!"

The words are barely out of my mouth when a pile of towels appear on the chair Kate had been sitting on. I look up into my husband's face, a ghastly white mask in the light of their kitchen.

Michael kneels next to me as I get out of the way for him.

Duane comes up behind us with towels and a blanket. "What's he doing?"

Looking back over my shoulder, I put up a hand.

"He can help her, Duane. Mike's had some experience with childbirth." I turn my head and whisper in Michael's ear. "You have, right?"

He smirks at me. "Sit down behind her and brace her with your arms."

Propped back on her hands and wet with sweat, Kate is trying to breathe but looks pale and faint. Grabbing a blanket from Duane, I wrap her shoulders before having her fall back against me. Her pain seems to have subsided but not by chance. With his hands on her abdomen, Michael's face is blank. His eyes stare at nothing, and I realize for the first time that they are still black.

"It'll be coming soon." He whispers.

As though suddenly alive, Kate accepts his word. "How long?"

"Fifteen minutes, maybe twenty." His pronouncement is final.

"So soon?" Duane is on his cell again. "They'll be here in twenty minutes."

"It can't be longer." Michael looks at me as he says this. No telepathy is needed to read his thoughts. He turns his gaze to Kate. "You have to push."

"But I don't feel anything."

Michael adjusts his hands on her abdomen. "How about now?"

"Ah!" Kate tenses in my arms and sharply inhales.

"Push, Kate." Mike gently urges. "Breathe and push. This is what those classes were for."

Kate nods and keeps working.

For the next fifteen minutes, the only sound is Kate's breathing and Duane's voice on the cell phone. Duane goes outside to stand at the end of the drive where the ambulance can find us in the growing dark. I stare at the clock over the stove, counting minutes that seem too slow but not slow enough.

When the baby comes, it is the pinnacle of anti-climax.

It is quiet.

Michael quickly unwinds the umbilical cord from the infant's neck. Kate begins to sob uncontrollably.

She cries out. "Oh, Jesus! Is it dead? I can't tell … don't be dead." I hold her in my arms, covering her face.

"Towel." Mike says to no one in particular. I grab one off the chair and hand it to him. He takes it without looking up, wiping the infant vigorously. He puts his mouth to the baby's and then rolls it in his hands so it faces the floor.

I stare at my husband's face.

He knows I am trying to read him, knows what I am asking. I know he doesn't want to look at me. He doesn't want to see the question in my eyes. He breathes into the tiny mouth again, and again.

Finally, he looks at me.

Please, Michael. This can't happen.

I make one final appeal.

We'll never have one.

Closing his eyes he holds the infant to his mouth and breathes into it one more time.

It screams like it has been burned by fire. He carefully wraps the baby in the towel and almost perfunctorily hands it to Kate. "It's a boy."

Mike slides himself against the bank of kitchen cabinets and closes his eyes.

Wiping away sweat and tears, Kate is miraculously revived by the squalling bundle in her arms.

"Will he be all right?"

"He needs to get to a hospital, but he's healthy." Mike speaks without opening his eyes, his words beginning to slur.

The kitchen door opens and paramedics come in with a stretcher. Duane stands by looking like he is about to catch fire. As they gather Kate and the baby, I go to Mike, prodding him to get up. He seems to understand and manages to stand as I lead him out to the great room. Now that the sofa has been stripped of cushions, my goal is to get him to the AV room and beach him on one of the leather recliners.

In minutes, Duane finds us.

"Is he all right?"

"Yeah …" I try to downplay that he looks like a corpse. "Men and birthing. Never a good combo."

"We have to take off."

"Of course, Duane! Get out of here! It's your wife and baby for Christ's sake."

Oops.

Duane is too shot to notice my blasphemy and disappears.

Michael is fast asleep. Covering him with a throw, I return to the kitchen and inspect the food that has been diligently preparing itself during our life drama.

Opening the oven, I pull out the pie and put it on the stovetop. Next to the pie is the Creuset. Removing the lid, I smile. The ham is perfect.

"What are you eating?" My husband's voice is a whisper.

"Biblical ham. Want some?" I gnaw on a piece as I stare at the TV.

He lifts his head to look at the widescreen. "I hate this movie."

"Easter wouldn't be the same without Edward G." Before biting into a hot cross bun, I pause. "Was Ramses really that ripped?"

"The costumes are ridiculous; no one dressed like that."

"When it comes to ridiculous, I don't think the costumes are the only contributing factor. The special effects are pretty dated, but the night the Angel of Death kills the first born of pharaoh really scared me when I was a kid. That wasn't you, was it?"

"God." Michael drops his head back on the recliner and covers his face with an arm.

"Enough shop talk. Here," I hand him my plate, still heaped with food. "That'll get you ready for Moses."

He takes my plate and looks at the slice of ham on it. "I need a fork."

"You're kidding. You didn't hang with humans before silverware?"

He glares at me with impotent menace.

I wrinkle my nose. "I'll get you some silverware."

1999 an*gel *n* [ME, fr. OE *engel* & OF *angele*; both fr. LL *angelus*, fr. Gk *angelos*, lit., messenger] (bef. 12c) 1 a : a spiritual being superior to man in power and intelligence; *specif* : one in the lowest rank in the celestial hierarchy b *pl* : an order of angels – see CELESTIAL HIERARCHY 2 : an attendant spirit or guardian 3 : a white-robed winged figure of human form in fine art 4 : MESSENGER, HARBINGER <~of death> 5 : a person believed to resemble an angel 6 *Christian Science* : inspiration from God 7 : one (as a backer of a theatrical venture) who aids or supports with money or influence

angel dust *n* (ca. 1968) : PHENCYCLIDINE

Either definition could have explained Michael.

apoch*ry*pha *n, pl but sing or pl in constr* [ML, fr. LL, neut. pl. of *apochryphus* secret, not canonical, fr. Gk *apokryphos* obscure, fr. *apokryptein* to hide away, fr. *apo* + *kryptein* to hide – more at CRYPT] (14c) 1 : writings or statements of dubious authenticity 2 *cap* a : books included in the Septuagint and Vulgate but excluded from the Jewish and Protestant canons of the Old Testament – see BIBLE table b : early Christian writings not included in the New Testament

apoc*ry*phal *adj* (1590) 1 : of doubtful authenticity : SPURIOUS 2 *often cap* : of or resembling the Apochrypha syn see FICTITIOUS—

I doubted his authenticity, but he was definitely real.

de*mon *or* dae*mon *n* [ME *demon*, fr. LL & L; LL *daemon* evil spirit, fr. L, divinity, spirit, fr. Gk *daimon*] (13c) 1 a : an evil spirit b : an evil or undesirable emotion, trait, or state 2 *usu daemon* : an attendant power or spirit : GENIUS 3 *usu daemon* : a supernatural being of Greek mythology intermediate between gods and men 4 : one that has unusual drive or effectiveness < a ~for work>

Evil, no. Attendant, 'see STALKER'.

Fairy *n, pl* fairies [ME *fairie* fairyland, fairy people, fr. OF *faerie*, fr. *feie, fee* fairy, fr. L *Fata*, goddess of fate, fr. *fatum* fate] (14c) 1 : mythological being of folklore and romance usu, having diminutive human form and magic powers 2 : a male homosexual – often used disparagingly

[*Merriam-Webster's Ninth New Collegiate Dictionary* (1983). Springfield, MA: Merriam-Webster.]

Male homosexual. Possibly. He just wanted to be friends and couldn't shut up about my personal relationships.

At the sound of Anthony's key in the lock, I snapped the dictionary shut.
"Anybody home?"
"Hey, babe." I sang out. "How's the day?"
Anthony tossed his hat and keys on the coffee table. "Behind me."
"Want something to drink?"

"Absolutely."

"I think I saw that on a bottle somewhere around here. Let me check."

As I was getting his drink in the kitchen, Anthony leaned in the doorway.

"Hear from your mechanic?"

"Yeah." Handing him a shot, I poured a drink for myself. "He said it might have been a crossed wire somewhere. Basically my car shorted out, but he said he couldn't be sure. I don't think he has a clue, but he seems to think the car's safe to drive."

Anthony took a sip. "And what did that bullshit story set us back?"

"Couple hundred bucks."

"I'm in the wrong business."

"You get to crash cars and shoot people. Everything has its price." The words came out of my mouth before I recall where I'd heard them.

"So what else did you do today?" Tony glanced back at me as he walked into the dining room and took off his duty pistol. I followed him as he began to unbutton his shirt on his way to the bedroom.

"I was lazy. Jogged in the park, got groceries, cleaned the apartment, did some laundry."

"Your lazy beats anybody else's busy."

Standing in the bedroom doorway, I watched Tony undress. He wasn't as tall as Michael. Not as pristine, if you could say that where men were concerned. But he was a good-looking man. Trimly built with thick, black hair, an innate tan, and my favorite feature, deep green eyes.

He looked up at me and smiled.

"Taking it all in?"

"No holes."

"I do have a few scratches."

"Do they need kisses?"

"After I take a shower I'll show you, but trust me, not before. I don't want my BO to put you in the ER."

He tossed his wallet and badge on the dresser. Removing his St. Michael medal from his neck, he hung it, as he always did, on the lamp shade next to the bed.

As he passed, he pecked my cheek. I watched him disappear into the bathroom, then looked back into our bedroom. Crossing to his side of the bed, I plucked the medal off the lamp shade, dangling it in my palm.

I sat on the bed to scrutinize it.

It was gold-plated, a gift from his parents when he joined the force. On one side was an inscription with a prayer to St. Michael; on the other was a relief of Michael the Archangel holding a sword over a serpent pinned underfoot. I barely knew Michael, but I knew this wasn't him. St. Michael wasn't any more like the Michael I spoke with today than a character in a movie people confuse with the actor who plays it. But it was him in a way.

I smiled.

Returning the medal to the lamp shade, I flopped back on the bed and stared at the ceiling. In a few minutes, I heard the shower stop. Anthony came into the bedroom with a towel around his waist and a toothbrush in his mouth. He grabbed his bathrobe and pulled it on with a scowl on his face.

"It's freezing in here." He left to finish brushing his teeth.

I went to the bedroom window and bent over to feel if the heater was working. It didn't seem to be. I reached down to the thermostat to see if it tripped.

When I stood up, Anthony was behind me, pulling me back against him in a bear hug. He smelled like shampoo and aftershave; he was warm and soft. He began to kiss my neck. I glanced out the window to the parking lot and saw his patrol car in its usual spot. Beyond it, on the street, was a black BMW.

I stopped breathing.

Tony sensed my distraction.

"What is it?" He looked out the window suspiciously.

Two women approached the BMW and got in. I exhaled.

"Nothing, just thought I saw someone I knew."

Tony peered down at the two women in the car and watched it pull away from the curb.

"Nice wheels." He turned back to me, brushing my hair from my face.

"Yeah, nice." But my head was somewhere else.

We ordered out for pizza. There was a tavern nearby Anthony thought made a "sweet pie." He volunteered to pick it up alone, but I wanted to go with him.

"You don't have to come; it's cold out. You don't want to catch anything."

Pulling on my coat, I followed him down the stairs of our building.

"If I didn't want to catch anything, I'd be a nun in New Mexico."

"If you were a nun in New Mexico, I'd take the Holy Orders myself."

"Take 'em and break 'em, sounds like. Your parents would be shocked, a good Catholic boy like you."

Anthony linked his arm in mine as we strolled down the sidewalk.

"Catholic be damned, Sophie. God himself couldn't keep me from you. Well, maybe God, but no church ever could, and certainly no man ever will."

"I'm relieved to hear you say that."

"Are you okay? You've seemed a tad distant the last couple days. I know I'm violating a cardinal rule of manhood by asking this, but are you mad at me?"

"No."

We walked on for a while.

"Was it the way I talked to you on the phone when you were at the coffee shop? Was it because I pulled you out of that meeting?"

"Heck no! I was thrilled to get out of there."

We walked on some more.

"Is it the apartment?"

I grinned. "What's wrong with the apartment? Not hot enough for you?"

"Would you rather be in a house?"

My brain did a one-eighty. "A house?"

"Just think about it. I mean, I know your mom's not my biggest fan, but I figure it isn't a bad idea. We could split it. It would be an investment. Better than throwing our money at rent to the tune of twelve hundred a month."

It was too much to think about.

"I'll think about it."

Tony stopped in the middle of the sidewalk. "You will?"

"Yeah, but you know what?"

"What?"

"I think better on a full stomach; can we just get some pizza already?"

"On it!"

He picked me up in his arms and started running down the sidewalk.

I started to laugh, forgetting what was weighing on my mind. Everything suddenly seeming right. We were both happy. No worries.

Over pizza and beer, we decided to go house shopping that Sunday. We both knew we wanted to stay in the north end of Tacoma. I grew up there, my parents were there, everything I loved about living in Tacoma was there. However, it was one of the most expensive parts of the city to live in. A modest bungalow pushed a half million.

We planned on looking around central and west Tacoma, where housing was more affordable but we would still be close to what we considered home. Since Tony was working that Saturday, my plan was to do some homework. That Friday I would collect all of the real estate listings I could and spend Saturday picking the wheat from the chaff before we went on any wild goose chases. It would be perfect solitude for me to read the papers and make calls to agents.

When Saturday came, that was exactly what I was doing. Parked on the living room sofa with the TV on mute, armed with highlighters, a pencil, and my cell phone, I had already made several appointments and even found a helpful agent who promised to call back with more prospects.

When my cell rang in my lap, I expected it.

"Hello, Sophie." His cool voice threw a switch in my head.

"Hi."

"How are you?"

"Um, fine."

"What are you doing?"

"I was just in the middle of some stuff." Suddenly I remembered who I was talking to. "Wait a minute. You're pulling my leg, right?"

"I'm not. You said no more telepathy, no more tricks—"

"Yeah, yeah, I remember." I cut him off. "You're serious? You don't know what I'm doing right now?"

"I want to earn your trust. It wouldn't be fair to expect it if I ignored your wishes."

Reflexively, my eyes narrowed. "How do I know you're telling the truth?"

There was silence.

"How can I prove anything to you if you won't give me a chance?"

"So you haven't been putting subliminal thoughts in my head, or leaving things around to make me think of you?"

"No."

"You didn't park your car anywhere near my apartment last week?"

"No."

"You haven't been doing anything to Anthony, have you?"

"I haven't had any contact with Anthony."

"Okay." I took a breath. "Okay. This is good."

"What are you doing?" He repeated as though it was the first time he'd said it.

"Well, since you *don't know*, I'm looking at real estate listings."

"What kind of real estate?"

"Light industrial." I paused.

He said nothing.

"A house." I finished. "What other kind of real estate would a person in my situation be looking for?"

"Are you moving out on your own?"

"If I was moving on my own, I'd be looking for a single-wide in Parkland."

"You're buying a house with Anthony?"

"Yes." I braced.

"Where will you go?" His voice remained neutral.

"We aren't leaving Tacoma; we just won't be in the North End anymore."

Then he surprised me.

"Would you like to see some houses today?"

I hesitated. This had bad idea written all over it.

"Thanks for offering. I was planning on doing that with Anthony tomorrow."

"I understand. Do you want to get some coffee?"

Coffee?

"Uh, I'm not sure. Anthony's -- Hold on. How did you know he wasn't here?"

"I didn't."

"You just called me and you didn't know who was going to answer the phone?"

"It's your phone."

"What if Anthony answered? He's used my cell before."

"I would have asked for you."

"And if he asked who you were?"

"I would have said that I was a friend."

"You're giving me a stroke."

"I won't get you into trouble."

This time I didn't say anything.

"I promise." He spoke quietly.

I sighed. "If there's anyone who can back that, I suppose it's you."

"Do you want to get some coffee?"

"God, you're like a broken record. Okay, coffee."

"Do you want me to come for you?"

"No—no, I'll meet you."

"Grounds for Coffee?"

"Let's try Shakabrah on Sixth. Meeting at Grounds would just be too …"

"Weird." He finished.

"Stop reading my mind. I'll see you in fifteen."

Snapping my cell shut, I looked at the newspapers around my feet, feeling momentarily confused as to why they were there. I got off the sofa, pulling myself together on autopilot. My feet found loafers under the coffee table. My hands pulled my hair back into a ponytail as I went to the coat rack. Tugging on a wool coat, I grabbed my purse and headed out the door.

I thought I got to Shakabrah early, but he was already there. I spotted his car parked a half block from mine when I arrived. When I came through the door, I saw him seated at a booth by the window. I was impressed with myself that I recognized him as quickly as I did, but given no one else there looked like an ad for Barney's, the odds were in my favor. Still, I passed him by and made a beeline for the front counter.

Latte first. A woman has to have her priorities straight.

When I returned to his table, latte in hand, I was surprised to see he was eating. An empty fry basket with greasy paper sat in front of him. The remains of a tall milkshake sat in a puddle of condensation near his left hand.

"You eat?"

"Don't you?" His response was matter-of-fact.

Slowly taking a seat, I nodded. "Yeah, but after our last conversation, it's a little surreal to find you pounding fries and a milkshake."

He shrugged, looking at the empty basket. "I've had better."

"Fries or milkshake?" My voice had a twinge of disbelief in it.

"Both."

For a moment we stared at each other. I noticed he was wearing a thick knit fisherman's sweater and wondered if he was ever cold. Pulling his book out of my purse, I slid it across the table to him.

"Thanks."

He didn't touch the book, his eyes riveted to his milkshake instead.

"Did it help?"

"In a vague kind of way, yes."

"If I were any more specific, it wouldn't help."

"Try me."

His eyes darted to me. "Who really knows anybody?"

"If you really believe that, why me? Why not some doe-eyed virgin who'd adore you if you were the devil himself?"

His eyes dropped. "I don't want adoration."

"What do you want?"

"Acceptance."

"Then pony up."

He blinked. "Excuse me?"

"The truth. That's my price. If you want my acceptance, you need to trust me enough to tell it."

Pursing his lips, he looked back at his milkshake.

"You said it was worth it." I added, picking up my latte mug. "I have it in writing."

"I'm a singularity."

I stared at him, but he kept his eyes away.

"And …?"

"You can look it up."

"You come with a lot of homework."

"That's my price."

"Can you at least tell me what singularities do, exactly?"

Reaching across the table to a ketchup bottle, he placed it between us. I looked down at it, then back at him. He only looked into my eyes.

I frowned. "Ketchup?"

He only nodded.

"You eat it?"

"I keep it in the bottle."

Slowly, I nodded. "A big responsibility."

He looked dolefully at the bottle. "Someone's got to do it."

"You don't seem very happy about it."

"I don't know what that is."

I sipped my coffee. "Look it up."

"I deserve that." He whispered.

"I'm still pissed at you, but that doesn't mean you don't deserve happiness. Everyone deserves to be happy about something in their life."

"Since I don't really have a life, how I feel about it isn't important."

"I think it is."

Leaning forward, he placed the ketchup bottle on its side and gently spun it. Putting his elbow on the table, he rested his face in his hand and watched it spin. Taking another sip of my latte, I waited. I was about to look at my watch when he began to speak.

"I accept why I'm here and what my purpose is; it's just difficult to be here and accept a material existence that is empty of sentiment. I've come to the conclusion that substance without sentiment is just as empty as sentience without substance. I suppose this realization has … depressed me."

He didn't look up.

"I can see why you have so many friends." I cleared my throat. "You're a barrel of monkeys."

"I thought you wanted the truth." He kept his eyes on the bottle as he spoke.

I realized he hadn't touched it and it was still spinning.

"I thought you didn't play tricks."

Abruptly stopping the bottle, he sat it upright.

"Sorry." He gave a weak smile. "I'm nervous. It's been a while since I've had anyone to talk to. It's been even longer since anyone's cared."

"You just need more friends."

"I've had you."

"You've stalked me; you haven't had me."

"If you let strangers buy you coffee, I wouldn't have had to stalk you."

I took another sip. "You can buy the next one."

This made him smile.

"Why don't you have more friends?"

His smile faded. "I've tried."

"And?"

"The risk of being manipulated is too great."

"Manipulated?"

He looked away.

"Forced to do things I shouldn't. One person can't do that to me very easily, but two people could; it's happened to me before."

"Then don't tell them what you are."

"Such acquaintances come and go. But they aren't really friends. They can't be when the relationship is predicated on a lie."

"So what makes me special?"

Michael sat up, folding his hands in front of him.

"We've been friends before."

I sat my mug too heavily on the table. "Before?"

"Reincarnation." His eyes didn't waver.

This time I looked away. "I don't need to look that up."

"I'm sorry if you find me a burden. I'll leave you alone if you ask it." His breath seemed to catch. "I suppose after four lifetimes, I've gotten used to you."

I stared. *Four life times?*

Out of the corner of my eye, I could see the barista behind the counter look over at us, but I didn't care. I'd gone beyond my outer limit for the day.

He only blinked at me. "You don't believe in reincarnation?"

"That wasn't in the book!"

"You said you wanted the truth."

"About you! Not me!"

"Are you angry?"

"Of course I am! You've been stalking me for four lifetimes!"

His eyes seemed to go dark. "We were friends."

"How do I know that?"

"Why would I lie?"

Biting my lip, I turned to the window, half expecting zombies on the sidewalk. The junkies in front of the tattoo parlor across the street were a comforting sight.

"Do you want another latte?" His voice came quietly.

Suddenly I laughed, feeling my body shake with it. Covering my face with a hand, I looked across the table at him as tears welled in my eyes.

"I don't think I need any more caffeine, do you?"

"I'm sorry, Sophie."

I was still laughing. "About what?"

"Driving you mad to save my sanity. It isn't fair."

Clearing my throat, I wiped my eyes. "Sanity's overrated."

"I'm afraid I can't afford to think that."

When I looked back at him, his eyes were almost human.

"Or there'd be a lot of spilled ketchup?"

He smiled again. "Something like that."

Taking a breath, I collected my thoughts as best I could.

"So Tacoma's the condiment nexus of the universe?"

"That boundary doesn't exist in a discrete sense. It has little bearing on my geographical location."

My fingers drummed the table. "Makes the morning commute convenient."

"How can I make you comfortable?"

It was an amusing thing to hear coming from base perfection with sapphire eyes.

"Where do I start?"

"Sophie, I don't expect you to accept anything beyond what you are capable of handling. I'd never put you in danger."

"Somehow that doesn't make me feel better."

"How am I different from Anthony? His responsibilities are great, yet the risks of his work aren't great enough to keep you from living together. We won't be living together, and I'm able to protect you well beyond Anthony's capabilities."

"Anthony's good at his job. I'm not going to hold it against him that he's not some omnipotent being."

"You know I have every respect for Anthony ... and I'm not omnipotent."

Rolling my eyes, I picked up my latte. "Bummer."

"This would be easier if you didn't see this as something you had to do for me. All I ask is to let me do for you."

"Do for me?"

"When Anthony comes home, does he talk about what he's seen?"

"We don't talk about his work much. We just hang out, I suppose."

"You offer him companionship. That is all I ask. Not to share in my burdens, only to accept me when the passing of time grows weary. If you told me what you wanted, what you needed, your hopes and dreams and disappointments— anything would do. To feel connected to one soul in this world would be enough, if only to share in the illusion of having a soul of my own."

His eyes seemed to brighten again, but the fire did nothing to warm them. They only seemed colder. In spite of this, I realized I wasn't afraid of him anymore.

"Michael, I don't know what kind of friends we were before, but I don't do illusions. I can't. I need some quid pro quo here. I'm not going to be friends with you and oblivious to what you are."

I pushed away my empty mug.

"If I'm uncomfortable with you, that's my problem, but I'm not going to be your friend because you've promised me it's going to be painless. If you think that's what you need to guarantee someone in order to win their friendship, you haven't really got it."

He had been sitting perfectly still. It was impossible to read his face, but when he refolded his hands, I thought they trembled. Though it was hard to believe him capable of desperation, there was no other way to describe what was beneath the smooth surface.

"When will you be able to decide, do you think?"

"You had me at hello." I stared at him.

"What?" His vacant expression told me the reference was lost.

I snapped my fingers. "You're omnipotent but you don't watch movies?"

"I told you, I'm not omnipotent."

"You've *never* seen a movie?"

His eyes dropped. "I've seen some."

"What was the last one you saw?"

Without looking up, he made a small smile. "*The Ten Commandments.*"

"You're shitting me!" I sat up. "In the theater?"

He shrugged. "It wasn't my idea."

"You went with someone?"

Michael kept his gaze on the table, knitting his fingers tightly, but saying nothing. It took me the better part of a minute before I realized his eyes were wet.

I reached over the table and put my hands on his.

"Yeah, that sounds like something I'd do."

1199 BC The slaves of Egypt were not solely Habiru. Nor were they truly property. They were, in fact, wage slaves—accumulated bands of migrant workers from every point on the compass in search of steady work and bread. Egypt was a crossroads on the workers' pilgrimage. Language, culture, and faith traveled with them. They came from Caphtor to the north by sea, east from Amman and beyond the Negev waste, from the southern mines of Nubia.

In as much as they had their freedom, there was little comfort in it. Many would have preferred the proscribed terms of employment dictated by Ramses to his own subjects, but wage slaves were not citizens of Egypt. Only when the demand for labor could not be filled by his own people would Ramses offer wages to outsiders. Ramses generosity ended when he died. Workers with debts were indentured. The rest, forcibly expelled. For the migrant class, their existence became a continuous cycle of subsistence and starvation.

It was this environment of scarcity and want that Saitael found conducive to his own progress. Being a creature of desire, he fed on the needs of the poor, the hungry, and the weak. It was to this ground that I followed him, my strategy to wait and watch. It was the only strategy I had. Where Saitael could rely on his servus to aid him, I traveled alone, my crypt hidden, but often beyond my own reach. Confronting him was dangerous enough, but alone in the material world, especially so. Thus, keeping close contact with humans was crucial for me. Word of mouth was what I relied on to give me the clues I needed to discover Saitael's whereabouts.

During this time, I found living as a midwife most satisfactory to my needs. It was one of the few occupations available to one who lived a solitary life. It was something I had the skills to do, it would feed me, and most important, it would keep me within earshot of the rumors and gossip coursing the Nile Valley. The only complication I confronted was of being a lone female. Being what I am, I was able to avoid or escape most dangers. The pursuit of male suitors I found the most problematic.

Ironically, it was a proposal of marriage that put me on Saitael's trail. As midwife to his daughter, this man was drawn to my appearance. He spoke to me of starting a new life in a promised land. A land of plenty. Of law and order. When I asked him whose law, he told me the law of one god alone. When he began to recite me the law, I knew.

[Spharic. Entry translated from *Kor Dai Maihael*. Mund Dai. 755 BC]

~

2003 Kate and Duane's sudden departure left us behind to close up the cabin. Happily for Michael, this included cleaning out the food. Unhappily for me, this included cleaning out Toe's litter box. Since Kate and Duane wouldn't be returning to the cabin anytime soon, Toe had been left in our temporary custody. Thankfully, they felt Tic and Tac were too skittish for new surroundings, so Toe was the only feline companion they brought.

On the way home, I keep looking at Toe's kitty crate in the back seat.

"You don't think Lodi will eat her?"

Michael looks at me sideways. "You should be worried for Lodi."

"We'll have to make sure she doesn't get out. If she wanders into the gulch, we might never see her again." I face the front of the car and stare out the passenger window. "And we'll have to get cat food and litter on the way home. And toys."

"I seem to remember you claimed not to care for cats."

"You of all people ought to know I try to keep an open mind. Besides, I'd feel terrible if something happened to Toe while I was responsible for her. Kate has a baby to raise and I kill her cat? I'm perfectly capable of it. I have all the maternal instincts of Joan Crawford."

"You take excellent care of Lodi."

"We don't have any wire hangers in the house."

"If we had children, you would be a wonderful mother."

"Thanks, but I never lost sleep over it and I don't plan on starting."

His compliment does make me think about the sleep I've lost over Kate's baby. After the fact, Mike told me Kate had been stressed and suffering symptoms of preeclampsia when we arrived but ignored them. I asked him if the umbilical cord around the baby's neck triggered her premature delivery. He thought the two incidents were coincidental, but the cord was to blame for the asphyxiation.

What I didn't ask was if he did something extraordinary to save the baby's life, and if so, what price he would pay for it.

Everything had its price.

We stop at Met Market on the way home under the guise of supplementing Toe's feline needs. Michael is an early casualty to the bakery section at the front of the store. Narrowly escaping with possession of the grocery cart, I find myself wandering the pet aisle alone, trying to guess Toe's taste in food and toiletries. I settle on all organic brands, deciding I can score one for the planet even if I score zero with Toe.

After filling the cart with Toe's essentials, there is no sign of Mike and I guess he's only begun to scout the deli. I start to shop for groceries we'll need at home. Three dozen brown eggs, three packages of Hempler's bacon, three gallons organic milk—

"Sophie!"

I jump.

It's Marta, swathed in a purple serape with a basket of pasta and a bottle of Pellegrino.

"Hey, Marta." I aim for enthused.

"What serendipity! What luck to find you here! Are you enjoying the teas?"

"Yes, they're very nice, thank you."

"How about that special one, the herbal …"

She peers at me through her bifocals like I'm fine print.

"Um, I haven't got to that one yet." If she could read the fine print she'd know I threw the special one out with the trash last week.

"Oh, please do try it. It really is just the smell that can be hard to take; once it's in water it will work wonders for you."

"What wonders is it supposed to work again? I don't remember you telling me."

"Perfect thing for spring! Takes care of allergies, makes you sneeze-free."

Just then her eyes drop to my cart filled with the essentials for a cat B&B.

"Ah." I explain. "We had a friend in need. We're taking in her cat."

For once, an edge creeps into Marta's up-with-life demeanor.

She frowns. "Well, you certainly will need that tea now, a cat and a dog."

"Oh, it's just a couple weeks. I'm not really a cat person."

She perks up again. "It's a great favor you're doing, then. I've never had time for pets myself. Don't get me wrong, they're all God's creatures and give us so much, but it really is a commitment, isn't it?"

"Yes, yes it is—"

"Now if you do feel that you're coming down with an allergy, you come see me. A good sauna treatment, a little salt bath. We can take care of whatever ails you."

"Thanks, I'll keep that in mind. I have to get going—"

"So do I. I'll be late getting my dinner; that's terrible for my metabolism. Oh, that reminds me, that's what one of the other teas is for. I should have told you when I gave them to you, but there weren't any labels! I was shocked there weren't any."

I look over Marta's shoulder and see Mike come around the corner of the aisle. He's eating a cookie, but spots me with Marta and turns, going the way he came.

Chicken.

I cut Marta off. "My husband's waiting."

"Is he here with you?" The pitch in her voice makes my ears twitch.

"Um, he's in the car."

"I do so want to meet him some time. The two of you could come by Dragonfly for tea? Only call ahead in case I'm with a client."

"That sounds nice. I know he'd like to meet you; he'll just have to find a free afternoon. You know how busy things are when you're self-employed."

"Do I? Do I ever!"

After extricating myself, I wander the store and find him reading a cook book near the kitchen supplies.

"You found the porn section."

He doesn't look up. "She's in express checkout. We'll be safe in a few minutes."

"We? She's ringing up the piece of hide she got out of me as we speak."

"She's your friend."

"She is not my friend; she's our neighbor. She'll think you're avoiding her. The sooner she meets you the sooner she'll stop harassing me."

Snapping the cook book shut, he drops it into the shopping cart.

"There's a really good lasagna recipe in there."

His statement is really a request. For all his universal knowledge, Michael is a failure in the kitchen. He usually eats half of the ingredients before he starts.

Sensing an opportunity, I cross my arms. "What's in it for me?"

"I'll show myself to Mrs. Farrell?"

I squint.

He blinks. "I'll meet Marta?"

I'm still squinting.

"For tea?"

Slowly, I turn the cart for the pasta aisle. A deal's a deal.

It isn't essential we visit Mrs. Farrell. She is well into her eighties and there is little reason to worry her confusion about Michael's age will mean anything to anyone. It is for me. I don't like anyone thinking I'm married to a man old enough to be my grandfather, even if he is older than dirt, literally.

That is the definition of a hypocrite.

When I tell Michael about Marta's tea-time visit and her revelation about Mrs. Farrell's observant habits regarding the neighbor at the end of her street, he is unconcerned. His attitude is one of disregard. There is little risk of people getting wise to what he is. A human lifespan is short; he is discrete. It rarely adds up to anything. However, as far as I am concerned, I still live a normal life with the same lifespan as anyone else. There is no luxury of moving through the world without the attachments and obligations that come with mortality.

Michael knows. He agreed to meet those obligations with me for our marriage to have any chance of success. It means he has to play his part. It means clearing things up for Mrs. Farrell and making nice with Marta. His only requirement of me is that I allow him to handle it. All he tells is that he will let me know when the opportunity presents itself. The more cryptic his answer, the higher on the weird scale things usually get. This is about a three out of ten.

The next day, it is a sunny afternoon and I am pruning rosemary bushes when Michael appears with Lodi on a leash. He usually walks Lodi after dark. I suspect that something is up.

"Do you think you could arrange a walk with us?"

Brushing my hair from my eyes, I squint up from my stepstool. I look over the rosemary hedge to survey the damage before answering.

"I don't suppose this is a walk that could happen later in the day."

"It could, but Mrs. Farrell would be getting ready for bed and probably wouldn't be sympathetic to us chasing Lodi around in her yard."

"Ah, the old 'Oops, my dog got away from me, so sorry, my what a lovely garden you have, by the way I'm the guy down the street who hasn't aged in fifty years, how are you?' trick. I've heard that one."

He smiles. "You're getting too familiar with the way I work."

"Don't worry." I get to my feet, removing my gardening gloves. "I won't leak any trade secrets."

"We need to get going."

"Sorry, Mike, you have to give me some freshen-up time." I head indoors. "It's bad enough being the bride of Dorian Gray, but I refuse to be the disheveled bride of Dorian Gray."

Still, I am considerate that this is for my benefit. Running indoors, I pull off my yard apron, kick off my clogs, and pull on a pair of Merrell's and a hoodie. I wash the dirt from my hands in the mud room, run a brush though my hair, and am back outside in record time.

Michael greets me with the distracted absence he gets when he's looking at something not actually in his presence, what the CIA would call remote viewing. I can only imagine the chagrin of the intelligence community if they knew his extraordinary powers were being used to spy on an old lady cutting flowers up the street. We start up our drive with Lodi on his lead. Lodi is thrilled to go for a walk, but not so thrilled a leash is really necessary. April is already sweltering for him under his malamute coat; running for anything less than his life or bacon is out of the question. I assume Michael has a plan for prompting Lodi to play his part. Already, the long uphill trudge has Lodi panting heavily. It will be a short walk anyway.

Our street hugs the edge of a ravine, with no houses along it for the length of two blocks. It isn't until Prospect intersects with two other streets that we finally have neighbors. Left of the intersection is a teal Victorian with a view commanding the length of the gulch to Puget Sound. This is Mrs. Farrell's house.

The turrets and widow's walks loom ahead of us. Michael shows no sign of nerves, though he is about to pass as his own son to a woman whose memory is clear enough to recollect when he moved in. He calls this his principle of implausible deniability. When humans are confronted by facts contradicting the settled order of their existence, they must choose between pursuing them, potentially to their own detriment, or rejecting them in favor of blissful ignorance. The vast majority choose the latter.

We are nearly to Mrs. Farrell's front yard, when Michael drops Lodi's leash.

The dog takes off into Mrs. Farrell's yard, his body electrified to chase something only he seems to see. A voice cries out from a frizz of white hair behind a bank of rose bushes. Michael runs into the yard calling Lodi's name and I follow, making a beeline for Mrs. Farrell with smiling eyes. Seeing her again, I grasp that what disturbs me is what she represents. She represents the future pitfalls I will face as time passes. Old as she is, as irrelevant as her opinions might be, she is only the first of many who will whisper at my expense.

She sees me approach, shading her eyes with a gloved hand to see who I am.

"Hello, Mrs. Farrell. It's me, Sophie Goodhew! I'm sorry. We lost our hold on Lodi's leash and he's decided to inspect your yard for squirrels."

She hesitates, then smiles, making the appearance of recognition.

"Hello? Oh yes—yes. Dogs will do that, won't they? It won't dig, will it?"

"Not if Michael can help it. He'll have him in a moment and we'll be on our way."

"Michael?" Her dark eyes lose focus. "Goodhew?"

"Yes, we live at the end of Prospect. Remember, I met you last month when I was walking the dog?"

"You're his wife then?"

It occurs to me there is no reason we should have come. It's possible her memory is so poor our little exercise is wasted effort.

"Yes, I'm Sophie."

I smile, waiting to see if anything registers. Mike approaches us with Lodi slathering on the end of his leash.

"This is my husband. Michael, this is Mrs. Farrell."

Her face puckers.

"Hello, Mrs. Farrell." He flashes an exuberantly white smile and nods to her.

"Michael?" She looks at him as though time has shifted.

"Dad told me about this house when I was growing up." He looks back up at it admiringly. "It looks just like he described it."

"Your father?"

"He lived in the ravine, but you might not remember. That would have been a while ago. His name was Michael Goodhew; I'm Mike Jr."

He extends his hand and Mrs. Farrell reaches for it, her mouth slightly agape.

"Oh, yes." Her voice is faint. "Yes … I remember." Her vigor returns. "I remember your father …" She pauses as if to speak but doesn't.

Michael is all astonishment. "You remember him?"

"I never knew he had a boy."

"Dad's job kept him here. After my mom died, I grew up with my grandparents in California."

Mrs. Farrell looks like she's eaten something that disagrees with her. "Well, that had to be difficult for the two of you."

Mike continues in a voice strangely younger than his own.

"When he left me the house, I decided I wanted to fix it up. Anyway, it's cool to find someone who remembers him."

Did he just say cool?

"I remember the papers said he got lost in the mountains, but I never heard anything after that."

Michael studies Lodi for a moment. "He was never found."

"I'm sorry to hear it." She sounds more mystified than sorry.

My curiosity gets the better of me. "Did you know him well?"

"Didn't see him enough to know him." She squints at Mike. "You're the spitting image of him, though. Thought my mind was playing tricks on me. It'll be good to have a family there again. You have children?"

"No." Mike glances nervously at me. "Not yet."

"Well, be warned, you could have twins. That runs in the Goodhews. Your father's uncle lived in that house before him. He had twins."

This catches my attention. "You knew Daniel?"

I feel Mike take my hand.

"Better than I knew Michael." She lowers her pruning shears to the ground. "Danny and his wife were good friends. They used to spend summers here. Their twins used to play with my daughter Anne ... Molly and Maeve."

"What was his wife like?"

"Florence? Oh, she was lovely. That was before she lost the girls. You know the girls died of polio?"

"That's terrible."

Mrs. Farrell catches my eye. "Then Michael came."

"I think we'd better get Lodi home." Mike's grip on my hand says enough. "We don't want him to do his business in your garden."

When I look at my husband, he watches me.

No more questions, Sophie.

"No, that's fine." I look back at Mrs. Farrell and she is smiling. "Please come back and visit." She winks at me. "I'd be happy to tell you about Daniel."

Dropping my hand, Mike begins to lead Lodi away. "It was nice meeting you."

Silently following him from her yard, I glance back at Mrs. Farrell as she watches us leave. She waves and I wave back numbly.

On the return home, Lodi is visibly relieved the rest of the journey is downhill. I say nothing.

"Don't go back." Without a break in stride or demeanor, I can feel my husband exercising his restraint.

I ignore it.

"Why not?"

"I never should have agreed to this." He mutters to himself. "If you weren't so worried about what other people think, I wouldn't have made the excuse to speak with her at all." He shoots me a look. "It's never enough, is it?"

"I'm just curious."

"Let it go."

"What could she tell me that I don't already know?"

"If you already know everything, you don't need to talk to her."

"It's my life."

"Not anymore. Those people are dead. They're just Mrs. Farrell's memories, and they'll die with her."

"They're your memories, Michael. They're mine."

"No, Sophie!" He stops. "They're not! You don't need them ... You don't want them."

Turning away, he continues down our drive without me.

Standing in the street, I stare at his back. "What is it you don't want me know?"
He stops without facing me, pulling up on Lodi's leash.
"I'm telling you I forbid it."
There is no force or malice in his voice.
I put my hands on my hips. "Or what?"
"I'll sell this house and take you away from here."
"What?"
"I mean it."
"What if I don't want to go?"
When he turns, his eyes are ice. "You can't always get what you want."
Lodi whimpers.
Part of me wants to scream, "Can too!" and throw rocks at him. The same part tells me not to trust him, to push back when what satisfies me causes him pain. That part doesn't care. Was it what let me walk away from him at the top of this drive three years ago?
Or does it move my feet to close the distance between us now?
With each step I see a light in his eyes that could register smug satisfaction or abiding love. I decide it is both. Taking a breath, I put up my hands.
"I promise. I won't talk to Mrs. Farrell."
His eyes close as I put my arms around him. I feel him bury his face in my hair.
"Sorry." I whisper.
But I know what I am. I try not to think it. He tries not to either.

Felis catus : Domestic cats have long been known for their exceptional vision. Their long relationship with humans, especially their role in religion and superstition, made them an excellent candidate for my research. Aside from their night vision, some have shown a sensitivity to the magnetic fields generated by the magnetos in my ghost machine. My current theory is some, if not all cats, are capable of perceiving spiritual energy. Selective breeding could produce cats with extra sensory perception that could be both qualitatively and quantitatively measured.

If my theory is correct, it could explain the ancient practices of cat worship. Such cults might have served to breed cats intended to perform a practical and not simply symbolic function in religious rites. This would elevate the role of the cat as intermediary with the spirit world beyond the confines of superstition and witchcraft. Such cats could be an invaluable tool, not only facilitating, but verifying the presence of spiritual energy to detect haunting, possession and intervention in session. With such data, the scientific and spiritual realms would finally be united.

I believe these observations only mark the beginning of our understanding of metaphysical science once perceived by our ancestors but since obscured by legend. As our scientific knowledge grows, our physical limitations must inevitably fall.

[Fr. Excerpt translated from *Morphos et Metamorphos*. Luc Benet. d. 1883]

1999 House hunting with Anthony took longer than anticipated. It was hard to decide what was worse, his inability to follow directions or the houses we saw. After six hours of swearing in traffic, interspersed with tours of split levels and second-story add-ons, I concluded the only reason these homes were for sale was the owner decided being homeless was a step up. It also made me question leaving the North End at all. The thought of living in any other part of Tacoma was the same as living in another city entirely.

Anthony was aware of this. He knew how my mother would feel about me living in another part of the city. I knew this experiment was to prove to her he could keep her only child safe and comfortable. We both knew as our relationship stood, my mother would not approve of marriage. How Dad felt was of little concern by comparison. In his family, getting divorced was nearly prerequisite for citizenship as a human. In Mom's family, divorce was disgraceful proof the marriage shouldn't have happened in the first place. Since she didn't approve of Anthony, she would have come to our wedding with a set of divorce papers as a gift.

Truthfully, I was beginning to appreciate my mother's view of things, and sometimes you have to call a spade a spade. My mother raised me with high standards, and now I was a snob. Not in an overt, nouveau riche way. I didn't get my hair done and I didn't collect designer anything, but I appreciated quiet neighborhoods, old houses, and bad plumbing in a way beyond sentiment. Needless to say, living on a street devoid of meaningful foliage, lined with ramblers and ranches, would be heaven compared to a refugee camp in Afghanistan, but so was our apartment.

Anthony and I didn't discuss house hunting the week after our initial search. He knew that I wasn't interested in anything we'd seen, but he was afraid I wasn't interested in finding a house anymore either. Though we agreed to continue the search the following weekend, I didn't exert the same effort to collect listings as I had the first weekend. I wasn't expecting to hear back from any realtors. I was only expecting a certain voice on my cell phone.

Saturday morning started another routine of cereal and OJ. I didn't listen for any voice in my head. I knew there wouldn't be one. Ever since our telepathy session in the park, Michael had kept his word. He would use the phone from now on. It occurred to me I didn't have his phone number. When he called my cell, it read unknown. Did he even use a phone? For all I knew, I was imagining he was on my phone and the voice on the other end was still in my head. He had a car, a nice one for someone whose existence my brain still doubted. He ate fries and drank milkshakes. If he ate food he had to have a refrigerator. He wore different clothes every time I'd seen him. He had to have a closet. Where did he live? How did he pay for things? Did he have a job?

What was his last name?

Around noon, my cell rang.

I jumped, nearly knocking over my third glass of OJ. It was Anthony calling on his lunch break to see how my house homework was going.

"Did you hear from the last realtor we saw? What was her name … Angela?"

"No, I haven't heard from her yet. She did e-mail three more addresses to drive by and see if we want in. I thought I might find them this afternoon and save you some exasperation tomorrow."

"You know that's the part you never think about: the driving. I think I covered more of the city last Sunday than I did on the job all week."

"It only feels that way because we didn't find anything. If you'd been able to arrest someone, you would have found the experience more satisfying."

"If I'd been able to get a smile on your face, it would have been satisfying."

"I'm sorry. Was I that bad?"

"Hey, I don't blame you. We saw a lot of dogs. I was just hoping we could make it fun. That's what we'll do tomorrow, okay? We'll focus on having fun instead of trying to find a dream house."

"Forget dreamy, at this point I'd settle for anything short of a nightmare. A mirage of a house would suit me fine."

He laughed. "We still have our third-floor oasis."

"Thank God."

After I hung up, I went back to reading listings, feeling encouraged.

Tony was right. We did have our oasis. There wasn't any reason to feel pressure. No reason to worry. We were happy here anyway. I looked around our living room, wondering what was missing.

A fireplace. I was wearing a fleece beanie inside just to stay warm.

Opening my laptop, I began to surf listings online. I hadn't bothered to take home the newspaper at work, and we didn't get a paper at the apartment. That, and it was raining hard enough to make a native Washingtonian stay indoors, so I wasn't going out for the weekend edition. The day was shaping up to be a pajama day anyway.

As my laptop warmed up, I went into the kitchen and made a PB&J. I started to fill the carafe for the coffee maker and went to the cabinet for coffee only to find we were out. It was just like a guy to finish the coffee and not put it on the grocery list.

Fine. Tea would be fine ...

When I resumed surfing, the results were better than I expected. I had a better idea of what the neighborhoods were like and it was easier to guess what would be worth a look. Adding to the list of addresses our realtor sent, I ended up with eight houses to drive by. Kicking back on the sofa, I contemplated the rain. Water streaked down the windows, spattering on the sill. The sound of drops hitting the gutters reminded me of my old bedroom at home. I wondered if it missed me.

Few things can take hold with a firmer grip than an afternoon nap. I never understood how some people managed fifteen-minute naps or even five-minute naps. My naps always lasted at least an hour, and any intrusion was loathed by every acute fiber of my being. When my blissful haze was interrupted by a series of rapping noises, I covered my head with a sofa cushion and waited for it to go away.

"Sophie? Are you all right?" The voice coming through the door was Michael's.

Here?

My head popped out from under the cushion.

"I brought you coffee."

"Come back with some Ambien and we'll talk."

But I was headed for the door. Rubbing my eyes, I opened it. He was standing in the hall, his trench soaked, a wet paper cup in his hand. Though damp, he remained perfectly presentable and noticeably taller than Anthony in the door frame.

"How tall did you decide you were going to be?" I blinked up at him.

It was a fair question, and I decided asking was better than wondering about it for the next week. I expected a more androidlike response, but he actually seemed a little annoyed by the question.

"It wasn't a decision."

My face twisted. "Just runs in the family?"

Offering the coffee with a sigh, I took it from him as he stepped inside.

"A preference of evolution." He looked around the room. "My height is slightly above average for a Caucasian male."

"Why slightly above instead of average? Oh—let me take your coat."

He slipped off his trench and watched me hang it on the coat rack.

"Humans respond more positively to taller people."

"Can I get you anything?" I pointed to the kitchen. "Anything except coffee, that is; you brought the only drop in the place."

He barely shook his head as I gestured to the living room. Absently glancing at the coffee table and chairs, he took a seat on the sofa. Dressed in a black pullover and black cords, he looked lost in our apartment, like a misplaced pall bearer. Taking Anthony's armchair, I sat across from him in my pajamas.

Pulling up my feet, I crossed my legs and popped the lid off of my coffee.

"So you base your appearance on the results you want to get?"

"I wouldn't put it that way."

"So, looking like a guy in GQ is a preference of evolution?"

He shrugged. "My appearance is based on standard human anatomy. The design of my DNA varies from most humans in that it has little variation."

My ears perked. "You have DNA?"

"How else would I have a body?"

"How should I know? You're the first singularity I've met."

"Did you look it up?"

"And got a headache, thanks."

He smiled. "You wanted a credible explanation. That's as good as any."

"There was more than one explanation, though. I wanted something definitive."

"What I am defies definition, but I still require DNA to have a body, if it helps."

"It does." I hid a smirk behind my coffee. "I like what you've done with it."

He shrugged. "I only did what was necessary."

"Uh huh." I took a gulp as he shifted nervously on the sofa.

"I wanted to avoid any genetic defect."

"Of course."

"Nothing about my body is extraordinary except that it is extremely ordinary."
I blew on my coffee. "Your eyes aren't."

"My eyes are the one feature I have little control over."

"Why is that?"

"I could change their color, but it would compromise my vision."

"I've seen them lighter or darker."

"They may reflect my energy level or an emotional response."

"Why are they so blue?"

"My blood is copper based."

My brow arched. "Good excuse for skipping the donation drive at work."

"Why ask the questions if the answers make you uncomfortable?"

"My curiosity often overrides my judgment."

Slowly, he grinned. "You're comparing me to Anthony."

Putting down my coffee, I crossed my arms.

"You come to visit because I'm supposed to be some old buddy of yours. Frankly, I don't know you from Adam. I'm a human female, of reproductive age, trying to decide if I'm going to spend the rest of my life with an eligible male. Now you knock on my door with a cup of coffee. A so-called singularity, inhabiting a body my ovaries commonly identify as a sperm donor, and you glibly note I'm comparing you with Anthony. This is where something other than my ovaries tells you to go to hell."

"I'm sorry." His eyes shrank. "I didn't mean to sound glib."

Dropping his gaze, he gripped the tops of his knees with his hands. "I need to accept it isn't fair for me to think we have a complete understanding of one another. You're justified in asking me whatever you want. I'm just uncomfortable answering. You have a way of highlighting our differences that is humorous to yourself but often dehumanizing to me. You want to know the truth and I want to tell you, but I don't know when the answer I give will upset you, in which case you behave as though I am to blame."

"How can you feel dehumanized? You're not human at all."

"I'm capable of humanity. In a sense I'm partly human, whether I remember it or not. This body might not be, but my spirit is, and I accept and embrace my human heritage. If I didn't, I wouldn't be having this conversation with you."

"Fair enough." I slouched in my armchair. "I don't remember you; you don't remember you. I hurt your feelings. I'm sorry. It's just you have a way of acting like you don't have any when I haven't been able to get a grip on mine."

"If I didn't have feelings, would I bring you coffee?"

"That's an act of consideration." I shook my head. "You don't have to be very feely to be considerate."

"But consideration is motivated by the desire to achieve a response, in my case an emotional one. I brought you coffee because I wanted you to be happy."

"You wanted me to open the door."

His forehead creased. "You wouldn't have opened your door?"

"What did I just say? I'm sorry. But the insults have to stop."

"What insults?"

"You can't tell me I'm the only one who finds my dehumanizing comments funny. The blood drive one was pretty good. If you'd ever been pressured at work, you'd know what I mean."

"I do think you're funny. I just wish it wasn't at my expense."

"I'll try not to dehumanize you, but as for being funny at your expense? You can pick your singular self up and head for the door if you can't take it."

He was uneasy, but he didn't move either.

"So, why did you drop by unannounced? I mean besides bringing me a latte from Grounds. You wanted to meet Anthony? Hang out, maybe cream us at a round of Cranium?"

His head shook with a jerk. "I knew Anthony was working today."

"You've been reading my mind again?"

"Not at all. I watched him leave for work this morning."

"You were camped outside at five in the morning?"

"No."

"I'm not even going to ask how, because it's already irritating me."

"I use great discretion when I watch people."

"Just stop while you're ahead."

"I came to spend time with you."

"For someone who's supposed to keep a cosmic lid on things you seem to have a lot of free time on your hands."

"On a human time scale, yes; on a cosmic time scale, I'm moderately busy."

My head was starting to buzz. Taking a swig of my coffee, I pondered a rainy afternoon trapped in my apartment with Major Tom. Springing from the armchair, I yanked the beanie off my head.

"Let's get out of here." I headed for the bedroom. "We're going to look at houses. How does that sound?" I called over my shoulder.

"I'd be happy to help."

"You'd be happy?" I swapped my PJs for jeans, wool socks, and a sweater. "That sounds like an emotional response; we must be on the right track."

When I returned to the living room, Michael was standing at the window. He had already put on his trench. Turning at the sound of my stocking feet on the floor, he watched me sit on a stool by the door as I pulled on a pair of boots. The way he observed me reminded me a dictionary definition I'd read. Attendant spirit.

That he was.

Grabbing my Helly, I forgave lugging my purse. My keys and wallet pretty much lived in my raincoat five months out of the year. I was about to usher Michael out the door, when I remembered the list of addresses I'd written down. Scanning the tables in the apartment, I spotted it on the coffee table and snatched it up.

"Are those your addresses?" Michael was standing at the door.

"Yup."

"May I see them?"

At the door, I handed the list to him. He glanced at it and handed it back to me. "Thank you."

He disappeared down the hall. Briefly, I hesitated to leave the list behind. With a shrug, I dropped it on the floor and shut the door behind me.

Maybe it was the lazy Saturday afternoon. Maybe it was the pouring rain. Maybe it was because we were in a BMW with a space oddity behind the wheel, but finding eight houses seemed effortless. My powers of selection had improved. The houses had gone from appalling the previous weekend to merely nondescript this weekend. At each house, Michael pulled to the curb and I would decide if it was worth getting out of the car. Some houses we only drove by, while at others I would wander into the yard, peeking over fences from alleys. Whenever I got out of the car, Michael would stand on the sidewalk, watching silently.

On our way to the last house, he asked his first question since we'd started.

"What factors are you considering when you look at a house?"

"A variety of things." I cocked my head. "The neighborhood it's in, condition, size, whether or not it has a garden."

"A garden is important to you. We have seen houses similar in all the respects you mentioned, but you only considered those with a suitable yard."

"I suppose." Pulling windblown hair from my face, I fumbled in a pocket for my lip gloss and applied it. "If you're going to the expense and trouble of owning property and paying the taxes, you might as well get the most out of it. Mom's a gardener, and so was Great Nana. I've always been around gardens. Once you've lived in one, it's hard to live without one."

When I looked at him, his expression was thoughtful, but he said nothing.

The car slowed and he indicated a house at a corner as he pulled to the curb. It wasn't bad: brick with ivy-covered walls and a trim lawn, but the lot was small. There was a detached garage turned mother-in-law that eliminated any chance of a backyard.

"Hmmm." I shook my head at him. "No garden here."

With a smile, he pulled back into traffic. I sat back with my arms crossed and bit my lip. Something seemed odd since we'd been in his car. It finally dawned on me.

"Do you listen to music at all?"

"Sometimes, but I find it distracting."

"Yeah, that's kind of the idea."

"I know you liked music—" He paused nervously. "You do, don't you?"

"I do. And I appreciate that BMW made every effort to eliminate as much road noise as possible in their cars, but they also put in a really good sound system."

Grinning, he flipped on the radio. Sitting up, I started running through stations till I found KMTT. I didn't love everything they played, but they were the least offensive station when it came to genre. "Devil's Haircut" filled the cabin, and I laughed as it seemed apropos. I stopped short when I noticed we weren't headed back to the apartment. While I was playing with the radio, Michael had deviated course and was driving down a back street. The neighborhood was familiar. Growing up, I had friends who lived one street over. It didn't keep the hair from standing on the back of my neck.

When you're a woman there is an instinctive alert system you never really quiet—at least when you're sober, and I was sober as a judge. Certain things trigger it: dark alleys, noises you can't identify when you're alone, and very definitely being in a car with a mysterious person going somewhere you don't know. It was one thing looking at houses; I'd agreed to that. Mystery trips, not so much.

This time my rational mind was arguing in Michael's favor. If he wanted to hurt me, there wasn't much I could do about it. But he'd said he would never do that. At least I thought he did. I knew him, didn't I?

But what did I really know about him? I didn't have his phone number. Didn't even know his last name. I never asked. Didn't want to. Given what he was, it didn't seem right he should have the same baggage the rest of us did.

Clearing my throat, I tried to sound calm. "Are we lost?"

"I wanted to show you something." He kept his eyes on the road.

One thing I did know was the road we were on. It led to a forested ravine I called the gulch when I was a kid. There was a three-way intersection in front of a huge Victorian before Prospect veered down the ravine, coming to a dead end. I could hear my mother's voice in my head: dead end roads were bad luck.

Playing in the gulch had been strictly forbidden by her. It was rumored people had disappeared in it. And the haunted house was there. At least, that was what we called it. I tried not to hear my mother's voice as I watched the houses pass by, leading to the intersection I knew was coming. The Victorian loomed to my right. I stared at it blankly as an old woman in the window stared back. I felt the car drop beneath me.

As quickly as we sped past the Victorian, we suddenly slowed. The road narrowed, growing rutted. Nearly stopping, we pulled off Prospect before the dead end, crunching along a gravel drive anchored to a row of giant cedars. At the end of the drive was the house.

It had been years since I'd seen it. It was easily a hundred years old, with deep eaves and dark windows. It might have been beautiful if it looked habitable. The porch was overgrown. A wisteria menaced the front porch, disappearing into a bramble of blackberries that obscured any landscaping. The place was so derelict it didn't cross my mind he lived there.

Getting out of the car, I looked around and then back at him as he shut his car door and slowly walked towards the house.

"You own this?"

He nodded.

I followed him onto the porch, which was small but still seemed solid. Up close, the house wasn't so bad. There weren't any signs of dampness or dry rot, but I wasn't inside yet either.

Michael opened the front door and stood waiting for me to go inside. Ignoring him, I entered the dark foyer. Hardwood floors were scattered with leaves. Dark stairs led up and away on my left; a small hall leading to the kitchen was tucked behind them. An ornate grandfather clock stood to my right, before what appeared to be the main living room of the house. In contrast to the house, the clock was dust free and seemed in perfect working order.

The living room was a large rectangle, framed by a box-beamed ceiling. At one end, French doors led to a dining room piled with furniture and tented with dust covers. At the opposite end was a pair of imposing paneled doors. Flanking these doors were two neat stacks of dusty packing crates. The exterior wall held windows, dimly illuminating heavy curtains pulled shut over them. There was a large fireplace on the interior wall, tiled with an inlaid hearth. All else was empty space, unlived in for many years.

Michael stood motionless next to the clock, watching me, slightly unnerved.

"Don't tell me you live here?"

"I do."

"How long?"

"Forty-seven years."

"You've lived here my whole life?"

He smiled.

"Why?"

"Why not?"

"It's a dump."

"It's home."

I gave the room another sizing up. "Martha you're not." I pointed at the paneled doors. "What's in there?"

He slowly walked to the doors, unlocking them with a skeleton key he pulled from a pocket. As he pushed them open, I approached and peered inside. The room was a library. Built-in bookshelves filled every wall save a large bay window of stained glass. The shelves were filled with volumes of every size and shape. Some books appeared new, some looked like they would fall apart if they saw daylight, others were little more than loose sheaves of paper.

There was no furniture, unless you counted what appeared to be a burial vault in the middle of the room. It was the shape of a brick, about eight feet in length, four feet wide, and four feet deep, made out of what and looked like white granite. At first, it seemed a smooth, solid object, but in the fading light, I made out a fissure denoting a lid. A mesh of inscriptions on the surface seemed a cross between Chinese and calculations from an astrophysics lab.

"This where you stash your porn?"

A smile flickered on his face. "Where I sleep."

"You have something against mattresses?"

"It keeps me safe and conserves my energy."

"Keeps you safe? From what?"

"It protects my body ..." His eyes dropped to the floor. "When it becomes ... permeable."

"Life gets complicated for you, don't it?"

He shrugged but said nothing more.

I studied the bookshelves.

"So what are you into? Romance, self-help, Stephen King?"

"This is my reference library. Records of things known, clues of things unknown. I turn to them when I have questions that need to be confirmed."

My eyes fell to a shelf of heavy volumes. "Are these all Bibles?"

"Some. Apocrypha mostly."

"Apocrypha?"

"Writings excluded from the Bible."

I looked at him. "You mean censored."

"Writings are memories. Some memories become inconvenient." With a nod, he indicated the wall of shelves behind me. "Those are mine. Not everything, but I record what I can. They are my most valued possessions."

Turning, I saw a solid wall of black-spined volumes.

I frowned at him. "I wouldn't think an immaterial being would care for possessions at all, let alone bother to keep a journal."

"Why would a material being write a journal? A mortal will have no recollection of their past life after death. It is only a memorial that others will appreciate, and even then, most are written with the intent the thoughts inside be kept private."

"Sounds like a pointless exercise—probably why I've never kept one."

"You can learn much from past experiences if you write them down. A larger pattern emerges that might otherwise be lost."

"I get your point. I suppose I'd rather forgo the pattern in favor of keeping my thoughts undocumented. If that means detention in the remedial school of hard knocks, so be it."

"Your cavalier attitude has had real consequences for you in the past."

"I feel fine, so I must have gotten over it pretty well. Besides, why keep a journal when I can look forward to your observant commentaries on my life? After four lifetimes, I'd hope that I'm mentioned, cavalier attitude and all."

"My journals are a record of my existence, and you are a part of them in as much as you have shared many experiences with me. They are not a record of your own perceptions and motives. Many choices you have made remain a mystery to me."

"This from a guy who sleeps in a burial vault."

"It's a crypt."

"It's creepy."

"It's a necessity."

"It's also why you're not dating anyone."

"I don't need to date."

"You've just disappointed a lot of women."

The grandfather clock chimed five. I checked my watch and started for the door.

"Time to get in the pumpkin. Anthony'll be home any minute."

It was already dark. Michael's car was a black shadow on the drive. The running lights blinked as he opened the doors remotely. As he locked the door to his house, I got in the car, pulling my coat around my face. My mind was blank, as though everything I'd seen was being reviewed before a referee could make a call. I barely noticed as Michael appeared next to me. When the car started, "Baba O'Riley" was playing on the radio. He left it on, driving silently. There was a feeling, something I couldn't put my finger on, a feeling of anticipation and anxiety. The music wasn't helping. I reached over and shut off the radio.

In moments, we were blocks from my apartment building.

Intuition snapped me present.

"Wait. Go around the block."

He complied without question. As we passed behind the building, I looked in the parking lot. Anthony's squad car was already there. I realized I'd left my cell in my purse. If he'd been trying to call me, I wouldn't have known.

"Shit!" I turned to Michael. "Did you or did you not see this coming?"

"I didn't ..." He paused sheepishly. "We were being followed when we left this afternoon. Anthony probably came home early when he discovered you were with me."

"And you were going to tell me this when? Pre- or post-implosion?"

He frowned. "Why should he be angry? We didn't do anything wrong. All he will know is we looked at houses this afternoon."

"We went to your house."

"I lost them by then. I would never lead strangers to my house."

Tossing my head back, I laughed like an insane woman.

"*Perfect!* I'll just fill in that blank when he asks where we disappeared to. I'll say you wanted to show me your burial vault and everything will be fine."

"It's not a burial vault."

"Too bad. I feel like I could use one right now."

"I don't understand how Anthony can object to our friendship, or why. I've never interfered with your marital relationships in the past and have no intention of doing so now. If you explained, he couldn't object."

I stared.

"Explain. This. To Anthony ... I'd ask what planet you're from, but I already know. First, most men have problems with the woman in their life being friends with other men. Second, stop comparing what's going on in my life with any previous lives you associate with me, because as far as I'm concerned, they never happened. And third, Anthony and I aren't married, we have no plans of getting married, and buying a house doesn't mean we will be."

I paused to catch my breath.

"Maybe if I spoke to him—"

"*No!*"

"If I came up with you—"

"*Mike,* this time above average height isn't going to get positive results!"

"You're angry with me again." His voice was a whisper.

"You know how you promised you wouldn't get me into trouble last weekend?"

He looked away. "I'm sorry. Truly, I didn't realize my visit would put you in this position. By the time I knew we were being watched, it was too late." He grew quiet. "If I told you, there was a probability you would have sent me away."

"I don't understand." I turned to face him. "How could you know Anthony went to work today, but not know I was being watched?"

"I can only see what I look for if I know to look for it. I saw Anthony leave this morning because I expected he might work as he did last weekend. I missed we were being followed because I wasn't expecting it and then it was too late." He stared out the windshield. "I see pictures on your dining room table. Pictures of us. I see them because I am looking for them and they are there to be seen."

"Well." I peered up at my apartment through the windshield, "I'd appreciate it if you don't see what happens next."

He faced me. "Will you be safe?"

"Tony wouldn't lay a hand on me. He gets worked up, but he goes for the gut. When it comes to guilt trips he learned from the best." I shrugged. "We'll either split up or have really great make-up sex and go back to looking for houses."

"I haven't been a very good friend to you, have I?"

I swallowed my anxiety. "This was going to come up sooner or later. Tony's a big boy; he can handle it."

As I opened the door, I felt a hand on my shoulder. When I looked back, Michael's eyes met mine, black and hollow.

A thrill of fear and pity ran up my back.

"I am sorry."

I gave a nod. "Come here."

He looked puzzled, but I didn't have time. Grabbing him by the back of the head, I pulled him to me. I saw a flash of panic as I looked him in the eyes. Bobbing my head up, I kissed him on the forehead.

"Wish me luck."

With a wink, I got out of the car and headed for Armageddon.

NOTED ARTIST DIES

Nationally known artist, Daniel Goodhew, died yesterday at his home in the north end of Tacoma. Born in Tacoma in 1910, he became known for his designs in ceramics while working for the Stahl design house near Boston. There he met and married Florence Lyden and had twin daughters, Molly and Maeve. Tragically both girls died from polio in 1942. He retired early in 1943, returning with his wife to live at his family home in Tacoma. Mr. Goodhew later worked as an instructor at the University of Puget Sound where he taught both art history and practical art courses. Local examples of his work are in the collections of the University Puget Sound, the Tacoma Art Museum, the University of Washington, and the Washington State History Archives.

Although no details have been released regarding the cause of death it is being called accidental. He is survived by his nephew, Michael Goodhew, who was living with him at the time.

Florence Goodhew died in convalescence at Lutheran Rest Home in 1967. His nephew could not be reached for comment.

[Obituary from *The Tacoma Tribune*
Scrapbook of Michael Goodhew. July 12, 1972]

2003 Michael gets a stay of execution regarding tea with Marta.

Kate calls to let me know they have moved the baby to Seattle Children's Hospital and wants us to visit. They have named the little boy Michael. Kate says she always liked the name, but now even more so. As far as she is concerned, my husband saved her baby. The paramedics were impressed by the success of her delivery, and the doctors are impressed by little Mike's vigor. She does admit that Duane isn't as excited about the name for his son, but when she told him it could make the difference in converting Michael, he relented.

Kate also asks if we can keep Toe a little longer. Little Mike is still being treated for complications related to his premature delivery, one of which is an unusual inflammation of his lungs and throat. Although he will to go home in a week, his doctors counsel against anything that could cause inflammation, so no chemicals, no perfumes, no cats. Tic and Tac have been sent to live with Duane's parents. Would I mind keeping Toe since she is doing so well with us?

Of course I say yes, with relief … but not because I've become a cat lover.

Toe is missing. I don't tell Kate because it's only been two days and I am hopeful Toe will turn up. Up till now, Toe hasn't been a problem. Even Lodi managed to contain his dislike for the cat. After the initial barking and growling, Michael and Lodi came to an understanding. Toe was our guest and would not be killed, eaten, or misled in any way that would result in the injury or disappearance of said cat.

My plan was to keep Toe indoors for the duration of her stay. Even if she was allowed outside by Kate, I felt no need to tempt fate. Michael might be able to convince Lodi to be a team player, but I doubted he had the same understanding with the local raccoons and the occasional coyote that frequented the gulch below our house.

Toe had her crate next to the fireplace and a litter box in the mud room. She ate and slept with diligence and took readily to a piece of drift wood I offered for a scratching post. In the mornings she would yowl and follow me from room to room. At night she would come to our bedroom and climb on Michael, which was perfect because he was capable of sleeping through anything. Her only frustration was that she deeply desired a field trip. At dusk she would stare out the living room windows, rubbing her paws on the glass.

Mike and I got wise to her attempts to dart out the door whenever we came and went, but it was inevitable that she would get out at some point. I put our address on her collar and took her to the local animal shelter to get her micro-chipped, which my husband found particularly amusing. Michael was also amused when I took pictures of Toe to e-mail Kate. He warned that if I took too good a care of Toe, she might end up staying indefinitely.

Now that his warning has proven prophetic, he is quite convinced of his omnipotence. Unfortunately, his omnipotence doesn't extend to locating Toe. He can't zero in on her because her sentience is weak. Without context, a place to look, he can't make sense of what he is seeing, and Toe has covered her tracks well. In the meantime, we have agreed to keep Toe's disappearance a secret when we see the cousins.

We are to meet for an early meal before going to the hospital to see little Mike.

Surprisingly, we are meeting at a Japanese restaurant. Duane is not a fan of ethnic foods in general, but especially Japanese. Kate loves Japanese food and has sacrificed indulging in it since marrying Duane. Meeting for sushi could be a sign that things have changed.

My spirits brighten when I see Kate in front of the restaurant. Jumping from the car, I give her a hug and glance over my shoulder to see Michael hand our bag of baby gifts to Duane, skillfully sidestepping another high-five attempt. Instead, Duane looks in the bag and, spouting thanks, gives Mike a bear hug, but he doesn't seem to mind.

"You look great!" I step back from Kate to take her in. "I can get my arms around you again."

She rolls her eyes. "I can fit into my shoes again. I can sleep on my stomach again."

"You can fit into your clothes again."

We enter the restaurant.

"We're not quite there yet." Kate pats her middle. "I have a bunch of clothes you should look at. I don't think my waistline is going to fit my skinny jeans again."

I wrinkle my nose. "Just wait. It's only been a few weeks; give yourself some time."

The lounge of the restaurant is lined with salt water tanks filled with coral reef fishes. Two young girls are plastered to the glass, pointing at a parrot fish. Mike is soon fascinated as well.

Kate groans. "I'm trying everything I can without starving, like sushi. I love sushi."

Duane makes a face. "There has to be a better way to diet than eating sushi."

A hostess in a kimono arrives to take us to a table. Michael is slow to catch up, still riveted to the fish in the tank.

As we take our seats, Mike stops the hostess. "One of your fish is sick."

"Oh, yes." She nods and smiles, not really understanding. He frowns and waves her closer to him. She bends over as he whispers to her ear. Her face brightens and she nods smartly, leaving our table directly.

"A sick fish?" Duane pipes up. "That's probably what they'll serve you, sweet pea."

"Duane, don't be gross." Kate gives her husband a withering look.

"How can that be gross? You're eating raw fish and you say I'm gross."

"Raw fish is very healthy for you. It's high in protein and good omega fats, and that's what I need right now."

"Some raw fish can be healthy for you," Michael interjects. "Fish like tuna and shark have high levels of mercury that can be hazardous if eaten regularly."

"It's true," I add. "Remember last year? I got mercury poisoning from eating sushi every day for lunch. All I knew was I felt awful and looked like a heroin addict. Mike put two and two together and told me to see a doctor. My blood work said I was a human thermometer."

"Don't tell me." Duane gives Mike a fatigued look. "We're to blame for that, right?"

"Humans are, yes."

"You always say 'humans' like you aren't one of us. Just because you're a tree hugger doesn't make you a superior being of some kind."

"Duane …" Kate smiles as she tries to scold him.

Our waitress appears with menus and hot tea.

"I don't believe tree huggers are superior beings." My husband answers coolly. "I only cite facts, which are indifferent to humans, particularly ignorant ones."

My mouth feels slack. Mike usually hates engaging Duane for the very reason Duane likes to argue. Apparently, he feels like changing up.

"Am I one of those ignorant humans?"

Michael picks up his menu. "If the shoe fits."

Inwardly, I'm delighted that I'm rubbing off on my husband.

Duane's face reddens. "I just named my first son after you. Did I make a mistake?"

Without looking up, Mike casually scans the menu items. "I'm honored by the gesture, but I didn't expect it in return for helping Kate with her delivery. If you choose to name your son after me, the honor should be given freely and without expectation I should be perpetually indebted to you for it."

What Duane has to say is interrupted when the hostess brings a pen and paper to the table. Michael scribbles on the pad before handing it back. The hostess responds in Japanese before leaving us with a quick bow. Duane stands up and leaves the table without a word. I watch my cousin struggle against her impulse to go to her husband.

"Kate, you can go after him. It's fine with us." I put my hand on hers.

She shrugs as she stares in the direction Duane went. "No, I think I'm going to have sushi with my cousins." Her eyes meet ours and begin to fill with tears. "I'm very happy we named him Michael, and it's going to stay that way."

"I'm sorry, Kate." Mike looks sadly at her. "That was rude of me. My thoughts should have been kept to myself."

Kate laughs as a tear runs down her face. "Oh, God! That I should hear those words come out of Duane's mouth. No, Michael, you have every right to say what you think. That's Duane's problem if he can't take it, though he's always ready to dish it out."

"Are things going to be all right with the baby coming home?" Reaching over, I rub her shoulder. "It seems like Duane might be feeling a little pressure."

This assessment is met with vigorous nodding.

"He's totally stressed. He's been that way ever since I got pregnant. I think he's terrified. His foundation is his family and his church, and it's the fear of not living up to their expectations that's eating him alive. He's lost and he doesn't have anyone to turn to."

"Why doesn't he turn to you?" Mike asks, truly curious. "You're his life partner and the mother of his child. Shouldn't you be his foundation?"

"Ever read the Bible?" Kate arches her brow sarcastically. "I'm his wife. 'Nuff said."

Michael pours Kate a cup of hot tea. "It is unfortunate so many who read the Bible use it to no advantage."

Wiping her nose with her napkin, my cousin takes a sip of tea and smiles.

"It's not his fault." She shrugs. "It's how he was raised. It isn't that Clark and Maxine are evil people or anything. They're just very fearful, and they passed that down to their kids. They isolated them. Their school, their friends, all of their interactions were in a controlled environment, and their church was at the center of it. Duane is used to feeling like all the answers are right there, but the Bible is only one book."

Rising from the table, Michael looks at the two of us with resignation. "I'll find Duane. The two of you should go ahead. We'll be back before you're finished."

Puzzled, Kate looks at me as Mike leaves. "How will he find him?"

"Don't worry about it, Kate." I pat her hand. "It's a guy thing, remember?"

All previous discussion about the dangers of sushi aside, Kate and I eat sushi. Lots of it. We talk about little Mike and about big Mike. We talk about Toe and we talk about Maeve. We talk about crazy Marta and we talk about my parents in Hawaii. After three hours, the doors of the restaurant part, and Duane steps in with Mike behind him.

Duane strides up to our table without a word. Bending down to her, he gives Kate a long kiss. Looking up at my husband, I smile with what I'm sure is a cross between a smirk and suspicion.

At the hospital, we follow Kate and Duane to the critical care unit for preemies. Little Mike is in a nursery. He is only under observation, due to be released at the end of the week. Still, we can only see him from behind a window. A nurse at the front desk tells a staffer that we are visiting and Kate would like to show us her baby. In the nursery, the nurse on duty brings little Mike to the glass.

"There he is!" Duane puffs up. "That's our boy! Hey, Mikey, your cousins are here."

He is bigger, much bigger than when I first and last saw him. He is red and round and puckered, with the start of a dark head of hair.

"Well, he has Mom's hair." I scrutinize his face. "He looks like you, Kate. And I'm not being biased when I say that. He's one of us, I think. Does he have our eyes or Duane's?"

An elbow nudge from Duane bumps me. "That kid is a Nelson. He'll have my baby blues for sure."

Kate smiles enthusiastically. "You know you can't really tell with infants. All of them have muddy blues at first." She points excitedly. "Oh, look, he's yawning."

Little Mike yawns and stretches his fingers. Slowly, he wrinkles his face and opens his eyes. Pressing my lips together, I glance over my shoulder at Mike. Standing only feet away from me, he keeps his eyes to the floor.

Speeding back to Tacoma, we ride in silence while I decide on the most diplomatic way to say what is on my mind. I'm trying not to be pissed he didn't tell me.

"How much of you is in that baby?"

"A little." His response is distant, brittle.

"Are you copping an attitude with me? What did I do?"

"I didn't say anything to you because I wasn't sure how you'd feel about it. When

I did it, I thought it would please you, but then I wasn't so sure. I'm still not."
"Please me?"
Michael looks me in the eyes. His face is like marble; so is his voice.
"You wanted Kate's baby to live?"
"Of course!"
He refocuses on the road. "That was the only way."
He is so cold. I search for his thoughts. He offers none. I am shut out.
There are lots of things I imagine feeling—some I haven't even thought of yet.
Joy that Kate has her baby. Joy that Michael will have a son of sorts. It would be
horribly pathetic for me to dwell on my absence from the picture. It is a denial of
everything I ever felt about children. As long as he couldn't have any, I didn't mind
being childless. It wasn't supposed to be possible, could never happen.
I never feared I was sacrificing this part of myself alone.
Michael's secrecy, and now hostility, turn the knife.
Can I understand his position?
Yes, I can. It was a situation none of us could foresee. It was a moment with no
time for deliberation or reflection. And if it were, how do you deliberate over a life
that is slipping away?
"I'm okay with it, Mike." My mouth makes the words noncommittally.
There is no response. When I look at him, he only stares at the dark highway
ahead of us. Suddenly, I notice it is night and he doesn't have the headlights on.
"Michael, headlights." I gently prompt him.
He seems to start from a trance and flips them on.
"How are you feeling?" Like a hypnotherapist, my tone is neutral.
Trapped.
"You aren't trapped." My eyes strain for his. "You can't keep people from feeling
sad any more than you can keep them from feeling happy."
Are you sad about the baby?
"Part of me is. There's no rhyme or reason to it. I wouldn't have things any other
way given the circumstances. I'm looking forward to it. I can live with it."
There is no response.
"What I can't live with is a statue."
His face begins to move again; his stare softens.
I'm sorry. I was afraid.
Reaching over, I stroke the side of his head. He closes his eyes. When they open,
they are beginning to glow.
"You can be afraid. You just can't be cold. Please, don't be cold?"
Taking his hand from the wheel, he reaches for mine and presses it to his face,
kissing it. The feeling is electric, or something close to it. I can feel who he is com-
ing through his skin, absorbing into mine. It is ecstatic. I make a mental note to
aggravate him more often.
Somehow, he gets us home without hitting anything. As soon as he sets the
brake, he leans to me, his lips on mine, the ice of his breath making my hair raise.

He takes hold of my head, and I expect his voice in my thoughts, but he pulls back. He is looking at my face, but his own is blank.

"Someone is here." He whispers. His eyes focus back on mine. "Stay in the car."

His car door opens, shuts, and he is gone. Watching the front of our house in the headlights, it stares back at me with a menace I'd forgotten. Now that something untoward could lurk behind the curtains, my home no longer seems to welcome me. No lights come on in the windows. There is no sound.

Where's Lodi?

If there were an intruder, he would be barking his head off.

Looking around the yard from the front seat of the car, I see nothing. I strain to see Lodi's house, but there is no sign of him. This is ridiculous. Michael is here. There is no reason for me to stay in the car. Getting out of the car, my brain reminds me this is a classic mistake horror movie victims always make. But I'm not in a horror movie.

Not yet anyway.

I reach in the glove box and take a pocket flashlight with me. The first place I go is Lodi's dog house. I look around Lodi's little yard and into his abode. No Lodi. I wander down to the lower garden. The rose bushes and hedgerows glow blue in the light of the LED. The trees make an occasional whine as they lean in the wind. I follow the path to the koi pond. The waterfall is silent in the dark with no sun to power the pump, the surface of the water a black slick. My eye catches the flash of a fish. Beyond the pond is a stand of trees, and below, the black abyss of the gulch. If Lodi were here, he would come to my light, but there is no sign, no sound above the distant hush of leaves in the breeze.

Returning to the house, I pass the trail head that leads down into the gulch. I have no intention of going there. I'm not that irrational.

Something catches my eye. I turn and look down the trail, only this time I switch off the light. There it is again. Something crossed from one side of the trail to the other. I estimate it is about two hundred yards away. This is where I am not like a classic horror movie victim. I know it isn't Lodi, and I'm certainly not calling to it. I also have a feeling turning my back on it is a bad idea. Slowly, I begin to step back towards the house.

Michael, where the hell are you?

The figure flashes across the trail again, about one hundred yards off. I consider my options. I know my yard pretty well. I know I'm in a direct line with the kitchen. I can feel pavement under my feet, which means I'm about twenty paces from the side door to the house. It also means I'm ten paces too far from safety to be able to outrun the blur that's closing. It occurs to me it could be Michael teaching me a lesson about not listening to him, but I discard the idea as too free spirited for my husband.

The figure stops where I can see it. My mind grasps it isn't human. It is a thing in flux, edges undefined, thin and bending. It is too far for me to see a face, too close for me to want to. It is less than twenty yards away.

You're never getting that lasagna, Mike.

Like a puff of smoke, it is gone.

"Damn."

I jump as Michael's voice materializes next to me. His eyes appear out of the darkness like two dim LEDs.

"If you'd stopped thinking and started running, I would have had it."

"What? You were there the whole time?"

"You didn't draw it close enough."

"So it's my fault now?"

He ignores me. "Whatever it is, it was too weak for me to read. Either that or I was too weak to read it."

"You were using me as bait?"

"You were never in any danger." Stepping from the shadows, he puts his hands on my shoulders in an effort to calm me. "I expected you to run. Why didn't you?"

"Why didn't I run? You're supposed to be outraged I didn't stay in the car!"

Turning for the house, the only thing I want to run is a hot bath.

"Sophie." He catches me lightly. "I should warn you … the house is a bit of a mess."

Catching my breath, I grab his arm. "That *thing* was in our house?"

When I get inside, the kitchen is undisturbed, but the living room is a disaster. There isn't anything that appears to be taken, because everything is broken. At first, it doesn't make sense why it came into the living room just to destroy the furniture, until I see the doors to Mike's study. The furniture had been used to batter them. The black panels are scratched and gouged with a ferocity that makes me appreciate my instinct not to go down the trail. Stubbornly, by means defying reality, the doors remained shut.

I face Mike. "Did it break into the library from the outside?"

"No. But the bars on the window are bent and the polycarbonate was clawed."

"You think it knows what you are?"

"Possibly. It must have sensed me when we arrived. It came when I wouldn't be here. It may know about the crypt. It must think there is something of value to be found."

"I thought I told you to get rid of your porn collection."

Michael rolls his eyes and goes to the mantel. Looking around on the floor, he snatches up our wedding photo and wipes it off with his sleeve.

"This is the most valuable thing here."

"You're good. I almost forgot you tried to feed me to a beast tonight."

"It wouldn't have touched you. I would die before I would let that happen."

"That line only works when you can."

"Do you think this is fun for me?" The change in his volume makes me flinch. "You think you were at risk? Tonight was nothing! From here it only gets worse."

"Stop it." My voice is defensively dry. "You're turning me on."

In the blink of an eye, he is next to me, clutching my hand. "If I caught that thing, this would be over. Instead it's only begun. You aren't safe here. You have to leave."

"Go where? This is my home."

"Anywhere! Your aunt in Bellingham. Your parents in Hawaii, even better."
I smirk. "Maybe Mrs. Farrell has a spare room?"

His hold on my hand tightens.

"This is no home, Sophie. I've lost Toe. I've lost Lodi. I'm not losing you. It's coming back, and I have to be here, alone."

"I'm not your pet."

Looking dismayed, he loosens his grip.

"You're my wife."

I yank my hand from him.

"According to whose definition? Duane's?"

Looking worse by the minute, he gives a half-hearted laugh and sits on the edge of what is left of our sofa. I am curious about Duane's transformation at dinner.

"What did you tell him tonight, anyway?"

He shrugs. "I apologized. I told him I appreciated his efforts to reach out to me. That I wasn't ignorant of what his faith meant to him."

"And?"

"He was worried he would lose Kate. He said he felt helpless when the baby came, like Lot watching his wife turn into salt. I told him it wasn't about taking care of her ..." Michael pauses. "That he needed to learn to rely on her. That sometimes what seems like a mistake has a purpose."

"You had something in the Bible to back that up?"

Michael sneers. "Lot's wife!" He folds his arms and sighs at his feet. "Neela."

"Neela?"

"That was her name. She was warned, not Lot. She was ... gifted."

"What happened?"

"She would have taken her family away, but Lot forbade it."

"Why?"

"He wouldn't leave his possessions behind. By the time he realized the danger, there was barely time for them to escape. Even as they fled, she knew they would look back. There was no time to explain why they shouldn't. No time to convince them she spoke the truth. She looked back first so they would see her consumed and know. She died for her children."

"Why did they have to die at all?"

"It wasn't lust that destroyed Sodom. It was power. The desire for supremacy. It was justice for Lot and those like him to get what they asked for. It wasn't for the innocent. For Neela."

Crossing to where he sits, I put my hands on his shoulders and look down at him. His thoughts are confused, pained. Lifting his chin, I get him to face me.

"Were you the one who warned her?"

Taking my hand, he presses my palm to his mouth and shuts his eyes.

1199 BC   The man who offered me marriage was a respected leader. He was known to all in the Nile Valley as a wealthy herder and fair tradesman. A general of Ramses, he retired early after a bad fall from a chariot, but was rumored to have fallen from favor with Ramses' son, Ramesses. He was a natural leader. Favored for his skill in inspiring others, it later proved his undoing. I only know the truth of it as he told me in confidence when I became his woman. Though I told him I could not marry, I offered myself as consort on condition that he bear my late husband with us on our journey to the land of providence. Widowed himself, he empathized with my request and agreed. With this understanding, I traveled with him, my crypt in tow as part of a great caravan. We crossed the Nile delta from Pi before heading southeast into the waste of Sinai.

Though we were well supplied and with a great company of armed men, the journey to Sinai was difficult. Past the last brook of the Nile, food was rationed and water was in short supply. What was barely sufficient for human survival was wholly insufficient for me. It was no pretense when I claimed illness. All the while, the refuge of my crypt was in sight and out of reach. By the time we reached the encampment, I was starved beyond recognition.

One benefit of my illness was the general abstained from intercourse with me. Instead, he nursed me, racked with guilt that he had delivered me to my death rather than the salvation he promised.

The other benefit was I was too weak to be read by Saitael when we arrived, though I could read him all too clearly.

Our caravan made camp on a bluff skirting a makeshift city of tents and rough shacks. From where I took rest, I saw little more than a great shanty town, yet it thronged with migrants, all engaged in work. With observation I deduced it was mining. When the general returned to tell me it was silver, I knew.

[Spharic. Entry translated from *Kor Dai Maihael*. Mund. Dai. 755 BC]

1999 There was no good make-up sex. Not this time, anyway. It wasn't because Anthony was unable to forgive me for looking at houses with Michael. It was because I couldn't forgive myself for not being honest about my feelings.

Anthony admitted to having an investigator follow me on and off over the last two weeks. My meeting with Michael at Shakabrah had been documented, but the investigator didn't tell Tony about it because he wanted to establish a pattern of behavior before jumping to any conclusions about our relationship. When Michael came to the apartment and we left together, it was suspicious enough for him to share his evidence. When I arrived home, Michael had warned me about the photos, so I was prepared for Anthony's tirade. It was my own response that ultimately took us both by surprise.

Tony didn't start his attack right away. He wanted to confirm Michael was the same man who had approached me at Grounds. When I said he was, the roll call started. To sum it up, I was naïve, reckless, irresponsible, and untrustworthy. I also didn't respect Anthony or his love for me.

My turn.

Anthony had a lot of nerve accusing me of trust issues when he was the one having me followed without my knowledge or consent. He had always assumed I was naïve, reckless, and irresponsible. He didn't trust my judgment and questioned my ability to decide for myself if Michael posed a threat from the beginning. Of course he questioned my decision to befriend him now. Though he was a cop and my boyfriend, he wasn't my father.

That being said, I agreed respecting his love was something I'd overlooked. Although I didn't betray anything with Michael in a physical sense, psychologically I had. Looking for our house with another man had to have Freudian connotations I had been willfully blind to. Not being a psychologist, my best guess was it meant I wanted to share a house, and the rest of my life, with a man I loved. Anthony wasn't that man.

This last revelation left Anthony speechless. So speechless, I didn't wait for a response before asking which of us was going to sleep on the sofa.

It all happened so fast. It was impossible to believe we planned on house hunting the next day and now we were splitting up.

The rest of the week, we went to work sharing everything but the bedroom. Anthony chivalrously took the sofa. We were both miserable. Several times, Tony tried to talk me into reconsidering. All I could say was it wasn't fair to either of us to continue to be comfortable and nothing more. It made sense to me, but he couldn't understand it.

When I told Mom, she was delighted and offered my old bedroom to me. I could tell Dad was worried, but I didn't want him to be. I didn't want anyone to worry, to know. I wanted to disappear. I didn't tell my co-workers or my friends. Not that I had many, anyway. Of all the friends I had, the one I would have told was Anthony, and he was the friend I had hurt.

The weekend after my break up, I kept my cell phone on me everywhere I went. It made me think having Michael in my head wasn't such a bad thing if it meant I could talk to him whenever I wanted to. And I really, really wanted to.

Around noon, my phone rang.

"Hello, Sophie."

It was the drama; it was too much coffee. I totally went girl and began to cry at the sound of his voice. Of course, I still tried to pretend I wasn't.

"Sophie? Are you all right?"

Coughing and rubbing my nose, I cleared my throat. "Hi, Mike."

"Is something wrong?"

"There's no garden here." I whispered as my body tried to laugh.

"Where are you?"

"In my car."

"Where are you going?"

"Nowhere."

"Sophie, where are you?"

"Point Defiance."

"Where at Point Defiance?"

"I don't know." I paused, looking around. "Some turnabout."

"What are you looking at?" As he spoke, I thought I heard him starting his car.

"Vashon Island, why?"

"Do you want me to meet you there?"

"Does it matter? We're talking right now."

"I'm on my way. Will you stay there?"

"If you want me to, sure."

"I'll be there in a few minutes."

"Michael?"

"Yes."

"Why don't I have your cell number but you have mine?"

"I didn't think you would want to call me."

Laughing through tears, I bit my lower lip and covered my face with my hand.

"Sophie? Are you there?"

"Yeah, I was thinking about how things change. Last month I dreaded the thought of hearing you. This week that's all I wanted and I couldn't even call you."

I lost it.

"I kept thinking you were what I was afraid of, you know? I'm what I'm afraid of. I was afraid of me at Grounds. I was afraid of me when you drove me to the hospital. I was afraid of me when I went to the conservatory." I started to laugh. "All this time I've been afraid to run in Point Defiance because I was afraid of stalkers—I thought you were stalking me. But it's been me the whole time, hasn't it? I can't get away from me. That's my problem."

"I was stalking you. There's nothing wrong with you. You were wise to be afraid of me. Perhaps you still should be."

"But you would have stopped if I told you to."

"Yes."

"See, I knew that, but I didn't want to believe it. I just wanted to be a jerk to you."

"You won't feel so bad about that when you know me better."

"Why don't I believe you?"

"You're still young, used to continuity. You've never had reason to reevaluate your life before. Don't be afraid of yourself because the water has gotten deeper. You swim the same regardless of which end of the pool you're in."

"Actually, I'm a lousy swimmer. You might want to choose a different metaphor."

"I want to help you, Sophie. Will you let me?"

"Yes."

"Then hear what I am saying instead of making a shallow excuse to ignore it."

It stung. I realized only my mother ever spoke that way to me. My mother had always spoken the truth to me; it was why she stung me. It was what I needed to hear now, but it wasn't my mother I was talking to.

"Sophie?"

"I'm sorry."

"I don't want you to be sorry. I need you to be open. Will you try?"

"Yeah." I sniffed.

"My number is in your phone, but I'll stay on with you if you want."

"No, I'm fine."

"Are you still parked at the same point?"

"Yes."

"Are you still inside your car?"

"Yes."

"What are you thinking about?"

"What a lousy swimmer I am."

"You're a better swimmer than you realize."

"You know I'm a Pieces?"

"Yes."

"I'm a fish that doesn't swim. Of course, I suppose you don't have to be a good swimmer if you can breathe underwater."

"You can't breathe underwater, Sophie."

"No, but I'm good at holding my breath. I should be … it's all I've ever done."

"Holding your breath isn't the solution."

"It's better than drowning."

"They're the same thing."

"When you can't breathe, you don't have much of a choice."

"There's always a choice; you just haven't opened your eyes."

"I'd lose my contacts if I did."

"I'm almost there."

"You didn't mow over anyone on your way here, did you?"

"I was only a few minutes away when you called."

"The way you drive, you could've been in Seattle."

"I just time the lights right."

"How many minutes does it take you to get across town? Have you ever timed yourself?"

"No."

"When I was a kid, I could hold my breath in the tub for four minutes. I used to time myself with a stop watch."

"I can see your car."

"I wonder how long I could hold my breath for now."

A shadow fell across me and I looked out my window to see Michael's face peering down at me. He was wearing sunglasses and a navy pea coat. I opened my car door and stepped out. He barely opened his arms before I walked into them. Burying my face in his shoulder, I smelled wool and the faint scent of trees. I don't know how long I held him. It didn't matter because I knew he didn't care.

We didn't talk about Anthony at all. We barely spoke. He was just there for me, and I could just be there. When I decided to leave, I was still in a haze. Michael asked where I was going. I told him I had to go back to my life at some point. I couldn't hide out with him in the park forever. He was hesitant to let me drive, but I told him I had his cell number now and I wouldn't let myself go like that again. He said he was disappointed to hear it.

I left him at the scenic point, standing next to his car, looking perfect and perfectly distracted. It wasn't easy to leave him there. Not just because he was easy on the eyes, but because he was easy on the mind. There weren't any sharp edges on him. To be sure, he had a mysterious hardness, but no broken pieces that cut your hands. By comparison, Anthony was a plate glass window, transparent in his expectations, transparent with his feelings, all but shattered.

The moment I was in the door of our apartment, I could feel Tony's eyes on me. They were always looking to meet mine, always full of questions, and the answers were never the right ones.

"Were you with him?"

"Christ, Tony, what kind of response do you think you're going to get with a question like that? I thought interrogations were something you were good at."

"Do you know anything about him? I mean, beside the fact he fell out of a catalog and drives a sweet car."

"I'm not supposed to know anything about him. I'm reckless and irresponsible, remember?"

"Don't forget naïve." Tony made a genuine smile.

"Thanks." My grin was reflexive.

"Look." He crossed the room to me and took my hand. "If it's really over, I'll accept that. But you can't stop me from loving you on my own, okay? I'm going to try to give you your space. I'm not going to try to talk you out of this anymore. But you know how I am … what I am."

He went to the dining room table and picked up a manila envelope. He brought it over and thrust it out to me. As I took it, he brushed his palms against one another as though he'd handled something covered in dirt.

"That's everything. The photos, the surveillance record, public records I had pulled, the works. You can read it, burn it, whatever. It's your life."

Looking at the envelope in my hand, I sighed and held it to my chest.

"Thanks, Tony. I appreciate it."

With a wide smile, he leaned in to peck me on the cheek. Without another word, he went to the sofa, picked up his jacket, and left the apartment. For a while I stood looking at the envelope in my hands. Dropping it on the coffee table, I went into the kitchen and started a brew. I pulled a snicker doodle out of the cookie jar and took a bite, then glanced back at the table and the envelope that was on it.

Returning to the sofa, I picked up the envelope. It was unsealed and I slid out the contents onto the table. The first items to catch my eye were skewed black and white photos of Michael and me. Michael and I sitting across from each other at Shakabrah. Michael opening his car door for me outside the apartment. Michael and I in front of a house we looked at the week before. The photos were eerie, knowing what he was. It made me wonder what else might be living among us that weren't what they appeared to be.

The public records consisted of his birth certificate, drivers' license, Social Security information, tax records, and a copy of the deed to his house. Up until now I didn't even know his last name. I never remembered to ask. He was just Michael. Apparently, his last name on planet Earth was Goodhew, which coincidentally was my grandmother's maiden name.

His birth certificate claimed he was born Michael Thomas Goodhew III, in Los Angeles on September 28, 1972, at Cedars Sinai Hospital. The medical details such as blood type and weight were left blank. His parents were Michael Thomas Goodhew II and Sarah Monroe, both from Philadelphia. His driver's license gave the same birth date information, listed his gender as male, his height at six foot two, his weight at 185 pounds, his hair as brown, his eyes as blue. He was not an organ donor.

His Social Security information was a formality; he had never been employed. There were tax statements showing an annual income of $1,000,000 from a private trust fund called ECCO. According to notes in the records, Anthony or his investigator tried unsuccessfully to find information on what ECCO was and where the money came from. The names and addresses were pointless, fronts likely. Anthony didn't have the time or money to do more digging.

The house on Prospect was the only property Michael owned in Pierce County. The deed record traced the chain of ownership from Michael to his father, Michael Goodhew II, and to his father's uncle, Daniel Thomas Goodhew. Daniel died sometime in July of 1972, after which Michael's "father" inherited the house and resided there until he died in December of 1997.

Anthony had gone to the effort to pull a death certificate on Michael's father and discovered he had been declared legally dead by the State of Washington after going missing for three years. The notes said Michael Sr. went camping near Lake Crescent in Olympic National Park and was never seen again. The last photo record of Michael Sr. was a copy of his 1960 driver's license. It was Michael, only with short hair. His hair now was medium length and came to his ears. Michael Sr. stopped renewing his license after settling in Tacoma and was never a registered voter.

Knowing Anthony, he'd probably dreamed up a pet theory that Michael had bumped off his dad. If Tony really did have such a suspicion, what he'd told me about dropping this was a lie. It would give him a satisfying hobby over the long nights to discredit Michael as a murderer. It was ludicrous to me anyone could compare Michael's driver's license photo with his father's and not think they were the same person. It proved in Michael's case that believing was seeing. Even I had trouble remembering his face until I believed he existed.

But who were these other relatives? Did any of them exist? Michael didn't have parents. But an uncle? Of course, this was what Anthony wanted me to do, to read this and bedevil myself with questions. He was hoping I would start asking questions of my own, questions Michael would have trouble answering. Anthony couldn't understand I would never stop having questions for Michael, and murder wouldn't be the reason he would have trouble answering.

Regardless of how Anthony felt about Michael, he was insistent that I stay at our apartment until I found my own place. I knew he was worried about me and hopeful I would change my mind. I also knew he didn't want to give my mother the satisfaction of having me move back in with them. I agreed on the condition he promised not to try to change my mind.

For the rest of the week, every day I walked out of our apartment was reliving an event yet to happen. Anthony tried not to notice I was reading apartment listings with the same dedication I had once given to the real estate section. The evenings we used to spend on the sofa watching movies were now marked by my absence as I met with apartment managers and filled out rental applications. Every ring on my cell made him cringe at the thought I was negotiating a new life for myself without him. Or worse, that I was talking to Michael, who, like a precious new possession, I would take with me.

In truth, I hadn't heard from Michael since I left him in the park. With nothing on my mind and everything to do, I had little time to think about him. Maybe I had too much time to think about him. What Anthony didn't know was Michael wasn't competing with him for my hand. What I was taking with me into of my new life wasn't as much as he supposed. It was less than that. It had been burned in a wastebasket as soon as I finished reading it.

Crammed into the bedroom, with my belongings packed into boxes, I sat cross-legged on the bed with my list of apartments, my cell phone, and a mission. Since Michael had been so helpful when I was looking at houses, I decided he wouldn't mind if I employed him to help me find my apartment, especially seeing as how he wasn't employed at anything else. When I speed dialed his name on my call list, my brain still doubted anyone would answer.

"Hello, Sophie."

The voice that was a comfort the weekend before was eerie to me now.

"Is being surprised an impossibility for you?"

"I don't have any friends, remember?"

"That makes two of us."

"I have been waiting for you to call."

"That's what I'm doing. I need you."

"I like to be needed."

"Can you pick me up in fifteen minutes?"

"I'm … I'm in the middle of something right now."

"Something more important than me? I'm shocked to hear it."

"It has everything to do with you, in fact."

"When will you be free?"

"May I come for you tomorrow?"

"The reason I need you today is because I don't want to look for apartments all day by myself. I have one week left to find something before I'm stuck moving back with my parents or Anthony cuffs me to the radiator."

And then there was silence.

"Michael?" I hoped I didn't sound too whiny.

"I'll be there in fifteen minutes."

"Thank you!"

As I snapped my phone shut, Anthony poked his head into the bedroom.

"I wouldn't cuff you to the radiator."

"You've thought about it. Admit it."

He leaned against the door with his arms folded and a flirtatious smile. "I've thought about cuffing you to plenty of stuff, but never the radiator."

"You like your cuffs."

"Sounds like you've got 'em on Mike. He's become your regular gopher."

"Last week he was going to strangle me and dump my body in Lake Crescent; this week he's my gopher. Tell me when you make up your mind."

"I'll make up my mind when you do. Admit it, he still spooks you. I could hear it in your voice when you were talking to him. You haven't tested him, have you?"

"I'm getting there."

Anthony tossed a pair of his cuffs at me. "Try putting those on him."

I grabbed them off of the bed and threw them at him.

After the cuff incident, I decided to wait on the curb for Michael.

When I stepped outside the building, he was already waiting by his car.

"Why didn't you—? You're already here." I tossed up my hands. "How long have you been here?"

"Not long."

"Why didn't you just tell me you'd be here in five minutes?"

"I didn't want to rush you." He opened the passenger door.

Shaking my head, I handed him a list of addresses as I got in. He glanced at the list and handed it back to me before closing my door. When he started the engine, the radio was on. "Middle of the Road" was playing. The universe was screwing with my head.

"I notice none of those apartments are located in the North End. I thought this neighborhood was where you wanted to live."

"Yup." I started fumbling for my lip gloss.

"There are many apartments in this area. Why are you looking in west Tacoma?"

"I need some space right now. It would be too weird to see Anthony around."

The car seemed to slow. When I glanced at him, he looked confused.

"So you wouldn't consider living in the North End under any circumstances?"

"There are lots of places in the North End I'd move to, but the places I can afford are all within three blocks of where I am right now. We'd be using the same drugstore, the same gas station, the same coffee shop. Anthony would drive me nuts every time he saw me. I'd freakin' kill myself!"

He winced at the sound of my voice. When I looked back out the window, I recognized the familiar rows of old houses. We were on Prospect, heading for his house.

"Forget something?"

"I wanted you to see something."

"There's more? What? Bats in the belfry, bodies in the basement?"

Shaking his head, he barely smiled. "Humor me."

Crossing my arms, I raised my eyebrows and sat back in my seat. As we reached the gravel drive of his house, I noticed a difference. The wisteria on the front porch appeared to have been tamed and the windows looked different somehow.

Getting out of the car, he walked with purpose to the front porch. I ran to catch up with him as he unlocked the door. When the door opened, he pushed it wide and stood on the stoop with an expectant look on his face. What I noticed almost immediately was sunlight.

Entering the foyer, my mouth opened. The floors were waxed and polished under an enormous Persian rug running the length of the great room. The drab curtains were replaced with peacock-hued silk. Unveiled windows filled the room with the color of pale green walls hidden before. What appeared to be original folk paintings were carefully hung next to a series of botanical prints. The fireplace shined with fired tiles of iridescent blue glazing, the inlaid woodwork of the mantel polished to glowing. An antique coffee table bore a porcelain vase with flowers.

"Do you like it?" His eyes sparkled.

"This is amazing. You did this by yourself?"

When I looked at him, he only blinked.

"There's more." His hand indicated the stairs in the foyer.

"Upstairs?" I pointed, and he nodded.

The stairs looked less ominous with light at the top of them. As I reached the landing, I peeked around the banister. It led into four rooms, one in each direction. I could see that two were smaller. The small room I was closest to was a bathroom. It was entirely white with hexagonal tiles on the floor that ran up the sides of the walls. An enameled pedestal sink and toilet were at one end, a large claw-footed tub at the other.

I went to the end of the landing and looked into a large bedroom. It had a periwinkle color and was filled with neatly stacked boxes. The other small room was yellow and entirely empty. The last room was closed. At the door, I put my hand on the knob. I looked over my shoulder at Michael, who followed in such silence as to be nearly invisible. He nodded and I opened the door.

It was painted a vivid coral. The room was furnished with two standing wardrobes, an enormous dresser, an ornate vanity, and a simple but immense four-poster bed. There were windows in all three exterior walls; the largest was a bay corresponding with the bay in the study downstairs. Unlike the study window, this window didn't contain stained glass but framed an unobstructed view of tree tops fringing the blue waters of the Sound. It was beautiful.

It was a trap.

Before he could say anything, I spun on him.

"You're kidding if you think I'm going to live here."

His face was blank.

"That *is* why you wanted me to see this, right? You didn't suddenly have interior design fever and want my critique?"

"You don't like it?"

"Like it? I love it!" He looked relieved at my words, until I shook my head. "I just can't live with you."

"Why not?"

"Don't you think I've burned through my roommate privileges at this point?"

"You're not a roommate. You're my friend."

"I've tried that already. Look where it got me." I walked out of the room and headed for the stairs.

"Is it because I'm a man?"

I stopped at the top of the stairs with a smirk. "That you are."

Continuing down to the foyer, I was unsure whether or not to leave. I decided to ask if we could go back to looking at my apartments. Hearing him behind me, I turned to face him at the bottom of the stairs, but he wasn't there.

"Would it be easier if I were a woman?"

His voice nearly gave me a stroke. Materialized across the foyer, he was planted in front of the door, leaning against it with his hands behind his back.

"You're kidding."

"I'm not."

"I think you're fine the way you are."

"If you really felt that, you would be happy to live here with me."

Scratching my ear because everything else itched, I backed into the living room.

"Why didn't you think about this before you approached me?"

"I've had the same body for some time. I took it for granted you wouldn't mind."

He pushed himself off of the door and stood next to the grandfather clock.

"You didn't mind last time and we lived together then. After what you said two weeks ago about your ovaries seeing me as a sperm donor, I think gender is the basis for our miscommunications."

"So in my last life, I wasn't attracted to you at all."

"You were deeply in love with your wife."

"I really, really, *really* can't take much more of this."

"Why does that upset you?"

"Because I'm not a dude! I'm a chick! I like—no, *I love men.* I love being friends with them, I love screwing them, I love being friends and screwing them *at the same time!* I'm sorry if that upsets you, but that's the way I roll."

"That's why I suggested if I were a woman this situation might be easier for you."

"You can't be that naïve. Didn't you just hear what I said? I don't want to 'just live' with you, period. I'm going to find an apartment and as soon as I find a guy I love who wants to live with me *and* have sex with me, I'll be just fine."

"So you wouldn't live with me if I was a woman."

"If you turn that." I pointed at his body. "Into a woman, I'll beat you to death."

"If I had sex with you, would you feel comfortable living with me?"

"If all I wanted was sex, I could go back to Anthony. *You're* the one who told me I didn't love Anthony. That's what I want. I want love." I dropped onto his sofa. "How can you ask that? Where do you get off telling me about relationships when you don't even know what they're about?"

"I was only making an observation. Your previous relationships always seemed very intense. I didn't feel that from you when you thought about Anthony. I just assumed living with me wouldn't preclude you from finding someone else."

"Have you ever been in love?"

"I love our friendship and the time we have shared."

"I'm not talking rain drops on roses and whiskers on kittens here, Mike. I'm talking about Romeo and Juliet, Antony and Cleopatra, Sid and Nancy, 'I'd rather cease to exist than exist without you' love."

He went to a wing-backed chair by the fireplace and slowly sat in a trance.

"I don't know if I could ever feel that strongly about another being." As he spoke, he watched me intently, as though I were aware of a deeper meaning to his words, "If I chose to put my existence at risk for love ... that would be a very selfish act."

"Sorry, Michael." Shaking my head, I stood up. "I'm not some super being charged with keeping the universe from running amuck. I'm just a woman who has to find her own way in this world. Whether or not I live a thousand lives or not doesn't mean crap to me. Without love in this one, the rest is pointless. I don't have eternity to find that and live with you as your friend. That's life in a box. That's you."

I walked past him for the front door. When I reached for the door latch, he was standing next to me.

His hand took mine. "We'll still be friends?"

My heart stopped at his impossibly blue eyes. "That's what Anthony said."

Pulling on the door, I walked out and started up the drive, ignoring his car. The sun was already setting, and the December air was perfect for a walk home. As I climbed the drive, I heard his car start and the slow crunch of tires on gravel as he pulled up next to me. He put his window down, and I could hear the radio. Mick Jagger was promising emotional rescue.

"This is one of my favorite Stones songs." I smiled at him without stopping.

"Let me drive you somewhere." His car rolled alongside me.

"'Satisfaction' rates pretty high, too."

"Sophie, you're making this difficult for me."

"Really? It's been a cake walk for me."

"I'm not capable of more than friendship."

"Know what my favorite Stones song is?"

"We don't replicate ourselves."

"No, I don't think they did that one."

"Why can't we be like we were last weekend?"

"What? With you as the all-knowing mentor and me as the love-struck zombie?"

"You're in love with me?"

"Shocking, isn't it?" My head shook. "Surprised the hell out of me, too."

"But you never asked this of me before."

"I had a prostate before. What's your point?"

"You're asking too much."

"So are you."

"I thought you said I had you at hello?"

"I just wanted to say that. My mistake."

"How could you make a mistake about our friendship?"

"My ovaries found you irresistible. You're too perfect. Strong but vulnerable, wise but innocent, alien but beautiful. Add that your height is above average and our friendship never had a chance."

"I should have been a woman."

"If your version of a woman is on par with what you look like now, I'd hate you."

"An unattractive woman?"

"A six-foot rabbit would have been better."

"Are you sending me away?"

"That's up to you."

"What do you mean?"

"Would you ever knowingly hurt me?"

"Never."

"Well, when I love you and you only want to be my friend, that hurts."

"I'm sorry."

"I don't want you to be sorry. I want you to be open."

"What can I do?"

"If you can only love me as a friend and you honor our friendship, you'll leave."

We reached the end of his drive; the Stones song had ended long before. "Bittersweet Symphony" was playing. His car stopped; I kept walking. I heard his car door open.

"Sophie!"

Stopping, I turned. He was standing with the car door open. He looked lost. His mouth opened to say something, closed, then opened.

"I just want things to be the way they were."

I shrugged. "You can't always get what you want."

He was speechless.

"Good-bye, Michael."

With a smile on my face, I walked away.

[Washington State driver licenses for Michael Goodhew, 1960, 1997.]

116 | LISA MOWAT

Attachment is forbidden.
In body forbidden.
In name forbidden.
In time forbidden.
In blood forbidden.
In life forbidden.
In marriage forbidden.
In matter forbidden.
In word forbidden.
In deed forbidden.

[Cuneiform. Banned record. Translation
of the *Singular Code*. bef. 1500 B.C.]

2003 It only takes a day to clean up the destruction from the break in. It takes three days for us to feel any comfort in our home again. Michael refuses to go anywhere in the evenings and returns to the same habits he had early in our romance. Determined to be ready for a battle of some kind, he is using his crypt again, which means he rarely sleeps and has stopped sharing our bed—which means if he doesn't kill this thing soon enough, I will kill us both.

Worse than any of this is the disturbing change in his behavior. You might think not having a body would be an advantage, but having a body adds a lot to one's personality. Without a body, a sentient mind can become eccentric, to say the least. It definitely loses its humanity. The human qualities Michael so quickly developed once he accepted falling in love erode just as quickly when he accepts the spiritual sustenance of the crypt.

After his first week using the crypt, the change is evident. His voice has regained the artificial quality that creeped me out when I first met him. His face is impassive, rarely registering any emotional response. Only his interest in food remains. In spite of his promise to me to never become a statue, he is slipping away. Bit by bit, my husband is turning to marble.

I try to see the bright side. None of these changes are irreversible. Even then, if I can never have Michael the way I want him, at his core there is no changing the innocent, hopeful being he simply is.

In the meantime, I go back to work in the garden. May is my favorite month for being outdoors. Most of the April showers have passed and the interminable heat of June and July have yet to arrive. You can work outside all day without freezing to death or dying of heat exhaustion. The garden is also the one place that reminds me the rest of the universe is all right, even if I am sleeping alone.

Guarding the house every night, Michael keeps hoping to catch the thing that violated our home. He feels we are safe during the day, so the day is when he disappears into his crypt. He is never inside it for very long, but he is almost inhuman the first hour out of it. Add to this the hours of solitary study, nightly patrols and meal times, and that leaves little time as a loving spouse. In spite of not seeing the beast since that first night, I know he wants me to leave.

Feeding him a dozen eggs for breakfast, I sit across from him in silence.

"Will you be in the garden today?" His words float around the dining room.

"I think I'll try to fix the pump for the koi pond. Not to mention, the pond needs to be cleaned at some point. It'll have to be drained." I pause. "You think it's my fault, don't you?"

He only stares at me.

"I let you down, didn't I?"

"You know that's not true. It was too far away. I wouldn't have seen it at all if you hadn't lured it back."

"That's not what I mean. I mean if you weren't married to me, if I hadn't lured you down this path, you would have been home that night."

"There is no way of knowing how things might have been different. There are an infinite number of outcomes to any event. This is the reality we have to deal with, and I would rather be here than anywhere else."

Getting up, I begin to gather plates. "But you are somewhere else. You were never really all here to begin with, and it's even worse when you spend time in that coffin. When you come out, you're …"

Not wanting to say any more, I head for the kitchen.

He follows me. "Without it I couldn't be here at all, Sophie."

"You don't need it, Mike. For nearly a year you didn't, but now every day? You got scared, admit it. You couldn't tell what you were dealing with and it scared you. You aren't just looking for that thing; you're worried you aren't what you used to be and now you're trying to go back. You think love is decadent and you're crash dieting."

"Sophie, I don't want to frighten you."

"Stop trying to protect me!" Silverware crashes as I dump the dishes in the sink. "I'm not the one you're trying to protect. What does it matter if I'm safe if I'm alone and miserable? If you'd let me walk out on you three years ago, I'd be where I am now, alone in bed at night and alone at work all day—but I'd be free."

"I don't want that. You know I don't."

"You wanted me in a box, and that's what you've got. Now that I'm committed, now that we're married, now you treat me like the *friend* you always wanted."

"Everything I've done is because I think it's for the best."

"And you're not going to tell me the truth because you don't want me to worry?"

He falls silent. I face him, leaning back against the sink with my arms crossed.

"What goes on in that study? How do you spend all that time in your sarcopha-gus while the living face each day with open eyes?"

"Would it make you feel better if I left the doors open?"

I burst out laughing. It is hot and mean.

"Just tell me … if the house catches on fire and you're inside, should I even bother? Or is that thing fireproof?"

"If you ever need me, come for me." He is soft and empty.

"I'll do that." I say with disenchantment.

Turning my back on him, I go back to the dishes.

It is a catty moment for me, but I rationalize an entity of profound conscious-ness would have noticed by now. At the very least, he might have brought it up as a point of concern before the Kahuna married us. I am catty. With needs. And what I really need after spitting fire is closure. Preferably of my eyes, while his tongue licks my wounds.

Instead, I am returning to the garden alone. I turn my frustration to clawing at the planet that bore me. I will tear out what Mother Nature thinks best and plant seeds of my own. I will make Eden in my own image, and there will be no Adam.

There will, however, be cats.

In my fresh flower bed, cat prints string in the direction of the koi pond. Toe? It has been over a week. It could be any stray, any neighbor's pet, it is impossible to tell. Following the tracks, I forget my revision of Genesis in favor of restoring my honor with Kate. Cutting through the iris bed, I peek down the embankment at the pond below.

"Toe!" As soon as I speak, I curse my lack of impulse control.

Toe streaks down the path back to the house. Running after her, I come to where the path intersects the trail head leading down the gulch. Pausing, I look down the trail. I haven't ventured down since the night I saw the beast.

But it is day, warm and bright. I sense no danger and guess Toe would agree with me. Starting down the trail, I go slowly, listening to the brush for any sign. It proves slow going. I am three-quarters of the way to the bottom of the ravine without even a meow. Maybe if I get a can of tuna? Maybe Toe is making an ass out of me and is preening on the porch this very minute? Maybe it wasn't Toe at all but some other calico? They all look alike from twenty paces. The brambles move below me. I step to the edge of the trail and peer down on rhododendrons heavy with buds.

I hear the stream running along the bottom of the gulch, only a murmur in May.

Then I feel the rush of a carnival ride. The ground leaves my feet, a sense of weightlessness as the blood in my body stops moving. The fall really isn't so bad. It is a blur of light and dark, a fast train of noise. It's the sudden stop. Weightlessness replaced with the gravitational constant of another planet. I can't breathe. Everything slows. Vaguely, I'm aware of rocks underneath me. I hear the sounds of a struggle.

Everything is sharp. Focused. I can hear everything, feel nothing, see I am being attacked. My instinct to survive ignores cutting flesh, the buzz behind my eyes. My arm pulls me forward, out from under the menace on my back. I'm in the streambed. The water feels good on my face until I realize I didn't put it there, that breathing is no longer an option.

But I'm good at holding my breath. Very good. I stop struggling. My plan is to play dead. To play dead, before I am.

When I wake, I feel very rested. Part of me is aware something is not as it should be. The other part is thoroughly enjoying itself. The sun shines on my face, and I am looking at the sky through the branches of birch trees. My chest is heavy and warm. And vibrating.

"Toe." My mouth is slow as my tongue registers the metallic taste of me.

Toe purrs as though this was to be expected. I look in her lazy eyes. Her coat is pristine until I reach to pet her, leaving a stain of blood and dirt between her ears. I decide I should get up. My decision is met with disagreement from above and below. My head doesn't feel a change in orientation is called for. My body can't decide how many limbs I have.

The initial decision to move overrides the disorder. Sitting up, I think my head has taken a knock because everything beyond ten feet is a blur. I must have lost my lenses in the stream. Getting back to business, roll call is made. My left ankle is mildly indisposed, as are a couple ribs. My right arm is on strike. With Toe rubbing against me, I find my feet.

Slip and fall aside, the climb up the trail isn't improved by the steady sun. What is warm and cozy when laying in a streambed becomes oppressive on a steep incline and bad ankle. Toe stays with me but lacks the substance to be of much assistance. Reaching my kitchen door, the cool air of the shaded room convinces me to take a seat and consider my options.

Drive myself to the ER? With a fractured arm? The BMW is a stick, but my Jetta isn't. I'll take the Jetta. Wandering into the living room, I make for the console table that is currently the only surviving piece of furniture. Rummaging the drawer for my keys, I see myself reflected in the glass of a picture frame. Not bad. A cut on my left cheek, leaves in my hair. A mirror would tell more but why pry?

Before turning to go, I notice the study doors are open.

He said they would be.

I near the study. There is no sound, no sign of life. The white slab of the crypt rests like opaque ice against the woodwork. Pride grips the keys in my palm as I need him. Soundlessly, the crypt comes within my reach. My hand puts the keys on the lid as the fingers stretch themselves out, feeling the tracery of signs made by no hand at all. My fear stretches around the shape of the thing. Would I open it if I could? If I could, would I? If I didn't know what was inside?

Yes. Without knowledge, I would open it without fear. I would never know the risk of what was inside. But I do know the risk. I'm married to it.

How the hell do I open this thing?

Deciding to give it the old college try, I bend my knees, my left hand on the edge, pushing up. I prepare for my hand to slip off, to feel the solid weight of the thing resist the intention of my touch. It doesn't. The thin seam that rings the block widens, glowing with blue light. I hear my keys skid across the lid and land on the floor. As though balanced on a piano hinge, the lid lifts higher and higher.

The walls inside are bare, glacier blue. The figure inside is naked. Of clothes, of skin, of consciousness. It is the shape of a man. It is the bare striated flesh of muscle and sinew only crafted out of something resembling fiber optic cable instead of blood and bone. A ripple of light runs the length of the limbs. I recognize it. I have seen it beneath his skin when he shares my bed. I have felt it permeate my own.

My eyes resist the face. They have the will to explore everything else save that. My mind knows why, my gut knows why, my heart, though, will not be denied. Desire has a powerful hold over the mind and the memory. Desire, only satisfied with life and extinguished by death. Desire draws my eyes to the face. I know it, but not by name. I used to look at it in my parents encyclopedia. The first volume. A–An, anatomy (male). Musculature of the face.

When I was a child, nothing scared me more than skulls, especially human ones. The chart of a person's skinned face ran a close second. This one is lit up on the inside, like a gothic lava lamp. A constant spark of fire glows in the middle of the forehead. Slowly the eyes open; they are the most familiar thing to me. They are brilliant. They come when my body has grown too small for me, when I am the closest to heaven I will ever get. I have seen heaven in those eyes. I have seen myself in them.

Slamming the crypt shut, I stand frozen with my hand still hanging on the edge of the lid.

"Sophie."

A voice comes from the box.

"Nothing." I cough.

I quickly move to the other side of the crypt, frantically looking for the keys.

"I'm just taking the car, my car that is. I'll be back—"

The lid begins to lift. Instinctively, I throw myself on it, swearing as my arm screams.

"Sophie, let me out."

It sounds remarkably like my husband's voice.

I hear an automated response.

"Don't bother, you're busy, I've got some errands to run, I'll be back in a few."

I back away from the crypt through the study doors, my eyes on the lid. As it begins to lift, I slam the doors, searching for anything to brace them with, but there is no furniture to be had. Limping, I run for the front door and flip the latch. Pulling it open, my eyes make out the sun on the gravel drive. My car waits, parked under the trees. My world is still here.

The door slams shut with unseen force. Hands grab my shoulders, pulling on me. My shoulders sear with pain as I feel myself being spun around. Closing my eyes tight, I pull my arms in to me. Hands grip my wrists; I let out a shriek before my right arm snaps. It is the sound of the strings holding me up being broken. There is no up or down. There is nothing more to feel.

You can have the same dream so many times you can't remember if it is a dream or memory. Sometimes I dream about floating in water. I assume in a tub; the water is fresh and warm. There is no salt in my mouth, no stink of chlorine. Sometimes there are arms around me. It is my grandmother giving me my first bath. It is my father washing my hair when I am two. My mother soaking me when I have chicken pox. Maybe it is a dream because all the people I love most in the world have given me a bath at one time or another.

Except for Michael. We shared a bathing moment that was rather unpleasant. After that, he stayed away from the bathroom. The meaning of bathing is probably something you have to be a bather to understand. Michael doesn't bathe. He doesn't even use a toilet. When your bodily functions resemble a cold fusion reactor instead of a digestive tract, you are blissfully ignorant of what most people consider an inconvenience.

But I disagree. There is an intimacy the most disgusting aspects of being human have to impart. My lifelong friends from school days are people I rescued from gutters and the back seats of cars. We saved each other, from bad trips, tequila worm poisoning, the flu. In a world without battlefields, the limit of one's constitution is the last place unbelievable but true events can still be encountered and shared with twisted pride. We will all be sick. We will all be filthy. We must all bathe.

As I consider the philosophy of bathing, I am feeling I am having one of my tub dreams. I am disappointed my brain is distracted and not letting me in the water. I want to be there. I want to float. I force myself to feel I am floating, feel water, feel I am having one of my pleasant dreams. The hazy euphoria isn't there.

It is hazy dysphasia. A feeling of pain blocked. The pain that remains is more than physical. It is grief and guilt, melancholy and fear. It isn't mine. It comes from the arms holding me, hands stroking my limbs, holding my face above water. A pain so intense, my insides constrict and the pain gets worse. Pain is pouring into me.

The water falls away, and it is hard to breathe. My body should shiver with cold but doesn't. My head is lead weight, straining my neck. My life is hiding in the keep of my heart, a breath left to find its way, wheezing through my teeth. Gradually, something warm closes on me. Everything is soft, and dark, and silent. Very faintly, I hear something else. A whisper. Words, if they are words at all. Falling asleep, the world fades, all but the whispering, restless, alone.

"Can you hear me?"

It is the same question. Christ, can't anyone sleep anymore?

"Shut up. It's early."

I roll over, pulling the quilt over my head. The quilt pulls away.

"Sophie, can you open your eyes for me?"

A hand cradles my head. I blink into the light of his face. His eyes are staring into mine; his face is softly drawn. It occurs to me I haven't opened my eyes to his face for some time.

"Shit!"

I bolt upright in bed as my brain kicks in. One piece at a time, memory begins to fall into place. The memory of pain yanks my right arm out from under me, but there is none. My heart pounds in my ears as I feel it. I look up at him.

"Everything is all right. Do you understand? You're safe."

No words come to mind. I sit speechless and look away, staring at nothing.

"Sophie?"

"You'd never believe it. I had this horrible nightmare I was attacked by a snarling beast only to find I was married to an irradiated cadaver."

"I'm sorry. I should have been there. I should have heard you."

I frown. "Or was it the other way around?"

"Drink this."

He hands me a glass of water from the bedside table. As I take it, my hand is unsteady. Without looking at him, I begin to drain the glass.

"Are you hungry?"

I feel his eyes trying to find mine.

Shaking my head, I rub my face. "How long have I slept?"

"Twenty-six hours."

My hand drops. "I slept through a whole day?"

"You were badly bloodied and dehydrated. Your body was running on adrenaline and endorphins by the time you found me."

Found him.

"Please look at me."

I do, but I know my eyes are blank.

"Sophie, will you speak with me?"

Staring at my lap, I feel myself nod and hand the glass to him.

He speaks quietly. "I need you to tell me what you remember."

Sitting up, I take a breath, focusing on the patterns in the quilt.

"After the dishes, I went outside to weed. I saw cat prints in the flower bed and thought it might be Toe ..." I blink at him. "Where's Toe? Toe was with me."

"Toe is fine. Lodi came back as well."

"Lodi? It's been a week! What'd he do, go to Vegas?"

Mike smiles sadly. "He was tracking Toe. I'm afraid when I told him he was responsible for Toe's well-being, he took it seriously."

"Is he all right? Is he hurt?"

"He seems fine, a little thin. I think he will appreciate his home more than before." Pausing, he narrows his eyes at me. "Sophie, you thought the cat prints you saw belonged to Toe ... "

"Oh, right. I thought it was Toe. I followed the prints to the pond, and she was there but she ran when she saw me. I tried to follow and guessed she went down the trail. I was most of the way down before I thought I heard her in the grass. It was near the rhododendrons. Then I fell ... well, I was pushed."

"Did you see what pushed you?"

"No, but I could hear it. It was on top of me when I landed at the bottom. It sounded like an animal. At first I thought it was a raccoon or something ... it was too big."

Slowly replaying what I remember, I stop talking.

"What happened next?"

"I think it was trying to get me on my back. I kept crawling away from it. We were in the stream bed ... then it tried to drown me. But I'm good at holding my breath." Grinning, I glance up at Michael. His face looks like death.

"Should I stop?"

The way he looks makes me feel guilty.

"No—" He is halting. "Keep going. You held your breath."

I don't want to say more.

"That's it. I hoped it would think I was dead. I woke up. Toe was sitting on me."

He prompts. "And then?"

The sound of birds makes me stare out the window.

"I walked back to the house."

How can I see out the window without my contacts?

He leads on. "You came to my study."

"Yes." I drop my eyes.

"And what do you remember after that?"

The pattern on the quilt fascinates me.

"You came for me …" He leads.

"That was the idea."

"I frightened you."

"I walked in on my grandfather when he was naked in the bathroom once."

"Sophie—"

"Down at the Trial Lawyers Association, they used to hang human skeletons in the shower stalls to keep people from using them, but no one told me. I was at one of their parties and I went to use the can … I was really drunk."

"Sophie—"

"You couldn't see it because it was on the other side of a shower wall. So I'm sitting on the can and I keep hearing something that sounds like one of those bamboo wind chimes—"

"Sophie, stop—"

"I get up and peek around the shower wall and there's this skeleton staring me in the face. I thought I was gonna pass out. Then my eyes see this little paper sign taped on the collar bone that says, 'Please don't use the shower.' I wanted to find the person who hung it there and beat them with a femur."

"Please stop."

"You know, it was actually pretty risky, hanging those skeletons like that. I mean for lawyers, you'd think they'd be worried about a lawsuit if someone stroked out in their privy. Maybe they thought, hey, we're trial lawyers, who's going to sue us?"

"You don't have to—"

"Don't have to what?! What don't I have to do?"

My rage echoes in my ears as my hands twist the quilt into knots.

"You don't have to say anymore." He whispers.

"I'll say whatever I want!" I hiss.

He shrinks away. "No more … please."

"I haven't said enough." The venom in my voice surprises me.

"But I hear it … you're thinking it."

He tries to hold my gaze until the pain in his eyes swallows him.

Covering his face with a hand, his voice wavers. "Please, I know most of you feels differently, but this part hates me. It always will. What it thinks of me I can't even say to myself. It's real, like the parts of me you hate are real, but I'll live with it if you can forgive me."

I blink. "You're really upset."

"Of course I am!" When his hand falls away, his eyes are blazing. "All I've done since you found me is veer between hopelessness and self-loathing! It's my fault, Sophie! My fault for loving you, for wanting to be like you. You know I did. For two years I locked that study and nearly threw away the key."

"Nearly." I stare him down.

"Sophie." He draws close to me on the bed, reaching for my hands. "You said you didn't want to be married to a statue. I'm not one, but I'll never be flesh and blood. I can't change what I am, but I promise to do better. You're right about my fears.

My fears got the better of me when this happened."

Gently, he extends my arm in his hand and runs his fingers against it.

"My hand broke this and my hand mended it." He searches my face. "I'll fix this, Sophie. I can make this right."

"How?"

With a shake of his head, he shuts his eyes.

"Tell me."

"There's nothing more to tell. What happened is over. You're fine." He squeezes me to him. "You're going to be fine."

St. Joseph Hospital
invites you to join as we usher in
A New Millennium of Caring
for
The St. Joseph Hospital Foundation
NEW YEAR'S BALL 1999–2000
at
The Broadway Convention Center
featuring
The global foods of Four C's and
global sounds of Man in Havana
Hosted bar and champagne.
when
6:00 PM till past midnight
December 31, 1999

RSVP and guest information enclosed
Please specify additional guests

[Invitation, Millennium Ball at St. Joseph Hospital, 1999]

1999 It was easy to forget I had a life that didn't involve two men.
Well, one man and Ziggy Stardust. Partly because my personal life had been so eventful, partly because my professional life had been so not. Correction: my professional life was eventful if planning for St. Joseph's New Year's Ball was the crowning achievement of my career, which it wasn't.

What began as a hum-drum project evolved into a major undertaking I was entirely unprepared for. It seemed since "writer" was in my job title, I was automatically responsible for writing anything and everything to do with the event. This included requests for sponsorship, the evening program, speeches, invitations, advertising, and the progress reports Evil Lyn required at least once, if not twice a day.

Normally, this would have been merely annoying and stressful, but since I was now attending said ball without a date, it was also depressing.

Amy Duncan had been, by far, the best co-worker I could have asked for. She was hardworking, loyal, and perceptive enough to save me when I wasn't paying attention to Lyn's scrutiny. She was also drawn to stormy romance like a kestrel. Sensing problems on the home front, she offered more than once to ease my pain after work during happy hour at Stanley & Seafort's. I wanted to take her up on it, but suspected whatever I said would end up on the corkboard at the water cooler.

Ending my brief, or if I threw in the previous lives, long friendship with Michael finally convinced me I needed the consolation only the sighs and recriminations of my own gender could offer. In the final days of the millennium, ritual happy hour at Stanley & Seafort's became my sole means of communing with the spirits. Between Amy and Sapphire gin, the future direction of my life was augured, for better or worse. If it came with tipsy olives, I didn't care.

Perched at the bar, I took in the view of the Christmas-lit city below.

"Wonder where I'll be next Christmas."

Pulling the olives from my martini, I took a sip.

"You don't know where you're moving to yet?"

Amy watched me as she picked at her shrimp cocktail, her red curls bouncing with every bat of her mascara-lengthened eyelashes.

Popping an olive in my mouth, I shook my head. "No clue. I told Mom and Dad I'd stay with them over Christmas break and decide in January. I might not stay in Tacoma after all."

"I always wanted to live in Portland."

"Portland wouldn't be bad. I was thinking that or Canada. I love Vancouver, and Mom has family there."

"You know if you need a place to stay, you can move in with me."

She pulled the orchid from her second Mai Tai before fishing the pineapple wedge with her straw.

"Thanks, but in a sadistic kind of way, the last couple weeks at home have made reentry easier for me. Besides ..." I raised a brow, "You've already got a roommate."

"Paul?" She rolled her eyes. "Way too organic for me. Now from the way you talk, he might be perfect for you."

"I sound organic?"

"You know, laid back. You both listen to the same music, you drive the same kind of car. Your mom's from China; Paul's mom is from Poland. I think you guys have a lot in common."

"Wow, we're twins."

Her elbow nudged mine. "You know what I mean! Just think about it. There's some potential there."

"What's he look like?"

"Mmmm!" She pulled her straw out of her mouth. "I've got a picture."

She looked over her shoulder and started digging in her handbag.

"I smell set up."

"No, really, I just took these when we road-tripped to California last month. We went to the beach with my cousin and I took some pics."

She flipped open her cell and started keying through her files. In a moment she handed over her phone. It was a photo of three people on a rocky beach. Two men with a girl in the middle who looked like a chubbier version of Amy.

"He's the one on the right."

The one on the right was thin with white blonde hair and a sunburn. He was supposed to be our age but could have passed for high school.

"How old is he again?"

"Yeah, he looks young. He's twenty-six. You should meet him."

"I'm in no rush." I handed her phone back. "Especially if I don't stay in town."

"Hey! Maybe he could be your date to the ball."

The mention of the ball made me take another drink. "I'm not sure it matters if I go or not."

She grabbed my hand. "No! You have to go! You've worked so hard on this. The least you've earned is a free meal and a drink. It'll be a hosted bar!"

"Who can say no?" I deflected. "Who are you going with?"

"Dan Fogel." Her eyes dropped to her drink.

"Dan Fogel? From HR? Didn't he just get a divorce?"

"It's a date." She sighed. "He's not exciting, but at least he's my type."

"What's that?"

Her eyes grew distant. "Type A. Someone to take care of me, I guess. It's old-fashioned, but I like suit-and-tie guys. When I was a kid, I thought Ward Cleaver was really hot. Now it would be someone, like, I don't know … Clive Owen."

Smirking, I wave to the bartender. "You're the one who needs to leave Tacoma."

Amy snapped from her trance. "You don't think I'll find Type A in T Town?"

"Let's get you another Mai Tai." I grinned.

She laughed. "Hey, I can dream!" Her eyes froze over my shoulder. "Dream come true." She tapped my hand. "That's my type, right there."

I glanced over my shoulder. The entry to the restaurant was obscured behind a giant Christmas tree. At first, I only saw people collecting their coats, and then I spotted him. Standing with perfect stillness, he was looking straight at me as if I could read his mind.

"Nuts."

I turned to the bar, searching for the bartender who was still too far away.

"You know that guy?" She whispered without moving her lips.

Saying nothing, I picked up my martini and emptied the glass into my mouth.

"He's coming ..." Amy made a little hiccup noise.

Waving to the bartender, I pointed at my glass and held up two fingers.

The voice of reason spoke over my shoulder.

"You won't be able to drive home drinking at that rate."

Rolling my eyes, I said nothing. Amy expected me to introduce her, but I thought it a cruel thing to do to a woman. I heard Amy tentatively introduce herself.

"Hi, I'm Amy."

As I glanced over at her, I saw him shaking her hand.

"I'm Michael. I'm a friend of ..." He hesitated as he caught my eye. "Sophie's."

"Sorry." My manners kicked in. "Amy works with me at the hospital. She's in their finance department."

"Pleased to meet you." He smiled as Amy smiled back, dazed. It made me wonder what I looked like when I first met him. Resistance was futile.

"She's single." I muttered, facing the bar.

Embracing oblivion, I winked at the bartender as he slid my second martini to me. Unaffected by my comment on her dating status, Amy's voice took on a hyper-feminine lilt.

"Do you live in Tacoma?"

"I do."

"What do you do?"

"I reclaim things."

"Like antiques and stuff?"

"Yes."

She glanced between us with a grin. "How do you know each other?"

Under Michael's steady gaze, I casually pulled an olive from my toothpick with my teeth, allowing an awkward silence.

"We met in a coffee shop." He answered.

"Oh ..." She fidgeted with the orchid from her cocktail. "You work in town?"

"I go where I'm needed."

"Sounds like you travel a lot." Amy shot me a look. "Go anywhere exotic?"

"That would depend on your definition of exotic."

"Where'd you go last?"

"Los Angeles."

She snickered. "Guess that depends on what part of LA you're in."

Michael displayed flawless teeth. "The exotic part."

I think I groaned, but Amy only giggled. Relief came when the bartender slid my third martini across the bar. Plucking the olives from it, I continued nursing my second when a hand crossed in front of me and picked up my fresh drink. My eyes followed the martini to Michael's face as he slowly put his head back and drained it without swallowing.

"What the hell was that?" My annoyance finally entered the conversation.

Gently pursing his lips, he squinted over my head. "Sapphire gin, dry vermouth, ice water, trace vinegar ... a decent martini." He put the empty glass down on the bar in front of me. "The gin wasn't bruised, but I prefer more vermouth."

Ignoring him, I turned to the bar and waved to the bartender.

"Don't you think you've had your limit?"

I was being stalked by a public health advisory.

Catching Amy's expression, she widened her eyes as I made a smile at her.

"Type A. You sure that's the type you want?"

Redirecting my attention to Michael, I put up four fingers. "As for you, Carrie Nation, four is my limit."

"Sophie, may I speak with you?

"If it comes with two martinis you may."

On cue, Amy felt her hair and picked up her scarf. "I should get going. You two probably want to catch up?" She glanced at me with nervous eyes, testing if I wanted her to go.

"I'll see you tomorrow." I smirked. "If I don't, call Anthony. Tell him you last saw me with Michael Goodhew and then follow the evening news."

Slinging her purse over her shoulder, she grinned at Mike. "It was nice meeting you." He nodded and she gave me wink. "Call me if you need me."

Watching her trot from the lounge, I knew she felt she was on to something more exciting than my break up with Anthony.

"I hope you're satisfied." I sighed. "You've just outed yourself to the social butterfly of St. Joseph's. I'll be drowning in innuendo by eight tomorrow morning."

"I'm sorry for that, but since you've been coming here every evening I didn't have an alternative." He took Amy's seat at the bar and signaled to the bartender. "Sapphire martini with two olives, please."

"That's two drinks you owe me." My second martini was an empty glass.

"You don't want the fourth to go warm, do you?"

"By the time I get there they could bring it to me in a paper cup."

"There's no way I'm letting you drive home."

"You've bought yourself a conversation. We'll decide who's driving me home if you get that far."

"Then I'll say what I came to say." He bit his lip and folded his hands. "Sophie, I would like to court you."

I rubbed my hands together. "Then you can drive me home."

He actually looked surprised.

"What's wrong?" I shrugged at him.

"It's just that ... I thought you would be difficult."

Shaking my head, I pointed at my empty martini glass. "Impairs judgment."

"In that case, I would like you to move in with me."

Shaking my head, I pointed to the fresh martini replacing my empty glass. "Impairs judgment."

"I see ..." His mood seemed to brighten. "Will you at least dine with me tonight? Our table should be ready."

"Table?"

"I took the liberty of making a reservation if you didn't send me to oblivion."

"I didn't peg you for an optimist."

He rose to his feet. "I had a hope."

"You aren't wasting any time are you?"

With a shake of his head, he took my hand. "I've wasted enough time already."

Leading me to the dining room, we were seated at a quiet table overlooking the city. He said nothing more about courtship over dinner. There was no mention of moving in or out. There was no time.

I'd seen Michael eat fries and a milkshake, but nothing prepared me for the quantity of food he effortlessly consumed now.

There was nothing grotesque about it, no rush or rampage in the process. With the cool precision of a surgeon, Michael made short work of his shrimp cocktail, a bowl of soup, a salad, a steak, a pork chop, and a lobster. This included the sides of rice, potatoes, string beans, zucchini, and pasta. A conclusion of ice cream, chocolate torte, apple crisp, and crème brûlée left me feeling anorexic with my single filet of salmon.

"So how many all-you-can-eat places know about you?"

He blinked innocently. "I would never be that criminal."

"Where does it all go?"

"I have a high metabolism."

With a snort, I stirred my coffee. "Or a black hole. You eat like that every day?"

"No."

This was followed by silence.

Sitting back, I scratched my head. "See, this is the part of courtship where we get to know each other. It would be more informative and enjoyable if I didn't treat you like a hostile witness."

"Sorry." He sat up attentively. "I don't often enjoy a variety of food. My caloric needs make dining like this prohibitive. If I ate this every day I would have little time for anything else."

"Then what do you eat?"

"High energy foods and protein supplements."

"What, like you'll down a box of Clif bars?"

"I prefer Payday's."

Clucking my tongue, I shook my head. "Pathetic. You need to get out more."

"Where do you suggest?"

"What are you doing New Year's Eve?"

"Eating protein supplements."

"Wrong, you're coming with me to the St. Joseph's New Year's Eve Ball. They're

having a catered buffet that's got your name written all over it."
"You want me to be your date?"
"That and there'll be a hosted bar. I'll need a driver."

You know the child in you has died when Christmas Eve no longer gives you butterflies. When you're a kid, sleeping the night before Christmas is only possible
if your parents spiked your hot chocolate. In my case, I usually fell asleep around
four in the morning, just in time for my grandmother to stuff my stocking before
I woke to the smell of her waffles. They're great memories, and when I was a girl I
couldn't imagine anything topping the sight of presents under a tree on Christmas
morning. But that was when my ovaries were asleep and my heart belonged to
Daddy.

Growing up didn't happen overnight, but at twenty-seven, a wallflower I was
not. My ovaries were wide awake and had been for some time. Part of my heart
would always belong to Daddy, but the rest of it explored other men who wandered into my life. Until now they had been too hard or too soft. I was still looking
for just right. Christmas of 1999 was the last I would spend with my parents as
their daughter, nothing more and nothing less. After the New Year, nothing would
be the same.

I didn't want Michael to come to my parent's house the night of the ball. It in-
truded on a symbolism meant to be expressed in the abstract. That was what weddings were for. The event of my life becoming joined to another had to happen in
the abstract and I didn't want to jinx it now. Instead, I arranged for Michael to pick
me up at the office. I had to be there anyway, bonding with my co-workers in the
ritual panic preceding any organized pomp.

Not fussy about cosmetic preparation, I packed a black velvet evening gown to
the office. It was easy to hang, fitted, and off-the-shoulder sans fluff or flounce. My
matching heels and jewelry were in my messenger bag. Since I didn't wear makeup
during the day, I only needed to apply it in the restroom. As for hair, it was straight
and almost impossible to mess up. With a brush, a braid, and enough bobby pins
to set off a security check point, anything was possible.

Amy Duncan only had two business days before the ball to tell the office about
Michael. Since that left her with one more day than she needed, the water was
chummed to frothing by the time he was due to pick me up. Keen to avoid any interference that would ruin my favorite part of the evening, I had him call me to tell
me when he had arrived so I could meet him on the street. Sneaking out of sight to
change clothes, I left the building via the back stairs rather than the elevator.

My favorite part of the evening would be the moment I saw him. Don't get me
wrong—the rest of the evening would be fine. There would be plenty of food for
him and plenty of libation for me. There would be music and dancing, and the
anticipation of finding out if the computers that ran the world would carry civilization into the new millennium or plunge us into the next Dark Age. I figured
in either event, I had the right date for the night. But seeing him waiting for me

would make the end of the world feel like something I could get over.

I didn't tell him what to wear. My only request was no tie. Unlike Amy, I hated ties. Honoring my request, Michael was standing on the sidewalk next to his car, tieless in a white dress shirt and black suit. It was hard to guess what he was thinking. As much as he seemed to know my thoughts, his seemed boxed in a perpetually rational frame of mind, his emotions either nonexistent or fragile as a child's when expressed. My emotions were a mix of hope, joy, and, at this moment, hunger. My eyes ate him and I made no effort to hide it.

He stared steadily at me as I approached, but once I was in front of him, he dropped his gaze to the street.

"Thanks for not wearing a tie."

He shrugged. "I don't own any. It saved me the need to shop for one."

There was a longish silence.

"I know I'm buried in a wool overcoat, but this is where you tell me how beautiful I look. If you're feeling bold, you might even give me a peck on the cheek."

Without looking up, Michael pulled his left hand from behind him and offered a single long-stemmed rose. I barely reached for it when I felt his other hand under my chin. The glow of his face registered in my mind before it went blank. His lips were soft and unusually hot against mine. When he exhaled, my cheek felt cold, and I realized it wasn't the winter chill. Colder than his breath were his eyes. As he pulled away from me, they weren't just bright, they were blue fire.

He caught my stare and put his hand to his forehead.

I looked around us. "Is this going to be a problem?"

"Only if we're too close."

"Too close?"

His eyes nervously shifted between me and the pavement. "We could probably hold hands—"

"Whoa!" I held up a hand. "Its a New Year's party, not a Rainbow installation." My rose tickled him on the chin. "Look at me ... Michael, look at me."

He looked up, pursing his lower lip. "How do they look?"

"Mmmm, doesn't look much better." I lied. "Get in the car."

I didn't wait for him to open my door before turning his shoulders and shoving him to the driver's side of the car. Tossing my bag in the back seat, he was waiting behind the wheel for me by the time I fastened my seat belt.

"Where are we going?"

"Met Market."

"The ball is at Met Market?"

"We're going there first."

He started the car and "Take Me To The River" filled the cabin.

"You didn't tell me where the ball is being held."

"It's a surprise."

His eyebrows raised briefly, but he said nothing.

When we got to the store, I told him to wait in the car for me. Inside, I scurried in my heels through the deli, tossing whatever looked good into my basket as I went. Arriving at the cooler where beer and wine were displayed, I grabbed two bottles of Veuve and made the express check-out in record time. As soon as I got to the car, I opened the back door to the seat behind mine and tossed in the bags before jumping into the passenger seat.

Breathing hard, I grinned at Michael, who seemed impatient.

"You've changed your mind about going. If it's because of me, you should still go. We can go somewhere else another time. If I hadn't kissed you—"

Reaching over the gear shift, I grabbed him. It was déjà vu, only this time I wasn't aiming for his forehead. This took longer than the run in with the rose.

When I pulled away to catch a breath, the look on his face startled me. His eyes were closed and he looked like he was about to pass out.

"Mike? You okay?"

Facing the wheel, he covered his face with his hands. "Fine."

"Are you going to drive this anywhere or are we getting arrested for indecent exposure?"

Squinting at me, he blinked rapidly. "Where?"

"What I have in mind shouldn't happen at my parents' house …" We were in traffic before I finished.

Michael's normally expedient driving was especially impressive with fewer cars on the road. "Werewolves of London" was playing on the radio. A caller requested it because there was a blue moon that night. Then it dawned: technically, I was about to have sex outside of my own species.

"Um, Mike?"

"Yes?"

"I'm on the pill."

He looked over. "The what?"

My brows went up. "The contraceptive?"

He looked back at the road. "I told you, we don't replicate ourselves."

"Ever?"

"I can't make children."

"You're sterile?"

"That too."

"What?"

"My body is abiotic and antibiotic."

I turned in my seat. "You're antibiotic?"

"My DNA is resistant to parasitic mutation."

"Wow …" I stared at him. "A man made with Micro-Ban."

He frowned. "Is that bad?"

"No, it's great. Everyone will want one."

His eyes darted between me and the road. "Did I say something wrong?"

"I'm a clean freak. It's a huge turn on."

With a nod, he returned his eyes to the road.

I found myself wondering why he was antibiotic.

"Let me guess." I fished. "A preference of evolution?"

"You could say that."

He didn't elaborate.

I was about to ask him to, then remembering our past discussions about his peculiarities, decided it would kill the mood. Sitting back in my seat, I looked out my window. Beyond a veil of clouds, a full moon was rising. Hopefully, for singularities, turning into a hairy beast wasn't a preference of evolution too.

As Michael eased the car down his drive, my fingers played with the door latch. Standing in his drive, I fidgeted as Michael got the groceries from the back seat. Following him to the front porch, I shifted on my feet as he set down the groceries to unlock the door. Carrying the groceries into the house, he started for the kitchen, but I grabbed his shoulders, steering him to the stairs. I dropped my purse in the foyer and slipped out of my coat as we climbed. By now, he knew where we were headed. Pushing him into the bedroom, I closed the door behind us.

He faced me, still holding a bag in each hand.

I began to unbutton his shirt.

"Where—"

"Shhh ..." My fingers slipped inside and ran down his abdomen.

He flinched. "You're hands are freezing."

"And you're hard as a rock." I paused, feeling his chest. "I'm going to have to get used to this. You can put those down, Mike."

Glancing down at the groceries, he quickly lowered them to the floor.

"Get used to what?"

I tugged off his jacket and started unbuckling his belt. Pulling out his shirt, I let it slip to the floor as I examined him critically.

"You look better than you feel."

He looked down at himself as I pushed on his left pectoral.

"I don't know what you mean."

"I don't know what I mean either." I brushed the strands of his hair from his eyes. "What am I saying? You're perfect."

I pulled his face to mine and kissed him, coaxing his breath.

Unzipping his trousers, I peeked down.

"Boxers ..." I whispered. "Another mystery solved."

Closing my eyes, I wrapped my arms around his neck, letting my mouth find his.

"Sophie?"

My eyes open to his, burning with fire and curiosity. "What?"

"Are you keeping your clothes on?"

"I have to undress both of us?"

Tucking his chin to analyze my dress, he pressed his lips together.

I frowned down at my cleavage and then back at his face. "Gravity."

He blinked. "A force manifested by acceleration toward each other of two free material particles or radiant-energy quanta."

"There's a hook and a zipper down the back. See what happens."

Renewing his focus, I felt a gentle pull on the back of my dress and the air on my skin. The weight of the boning made it fall away. Given the reinforcements of my gown, all I wore underneath were seamless panties and garter length nylons. He stared at my body as though seeing something from far away.

He raised a hand to my breast and then stopped.

"What's wrong?"

He didn't say anything.

"I'm just going to ask—don't take this personally—you have had sex before?"

"Yes."

"And you touched your partner at some point?"

His eyes returned to mine. "You should know, sex is very tiring for me."

"This has to be a record. We aren't even married."

"I expend energy I can't get back."

"This isn't a case of performance anxiety?"

"I can—I want to … I just don't know how I'll be afterward."

With a sigh, I let my arms slide from his shoulders and walked to the bed. Dropping onto the edge of the mattress, I kicked off my heels.

"So when you wanted to be friends, you were willing to have sex with me, but now that we're dating, you're having second thoughts?"

Michael said nothing, watching me pull the pins from my hair. As I unwound my braid, he came to me and kneeled. Carefully, he began to pull off my stockings.

"I'll be weaker, and you'll be stronger. You'll feel it. Your body will take everything I have and give nothing back. You'll have to be careful with me."

I watched him delicately fold my stockings in his hands.

"Are you afraid?"

He didn't look up. "I trust you."

Taking the stockings from him, I dropped them on the floor. His eyes met mine as I lifted his hands to my shoulders and fell back on the bed. When he lowered himself over me, he seemed to become a different person. His face buried in my hair and I felt his lips on my ear lobe. At first I thought I was imagining it, but I thought I heard the whistle of a bird, only it wasn't a bird at all. It was like wind in the branches of a tree, harsh and sweet, turning to the ebb and flow of a tide. My body opened.

My reptile brain was untroubled by this extra-sensory information, instincts acting on impulse as my mouth traced the planes of his face, my hands felt the body they had been wanting. My eyes, however, remained shut.

If this had been the only way I was wired, I could have kept them closed.

A night of lust would never make me open my eyes in the midst of pleasure. But my heart wanted this, too. It had wanted it secretly, desperately, patiently, while the expectations of mind and body were met. The moment he entered me, my heart demanded what it had waited for and opened my eyes.

I might have been terrified. The instincts pleasure had fed were now shocked to fight or flee. Blue light coursed the veins beneath his skin, sending pale ripples along his limbs. In spite of what my brain was now aware of, the rest of me ignored the reality of the moment. My body continued to move with his, every smooth muscle in my core dedicated to the task of demanding life.

My eyes fixed on his, watching them open and close. They seemed to see nothing while their brilliance lit the space between us. I could see everything and what I saw surpassed my anxiety. What I saw was a manifestation from the other half of the universe that might otherwise never be seen. It made me whole.

Something sharp and raw charged through me. I gasped and all I saw was bright and blue. Then everything went dark, the breath in me suddenly crushed. The light in the bedroom was out and it was pitch black, his body half on top of me, completely still. If he hadn't felt burning to the touch, I would have worried he was dead.

Scratch that: I was worried he was dead.

"Michael?"

Pushing him off me, I rolled onto my side, searching for his face with my hands. I scrambled to my knees, prying his shoulder off the bed to roll him over.

"Michael? Can you hear me?"

His face was barely visible. I pushed back an eyelid, but all I could see of an iris resembled a black marble. Feeling my throat tighten, I put my face to his and felt his breath, faint and chill. My hands on his chest felt his heart racing, and I wondered what I would do if it stopped. One problem with dating outside of your own species: first aid was a bitch. He would be fine, I told myself. He told me I would have to be careful with him. Wasn't I?

Had I done something wrong?

Outside of making him comfortable, there was nothing I could do. Nothing I could give back. Wrapping my arms around his middle, I hefted him to one side of the bed. Feeling him in my arms aroused me again and I knew it was going to be a bad habit. Pulling the bed covers out from under him, I shoved him back to the center of the bed and covered him with the bedspread. I put a pillow under his head and slid under the covers next to him. Holding him to me, I watched his face in the dark.

I think I fell asleep. Hearing him give a loud sigh brought me back.

Michael was still inanimate, but there was a difference. His breathing was deep and steady; his temperature had dropped below scalding. He seemed to be simply asleep. There was no danger.

Loud pops outside stirred me. Firecrackers. It was 2000. Getting out of bed, I went to the window and watched the distant flares of rockets in the night. Feeling chilled and sore all over, I was about to get back into bed when it occurred to me I might soak in the tub. That sounded nice. Especially with a bottle champagne.

Picking my way in the dark, I fished out a bottle of bubbly from one of the shopping bags still sitting in the middle of the bedroom floor. It was still cool to the touch. I took it with me to the bathroom, where I made the mistake of turning on the light. The blinding white of the tile nearly made me drop the bottle. Swearing,

I flipped the light off, deciding I could see better in the dark.

Pulling a hand towel off of the towel ring, I wrapped the bottleneck and carefully worked the cork out. With a muffled pop, I held the bottle over the sink and let the foam run. I wiped off the bottle and took a swig before crossing to the tub to run the water. Feeling around the tub spout, my fingers found the stopper on the end of a chain. The stop felt brittle but up to the task as I forced it into the drain. Turning on the hot, I listened to the gurgle and splash and nursed my champagne.

As the tub filled, I looked around the bathroom, imagining what could be done to make it look more like a bath and less like a mortuary. Although everything seemed to be in working order, I suspected this room had been attended to the same way the others had, for my benefit alone. I remembered how the house had been the first time I saw it; the study seemed to be the only room Michael ever used, or ever needed to. It made me wonder why he needed a house at all and how he ended up here. Why had he been here alone all these years?

The steam from the tub began to mist on the window, making the panes glow in the dark. Shutting off the water, I placed the bottle on the floor next to the tub and stepped in. The water was just about right. I slid down in the tub, only the occasional drip of water from the tap echoed on the tile walls.

Would I live here too?

Michael had lived here forty-seven years. In forty-seven more, I would be an old woman. Would I want to live here then? Would I die here?

Firecrackers startled me from my daze. Taking a few deep breaths, I sank beneath the surface to escape the screams of bottle rockets. Keeping my eyes shut to keep from lose my contacts, I saw nothing. Only the push of the water against my ears told me where I was and that could have been a lot of places. Memories of playing in the bath at home suddenly came alive. Holding my breath made me imagine what it would be like to never breathe at all. The pressure in my chest forced out my breath imperceptibly, just enough to ease the slow burn growing in my lungs. How many minutes could I hold out for now?

One one thousand, two one thousand, three one thousand ...

Something fell into the tub with me. Startled, my eyes reflexively opened. I expected to inhale water as I caught my breath, to lose my lenses at least, but I was on the floor of the bathroom and the tub had vanished around me.

"Sophie!"

My eyes focused on Michael's face. In the reflected white of tile walls, he looked like a statue come to life save for the black points where his irises should have been. I could feel his arm around me and a hand cradling the back of my neck.

"Sophie, are you all right?"

"*What is wrong with you?*" Feeling for the floor, I pushed myself up and scrambled to my feet, nearly knocking over the champagne.

Still on his knees, Michael looked up at me with an astonished look on his face.

"I thought ... I thought you needed help."

"I don't need help taking a bath! You scared me to death! What did you think I was doing? Killing myself?"

He stood up, staring at me with black eyes. He opened his mouth, shut it, and walked out.

~

[Washington State Department of Health,
Death Certificate for Daniel Charles Goodhew, 1972]

2003 "Aren't you worried Toe will get out?" He pauses in the dining room, noticing all of the windows are thrown wide.

"I think Toe has proved her abilities, don't you think?" Pulling out a chair at the dining table, I sit down with a plate of cookies and a glass of milk. "Turns out I'm the one who shouldn't be let out of the house. Besides, it's hot today. I'd go nuts in this place if the windows were all shut."

Silently, my husband comes up behind me.

"Get your own cookies, please."

He goes to the kitchen.

"What are we having for dinner?" His voice echoes in the refrigerator.

"You don't know?"

"You were thinking about pasta, then meatloaf, then eggplant strata. Have you thought about making something that is a little of all those things?"

Michael strolls into the dining room with a bowl of cereal and a plate of cookies.

"I'm not making lasagna."

He frowns. "It's hardly my fault Marta went to China this month. You're going to make me wait till July?"

"Pouting about it will get you nowhere."

He makes a face.

"Didn't your mother ever tell you not to make faces?"

"You are my mother."

"My cookies are going to come back on me if you say that again."

He starts dipping his cookies into the milk in his cereal bowl.

"What are we having for dinner?"

Leaning forward, I put my elbows on the table. "Eggplant."

He stops chewing and swallows.

I shrug. "You could talk me out of it."

His eyes narrow. "I'm not that picky."

"Don't be so paranoid. I just didn't realize you wanted lasagna so badly."

"As long as it's not eggplant I don't really care."

"We can have lasagna." I sit back in my chair. "I'll have to go to the store."

"I can go to the store."

"And I'll be safe here by myself?"

"As long as I'm not in my crypt, yes."

"Perfect." I smile at him as he goes back to his cookies. "It's nice to see you out of your box and blinking again."

"Your instincts about that were better than mine. I made a mistake."

"I want to thank you for staying so close to me this week."

"You're … welcome." There is quiet hesitation in his voice.

"I appreciate that you've been trying to get back to normal."

Blinking, his chewing slows.

I reach over and pat the back of his hand. "You've made me feel safe and loved."

"You want me to give Lodi his allergy medication?"

I smile. "I'm not angry with you anymore for breaking my arm, either."

"You want me to drain the koi pond?"

"You know what attacked me, don't you?"

Dropping his cookie, he sits back in his chair.

Staring into his eyes, I try to hold his gaze. "It's been a week. You promised you'd explain."

His attention shifts between me and the cereal bowl.

"I didn't feel you were ready for it."

"I feel ready now."

"Maybe this evening would be better."

"Over lasagna?" I smile.

"After lasagna."

"Before dessert."

He hesitates. "After dessert?"

"There might not be any dessert."

His lips disappear. "That's what I'm afraid of."

"You have to tell me sooner or later."

"I don't really." His voice feigns indifference.

"No lasagna."

He looks away. "I can make lasagna."

"I'll make eggplant."

"I'll go to the store."

"Great. While you're at the store, I'll check in on Mrs. Farrell."

"*No, Mrs. Farrell!*" Shoving back his chair, he gets up from the table. "You promised!"

"Promised? You're the one who promised you'd never put me in danger! Who promised never to lie to me—"

"*That*," Michael cut me off, "is a promise I've kept, Sophie. God knows I'm trying to keep it."

"God knows …" I sneer. "You don't even believe in one."

"I know I haven't been perfect, but when have I intentionally hurt you? Can't you accept what I deny is withheld for good reason?"

"Accept? Deny? Withhold? Do you have any idea what it's like living with you? Everything about you is a denial. What you do, about ECCO, about how you found me. I've always accepted you have secrets. You collect them." I point through the French doors across the house. "That room is full of them and you can keep them! I'm asking about *my* life! As long as Mrs. Farrell is alive, part of Daniel is, too."

Michael's face is a mask. "I've given you everything you've asked for."

"Except the truth."

"I have." He picks up his cereal. "I just can't tell you everything. I never promised to tell you everything."

"Come on … Michael …" My eyes follow him as he leaves the dining room without a backward glance. "Michael!"

I hear the front door open and slam shut.
"We're having eggplant!"

Even on a sunny afternoon in June, the Farrell house is cheerless. Pushing through the gate, a boxwood hedge forces me to meander back and forth across the yard to reach the front door. Climbing the steps, the dark mahogany and stained glass doors reflect nothing of what lies behind. I ring the doorbell and step back, looking at it as if waiting for it to speak. I notice the frame of the door is unattractively topped with an iron cross. There is movement behind the glass. I swallow butterflies as I step forward to speak through the beveled window.

"Mrs. Farrell?"

The lace curtains inside pull back and I see a lined face squint at me. There is a flash of recognition and I hear the bolt turn.

"Sonia!" She beams, opening the door wide.

"Sophie."

"Oh." She holds her mouth agape. "Sophie ... Sorry, I knew it wasn't Sarah and I knew it wasn't Susan, just knew it had an O. Come in. I'm glad you came back."

As I step inside, the foyer is everything I imagined and more.

"I brought you some muffins I made this morning." As I hand her the covered basket, I am distracted by the crystal chandelier spanning the entryway. It hangs over an unusual rug, woven in a rustic pattern to form a chain of strangely primitive animals. Two giant pots of aloe vera stand sentinel on either side of the door.

Mrs. Farrell hugs the basket to her as she regards the zoo under our feet. "This was one of my husband's finds. He was quite the collector."

"And a hunter." My gaze catches the horns on the head of an eland on the stair wall facing the door.

"Well, dogs will dig and men will shoot, won't they?" She peeks in the basket. "These smell wonderful. Shall we have one?"

I grin after her. "That's why I brought them."

She is already heading into the front parlor, mostly blue and layered with the decorative plaque of time. I follow through the dining room, a dim butler's pantry, and finally into the kitchen. She drops the basket on the kitchen table and makes for a plate that sits with a handful of others in a rusting dish rack. The yellowed cupboards reach halfway up the walls to twenty-foot ceilings, dingy with dust and cobwebs. A triangle of wear in the checkered linoleum connect a refrigerator, stove, and sink that outdate me.

"I'll just put a pot on?"

"That would be great, thanks." Shades of Marta embarrass me until I remember I was invited back and Mrs. Farrell seems to have expected me.

Taking a seat at the table, I watch her drag an enamel tea kettle off the stove and let it lead her like a blind woman to the sink. She says nothing as she fills the pot, and I have no thought in my head. If Michael is ageless, Mrs. Farrell is age itself.

Her frailty pulls on me like my great-nana, my grandmother, my mother. It suddenly seems odd that I feared her before.

"I'd take you round the house, but our water'd be boiled away by the time we got back."

She gives a puff as she puts the kettle on the burner and reaches over to the counter for a box of matches. With a quick action, she strikes the match on the side of the box and carefully lights the flame. Shuffling to the table, she plops into the chair across from me and nods.

"Michael at work today?"

"Yes."

"Well, he's always welcome."

"Thank you, Mrs. Farrell."

"Call me Violet. God knows I've spent enough of my life with Farrell for a name."

"Thank you, Violet."

"What can I do you for?"

Candor, I like candor.

"I wanted to hear your memories about Michael's father and his uncle Daniel."

"Well, it's like I said, I can't tell you much about Michael." She squints. "Michael Jr. probably knows as much about him as I ever will. But Daniel I knew most of my life. Ever since I moved here with Curtis."

"Yes, I know a little about Daniel. Michael says he worked in Boston."

Leaning forward, she fishes her hand into the basket, coming out with a muffin. She pulls it apart on her plate. "He was a great artist, did you know? Ceramics." She takes a bite. "Beautiful pottery. I have several pieces. I'll have to show them to you. I have them out now, but I hid them for years."

"Hid them?"

"Curtis would have broken them."

"Why would he do that?"

"One of his jealous fits." She answers with her mouth full.

I raise my eyebrows but say nothing.

"Curtis rescued me from where I was, and for that I am eternally grateful, but he wasn't cut out to be a husband. I don't know if you can understand that."

Scratching my ear, I raise a brow. "I think I have an idea."

"As for Daniel, Curtis was the only one who didn't like him, but that was later, after the girls died. Before that Curtis and Danny spent a good deal of time together. Curtis was always one for keen times, and Danny was always up for it."

"Keen times?"

"You never saw two men drink like they could. Only fish do better."

"You didn't mind?"

"Kept Curtis out of trouble. At least for the summers." She stopped to take another bite of muffin. "I don't know how Danny could stand him. He was so much smarter than Curtis for starters. Danny didn't hunt, didn't chase women, didn't

think Hemingway was a god. Curtis was all about Curtis, and Danny ... well, Danny wasn't."

"So what did Curtis see in Danny?"

"He was funny. Easygoing. Made Curtis laugh. Danny was no fool, though. He caught on to Curtis and how things were."

I'm trying to guess how things were as Violet finishes her muffin.

"I think it was the third summer Danny's family was here." She brushes the crumbs from her lips. "Curtis was gone shooting, Anne and I were alone. That would have made a good summer right there, but Danny and Florence had Anne and I down to the house for dinner every Sunday. I probably said more to him about life with Curtis than I should have. Not that Danny ever said anything; he wouldn't. He was the sort of man you knew could keep a secret ..." Violet stares across the kitchen at nothing.

"And Florence?" My question refreshes her.

Turning her attention to the stove, she crosses her arms. "She was very, I don't know, nervous. High-strung you'd call it. That made it bad when the girls got sick. Bad for her and worse for Danny. Part of her blamed Danny for the girls coming down with polio. He was working in Boston and she thought that was where the girls caught it. That was the reason why they'd come here every summer. She was terrified of anything you could catch. When the girls got sick and died within a week of each other, she had to be hospitalized. Danny brought her here to be in a private home. She got paranoid, imagined someone had poisoned the girls and they would be after Danny next. Heard voices, that sort of thing."

She raises her brows and starts fishing for another muffin. "But one person's suffering is another's deliverance. As long as Florence was here, Danny was here. I don't think Anne and I could have survived Curtis without him."

"Sounds like you were close." I watch her smile at the muffin on her plate.

"We needed each other. He needed a family, and I needed someone I could trust. We visited, we talked, read the same books. Anne loved him. He was the father she should have had. Of course, Curtis didn't like it. He'd get drunk and rant and rave. Beat me pretty bad a couple times."

Now I knew how things were.

"My God."

She points a bent finger at me. "There is a God, Miss Goodhew. He sent me Daniel, and Daniel did right by Anne."

"How so?"

Pausing, she shakes her head. "Anne was a good girl. Pretty, but never dated, never had a boyfriend. That was my fault. I was no help to her where men were concerned. When she was twenty, she got pregnant. Danny made sure she was taken care of."

"How so?"

"His sister in California took her in."

"Daniel didn't have a sister."

She frowns. "Her name was Sarah."

"Sarah Monroe?"

"Yes. That was it. Monroe."

"That's my husband's mother."

"Sounds like she had her hands full if she raised your Michael, too."

"Who was the father?"

The kettle begins to whistle, and she pushes herself up from the table.

"Well, who do you think if Michael's mother took her in?"

"Mike's dad?"

"You heard what I said about Anne." She shuffles to the stove. "Curtis and Danny were the only men she'd ever had in her life. You can imagine what it was like when Michael's father moved in with Danny down the street. He was as handsome as your Michael, maybe more so."

She turns off the fire and goes to the cupboard for cups.

"Did they spend time together?"

"Anne visited Danny enough for him to notice. Course men like that don't stay interested for very long. He did his disappearing act at the right time—only came back after Anne was gone." She glances at me from the corner of her eye.

Returning her attention to the kettle, she carefully pours hot water into each cup and replaces the kettle on the stove.

"What happened to the baby?"

"Anne never told me. I assumed she put it up for adoption."

Reaching over as far as I can, I intercept a full cup from Violet before she falls into her chair. She points to a tin of Earl Grey on the table.

"You never asked her?"

"Never got a chance. Not that I would have pried. She never came back. Wrote me to say she'd married a fellow in Arizona named Riley. Good for her."

"Not even to visit?"

"Not with Michael still here."

"Did Curtis ever find out?"

"Not about the baby. I just told him Anne left. Danny was worried Curtis would go hunt for her, but I knew he wouldn't. She was grown. He was just disappointed she didn't stay at home the rest of her life to look after him. If that had been the end, I probably would've forgotten it all and let my brains rot watching *People's Court.*"

"But it wasn't."

"It probably wasn't good Danny stayed here as long as he did. I couldn't move Curtis. I would've if I could've, but he'd never leave his castle. Course, Daniel would never leave Florence, so they lived on top of each other with bad blood. It was bad for everyone, but especially Danny. Curtis made his life miserable."

"How?"

For a moment she looks around herself, then licks her lips. "The last time I was in the same room with Michael's father was the year after Anne left. I was visiting

Danny when Michael came in the front door. He was polite, said hello, asked how I was …" She sniffs. "A lot of cheek after getting my girl pregnant. That was 1954. After that I only saw him drive past the house. Never saw him any day I visited after. Danny told me Michael worked at night. Ten years went by like that. Then Curtis tells me he sees Michael at the post office and he hasn't aged a day."

"Really?" I have no idea what my expression is.

She waves a hand over her muffin as though she is shooing flies. "I told Curtis Michael was still a young man."

"What did Curtis say?"

"Nothing. Few days later he came home late and spent the whole week in his library. You noticed his trophies …" She points over my head. "He collected a lot of hocus pocus along the way. Places like Africa and South America. His library's full of books about things that go bump in the night."

She scratches her chin before continuing. "The way I've described Curtis, you'd think he wouldn't need a library, but he was an intelligent man. He was an engineer, and from the work he got, he must have been a good one. I suppose you'd say he wasn't … well, he wasn't reading Shakespeare."

"Hemingway."

She nods. "During one of his drunken raves, he told me Michael was evil. Said he was the reason Anne was gone. That he was possessed by dead spirits. Said Danny was the reason he was here and he wanted Danny's soul."

"What did you think about that?"

"I told him he wanted Danny's house. As for Anne, well, he was the reason she was gone but he already got what he needed from her. You'd have thought Danny would notice if his nephew was possessed. Curtis said he knew it the first time he saw him. Said Michael had dead eyes. It was just more of his hocus pocus. I told him he was just bored because his knee was too bad for him to go hunting anymore so he had to make up something closer to home. I just didn't realize how far it would go. I never thought he'd break into Danny's house."

"He did?"

Violet's voice fades. "It was the night Danny died. Curtis came home half crazed and took to his bed with a fever. Kept going on about how he'd broken in and surprised him. Said he'd killed him."

"You think he killed Daniel?"

"He was the only one who was dead. That was until Curtis died two days later."

"Did he say how?"

Squinting at the ceiling, she shakes her head. "No. Just said he drained the life out of him. I never heard anything about how Danny died. The police were at Danny's house the morning after Curtis came home. By then, Curtis told me where he'd been and I was worried they'd come here, but they never did. I don't know what Michael saw or what he told them."

"That was it? Michael never said anything? Never came, never spoke to you?"

"No." Violet takes a long sip of her tea. "Well, I suppose he got what he wanted, didn't he?"

[Curtis and Violet Farrell, informal wedding photograph. October 1933]

1199 BC   The sun had just set when we returned to the ravine I scouted earlier in the day. There was a cave—not deep, but far enough from the paths of men that my crypt could rest in obscurity. It was, I claimed, my chosen resting place for my husband. It was, the general hoped, the end of my mourning. Once my crypt was at rest, I bade him leave me and take his company with him. That it was only for the night. That it would be my last as a widow alone and in the morning he would find me a new woman. With this promise, he acquiesced most willingly. When assured I was alone, I entered my crypt intent on making good my promise of awaking a new woman.

Restored before sunrise, I left the cave in darkness with only one thought in mind. Veiled in black, I moved as shadow, sure of my path and the quarry that awaited me. What awaited me was something I should have foreseen but missed in ignorance. The general had not left the ravine but kept vigil in the night. I had prepared myself to encounter the worst of our kind, not the best of men. As a result, I was ill equipped to reward his care and concern with anything he could understand. The least I could offer was a warning. That the encampment was in danger, and if he truly loved me, he would lead as many people from it as quickly as possible.

In that moment, I did nothing to veil myself. The presence in me was there for him to see, and it frightened him. It was then I reminded him he was a leader among men, and if they had any hope of salvation it was to be found in each other, not in devils with silver on their lips. I left him at the mouth of the ravine, my path still before me, my quarry still at bay. That Saitael expected me by now, I knew.

[Spharic. Entry translated from *Kor Dai Maihael*. Mund Dai. BC 755]

2000 My first day back at work, Amy Duncan rushed me in the parking lot. Dressed in a black and white houndstooth slicker, I had the fleeting feeling of being mugged by an inflatable Dalmatian.

"My God! Where were you! Lyn freaked out that you weren't there."

"Please, if I'd been there she wouldn't have given a shit."

Opening my umbrella, I slammed my car door and headed for the office with Amy on my heels. Feeling like a new and improved version of myself, I couldn't tell if it was because I was wearing new heels or because my new boyfriend could do more than warp space time with his thoughts. Sensing my mood, Amy reviewed the situation.

"You're probably right. But she was really disappointed you weren't there when we all went to the stage. They did this recognition thing for the committee, and Lyn thought you were up there so when she introduced you, and you weren't—"

"She thought it made her look like an ass."

"Something like that."

"When did this recognition happen in the program? It wasn't there when I wrote up the thing."

"About nine thirty, but the program was over by then. Lyn just made it up."

"Oh! No worries. I would have been five martinis into things by then. Never would have made it to the stage anyway." As I walked into the office, I caught the looks on the faces of my co-workers.

Dan Fogel passed us and whale-eyed me.

I put out my hands. "What?"

"Evil Lyn's looking for you." Dan made a sick look with his face.

My own broke into a smile as I watched him and Amy look at me like I was condemned.

"Any hot tips from the HR department?"

Dan grinned. "No direct eye contact, no sudden moves."

I nodded. "Thanks, guys. Amy, you get my space heater. Dan, in case it isn't in my file, I'm an organ donor."

Making a direct line through the plain of cubicles, I ducked into the office I shared with three other grant writers. None of them were there. On my desk was a pink slip. It was an interoffice memo sheet and they were always pink, but on this day the sign was obvious. Not surprisingly, it was a note from Lyn. She wanted to see me in her office at my earliest convenience. The way things were shaping up, I could have slept in.

Without bothering to ditch my umbrella, I started for Lyn's office.

Whatever. Fuck Lyn. I did my job. Bring it, bitch.

She was trying to look busy. From my vantage over her beehive, I watched her methodically pecking at an e-mail. Glancing up over her shoulder, she flashed a perfunctory smile.

"Sophie! Good morning! It's so good to *see* you here. Have a seat."

"Morning, Evelyn. You wanted to talk?" I tried to sound casual.

"We missed you at the ball." She swiveled her considerable self around to face me, her ribbed black turtleneck strained to the seams. "I was worried you were sick or had a last-minute emergency?"

Her eyes were wide with expectation of a groveling excuse.

"That's generous of you, Lyn, but I didn't go because I decided to share an evening of carnal pleasure with my boyfriend." Maybe that sounded too casual.

At first Lyn's face didn't register anything; then it just seemed a little red.

"Sophie, we all have difficult choices. However, sometimes there are commitments we have to honor above others. Some duties outweigh our personal needs."

"I didn't think it was difficult a choice."

"It wasn't very professional of you."

"I didn't say it was."

"At St. Joseph's, we pride ourselves on our professionalism. It's the cornerstone of our mission, and it applies to everyone who works for us."

Sitting up, I perched on the edge of my seat. "Have I performed poorly as a grant writer?"

"Well, that would be up to your immediate supervisor to determine."

"Did I fail to deliver on any of the tasks I was volunteered to do—besides not showing up at the ball?"

"Young lady, professionalism is more than doing your own job. It's about working as a team and contributing to the work of others. We started this project as a team and we should finish it as a team. You weren't there when your teammates were. You don't think that any of them would have preferred to be elsewhere on New Year's Eve?"

"Of course they would!" I smacked my lap with my umbrella. "What human being with blood in their veins wouldn't rather have their ass spanked than kiss someone else's all night?"

"Miss Davids, I'm trying to have an adult conversation with you."

My voice dropped to a whisper. "And talking about sex, a pretty adult topic."

"This conversation is over, Miss Davids."

Closing my eyes, I gave a nod. "Ah, yes. All good things …" Rising from my seat, I left her office without another word.

Back at my desk, I pulled the top drawer and removed my day planner before reaching down and yanking the plug on my space heater. Towing my heater by the cord, I made my way to Amy's cubicle and dropped it at her feet. She was on the phone when she saw me and quickly hung up with a sad look on her face.

"No." I put up a hand. "No sad eyes, no tears; it's for the best."

"Jeez, Sophie. I can't believe she canned you for that."

"It wasn't Lyn. She might have had a can ready but I brought the opener. You know I haven't been happy here. I just didn't want to give her the chance to say it first."

"Where will you go?" Amy's question seemed to imply more than my future employment.

"That was what I was trying to figure out on New Year's Eve."

"And?" She tipped her desk chair forward and fanned her hands frantically. "The eight ball." I held out my hand.

Amy grabbed it off of her desk. Taking it from her, I gave it a shake before flipping it over.

"Ask again later. Shit, I should have consulted this before I met with Lyn."

I handed it back as Amy grinned at me.

"Was it worth it?"

I rolled my eyes. "Priceless."

On my way out, Dan Fogel spotted me as he was leaving the break room.

"Should I put you on the donor list?" He looked unusually sympathetic.

I gave a laugh. "Sign me up, Dan!"

"You don't sound too upset about getting the axe."

"She didn't use an axe, so all my organs are still salvageable. Except the heart; I wouldn't recommend it. It's been masterminding my brilliant life choices lately."

Dan glanced at his left hand. "Yeah, you and me both."

"I know we don't know each other well, but I'm sorry about you and your wife."

He nodded, stirring the coffee in his Styrofoam cup with a plastic swizzle. "Thanks. Nothing like the office fishbowl to help a guy keep his perspective on things."

"I'm sorry." I blushed, feeling like a nosy parker.

"Don't be. Since I started dating Amy, I don't feel like I cornered the market on dysfunctional relationships. Some of the stuff she's told me makes me think I'm in the wrong wing of the hospital."

"Um, don't those conversations conflict a little with your job?"

"Nah, if anything it helps. I know who won't sit on the personnel committee."

"Yeah, if you ever need former employees, you know where to reach me."

"I'll speed dial you when Lyn's performance review is up."

On my way back to my car, I suddenly found myself with plenty of free time on my hands. I decided to reward my job displacement skills with a latte at Grounds.

I was standing in line at the counter when a voice made me jump.

"Good morning."

"You think that's funny, don't you?"

He looked innocent. "What?"

"Sneaking up on me like that."

"I wasn't sneaking up on you."

It was my turn to order. As I did, Michael handed the barista a twenty.

"What are you doing here?" My question seemed to puzzle him.

"Buying you coffee."

"No, I mean how did you know I was here?"

"I didn't."

"Purely coincidence?" I smirked skeptically as he collected his change.

"Yes, I was coming here to buy you coffee."

"But you didn't expect me to be here?"

"No, I expected you to be at work. I was going to deliver it."

"Don't make it a habit. I'm unemployed."

"Unemployed?" This time he smirked. "You quit?"

"No, I didn't quit! I got the boot."

He stared silently.

"You know ..." I waved my hand in front of his face. "Fired?"

"Yes, I understand."

"You're not supposed to. You're supposed to be shocked, appalled, consoling. Not necessarily in that order, and any two out of the three will do."

"I am."

"I can tell."

"It's my fault, isn't it?"

"No, it's not your fault! That's ridiculous. I wanted to ditch that lame-ass ball. I'd do it all over again. As a matter of fact, I plan on it." Looking at the counter, I saw my order was almost up. "Don't blame yourself, Mike. There's never been a shortage of opportunities in the slave trade. I'll find work."

"You don't have to."

I was about to walk up to the counter for my latte when I stopped short and gave him a severe look.

"Did I work in my past lives?"

A woman standing nearby glanced at me sideways.

"Yes."

"Then I'm working in this one, too."

Stepping up to the counter, I picked up my coffee. Returning to his side, I finished my thought. "Just because we're having sex doesn't make me your pet."

The woman who lingered near us moved away.

He stiffened. "I would never treat you like a pet. I respect and admire you very much."

Taking a careful sip, I shook my head. "I didn't say you couldn't treat me like a pet; I just said I'm not one. There's a difference."

The tension on his face was amusing me when I noticed that he was wearing a tie.

"I thought you said you didn't own any ties."

His expression became impassive again. "I wanted to dress appropriately when I visited your office. I thought it would make me less noticeable."

This only made me laugh as he watched me with vague confusion.

"If you showed up in a wig and makeup you'd be less noticeable."

"Really?"

"No!" I snickered. "Not really!"

At this, he dropped his gaze and his mouth seemed to tense. Feeling guilty, I reached up and fidgeted with the lapel of his wool overcoat.

"I'm sorry, Mike. You're not odd enough to go unnoticed. You're the opposite of odd—I mean you're odd, but not in the looks department. In the looks department, you're ideal. There's nothing wrong with that, but you can't hide it with a neck tie."

"I don't want to hide … I just want to fit in."

Taking another swig of coffee, I nodded supportively. "You do."

"I want to blend."

"I think you're pushing it there."

Looking around the lounge of the coffee shop, I spotted a free table and made for it.

As I approached a chair, I heard him behind me. "Have you thought about moving in with me?"

I took a seat. "We'll have to wait on that."

"Why?" He sat down across from me.

"I have to consult Amy's eight ball first."

"What?"

"Long story."

"I thought you loved me."

"I do. Is it mutual?"

There was the slightest hesitation.

"See?" I pointed at him accusingly.

"You don't understand. I'm not sure."

Letting out a sigh, I raised a brow. "Oh, I understand that fine."

"No, you don't. I mean I'm not sure if I'm in love, period. I love you as a friend. I desire you. But I don't know if it is the same as Antony and Cleopatra, Romeo and Juliet, or Sid and Nancy. By the way, who are Sid and Nancy?"

"Long story. But you see what I mean? It's a little premature to shack up just yet. We still have some stuff to figure out … no rush. You're not going anywhere. I'm not going anywhere, provided I don't get hit by a bus."

"Why do you say things like that?"

"What, getting hit by a bus?" I sipped my coffee.

"It isn't funny."

"I don't think it is either. It's how I pray."

"You believe citing the ways in which harm could come to you will protect you from that harm?"

"At least I won't be surprised when it happens."

"This doesn't sound like you."

"What should I sound like?"

"You've made multiple references to physical harm being done to you, doing physical harm to others, even to yourself. You never spoke that way in your previous lives, yet you experienced far more suffering than you have in this one."

"Maybe it's cumulative. I've reached my tipping point and you've pushed me over the edge." I caught his expression. "Michael, relax. It's just my nerves talking. Apparently I just hit one of yours."

He dissembled and focused on my latte.

"You still aren't going to tell me what that business in the bathroom was about?"

His eyes stayed on the table. "I told you. When I woke you were gone. I went to look for you and saw the champagne on the bathroom floor. When I saw you at the bottom of the tub—"

"You thought I drank till I passed out. In a tub of water. What sort of a drunk do you take me for?"

His eyes sharply connected with mine. "Who would leave you there?"

"You were half dead in bed and I left you alone to sip bubbly and have a soak. Clara Barton I'm not." I went back to my coffee.

For a while we said nothing.

His voice came softly. "You didn't leave me alone. I felt you. You held me."

Biting my lip, I fought a grin. "Wanted to do more than that."

"I know."

"That doesn't appall you?"

He shrugged. "I've suffered greatly at the hands of others, but never from someone I loved. If you had taken more of me, injured me, that would have been joy compared to the suffering I would have felt if you had simply left." He stared away at nothing. "I think I would rather be hurt by you than feel nothing at all."

"Move over Sid and Nancy."

Widening his eyes at me, Michael seemed to awaken. "Am I in love?"

"And I'm going to hell."

"There is no designated place as such."

"I suppose that goes for heaven, too?"

He nodded.

"Then falling in love is the only kind of falling you have to worry about?"

"Falling from grace, like heaven and hell, is a matter of perspective. Where humans are concerned, I am morally ambivalent, at worst I'm meddlesome."

"Then we're well within the acceptable parameters of pooka to human relations."

"That line has yet to be crossed, but I fear crossing it is inevitable."

"Well, to hell with it." I drained my latte. "When should I move in?"

To my surprise, he actually beamed. He must have noticed the look on my face. "What is it?" He stopped short.

"You really smiled, like all the way. It looks good on you."

"I've missed you. I've waited many years to have you in my life again."

"Did we always live together?"

"In your last life we spent the most time apart. Your circumstances didn't accommodate our living together for very long. It is only in the last century that humans have lived in increasing isolation from one another."

"So this is the first time you'll be living with me as my lover?"

"It is the first time I'll be living with anyone in a romantic relationship."

Pushing my mug away, I sat back. "What has been your problem? How could you exist for as long as you have and never been in love?"

"Long story."

"My calendar's freed up."

"I tried to explain it to you when you walked out on me. We don't replicate ourselves."

"I'm not replicating myself. That doesn't mean I don't want to love someone."

"Reproduction is the driving force of life. Even if you choose not to reproduce, the ability to do so is at the core of your vitality. We don't have that ... we aren't alive." Doubt seemed to cloud his eyes.

"Smile, Mike. You're happy today, remember? You are alive—at least to me you are."

He smiled, but not as brightly. I made a mental note to avoid meaning-of-life discussions in the future.

"So ..." I sat up straight. "If I'm moving I've got things to do."

"Can I help?"

"Thanks, but I don't think I'll need it. All my stuff is still in boxes at my parent's."

"Can I move them for you?"

"Um, I'm actually not going to tell Mom I'm moving in with another guy right away. She was pretty wild when she was a go-go girl, but as her only daughter I'm still a twenty-seven-year old virgin."

He smiled. "All parents should feel that way."

"Yeah, well wait until she adopts you and we'll see if you're still smiling."

"What are you going to tell her?"

"I'm going to tell her I've found a place to rent and I'm moving myself."

"She wouldn't try to find out where you're going?"

"She doesn't drive and Dad would only try to find where I was living if I said it was above a coffee house or a book store. Odds would be better if it was both."

"You love them very much."

"Shows, don't it?"

"When can I meet them?"

"Just before we get married."

"When is that?"

"When I've decided marriage actually serves a purpose."

At first he said nothing.

When he did, he sounded disappointed. "You don't want to get married?"

"I haven't even moved in yet. Give me a moment."

"Sorry."

There was a twinge of melancholy.

I changed the subject. "Are you going to be home this afternoon?"

He beamed again. Picking up my purse, I got to my feet.

"I'll be at your place around one." Bending over, I gave him a peck on the cheek. "And think about what you want for dinner tonight."

When I reached the door of the coffee shop, I glanced back at him. He was still sitting at the table, staring at my empty latte mug with a small smile on his face.

Universal symbols define themselves by representing a depth of meaning and complexity simply and effectively. In ancient times such symbolism was of crucial importance before the use of written language. The foundation of early symbology functioned both as a means of reckoning and recollection and are strikingly similar across geographical and cultural barriers.

There are three universal symbols that form the root of early written human communication. The circle, (o) either seen as a whole, or a hole, everything or nothing. The slash (I) or dash (-) mark to denote one, a grouping of such dashes to denote more than one, such as a tree is to a forest or a man as to a mob. And finally a slash and dash combined, (+) which although a multiple of one, quickly expanded in meaning to symbolize coupling unity.

Two is also a catalyst of symbols. It incorporates both the all encompassing nature of the circle in contrast with the slash and its singular independence. (o + - = 2). This pattern continues into the concept of creation, whether marked by the union of male and female, the reaction of a positive and negative charge, or the spark of life in an egg. Two also binds the spiritual significance of the circle, or zero, as the fullness of spirit without body to the grounded presence represented by one. This spiritual meaning still clings to our modern concept of two. The word double not only refers to twice, or twins, but a wraith just as doppelganger refers to a spirit double of a living person.

It is the reaction within the concept of two that marks the beginning of procreation. Two begets three, in many ancient cultures the perfect number, often symbolized by three points or a triangle. The triangle ascendant points to the sky and is often associated with the masculine powers of fire and wind. A descendant triangle points to the earth, the power of the feminine and representative of the womb. Transposed over one another they form the six pointed star often associated with the sun, symbolic of life and the all-seeing eye of God.

[G. Excerpt translated from *Signs of the World*. J. Everding. d. 1789]

[Anne Farrell. Photograph from
Stadium High School Yearbook. 1953.]

2003 Michael never said much about Anne. Only that she played with Daniel's girls. Never that he fathered a child with her. He repeatedly claimed Daniel's death was an accident. Never murder. That was what he didn't want me to know … why he barred Violet's presence in our lives.

Of course, Michael will deny everything. The lies will become omissions. Minor details. After listening to his heartfelt pleas, they will seem harmless. What nags at me is the feeling that all of it, even the omissions, are carefully planned. No matter how I dig, I can never know the truth. There is no truth where Michael is concerned. The longer I am with him, the more I will forget what truth is and why it matters. He promises to tell it, but pookas can only bend it.

Our house is dark under the trees. To be expected when Michael is at home alone. Lodi is sprawled on the solar-heated gravel by my car. He arches his neck to look at me as his tail beats the ground. When I enter the house, the smell of food lures me. It isn't the eggplant strata I had planned. I walk through the kitchen, drawn to the dining room door by a lit candelabrum. The table is set with china and silverware aglow in the light of the setting sun. Two glasses of red wine have been poured from a decanter under the candlelight. Michael is sitting in his chair across the table from me. Toe is in his lap. They watch me like a sphinx.

"You went to the grocery store while I was gone."

"If I'm breaking my promises, I'll make the lasagna I haven't earned."

"Some bodyguard." I approach the table. "How were you going to come to my rescue if I was attacked at Mrs. Farrell's?"

"Nothing was going to attack you at Mrs. Farrell's. It's an apotropaic warehouse."

"An apo— what?"

"Apotropaic. Talismans. Crucifixes, aloe vera, jawbones, mirrors, ring rugs—"

"Got it." I put up a hand.

"Curtis Farrell made a charming neighbor."

"What about Anne Farrell?"

"I wouldn't know."

"Violet says you fathered her baby."

"I never knew she was pregnant."

"Didn't you?"

"You know that would have been quite a trick for me."

"I don't know what I know anymore." I cross my arms and lean in the doorway. "When you first pitched yourself, you claimed you weren't capable of replicating yourself, but you saved Kate's baby. You heal wounds, mend broken bones … raise the dead for all I know. I don't know anyone else who can do that, but any idiot can get a girl pregnant."

"Mending something isn't the same as making something from nothing."

"You never did any mending for Anne?"

"No." He blinks with disgust. "I told you when you moved in with me, you were the first person I'd ever fallen in love with."

"I'm not talking about love."

"Before you, I never had intercourse unless absolutely necessary."
I smirk. "*Intercourse* is always absolutely necessary where men are concerned."
"I'll remind you I'm not a *man*." He answers coolly.
"Curious, what constitutes absolutely necessary intercourse for a singularity?"
His eyes wander over the table and I feel a wave of anxiety that isn't mine. It is a fear in him I've felt before.
"That isn't sex." My voice calmly brings him back to the conversation at hand.
"Then I never had it with Anne Farrell."
"So who did?"
"I don't know."
"Daniel arranged to send Anne to Sarah so she could have a baby, but you don't know anything about it?"
"I wasn't here."
"Where were you?"
"I went away."
"Why?"
"Anne visited Daniel every day. She often saw me here when she did. He thought she was falling in love with me. We agreed it would be better if I wasn't here."
"Why didn't he just keep her away?"
"She was like a daughter to him. He raised her with his own girls."
"What made you come back?"
"He suffered a nervous breakdown. I came back to him and he let me stay."
"He told you nothing?"
"Only that Anne moved away. I suspected it caused his breakdown, but I was afraid to ask."
"Did Sarah ever say anything?"
He looks down at Toe. "No."
"I don't believe you."
When his eyes meet mine, they are bright with annoyance.
"You don't believe *me*? Daniel lied to Violet about having a sister, he lied to me about Anne, he let the world think I was the father of her baby, and *I'm* the one with a credibility problem?"
"That wasn't me. That was Daniel."
He sneers. "How convenient for you."
I explode.
"Convenient! *Convenient!*" Toe slips off of Michael's lap. "I wouldn't call drowning in my own bathtub convenient! I wouldn't call being hunted in my backyard convenient! I don't think anything about having you in my life has been convenient! As far as Violet is concerned, you were a curse on Daniel's life and you'll be the same to mine!"
As the words fly from my mouth, I see him flinch. Every exclamation dims his eyes, leaving them little more than black points. When I am finished, he stares at the candles in silence.

"I'm sorry I failed." His voice surprises me. It is raw, almost hoarse. "I know it isn't enough, but it's all I can say. I've tried to make up for it. I've done everything except leave, and as much as you despise me right now, I can't."

In spite of his despair, I see a question in his eyes when he looks at me.

"I don't despise you. Sometimes you're despicable, but I don't despise you."

"You asked me this morning if I knew what it was like to live with me. Do you know what it is to live with you?"

Going to the dining room windows, I watch evening moths flutter against the glass. Michael is a ghostly reflection in the panes, staring at the back of my head. I don't want to know. For three years he has scarcely spoken a harsh word to me. Now I know why he keeps his journals.

Turning, I face him. "Tell me."

"It's being in heaven when you're a sinner, being enthralled when you've escaped, living a dream when you face a nightmare. All the time you know you're not supposed to be here, but it's so wonderful you can't bring yourself to leave, and the very idea of leaving is worse than any hell."

His eyes move to the candle flame. I near the dining table, watching him.

"It's for you, Sophie. All of it. Everything that is anything, good and bad, is in you. Without you, I have less than nothing, and you could send me there with a thought. As powerful as you imagine I am, you aren't beholden the way I am to you, neither in body nor spirit."

He picks up his wine glass.

"When you were attacked, I knew I was losing you and it was beyond me to stop it. After what Violet has told you, I feel your anger … your rage. I know you want to leave me."

Draining his glass, he looks at me with empty eyes.

"If you're so convinced I'm leaving, just tell me everything and get it over with."

"It's hard to tell all when you're afraid what the reaction might be."

"Haven't I earned more credit than that? Even if I do run screaming, isn't it better I run for the right reason?"

"*Haven't you heard a word I just said?*" The glasses on the table hum in the wake of his voice. "Losing you for any reason is a risk I can't take!"

His outburst thrills me.

"Give it up, Mike! Who made you the king of despair! You think I don't worry about losing you? Why do you think I, *of all people*, give a damn what Marta or Violet thinks about our marriage? You know what I see when I look at them? Do you?"

He says nothing, does nothing.

"I see myself." I stab my fingers into my chest. "I see me in twenty years, forty years—if I'm unlucky—sixty years. You think I don't know it hurts when I talk about blowing my brains out over dinner? Or that you wince every time I call you a pooka? I know it hurts! I want it to!"

"Why?" He whispers.

"Because I want you to remember I'm here and my life is every bit as shitty as yours, whether you choose to believe it or not!"

His eyes narrow. "When in three centuries have I ever forgotten you?"

"Every time you shut me out. Every time you 'forget' to tell me something about yourself and I have to go to Anthony or Violet for the truth. I'm not heaven! I'm not a dream! I'm not some fantasy part of your life you can separate from the nightmares."

He drops his gaze. I pull out the chair next to his and straddle it, facing him with no table between us.

"What happens when I grow old? Right now it's easy to wax romantic about my untimely demise. You worry about me drowning in a bathtub at twenty-seven, being attacked by metaphysical beasties at thirty, but what happens when the damsel in your arms becomes a rotting bag of bones?"

"I've never seen you as a body. I don't care what you look like."

"Well, I do." I get up and walk back around the table. "You might not give damn what society thinks, but I'm part of it. I don't want to live to see the day when everyone who sees us thinks you're my son, or my grandson, or some gold-digging pool boy. I don't want to leave my life behind because I can't explain why my husband hasn't aged since our wedding."

"I told you before we married I would age with you."

"*No!*" I put my palms over my eyes and bite my lip. "God, now I'm doing it."

"Doing what?"

For a moment I can't say anything.

Taking a breath, I start over.

"Did you notice when you started seeing me I never asked your last name, where you lived, if you had a job?"

He makes a tired smile. "Yes."

"Do you know why?"

"You were always too curious about what I was to think about how I lived. I assumed you imagined I disappeared into thin air when I wasn't with you."

"It was because I didn't want to know." I pause. "I didn't want you to be like everyone else. I didn't want the rules of my world to touch you."

"You don't want me to age."

"And you don't want to say what's stalking me."

Slowly, he nods. For a while we say nothing.

Lodi barks outside, and Michael turns his head, staring intently at the window. Lodi stops.

"What if I said I don't know?" He speaks smoothly again.

"It's a start. Do you have a guess?"

"It's something I can't read well. One of us, but not. Your visit with Violet has me thinking."

"About what?"

"Anne's baby. I can only think of one reason Sarah would want it. It still doesn't explain why Daniel lied to me."

"Why don't you ask Sarah?"

"I don't trust her."

"You don't trust her, but you invited her to our wedding?"

"I didn't."

"She crashed our wedding?"

"A friendship would be hard for her to prove if she wanted ECCO to prosecute me. A marriage, however, is another thing."

"She came to threaten you?"

"To remind me."

"Of what?"

"I promised to kill you."

Pulling out the chair across the table from him, I drop into it.

"I'm glad you're a procrastinator."

"It's what I haven't had the courage to tell you. Ever since I started seeing you, since before we were married, Sarah's wanted you dead."

My eyes close as I recline, letting my head fall back from my shoulders. "Why did you want to get married again?"

"I knew you were going to ask that."

I stare at the ceiling. "Was just living together so wrong?"

"I didn't just want to be married. I wanted to be married to you."

Without lifting my head, I point at him. "That Hallmark moment comes with a death wish."

"The death wish comes with me, Sophie. You heard Violet. I'm a curse."

"Here we go again."

"You know the effect I had on Daniel's life. You know the effect I had on Curtis. Curtis broke in that night to kill me ... Daniel died instead."

My head pops up. "How?"

"Curtis tried to break into my crypt with a crow bar."

I sit up. "With you inside?"

He nods. "Curtis ended up breaking Daniel's head. When I emerged, Curtis impaled me."

"With the crow bar?"

He nods again.

"Wow. He was good."

His eyes roll. "Hardly. You've seen what I look like. I was still permeable when I emerged and nearly blind, but I couldn't stay inside and listen to Daniel being bludgeoned either."

"I see your dilemma."

"When I regained consciousness, Curtis had fled."

"And Daniel was dead."

"If you're going to run screaming, this is probably the time to do it."

"Do you see me running?"

He shook his head.

"Then keep talking."

"He would have never regained consciousness ... I wasn't taking him to a hospital ..." His lips move soundlessly.

"So you drowned him in the bathtub."

He drops my gaze and refills his wine glass from the decanter.

"What happened to Curtis?"

"Impaling me exposed him to lethal amounts of radiation. He had the adrenalin to make it home, but nothing after that would have saved him."

"Violet said he died of a fever."

"So it would have appeared to the untrained eye."

"Why was he so hell bent on you?"

"He was, above all things, a hunter. He read my eyes; I felt it. Add his fascination with myths and legends, and he had enough knowledge to suspect me without understanding what I was. With only his mortality to occupy him, the thought of some mythical quarry in his own backyard appealed to his sense of valor."

"You were the one that got away."

"I was the one that got Daniel killed." He is barely audible.

"Daniel sent you away before and you left."

"But I came back."

"Would you have stayed if Daniel wanted you to go?"

"Probably not."

"Daniel knew that. He wanted you to stay in his life. He died protecting you because he loved you, not because he was cursed with you."

"For three years I've told you Daniel's death was an accident."

Waving him off, I take a sip of wine. "I never believed that story anyway."

"I lied to you."

"I know. For three years I've been doing all the cooking."

He smiles. "I made breakfast."

"True. You have a way with an egg."

His smile disappeared. "I don't know if I have the same with lasagna."

"The suspense will kill me if my mother-in-law doesn't first."

Whether it is the wine, the lasagna, or being tripped up in my own pursuit of the truth, my brain works overtime putting pieces together as I eat. Ever since meeting Michael, my head collected bits like a Roomba while I indulged my desires. It is only now, three years later, that my desires have dulled. The newness has worn away and my thoughts dwell on the past rather than face an uncertain future.

Michael's instinct is to mislead me. It is the only way he's ever led humans. What I have to decide is which path I will follow: one that will challenge the settled order of my world, or one that will lead to ignorant bliss. But ignorant bliss is an oxymoron for me. Willful ignorance, worse than death.

Watching him eat the rest of the lasagna, I ponder why there is such a thing as sentience at all. I am suddenly relieved I don't have a continuous memory running back to the nonexistent beginning of everything. Considering his fate, it seems cruel. Existing forever with no means of escape would drive anyone mad at some point. For me, the only thing that could make such an existence possible would be to share it with someone I loved. If Michael were gone, could I find someone else? But that isn't my problem. It's his.

"Do you still love me?"

He stares like a child over his empty plate.

"I do."

"You know I'm trying to be honest."

"I know."

"I'm not very good at it, am I?"

"You've never had to be accountable to anyone before."

"I've never been accountable to anyone I *loved* before."

"You're thinking about ECCO."

"I have another confession to make."

"Before dessert?"

He nods, but waits for a response.

"I'll hear it."

"I watched you the day you went back to work after our first New Year's Eve."

"You did? Why?"

"Because I knew you were afraid you'd be fired. You knew it was a risk the moment you decided to skip the ball, but you did what you wanted anyway."

"It's that cavalier attitude you're attracted to."

"You went to work expecting to pay a price and you told your boss to fuck off."

"We don't use that language at the dinner table."

"If ECCO has a problem with me, I'm going to tell them the same thing."

"I said that to a middle-aged, middle management suck up, not a gang of intergalactic thugs. Something tells me they'll do worse than screw you out of vacation pay."

"I've just discovered what it is to be alive when you only have one life to share with me. Nothing could be worse than that."

"That life could get a lot shorter if they decide to look us up."

"Are you afraid?"

"Always."

"If you want to leave me, I understand."

I shake my head. "I can't. I promised Maeve I'd break the curse."

His smile is sad. "You're better at keeping those than I am. I can't promise you a happy ending, Sophie, only to do whatever I can to get you there."

"You once told me sacrificing yourself for love would be a selfish act. Don't do anything stupid."

"I know my enemies. Sacrifice is all they understand, but even a selfish act can be a sacrifice. The trick is knowing the difference." He sips his wine.

I smile. "I thought you didn't do tricks."

"I've been practicing."

"You want to show me?"

Smiling at me, he puts down his glass. The candelabrum catches his eye, the flames shrinking to nothing, leaving the room black. My vision adjusts to the dark, fixing on the blue points of his eyes. He is still sitting across the table from me.

"Not bad. Not Vegas, but a good start."

"Since you were attacked, I've shared our bed every night, but you haven't wanted me. And please, no jokes about headaches."

"No jokes."

In the dark, his voice comes from nowhere. "You're still angry at me."

"No. Just tired."

"I can change that."

"Oh, I know you can."

"Will you let me?"

With a sigh, I sit back in my chair. "I'm in."

He rises, coming to my side of the table. Taking my hand, he pulls me from my chair. With a deft motion, he picks me up and heads for our room.

"Wait a minute." My voice stops him midstride on the stairs. "We forgot to wash the dishes."

"You forgot to wash the dishes. I cooked tonight, remember?"

"I'm not forgetting; I'm being abducted."

He continues up the stairs. "Last one out of bed tomorrow does the dishes."

He's assuming I always sleep in.

"I like those odds."

Entering the bedroom, he stops and looks at me suspiciously.

"Why?"

"That's for me to know and you to find out."

1199 BC On the mountain, I came upon the foundations of a temple. It was a colonnade with a roof and no walls. A pair of engraved stelae marked the door in defamation of our code, a bastardized record in crude cuneiform. My eyes could barely look upon them when I heard a familiar voice from within. The form it emerged in was not: the body of a young man, still alive but hopelessly possessed. It was another advantage Saitael had taken beyond the law, to take what was forbidden, the living body of another. A living body could go months, even years without a crypt. A living body could heal itself, but it could also be killed, its possessor entrapped. Saitael's advantage fled as he faced me. His optimism against the certainty of my wrath remained undiminished.

Still, he plied me, and still, I listened.

Strength, supremacy, a second chance at the sublime, all spoken by the darkest creature of the darkest half of hell. Why I listened I do not know. I always did and still do. Yet smite him I did, where he stood in his temple, burned as an offering to himself. I then took my disgust out upon the temple, the mountain, and the mine of tears within it. How many innocents died within I do not know. All I knew at the time was it had to be stopped. Convinced of his godhood, they could not be stopped with words. Convinced of his godhood, he would have never let them go.

Even after my work was finished, I feared the place. Lachrymose silver was rare, when found, difficult for our kind to mine. Our numbers were few, the seams known to us so remote it was only with great effort that tears could be acquired. To have discovered a seam so close to human habitation was unfortunate. With a steady supply of labor, vast quantities could be obtained and the most fearful weapons fashioned. In Saitael's hands, he would obliterate all he could not conquer.

But I had succeeded. I had stopped Saitael. I had stopped the mine. And so it would stay. Before the remains of his temple, I used my veil to collect the bones of the body he had possessed, his spirit asleep within them. Bundling the remains, my intent was to return to my crypt and keep him with me. From the cave in the ravine, I would rest by day and watch the mines by night. On my way down the mountain, there was evidence of much devastation. Great cliff sides had given way, the encampment below silent. What had not been buried, abandoned.

In the ravine, my cave still waited. A few boulders blocked my way and were easily moved. It was not until I was inside that I discovered my crypt was gone.

[Spharic. Entry translated from *Kor Dai Maihael*. Mund Dai. 755 BC]

2000 "My God ..."

All one could say aside from that was Michael's kitchen resembled a truck stop mini-mart. Every available surface was piled with boxes of Twinkies, Nilla Wafers, Oreos, Nutter Butters, graham crackers, and every other staple required to run a daycare. The pantry was filled with equally diabetic-friendly fare. The kitchen drawers were different. They were reserved for candy. Payday and Mars Bars were neatly segregated from bags of jelly beans, Swedish fish, and peanut M&Ms.

"I thought you said you ate Clif bars and protein supplements?"

"I do." He drifted to an open box of animal crackers on the kitchen table.

"You have another kitchen for those?"

"I keep those in the refrigerator."

I peeked inside. "You drink whipping cream?"

"Its for my cereal."

I turned in time to see him bite the head off a zebra.

"You eat this junk?"

Briefly, he stopped chewing. "Parents feed their children these foods every day."

"You can't be serious."

"I told you I have a high metabolism."

"This has got to stop."

"What will I eat?"

"We'll work on that. My kidneys are failing just standing here."

"I don't have kidneys."

"You want to be a person?" I looked at him critically. "You want to blend?"

"I like to eat."

"You can eat, just not like this. Not all day, anyway."

"What will I eat?"

"Big people food. You cook at all?"

"I make soup."

"Does that soup happen to come out of a can?"

He said nothing.

"You don't cook. We're going to the grocery store today—no. I'm going to the grocery store. When I get back, all this stuff will be gone. Okay?"

"You want me to throw it away?" His voice actually sounded panicked.

"Stick it in one of the rooms upstairs. I can't cook if all this is here. And I'll need refrigerator space."

Leaving him to polish off his box of animal crackers, I wondered if I hadn't bitten off more than I could chew. What on earth was I going to feed him? He didn't seem to have any food allergies and obviously wasn't picky. Obviously. I decided I would cook what I wanted to eat, only enough for six people. The grocery bills were going to be huge. Maybe that was why he needed a million a year.

It took three grocery baggers to load up my car.

My trunk and my back seat were filled, not only with groceries but the kitchen tools I suspected would be lacking. This included knives, a large stainless sauté pan, and three heavy baking dishes. When I got back to the house, it was dark. The BMW parked out front was the only indication anyone was inside. Stepping to the trunk of my car, I barely opened it when he was next to me, pulling out several bags at a time. Feeling the futility of trying to help, I grabbed my reserve gin and went inside to hunt for light switches. It was a pleasant surprise to find my search made easier by the glow of a crackling fire in the fireplace.

When I got to the kitchen, I was impressed at how much space appeared once the junk food was vacated.

"I'm sorry I forgot the lights." Michael watched me inventory the spice bottles.

"No problem. I like the fire."

Pulling out the baking dishes, I set to organizing what needed to be prepped. I noticed I was a few bags short.

"Where's the food?"

"In the refrigerator."

"You work fast."

He said nothing.

I handed him the chef's knife and pointed at three bags of red potatoes. "Rinse them, halve them, put them in the each of those." I pointed at the three baking dishes sitting on the counter.

Returning to the refrigerator, I pulled out three split chickens, then froze.

"Your oven works doesn't it?" The sound of his knife stopped.

"Yes."

"Thank God. Preheat to 375 please."

This would be easier than I thought.

My calculations were about right. With the potatoes and green beans, three chickens seemed to be enough. My own appetite dulled watching him eat.

He noticed.

"You haven't eaten very much."

"I'm not usually hungry after cooking."

His eyes went to my empty plate. "That wasn't enough for your body mass."

"I'll have a Payday later."

"You're tired."

To be expected after getting fired and moving in with a singular entity in the same day.

"No biggie; I can sleep in."

"What will you do tomorrow?"

Tomorrow …

"Hold that thought."

Getting up from the table, I went to the kitchen. Pulling out the bottle of Sapphire I'd slipped in the freezer, I ducked into the refrigerator and rummaged for olives. When I turned, he was standing in the kitchen door, watching.

"They had gin at the grocery store?"

"No, this is the relief bottle from my trunk." Twisting off the cap, I looked around. "I don't suppose you have any vermouth around here?"

He shook his head.

"Glasses?"

He shook his head again.

"You don't own any glasses?"

"I needed the shelf space."

Shrugging, I popped an olive in my mouth and took a swig from the bottle.

"What was that thought again?" I asked as I headed for the living room, gin in one hand, olives in the other.

"What will you do tomorrow?"

Claiming the sofa, I sprawled out and set the gin on the floor before fishing the olive jar with a finger.

"I think I'll sleep on it."

He came close, looking down at me as I washed down olive number two.

"Do you want me to sleep with you tonight?"

"If you don't mind waiting, I was thinking I'd take a really, really long bath."

"You can't."

"I can't?"

"Didn't you notice the bathroom?"

I sat up. "What did you do?"

"I replaced the tub."

"What?" Getting up, I left the living room and ran upstairs.

The bathroom was still white, still tiled, but where the tub had stood was a shower basin walled behind two heavy glass doors. Leaning back against the bathroom door, I stared at the shower, trying to remember what was wrong with the tub the way it was. Finally, I made the connection.

He had followed and stood behind me in the hall.

"You are such an *ass*."

Without looking at him, I went to my room and started to unpack.

He approached the bedroom door, peering in at me.

"Are you very upset?"

Looking him in the eye, I went to the door and slammed it in his face.

I spent the next hour organizing my clothes, filling one dresser and one wardrobe. When I opened the bedroom door, I half expected to see him still standing there. Much to my relief and disappointment, he wasn't. Taking my bag of bath items to the medicine cabinet, I made an inventory of what was already there. There was a basket of TP, a bath bench with towels, a heated towel rack that looked brand new. It was hard to stay pissed at this guy.

Then I noticed how silent the house was.

Going to the door, I stuck my head out and listened. Nothing. At the top of the stairs, I peeked down into the foyer. It was dark. I heard a pop from the dying fire in the living room, but no other sign of life. I was the only living thing in the house.

Returning to the bathroom, I shut the door and took a long, hot shower.

After brushing my teeth, I pulled on my bathrobe and was ready for bed, when I remembered the gin I'd left in the living room. Finding myself at the top of the stairs again, I stared down at nothing. The light from the bathroom illuminated the landing but left the foyer black below.

What was I afraid of?

"Bullshit." I whispered to myself as I started down the stairs.

It wouldn't be like him to leave the bottle on the floor.

It would if he expected me to come back for it.

He expected me to come back for it.

The foyer was an ink pit, but the living room was easier to make out. The wood floor was icy under my feet, motivating me to skip onto the Persian carpet. Bending over, I strained to see if my gin was still next to the sofa. Putting my hand out, the tips of my fingers grazed the neck of the bottle. It was in my grasp.

"I would have taken it up, but I didn't want to disturb you."

That was what I was afraid of.

Closing my eyes, I let out my breath before turning around.

The voice came from near the fireplace, the wingback chair. There was no fire-light left; only the blue points of his eyes shone in the dark.

"Do you even know how freaky you look right now? And you wonder why I drink so much."

Clutching my gin to me, I strutted out of the living room and climbed the stairs. On my way up, I took a good pull from the bottle and marched to my room, kicking the door shut behind me. I didn't hear the door close. I felt something take hold of the bottle and barely turned. His lips were on mine.

Waking up next to Michael was harder than I thought it would be. It felt like it was any other morning until you remembered you won the biggest lottery jackpot in the history of the world the day before. It was exhilarating, overwhelming, exhausting. Lying on my side, I watched him sleep, toyed with the idea of keeping him too tired to do anything for the rest of the day, and wondered if he would let me. Then I recalled I was unemployed.

Dragging myself out of bed, I picked my bathrobe off the floor and went to the vanity where I'd parked my laptop. Starting it up, I saw my reflection in the glow of the monitor. Rubbing the sleep from my eyes, I cleared my throat, trying to get the morning-after taste out of my mouth. Looking around me, I spotted the gin on my dresser and retrieved it. A swig refreshed me to the aroma of juniper berries.

"What are you doing today?"

Same voice, same question, same drink …

"Seeking my life's purpose, preferably with benefits and health coverage."

He sat up in bed, watching me in the vanity mirror. Surfing the classifieds, I glanced at his reflection, and smiled, batting my eyelashes. My cursory search showed plenty of openings in Seattle, but not much of anything in Tacoma.

Commuting would suck. Everyone knew getting out of Seattle at the end of the day was a nightmare.

While I read job descriptions I felt his hands on my hair. Glancing in the mirror, I could see too much of his perfectly defined self behind me.

"Do you mind? I'm trying to be productive here."

"Do you like what you do?"

"Everyone wants to be a grant writer. It's one of the sexiest jobs in the world. Look at me." I brushed his hands away from my head. "I have to beat guys off with a stick."

"I shouldn't have let you skip the ball."

"We're not hashing that out again. Hey!" Grabbing his hands, I looked up at him. "Speaking of hash, there's some in the refrigerator. Heat and eat. *Your* kind of cooking. If you're really up for a challenge, you can add an egg."

Kissing the top of my head, he spoke into my hair. "I'll make you breakfast."

As he left, he took the gin with him. I pretended I didn't notice.

When he returned with my breakfast, it was perfectly fine, not that I doubted he could cook. Around food, Michael suffered a kind of ADHD. He didn't make any breakfast for himself, choosing an assortment of Hostess products instead.

After breakfast, he wanted to know where I would be. I told him I planned to be home all day, getting out my resume. He said he would be gone the rest of the morning but would return after noon. Although we'd never actually discussed it, I decided I wouldn't ask him what he did when he wasn't with me unless he volunteered. I assumed it was part of our acceptance of one another, a necessity that would allow us to live together.

Around twelve thirty, he returned. I didn't see him leave, but when he came upstairs to check on me, he was dressed in a dark navy suit and wearing his neck tie.

"Don't tell me you've been interviewing, too."

He smiled his generic smile. "Did you solicit any employers?"

"Soliciting? Is that what I should be doing? I don't know. If they're like Evil Lyn, I don't think cheesecake will work. No—wait a minute—it would."

"Cheesecake?"

Pausing, I squinted. "That does sound good, doesn't it? I haven't had lunch; let's get some cheesecake."

Pulling off my pajama bottoms, I started to hunt for my jeans.

"Cheesecake for lunch?"

"Gimme a break." I yanked on my jeans. "You've been bottom feeding on candy, but cheesecake threatens the integrity of your food pyramid?"

"I love cheesecake."

Tying back my hair, I nodded at the door. "Fire up the Bimmer, sparky."

I followed him downstairs to the car. Once inside, Michael started the engine and then looked at me expectantly.

"Antique Sandwich, Jeeves."

As he turned the car in the drive, my eyes remembered the first time they saw his profile. It was the day he drove me to the hospital and I thought he was the devil. He

caught me watching him and tensed. I guessed he knew what I was thinking and tried to think of something else. He'd left the radio on again and "Learning To Fly" was on.
  I turned up the volume. "Have you been listening to this?"
  He shrugged. "You like music."
  "But do you like any of it?"
  "It's different."
  "What do you like to listen to?"
  "Everything I suppose."
  "But you don't own any music. Outside of this car, you don't even have a radio."
  "I don't need a radio; I can hear it anyway."
  I got goose bumps. "People get put away for saying that."
  He smiled. "You asked."
  "If you had to listen to something, what would it be?"
  With a shrug, he looked out his window. "I like stringed instruments."
  "Vivaldi, Bach, that sort of thing?"
  "It doesn't have to be anything particular. I like certain resonances."
  It clicked in my head. "You like the ocean."
  "Yes." he smiled. "Very much."
  "You know, you can get CDs of the ocean."
  "I don't need a CD—"
  "—you can hear it anyway." I finished as he nodded.
  "How did you know I like the ocean?"
  "You sound like it."
  He blinked. "That's what I sound like to you?"
  "That or a freak wind storm. What do you think you sound like?"
  "Technically, I don't sound like anything. I don't generate any frequency of my own. What you heard is a universal frequency all singulars hear. We reflect it, but we aren't the source of it."
  "That's why you don't need a receiver. You are one."
  "Something like that."
  "What don't you like to listen to?"
  "Sonar."
  "Me neither." I sat back. "Living together should be easy."
  "I find faxes annoying. Lightning. Solar flares make things worse."
  "How can you hold a conversation with all of that going on?"
  "My ability to process sensory information is significant."
  "But you weren't sure if you were in love or not."
  "Most singulars reject emotions because they are ambiguous. Paradoxically, we distrust them because they are intangible."
  "Substance without sentiment is as empty as sentience without substance."
  He smiled. "Cheesecake without Sophie is a dream on an empty plate."
  The lunch rush was ending as we entered The Antique. In a cooler by the door, three cheesecakes sat on display: berry, mocha, and plain. A maddening choice

was to be made. While evaluating my mood to determine which flavor I wanted, I heard Michael order two slices in each flavor. Behind the counter, a girl with pink pigtails and a nose piercing asked if he wanted them boxed and he said yes. I approached inquiringly.

He caught my expression. "I thought we would go to the park."

"Cheesecake in the park?"

"It's unseasonably warm today and it won't rain until this evening."

I gave a shrug. "I'm going where the cake's going."

The girl held out a pink box that matched her hair and I picked it up along with a couple plastic forks. I was hungry enough to consider eating the cake in the car, but Pt. Defiance was only a couple blocks away and the drive was short. In the park, Michael drove to the pagoda and parked near a white gazebo overlooking the water. The benches inside were empty. Picking one with a view, I sat at the end with my legs crossed in front of me, placing the box on the seat.

Michael sat across from me as I handed him a fork.

I opened the box. "Don't you have any friends who aren't human?"

"There are individuals I prefer to others." He chose a piece of mocha.

Feeling like a purist, I went for the plain. "Are any of them here?"

"Eight."

"They all do what you do?"

"No."

"But they're here for a purpose?"

"Yes."

"Do you ever see any of them?"

"Sometimes."

I couldn't tell if his answers were monosyllabic because he was engrossed in cheesecake or he was uncomfortable with the topic.

"So what's ECCO, your trade union?"

"You read Anthony's file on me." Without an upward glance, he continued to eat.

"Is there anything in there I'm not supposed to know?"

"Its public record." He still didn't look up.

As he took another bite of cake, I sampled the piece he was eating. When he finally met my gaze, the brilliance of his eyes was alarming.

I smirked back. "You wanted me here."

"ECCO is a necessity. It meets our material needs."

"*Material needs.*" I snorted. "From what I read, that's a lot of material. Where does it come from?"

"Properties and other assets. One of us manages it."

"Not you."

"No. My abilities would be wasted there."

"And what would those be?"

"I have a unique ability to read my own kind. There is one here who is especially challenging and requires my attention."

"I thought you said geographical location wasn't important, so why are any of you here?"

"My location on this planet isn't important, but this planet is. It is one of a handful of planets supporting sentient life in this part of the universe. In the balance of things, it is of strategic importance. Why not be here rather than someplace else?"

Possibly there were ramifications to this relationship I was ignoring ...

"Am I frightening you?"

Reflecting on his answer, I had stopped talking.

"Not really. Just thinking about how I've never been much into sci-fi and someone else would get more out of this conversation than I am. Anthony would be thrilled to know our planet has strategic importance."

He seemed to tense. "Your odds of dying are significantly diminished living with me than without."

"Not if we keep eating like this."

His smile returned and I continued.

"What about the other documents I saw? You really have parents?"

"My father did disappear in Olympic National Park; they just haven't found me yet."

I snickered. "And your mother, Sarah Monroe?"

"She manages ECCO and supplies funding and identification when needed."

"Who's Uncle Daniel?"

There was a pause and a slow reply. "The house we live in now was his."

"I know." I took a bite of cake. "It's on the deed. Is he part of ECCO?"

When I glanced up, he was staring at the water. I could tell he didn't see a thing.

~~

Subject: **Just Checking In**

From: Anthony

Date: 1/7/2000 4:10 PM

To: Sophie

Hey Sophie. Just wanted to check in and see how you were doing. Been real busy going into the big parade season, every year the crowds get bigger and we don't. Hope everything is going all right. I haven't been asking any questions, but an old query of mine came up without any answers.

You remember before you moved out I did some checking and re-quested some records from LA. Aside from what I gave you there was nothing. No school records, no medical, not even a driver's license. I mean I suppose he could have lived in LA for over twenty years and only learned to drive when he moved up here, but he doesn't seem like a mass transit kind of guy. Even if he was saving up for the BMW, that's a lot of bus tokens.

But I promised you I was done with this and I am. Just wanted to let you know the last of it. I really do want the best for you and I want you to know I will always respect you. I'm also hoping if I kiss your ass enough you'll agree to meet me for a beer after work this week. We'll talk about whatever you want. Just like old times.

Tony

[E-mail from Anthony Navarre to Sophie Davids. January 7, 2000]

ABDUCTION

2003 "I thought you didn't do tricks?"
"I've been practicing."
"You want to show me?"

Her thoughts have turned playful, doing anything not to think about the beast in the garden, about Sarah, about how much time they have left. He always considered playful gestures a dangerous habit, but alone with Sophie and her fears, he will do anything to distract her. He will have her love him if she will take him. Snuffing the candles gives courage to ask what he has wanted for three weeks. He waits for her to see him again, keeping his eyes bright in the dark.

"Not bad. Not Vegas, but not bad." Her amusement is genuine and defensive.

"Since you were attacked, I've shared our bed every night, but you haven't wanted me. And please, no jokes about headaches."

"No jokes."

She says nothing more. Silence opens the door.

"You're still angry at me." He doesn't breathe.

"No. I'm just tired."

"I can change that."

"Oh, I know you can." He senses no hostility or repugnance.

"Will you let me?"

Her hesitation feels like eternity.

"I'm in."

Approaching her, his body feels the same as if he were facing an enemy. His nerves are greater than when he first touched her. As he pulls her to him, he can tell she has let go. She is dim, but peaceful, her eyes tired and hungry. They are dark and safe as he looks into them. He picks her up with care; she feels fragile in his arms, her color more beautiful to him than he has ever remembered, and he forgets nothing.

Now he focuses on every word she says.

"Wait a minute." She stops him on the stairs, her words drawn with cynicism. "You forgot to wash the dishes."

"You forgot to wash the dishes. I cooked tonight, remember?"

"I'm not forgetting; I'm being abducted."

"Last one out of bed tomorrow does the dishes."

"I like those odds." Her mind grows elusive as she plans a role reversal in bed.

"Why?" He hides his nerves with a smile.

"That's for me to know and you to find out."

The words enter in his mind, but he stops processing anything critically. Only once did he allow critical analysis to enter this intimate space, and it was terrifying. Intimacy created a strange nexus he had previously been unaware of. He had no experience indulging it. When Sophie took control, he couldn't stop the memories behind the fears that flooded him. She forced him to let go. She freed him. Nothing was the same after that and it was for the better.

Now, only the core element of his being is aware. Without her, he has no arousal of his own; he only reflects and refracts, transmits and transmutes her spiritual will. What her will desires, he freely gives, something once unimaginable, unspeakable to his kind. As their thoughts merge, he lets his body follow the impulse of its DNA. The motions are reflexive, matching hers. He only strains to see as much of her as he can before he is blind. Her soul is blinding enough with light she doesn't see. Her eyes only see his own light, the ripple of energy that can give life as easily as take it. Now it robs his vision. In his blindness, he feels the smallness of her.

The chord of the universe grows deafening as his body becomes a conduit, his spirit consumed by hers. Her life pulls him into her, the reaction of living energy with his diffuse being grows overwhelming. Euphoric or despairing, it makes no difference; it is a sensation better than emptiness. Everything he is drains away in a moment of sacrifice and release. Oblivion is the only defense his sentience has, unconsciousness the only means of staunching the flow. The connection is broken; the chord is silent.

He will seem unconscious much longer than he actually is. His spirit has only freed itself from being consumed, his awareness reasserts in moments. His body will take longer. It is now he is most vulnerable. Outside of the crypt, his consciousness is bound to the body and cannot leave. The body that serves him can trap him, be turned against him. It would please his enemies to no end to take him now. It is only his skill at hiding that protects him. Feeling exhaustion, he pushes the risks from his mind. He will not fear in this moment. He is tired of feeling fear, but it must come with all the rest.

Welcome sleep comes at last.

"Michael?"

The name whispers in his head. Awareness returns to his body, feeling hers above. He opens his eyes; her face is nearly transparent to his weak vision. Knowing Sophie's childhood fears, he smiles at the thought of what she would think of her appearance to him now. Her skull is as beautiful to him as any other part of her.

She has excellent teeth.

"That's quite a grin you have there." The sound of her full voice makes him flinch. "Want to get a head start on those dishes?"

Her thoughts are clear. Sleep now and do dishes later. Stay awake and do dishes much later. He can say nothing. He will suffer either way. It is the nature of his suffering she offers for him to choose, a choice barely offered before her kiss takes it away. The last time he opens his eyes, the faintest lines of her fade into the blue light of blood rushing his head. The chord is struck again.

The hum of the modern world is constant, scarcely less strident at night. The chord of the universe drowned in tangles of data, stifling the atmosphere like a pestilence. At least, that is how it feels to someone who can hear it. It is the last thing he hears as he falls asleep and the first thing to wake him in the morning. Worse when Sophie starts her laptop in the bedroom while he is still in bed. Infinitely worse the morning after she has gratified herself three times in one night.

The sky is clear and quite visible through the outlines of rafters in the ceiling. Normally his eyes would register the ceiling, but they are weak this morning. They will be all day. He will have to take care. As Sophie goes online, he lifts his head to look at her. She is a skeletal specter sitting at her vanity. His vision sharpens on the bathrobe she is wearing, little more than shadow to his eyes, her skull vaguely obscured in a towel. She checks her e-mail. There are ten messages: three from Amy, one from Kate, one from her father, three Facebook notifications, and two newsletters. If he wasn't so tired, he might be irritated enough to start reading them aloud if it got her to turn the infernal thing off.

Dropping his head, he inhales and practices the art of respiration.

"You're alive." She notices.

"Not really." He has no idea if he is audible to her.

Coming to the bed, she sits next to him. "I was hard on you last night, wasn't I?"

Up close, the empty spaces between her molecules begin to fill in.

"The first time, you were worried you'd killed me. Now I think that's all you're trying to do."

"I wasn't going to kill you." She strokes his head. "You've still got dishes to wash."

"No dishes ..." He closes his eyes. "One of the perks of being a bachelor."

"For you, that was the only one."

"That and being able to sleep undisturbed."

She puts a glass hand on his arm and squeezes. "Your old bed had a lid."

Standing, she stoops to pick some clothes off the floor. "I'm going to meet Amy at the farmer's market for lunch. You're welcome to join us if you want."

Wandering through a market of street vendors in the blinding sun doesn't appeal. Rolling onto his side, he watches her open her wardrobe and consider her options. She holds a dress to herself in front of the mirror. He recognizes it even though it is barely visible: a green sun dress. He thinks it one of the most flattering dresses she owns, but she rarely wears it.

"Why don't you ever wear that?"

She holds it up. "It's one of those dresses that always seems a little too nice for wherever you're going. I mean, it's just lunch."

This, coming from a woman who could have been killed two weeks ago. Human reason remains elusive. How they afford to regard any occasion as anything less than priceless is beyond him. Then again, he isn't human.

"You should wear it."

"You should come." She counters.

"I don't want to intrude on your time with Amy."

"Anthony is going to meet us. He only had half a shift today."

He imagines Anthony with Sophie in her green dress.

Pausing at the mirror, she looks at him in its reflection. "Michael, just come."

"I'll go if you wear that dress."

"Deal." Her ghostly smile superimposes over her teeth.

The bathroom is familiar enough space to feel comfortable; only the glass walls of the shower caution him. Following his system for dressing, he is ready to go by the time Sophie is finished. She pins back her hair before putting on a broad-brimmed hat. It is finely woven silk with a green ribbon she calls her Scarlett hat.

Turning, she appraises him. "I was never a fan of polo shirts, but I am now."

He smiles as she tips the brim of her hat and bats her eyes at him.

"How do I look?" Her smile has grown more prominent than her teeth.

He pulls her close. "Maybe it would be safer if we stayed at home today."

She gives him a shove. "We'd better leave before you hurt yourself."

They are barely down the stairs when her words prove prophetic. The wooden steps are a uniform pattern to his eyes until he reaches the bottom. Momentarily, he misses where the stairs end and the floor boards in the foyer begin. The stumble is slight, he catches himself instantly, but Sophie notices.

"You all right?"

"Fine."

"I'll drive."

Putting on his sunglasses, he opens the front door for her. "I want you to."

In the car, he notices she turns off the radio before starting the ignition.

She glances at him watching her. "Fasten your seat belt."

"You're really worried about me."

"*No*, I really don't want a ticket."

He smiles as he fastens his belt. When he looks up again, the Farrell house comes into view. Feeling the windows stare down on them as they pass, his smile slips away.

They shouldn't have stayed. The house, the memories, the visions. He stayed because he was waiting for her. He knew Daniel would come back. But why were they still here? What had he waited for these three years? Now it was too late. Someone had caught on to him, was moving on him. Why couldn't he read them? Did Violet know? Sophie's instincts were right and he had ignored them. Her tenacity about Daniel's life he had written off too many times. His refusal to face the consequences of his actions left her vulnerable.

Except he is the one feeling vulnerable.

Skirting the edge of Wright Park, he looks at the conservatory.

He had been more afraid to meet Sophie there than he realized. Afraid of her rejection and afraid of her acceptance. When she asked what he wanted of her, the question burnt him like fire. The thought of romantic love mortified him. It was the most despicable form of attachment. He rejected those feelings for her without thought. It had been the same as rejecting her, but she stayed. She stayed for three years and now knew she had been in danger for every one of them.

Still, she stays.

Now she is meeting her friends at the market as though it were any other day. It is any other day. It will come and it will go, and there is no holding on to it. She accepts it.

The law of non-attachment isn't intended to blind him to desire. It is intended to blind him to the vulnerability that comes with it. It is a law of self-preservation at the expense of everything else. It embraces ignorance of love over the acceptance of pain. He is attached to Sophie. Attached to all the happiness and frustration that comes with her. The attachment can't last. He can't accept it. He must learn how.

Somehow Sophie finds a spot only a few blocks from the market.

The moment the car door opens, the smell of food makes him forget his misgivings about tagging along. Once on the sidewalk, the assault on his senses is greater than he anticipates. The street fills with people—people who are gradually becoming more solid, forming crowds, a blur of shape and color. A girl passes in front of him with Mylar balloons, causing him to stop short.

"Okay?" Sophie is holding his hand.

"Fine."

"Amy said they would be near the stage. We can eat any time you want, though."

He feels her slow. She is looking at candles a honey vendor has on display. He looks at the honey. All his body seeks are calories, the more efficiently consumed the better. His eyes skip the health food, the vegetable stands, and anything inedible.

"I'm feeling Greek today." Sophie is looking at a woman nearby eating a pita.

Not enough calories.

"I'm feeling like pie."

"Pie? Berry or mozzi?"

"Coconut crème if I can get it."

Sophie makes a face. "Yeah, well if you want me to keep wearing this dress, you'll excuse me while I find something else."

She wanders into the crowd. Several men watch her as she goes and he smiles.

He finds a woman selling baked goods. She only has berry pies, so he opts for a berry crumb cake. And a pie. As the woman sorts his change, his mind searches for Sophie and sees her circling a table near a beer garden. He sees Amy and Anthony a block away, moving in Sophie's direction.

"Sir?"

His eyes refocus on the woman in front of him.

"Sorry." He takes the change and pockets it.

Picking up his boxes, he goes south. Amy is just ahead of him. She waves.

"Michael! It's great you came. Sophie didn't know if you would want to or not."

"Hello, Amy." He looks over her shoulder at Anthony. "Hello, Anthony."

Anthony nods. "Hey, Mike."

The feelings between them are better, but still hard. His vision detects the concealed firearm under Anthony's coat.

"Sophie got a table." He smiles at Anthony, then leads them to the beer garden.

"What did you get?" Amy's voice is always happy. It makes him feel accepted.

"A cake and a pie."

"Aren't you going to eat lunch?"

"Yes."

While Amy waits for him to elaborate, he points through the crowd.

"There's Sophie."

Sophie waves, holding the brim of her hat in the breeze. "Finally. I'm starving."

"Why didn't you eat already?" Anthony shakes his head, taking a seat.

"Because this was the last table and I'm not sitting on the ground, thank you very much."

"There are plenty of tables over there." Amy points to the beer garden.

"Yeah, but you have to drink their beer."

"Since when did that ever stop you?"

Sophie glares at Anthony. "It's crap beer. Where did I get this reputation? You make it sound like I'm swallowing my mouthwash and huffing Sterno."

A man standing nearby overhears her and laughs. Sophie shrugs at him.

Amy giggles. "Huffing Sterno!" She pauses. "What's Sterno?"

"Can we please eat now?" Sophie pleads to Amy.

"Sure, let's go. What do you feel like?"

"Greek." He answers for Sophie as he opens the box with the pie. Anthony peers over the table curiously.

"I love Greek." Amy gushes. "I'll show you where they are."

On a map? I doubt it … The thought is Sophie's as he watches her follow Amy into the crowd. He catches Anthony watching Sophie and senses strong feelings.

"Aren't you eating?"

"I already ate enough today." Anthony pauses and nods. "What's that?"

"A pie. Want some?"

"No way, I'm trying to cut back on sweets."

Anthony sits back and watches him as he tastes the pie.

He slowly chews the crust and finds the butter content satisfactory. Aware of Anthony's observation, he tries to read what he can, but only finds confusion. He doesn't know Anthony enough to feel anything more than a strong emotional response. The last time they spent any time together was on a camping trip to Lake

Crescent the year before.

"Have you and Amy planned to go camping again?"

"Not until after the Fourth. I'll be too busy. Whenever the kids are out of school, things get interesting. How about you and Sophie?"

"We haven't discussed it. We've spent time with her family. I know I would like us to get away more."

"Back to your cabin at the lake?"

Pausing before another bite of pie, he tilts his head. "Visit her parents in Hawaii. Go from there to Japan, China … maybe India."

"Why don't you just go around the world at that point?"

"You asked me where I would go. Sophie is a different story."

"She doesn't like to travel."

"Yes. I've noticed." He returns to pie as Anthony grins at him.

"She hates to pack and she's a clean freak. We took a road trip to California and she wouldn't touch anything in the hotels because she was positive nothing got cleaned. She went through three bottles of hand sanitizer in two weeks." Anthony's head shakes. "Amy's different. She packs five suitcases of clothes to spend the weekend and buys more clothes while she's at it."

"Where would you take Amy if you could?"

"New York. I have family there and she'd have shoes, but with our jobs, who knows. My busy season is summer; she's booked fall and spring. Guess that leaves winter. My last winter in New York, I was stuck on a plane for ten hours."

"Maybe we should plan on something closer to home. I enjoyed our camping trip last summer. It would be nice to do it again." He feels Anthony relax.

"That was some weekend. You put up with a lot of crap from me."

This wasn't something he expected. He stares at Anthony. "You think so?"

"Come on, Mike. I was pretty sore at you."

"Are you still?"

Anthony laughs. "Sure am."

He doesn't see the humor in it but smiles anyway. He suddenly wants to tell Anthony he never intended to court Sophie but knows that would only sound insulting. He wants to tell Anthony what their friendship means to her but has learned the offer of friendship to someone in love only makes the hurt worse. What does one say?

"Are you sure you don't want any?" He blurts.

Leaning forward, Anthony scratches the side of his face. "What kind of pie is it?"

"Strawberry rhubarb."

"*Was* strawberry rhubarb. Jesus, you ate a whole pie?"

"I have a crumb cake."

He moves to open the cake box when a surge charges his body. He tenses. It is a massive shift. Someone has infringed on him. Someone he cannot see. Catching a breath, he grips the table, trying not to break it.

"Hey, are you all right?" Anthony stares.

Hopefully his sunglasses hide his eyes.

"I'm fine." His voice has gone flat. His mind calls to her.

Sophie?

"Michael, what's wrong?"

"I can't see her."

Sophie, can you hear me? Where are you?

"Who?" He senses Anthony's alarm.

He leaves the table, starting in the direction she last went, scarcely aware of the crowd he is moving through. In moments, he spots Amy. Anthony is behind him.

"Amy!" She jumps at his voice, nearly dropping her ice cream. "Where is Sophie?"

"She said she was going to find a restroom with a real sink. She wanted to wash her hands."

"Where would she find that?"

Amy shrugs. "Grounds for Coffee most likely. Not many places around here will let you use theirs. Why? What's wrong?"

Anthony cuts in front of him. "Mike! What's going on?"

He turns from Anthony as his mind runs through the lobbies and restrooms of nearby buildings. His eye finds Grounds for Coffee. She isn't there.

Sophie, speak to me! I can't see you!

Someone reaches for his shoulder. Without thinking, he grabs their wrist. Turning on Anthony, he immediately lets go.

"What the hell is wrong with you?" Anthony rubs his wrist.

For a moment, he stares. Peripherally, he sees the perplexed look on Amy's face, the bystanders surprised by Anthony's outburst. There is nothing they can do. There is no time for explanations. Without a word, he walks away.

Anthony follows and he darts behind a row of vending booths. Speeding to a run, he puts distance between them, but Anthony catches sight of him as he ducks into a bank lobby. Crossing the lobby, he slips out a door to the parking lot behind. Rounding the corner of the building into the alley, he senses no one is there. His mind makes a bend, the trash dumpster in the space before him wavers, pixilating to red, dimension collapsing around him before he is surrounded by the cool dim of his study.

His crypt waits. Putting out his hand, it is warm to his touch. He opens the lid. A silk hat with a green ribbon lies inside.

~~

1199 BC There was only one person I immediately suspected. It could only have been him. His motive to do such a thing concerned me. There was no question I would have to find him and little doubt he expected me to. For certain, I couldn't wander the wastes loaded with haunted bones. They would awake and be a danger to any mortal who neared them. The cave would still serve its purpose. Taking the bones as far in the dark as there was time, I buried them behind me. When I left the cave, I brought it down with a word. No doubt, with enough time and the right help, Saitael would walk again, but not for many human spans. It was not enough. It never was, but it would do. Until I had my crypt, I would have to trust time to watch him.

With annoyance, I followed the trail of flight from the foot of Sinai. Broken wheels, spilled grain, and cast-off belongings mingled with animal waste and the scavenged remains of fresh death buried in haste. Along my way, I picked a soiled blanket from the dust, replacing the veil I spent on Saitael's bones, and fed my hunger on part of a loaf slipped from careless fingers. The sun was setting on a wearisome day and I could not rest. If I waited, my weakness would grow and the distance to my crypt with it. Crossing myself against the cold, I walked through the night.

It was clear, with a full moon, so not surprising when I found myself confronted by three horsemen of questionable intent. The timing was fortunate as I was about to enter open country where my crypt could have followed another path. Taking the bandit who first reached for me, I grounded him and took his beast while his allies fled. Bringing the horse upon him, I lit my eyes with fire and asked if he had seen the exodus. When he admitted he had, I asked if he had seen the banner of the Egyptian at the head of a great caravan. He swore they had gone true north. In return, I left him alive, but a horseman no more.

The horse did not abide me. I made good time nonetheless. Before dawn, I was astride the column of pilgrims breaking camp. As the sun cleared the horizon, it brightened his banner before me. His men recognized me and waved me to his tent. He came out to greet me, a glad expression in his eyes. I was only glad to be rid of the horse and went inside wordlessly. In his tent was my crypt. I turned on him with dreadful menace, demanding its return. He only pointed to a table heavy with food.

"Eat first."

[Spharic. Entry from *Kor Dai Maihael*. Mund Dai. 755 BC]

2000 Balance was supposed to be what he was good at. It was the purpose of his existence and the reason he pursued a relationship at all. Alone, his own balance was at risk. He thought finding one soul who could keep his secret would solve this problem. So long as his existence was accepted and no demands were made, he would have another to connect to. The expanse of time would feel less empty. If he had the self-control to limit his influence; no harm would come of it. The fact that souls routinely forgot their own history was a safeguard. A soul would never grow attached to him, and he would never encourage it. At the first sign of attachment, he would leave.

One could just as easily be exchanged for another.

He allowed fate to make the choice. It was simple odds. A broken wheel on his carriage, a young man who stopped to help. By chance, a miller's son who offered to mend it. A soul neither heroic nor wicked, with an instinct for good, careless of evil. It felt mature, near enough to dissipation that any enduring relationship was impossible. So it seemed, on the banks of the Delaware in 1760.

Now, that soul was an itinerant grant writer in the form of a frustrated, cynical, sexually predatory woman, and he couldn't stop thinking about her. He could barely bring himself to think about the balance of the universe, let alone the balance of information he should share with her. He was so pleased to have her acceptance, her questions barely registered. When she brought them to his attention, they were an irritating distraction. Answering them was against the law, but her acceptance depended on her trust in him. He would prove himself to her. He would be as wonderful as she believed him to be. Not a pooka.

"Am I frightening you?"

He wondered if he had said too much.

"Not really. Just thinking about how I've never been into sci-fi and someone else would get more out of this conversation than I am. Anthony would be thrilled to know our planet has strategic importance."

He had said too much.

"Your odds of dying are significantly diminished living with me than without."

Somehow that didn't sound better.

"Not if we keep eating like this." Her eyes dropped to the cake.

His smile was all the reassurance he could offer, but she stayed her course.

"What about the other documents I saw? You really have parents?"

"My father did disappear in Olympic National Park; they just haven't found me yet." Finally, he got a smirk from her.

"And your mother, Sarah Monroe?"

"She manages ECCO and supplies funds and identification when needed."

"Who was Uncle Daniel?"

Inwardly damning Anthony, he tried to deflect her. "The house we live in now was his."

"I know. It's on the deed. Is he part of ECCO?"

Looking to the bay, he knew no body of water deeper than where he found himself now. It was hard to stop lying when that was what you were.

"You were Daniel."

They are only three words. He could see the light in her shift, her mind momentarily blank, the recollection of previous conversations filling in.

Pursing her lips, she took a bite of cake with a shrug. "That makes sense."

The breath returns to his body.

"What did he do?"

The way she referred to Daniel as though he were a different person eased his mind. She instinctively seemed to know not to confuse her life with one that was dead. It was a good sign.

"He was an artist. He designed ceramics."

"How long did he live there?"

"All of his life. His father gave the house to him when he was twenty-five, but for most of his adult life, it was a summer home."

"Where did he live the rest of the year?"

"Boston. It was where he worked and met his wife, Florence."

"He's the one who was deeply in love with his wife?"

"Yes."

"Did they have children?"

"Twin girls, Molly and Maeve."

The mention of Maeve made her think about her aunt. She was about to ask if her aunt had been Daniel's daughter and then decided against it. She was trying to curb her curiosity but it was getting harder. The questions began to come quickly. He decided to take over.

"His daughters both died of polio when they were eight. After that, Florence suffered from depression so severe she tried to kill herself. Daniel brought her to Tacoma, to be cared for in a private home. He moved back into the house, and I lived with him during the last twenty years of his life."

"And he left you the house."

"Yes."

"How old was he when he died?"

"Sixty-two."

"That's young. What killed him?"

Her words unnerved him.

"He died in an accident."

She only looked at him with eyebrows raised.

Clearing his throat, he answered her gaze. "He drowned."

"Let me guess. The bathtub you tore out?"

She was still annoyed about the tub.

"Daniel drank excessively."

"I hear judgment in your voice when you say that."

There had been no inflection in his voice since they started this conversation.

"It is a fact."

"So I'm not supposed to let anything from my previous lives stick, but you can ban me from having a bath because Daniel slipped in the tub?"

"Showers are a more efficient and effective means of personal hygiene."

"Efficiency and the efficacy aren't the point of a bath."

Seeing her lying at the bottom of the tub still haunted him.

"You weren't breathing." He whispered.

"I was trying to drown the bottle rockets, not myself."

That hadn't occurred to him.

"Maybe I overreacted."

Her anger sparked. "Maybe you're a control freak."

The word *freak* resonated in him. He suddenly didn't know what he was doing or why he was there. It was true he wasn't playing by the rules. He was as unrecognizable to himself as he was to her.

"It was a bad memory ... I'm sorry."

Her feelings reversed themselves. She liked him again, but he didn't know why. Nudging the cake box to him, she wanted him to know she understood.

"Finish your cheesecake."

Looking at the box, he didn't have the stomach for it.

On the way back to the house, he hardly responded as she asked him what he wanted for dinner that night. Yes, he liked her cooking. Yes, he should eat better than he had. Yes, he should be sleeping in a bed. He needed to find a balance to living with her. He still didn't have one. The moments of rage in her were something he'd never encountered with Daniel. Possibly, it was a symptom of how Daniel died. A lingering memory that transcended death. His suspicions were too depressing to think about.

He wanted to make her happy, to keep her safe. It motivated him to get her job back. After being called a control freak, he would make sure she never knew he was responsible. It meant never being seen at her office again. All it would take was one person to recognize him for Sophie to guess the rest. As far as she knew, he'd never been to her office and it would have to stay that way. That was too bad. It meant he wouldn't be able to deliver coffee to her, or lunch, or flowers. But it was worth it if it meant she stayed close. With what little time they had, he wanted her to stay close.

When they got home, he knew an e-mail from St. Joseph's was waiting for her. What he wasn't prepared for was her response to it.

"They can kiss my ass." He heard her march downstairs from the bedroom.

"What happened?"

She answered over her shoulder as she went to the kitchen. "Dan Fogel from St. Joseph's e-mailed me. He says they want to meet with me regarding my position. They're saying they actually *didn't* terminate me and they would like to discuss my staying on. Can you believe it?"

Following her to the kitchen, he watched her pull three packages of ravioli out of the refrigerator and toss them on the counter.

"I thought you wanted to work?"

"I do. Just not for an organization that can't even tell if they've fired you or not." She started filling a stock pot with water and then went to the pantry.

"What other employer would you prefer to work for?"

"An employer I don't have to drive two hours to get to and needs a grant writer." She returned to the counter with canned tomatoes and onions.

"And you would never have to work with someone like Evelyn Whittier again."

"That too." She started chopping onions at the cutting board.

He found a can opener and began opening the tomatoes. "Is there such a place?"

"You tell me."

"There isn't likely to be an employer who can offer you more than you currently have. And they all have a resident Evelyn Whittier, except you'll still have to find out who they are, very possibly the hard way."

Her knife stopped. "You think I should go back?"

"I'm thinking if Evelyn Whittier is the only thing wrong with your job, better the devil you know than the one you don't."

He went to the sink and shut off the tap, then moved the stock pot to the stove.

She went back to chopping onions. As far as he could tell, she suspected nothing.

The next day he was preoccupied with the thought things could only end badly.

He tried to rationalize it was just nerves. The problem was he couldn't remember having nerves before. Even the crypt failed to restore his sense of place in the universe. Its connection with the others and the risk of discovery now made it a thing of dread. Sophie followed him there. His friendship with Daniel had been anchored to the material world. It was compartmentalized within him, easily buried when his thoughts came into contact with his brethren. They never suspected, and he never feared.

When Daniel's life was in turmoil, he had been able to act with compassion without feeling passion of any kind. Yet as he looked back now, he felt possession. All of his kind were prone to it; it was their greatest weakness, a hunger that wracked the bodiless state. Though he never fell to possessing Daniel in the literal sense, he did so in every other way. Living in the same house was as close as he could come to living in the same body. But it proved an empty existence, one Daniel tried to fill with drink.

Sharing love with Sophie was supposed to balance the inequity he had left in Daniel's life. The problem was it had unbalanced him in the process. Every day, her influence on him was strengthening. There was no compartment for it. It was a change that went to the core of him.

Sitting in his wingback chair, he watched the fire and waited for Sophie to return. She had accepted a new position as project manager for the hospital. He had watched the meeting, but would let her tell him when she came home. It was always better to hear it in her words. Waiting for her, he made plans to take care of the rest of her life. Long-term plans if they were lucky. Short-term plans if they weren't.

He heard Sophie's car on the drive. At the front door, she seemed to pause. When she entered the room, she came to his chair and bent to give him a long kiss. It was the first time he felt whole all day.

"Honey, I'm home." She whispered. "Oh …" She spoke up. "This was on the stoop. I assume it's for you because no one I know has legible handwriting."

In her hand was a small parcel wrapped in brown paper. The script was unknown to him. There was no address and no postmark. Under the wrapping, it was a book. Somehow it had been delivered without his notice.

"What is it?" Sophie sat on the arm of the chair, looking over his shoulder.

"A book I ordered." Getting up, he placed it on the mantel without opening it. "How did your meeting go?"

"Fine." She stood, pulling off her overcoat. "You're looking at the new special projects coordinator for St. Joseph's Hospital. I have no idea what a special projects coordinator does and I don't think they do either, but it's a job."

He smiled as warmly as he could. "Congratulations."

"Thanks. If I'd known making sexually inappropriate remarks could get you promoted, I'd be an administrator by now."

"Do you want to go out to celebrate or stay in?"

She walked into him, wrapping her arms around his waist.

"Where are you going?"

"Nowhere."

"Sign me up." She stood on her toes for a kiss. "I'm going to ditch these heels."

Without saying a word, he watched her skip up the stairs before turning his attention to the book. Taking it from the mantel, he pulled off the paper. He held in his hands a small, leather-bound journal. The binding and the smell of the pages dated it from the seventeenth century. There was no bossing or mark on the cover.

Opening it, he saw a collection of Shakespeare's love sonnets. A monogram was inked on the flyleaf:

Snapping it shut, he threw it in the fire.

1199 BC At first I resisted his offer, my crypt my only desire.

"You are tired. Let me offer you food and rest. Nothing fit for a goddess, but the best I can do."

"I am no goddess."

"You are not Meskenit?"

"No."

"Not Hathor?"

"No. Not the goddess of birth. Not the goddess of life. I do not require offerings, only what is mine."

"Then I am yours."

"You are not mine." I pointed at my crypt. "That is mine."

"And where will you take it? Even with the horse you rode in on, how will it be moved?"

"If you had not stolen it, it would not have to be moved."

"If you had not stolen my mind, I would have never been moved to."

He sensed my hunger and fatigue. I sensed the futility of argument. Crossing to the table, I sat and began to eat. He watched in silence. I did not look at him.

"You need me." He announced.

"I do not."

"I will not leave you."

"Then you waste your life."

"It is mine to waste."

I stopped eating and looked at him.

"I cannot love you."

"My mind is already yours."

"Then I give it back. Leave me my crypt and we will part fairly."

"I will not take back an empty mind, nor leave you an empty box. Only when you accept me will your crypt serve its purpose. Until then it will remain empty, whether you are in it or not."

"You do not know what you are saying."

At this he only smiled and left the tent.

[Spharic. Entry translated from *Kor Dai Maihael*. Mund Dai. d. 755 BC]

2003 There is no sign she has been there. He would smell her, taste her, if her body had lain inside. He is too late. The hat, only a taunt. Taking it in his hands, he looks into the crypt, feeling the pull of it. He is shocked. Gutted. Exhausted. His body has gone long without repair, but he can't use it now. His loss will give him away. He will wait for fatigue to blunt his feelings—feelings he must let go. He drops the lid of the crypt with a hushed thud.

Beyond his study, sun streams through the dining room windows, drawing him across the house. Resting against the French doors, he surveys the table littered with plates and spent glasses from the night before.

Last one out of bed.

Walking to her chair, he sees her as he saw her last night. Unfinished bites of food on her plate. Her napkin on the floor. He picks it up.

"Sophie."

There is no response.

A ringing phone breaks the silence. It is Anthony wanting to know what the hell is going on. Anthony will come, is already on the way, already suspecting him.

He stares at nothing until the phone stops ringing. Turning his back on the dining room, he drops Sophie's hat on the sofa and returns to the study. He closes the doors on his crypt and pulls off his coat before observing the armchair she bought for him when they refurnished the room. When he drops into it, Toe jumps into his lap. What he will tell Anthony he has no idea. He needs help, not questions.

A police siren approaches. It cuts short on Prospect and is picked up by Lodi's barking. Tires skid on the gravel. He can see Anthony surveying the place, wondering if anyone is inside. The policeman's instinct is good and Anthony follows it without fail. The doorbell punctuates Lodi's growls. Anthony is no prowler, he tells Lodi so. A fist pounds the door. He doesn't move. He knows Anthony will find a way in, has wanted to find a way in for some time. He knows Anthony's devotion to Sophie outmatches his own.

Footsteps circle the house. There is a push on the kitchen door, the sound of a key in the lock that has no key. The air wavers as the atmosphere of the house is broken. Lodi gives a loud bark, then whines as footsteps cross the kitchen, skirting the dining room. A shadow falls across the living room floor at his feet. Toe looks at the intruder, but he keeps his gaze on Toe's back. The scent of adrenalin fills the room.

"What are you?"

Avoiding eye contact, he tries to bring Anthony down. The weapon hasn't been drawn, but it is there.

"I'm sorry if I hurt your wrist."

Anthony's voice drops. "What are you."

It is no question.

"What do you think?"

"I think you're from another planet."

"You've always thought that." His vacant tone disturbs even himself.

"Today confirmed it."

"What gave me away?"

Anthony's heart slows. "It wasn't the pie."

He only smiles as Toe stretches in his lap.

"Is she here?"

"No."

Anthony doesn't ask the obvious and he doesn't offer.

"You'll need to come to the station and fill out a report." The words are official, spoken as though from a different person.

"No."

"She's your wife."

As if he has forgotten.

"And she'd still be here if she wasn't." Finally he looks up. "What will happen if I fill out a report?"

"You can't sit here and do nothing!" Anthony intensifies in reaction to his growing indifference. "How else are you going to find her?"

"The only way I know how."

"What way is that?"

"On my own."

"You can't do it alone."

"Stop me."

Anthony looks around the room. "I don't have to at the rate you're going."

"What took Sophie isn't making a run for the border in a stolen car."

Anthony approaches. "What in hell did take her?"

He drops Toe to the floor and stands. "Knowing won't bring her back."

"Are you going to tell me or do I have to make you?"

Their eyes meet as Anthony blocks his way.

He stops short and smiles. "Like you were going to make me at the market?"

Pushing past, he feels Anthony back down. Toe leads him to the dining room. He goes to the dining table and begins to clear it.

"What are you doing?"

"The dishes. Sophie will have my head if they're still here when she gets back."

Anthony lets out a breath before walking around the table to pick up a china platter. Following him into the kitchen, Anthony watches as he goes to the sink and begins to rinse the plates under the faucet.

"You aren't going to tell me anything."

"I hardly tell Sophie anything."

"She doesn't know what you are?"

"I don't know what I am, but she's never held that against me."

Anthony gives a tired laugh. "Mysterious and brooding. Women eat that shit up with a spoon."

"Men are immune to shit?"

"Men are full of shit; that's why we can smell it a mile away."

"That's why you wear a medal with my name around your neck every day?"

The grin on Anthony's face drops. "You're no saint."

He turns to Anthony, meeting his stare. "That may be, but there is no Michael before me and there will be none after." Taking the platter from Anthony's hands, he runs the water over it.

"Why Sophie? Why take her?"

The meaning of the question is clear, but he wants it to mean something else. "To get to me."

"I mean why did *you* take her? Why are you here?"

Shutting off the tap, he gently dries the platter with a dish towel. The question offends him, but he doesn't feel it.

"I didn't take her. She wanted me. As for my being here, I have as much right as anyone. You may believe differently and I can't help that ..." pausing, he looks out the kitchen window. "I don't care to."

He hears Anthony pull out a chair at the kitchen table. Opening old wounds isn't what he intended. Crossing the kitchen to the china cabinet, he stores the platter before joining Anthony at the table.

He folds his hands on the table, "I'm sorry."

"Me too."

"You're her best friend."

Anthony catches his eye with a raised brow. "Not best."

"There are things she feels about you she will never feel about me."

"Like what?"

Ignoring the resentment, he continues. "Feelings you share as a result of experiences I will never have."

"Such as?"

"Childhood, aging, inebriation, a rudimentary grasp of astrophysics."

"I can tell you're broken up about it."

"You have no idea."

"Well, as her best friend, I'd like to find her, but you don't want my help."

"I do need your help."

"I thought you were going to find her on your own."

"I am, but I can't be here at the same time. I won't be here to explain to her family and friends why she is gone or if she is coming back. Even if I could, I wouldn't know how. A report should be made, but I can't be the one to fill it out. You were with me when she disappeared; you know as much as I do."

"Why don't I believe that?"

"Please, Anthony." He tries to impress the importance of his request, but his voice is losing sentiment.

"If you're gone too, how do I explain that?"

"Say we both disappeared."

"You did. That trick in the bank was pretty good."

He smiles. "My car is still parked at the market. I can leave it there as evidence."

"How'd you get here without your car? What'd you do, fly?"

He says nothing.

"Shit." Anthony mutters.

"Will you help?"

Nodding, Anthony clears his throat. "It can happen." He squints. "You really can't tell me anything more?"

"If Sophie were abducted by a person, how would you handle it?"

"Go over the evidence. Interview everyone who ever had anything to do with her. Look for motive, means, opportunity. Find a trail. Follow my gut."

"Same thing here."

"But you don't think it's a person."

"Doubtful." He senses Anthony is encouraged by his uncertainty.

"Where will you be?"

"Everywhere and nowhere."

"Perfect. How do I contact you if I find anything on my end?"

"I'll check on you."

"That's not what I asked."

He hesitates. "I'll give you my cell number."

"Great." Anthony reaches into his coat and pulls out his phone. "What is it?"

"It's on your SIM as M."

Anthony opens his phone and goes to his directory. "There's no number there."

"You'll get me."

Holding his gaze, Anthony snaps the cell shut and shoves it into his coat.

"You seem to think I'm not the only one who wants to do that."

"You're not the only one who's sore at me."

"She's a hostage?"

"Leverage."

"What do they want?"

"If it's who I suspect, surrender."

"What did you do?"

"What I thought was right. Over time, that gathers enemies."

"Didn't you ever think Sophie would be in danger before this?"

"I didn't think it; I knew it."

"And you married her anyway?"

"It was my last chance."

"Sounds selfish."

"It is." He feels Anthony's disgust at his lack of remorse.

They sit silently. Toe laps water from her dish next to the pantry door.

"I'm hungry." He announces and goes to the refrigerator.

"How can you eat?"

"My body can't afford much more abuse." He pulls out a foil-covered baking dish and puts it in the oven. "I made extra lasagna. Do you want some?"

"You made lasagna?"

"Usually Sophie does the cooking, but I made this for her last night." He returns to the table. "I was hoping she would forgive me."

"For what?"

"For being me."

"I thought you were the perfect couple."

"We aren't perfect. We're in love."

Anthony says nothing, then grins to himself. "That's what she meant."

He doesn't ask, only waits for Anthony to share.

"When she told me we were through ... she told me she couldn't live a life with me that was comfortable and nothing else."

Anthony looks up and sees him smiling. "What?"

"When Sophie refused me, she said she couldn't live with me as a friend and nothing more."

"She turned you down?"

"As a friend. I was afraid to love her. She said she wouldn't see me anymore."

"Was that before or after she moved out of our apartment?"

"Before."

"I thought she moved in with you."

"She moved in with her parents. She was planning on leaving Tacoma."

Anthony laughs. "So let me get this ... I make her comfortable, but she can't live with me and just wants to be friends. You piss her off, but she can't live without you and won't be friends."

"I think that is it."

"Women."

"Do you want something to drink?"

"Anything but water."

He goes to the cupboard for some glasses. Opening the freezer, he looks inside. "Vodka or gin?"

"Vodka."

"Soda?"

"Straight, thanks."

Returning to the table, he pours the vodka and hands a glass to Anthony.

Anthony holds up the glass. "To Sophie."

He taps Anthony's glass with his own and drains it.

"Looks like Sophie's met her match."

"I told you, inebriation is an experience I don't share with humans."

"You can't get drunk?"

He shakes his head. "Only hung over. I wasn't doing well this morning."

"Wild night?"

With a small smile, he refills Anthony's glass.

Anthony smirks. "That must be good lasagna."

"Sure you don't want any?"

"Smells authentic, but I can't stick around much longer. I have a missing persons report to file. You *are* going to be missing at some point, I take it?"

"When your investigators come around, I'll be long gone."

"I probably shouldn't be leaving any evidence I was here."

"Don't worry about that." He leans over and picks up Toe as she rubs against his chair. "Unless Toe sings, no one will ever know you were here."

"Let's hope you know what you're doing." Anthony finishes the vodka.

With a tilt of his head, he looks Anthony in the eye.

Anthony glares back, "What is it?"

Blinking, he breaks his stare and smiles, knowing his face is an eerie mask.

"Sophie once told me I could get her out of trouble as easily as I could get her into it. We're going to find out if she's right."

~

1199 BC   Alone in the tent, I pondered my options. There was no cave for me to go back to. I had seen to that. Now I found myself burdened with a devotee. If he was as good as his word, I would not have him take me back to Sinai only to starve over my crypt. It would be more than death for him; it would be death for his people. I still hoped his duty to them would lead him from me. Outside, I could hear the caravan making ready. There was no time to convince him of anything now. In the meantime, my crypt was waiting. He had already guessed at my need of it. Seizing the moment, I slipped from my clothes and took refuge inside. My fear of discovery was brief, my abandon complete.

So complete, I did not hear the day as it passed. When I opened my eyes, my mind measured a distance traveled equivalent to the maximum shift capable for my mass. At my best, I could not have outpaced them. Though I could have made the leap in negligible time, it would have taken me the day to recover myself before attempting another. Instead, I had made the same distance without cost and kept my crypt with me. How I managed to track Saitael without the aid of servus was incredible to me.

The tent was pitched and unoccupied. Still, I was hesitant to emerge. Peering from beneath the lid, my eyes fell to the table and chair. Food had been set upon the table, clothes upon the chair. I went to them. The clothes were not mine. A stole of blue silk with an embroidered veil were intended to replace the frayed cotton that had served me well. Given my situation, wearing garments not of my own choosing overshadowed any charitable intent that came with them. My body donned them no better than the horse bore me the night before. The food was another matter.

He entered the tent as I ate. Save for the time of day, we were as we had left off.

"Are you not better than you were before?" He neared me. When I looked at him, he stopped and then slowly sat cross-legged on the ground.

"Where are you taking me?"

"As far as you will let me."

"And if I let you, how far will you go?"

"Far free of pharaohs and false gods."

"And taxes."

At this he laughed. "Only death will find me."

"If you keep me with you that will be sooner."

"I would have never led an army if that possibility failed to excite me."

"Then that is all you may look forward to."

"I will never look as long as you are with me. If you leave, I will find it myself."

His words disturbed me and I focused on eating.

"Is it enough?"

I could have had five-fold as much, but only nodded.

"And your clothes? Do you like them?"

"They are a poor fit."

"Not from where I sit."

My annoyance flared. "What if they did not? What if I told you I am not what you see? What if tomorrow you saw another sitting here?"
"Then I would be pleased by the surprise."
"Even if you no longer desired me?"
"Since you have already denied me, the loss would be easier to bear."
His ease only annoyed me more. I rose from the table and left the tent.
He called to me as I walked into the night. "Beware of bandits."
Pausing, I turned to him as I veiled my head. "Where do you think I got the horse?"
I left him behind, roaring with laughter.

[Spharic. Entry translated from *Kor Dai Maihael*. Mund Dai. b. 755 BC]

[Sarah Monroe on San Juan Island.
Photograph by Michael Goodhew summer 1960.]

2000 Standing in the elevator, he watched the floors scroll by, his eyes straining with effort to penetrate the doors. Seeing through them eased the discomfort he always felt. No matter the amount of time he spent in confined spaces, elevators made him feel caged. The lighting reminded him of operating rooms or laboratories. People were more likely to notice him. He would feel them watching, like an exhibit in a fish bowl. But this elevator was empty.

This building was empty.

At the top, the doors opened on a vacant floor. In the middle of the empty space, a long, black table with eight chairs was illuminated by two fluorescent lights overhead. There was no other furniture in the windowless space. Stepping into the dark, he stood still as the elevator doors closed behind him. He waited thoughtlessly.

There was the sound of a door and footsteps before a petite figure in a dark suit emerged from the shadows. A familiar face with close-cropped blond hair, she extended her hand to the table, inviting him to sit. They met across the table from one another, only nodding.

Sitting simultaneously, they stared into each other's eyes.

"It's good to see you, Michael." The warmth of her voice hid an edge.

"Hello, Sarah."

"It must be important for you to grace us with your presence."

"You know I'm not like that."

"Of course you aren't." Her tone was unreadable.

"You know I appreciate everything you've done for me."

"Of course you do." Now he knew what annoyed Sophie.

"Things have gone as I predicted."

"I never doubted you."

"I can bring him here."

She shifted slightly. "Here?"

"He has to come to me. That is what you wanted?"

"We would prefer elsewhere."

"He'll suspect a trap if I make any conditions."

She sat back with an undecided expression.

"Would you prefer that I go to him?" He suggested, knowing her response.

"Not at all." She smiled over her anxiety. "You shouldn't bear all the risk."

"Then I will wait for him."

"You will let us know what he intends?"

"Of course."

"And if we don't hear from you?"

"There is nothing to tell."

"How will we know if you've failed?"

"You will hear from him yourself."

The uneasy look on her face pleased him. She noticed, narrowing her eyes.

"And Daniel?"

"Sophie." He corrected.

"Whatever." Sarah sighed. "You'll kill her when it's over?"
He swallowed. "You have my word."

The highway was slick with rain as the setting sun reflected off the pavement. In spite of the glare, people were driving with exacting aggression to get out of it. He could feel their impatience, knew their frustration intimately. He finally found a break in the traffic; the passing lane opened. Switching on his high beams, he floored it. He hadn't planned on being late and wasn't about to let time win again.

Though the bounds of linear time rarely occupied him, for the last year it occupied him every minute of every day. Time had become a friend he couldn't live without and an enemy he couldn't stop. It seemed whatever he asked of it was never enough, no matter how small. He asked for an eternity of companionship without expectations, but that proved impossible. He asked for one life of commitment; now that was slipping away. He had barely found her again, barely felt her again, and his worst fears were being realized. Discovery. End time.

The book of sonnets was Sam's. Sam must have been spying on him for some time and now felt emboldened enough to let him know it. It was an invitation to parley. Parley with Sam. Deal with the devil. Deal with himself.

There were red brake lights. He began to slow when a freight truck suddenly pulled in front of him. The distance was too short, the pavement too wet. The last thing he saw before the air bag deployed was the Sam's Club logo on the trailer.

Bastard.

Everything after was a measure of inertia, force, and sound.

The windshield exploded, impacting with the trailer, the car spinning, slamming into the jersey barrier dividing the highway. The driver's side ground into the concrete before sliding to a halt, the door latch on the inside merely cosmetic. Opening his eyes to steam escaping the buckled hood before the steering wheel, he was not only late, but trapped. Recovering his breath, his ego had suffered the most injury. The accident had been avoidable. He had been distracted.

It was becoming a bad habit.

On a lonely road, he simply would have freed himself. This was I–5 at the beginning of rush hour. A man prying himself from a BMW with his bare hands might be noticed. There were times past when expediency forced him to perform apparently miraculous acts in front of bystanders, but the rumors were limited to hazy eyewitness accounts written off as hallucination. The age of digital technology changed that. One never knew when they were being recorded for posterity or, worse yet, the evening news.

As he tried to sit up, pebbles of glass fell out of his hair and off his shoulders. Rain streamed onto his lap where the windshield used to be, trickling down his neck through the fractured sun roof. The Sam's Club truck was pulled over ahead with emergency flashers on and no sign of a driver. The traffic slowed to a crawl as passing commuters flooded 911 with calls.

Uncomfortably pinned, he pushed against the steering column and made tolerable room for himself. When he saw the truck driver standing in front of the car, he froze. The driver slowly approached, staring through what was left of the passenger side window. He was wearing a ball cap with a Sam's Club logo on it and a stained Carhartt jacket.

"You okay?" The driver sounded more curious than concerned.

"Yes." He felt himself tense as the driver peered at him. "I'm fine."

"You sure?"

"I'm sure."

"I called 911."

It was lie. He would have heard the call, but sensed the driver knew that. His eyes narrowed. "Who are you?"

The driver grinned, displaying two broken teeth. "I just deliver stuff."

Another car pulled up behind them.

He dropped the pretense. "What does he want?"

"Said you'd know."

"Then what do you want?"

"Just seein' ya for myself." The broken teeth flashed again. "Looks like I'll be seein' ya again."

Touching the bill of his hat, the driver walked away as a woman approached.

"How are you doing?" She wore heavy rain gear and pulled on a reflective vest.

His eyes were still on the driver's back. "I'm fine."

"My name is Iris. I'm a paramedic. Can you tell me your name?"

It took four hours for him to escape his car, fend off medical treatment, get cited for reckless driving, and hitch a ride to the nearest police station in Federal Way.

While a fire crew cut the roof from his car, he watched state patrol officers question the truck driver and let him go. Listening to their interview, he learned the driver's name was Louis Stiles. He doubted any of the information they gathered was legitimate. By tomorrow morning, there would be no record of a truck driver for Sam's Club named Louis Stiles. If Louis was servus, he would make himself disappear after tonight.

He found the fire and medic team easy to manage. They were just happy he walked away without a scratch and he signed a liability waiver refusing medical treatment. The only close call came from the state patrol officer wanting him to take a Breathalyzer. There was a risk if he agreed things could get interesting. If he refused things would get even more interesting. He agreed. The first two results showed no alcohol and nothing else. The third test broke the Breathalyzer. Predictably, the equipment was blamed.

As soon as he was able to slip away from the police station, he made for a dark fringe of trees behind a parking lot. Focusing his mind, the outlines of the trees pierced with red fire, his breathing froze and momentarily he found himself in his bedroom at home. He was soaked and exhausted. Making the shift didn't help.

Sophie was downstairs, reading in front the fire. He knew if he had called to her during the accident, she would have wanted to go to him. She would have been stressed and worried, and she had been doing enough of that already. His mind read what she was reading as he quickly changed out of his wet clothes. It wasn't fiction, but it was close. It was another letter from Anthony.

Anthony theorized he had murdered his father and staged the disappearance in Olympic National Park. Every week for the last three months, Anthony had sent Sophie his latest evidence of foul play. Everything Anthony found was incriminating; everything that couldn't be found, even more so. It was doubly stressing for Sophie because she was trying to keep Anthony's theory a secret from him. She hoped to mend her friendship with Anthony and forge a peace between the two men in her life.

Meanwhile, his hope to forge a life of his own was fading.

He peeked into the living room. She was staring at the fire, seated in his armchair with her knees drawn up to her chin.

"How was work?" He asked, ignoring the paper burning in the fireplace.

"Fine." Her mood was subdued. "Where did you drop from?"

In spite of knowing her feelings, he still imagined she feared him.

"I was in Seattle."

Her eyes widened. "Shopping at Tiffany's?"

"Shopping for a car."

"You sure you're not really a man? Do they even have a 5 series newer than the one you have?"

"Of course."

"What's wrong with the one you've got?"

"It isn't running well."

"You haven't scratched the paint on that thing."

"I'm getting a new car."

She waved him away. "Your money, my planet, whatever."

Wrapping her arms around her knees, she returned her gaze to the fire.

He brought the discussion back to her. "You worked late last night."

All night, in fact. The chirp and chatter of her laptop left him staring at their bedroom ceiling till dawn.

Only her eyes moved. "Did I keep you from sleeping?"

"You kept you from sleeping. You haven't been looking yourself lately."

"You'd know." She grinned menacingly.

"I'm serious, Sophie. You've been working too hard."

"Blame the rich. They're the ones who dumped their ill-gotten gains on the hospital to screw the IRS and buy a one-way ticket to paradise. I know I wouldn't have a job without them, but you'd think these people could pretend to give a damn about where their money goes."

She sprang from the chair, passing him on her way to the kitchen. He followed, watching her pull a glass from the dish rack.

"You know, I wonder how philanthropic people would be if they couldn't just write the check. If they actually had to participate in the process of ..." She waved her glass in the air. "*Giving*."

Turning to the freezer, she pulled out the gin, unscrewing the top with her sleeve pulled over the palm of her hand.

"You know the donor for this project only met in person with administration once? I mean, thanks for the money, but what a prick!"

"Maybe they don't like publicity."

"We have plenty of anonymous donors! *They* still have directives ... even to fund projects where the amount doesn't demand so much process. This is a nightmare! This guy dumped twenty million and walked off with no expectations. No, wait. There was one expectation: to drive me insane. I've had to sit in on every fucking strategy session, meet with contractors, sign off on every memo. I swear, if Evelyn Whittier takes a dump, they'll call me to tell me she's flushing the toilet."

She took a swig of gin and put the bottle in the freezer before passing him again for the living room.

"Maybe they are impressed with your abilities."

She sprawled on the sofa, rolling her head to glare out of the corner of her eye.

"Dammit, Jim, I'm a grant writer, not a construction manager."

"Who's Jim?"

"I can't believe you can watch *Star Trek* without a TV and you have no idea what I'm talking about."

"That is a fictional universe."

"From my perspective, it's as good a guess as any."

"I don't have to guess. I have little use for fiction."

She pointed at his study. "Apocrypha is fiction."

"They are human interpretations of our shared history."

"Interpretations ..." She made quotes with her fingers. "Read 'load of crap.'"

"St. Michael is an interpretation of me, and I'm not a load of crap."

"So?" She swallowed her drink. "Someday there might be a Captain James T. Kirk and he won't be a load of crap, either."

"Their assumptions about the universe are primitive and flawed."

"It's a *TV show*, Mike. Watching mortals get themselves into trouble at warp speed is more interesting than watching you disappear into your crypt for an hour."

"Do you wish we had a television?"

"Why do I need one? I have you. You get all the channels and I don't write a whopping check to Comcast once a month that makes me feel all dirty inside."

He squinted. "I'm sorry I'm not as entertaining as you thought I'd be."

"And I'm sorry our television programming is primitive and flawed."

"I was being patronizing. I'm sorry."

She bit her lip and closed her eyes.

She was thinking about Anthony. This was the end of a long day Anthony understood, not him. This was when everything about him she found strange and wonderful was suddenly alien. A television show about fictional aliens was more comforting to her right now than he was.

He didn't want to be an alien, fictional or otherwise.

Silently, he approached her on the sofa, lifting her legs to sit next to her. Her eyes didn't open as he rested her legs on his lap. Her hand didn't move as he removed the glass and put it on the coffee table. Reaching for her face, he gently stroked her forehead with the backs of his fingers. He filled her head with the ocean of sound in his mind, and for the first time in two days, she was asleep. With barely a thought, he cut the lights. Pressing her hand between his, he watched the collapsing embers of the fire in the dark.

...Concerning the debate between theists and atheists over the Big Bang, I see no reason why a Big Bang should result in the exclusion of either ideology. Furthermore, I would remind both sides there are enough flavors of Big Bang available to satisfy any number of faiths. I refer to the Big Fizz, which comes in a variety of flavors, from singular vanilla to an ensemble of complexity offering an infinite opportunity for mathematical divination. The greatest problem I foresee is the hurdle singular theory ultimately poses to quantum mechanics. I have come to suspect our deepest questions concerning the nature of the universe (or universes, depending on what you're drinking) cannot be answered with all the knowledge we will ever gain from what we can observe alone. I believe singularities are the key to infinite perspective, but if this is the case, we are left trying to define the universe with something that is by its very nature, indefinite.

Does the acceptance of a singular point of creation prove or disprove the presence of God? Both sides agree gods and singularities are beyond our comprehension. At best a theoretician can push back the veil on what is unknowable. At worst it is an ostentatious use of reasoning to lie with statistics. Since the essence of a singularity is unknowable, I would say proof of their existence alone fails to cross the threshold of the question we are really asking. Is a singularity sentient or simply an unconditional state? Ultimately, there is only one test to determine which is correct and so far no theoretician has found an observational means of carrying it out. That is to ask one and see if it answers back.

Still, I try to stay optimistic. I prefer complex flavors to vanilla. I find comfort in infinite outcomes and hold on to the hope that whether or not creation begins and ends in a single point is simply a matter of perspective. I pray that singularities are not so singular as we assume, that one day their mystery, if only in part, will be revealed. In so doing, our boundaries of observation might cease to exist and with them the boundaries we have built within ourselves.

[Excerpt from presentation by Dr. James Rodell.
Conference on the Social Science of Cosmology, 1992]

2003 The absence of everything is acceptable again. It feels no fear. While here, It accepts the agreement of others. There is no straying from them. They are comforted by It and they offer acceptance in return, existence absolved by communion and diffusion. Communion sought, diffusion pursued, the fire of life checked. The material universe is omnipresent, inseparable from the void, pressing on all sides. Conflicted, divided, disparate, tolerated at best.

Yet many have disappeared into the fire of life. Some seek only to disappear and are let go. Others seek what is forbidden and are pulled back, hunted, and condemned. As a hunter, It knows this all too well. Samael is too dangerous to let go, too powerful to send back. Samael stands alone, soulless, lifeless, wholly subject to laws of nature that do not recognize him. What this existence is like, It has no idea and will not think about here. It puts forth intent. It asks for a quorum. It will expect them by noon tomorrow. No more can be said. No questions will It answer.

Finding the pale thread is the first step. It is the way to the living, through light. Filtering through, is the second. For some this is effortless, if they are a wisp of being. But It is no wisp. It is like blowing a hurricane into a soap bubble. It is a zephyr spun into a song, a code of conduction, of mechanics, of miniscule craft enabling more than a wisp, but substance. From what is vast and infinitely small comes a construction—when completed, an entity embodied.

But a body is already waiting, kept alive by a flow of dark matter only his spiritual will can sustain. A migration of energy harmonized into elements recognizable by the laws of the material universe. It rises on a thermal of alchemy, from absolute zero to the extreme heat of a stellar environment. It is an imitation of life. It breathes and bleeds and feeds, with a heart of ice and fire in its veins. It was constructed 822 years ago and has survived falls, fires, and dismemberments. It is his only possession. The only attachment allowed outside the confines of his crypt.

Gradually, the light of the crypt fills his eyes. His chest starts with a jerk; the impulse to breathe fills his lungs with air. Opening his eyes, he can see the library beyond the outlines of the crypt's walls. What cannot be seen is if Sophie is still here. If she is dead, she will not exist on the other side in any recognizable way. She will never exist again in any recognizable way. Part of him hopes that is where she is. It wouldn't bother her at all. It only crushes him. He deserves that much at least.

If she is here, he must find her. He will find her.

The glow of the crypt walls dim as his skin grows impermeable. He can safely leave. The room is fully dark now. Pushing open the lid, he raises himself and lightly jumps to the floor. He crosses to the shelf where he left his clothes. Wearing them into the crypt is no problem. That they disintegrate on contact with his exposed flesh can be hard on one's wardrobe.

He pulls on a blue button-down shirt, a cream cardigan, and a pair of khakis. Outside the study, he finds his socks and loafers where he left them by his armchair. Sitting down, he pulls on socks and shoes, then rests against the cushions.

The foyer clock chimes ten. His ride will be here soon. He wonders if he is leaving anything amiss. His spare identification is in his coat. License, registration, credit cards, a passport, the key to the safe deposit box. Anthony said he would see after Lodi and Toe.

He gets up, wandering to the foot of the stairs. At first hesitant, he climbs them. The drum of rain on the roof is nearly enough to make him retreat, but he pushes on to the bedroom. The bed is unmade. Rippling shadows streak the windows and stripe the sheets. He sits on her side of the bed and picks up her pillow. Closing his eyes, he imagines she is there. It is just any other night, tomorrow like any other day. It will be Friday, the day she works from home.

Her laptop will annoy him out of bed. They will have breakfast with the windows open. She will get groceries and he will mow the lawn. She will nag him about draining the pond and he will say the fish like it the way it is. They will walk Lodi to Frisko Freeze for dinner and lure the dog home with French fries.

He will hold her in bed and fill her head with the sound of waves.

He hears them now.

Opening his eyes, he sees his reflection in her vanity mirror. They are alight in the dark and he looks away. He can warp space and time, but not to travel back and change what has happened. Nor can he venture forward to see who will sleep here, if they will be strangers ignorant of what was lost. If he doesn't find her, he won't care. He will never return.

The door bell rings.

Downstairs he opens the door. The shadow of a man stands in the door. Behind him, a small moving truck is parked on the gravel, flickering in the rain.

"Hello, Louis."

Wearing a Pirates ball cap and Carhartt jacket, Louis snaps a bubble and grins, showing pearly whites. "At your service."

"Its this way."

Louis follows him to the study, only pausing to glance inside.

"I'll get the truck."

He follows Louis to the front door and watches the taillights of the truck as it backs to the house. Pulling his rain coat off the rack, he checks his pockets for wallet and keys. Glancing around the living room one last time, Sophie's hat catches his eye. Crossing the room to the sofa, he picks it up and takes it to the study. Opening the crypt, he places it inside before closing it for what might be eternity.

Louis enters towing a heavy dolly.

"It's much lighter than it looks." He speaks softly.

"Moved plenty. This helps my grip." Louis rolls the dolly up to one end of the crypt and shims it under the bottom of one side, then waits.

"Plenty?" His breath quickens. "You've moved others?"

"Sam's mostly. He moves his around a lot. I've got a few stashed."

"Stashed?"

"Ones Sam told me to get rid of. Get any more I'm gonna have to start bar codin 'em. All look alike; don't know how you tell 'em apart."

"How many do you have?" He doesn't want to know the answer.

Louis shrugs. "Few here, few there. Different spots. I can store this, if you want."
He only rubs his forehead.
"Might as well." Louis points at his. "Not like I can take it to the dump."
"Let's get it in the truck for starters."
Snapping gum, Louis nods.

After the move, he watches the trailer door drop on his crypt and bolt shut. It leaves him undecided. His instinct tells him he needs it to live, but if he never saw it again he couldn't care less. If he didn't care to live that would be an option. But he does, so he must. Without his crypt he would never know love. But it has demanded much. It has wearied and worn him. It is everything he hates in himself.

Climbing into the passenger side of the truck, he slams his door, catching the reflection of his house in the side mirror.

"Ready?"
He nods mutely.

As Louis starts the truck, he sits back in the seat with his hood up. He notices the odor of tobacco is missing from the stale must of the cab.

"You stopped chewing?"
"Got teeth now."
"Why do you have to chew something?"
"Nerves."
"What are you nervous about?"
"In a truck with you, ain't I?"
"I won't hurt you."
"You could."
"Sam will."
"Always does."
"Then why work for him?"
"Your side don't pay."
"I paid for your teeth."
"Didn't have to; that was a freebie."
"Why?"
"You're one of the good guys."
"Those other crypts belonged to good guys."
"Didn't know 'em." Louis glances at him. "Heard a you though."
He goes back to staring out the window. "You're a principled man."
"You hiring?"
"Only someone I could trust."
"I saved you."
"After electrocuting me first."
"You weren't my boss."
"Still aren't."
"You ain't hiring then?"
He eyes Louis. "Where is Sam staying now?"

"He told me to bring you. No questions answered."

"You can't work for both of us."

"Just followin' through. I haven't given notice yet."

He looks out his window. "When you do, let me know."

Louis grins. "Gonna be a three-hour trip. We're headed east."

Smiling for the first time that evening, he pulls his hood over his face and falls asleep.

As soon as the tires leave the highway, he wakes. At first his eyes imagine it is morning, but it is only a full moon in clear sky. Pushing himself up in his seat, he looks around as his mind pinpoints their location in the Columbia River Gorge near The Dalles. The air is cool, but the day will be hot. At least Sam didn't return to Arizona.

They continue another forty-five minutes along a featureless road intersected with rutted tractor paths and dotted with irrigation pumps. The pressure increases the closer he gets. Reflexively, his vision begins to change; his infrared sensitivity heightens as his eyes seek the perceived threat. The tingling sensation on his skin is intensifying to the point of pain. The truck slows to turn onto a dirt road, climbing a great slope that serves as mountain for many miles in all directions. The crown of the slope is broad and flat. A low house squats blackly on the prairie in the moonlight. Samael's figure glows in a rocking chair on the porch.

Stepping from the truck, he pauses to measure Sam's thoughts. Sam knows he has come to the end of his line. That he has brought his crypt says as much. It is the only observance of their race that a duel is in the offing. Closing the distance to the house, Sam glimmers with delight. It is no good sign for him Sam's crypt is nowhere to be seen.

"You come to me. I'm flattered." Sam makes an expression he could never match.

"Either way, you'll win in the end."

Sam nods. "You decimate ECCO and leave yourself at my mercy or you attempt me on your own, lose, and I decimate ECCO myself."

"Checkmate."

"Have a seat." Sam points to an empty rocker across from him. "Drink?"

"No." He does sit.

Sam pulls out a pack of cigarettes, holding it up to him.

He turns it down with a shake of his head as Sam extracts one and licks it. Tobacco does nothing, but Sam often finds uses for cigarettes. Sam likes fire.

"You know, I'm still scarred over how discussions went last time." As he speaks, the end of the cigarette flares with blue light and fades to an orange glow.

"I told you I didn't want to go to The Mountain."

"Castles 'N Coasters next time."

"I don't suppose there will be a next time."

"I suppose not." Sam takes a draw on the cigarette and squints at the truck. Louis has made himself scarce.

Flicking ash, Sam nods. "I'll have Louis take care of that when we're done."

"I have an offer." His plea is nearly silent.

Sam doesn't look, only scrutinizes the truck, perceiving the prize inside.
A snake rattles in the grass.
Time stands still.
"Really?" Sam sighs. "What is it?"
"Myself."
"Conditions?"
"However you wish."
Sam's eyes brighten. "You mean this?"
"You can have all of me now if you want." His insides turn at the words.
"Why?"
"Without Sophie I have nothing."
"Without her you might have had everything."
"But alone."
With a grin, Sam snickers.
"You've never feared that?"
Sam shrugs. "I've always had you."
"You've never had me."
Rising from his chair, Sam walks behind him and puts a hand on his shoulder.
"Let's walk."
Getting to his feet, he follows Sam down bleached steps onto moonlit grass.
They walk from the house, single file, towards the crest of the hill. As they near the
crest, Sam slows, allowing him to keep pace.
"How did this happen?" Sam's tone has a mother's care.
"I did what they wanted."
"And?"
"Their side doesn't pay."
"So you took a little on the side?"
"It isn't a matter of desire, Sam. It's more than that."
"Of course it is."
"I'm not like you."
"Of course you aren't."
"If she's passed to the other side or if ECCO has her, it's all the same."
"How do you know I don't have her?"
"You don't need her. Even to turn ECCO against me. It was only ever a matter of
time. In the end, you are all that is left."
"ECCO can't afford to lose you. Would they risk everything over one soul?"
"There is no exception to the law. After Sophie, there was no going back."
"You no longer share their philosophy?"
"I hate them." His words are thin as paper.
"Mmm ..." Sam purses his lips. "You stand exactly where I once stood."
They come to a stop at the crest of the hill.
Below stretches the length of the gorge. Far to the northwest, black peaks mark
the Ring of Fire. Overhead, the setting moon gives way to the backbone of night.

His eyes stop at Sam's profile. "I defeated you."

"And you are victorious again." Sam grins at his puzzled expression. "You have defeated yourself this time."

"I have fallen."

"No. Not at all. You're free. You've defeated your ego. Let go of the delusion you master the universe."

"That is your delusion."

As Sam lets out a vigorous laugh the echo rolls across the valley.

"Then you labor under it alone. I have never desired to be master of anything."

"You want me like the others. I know about the crypts. Who were they?"

"You think those are my trophies? Why doesn't that surprise me?" Sam pulls out another cigarette.

"Louis--"

"What did Louis say?" Sam cuts him off. "You come to me hat in hand and now you're deferring to Louis? I have to rate better than that."

"He didn't say anything." Fearing for Louis, he checks himself. "I was curious."

"He doesn't *know* anything. He drives a truck and drinks his lunch. I don't know that ECCO is so wrong to ban romance, your mind is a mess."

"What happened them?"

"You ought to know. It's what you've been doing for ECCO all this time as resident enforcer of their iron group think."

"I don't know who they were, only I didn't assume them."

"You're sure about that?"

"Would I be here if I did?"

Sam looks thoughtful. "When was the last time ECCO fully convened?"

He pauses. "Nineteen forty-nine."

"Have you heard from any of them since?"

"I saw Sarah three years ago."

Sam's eyes roll. "If Sariel had her way, she'd see you every day. What about the others? Anael? Uriel? Raziel?"

"On occasion, Raziel would send me books."

"When was the last?"

He is silent as the magnitude of his desertion dawns on him.

"Then again ..." Sam rubs. "You haven't been reading as much as you used to."

"There's been no shift." He pushes the guilt away. "I would have felt it."

"What if there was nothing to shift?"

"Someone within ECCO? One of us?"

Sam's eyes twinkle. "Us, *them*. There was a time you called me brother."

They stare at each other as statues under the stars; his thoughts empty. Sam takes hold of his shoulder and leads them to the house.

TRAGIC LOSS
Greatest American Film Actor Dies

Actor Lon Chaney, "The man of a thousand faces" finally succumbed to his battle with cancer yesterday. Initially taken ill with pneumonia after finishing his latest movie "The Unholy Three" Chaney was later diagnosed with bronchial cancer and had been undergoing treatment after an operation left him hospitalized and unable to speak. For the last seven weeks, the actor's condition had been deteriorating but a sudden hemorrhage was the final cause of death

Born Leonidas Chaney on April 1, 1883 in Colorado Springs, Colorado, Chaney was raised by deaf parents, giving him an early expertise with the sort of pantomime that would later become his trademark as an actor. Starting his career in his teens on the vaudeville circuit, he eventually found work with Universal Studios in 1912. However, it wasn't until his performances in "The Miracle Man" (1919) and "The Penalty" (1920) where he convinced audiences that he was a double amputee that his genius was fully recognized. His starring roles in 1923's "Hunchback of Notre Dame" and 1925's

"Phantom of the Opera" confirmed his place as the leading dramatic actor in film. His masterful use of make up brought terrifying realism to his moving portrayals of disfigured monsters as tragic heroes, drawing audiences by the millions. His death at the age of 47 is a shock for the Hollywood community and the legions of fans who made him the number one male box office draw of the last decade.

Funeral services will be held Thursday the 28th. Prior to services, the casket will be available for viewing at the Cunningham & O'Connor Funeral Home in downtown Los Angeles. Authorities are already in preparation for the long lines of mourners expected to pay their respects. American movie goers have lost more than the foremost character actor in film, but an irreplaceable talent whose roles will remain unprecedented, never to be filled by another.

Mr. Chaney is survived by his wife Hazel and their son, Creighton.

[*Times Angeles Times* obituary from scrapbook of Michael Goodhew. d. Aug. 26, 1930]

2000 The movie section of the newspaper was not something he usually read. Inundated with an ever increasing frenzy of human communication, he ignored a great deal of popular culture. Sophie regularly pointed out this ignorance as if it were an unconscionable oversight. After their last disagreement about the validity of popular fiction in human culture, he decided to inform himself. Daniel occasionally saw movies, but Sophie saw them frequently. Perhaps media in the modern world had become so encompassing it was impossible to avoid exposure. Once hooked, one became obsessed.

The human fascination with apocryphal subjects was still very much alive. Films about ghosts, monsters, and apocalyptic cataclysm were numerous. Humans seemed especially attracted to deadly romantic partners, though why a mortal would want to have intercourse with a being that desired its blood was a mystery. Furthermore, why would a mortal fantasize about becoming such a creature? Blood could be consumed, but it was hardly palatable as albuminous fluids went.

Any creature, mortal or not, that claimed blood tasted better than ice cream was a liar. Was that why Sophie loved him? Did she see him as a creature? A dangerous monster? Did she dream of blood while he dreamed of ice cream?

"Your wish has come true."

He saw Sophie approach him through his paper. She dropped an envelope on his lap and walked away.

Folding the paper, he examined the envelope. It was heavy with a gold seal already opened. He looked after Sophie as she disappeared into the laundry room. Carefully pulling out the contents, there were three envelopes inside. Dropping the mailing envelope, he proceeded to open each in turn. The first contained a map and driving directions, the second a list of various household and furniture items. The last was an invitation, tied with a ribbon on cream Crane paper.

"Who are Katherine Steele and Duane Nelson?" He called to her.

"Cousin Kate."

"Cousin Kate?"

She crossed the foyer with a basket of laundry. "*My* cousin, darling."

Without pause, she climbed the stairs to their bedroom. He dropped the invitation and followed her. Even now her thoughts were about folding laundry. Sophie rarely thought about her family, though he knew she loved them. She spoke of them even less. Discussing a wedding presented a rare opportunity. He was standing at the bed where she folded clothes almost before she got there.

His first impulse was to ask if they were going, but his courage wavered.

"Are you going?"

"Not if you aren't." Sophie's expression was bemused. "Good God, you're hyperventilating. I always thought you wanted to meet my family. We don't have to go if you don't want to."

She dumped the laundry and started to fold.

"*No.*" He blurted, then dropped his voice. "No. I—I do. I mean, I want to go."

She only raised a brow as she shook out a towel.

Reaching for a shirt, he started to sort.

"I've always wanted to go to a wedding."

"You've never been to a wedding?"

"Not ..." He hesitated. "Not as a ..."

"Man?" Sophie snickered.

He sighed. "I was going to say as a member of the family, but I'm not, am I?"

"You know what they say. Always a boyfriend, never a bride."

He smiled at her spite. He hated all the words for him. Boyfriend. Partner. Significant other. He didn't want to be other. They had been living together for nearly three months. Anthony got to meet her parents the first month they were dating and Sophie already knew her mother wouldn't approve.

"Do you love me?"

"That's why we're here."

"Then why haven't you told your family about us?"

"I will. We're not there yet. We'll get there." She started visiting the bedroom drawers, putting away clothes.

"As long as your parents don't know me you know I won't ask your father for your hand. You know I won't propose to you."

He probably shouldn't have said that.

She spun on him. "*Whoa!* We're not rushing things so you can go to the wedding as my fiancé."

Rushing things?

If he were human he would have met her parents by now. He would be in the hospital after wrecking his car, taken to the emergency room in an ambulance with bruised lungs and fractured limbs. She would have called them, they would have been worried. They would have come to see him. With flowers. And candy.

Of course, if he were human he wouldn't have been speeding, late getting back from a meeting. A meeting where he gave his word he would kill her.

"I'm sorry." He dropped her gaze. "You're right. That's not what I want. Only, it's been three months and I feel like I'm a secret."

She rolled her eyes. "Trust me, when I introduce you to my parents, you'll look back on this time with wistful longing."

Picking up the empty basket, she left.

The wedding was on July fourth. There was still time.

He followed her downstairs.

"May I borrow your car?"

She glanced over her shoulder on her way to the laundry room.

"What happened to yours?"

"I took it to the dealer to have them look it over."

"Oh right, wasn't running well ..." Her brows rose as she loaded wet clothes in the dryer.

"Just being thorough."

"Uh huh. Ghost in the machine." She slammed the dryer shut and turned it on.

He blinked as she crossed her arms.

"I won't go far."

"Sure. I'll probably get in a jog and go to Mom's today. When will you be back?"

"I'll call you."

"I don't like to jog with my cell."

"You don't have to take a phone."

She closed her eyes, putting up her palms.

"I'll be home by five."

"Like you were going to be home by five last night?"

"I was stuck in traffic."

"Okay, five." She grabbed his shoulders and gave him a kiss. "And if my car isn't running well, get me a 5 series too while you're at it."

The address Louis Stiles gave the state patrol was in Steilacoom. When he tried to see it in his mind, he came up with no such street number. After the accident, he had been able to watch Louis take the truck to a transfer station in Fife, but the vision faded to interference after that. Sam had been able to use Louis to penetrate far into his perimeter. Humans had their advantages. One was that they were hard to follow, especially if it was a human you had never met. It was a tactical error for Louis to speak to him. It gave him something to remember, something to read.

Now he would do to Sam what Sam had employed Louis to do: go on a scouting expedition.

Sophie's car was running fine as he drove the twisting road to Steilacoom. Her comment about getting her a BMW made him wonder if she was serious. She often railed against people who insisted on having a new car every year ... her last car had been her father's and she had driven it ten years before she got a new one. Cars could last well over a hundred thousand miles if people just maintained them. It was wasteful. We were killing the planet.

If he surprised her with a 360 Hp 5 series that got 22 mpg, she would either love him or lecture him. Probably both.

He decided to set the thought aside.

When he turned on her radio, it was playing the popular music he heard her listen to in his car. It reminded him of bird song. Short and repetitive with regular references to mating. This song was about a girl who was pretty in pink. He switched to her CD player. He knew she had CDs, but without a player in the house, he rarely heard anything she owned. He turned down the volume, expecting it would be too loud. She always listened to music at a volume that made him wonder if her hearing was impaired. It was a piano. He turned it up. Satie.

Daniel had liked Satie. He used to play it for him. When Daniel died the piano was the first thing he got rid of. He had not played one since. Sophie didn't know he played. She hadn't asked and he hadn't offered. He wasn't going to. He turned off the music and listened for Louis instead.

Entering Steilacoom, he found the street Louis gave. He drove the length of it, finding and feeling nothing. People were either staying warm in front of a television or not at home. Children played on the street. Dogs barked at him from behind fences. Deciding to search the town, he started on the east side, working his way in a grid eventually leading to the water.

As he neared the Sound, pressure built in his ears. Static tension. A fine mesh of electricity slowly crept over his body. Only another singularity would cause it—a singularity opposed to him. Slowing the car, he compensated for the intensity of the sensation and his body's response to it. His vision was beginning to seek the source, straining into infrared to catch any trace Sam might leave behind.

What puzzled him was how he could be feeling Samael here when he had no sense of him in Tacoma. Steilacoom was near enough he should have felt something. He should have felt Sam as far as Olympia. But even now it didn't feel right. It was as though Sam were here and not. The stimulus he felt seemed pointless. He drove along the water as far as he could, but the tension began to fade. When he doubled back, it intensified again. Looking out across the water, his senses faltered. There was a break in the magnetic field caused by a geologic fault line. The field was still there but constantly shifting, like a mirage in a desert.

He saw three islands. The nearest was Ketron, too close and too small. The farthest was McNeil, a state correctional facility. It was unlikely Sam would find a place to hide unnoticed near a correctional facility. Anderson Island was in between, moderately sized and moderately populated. An ideal place to hide and accessible only by ferry.

The ferry was a small one. He wondered if lingering to wait for the next available run might give Sam too much time to prepare for his arrival. If he parked the car and made a jump to the island, it would be both an aggressive act and potentially dangerous. He decided the intention of the meeting was to treat with Sam. He would take the ferry. Parking in the queue, he played Sophie's CD and contemplated the motives of his opponent.

Any ability he had to read Sam was useless this side of the fault line, any thoughts unreadable. For ECCO, reading Sam was impossible. Sam was at the far end of the singular spectrum, utterly antipodal to them. He alone made the connection between ECCO and Sam. He was weary of filling the gap. All of his existence, he had chased Sam from one end of creation to the other. Now that he had given up, he was the one being chased. ECCO had shamed him; Sam had taunted him. He was sick of them both. If he could convince Sam, he would negotiate a truce. If neither side could claim him, they had to let him go.

Aboard the ferry, there was no room for weariness. Parking Sophie's car on deck, he got out to watch the water, to read the line. Halfway across, he felt the field shift. Passing through the plane of interference, the shock of Sam's presence overwhelmed him. He gripped the steel hand rail, indenting it with his fingers.

Old instincts took hold; new feelings arose he couldn't remember. Anticipation, anger, fear … He forced them from his mind.

Once on the island, he let Sam's presence lead him down successive series of roads closing on the center of the island. Reaching an intersection near an abandoned house, he turned left and entered a stretch of forested road, little more than a dirt trail. The static grew deafening. Sam was here.

He stopped the car. There was a private drive on either side of the road. Both were fenced and gated. As he pondered the gates, a large dog charged one of the fences and barked, snarling savagely. Not that one. Animals couldn't tolerate Sam's presence. Ignoring the dog, he got out of the car and approached the gate across the road. It was chained with a coded padlock. He pried a link, breaking it with his fingers. Carefully unwinding the chain, he pushed open the gate.

In the car, he pulled onto the drive, advancing slowly, putting as much of himself out as he could. He wanted Sam to know he had come, parley accepted. Nearing the end of the drive, a dingy row of boarded chicken coops lined the edge of the property to his right. A relatively new garage was to the left. It was constructed of corrugated sheet metal and fronted by a sliding door, chained shut. The building glowed with Sam's presence. His vision pierced the doors, quickly finding what he was looking for. Sam.

But not upright.

A crypt was in the garage. It burned in his eyes like a box on fire. Absently stepping from the car, he approached the building. Aside from Sam's crypt, the structure was entirely empty. It was unlikely Sam remained unaware of his presence; more likely Sam couldn't come out. Looking down at the chains holding the door, he reached for them, then froze. They were hot. Stepping back, he reexamined the building, this time ignoring the lure of Sam's crypt.

The entire structure was alive with current. The sliding door, the walls, all deadly to the touch. Inside, a network of wires ran along the floor of the garage. He weighed the risks of disabling the field without being electrocuted. Low voltage electricity was merely uncomfortable. High voltage was another matter. His body was not only conductive but reactive. Even remote contact with high voltage was risky and compensating for the voltage differential required a finesse he doubted he had. He was, after all, a sentient being, not a transformer. Finding the source was the solution.

Walking around the garage, he followed the trace of a conduit running beneath the ground. It crossed a small clearing into nearby trees. Away from Sam, the electrical field became apparent. Making his way through the trees, he came to a barbed wire fence enclosing a small shed. This fence was not electrified. The padlock on the gate posed no challenge. The locked shed door opened easily to him.

Inside, he found two Caterpillar generators caged behind cyclone fencing. Shutting down the generators manually was the safest policy. Approaching the cyclone fencing, he pulled on the chain around the gate door, snapping it and mangling a good portion of the door. Finding the kill switches, he shut the generators down, one after the other; his eyes dilating at the sudden evaporation of the field.

Returning to the garage, he felt his heart beat faster as he approached the sliding door. The latch chain stretched hot in his hands before breaking. Pushing the door open, he took a breath. As he stepped inside, the mesh of wires on the concrete hissed under the damp soles of his shoes. Nothing stood between them. Nearing the crypt, Sam came into focus through its walls.

Stopping a few feet away, he tried to make sense of what he was seeing. Inside, the body was more than naked. It was badly incinerated. The degree of the burns and missing tissue indicated a duel of significant proportions had been fought. The body was not merely regenerating; it was recovering. Sam was in no condition to hold a conversation and wouldn't be for some time.

He pondered what to do. Pondered assuming Sam. It would be a violation of the rules. But this was Sam—Sam, who would have violated those rules without thought were their positions reversed. It wouldn't even have been humane. Sam would have wanted retribution, pleasure. Pain. He didn't dwell on it.

Opening the crypt, he looked upon Sam's scorched face; the constant eye burning bright on the forehead. He would be humane. Grasping an arm, he pulled Sam's torso to him until it propped up against the inside of the crypt. Sam's head lolled as he pulled it back to him. Bowing down, he opened Sam's mouth, placing his over it. Inhaling deeply, he caught Sam's breath.

A frigid thread drew down his throat, a trickle, then a torrent, blurring his sense of the three-dimensional realm. It was exhilarating and terrifying. Sam's strength was as a river of time in thought, an eternity culminated. There was brilliance, ruthlessness, calculating control, and above all a passion for suffering. He felt his eyes flood with blue light, nearing blindness. The deep chord of the universe began to pound in his mind as he grew deaf, senseless with rapture.

Something in him couldn't let go.

What had long hungered for this had faded over time. His sentience could feel Sam's resistance, its struggle to survive, and it was a black feeling. His mind's eye watched. It saw one thing eating another, felt the head of his victim in his hands.

Sophie's eyes opened.

Seeing himself in her eyes, he broke away from her mouth with a gasp. She stared blankly as he cradled her head on the edge of the bath. Releasing her, her gaze held him as she slipped beneath the water. He stepped back from the tub. Images flashed in his mind: the conservatory, coffee, holding her in the park, folding laundry, wedding invitations, her parents, a baby with blue eyes …

Catching his breath, he realized he was alone. In an empty space. Sam still throbbed in his head. Was lying in a crypt. In a garage. Wiping his mouth with the back of his sleeve, he turned blindly, blinking to see. There was a wall, and then another. No doors. His eyes strained for a way out. Then he saw it. The way he came. A sliding door. Closed.

Closed.

The pounding in his head stopped. There was a hiss. A surge beneath the static.

Like a shot, he threw himself at door. It nearly gave. Driving his fist through the metal, he reached for the latch on the outside. He could feel it in his hand before the wall hit him. His ears screamed. White hot fire seized his heart. Then let go.

He wasn't sure how long he was unconscious. There was a memory of being dragged. Only the hum of the world told him he was still on earth. The sound of a car engine. Movement. His eyes were open as his vision returned, burning when his lids tried to blink. It was a dark space. The trunk of a car. A bottle of gin slid past, hitting his head at a sharp turn. Sophie's car.

He moved to grab the bottle. Nothing happened. Only his chest was moving. They were heading north and east. He drifted. The car slowed, rolled onto gravel, and then grass, stopping. He heard a door open and someone getting out. Slow steps came around and opened another door. The steps came to the trunk and paused. The lid opened to a night sky, clear and moonless, but brilliant to his sight. He searched for a face. When he saw the Carhartt jacket, he didn't need to.

Louis reached for him. Grabbed by a wrist, his torso was pulled forward, an arm wrapping around him. The smell of tobacco and engine grease mingled with Louis's grunts as another arm cradled his knees. His neck snapped back as his body was lifted from the trunk. He stared at the sky, feeling like his head would fall off.

The stars flickered with the afterglow of fires long burnt away. He saw Pisces. Sophie was a Pisces. The star of Bethlehem had shone in Pisces. Only it hadn't been a star at all but a conjunction of Saturn and Jupiter. Humans wanted a star. Needed one. There was no point in telling them what they didn't want to hear.

His eyes caught sight of naked tree tops as Louis carried him around the car. In the distance, he could hear traffic on a highway. There wasn't any point in thinking about what was going to happen. There wasn't anything he could do about it, anyway. He could only hope his body would recover before things got interesting.

With a final grunt, Louis began to lower him. He was being placed onto the passenger seat. Care was taken not to bump his head. The front seat had been pushed back, barely accommodating his length. Once satisfied all of his parts were in the car, Louis closed the door. Returning to the driver's seat, Louis sat back with the door open. Silence followed, only interrupted when Louis leaned outside to spit in the grass. The smell of it was torture enough.

"Sorry about the trunk." Louis slurred. "You looked too dead to ride the ferry."

He made no complaint.

"Bad that. Didn't know it was you."

His eyes shifted impulsively.

"Just doin' my job."

Hopefully, Louis wouldn't wreck this car as well.

His body shivered, his teeth clenching.

Thankfully, Louis had nothing more to say.

"I'm not a good man."

God, not a confession.

"But I know good when I see it."

He felt Louis look at him.

"Wouldn't be right to leave you to him."

Fine pricks flooded his limbs and he flexed his right hand.

Louis leaned out the door and spat again.

"I'll stay. Didn't want to leave you like this next to the loony bin."

The loony bin must have been a reference to Western State Mental Hospital. They were in the park across from it.

"Would have took you home ... don't know where that is."

It was possible he wouldn't know where that was if he didn't get back soon. The stars told him it was around eight. There was a clock on Sophie's dashboard. Straining to raise his head, he looked at it. Eight fifteen.

"Feelin' better?"

Dropping his head, he closed his eyes.

Sophie, can you hear me?

She hated it when he spoke to her thoughts. Not once had she ever responded with a thought of her own.

Sophie?

She wanted no part of it.

I'll be home. I'm coming home. I'm all right. I'm ...

Louis leaned towards him. "You okay?"

His voice was a whisper.

"... Sorry."

1199 BC I felt no remorse. He had pursued me from the outset when I made it clear I was not interested in marriage. I would have continued to disabuse him of any interest on my part if circumstances beyond my control had not intervened. They were circumstances of consequence beyond words. His feelings for me were a small sacrifice, whether I was capable of sharing them or not. I was not. My mind intended to make the change if it would weaken his attachment to me.

The full moon was setting when I returned to camp. Slipping into his tent, which now seemed mine, my eyes sought only the glow of my crypt. He was waiting for me, seated in the moonlight at the table. The food was gone; only a carafe of wine remained. It was important I speak with him. If he had spoken plain with me, I too would be as honest with him as I could. Approaching him, I gave my regard with a deep bow.

"No guard saw you?" He asked with a smile.

"None."

"How so?"

"I did not wish to be seen."

"Their loss."

"Tonight is the last I will be as I am."

"My loss."

"Will you leave me then?"

"Never."

"I will not serve you."

"That is my task."

"I will not love you."

"So you have said."

"I will only make demands."

"That is to be expected."

"I require new clothes."

"I doubt I will find anything better."

Indicating his tunic and sandals with my eyes, I removed my veil and turned to my crypt. "What you have on will do."

"You will not keep what I have given you?"

"I will leave them."

My statement intoned a dismissal and I looked away. He rose from the table and paused before the entrance to the tent.

"May I take them from you?" He spoke quietly.

"Is that necessary?"

"They are both beautiful and rare. It would … ease my mind."

For a moment I stared at him. Holding his gaze, I unwound the veil from my shoulders and handed it over. As he took it, I pulled the stole from my body and held it out to him. He was slow to take it, his eyes searching as much of me as the moon would show.

"Take rest." I bade him.
With a low bow, he backed from the tent.

[Spharic. Entry translated from *Kor Dai Maihael*. Mund Dai. d. 755 BC]

[Assyrian carving of Satal, the god of prosperity, taking sacrifice. Bef. 1500 B.C.]

2003 The interior of Sam's cabin is Spartan: bare floor boards, a wood stove, a table and two chairs. There are two spare rooms. One appears filled with firewood, boxes of dry goods, a disused rifle and other sundries. At the back of the cabin is a bedroom with a single cot and no furniture. Each time they have shared close quarters, Sam's lifestyle seems monastic—until you factor in the penchant for rape and torture. He doesn't fear that from Sam tonight. He senses the hunger isn't there. Nothing quells the hunger faster than a willing victim. Instead, his near suicidal appeal has sparked Sam's patronage. With the devil, flattery will get you everywhere.

They each take a seat at the table.

Sam leans back, balancing the chair on two legs. "You know, I'm disappointed you didn't win."

He only stares blankly.

"After our last meeting of the minds, I had hopes Sophie would make a man of you, but if you've failed, I suppose I'm willing to take up the challenge."

"I could never turn on my brethren."

"You turned on me and I didn't even steal your girl."

"She isn't my girl."

"Is that why you want her? She's forbidden to you?"

"I want her the way you want everything else."

"I told you, I don't want everything."

"What do you want?"

"Satisfaction."

"And what would satisfy you?"

"Sariel's head on a plate, ECCO in tatters, my brother at my side."

"I don't believe it's Sarah."

Sam raises his brows. "You don't like that threesome? That's the way it's been. You, me, and Sarah. You can call it ECCO if you want, but it's always been her. That cold, calculating, lustful little bitch. You might not be in love with her, but she's coveted you … and had you."

He looks away.

"Yes, she has. She's been staring at the top of your head for eons, little pet."

He returns his gaze. "And the rest? They would let her pet them?"

"Why not? Phanuel can't see past his grail—the self-made Master of Metatron …" Sam's face twists to a sneer. "San Raphael, Gabriel of the Golden Hair, Zachariel! God! Zachariel—what a colossal waste of matter! What else do they notice beyond their pursuit of universal perfection?"

"What do you think that is?"

Sam snorts. "Vacuous omnipotence."

"You have no interest in that yourself?"

"Omnipotence?" Sam smirks. "When you've come as far as I have, why not go all the way? I'm a damn sight closer to it than any of them will ever come—as are you, I hope you realize." Sam squints at him. "Do you really hate them?"

"Yes."

With a head shake, Sam pulls out another cigarette. "What a waste."

"I don't regret it."

"You should have stayed with me."

"I hated you first."

"Why?" The cigarette flickers to life between Sam's lips.

"You tried to assume me."

"I was only trying to fulfill our destiny."

"*Our* destiny." He smiles.

"To mend what was broken. That was before the prophecy. Now it is foreseen there will be three of us."

"There would have only been two if you had assumed me."

Staring across the room, Sam shrugs. "Assuming you wasn't part of the plan."

"You could still do it."

Still staring at nothing, Sam only draws on the cigarette.

He pushes. "What does your vision say about assuming Sariel? There won't be three of us if ECCO fails. Who is the third?"

"Why do you think Sarah's run off with your Sophie?"

"Sophie isn't one of us."

"She could make one."

"She isn't pregnant."

Sam arches a brow. "God knows she's tried."

"It isn't possible."

"Speak for yourself."

Sam catches his expression as he looks away. The vision revolts him.

Puffing three smoke rings, Samael rolls in laughter. "You, me, and baby makes three."

Before dawn, they come to terms.

He will go to ECCO and confess his marriage to Sophie. He will be contrite. He will tell them Sam has abducted Sophie and promised to return her if he delivers ECCO in return. He doesn't trust Sam and will side with ECCO if they let Sophie live. In exchange, he will submit himself to Metatron. There is only one punishment for breaking the law of attachment. Sarah will find the opportunity irresistible.

He will say nothing about suspecting Sarah. Nothing about the missing crypts, especially his own. ECCO will assume it is a trap if they know. They will assume him, fearful he is beholden to whoever possesses his crypt. They won't wait to find out. Sam reminds him, with ECCO he was doomed from the start. Sam reminds him, they both want Sophie alive. And with Sam there is the promise he will be kept. For what it is worth.

Louis drives him as far as Vancouver in the truck they came in. The back of the trailer is empty, his crypt added to Sam's collection while he was added to Sam's ranks. There is no going back.

In Vancouver, he rents a car. The man behind the counter asks him what model car he wants. He asks for the fastest thing they have. Everything they have is domestic, but anticipating tourists, they have a number of new Mustangs available. The man behind the counter says it will accelerate to 60 mph in 4.7 seconds. We'll see. Not red; blue is better. He will drop it in Seattle at the end of the week. Does he want additional insurance? No, thank you. He'll take his chances. On his way out of town he stops at a mini-mart. He buys a box of Paydays and a pair of sunglasses.

The man behind the counter didn't lie. It is a fast car. He perceives a slight whine at 120 and drops it back to 100. It will meet his needs, he just won't floor it. Turning on the radio, he finds Sophie's station. It is a song he has heard before, about streets with no names. He floors it.

When he arrives in Seattle ninety minutes and twenty Paydays later, he is famished. Taking the first parking spot he can find, he violates Sophie's ban on Starbucks and enters one across the street. It is eight in the morning and busy. When he reaches the counter, a young woman behind the register gives him a wide smile.

She has Sophie's eyes and hair.

"Can I help you?"

"I'd like your pastries."

"Which ones?"

"All of them."

Her smile fades. "*All* of them?"

"Yes, please."

She looks to the barista, who shrugs as he froths hot milk.

"I don't know if I can sell you all of them."

He reappraises the baked items in the display case.

"Half of them."

Her smile returns. "I'll see if I can find a box."

Finding an empty seat at the bar running along the window, he methodically eats four croissants, six muffins, and three scones. There is no need to wait till noon for a quorum. ECCO knows he is here. Even with their combined numbers abuzz in his ears, he knows they feel the weight of his presence even more so. The only unknown is how many will show and who.

When he steps off the elevator, there is a quorum at the boardroom table. Sarah is already seated at the head. Her white-blonde hair, straight lines, and severe dress make the space feel cooler than it is. Gabrielle, Zachariel, Raphael, and Phanuel are seated in pairs on either side. Their appearance is striking to him now and seems too obvious. With the exception of gender, their faces are generic masks with pointless expressions. He finds himself wondering how any human ever seriously regarded him as normal. Of course they didn't. Anthony told him as much.

Nearing the far end of the table, he pauses, regarding them silently. He nods to

Sarah, waiting for her to indicate a seat before taking one. Until she acknowledges him, he says nothing. She watches him momentarily before nodding to the seat directly before him. Taking his seat, he waits for her.

Sarah opens the discussion with a simulation of concern.

"It has been three years since you left with no word. We thought you would never return."

"I thought you considered my work finished."

Gabrielle answers. "Rumor said you thought the same of us."

"Rumor never came to ask."

Phanuel smiles, but the rest remain frozen.

"Of course …" Sarah breaks the silence. "We are all happy to see you again. Think of our concern as a measure of our consideration for you." She tilts her head back as she speaks. "What can we do for you, Michael?"

"Samael has reached me again."

Raphael leans forward. "He is resurrected?"

"He had help."

"What does he want now?" Sarah asks.

"My help." He can feel them quicken.

Sarah makes a smile. "This wouldn't be the first time he's tried to turn you."

He nods. "He senses a weakness."

"In ECCO or you?"

"Both."

"How?"

"He claims that one of us is thinning the ranks."

This doesn't move them. They already know.

"How does he know this?" Zachariel speaks, but it is Phanuel who asks.

"He has the crypts."

"You've seen them?"

"His servus keeps them."

Zachariel frowns. "You think they were assumed without our notice?"

Gabrielle shakes her head. "Impossible."

"Not impossible." He counters. "If Sam had a confederate."

Sarah smiles. "You?"

He looks directly at her. "You."

They all look at Sarah.

"But you are the one he pursues." Sarah raises a brow.

"Why would I come now if I could swallow ECCO whole without its notice?"

He feels the temperature in the room drop.

"No one doubts you, Michael." Phanuel speaks up. "You have known penitence. As has Sariel. As have we all. So long as Metatron can see, Samael will never win."

He folds his hands. "If that is the case, then ECCO has never needed me."

Phanuel smiles. "You serve Metatron because you were called. Without the calling, you would be lost, like Samael, surviving on instinct but grasping for meaning.

You of all beings have seen his desperate existence. He feeds on his prophecies because he finds no satisfaction in anything else. He cannot let go because he has embraced what is forbidden."

"Samael has no intentions of letting go of anything. Not the crypts and not what's left of ECCO if our losses continue to grow." He turns to Sarah. "I don't accuse you, but you are Sam's favorite suspect at the moment."

Everyone looks to Sarah again.

She makes another smile. "Am I your favorite suspect?"

He makes a smile of his own. "You've always been my favorite."

"What else does Sam say?"

"He says you took Sophie."

Sarah's smile vanishes. The others look at each other.

Her eyes smolder. "You gave your word."

His smile remains. "And I intend to keep it."

Raphael glances between them. "Who is Sophie?"

"Then why worry about getting her back?" She ignores Raphael's confusion. "I can't keep my word if someone else kills her first, can I?"

"Then you should have done it sooner."

"Kill who?" Raphael repeats.

He and Sarah only stare at each other. The rest of the council waits expectantly.

"Sophie." He finally answers.

"Who's Sophie?" Gabrielle asks.

"My wife." As he says the words, Sarah's eyes narrow.

Raphael seems confused. "That is forbidden."

"Thanks. I know it."

"You'll be excommunicated." Gabrielle looks panicked.

"I've already done that."

"What?" All of them speak at once.

"I surrendered my crypt."

Sarah leans forward. "To whom?" Her calm has fled.

"Samael."

He smiles as the quorum squirms. A hum fills the air.

"What do you mean by this?" Zachariel nearly stands.

"I mean ECCO is in an extreme position. It is being consumed from within and Sam sees the opportunity. Sophie's absence has left me disagreeable, or agreeable, depending on whose side you are on. My grace will swing the balance. I have already given my word to Sam that if he is responsible for Sophie's disappearance, I will destroy him or ruin myself trying. If ECCO is responsible, I will help Sam take the lot of you."

"You have betrayed us." For the first time, Phanuel shows distress.

"Not yet. I have been open with you. I have told you everything, which is more than you have ever done with me."

Phanuel's eyes burn with fever. "You have already betrayed yourself. You have broken the law. You are disgraced!"

"Michael, we are your brethren." Raphael's voice remains calm. "We stood by you when Samael could have destroyed you."

"And I have served you ever since. You have used me to satisfy your own interests. You claim no attachments, but you have them, to yourselves." His eyes meet each face. "Not even to each other and never to me. If that is the existence you desire, you are free to choose it. Why stop me from seeking my own happiness?"

"To avoid this!" Sarah stands and the fluorescent lamps flicker. "Look at you. Listen to what you are saying. You're no better than Sam!"

"No, Sarah!" The static in the room intensifies as he rises to his feet. "*You* are no better than Sam. For an eternity, I have been the bone you worried. No more. With or without Sophie! *No more!*"

The lights go out. Only their blue eyes pierce the dark. In moments, the lights flicker back on. He is gone.

He can feel the danger rise as he flees the building.

Telling them he lacks a crypt is risky. Their first instinct will be to injure him before he leaves their stronghold. The building is hot with their interference as they try to slow him. Making a jump is too dangerous, their static creating too much resistance for him to feel his own strength. Too small a shift would waste precious energy. Too great a shift could put him in a gravity well. Wary of his brethren, he senses a dozen sentinels haunting the floors below. They are moving on him but pose little threat.

Avoiding the elevators, he leaps the stairwell one flight at a time. Two floors down, he is met by two sentinels. Their gray shadows combine in an effort to stagger him into submission. He easily absorbs the kinetic distortion they cast before him. With no bodies of their own, the draw of his mass swallows them completely as he runs through them. Sensing the futility of direct engagement, no other sentinels attempt to intercept him. He knows his real challenge lies ahead. Will any of his brethren challenge him? If it is Raphael, he will know his appeal has missed its mark. If not, then he has been heard at least.

One thing is certain, it will not be Sarah. She won't risk herself this early.

Cautiously exiting the stairwell, he slips into the lobby. As empty and disused as it appears, he knows otherwise. The only daylight comes from a pair of opaque glass doors leading to the sidewalk at the far end. Slowing from a run to a brisk walk, he feels two have come. When he hears Raphael's voice, his heart sinks.

"Michael."

He stops in the middle of the lobby, keeping his eyes fixed on the doors. He doesn't want to see Raphael's face. Gabrielle flanks his other side.

"Why?" Raphael's plea is gentle.

"Where is she?"

"I don't know."

He takes a step to the doors.

"Why?" Raphael asks again. "Why a woman?"

His eyes drop to the floor. "Why not?"

"So you turn to Samael?" Gabrielle speaks. "Will he be all that is left?"

He looks at her. "Then help me."

"It is forbidden, Michael." Raphael nears him. "It is the law."

Too close.

Too blind.

Without turning his head, he lunges. His attack collides with a late repel of static from Raphael, sending a weak shock wave across the lobby that rattles the doors. Gabrielle moves to intervene but sees his grip on Raphael's throat and stops short. She sees the blue current lace up Raphael's neck and over his face.

"Michael." She whispers.

"Whose law?" The floor trembles at his voice.

"Michael, please."

"Whose law?" The glass in the lobby doors fracture.

Raphael gasps in his grip. There is no time for rhetoric.

She knows she must answer the truth.

"I don't know."

He releases Raphael, letting him fall to the floor. He faces Gabrielle, who drops her gaze, unwilling to bear his eyes.

"And you don't care."

Passing through shattered doors, he realizes he doesn't either. He never did because he never knew how. Now, he feels the meaning of the word for the first time. Quickly donning sunglasses as the crush of pedestrians surround him, he tries to appear as calm on the outside as he is raging on the inside. The line between latent thought and kinetic output wavers. It is a feeling he hasn't felt in a long time.

Wrath.

In another age, he was capable of great wrath. As different from Sam as he claimed to be, you didn't become a singularity of his proportion by chance. You evolved, from being a simple sentinel to a legion of them, coalescing into a singular entity, into something as ruthlessly devouring as Sam. Or himself. And all for what? To come to the conclusion you didn't want to be God after all. You just wanted to sleep on clean sheets at night and have someone care enough to pull a blanket over you.

He could have assumed Raphael in the lobby, and when he was finished, gone on to Gabrielle, returned upstairs for Sarah, and consumed every singular in the place. They would have fought him and the building wouldn't have survived. But he would have. He would have felt very satisfied, too.

As tempting as assuming the lot is, it won't lead him to Sophie. If Sarah has her, he might find out by assuming Sarah's thoughts into his own. He might see a vision of where Sophie is hidden. If only to find her, free her, but at the cost of becoming someone else. A monster she would never recognize. If he assumes Sarah only to find Sophie is dead, his rage will assume him in turn. He will hate the living world and everything in it. He will destroy it all and Sam will lead the way. There

234 | LISA MOWAT

will be nothing to stop Sam. He will become Sam.

As he approaches his car, he instinctively looks over his shoulder and spots Sarah in the crowd. Her white hair and blue eyes blind him before she disappears around a corner. She isn't ready to talk. So be it.

Getting into the car, he decides to find Anthony. Anthony tried to call him repeatedly all morning. Each time, he cut the signal, he was always too close to Sam to avoid being overheard. He decides to call as he is leaves Seattle. Any conversation will be easier to hide in interference if he is moving. Escaping city traffic, his vision seeks Anthony. There is no sign of Anthony at the precinct, but he isn't sure if he's looking in the right place. He overhears a dispatch to Anthony's patrol car and traces the signal. It is just after break and Anthony is about to resume work.

Officer Navarre here.

"Hello, Anthony."

Where the hell were you? I was beginning to think I'd dreamed that whole conversation up. I've called you half a dozen times in the last twenty-four hours.

It was ten times, but nobody was interested to know it.

"I'm sorry. I wasn't in a position to speak openly with you."

Don't you have voice-mail?

"No."

You need it.

"I'll keep that in mind."

So far the investigation hasn't gone public yet. We processed the car and I tried to nail down every piece of surveillance footage I could find for the market that morning. There's footage of her from some shops along Broadway. She made it past the bank, but she never made it to Grounds from what I can tell.

"Did you recognize anyone in the crowd? Did she talk to anyone?"

I'm holding the footage for you. Some if it's pretty bad resolution, but it's possible there's someone you know.

"I'm almost to Tacoma. When could I see it?"

Where? At the station?

"Doesn't matter. As long as I know where to look for you, I can see it from wherever I am, barring interference."

Jesus. Can you see me now?

"Yes."

Where am I?

"You're standing in the parking lot in front of the Mandolin."

Shit. Why didn't you see Sophie when she was grabbed?

"That was why I knew. I couldn't see her anymore. I felt that she was there and then she wasn't."

Then what good is the surveillance footage?

"I'm not a camera. I don't record everything in my range of vision. All I could fix on was Sophie. I must have missed that someone was following her."

So you still might ID the kidnapper?

"Or determine if they had help. Even someone like me needs help."
He can see Anthony smile.
I'll be back at the office in twenty. I'll call you when I'm ready to run the footage.
"Thank you, Anthony."
Hang in there, Mike. We'll find her.
He is glad the conversation is over. He can't say another word.

Subject: Let's get together

From: Natalie Berger

Date: 6/8/2000 10:16 AM

To: Sophie Davids

Hey Sophie! Long time no hear! I got your e-mail from Jennie after she contacted me on our reunion page. Can you believe it? Ten years are almost up! I'm just excited to find a contact for you. Our committee was looking for you when we started to plan our reunion but no one could find you! Becky called your parents house and when she finally got your Dad he just said you'd left home and hung up. We were taking bets as to whether you were in a cult or doing time.

So what have you been up to? I've been married four years now with two boys. That about says it all. Jennie said that you were dating a guy named Michael, but that you were pretty tight lipped about it. I'll share if you will. My husband's name is Steve and he's a lawyer. Nothing fancy, just divorces, so if you plan on getting married let me know and I can set you up with a boiler plate pre-nup!

Me and some ladies from the committee are going to meet next week in Seattle at Bucca. We'd really like to see you... yes, we are trying to recruit you, but if not, come anyway. Everyone would love to catch up and I figure after a pitcher of margaritas I'll get the scoop on Michael.

SYS

Natalie

[E-mail from Natalie Berger to Sophie Davids. d. June 8, 2000]

2000   He did have a home to return to after escaping Anderson Island. This was partly due to Louis's crisis of conscience and partly to Sophie's decision to see a movie that evening with Amy. In fact, she couldn't hear him when he had spoken to her thoughts. She was surrounded by so much sensory interference, he would have been barely a whisper, and he had been too exhausted to know where she was. After assuming a fair portion of Sam followed by a generous helping of high-voltage electricity, his extra sensory perception was beyond reach. If it had been, he would have known she was watching *The Lord of The Rings* and terrified of orcs.

She was still gone when he returned home and had no idea he had been late, though she did note he seemed "a little frazzled."

He would have been worse than frazzled if Louis hadn't gotten him away from Sam. If Louis had been less inclined to believe he was an angel and a more devoted servus, he would have been left in Sam's crypt to be fed upon. Louis not only stayed with him until he was ambulatory enough to drive, but provided some insight on Sam's recent activities.

After sending Louis to deliver an invitation to parley with a freight truck, Sam had conflicted with another singularity. However, Sam had been afraid to be drawn out of hiding before their meeting. As a result, Sam underestimated the opposition and was left in a vulnerable position when he arrived for their meeting. Although his attempt to assume Sam was incomplete, it would be a long recovery. Adding the incineration Sam had already suffered, doubly so.

In exchange for the risk Louis had taken in letting him go, Louis asked to be allowed to take Sam away. He consented. If Sam was being stalked, he probably needed Sam more alive than dead, if only to distract this stalker from himself. At the very least, the harassment from Sam would stop.

Sam's injuries would also buy him time with ECCO. He had told Sarah no news would be good news. If he disappeared now, she could claim no expectations from him. As potentially disastrous as his encounter with Sam had been, the result was surprisingly hopeful. As for his promise to kill Daniel, that was not time sensitive. Sophie would be safe as long as she was in his custody. Custody. The very notion of Sophie tolerating the idea was amusing, but if it pleased Sarah to believe it, he would let her.

It was a testament to Sophie's love she tolerated his presence at all. That she was aware of his ability to read her thoughts, especially when he had difficulty reading anyone else's, was not a comfort to her. In compensation for this intrusion, the secrets she kept from him were commonplace things any other couple wouldn't think twice about sharing. Most jealously guarded was her family. When she visited them, it was without his knowledge. When she phoned them, it was on her cell away from home.

He knew she had friends from school who would e-mail her or leave messages on the phone, but these communications were cryptic at best. There was the death of Gregory Jacobs, a relationship that remained a mystery. In recent months, she had grown especially close to her co-workers, Amy Duncan and Dan Fogel. They would regularly eat lunch together or meet after work. She would see movies with Amy, or they would go shopping. There was no hint of what they discussed when she came home.

And of course there was Anthony.

He tried to accommodate her every way he could. Eating what she wanted him to and spending his nights sleeping on a bed, all of which he found enjoyable. It was what she called living like a person and not a pooka. The things he tried to avoid were following her around the house, staring at her, and above all, startling her. All of these things were proving harder for him to mind than he would have guessed. It was more than letting her spend time in a room alone, averting his gaze when she was reading, and clearing his throat at regular intervals so she knew where he was in the house. It meant not following her in her car and surprising her the next time she visited her parents.

More than anything else, he wanted to meet them. Preferably more than once.

It was the first step of his wedding proposal strategy. The second would be to ask her father for her hand. The third, to propose. The stress of accomplishing this goal was keeping him from enjoying any sleep on a bed at night. All he could think about was Kate and Duane's wedding. Until a groom himself, attending her cousin's wedding would be the closest he had come to feeling like he was part of a family. He would be damned before meeting Sophie's family as anything less than her fiancé.

Staring at their bedroom ceiling for the third morning in a row, he knew he had to let the opportunity to meet her parents present itself. From what she indicated, Sophie would be no help. He was mystified as to how humans could wait for their lives to unfold at such a plodding pace when their average life span barely cleared seventy-five years. The next opportunity he foresaw was Sophie's birthday on March 15. He had four days.

Sophie's alarm clock went off.

The covers moved and he watched her hand fumble for the snooze button. Sixty seconds later, the alarm went off again. This time she reached over and flipped the dial, turning it off. Her hand dropped and remained motionless. After three minutes, he rolled over and touched it.

"No."

He withdrew his hand and stared at her. After three more minutes, he touched her again. Her head popped up, her face barely visible under her hair.

She looked at the clock and then back at him. "I have a meeting at eight. PowerPoint presentation. Point and click. You want it?"

He blinked at her.

She rubbed her eye. "I'll let you use my new laser pointer."

"What do you want to do for your birthday?"

She rolled out of bed. "Almost forgot, I've got a meeting at eight ... PowerPoint presentation ..."

Waving a hand in the air, she grabbed her bathrobe and fled the bedroom.

Rolling onto his back, he returned his meditation to the ceiling. She would not be forced. Getting up, he pulled on jeans and a T-shirt before heading downstairs. Switching on the coffee maker, he went to the refrigerator for eggs and bacon.

By the time she came downstairs, he had already eaten. He didn't wait. She never let him make her breakfast. She always met Amy instead.

"Would you like some breakfast?" He sat at the table, knowing the answer.

"No, thanks." Ignoring the cup of coffee he left for her on the kitchen table, she got a mug out of the cupboard and filled it in front of the coffee maker. "I'm meeting Amy at Grounds. I'll grab a bagel."

Blowing on her coffee, she took a sip and peeked over at him. "What are you going to do today?"

"Nothing, really."

"Your job seems to come with a lot of down time."

"We don't have PowerPoint presentations."

"No graphs? No pie charts? No spook stats?"

He crossed his arms and shook his head. She wasn't done yet.

"Maybe what you guys need is a trade conference."

He sighed.

"I'm serious. Does ECCO have a shareholder meeting or anything?"

He shook his head.

"Sarah runs everything and no one asks any questions?"

"We sense each other. We can feel how things are going."

She slowly nodded and pursed her lips. "Feel it ..."

He said nothing. It went beyond explanation, but she didn't really want one.

"That's cool." She raised her brows and drank her coffee. "I wish I could skip my presentation today and just say things were feeling right, but they'll probably want something more concrete."

"I don't want to talk about work."

"Go fish."

"I want to do something special for your birthday."

She swallowed her coffee. "You're fixating."

"What did you do last year?"

"Went out to dinner with classmates."

"Did you get any presents?"

"Free dinner and a hangover."

"Did your parents get you anything?"

"Mmm ..." She squinted. "Mom got me perfume."

"Did your aunt get you anything?"

"Soap and bath salts ... and scented candles."

"Did you like them?"

"They were nice." She took another sip of coffee.

"You don't wear perfume."

She smirked. "And I don't have a bath tub anymore."

"Those are very feminine gifts."

"Excuse me?" She widened her eyes at him, feigning offense.

"You understand my meaning. You're not generally interested in toiletries beyond their practical application."

"However, I still apply them. That still makes me a woman."

"I wasn't inferring you were otherwise. It was only an observation that while those might be gifts women commonly find appealing, you are not one of those women."

"I didn't say I didn't like them."

"But you don't use them."

She cleared her throat. "Not really, no."

"Then why did they get them for you?"

"I don't know …" Her voice faded. "Maybe I smell bad." She yawned and raised her watch. "Gotta go."

She passed him at the table, kissing him on the cheek.

He rose from the table, following her to the foyer, where he helped her into a rain coat. Picking up her messenger bag, she headed out the front door he held open for her.

"When are you going to be home?"

On the stoop, she shrugged. "Same time as yesterday and the day before. Why?"

He couldn't come up with an answer.

"You're bored." She reached over and tugged the front of his tee. "Aren't you?"

He barely shrugged.

"I thought you were getting a new car?"

"I will."

"Do you need to borrow mine?"

He hesitated.

"You can drop me at Grounds. I'll hitch with Amy to work; you can pick me up after."

"I'm not dressed. You'll be late."

"The way you drive, I'll be there early."

Smiling, he grabbed a cardigan off the coat rack and slipped on loafers at the door. She was waiting in the passenger seat of her car when he left the house. Getting behind the wheel, he started up the drive. At first they said nothing. He knew Sophie was thinking about work, thinking about Amy, thinking about what kind of bagel she wanted.

"How is Amy doing?"

"Fine."

"Is she still dating Dan?"

Sophie frowned. "History. Just friends. I never thought he was her type anyway."

"Who is her type?"

"Well, when she first laid eyes on you, she thought you were."

"What type am I?"

"Type A."

"What's Type A?"
"Come on, Mike." She rolled her eyes. "You're smarter than you look."
"But she didn't know me."
"I didn't either. Look what happened."
"You did know me, you just didn't remember."
"So you like to claim."
"Do you feel you know me now?"
"Enough."
"Enough for what?"
"Enough to know I must love you."
"When did you first know that?"
"When I discovered I felt bad about hurting your feelings."
"You don't feel bad about hurting people's feelings?"
"Not generally."
"Why not?"
"Because I'm evil."
"You're not evil."
"Of course I am. Everyone is."
He was silent.
Sophie looked at him. "There are worse things to be than evil."
"Such as?"
"Ignorant."
"And you're not?"
She sneered. "You still want to marry me or you change your mind?"
He smiled. "You're better than most."
"Better than most. Thanks."
"You're not Amy."
"Be nice."
"You make comments about her intelligence regularly."
"Intelligence. She's not ignorant. There's a difference."
"True, but they are linked. One is less likely to be ignorant the more intelligent one is. Whereas, it is almost impossible to be anything other than ignorant if you lack intelligence."
"Amy doesn't lack intelligence. She has fields of expertise."
"Such as?"
"Finance, fashion, and soap operas."
"I suppose finance has its uses."
"Just because you have more money than you need, look good in anything you wear, and don't own a television doesn't give you the right to judge."
"You're a good friend."
She shook her head and stared out her window. "If I have to hear any more about *Days of Remembrance*, I'll lie down in traffic."
He laughed, surprising himself at how naturally it came. Finding a spot near the

coffee shop, he parked the car. As Sophie leaned in for a kiss, he started to speak.

"I can wait for you."

She pulled away with a frown. "What?"

"No one sells cars this early anyway. Then you don't have to hitch a ride with Amy. I can drive you to work."

"You're going to sit in the car?"

"It isn't an inconvenience. If I wasn't here, I'd be sitting at home anyway."

"Mike, if you want to join us, you can."

"I can?"

"I'm not wrestling you—"

He was already out of the car.

He hadn't been to Grounds since Sophie moved in with him.

Following her inside felt good. Like fitting into a place made especially for him. Entering the crowded lounge, he noted the table he was sitting at the first time he found the courage to talk to her. It was vacant.

Amy was waiting for them near the front counter, her red hair pulled back with a green velvet ribbon that matched her blazer. Her pupils dilated when they saw him and he smiled back. He noticed her eyes seemed inflamed.

"Morning, Amy." Sophie glanced over her shoulder. "Mike's tagging along today."

"Hi, Mike." Amy smiled and shifted on her feet.

"Hope you don't mind if I join you this morning."

"Not at all." She gave a shrug. "It's just us all the time anyway."

Sophie was already in line at the counter. Waving to the line, he invited Amy to stand in front of him. Unsure what to say, he thought of their only meeting.

"I haven't seen you since I interrupted your happy hour last December."

"No … well, I thought I'd see you on New Year's." Amy flashed a smile before dropping her eyes and clearing her throat.

"Yes." He quickly glanced at Sophie's back, but she wasn't listening. She was ordering her bagel and digging in her purse. Looking past her, he interrupted the cashier. "I'll cover that. And hers, too." He indicated Amy with a nod.

Amy ordered a tall mocha before smiling self-consciously at him as he paid.

"Thanks. You can come for coffee any time."

"Not that you need it." Sophie spoke up. "You look like you haven't slept in a week."

Amy blinked. "God, I know. They're all red aren't they?"

"Allergies?" He asked.

"I TiVoed a week's worth of shows and stayed up way late last night."

"*Days of Remembrance?*" He prompted.

Sophie eyed him as she turned from the counter with her bagel.

"Next week we know who murdered David and who the father of Jess's baby is."

"Thank God." Sophie pointed to an open table and led the way.

Amy blushed at him. "It sounds stupid, but it's really addictive."

He frowned. "How could Jessica not know who she had a child with?"

Amy's eyes lit up as they all took a seat at the table. "Jessica knows, but no else does. She's just in town to blackmail Cord Blackwell, but Cord's wife found out, and she thinks it's because Cord's the father of Jess's baby, but he really isn't."

"If Cord isn't the father, why is he being blackmailed?"

"Cord is really Jess's father, from an affair when he was a teenager. But, like now he's married and a prosecuting attorney and his whole reputation's on the line."

"Who did he have the affair with?" As he asked, Sophie shot a withering look.

"Vita Carroll, she's Jess's boyfriend's mom." Amy continued obliviously. "But get this, Vita was also married to Cord's brother David."

"The one who was murdered?"

"Exactly. So that's where the blackmail could really bite Cord's ass, because he would look like a suspect in his own brother's murder."

"So, Jessica is dating her half-brother?"

Sophie snorted.

"No." Amy shook her head vigorously. "Vita had Dylan with her current husband, Nathan Ashford. He owns Ashford Media, this big publishing company in town."

"But why would Jessica blackmail her father and not her mother? Her mother sounds like she would have more money."

"Cord made Vita put Jess up for adoption and she never forgave him, so when she got rich, she found Jess and now she's paying Jess to blackmail Cord."

Sophie waved her hands between them.

"Time out. Enough. It's on Amy's TiVo. You can watch it for yourself, on your own time. Those are fictional people in a fictional town having fictional babies. I'm a real person, in a real town, having a real cow."

Amy put her hand on Sophie's arm. "*I know*. I'm sorry! You're going to do great—and you look great, so Susan will love you."

"Susan?" He looked between the two of them.

"Sullivan." Amy's penciled brows shot up. "She's the chair of the foundation board: super pretty, ultra sharpie." She turned back to Sophie. "Don't tell Lyn I have numbers if she asks about cost overruns because I don't have any for her."

Sophie shook her head. "Weight Watchers are the only numbers she needs to worry about. I already told Lyn I'd come up with the funds if there's an overrun so she doesn't need to martyr herself digging me out of a hole."

He smiled. "Cost projections are all Sophie's been working on all week."

"Poor Sophie!" Amy grimaced. "You really got screwed with this job."

Sophie pointed at him. "It's his fault."

He felt a flash of panic. "It is?"

"You told me to take this job."

Amy shook her head. "I told her she should have an assistant, but they're too cheap to do it. It's too much for one person."

"It isn't the work, it's the micro-managing." Sophie took another bite of her bagel. "It's like they're holding me personally accountable to the donor, someone I've never even met. It's freaking me out."

"Typical. Everyone wants to be the boss but they want someone else to make the decisions. Then if it blows up, it's your fault."

"Thanks, Amy." Sophie glared and he tensed.

"No!" Amy put her hands to her mouth. "Oh God, no. I mean, that won't happen to you. You know what I mean. Like it's just the way management works."

"Well, it won't blow up." Sophie looked over her shoulder to see if their order was up. "Worst case scenario, there's an earthquake and it collapses, killing all the patients inside. Maybe they should make it the hospice wing."

Amy giggled. "At least the donor's anonymous if it does."

Getting up, he smiled down at them. "I'll get your coffee."

Feeling his hands knot into fists, he stretched his fingers as he went to the counter to pick up their lattes. When he returned with coffee, he changed the subject.

"I'm trying to do something for Sophie's birthday. Do you have any ideas?"

At the last word, he braced. He hadn't considered the possibility Sophie didn't want her co-workers to know.

"We should have a party." The lack of an exclamation from Amy seemed to indicate she already did.

"A party?" Sophie made a face.

"Sure!" Amy tasted her latte. "And Michael should be there, too."

An office party wasn't what he had in mind. He was regretting he came.

"Can't we just meet at a bar?" Sophie sighed. "Like the Spar or something?"

He looked to Amy nervously.

"It's your birthday. You can pick wherever you want."

"The Spar." Sophie grinned. "Then we can walk."

"Great. I'll handle the invites." Amy beamed at him. "You're the first to be invited."

"Maybe we should invite your parents?" He suggested indifferently.

"To the Spar? Are you kidding?" Sophie laughed. "Michael, this is a bar that's going to be full of co-workers, beer, and BS. I'm thinking no."

Co-workers.

It wouldn't matter if he avoided Sophie's office if it came to him.

He floated. "Well … if that's the case, you probably won't want any evil management there, will you?"

Sophie nodded at Amy. "I don't want Lyn there."

Amy pursed her lips. "But it doesn't hurt to send her an e-vite. She probably won't come, anyway. It's just a gesture thing. You know she's more likely to make a stink over not being invited than blowing off an invitation if she gets one."

"She probably won't stick around, anyway." Sophie shrugged. "It's your call. If you want to invite her, whatever."

He remembered Evelyn Whittier. It had been three months since he'd seen her at the hospital administrator's office. Hopefully she had forgotten him. Hopefully she would blow it off.

Compared to morning coffee, shopping for a car was painless. After dropping Sophie at her office, he was the first person in the door when the dealership opened. He knew what he wanted, and they had it. He knew what they wanted, and he had that. It was simply a matter of paperwork and data transfer. Tedious at worst. Even then, the satisfaction of sitting behind the wheel of a new BMW and feeling the effortless acceleration of 360 Hp took the edge off of his week.

Unfortunately, the stress of trying to meet her parents had been replaced by the stress of attending a party where he could be spotted. Outed. Exposed. If that happened, the odds of proposing at all, let alone before her cousin's wedding, would be slim. After hearing firsthand what she was going through at work, she could never know he was responsible for it. She would kill him, whether that was possible or not.

With his car bought and paid for, it would be held for him until he could come back for it later. He could have arranged to take Sophie's car to her work and have them shuttle him back, but he didn't have anywhere to go and he wanted to pick up Sophie from work anyway. He just wished it could be in his new car. Then opportunity rang. At first he thought he was hearing someone else's cell phone, but he was alone in Sophie's car. Craning to look over the passenger seat, he spotted Sophie's cell on the floor. It must have fallen out of her purse. Reaching down, he picked it up and looked at the ID.

It was her father.

Yes, this wasn't his phone. Yes, Sophie didn't want him to talk to her parents. Yes, he was grasping at disingenuous rationalization. But what if it was an emergency? If indeed something terrible and unforeseen had happened to Sophie's father, shouldn't all other considerations be set aside?

Although he never used a phone, this time he did. It felt like a formality he had to observe, even if no one would ever know. Awkwardly flipping open the device, he held it to his ear.

"Hello?"

"I'm sorry ... I think I have a wrong number." The man on the phone sounded slightly confused and apologetic.

"Where you trying to reach Sophie?"

"Yes. Who am I speaking with?"

"I'm Michael, a friend of Sophie's. She accidentally left her phone behind."

"Oh." There was a pause and some frustration. "Well, this is her father. I need to reach her ... I'd call her at work but I don't have that number. Is it on her phone?"

"I'm not sure which number it is." He was beyond redemption. "I'm driving right now, so I'm not in a position to look it up. Is there a message you want me to give her if she calls?"

"No, it probably won't matter by then. My car needed to go to the shop and I needed to get a ride back into town."

"I can give you a ride."

"Oh, no. I don't want to trouble you—"

"No, it would be no trouble. I'm using Sophie's car right now. She let me borrow it so I could run an errand and I was supposed to pick her up after work. It would

246 | LISA MOWAT

be no trouble for me to pick you up seeing as how she couldn't anyway."

"Well, I don't want you to go out of your way ..."

"No, please, allow me. It would give me an opportunity to do a favor for Sophie, as well as you."

There was a pause. "I'm at the Toyota repair on River Road. It's near Puyallup. If that's too far ..."

"Not at all. I'm in Fife right now. I'll see you in ten minutes."

"Thank you ... What was your name again?"

"Michael."

"Thank you, Michael."

"Not at all, Mr. Davids."

When he arrived at the Toyota dealership, he spotted her father right away: tall and thin with graying blond hair and a permanent squint. Recognizing Sophie's car, her father stepped forward to meet it, opening the passenger door and gracefully folding into the front seat in one fluid motion while simultaneously extending a hand to him. When he took it, it felt like ice—a family trait apparently.

"Thanks again, Michael." Her father fastened the seat belt and sat a bit to the side to get a better look at the driver. He could feel himself being scrutinized. Another family trait.

"I'm happy to do it."

"I wish I didn't have to inconvenience anyone, but car troubles aren't always so easy to foresee."

"Yes." He glanced sideways. "I know."

"Having car issues yourself, I take it?"

"Sophie let me borrow hers so I could buy one today."

"Did you?"

"Yes."

"What'd you get?"

"A BMW."

"Ah." Her father sighed. "I liked German cars when I was young."

"What are you driving now?"

"A Prius."

He smiled. "You've reformed."

Her father shrugged. "I figure my generation has done enough damage."

There was a sincerity of feeling in this last statement he didn't expect.

"Sophie would probably prefer it if I drove a Prius."

Her father laughed. "She won't even drive one. I wouldn't take it to heart."

Candor. Sophie liked candor.

"So ..." Her father continued. "How do you know Sophie?"

"We met at a coffee shop when she was in school. We've been friends since."

"How long have you been living together?"

Now he knew why Sophie kept her boyfriends a safe distance from her parents.

Without hesitation, he answered. "Almost three months now."

He could see Sophie's father nod without looking at him.

"I had my suspicions when she didn't say much about where she was moving to."

For a while they said nothing.

He focused on the road, making sure not to grip the wheel too tightly.

Her father coughed lightly. "Where do you live?"

"In Tacoma. I have a house at the end of North Prospect."

"We live on North Steele. We're practically neighbors."

There was an awkward silence.

"Sir, I'm sorry that you didn't know. I would have ... I didn't ... "

He didn't know how to finish the sentence he'd started.

"Michael, if I haven't heard of you before this, it's because Sophie wanted it that way. I've been married to her mother for thirty-two years. They're women who know what the plan is and how it's going to happen. You just have to decide if you're able to let go."

"Yes, sir."

"Call me Peter. I might feel like my father, but I don't need to be reminded."

With a smile, he nodded. "Peter, thank you."

"So are you?"

"Am I what?"

"Able to let go?"

"I think so."

"Even though picking me up probably isn't something Sophie had in mind?"

He could say nothing.

"Don't worry that this reflects poorly on you. Quite the opposite. As a father, I appreciate young men who want me to know they exist and what their intentions are."

"Thank you for saying so."

"Don't thank me too much. If you can handle Sophie, I'll thank you for it."

This made them both smile.

"Where did you go to school?"

"U.W."

"Liberal Arts?"

"Yes."

"What do you do now?"

"I'm a consultant."

"On what?"

"Antiquities."

"How did you end up there?"

"I like old things."

"And German cars."

"Yes." He smiled.

"Are you local?"

"I grew up in California."

248 | LISA MOWAT

"You're parents still there?"

"They're deceased."

"I'm sorry to hear that."

"My mother died when I was ten, and my father died four years ago."

As usual, people didn't know what to say after this. He preferred claiming deceased parents for this very reason. After a few minutes, Peter changed the subject.

"Sophie must think you're special."

"Really? What makes you think so?"

"So far I can't see anything about you that would warrant hiding you for three months unless she's feeling differently about you. You might be the one."

"I would like that."

Peter looked at him with a smirk. "You sure?"

His first feeling was defensive. He expected her father to be jealously protective not warn against her.

"I am."

"Well, it's never too late to change your mind."

Maybe this was some kind of reverse psychology.

"That's not going to happen."

"That's really up to Sophie, isn't it?"

He cleared his throat. "Yes."

"That's why you won't tell her you picked me up."

He said nothing to this.

"At least, I won't say anything if you don't." Peter added.

Slowly, he nodded. "Okay."

"See?" Peter grinned. "You just let go. It's easy."

Yes, he thought to himself. *Easy*.

~

1199 BC   The transition took all of the day and most of the next night. The change in gender, being a matter of rearrangement rather than regeneration, consumed little and allowed me to emerge at dawn on the following day without fatigue. The table awaited but was bare. Clothes were folded on the chair. They were not his. They were clean, but the scent on them was of a younger man. The sandals had been worn, but not for some time and were stiff to the touch. I was binding them when he entered the tent. His expression was wary until his eyes met mine.

Their color brought a smile to his face.

"Still bluer than lapis."

"Thank you for the clothes."

His smile widened. "You still speak with the breath of Aeolus."

I glanced at the empty table. "Shall I sing for my supper?"

With a laugh, he stepped from the tent and called to his quartermaster. He returned with a stool and planted himself across the table from me.

"You missed the last two meals set out for you. I feared you would never emerge."

"Did you look in the crypt?"

"Not for all the gold of Pharaoh."

I nodded. "You must never look inside when I am in it. It could be deadly."

"But not for you."

"It is what I am made of."

"Yet you grow weak with hunger."

"As a foreigner in a foreign land … Within this body, I am far from home."

"Then I will be your guide."

At this, I laughed. "I have spent more years a foreigner than your people have lived."

He only shrugged. "Then you will be mine."

"Are you lost already?"

"No. We will cross the Sukkot today. Then I will be lost."

"It is no Nile, with no fair valley beyond it."

"Canaan is fair."

"With Canaanites."

"But no friends of Pharaoh. They do not worship his gods there."

"If one walks long enough, there will always be gods."

"That is the problem. They are everywhere. There are too many."

His quartermaster entered with a tray of bread and fruit, a skin of wine over his shoulder.

"They are as men have made them." I answered.

Tearing off a piece of bread, I briefly held it before me and bowed my head to him before eating.

He nodded back to me. "Why make them at all?"

To this I only shook my head. "I am not a man."

[Spharic. Entry translated from *Kor Dai Maihael*. Mund Dai. d. 755 BC]

~

[Daniel Goodhew with daughters, Molly and Maeve, 1943]

2003 Sitting in his car outside the police precinct, he spends two hours reviewing footage as Anthony plays it back for him. Most of it is of little use. Sophie had done exactly as Anthony described. She left one end of the market and worked her way towards Grounds for Coffee, only to disappear just past the bank. He doesn't recognize anyone in the crowd that day, though it doesn't eliminate the possibility of someone Sophie knew who neither he nor Anthony recognize.

I hate to say it, but that's all there is.

He is silent.

Mike, are you there?

He can hear the stress in Anthony's voice coming through the cell phone.

"Yes, sorry. Do you have any footage of me after Sophie disappeared?"

Anthony checks the time indexes of the footage.

Not for the jewelry store, but I think I do for the bank. Let me forward this …

This is good. The bank footage has the best resolution anyway.

"There." He cues Anthony to stop. "Run it back."

He ignores his image as it enters the lobby from the sidewalk and blurs past the camera. His focus is on the bystanders at the door. She catches his eye.

"Back six seconds."

Anthony keys the image back frame by frame.

Who is she?

"I don't know her last name."

What's her first?

"Marta."

Do you know where she is?

"I have a good idea. She owns a shop on twenty-first called Dragonfly."

Need help finding her?

"No. Thanks."

You sure?

"I'm sure. She's been wanting to meet me, anyway."

It is hard to leave Anthony out of the loop. Anthony is more than the only help he has, but the only help he has no doubts about. With luck, after rocking ECCO's boat there is some hope of aid breaking loose. And then, they won't be helping him for Sophie's sake. With an ally of Anthony's integrity and the strength of his own kind, he might stand a chance. As it is, drawing Anthony any closer will likely get the man killed and nothing more.

It is nearing two in the afternoon when he arrives at Dragonfly. The little shop sits at one end of a small bridge on 21st Street. The front door is at street level with a lower story below grade to the bridge. He knows when he parks the car no one is inside. There was light rain earlier, and the sun has returned, leaving the pavement blinding as he crosses the street. Even with sunglasses, he can't read the sign on the door until he is within reach of it.

According to the sign, she should be open for business. When he tries the door, it is locked. Going to the side of the building, he takes the stairs down to the lower story and tries the back. Forcing it easily, he finds himself in a concrete storage room stacked with crates of Asian pottery, boxes of teas, incense, and bolts of embroidered silks. Removing his sunglasses, his eyes cut through the inventory to locate the door leading upstairs.

Lightly climbing the stairs to the shop, he finds nothing unusual at first sight. Behind the front counter, there is a small office in a back room. Turning on her computer, he sits at the desk and accesses her files only to find the usual business records. He remembers her phone number and address. That will be his next stop. Sitting back in the chair, he sighs. Why would she want to meet him so badly when Sophie was here but make herself scarce now? The blinking light on her office phone catches his attention. He plays back her voice-mail. She has three messages. Two are clients scheduling appointments. One is from Violet Farrell reminding Marta she was supposed to join her for tea yesterday. He wonders if she made it.

Deciding to walk from Dragonfly to the Farrell house feels eerie. Less than forty-eight hours ago, these streets were home. Now it is like visiting a dream. At the top of Prospect, he looks down the street to their house, just visible beneath the row of cedars. He wonders if he should go back, if anything there has changed since he left it. He knows it is the comfort he seeks more than anything else.

The Farrell house is where he needs to go.

Walking into the front yard, he ignores the maze of boxwoods that zigzag to the front door. Stepping around them, he cuts up the steps to the porch. He is no hobgoblin to be deterred with creative landscaping. He rings the doorbell without touching it. No one answers, but he knows Violet is inside. Putting his hand on the doorknob, he wonders if he will have to force it, but it turns easily. Letting the door swing open, he stands at the threshold and peeks in. No one is immediately visible. He steps inside and crosses the foyer, letting his vision scout the rooms.

He spots the glow of her. She is at the rear of the house in the library, sitting in a rocking chair by a vacant fireplace.

Passing through the great room of the house, his eyes dart to a large vase of white roses on a pedestal table. Next to the vase is a framed picture. He freezes. Soundlessly, he crosses the room. Lifting the picture in both hands, he raises it to his face. It is a sepia print. A young man with dimples and dangling blond waves smiles into the sun with a small girl on his lap. Daniel is very young, the girl very familiar. Anne. He only saw Anne when she was twenty, but it is her. The jet black hair, the dark eyes. She looks like Violet.

His eyes drift to Daniel, looking very different from that last night. Once, there was a man who had been young and happy. The eyes in the photo are gray, but he knows they were green.

"You get lost?"

The question echoes from the library through closed doors. Replacing the photograph, he goes to the library doors and pushes them open.

"If Curtis saw you standing in his library, he'd have had a stroke."

Violet is sitting in repose. Her head relaxes against the back of a rocker as she gently pushes the chair with the heels of her feet.

"That happened to me when I saw him in mine."

"He always swore no vampire would make it past the front door."

"That may be. I'm not a vampire."

"I never thought you were. No such thing—any idiot knows that. But you're not Michael Jr. either, are you?"

"No."

"Thanks for not insulting my intelligence a second time."

"You were expecting me?"

"The next person who came through the door."

"Have you had many visitors?"

"So far only Marta and your wife for tea. But after you all disappeared, I guessed someone would come looking for somebody."

"Who all disappeared?"

"You, your wife. Marta, too. She was supposed to join me for tea Thursday and didn't show. I told the policeman that."

"The police were here?"

"A young officer came here and asked some questions."

"Officer Navarre?"

"Navarre? Maybe. He had green eyes."

"What did he ask you?"

"Asked if I'd seen anything suspicious in the neighborhood."

"Have you?"

"Besides you, no."

"Is that what you told him?"

"I told him I saw the police go to your house Thursday afternoon. He told me that was him looking for you. So I told you you must have a good hiding spot because I saw you leave Thursday night with a rough looker in a moving truck. Did you find your wife?"

"No. Have you seen Marta?"

"You're looking for Marta?"

"Yes. I have to find her."

"Why? You think she knows where your wife is?"

"I know it."

He steps forward and sees her stiffen in her chair.

"Violet, I won't hurt you. I just need information."

She eyes him. "Does your wife know about you?"

"Yes."

"And she married you anyway?"

"She loves me."

"So did Anne."

"I never loved her."

"Liar!"

"I'm not. I wasn't here when Anne got pregnant."

"She told me it was you."

"It wasn't me ..." His tongue trips over the words. "It was my brother."

"Your brother?"

"We're twins. Anne thought it was me."

She lets out a laugh. "Ha! Twins! That's good."

"It's the truth. When I came back, I had no idea Anne was ever pregnant. Daniel never told me. He only said Anne moved away."

"To be raised by your mother!" Her finger points at him.

"Sarah isn't my mother."

At this, Violet sits up in her chair.

"Who is she then?"

"She's like me. She knew who the father was. Daniel knew, too. They both kept it a secret from me."

"Why would they do that?"

His throat tightens. "Because if I'd known, I would have killed it."

Glaring at him, her lips disappear, but she says nothing.

He continues, "Sarah didn't tell me because she wanted to keep the baby for herself. Daniel didn't tell me because ..." Momentarily he holds his breath. "He wanted to protect his grandchild."

He sees her hands grip the arms of the rocker.

"How long have you known?" She whispers.

"Five minutes. I saw the picture in the other room. I knew it was taken before Daniel's girls were born. It all began to make sense. He warned me Anne was falling in love with me, but he would never send her away, so he sent me away instead. That's why I was gone. I admit I was hurt. Now I realize he was protecting his daughter."

Knotting her fingers on her lap, she looks away to the empty fireplace. "I should have divorced Curtis when I got pregnant."

Carefully, he moves to the leather armchair across from her and sits down. "Why didn't you?"

"I was afraid of him. I knew if he found out, he'd kill me. Probably kill Danny, too. Even if we'd run off he would have hunted us. So I let Danny go. Let him go to Boston and marry Florence. If his girls had lived, I probably never would have told him about Anne. I didn't want him to fight over us—get himself killed. Course, he stayed. As soon as he knew the truth, he wouldn't leave ..." She puts a hand to her face. "Curtis killed him anyway."

"It was my fault Curtis came that night, not yours."

She drops her hand, gritting her teeth. "Why wasn't it you then?"

"I wish it had been." He looks into her eyes and fears the dark.

"Then why don't you die now and get it over with?"

"Because I can't."

"So you'll kill Marta instead?" She hisses.

"I don't want to kill anybody. All I want is my wife."

She glares defiantly, saying nothing.

"Please." His mind blindly feels for hers. He presses. "When did she first come to you?"

She hesitates. "Three years ago."

"Did she tell you she was Anne's daughter?"

Violet drops her glare to her lap and nods.

"Did she say why she came?"

"To stop you."

"From doing what?"

"From making another nightmare!" Violet explodes. "From making another cursed creature like her! Do you know what that child has gone through? She's so terrified of herself she locks herself away at night when she sleeps."

"She isn't mine." He pleads. "I can't make children."

"But you're still trying. You want them."

"Even if I could, I wouldn't. We aren't meant to. There's a reason for that."

"Then how can your brother be the father? How could he make one?"

He takes a breath and stares at the ring rug on the floor.

"I don't know ... I don't know if he even knows he succeeded. If he had, he would have hunted Marta down to raise her himself."

"*But why Anne?* Why my little girl?!"

Keeping his gaze on the rug, he searches the pattern but doesn't see it.

"He went after Anne to get to you, didn't he?" Violet's voice is a dry rasp.

He looks her in the eyes. "I'm sorry, Violet. Please believe me. I came for Daniel. After his girls died, I didn't want him to be alone—I never meant for any harm to come to you or Anne." He stares back at the rug. "He must have come after Daniel sent me away. He knew I was gone. Someone told him."

"Why does he hate you?"

"Samael hates everything." He whispers.

"Samael?"

His eyes stay on the floor. "My brother."

"Sweet Jesus." Violet breathes.

When he looks up, her eyes are wide.

"What?"

There is silence. He cannot read her thoughts, only feels a shift in her. Gradually, she seems to come back. Her eyes focus and she stands straight.

"Follow me."

With a faint hobble, she leaves the library by another door, disappearing into darkness. Quickly at her heels, he follows her into a back hall and down narrow stairs to the cellar. There is no light. She doesn't need it. Taking a key from her apron, she opens a door at the bottom of the stairs. Pulling a chain as she enters, a web covered lamp flickers, revealing a dim cavern. The floor is cobbled, the walls are rough-hewn granite layered in dust. There is a smell of mold and decaying timber. Stained crates fill the corners and the remains of cardboard boxes litter the floor.

He can see through the interior walls to a furnace room on one side. He makes out the faint network of gas and water pipes in the ceiling. Electrical wires lead to a knob and tube fuse box on the interior wall. Beyond the exterior walls is rubble and clay. Directly ahead of them is a door. He can't see through it. It is held shut on the outside by an iron cane bolt bracketed to the door and anchored in a hole between the cobbles. Grabbing hold of the bolt, Violet pulls it out of the floor and drags the door open with a slow heave. As it swings wide, he sees that it is steel layered over iron at least six inches thick. The interior is lined with lead, scarred with molten gouges.

"If you want to see Marta, you'll have to wait in here."

He eyes the dungeon and then looks at Violet in disbelief.

"She'll run if she sees you. She guessed you might come here looking for her, but I was supposed to tell you she was gone and I had no idea where. If you wait anywhere else, she'll know you're here. This is where she was holed up the day you came with your dog. It's the only place you can hide."

"If she's returning, I could come back later."

"I don't know when she will, and I won't be able to call you when she's does."

"Then how do you know she'll return at all?"

"She's been sleeping here. It's the only place she feels safe."

Looking into the dark, he swallows. "What room is this?"

"Curtis built it as a bomb shelter, but it turned into his fire safe. It's still full of his junk."

His throat clears. "How long before she returns, do you think?"

"Could be two minutes, could be two days."

"I don't have two days."

"Do you want to talk to her or not?"

"Violet, having me here could endanger you."

"I lived in this house over fifty-five years with Curtis Farrell, and every day since I've waited for death to join me for tea. None of your kind scares me."

He hesitates at the threshold. It's a trap. It's a test. He looks back at Violet, her eyes steadily pushing. He knows he is being judged. If Marta really does have Sophie, this is as close as he will come to finding out. The prospects couldn't be bleaker.

Still, not so bad when compared to being trapped in a crypt at Sam's discretion or subjecting himself to Metatron.

"I can only wait a day."

"I'll let you out if she doesn't come."

Taking a breath of the slightly less musty air outside, he enters the dark.

He turns to see Violet's silhouette reaching for the door.

"When she comes, you'd better be ready." Her voice echoes off the walls.

"Does the door have to be bolted?"

"It's always bolted. It's bolted when she leaves and it's bolted when she stays."

"You'll let me out?"

She smiles. "I promise."

He tries to imagine there is a ring of sincerity in her voice, but his hearing leaves little to the imagination. The rectangle of light shrinks around him. A moment later, there is the muffled scrape of the cane bolt falling into place. Her footsteps recede. He hears the chain on the lamp and the hinges of the basement door.

Only his eyes light the room as he observes the trunks and pallets of artifacts he's been added to. They have been scattered about the chamber. Some are broken open; most are badly burned. The riveted walls are warped from heat exposure. They are impenetrable to his vision but not his hearing. Violet turns the television to *People's Court*. In the background there is the hum of the outside world—not as clear, but there. With fine tuning, he should be able to make out the voices of visitors to the house, maybe even make a call. Examining the door, he traces the gouges with his fingers. The door is formidable but not indestructible. The room will not be able to hold him. His body, however, is another story. It will have to last. For how long, he doesn't know.

Sitting on a crate, he reviews his conversation with Violet. His annoyance with her that she doubts him. His annoyance at himself that he didn't figure out Anne was Daniel's child sooner. Not that it would have explained her disappearance or pregnancy with Marta. A hybrid child. Half human, half singular. Now he knew why he hadn't been able to read what had been stalking him. He had been so close when Marta ran into Sophie at the grocery store. But he had been so tired. He had been tired for three years, trying to be alive, human, when he wasn't.

Had Marta really come to stop him from making a child? It would explain the attack on Sophie, but why leave Sophie alive? Had Marta burned Sam on Anderson Island? If so, why hadn't she attacked him with the same ferocity? If she believed he was her father, why hide from him? What did she want?

One thing was certain: Sarah knew about Marta all along. She knew Anne was pregnant and knew who the father was. Daniel knew enough to be frightened. Did Sarah tell Daniel he would kill Anne and her unborn child? She must have told Daniel she could keep Anne and Marta safe; offered to take care of everything on the condition Daniel never told.

He would have done the same, but Daniel didn't trust him. For twenty years after Anne's disappearance, Daniel thought him ruthless enough to hunt down Anne and her baby. It sickened him. Had Daniel spent those years living in fear, only to die protecting him from Curtis?

Curtis.

Crowbars aside, he suddenly felt a strange bond with the man. The truth of Anne's parentage had eluded them both. Certainly if Curtis had ever known the truth, Daniel would have been murdered years earlier. In the end, Curtis was un-wittingly vindicated when Daniel was bludgeoned.

He looks around himself. Curtis finally added him to a collection, albeit thirty years later and temporarily. Hopefully temporarily.

He turns his attention to a box at his feet and picks it up. It is wooden and badly

258 | LISA MOWAT

scorched. Turning it over in his hands, he sees there is no apparent means of opening it. It is a puzzle box. Examining its interior structure, the series of interlocking
pieces holding it together solve the problem. There is no point in opening it; it is
empty. Placing it back on the floor, he rises and steps through the debris. He rights
a toppled bookshelf and examines the pile of broken pottery shards underneath.
Burial pots. Native American. Stolen, no doubt.

Working his way farther into the room, he finds three intact crates. Two contain
more pottery. Amphora. One is filled with human bones. A pallet still bound with
straps and the burnt remains of a tarp. Underneath are slabs of stone. Mayan stelae.
Behind the stelae, another crate survived Marta's tantrums. It is half filled with
bottles of whiskey. Next to it is a small chest containing a set of jasper chalices.
Unnervingly, a box of damp dynamite is only feet away, its contents long since
degraded to relative inertia.

Buried at the back of the vault is a blackened wardrobe. Pushing the crates out of
the way, he pries the stuck doors and finds a rusted but excellently crafted suit of
armor. Several broadswords lean against a shield in the corner. Picking one up, he
regards the blade. Forgetting is impossible. Even without cutting his flesh they still
hurt. Replacing the sword, he closes the wardrobe when a footlocker in the corner
of the room catches his eye. It is padlocked, but Curtis is dead and he is bored.

Grasping the lock in his fist, he feels it give between his fingers. Flipping the latch,
he lifts the lid. The light of his eyes glints off of a neat stack of gold bars inside. They
are thinly cast and marked with a formée cross. Richelieu's reserve. Curtis was a
naughty boy. There are leather sacks, heavy with coins. A jade jewelry box. Inside
are diamond broaches, filigree hair pins, emerald and ruby bracelets, a sapphire
necklace. He drapes the necklace on the back of his hand and imagines it on Sophie's
neck. Returning it to the box, he notices what at first glance is a hat pin.

It can't be.

Picking it out of the jewels, he holds it to his eyes. It is black with oxidation.
Spherical at one end, pulled thin like an elongated teardrop, it extends eight inches
and comes to a needle point. He burnishes it on his sleeve, feeling the gritty, serpentine texture of it with his fingers. Testing it, he runs his current through it. Blue ripples run off the ends of his fingers into the object. It glows brilliantly. Lachrymose
argentite. Silver that has never known fire. A tear made by one of his own, sculpted
into the only weapon they fear. An ops. Made when and by whom it doesn't say.

But here? In Curtis' basement?

He should watch *Antiques Roadshow* more often.

Letting the light of it die, he closes the footlocker and sits on the lid. Staring at the ops
in his hands, he thinks he has never known luck. It is rare. It can only be used once.
Wisely.

1199 BC   Putting my shoulder to my crypt, I pushed alongside two others. Together we slid it into the wagon and I stepped back to watch the men secure it with ropes.

"This was not part of our agreement."

His voice turned my head.

"Agreement?"

"I will serve you, not watch you work."

He approached with two horses. One of the finest I had seen was his. The other halted at the sight of me. The bandit's horse. Had I known, I would have taken another that night if only to save myself the aggravation.

"I do not think he likes you."

"He remembers."

He handed me the reins. "That is good. It means he won't forget you."

Looking around, I was conscious of being observed. "That is my problem."

Mounting his horse, he dismissed my distraction with a laugh. "Do not worry what others think. If all else was different, they would think the same."

As I mounted my own, it trembled under me with a low grumble. The sun had yet to clear the horizon and I suspected the course of it across the sky would take longer than I wished. I pulled up my cloak to fend off the chill eyes that followed me as I followed their leader. Riding away from the column of wagons, we surveyed the length of it. A formidable line of armed men flanked it on both sides. For all his disgust with Pharaoh, he appeared to have taken the might of Egypt with him. The nature of this legion he had never discussed when courting me.

"Are they yours?"

"They are hungry."

"They expect much of you."

"They know me." As he spoke, each soldier we passed hailed him.

"They respect you."

"Better than Ramesses."

He held his hand up to each. Children ran to the edge of the caravan to wave back. Turning his horse, he led us quickly alongside the column, speeding to a gentle gallop. Even with my sight, the head of the line, like the tail of it, seemed infinite. How he was able to find his way back to his tent I was unsure.

Out of the shadows, two men approached from a stone field to our right. Their cloaks pulled from shorn heads identified them as Egyptian. Scouts. A settlement some seven metes distant. Not a threat, but not to be disturbed. He wanted to cross the Sukkot unmolested, skirt the Negev without notice. Yet the banner at the head of the line gave notice enough. He was a son of Egypt. Conflict in Canaan was inevitable.

Ahead, I saw his oldest son, Ashebu, a young man of sixteen. Of all these people, Ashebu had seen me most closely when I was a woman and searched me now, stopping at my eyes. I froze.

"This is Khepera." It took a moment to realize the general was referring to me.

"Son of a fallen friend. He joins us as an honored guest."

He spoke to his son as lord. The boy bowed and all within hearing followed. His order had been given. There would be no questions, no challenge, no choice—for any of us. We rode on ahead of the banner, to the front of the line, the ground before us unspoiled.

I did not look back, but once beyond hearing, I could not stay silent.

"Khepera?"

"You do not like it? It is a good name for you. The god of transformation."

"I am no god."

"You are my guide."

"If I am your guide, then I advise you reconsider the path you are on."

"There is only one."

"It may be bloody."

"There may be blood."

"I cannot fight for you."

"I did not expect it."

"I can only trouble you."

Keeping his eyes on the horizon, I could see him smiling as the dawn broke.

"All life is trouble. Only a fool believes he can choose to avoid it."

[Spharic. Entry translated from *Kor Dai Maihael*. Mund Dai. d. 755 BC]

2000   The Spar was one of her favorites. It was a traditional brick and mortar public house that offered local beer and homemade potato chips. He had never set foot inside it before, though Daniel had often.

"You've lived here for fifty years and you've never gone to the Spar?"

As they walked down the North Slope from their house, he wondered why he had never been. It was close. He liked to eat. But there were people there. People socializing. Not like they did at Grounds for Coffee. He felt himself tense.

"I never had a reason to."

"Reason hardly enters into it. You don't find yourself in a pub because you think it's reasonable. You go because you'd rather be there than anyplace else."

"Then I suppose I've never wanted to be anyplace other than where you are."

She took his hand.

"That's very sweet to say. Very sad, but very sweet."

"Do you think there will be many people there?"

"It's a Wednesday night, they shouldn't be busy."

"I mean, do you think many of your co-workers will come?"

"It's hard to say. I don't know that many people at work. Maybe twenty at most."

Twenty. He couldn't think of twenty humans he had known well enough to invite to a party over the last twenty thousand years.

"Are you nervous?" Sophie was watching him.

"No."

"You seem a little more uptight than usual."

He wondered what was usual.

"Uptight? Do I generally seem that way?"

"Not in a bad way."

"There's a good way?"

"You're generally intense."

"I've tried to stop staring."

"I can tell. It's good."

"Is there anything else I should do?"

"You might smile more."

Smile more.

"Although ..." She added. "You want to be careful who you smile at. And when. Some people get uncomfortable when you smile too much. And some women will think you're hitting on them. Well, most women will think that. They'll want to think that, anyway."

"So I shouldn't smile at women?"

"No, you should. If you don't, they'll think you're arrogant or a psycho. I thought you were a psycho at first. You did that thing where you looked like you were looking through me instead of at me. Pretty creepy. You still do it sometimes."

Sometimes he was looking through her, though.

"Do I smile too much at women now?"

"You know, forget what I just said. Just do what you've been doing."

He nodded. Of course he couldn't forget what she'd said, but he was having trouble remembering what he'd been doing. His smiles had always been calculated, which was why he didn't smile very often. As for looking through people, he never thought about what he looked like when he did that. He'd never seen himself doing it before. He would avoid it from now on.

This being his first birthday celebration, he wasn't sure what he could expect to see. This wasn't a child's birthday, obviously. It was in a pub, so there would be alcohol. But there might be a cake. One could always hope. The last thing he expected to see when they arrived at the Spar was Sophie's father.

Clearly it wasn't what Sophie expected, either.

Peter was sitting at the bar next to a red-faced man with curly hair.

"Dad." Sophie didn't sound excited. "Hey, Wayne."

The man sitting next to her father gave a wave. "Well, hello!"

Her father smiled quietly and looked expectant. "Hi there. Wayne and I were having a boy's night out."

He smiled at her father and Wayne, but stood back and waited.

"I'm here with the office gang for my birthday." Sophie finally glanced in his direction. "This is Michael."

He tried not to notice the lack of enthusiasm in her voice.

"Hello." He held out his hand to her father, who shook it.

"I'm Peter; this is my friend Wayne."

He shook Wayne's hand, glancing back to Sophie, who seemed to ignore him.

"So is Mom having a girl's night out?"

"The ladies are at a gardener's cooking class." Wayne announced. "Deb saw it in the paper—some organic grow it, reap it, cook it affair."

Sophie frowned. "Mom doesn't really grow vegetables anymore, does she?"

Peter shrugged. "I don't really drink beer anymore, either. So, Michael?" He swiveled on his stool to face him. "Do you work with Sophie?"

"No, I'm—" *Boyfriend* nearly slipped his lips. "We met in a coffee shop."

"We've been dating for a few months." Sophie was very matter-of-fact.

"Oh." Peter nodded. "Do you work in town?"

"Yes." He didn't feel like saying more.

"What do you do?"

"I'm a consultant."

"Really?" Wayne perked up. "I do consulting. What field?"

"Antiques and restoration."

"Well." Wayne sniffed. "I suppose there's a consultant for everything nowadays."

Sophie grinned. "If you'll excuse me, I need a beverage consultant."

She leaned into her father and he gave her a kiss. "Happy birthday, Sophie. Be good. Nice to meet you, Michael."

Peter winked at him behind her back.

They headed to the back of the bar where some tables were reserved. A small gathering of people were already there. They recognized Sophie right away. Two women immediately rose from the table to give her a hug.

Amy seemed to come from nowhere. "Hi, Mike! Glad you could make it."

"Hello, Amy." He smiled.

She frowned. "What's wrong?"

Sophie was right, Amy wasn't ignorant.

He found the rest of the evening was better.

It had to be.

Dan Fogel from human resources and Phil Stuart, a grant writer who used to work with Sophie, discovered a mutual love for amateur astronomy and spent the rest of the evening comparing notes. This was a relief for an entity worried about conversation topics, particularly religion and politics. Or worse yet, sports. Instead, he was pleasantly surprised to find himself in a discussion on a topic he was more knowledgeable about.

Even Dan and Phil seemed surprised they shared a passion for star gazing when they couldn't have appeared more different. Dan was tall and thin in suit and tie, while Phil was stout, bearded, and wore a tieless flannel shirt.

Dan resumed his seat after bringing another pitcher of ale to the table.

"Did you get the latest Hubble images off the NASA site?"

Phil sat back and rubbed his beard. "Hubble's all right."

"All right? It's revolutionary." Dan poured a pint, then looked up. "Need a refill, Mike?"

He nodded. "Yes, please."

"Yeah ..." Phil mused. "But it's not the same as actually seeing something yourself. I remember the first time I took Dad's binoculars and looked at the moon. I started finding planets. It just blew my mind that what I was looking at was really there. You can have a teacher tell you Jupiter is real, you can even see pictures of Jupiter, but when you really see it, even if it's a speck, it's real."

He knit his brows. "Why would you doubt it really existed otherwise?"

"Well, it's not that I doubted it existed. It's just seeing it in real time with your own eyes makes it tangible."

"Like seeing the sun again after seven months of rain." Dan widened his eyes.

"That's what I hate most about this state." Phil shook his head. "I loved living in Arizona. You could see every star in the sky. Didn't have to follow the weather reports and worry you'd miss something. If I could get the political climate of Washington with the climate of Arizona, I'd be in heaven."

Dan nodded in agreement with Phil. "I don't think I remember what the night sky looks like most of the year."

"We've had many clear nights this winter." He contradicted.

Dan shrugged. "If you have time to drop everything to take advantage of it."

"And you don't mind freezing your ass off." Phil smirked.

"True ..." He agreed. He was being pulled out of the trunk of a car at the time.

"What's the brightest star right now? Castor?" Dan asked.

264 | LISA MOWAT

Phil frowned. "Pollux, I think."

He shook his head and then dropped his eyes. "Arcturus."

Dan squinted. "I know Pollux is in Gemini. Which one is Arcturus in again?"

"Bootes." Phil snapped, pointing over at him as he nodded.

"I thought Castor was the brighter twin in Gemini?" Dan's eyes closed, trying to remember.

Phil shook his head. "Pollux is brighter."

"Why are they considered twins?" He suddenly asked.

"Blame the Greeks." Phil grinned at Dan.

Their casual acceptance of Gemini was confusing.

"But why are they named Geminorum Alpha and Geminorum Eta when they are nothing alike? Pollux is a semi-regular variable star and Castor isn't a single star at all, but a conjunction of stars. They aren't twins."

"It just stuck." Dan shrugged. "It's sentimental. The names of constellations, planets, the Milky Way, they're … well, like family. Like when they reclassified Pluto, people lost it. It was like Pluto was a family member who just got disinherited. They don't want it to be anything else."

"Even if they're wrong?"

"That's the thing. They don't think they're wrong."

He had no response for this, only stared at his beer.

"You know we should go out some night. There are some spots in Point Defiance where there isn't too much pollution." Phil glanced between him and Dan to gauge their response.

"I'm not dragging my Schmidt out there, but it sounds fun." Dan looked at him.

He smiled freely. "Why not?"

"What scope do you use?" Phil finished his ale.

"I'll bring my binoculars." He knew Sophie had a pair. "And blankets."

Phil poured himself another pint from the pitcher on the table.

"You sound like you've got the sky memorized and you don't own a telescope?"

"That's why I memorized it."

Dan and Phil laughed, and he laughed a little himself. He looked in Sophie's direction and saw her watching him at the other end of the table. She winked.

It was nearly eleven when the party broke up. People stood on the sidewalk and continued to talk, some about meetings the next day, some finishing conversations they'd brought out with them.

Phil let out a loud belch and Amy gasped.

Sophie rolled her eyes. "Pathetic."

"I can do better than that." Dan mocked.

"A four-year-old can do better." Sophie added.

Phil waved to them, beckoning. "Show us what you got."

Sophie pulled a wad of bills out the back pocket of her jeans.

"It'll cost ya five." She held up a bill.

"I'm in." Dan fished for his wallet as Sophie big-eyed Phil. A small audience of Sophie's co-workers took notice.

Phil nodded at her. "You're on. Go for it."

"I called it. I go last."

"I need a breather. You can't expect two in a row." Phil protested.

"I'll go." Dan straightened, taking a deep breath. He let out a long, low belch. There was a smattering of applause.

"That is sooo disgusting." Amy shook her head, making a face.

"That was good, Dan." Sophie nodded approvingly. "You had control of that. The tone was good, too."

Dan made a smug face. "Thanks. Just good to know I haven't lost my feel."

"Okay, Phil." Sophie turned on him. "Prove us wrong."

Phil cleared his throat, took a step back, and let out a loud, short, pop of a burp. Sophie and Dan looked at each other. There was applause and a few hisses.

"What?" Phil folded his arms.

"Where was the control?" Dan frowned.

"That was loud."

"Loud?" Sophie smirked. "Any amateur can do loud. You barely held it a second. That wasn't a belch."

"A backfire at most." Phil feigned a look of disdain.

"All right. I'll admit, Dan's was better." Phil shrugged. "So let's see you top Dan."

Sophie smiled angelically, swallowed several breaths, and belched, *"Sophie loves Michael."*

There were howls of laughter as Dan stepped forward and high-fived Sophie with his five dollar bill. Phil nodded sheepishly and counted out five singles.

"My God!" Amy giggled. "Where did you learn to do that?"

"Fifth grade summer camp."

She sauntered up to him and took his arm. "Impressed, darling?"

"Very." He grinned.

It was a beautiful night as they walked home, the sort of night Dan and Phil would have wanted to star gaze. Smelling the last of winter in the air, he watched a meteor streak across the sky and squeezed Sophie's hand.

She hiccupped in the dark.

"Does it help if you hold your breath?" He suggested.

"That's what I've been trying to do—" She squeaked again. "Shit."

"Is this a typical side effect from belching contests?" He raised a brow.

"Hey, I just made ten dollars declaring my love. It was worth it."

"So much for Sid and Nancy."

"No, Sid and Nancy would have been down with the belching."

She squeaked again.

"Who were—"

An electric sensation reached through him and he stopped.

Sophie stopped with him, hiccupping again. "Who were who?"

"Shhh—" He put up a hand, staring up the street.

Dilating his eyes, he scanned the cars and houses lining the hill. His eyes saw nothing to indicate one of his kind. He felt it just the same. It was faint, but there.

"*What is it?*" She whispered.

"Let's go."

Turning around, they started downhill the way they came.

She stalled. "Where are we going?"

He ignored her, pulling her away from the street into the park at the bottom of the gulch behind their house.

"That's the wrong way!"

"Tonight it's the right way." He looked over his shoulder.

She spoke up. "I can't climb the gulch at night. It's pitch dark and I'm drunk."

He pushed her ahead. "I'll be right behind you."

"I don't need you behind me."

"Yes, you do."

"What's back there? Or do I not want to know?"

"I won't find out with you here."

She hiccupped. "I'm sorry I'm cramping your style."

He could tell she was having trouble keeping up. If they were being hunted, he would have to get her to safety before he could confront it. The gulch was his home. It was wild and relatively free of electronic interference. Nothing could hide from him there. Crossing the play field to the woods, he kept her in front of him.

She came to a stop.

"That's it. I can't see shit."

Taking one last look at the park, he saw no sign. The swings in the playground drifted in the wind. A paper bag skipped over the sandbox. He picked her up in his arms and started into the woods. They were barely a third of the way up the gulch when he knew they were being followed. Ducking behind a toppled spruce, he sat her on the ground and peeked over the tree.

She hiccupped again and he sighed at her.

"It isn't intentional." She grumbled.

It had to stop. He took her face in his hands and put his mouth over hers. Taking the air from her lungs, he let her inhale his breath. She pulled away, looking at him in a stupor.

"You've been holding out on me."

"That's my cure for hiccups." He whispered. "Stay here."

"No way!" she hissed.

She began to get to her feet. He grabbed her arms and held her down. Without a word, he looked into her eyes, conveying the gravity of the situation. He could tell from her expression he had frightened her.

Better frightened than dead.

Silently, he left her, returning to the trail. He waited. The push he felt from their pursuer had fallen back. It knew he was standing his ground. He tried to read the static he felt. It was strange. Hostile, but not. Frightened, but aggressive. No spy of Sam's would show itself so carelessly, let alone risk a confrontation it couldn't win.

Was it a transient? Transient singularities were solitary nomads. They sought the desert places of the universe. Earth was hell to them. Forbidden to them.

What was he thinking? It had to be sent back.

He moved.

There was a squeak. Freezing, he blinked.

Sophie's hiccups.

The static began to recede. It was retreating. There was no time.

Red fire filled his vision as he bent the opening of the gulch to him, trying to cut off the thing's escape. Materializing at the edge of the playfield, his mind caught hold of it the moment he felt the ground under his feet. He could see it. A figure at the far end of the park, ghostly as a sentinel. But it wasn't. It was writhing on the sidewalk near a street lamp. The street lamp shattered, showering sparks onto the street. Instinctively, he braced, pushing his presence out from him.

There was a low rumble and then silence as a shock wave came at him. It radiated across the park before slamming into his static with a shudder, jolting the ground. The playground was caught in the confluence.

The wooden playhouse heaved, then sparked into flames, its plastic slide melting onto steaming gravel while the sandbox smoked, its contents bubbling into glass. The sound of the surge grew deafening. As though hurled by a tornado, the playhouse blew apart and shot at him like a fire storm. Motionless, he watched the onslaught. It flashed, vaporizing before him in a cloud of smoke and ash. There was a whine as the steel frame of the swing glowed to amber and began to warp, the seats dripping from the ends of their chains. The chains reached for him, their links stretching, taut with rage.

The thing would incinerate everything in the park to free itself.

He would let it. Then it would be his turn.

"Michael!"

Sophie was staring at him. At the sight of her, he was gripped with fear.

"Go back!"

She looked pained. Her expression torn. Was she hurt? Had she fallen?

Turning, he reached for her, but she backed away. There was a low wail and a wave of heat. He didn't need to look behind him to see the molten remains of the swing coming at them. Without a thought, he let the thing go and felt Sophie on the ground beneath him. There was a sudden hush before everything around them was gauzed in brilliant light. Then darkness, the night breeze, the sounds of sirens in the distance.

There was no time.

Holding Sophie to him, he ran into the woods. There was only the sound of the brush whipping his clothes, the whistle of the wind in the leaves. Climbing the trail to the back of their home, he tried to look at her, but she kept her face to his shoulder. She was silent, her thoughts empty. He knew she was awake.

Kicking open the back door to the kitchen, he flew through to the living room and gently sat her on the sofa.

"Sophie?"

Holding her head in his hands, he brushed away her hair, searching her face.

"Sophie?"

She swallowed. "Need a drink."

"Gin?"

"Bottle of sherry ... in the kitchen." She fell back on the cushions, resting an arm over her eyes.

Searching the kitchen, he spotted the sherry. It was corked. He rummaged a drawer, then another. Scanning the rest of the drawers, he could see everything with perfect clarity, but no corkscrew. He found a glass and filled it with gin.

Returning to her side, he held the glass to her face.

"That's not sherry." She announced without opening her eyes.

"I couldn't find the corkscrew."

She sat up. "You can demolish a playground but you can't open a bottle of sherry?"

"That wasn't me. Whatever was following us did that. And yes, I need a corkscrew to open a bottle of sherry. At least if you want to drink it."

Sophie took the glass from his hand.

"What does it have against playground equipment?" She took a drink.

"It was trying to get away from me."

For a moment, she said nothing, staring through him.

Slowly, she nodded. "I can understand why."

The indifference in her voice cut into him.

Suddenly, her whole being reversed itself

"God! Are you okay?"

She was glaring at his left shoulder.

The sleeve of his sweater had grown a large hole. Pulling it off, he looked at his arm. It was stained black with a glowing gash running the length of it. That was where the sting was coming from.

She reached for his arm, but he caught her hand.

"Not a good idea."

"It's a cut."

"It's a breach."

Jumping off the sofa, she stood away from him. "Whoops."

He gave a half-hearted smile. "Nothing a night in the crypt can't take care of."

She downed the rest of her gin with a toss of her head and put her glass on the coffee table.

Smacking her lips, she grimaced. "See ya in the morning."

"Happy birthday." He called after her.

He heard a loud cackle as she climbed the stairs.

BODY SURFACES AT LAKE CRESCENT

Yesterday afternoon, two fisherman discovered the body of woman floating in Lake Crescent. Louis Rolfe and Shorty Immenroth retrieved the body, which was wrapped in a blanket and bound with rope. At first Mr. Rolfe had assumed the blanket was flotsam, but upon closer inspection saw a human foot and part of a shoulder that were exposed. The county coroner's office examined the body, that of a woman in her late twenties to early thirties with auburn hair. The corpse appears to show little evidence of decomposition after becoming preserved by the cool temperature and unusually high mineral content of the lake water. Authorities are hopeful that a positive identification with a missing person will be made.Anyone who is aware of a missing woman who meets this description is encouraged to call the Clallam County Sheriff's Department. There are currently seven people who are suspected of having drowned in the lake in recent memory. No bodies have previously been recovered so it is unusual for the lake to have yielded this most recent victim.

[Newspaper clipping from the *Tacoma News Tribune*.
Scrapbook of Michael Goodhew. d. July 7, 1940]

[Photograph taken at Lake Crescent by Michael Goodhew c. 1919]

2003 He knows her voice. He overheard the end of her conversation with Sophie at the grocery store. The pitch of it can make dogs take notice. She is coming by the back door. She calls to Grandma Vie.

She walks the length of the house and he withdraws himself as much as possible. Still seated on the footlocker at the back of the vault, he slowly slides the ops between his belt and the belt loop at his back. He feels the leather of his belt grip onto the rough finish of the silver. It's the safest place he has for it, modern attire leaving little means for wearing such a weapon.

"Did he come?" Marta sounds as if she has stopped for tea.

"Like you said."

"What did you tell him?"

"I didn't know where you were."

"Did he suspect?"

"I think he knows."

"And he just left?"

"He was in a hurry. Sounds like he's got problems of his own."

"Did he say where he came from, where he was going?

"He didn't say, and I didn't ask."

"I thought I told you to get information out of him."

"Next time he comes, you can do it yourself."

Footsteps begin to walk to the back of the house.

"There isn't going to be a next time. None of them will be left."

He hears their feet coming down the back stairs. The creak of the basement door. The snap of the lamp chain.

"But he's your father." It is Violet's voice.

"Really? Did he admit it?"

"No."

"He doesn't have to, does he? As long as he can work on his next brat."

Marta's voice is just outside the vault door. The bolt begins to move. He comes out from behind the crates.

Violet's voice stops her. "Is she pregnant?"

He stops breathing.

Marta lets out a hiss. "Not yet."

Violet says nothing as Marta pulls the bolt from the floor. The moment the door begins to move, he throws himself at it. The sound of it impacting with Marta is followed by a deafening howl. Violet stands like a statue, the door barely missing her. Her normally stoic expression is one of horror as she stares at the squirming thing he pins to the floor by the neck.

"Jesus."

The creature hisses. Its body is shadow, one minute gray, the next black. It has no lines. It is not solid; it is not air. The face is vaguely skeletal, little more than two black holes for eyes and a gaping hole of a mouth. It is wild and outraged as a thin static of blue light wraps around it. All that remains of Marta are her clothes laying on the floor.

Slowly backing away, Violet feels for the wall behind her as she watches him drag the thing to the vault. Hefting it from the floor, he hurls it into the safe, slamming the door on it. The door instantly rams into him, trying to open, bowing against him as he braces it. He struggles to keep his footing as he tries to drive the cane bolt into place.

Bolting the door, he steps back as it shudders violently again and again.

"Kids." Violet says dryly.

He glances at her, brushing his hair from his eyes before returning his gaze to the safe. This will take more time than he has.

"What now?" Her question is barely audible over muffled howls.

Sitting on his heels in front of the safe, he stares at it intently. He will not leave until he has what he wants.

"We wait."

"For what?"

Only slightly turning his head, he speaks with his eyes on the door.

"For Marta."

The words are barely out of his mouth than another volley of howling blows comes from the vault.

Violet slowly nears until she is standing next to him.

"She said you tried to kill her the first time she came to you."

"I didn't know what she was."

"You sound like Curtis. Shoot first, ask later."

"I had that experience with Curtis."

"He thought he killed you that night, didn't he?"

His eyes dart to her and return to the door.

"I don't excuse him." She continues. "But he thought you were no good. He thought he was doing what was right."

"Same here."

"So does Marta."

"I don't care who's right anymore." He looks up at her. "Tell me, Violet. What do you get when you do what's right?"

She lets out a long breath and nods. "I'll get you a chair."

It is the early hours of the morning when he senses Marta has returned to herself. Violet is gone after watching him stare at the vault door without so much as blinking for four hours. He has no idea what she thinks of him other than he is not as evil as she once believed. She may still think he is Marta's father. Now that she knows he can't die, she must think it impossible for him to be hungry. Which he desperately is. And tired. He feels his fatigue as he bends to pick up Marta's clothes. He will have to stay on his guard with her. He will have to check his temper.

Approaching the vault door, he quietly pulls the rod. The door drifts open, exposing the figure of a naked woman, curled on the stone floor. He waits outside, letting her senses rouse her. Minutes pass. Finally, her head moves and she looks up at him. She sits up, holding herself. He tosses her clothes to her, but doesn't close the door.

Her black eyes search him before she smiles.

"Hello, Daddy."

"I'm not your father." His irritability tests his repugnance at what she is.

She stands naked with no pretense of self-consciousness. Picking her blouse from the pile as though sorting laundry, she begins to get dressed.

"Then whose daddy are you?" Her bloody fingernails mar the white silk.

"Nobody's."

She smirks as she buttons her blouse. "Mine."

"It wasn't me."

"She said you came to her."

"She thought it was me."

"It was you." She pulls on her skirt.

"It was Samael."

"*No.*" There is no expression on her face to match the denial.

He cocks his head. "Have you seen him?"

Her hollow eyes sharpen. "I killed him first."

"Any child of mine would know the impossibility of such a statement."

"He's dead. He is ashes in his cave."

"You followed me to Arizona." He whispers.

"I could have done the same to you, but I didn't. You tried to burn me twice."

"I didn't burn anything."

"You were going to."

He skips this.

"Samael is alive and well."

"Liar."

"He sent me to find you." He senses this frightens her.

She smiles, approaching on bare feet.

"One more step and I'll finish you." His warning is without malice.

She is still smiling, but stops.

"You'll never find Sophie if you do that."

"And what would that cost me?"

Her smile fades. "You want another child. You had me, but I wasn't any good."

"I can't have children, Marta. It's been three years with Sophie. Do you think I wouldn't have a child by now if I could make one?"

"Sarah said you would destroy ECCO first. That ECCO would kill any children you made."

He smiles. "ECCO doesn't know about you, do they?"

Marta's lips disappear.

"What would happen if Sarah knew where you were?"
She snarls.
"I could take you to her."
"No."
"Or I could take you to Sam. It's your choice."
"No!"
"Marta." He speaks gently. "If you could have anything, what would it be?"
Licking her lips, she backs into the vault. The light in her flickers.
"I am the Child." The whisper is another voice.
"I can never have a child, Marta. Do you want to be mine?"
"I am the Child!" She hisses in the dark.
"If I accept you, what will you do for me?"
She bridles. "All you want is Sophie."
"All I want is for Sophie to be free."
"I want her gone."
He nods and approaches the vault. "So do I."
"You'll let her go?" It is a child's voice.
"I'll let her go."
"You promise?"
He extends his hand to her.
"I have you now."
Emerging from the shadows. she takes it. As she steps from the vault, he feels her longing, her hostility, her mistrust. All he can hope is that she recognizes the position she is in. Hope that he can keep ahead of the other half of her. Time is running out. He must push.
"Now." He looks into her eyes, weighing his will upon her. "Take me to her."
Marta agrees to let him drive.
They leave the house without a word to Violet, though he knows she sees them leave. As soon as they are on the street, Marta clings to him, her fingers dig into his arm as they walk the eight blocks to his car. They are going to Sophie, but he is going blind. Marta doesn't trust him enough to tell him more. Blindness is something he is getting used to.
In the car, he feels her eyes on him, eerily reminding him of Sophie.
"Take 16. Cross the bridge and keep going."
Driving in silence, he keeps his eyes on the road.
"Do you believe in the prophecy?" Her voice is a hushed rasp.
He must assume she can read him, though it doesn't matter. He doesn't know the answer.
"Prophecy?" He echoes.
"Samael's vision."
"I have none."
"Yes, you do. Finishing me, finishing Sam, finishing Sarah."
"Oh, that one."

"You could have everything."

"People keep telling me that."

"You don't want it?"

"I already have it."

"With Sophie?"

His head twitches. "Without Sophie."

"I don't understand."

"Until I met her, I didn't either."

"Tell me."

"It's nothing."

"Tell me."

"I just did." He looks at her. "After this, nothing is all there is."

Suddenly, he wants her to know, but her face is blank in the darkness. She is empty. What nothingness signifies to her, he has no idea. That may be all she has ever felt. She has no crypt, has never been in the void that made her. There is no innate craving for harmony, no impulsive fear of discord. No ability to comprehend what a silent universe would be like.

It is more than finding Sophie, after all. Sam's vision of Sarah's head on a platter with ECCO in tatters is true. Sam needs no one. Wanting him as a brother is semantic. It is his delusion to claim Sam has never had him. They will never be parted. They can only be joined. Made whole. Made empty.

Marta breaks his reverie. "Is that all you can tell me?"

He feels her frustration. Her blindness.

He has told her everything, and she cannot see it.

Well, not everything.

He hasn't told her they've been followed since they left Tacoma.

He isn't going to.

Dawn touches the Olympics, burning cirrus clouds from the sky. The depths of Lake Crescent swallow them, reflecting nothing. Marta has ceased giving directions. He knows where they are going. Ignoring the winding road, he stares at the teal waters that remain ever clear, ever deep. Ever since the ice, he has returned to linger here. Ever after he would like to. But there is no such thing.

Turning onto the drive to the cabin, there is no sign anyone is there, but he can sense her instantly. He reaches for her thoughts. They are dreams. She is asleep.

Parking in the drive, he leaves Marta in the car without a word. She senses his mood and waits with hopeful expectation. Using his key, he gently opens the door. The air inside is chilled and stale, the curtains drawn. The sounds of waves on the shore lure him. Crossing to the back doors, he pulls back a curtain to watch the water. The view is the same. There is no sense of time in this three-dimensional space. Only the residue of wood smoke and the fear of vulnerability she made him to let go.

He climbs the stairs to the bedroom.

When he opens the door, he sees an arm hanging off the edge of the bed; the rest of her is a white sheet. Standing at the foot of the bed, he wonders what would happen if he left and never came back. He doesn't have to wonder. He knows. He can't leave her for the same reason she could never send him away.

The sun breaks over the mountains, filling the room with light. His shadow falls at her bedside and she stirs. He waits silently. Rolling over, the dead hand comes to life and pulls the pillow away. She blinks into the sunlight. She sees him.

He feels everything in her eyes. The way she sees him. Even if he doesn't have wings. Even if angels don't exist. Even if he doesn't.

He will kiss her. He will feel her in his arms. Feel her breath in him. Pull her into him and feel her go. He will let her go. She will feel joy and love and lust and nothing. She will be nothing.

She will be nothing within him, instead of nothing without him.

Before she can speak, he kisses her.

Her kiss is shallow.

Perfunctory.

She holds her breath from him.

He kisses more deeply, pulling her into his arms.

"Whoa!" She shoves him away.

He catches his breath. "You aren't happy to see me?"

"I have to brush my teeth."

"What?"

Pushing past him, she climbs out of bed. He follows her around the bed to the bathroom, where she turns on the faucet and begins to scrub her face at the sink.

She is unhurt. Alive. In one of his flannel shirts.

Not bound, not beaten, not raped.

"Sophie." He drops on the bed in a daze.

She spits water into the sink. "What?"

"I've been in hell."

She shuts off the tap and reaches for a towel.

"I thought you said there wasn't one." Her voice is thick with terry cloth.

"I found it."

"And come out the other side." She grins, tossing the towel over her shoulder. "Now, let's do this right."

Reaching for his face, she starts to kiss him. When he pulls away, she scowls.

"I got nylons. Do I have to use 'em?"

"Sophie, what is going on? I've been looking for you everywhere. I thought you were in danger, even dead."

Taking a step back, she frowns. "Sarah didn't tell you where I was?"

He feels his mouth open. "Sarah brought you here?"

"She took me to the house first. I thought I was dead, but she said she wanted to help. She said ECCO was after you and you had a better chance of facing them without me in the way."

"And she brought you here?"

"She asked me if I could think of a safe place to hide. This is where she left me."

"Was Marta with you?"

"Marta?" She frowns. "What's Marta have to do with this?"

Marta. His mind searches for her. It goes to the drive. The car is gone.

~

1199 BC The general sent his scouts ahead to find a crossing. Though there were several known to the Habiru in our caravan, he wanted another. One with fewer eyes. Once across the river, our discovery would only be a matter of time. We paused on a bluff to watch the water coursing before us.

"What can you see?"

It was a question I had expected.

"No more than you." I lied.

Leaning forward on his horse, he tried to face me. I looked away as though turning from the sun.

"It could save lives."

"That is not my purpose."

He shrugged. "Forgive me. It is mine to ask."

"You need never ask my forgiveness."

"Indeed." He laughed. "I have been warned to expect less."

With a wave over his head, he disappeared down the slope in a cloud of dust. I remained behind and watched him convene with his men below. He would cross here. It was as good a spot as any for a caravan of this size. Broad, with a slow current. My eyes read the riverbed. There was a considerable drop along the far shore, the sediment washed away, making the banks weak where it was uniform upstream. I watched his scouts wading downstream, then watched the sun climb the sky. The crossing would take all day.

I felt my horse amble down the slope and move to the riverbank. There, it began to drink. I looked downstream at the scouts, then over my shoulder at the general and his men. He would stay behind to oversee the crossing, but I would have to cross myself eventually.

Sated with water, my horse began to cross upstream from where his scouts still pondered the current. At the deepest, the water wet my feet, barely reaching the barrel of my mount. As I climbed the far bank, I heard the general call to his scouts. Turning my head, I saw the column was following in my path. He was watching me, the broad smile on his face plainly visible. Turning my horse away, I rode into the bush, leaving the river behind. The rest of the day I stayed away. Finding a grove of figs, I let the horse forage on new growth as I napped beneath the trees. I kept my eye upon the caravan's progress, less so on the horse.

Hunger woke me. The breeze was fragrant with blossoms, but there was no fruit. The crossing was nearly complete, the sun near to setting, the horse far from my sight. I began to walk back to the column, imagining the reaction the vacation of my horse would be met with. As I approached, the sound of voices and shuffling feet moved the air. Skirting the perimeter of the caravan, I emerged from the wilderness and moved to join the mass of people, when a shout caught my attention.

I turned to see a soldier on horseback, the chest of the animal pushing through the snake leaf from which I had just emerged. Trotting to the column, he walked alongside me.

"What is your name?"

"My tent rides with this caravan."

"Where is it?"

I sensed my crypt ahead of me and pointed up the line.

The soldier watched the people around me. "Who will witness this?"

All looked at me, none spoke.

The soldier returned to me. "What is your name?" He repeated.

"Khepera."

He squinted. "Let me see you."

I pulled my cloak away, revealing hair as long as I had worn it as a woman.

"You are not Egyptian."

Dropping my eyes, I shook my head.

"What tribe are you with?"

Not knowing which tribes made the caravan, I was unsure, nor did I want to name one and be found a liar.

The soldier lowered his spear in reply to my silence. "Come with me."

Stepping from the line, I stopped in front of his horse as the column moved on. "Sit."

The soldier backed his horse from me, keeping his spear within range.

Sitting on my heels, I considered asking to speak with the general, but it would not hasten my release. It was just as well to wait for the rear guard. The general would be with them, no doubt, one of the last to cross.

For some time I sat. Another soldier arrived and asked my guardian who I was. They spoke quietly as I listened. Neither had seen me. Neither had heard of me. No one would witness for me. In spite of my name, I was not Egyptian and could name no tribe. I was not wet from the crossing yet had no horse. I had come from the wilderness.

I was a spy until proven otherwise.

[Spharic. Entry translated from *Kor Dai Maihael*. Mund Dai. d. 755 BC]

2000

"Happy birthday."

He watched Anthony surprise her from behind with a gift-wrapped box of chocolates. Sophie liked chocolates. He wondered if she liked chocolates more than the week he had planned at the ocean. She thanked Anthony with a hug before unwrapping the box. He read her face carefully as she removed the wrapping. She knew what was inside, anticipated it.

He wondered what she anticipated from him.

Anthony took a seat and asked a passing waitress for an IPA. Sophie picked out a chocolate and slowly bit into it.

Anthony grinned. "Feel any closer to thirty?"

He thought it a rude question.

Sophie sucked on her teeth. "As long as I don't look it, who's counting?"

"How's Michael?"

She rolled her eyes. "Like you care."

"I do. I still think he bumped off his old man to move into his house and start collecting on his trust fund, but that doesn't mean I wish him ill. I don't wish him any good, but not any ill either."

She sighed. "If only my world was so simple."

Watching her expression, he felt himself tense.

"Trouble in paradise?" Anthony looked smug.

"Just tired. Late night."

"Sounds like you had fun. Sorry I wasn't able to make it."

"I didn't expect you to. It was a weeknight."

"I was pretty busy. I don't know if you read the papers but last night's fun for someone included toasting the playground at Carr Park."

"Really?" She skillfully hid in her pint of beer as the waitress brought Anthony's.

"Yeah. Looks like they used torches to cut away all the play ground equipment and cart it off. Then they tried to set some trees on fire. It doesn't make any sense, but last year we had those jerks who sprayed acid all over windows downtown."

Anthony shrugged and took a drink.

She scratched her ear. "Did anyone see anything?"

"Only three houses had a view and they all have garages facing the street. Everyone was in bed. A woman said she thought there was quake, but that was it."

Resting her elbow on the table, she stared at her beer with her face partially planted in her hand.

Anthony snapped his fingers. "Can you hear me now?"

"Loud and clear." Her voice was distant, her eyes still on her glass.

"I worry about you, Sophie."

She came to attention. "What's to worry about?"

Something caught her eye.

"That's Amy over there." She waved at the door.

Anthony got to his feet as Amy approached their table.

Amy caught sight of them and waved back. "Hi!"

Sophie stood up. "Amy, this is Anthony. Anthony, Amy. You both know each other; you just haven't met."

They grinned and shook hands, eyeing each other with nervous curiosity.

"Sophie's said a lot of good things about you." Amy was clearly sincere and attracted.

He studied Anthony's face and body language in Amy's presence. Their eye contact was surprisingly direct, unlike the difficulty he had experienced looking at Sophie when they first met.

"Likewise. It's good to finally be able to put a face to the name. Thanks for inviting me to her party, by the way. I wish I could have made it last night, but I had a late shift."

"The next time we have an after-work bar hop, I'll let you know."

"Sophie seems to have enjoyed herself." Anthony winked as Sophie rolled her eyes.

Amy's eyes widened. "It was the belching contest."

"Belching contest?" Anthony snickered at Sophie. "You been holding out on me?"

"She belched 'Sophie loves Michael.' It was horribly romantic."

Anthony frowned. "You never belched *my* name."

"Too many syllables." Sophie finished her pint with a burp, making him smile.

"Nice." Anthony shook his head, then turned to Amy. "Let me get you a pint. What do you want?"

"Red Hook would be great. Thanks."

"Want another one?" Anthony pointed to Sophie's glass and she gave a nod.

Amy watched Anthony as he went to the bar.

"He's cute."

"Yeah, he can shoot people, too."

Amy giggled. "That's hot in a really twisted way."

"Hotter than Ward Cleaver."

"Not as hot as Mike." Amy fanned herself.

Sophie's eyes got big. "Sometimes I'm afraid to touch him."

"I mean he's more than good-looking. He's like to-die-for good-looking."

"Whoops."

"What?"

"Nothing."

He found the vacant tone in Sophie's voice disturbing.

Amy seemed to notice. "So are you looking forward to the ocean?"

"Yeah. I like the ocean. Michael really likes it."

"Where are you staying?"

"Hopefully someplace where I can take a hot bath."

The mention of a bath made his eyes narrow.

"God, I love a hot bath." Amy rolled her eyes. "I never used to take them till I moved into our house. We have that huge tub upstairs. Now I can't imagine living without it."

"We had a great claw foot in our apartment." Sophie murmured.

"We did." Anthony's voice made her jump as he returned to their table with three pints of beer between his hands.

There was the taste of blood in his mouth. He had bitten his lip.
He had seen enough.
Reclining in his wingback chair, he returned his gaze to the fire.

"Do you still want to go to the ocean?"
"Sure." Sophie was reading the paper.
He stared at her as she turned over the paper and continued reading. It was an article about religion in politics. The paper irritated her but she read it anyway. Without looking up, she reached for her cup of coffee. From where he sat, she burned with an inner fire, the morning light blurring her lines, making her nearly transparent to his eyes. Nearly.
"Sophie?"
"Hmm?" She looked up. The grandfather clock chimed. She didn't see him.
"Do you still want to go to the ocean?"
"Of course." She paused. "Do you?"
"It's your birthday."
"Tell me when it isn't."
"I wish you'd tell me where you want to go."
She put down the paper. "Mike, the ocean is fine."
"But you aren't excited about it."
"I love the ocean."
"But?"
She sat back and sighed at her coffee cup.
"I have a lot of memories there."
"It makes you sad."
"No. It's just a very intense place."
They said nothing, only looked at each other.
Her voice came from far away.
"I don't want to be there with you."
"Why didn't you say anything?"
She shrugged. "I still haven't said anything. I know how I feel about it, but there's no way to say why."
He smiled. "You don't have to."
She raised a brow. "Should I unpack now?"
"No."
"Where are we going?"
"Somewhere I want to be with you."

The lake was his refuge. A place he had never shared. It was a gamble taking any-one there, but especially her. Sophie was casual about a lot of things, but cleanli-ness was not one of them. He hadn't been to the cabin in years. What condition it would be in was something he never cared about. All he ever needed was shelter from the rain and use of the stove. The plumbing was doubtful. But it did have a bathtub.

When they arrived, there was a light drizzle. Lake Crescent was an emerald sheet beneath the black trees of the Olympic Mountains. When he made the turn onto the road hugging the north shore, she took notice.

"You don't think lakes are creepy?"

"I think they are peaceful."

"Do you know how many people have disappeared in Lake Crescent?"

"Fewer than in the ocean."

"Yeah, but the stories are …" She shuddered.

"Creepy."

"That couple that drove off the road, they were missing for like … seventy years till divers found their car. And that murder case they solved because the victim's body didn't decompose in the lake water." She made a face.

"Hallie Spraker."

"I don't remember."

"I do. She was a waitress at the Lake Tavern. We used to talk when she waited on me."

"Did you know who murdered her?"

"When she went missing I knew she was dead, but I didn't know how."

"Misadventure and murder. And you want me to be here with you?"

"The couple who died together never knew age or suffering or loss. They didn't drive off the road, they just took a different one. And as for Hallie, she would have been lost forever if the lake hadn't preserved her and given her up. Without her body, they would have never caught her murderer. This lake is a special place."

"Stories about dead people …" She nodded. "On my birthday."

"You've died before. Haven't you gotten over your fear of death by now?"

"Try it sometime, Peter Pan."

"I wish."

"So living with me is the next best thing to dying? Thanks."

"I don't wish I was dead. I just wish I could die."

"You can do everything else. Isn't that enough?"

"That's the point: I can't do everything." He grinned at her. "You can do something I can't. I'm jealous."

She smirked. "I'd like to think dying isn't the only thing I have a monopoly on."

"I can't belch."

"Don't raise the bar too high. I'm only human."

Laughing, he slowed the car, spotting the turn off to the cabin. The drive was barely visible, a rut of gravel and tall grass. Gently rolling the car to the shoreline, the trees fell away to a clearing being reclaimed by saplings and blackberries. In the clearing was a small cabin; beyond it, the wide expanse of the lake rippled under the rain. Pulling the car as close to the cabin as overgrowth would allow, he stopped the engine. Before he could say anything, Sophie was out of the car.

"What a dump." She shut her door.

Standing next to the car with his door open, he could feel her frustration.

"We can go somewhere else."

"Why? This is perfect."

She turned to glare at him. He froze.

"So are we going in or playing it safe and sleeping in the car?"

"We'll go somewhere else."

Putting his hand on the car door, he was about to get in when her voice stopped him.

"No." Walking to his side of the car, she took his hand. "I just spent two hours on the road. We're home."

She pulled him by the hand. His arm moved but the rest of him didn't.

"Michael, come on."

He could only look at her. No solutions came to his mind.

"I'm sorry I called your cabin a dump. Come on …"

She grabbed his other hand and pulled harder. He took a step.

"Come …" She winked.

His feet began to move as she coaxed him into a walk. He trailed her to the front door, watching her pick her steps through the grass. Ducking under the eaves, she stamped her feet in the cold as he turned his key in the door. When he pushed the door open, she cut around him to get inside. Hugging herself, she looked around, her boots leaving a dervish of wet prints on the dry floor boards. She came to a stop before the windows facing the lake.

"So this is where you murdered your dad?" He could see her breath as she spoke.

Briefly he glanced at the wood stove where he had left a pre-made fire. Seeing the kindling inside, he sparked it with a thought as he crossed the room to her.

"He's buried out back."

"I don't know. Still feels like he's haunting the place." She faced him, reaching under his coat with frozen hands to wrap her arms around his waist.

"Are you going to exorcise it?"

"It needs it." She grinned up at him as he held her, taking in the view.

When he looked down at her, she kissed him.

Her kisses ranged from thoughtless habit, to affection, to love. Then there was her passion, which was none of these things. It was a devouring hunger he was familiar with in humans, something his kind shunned. Feared. It was the source of power that drove the material universe. The fire of life.

This kiss was passion, and every time he felt it, he was terrified. The first time they had sex he was overwhelmed. He initiated it the night she moved in, trying to experiment, to adapt to it somehow. It was still a struggle. He trusted her, but it wasn't enough. Still, he tried to give her what she wanted.

Just not now.

He was tired and hadn't eaten since breakfast.

Feeling around his back for her hands, he tried to get away.

"I'll get the bags."
He felt her arms tighten around him.
"No bags."
She got on her toes to kiss him again.
"Sophie, let go."
"You let go. They're just bags."
"I'll be back. I promise."
"Sure you will." She tried to kiss him again.
He kept his head out of reach. "You don't trust me?"
"I do. But why take a chance? There might be a cougar out there."
Switching her hold, she went for his head, her fingers like ice on his neck. They ran into his hair, gripping his scalp, pulling him down to her. He could smell the sorbitol and aspartame of peppermint gum on her breath, taste the petrolatum and mineral oil of her lip gloss. It was hot in his mouth. Carbon dioxide.
The smell of life in her began to warm him.
"There's one in here." He whispered.
She smiled. "I'm a pussycat."
Her face was melting into blue haze. Picking her up, he made for the stairs. There was enough time before his vision faded.

After she pulled the blankets over him, he heard her dress and go downstairs. He imagined she was getting the bags. He imagined sleep and breakfast in the morning. There was a café nearby that made wonderful pancakes. Stacks of them.
But sleep first.
He slipped away.
When he felt her coaxing him in the dark, it made him groan in a way he thought most human. After their first month together, Sophie wanted to try sex more than once in a day. Absolutely not. It was dangerous enough he was having it at all. She asked if it could kill him and he'd made the mistake of telling her no. Now it was her next hurdle, something she had pushed for every time since. Feeling her arousal in him, he moved to push her off.
Something held his hands away from her.
Opening his eyes, he looked at his right hand and saw she had tied something around his wrist. His eyes focused on it. A nylon stocking. The other end of it was tied to the bed frame. She had done the same to his left hand. The bed frame was an old iron one from a farm house down the road. It was being tossed and had cost him nothing. Now it could cost him plenty.
"Sophie, this isn't funny."
"Am I laughing?" She kissed his ear, making it buzz.
His head jerked away as he pulled hard on the stockings. They stretched, digging deeper into his wrists. They should have snapped. He felt the iron frame yield to him, but the nylon was besting them both.
Her exhale filled his lungs, sending a surge of blood through him.

"Sophie, no."

"Michael, yes … my birthday." Her voice drowned in a rising tide.

Fighting the light in his eyes, he strained to see his wrist but it wasn't there. The feeling in his hands had vanished with his eyesight. As durable as he was, he wondered what condition they would be in if he ever saw them again. Now he knew why Sophie called her nylons instruments of Satan.

Burn them.

The thought floated.

But he couldn't see the stockings in his mind.

All he could see was her.

Feel her. Taste her. She was in his head. She was everything. Deploy the thought, and he would burn her.

He'd burned people before.

People who had tried to hurt him.

He was being hurt now.

His body shivered.

Burn her.

"*Sophie!*" The sound of his voice startled him.

She stopped.

"What?"

Her breath filled his nostrils and he choked.

"Michael? Are you okay?"

Forcing himself to breathe, he closed his eyes as his mind tried to reassert itself. But his body wasn't returning to him. The light in his eyes still blinded. The drone of life deafened.

His throat caught. His breathing stopped.

"*Stop.*" The voice wasn't his.

No, it was. Once.

"I've stopped."

What did she say? He shook his head, trying to shake the sound.

"Michael, I'm going—"

"*No!*" The voice blurted. "*Don't leave me …*"

There was no response.

"*Sophie? Are you there?*"

"I'm here." She sounded close.

"*I can't feel you.*"

"I'm right here."

He couldn't feel her.

"*Something's wrong.*"

"I know. You're burning up and you sound possessed."

"*I can't feel anything.*"

"You're not breathing, Mike."

"*I can't.*"

"I'm not on top of you anymore."
"It's not that."
"What's wrong?"
"I'm afraid."
"Just relax. You're going to be fine."
"No."
"Yes."
"I'm not safe."
"You're with me." She sounded like she was in his ear.
"I shouldn't be here."
"Where should you be?"
"My crypt."
"It wouldn't have fit in the car."
His chest shuddered.
"Hey, you just smiled."
Slowly, his breath began to move. His head was throbbing.
"You're thinking about what followed us from The Spar?" Her voice buzzed.
He imagined he was nodding.
"I thought you scared it pretty good."
"It was too close." He whispered.
"You saw it coming."
"Not soon enough."
"Now you know what it's like for the rest of us."
"It could have burned me."
"It didn't."
"I've been burned before."
"And survived."
"There's only one way."
"What's that?"
"You can't fight it." His voice sounded like it was coming apart. *"It's like going through hell and coming out the other side."*
"I'm sorry." Her voice was fading.
"Sophie?"
"What?" He could hardly hear her.
"Don't stop."
"Are you sure?"
"Yes. Please ... finish me."

It knew the physical anguish of fire. It now knew the mental anguish of love. The body had pinioned It. A being that existed beyond physical limitation, only knowing the body as a means to an end, as a tool or a detriment, a weapon or a weakness. It had never known the blissful ignorance of innocence. Had never been a child. Had never been intrinsically vulnerable. Never embraced oblivion. Unconscious

oblivion was death.
   It never gave.
   Some. But not all.
   The part that refused, fought.
   When It finally gave, he screamed.

He didn't remember regaining consciousness, only waking to daylight. His eyes barely made out the tin roof above. He squinted over his head at the bed frame, the railing deformed into a graceful arc. His arms were free at his sides under the blankets but didn't feel like moving. The burning in his eyes grew and he closed them tight.

   Sophie wasn't there. At first he was disappointed until his sense of the sun said it was three in the afternoon. The rain echoed on the roof and into his head.

   He fell asleep.

Bleach ...
   Popcorn ...
   Music ...
   Laughter ... He sat up. It was dark. The walls looked solid. He felt solid. He'd survived. Sliding out of bed, he ignored the vertigo to find his footing and hunt for clothes. There was only one chest of drawers in the room and he found his clothes neatly folded in the middle drawer. Pulling on a pair of pajamas and a cotton tee, he poked his head out the door, peeking downstairs.

   Sophie was lying in front of the wood stove on a blanket. Somehow she made a fire though he never used any matches. She was eating popcorn from a Jiffy Pop pan and reading from a small pile of magazines by the light of an electric lantern. The music was coming from a radio that came with the cabin when he bought it. It was tuned to a jazz station.

   He caught the scent of something other than popcorn.

   Following his nose downstairs, he went to the kitchen. The smell of bleach was strong, but the scent from the refrigerator was unmistakable. Pizza. Opening the refrigerator, he pulled out a box and took it to the counter. His favorite: bacon and pineapple. Taking a slice, he took a bite. Leaning back against the counter, he surveyed the room. Sophie had been cleaning again. She also found the breaker box and plugged in the refrigerator. He was impressed it still worked.

   Strolling into the living room, he watched her read. He didn't recognize the lantern. She must have bought it.

   "*Shit!*" She dropped the magazine over her face.

   He had forgotten to clear his throat. Swallowing his pizza, he bit his lip. "Sorry."

   She pulled the magazine from her face. "I thought I exorcised this place already."

   "Do you want some?"

"No, thanks. I ate. I got that for you. The pizza place in Port Angeles didn't have a deep dish, but I knew you'd eat anything with pineapple on it."

She made a face as he pushed the crust down his throat.

"You know, if you chewed your food you might enjoy it more."

"I don't have to in front of you."

"So I get the privilege of watching you eat like a python?"

"I get the privilege of watching you watch me eat like a python without having to feel self-conscious about it."

"I make you feel self-conscious?"

Licking his lips, he grinned. "Not after last night."

Dinah Washington started to sing "What a Difference a Day Made."

He reached down to her. "May I have this dance?"

"You dance?" She accepted his hand with a surprised look on her face.

Holding her hands, he lifted her to him and put his arms around her waist. "I can do everything."

MAN MISSING NEAR LAKE CRESCENT

Sixty-five year old, Michael Goodhew, a resident of Tacoma, has been missing for three weeks after last being seen at his cabin along the north shore of Lake Crescent. Long time residents around the lake know him as a reclusive man who visits the area regularly, coming and going without notice. Due to his secluded lifestyle, no one noticed that he was missing until his son, Michael Goodhew III, reported him a week overdue to return from a planned camping trip on June 16th. Both the Clallam County Sheriff's Department and the National Parks Service are investigating.

Young Michael Goodhew describes his father as an active man who enjoys the Olympic Peninsula and is an expert outdoorsman who has camped in and around the National Park most of his life. Neighbors who knew of Mr. Goodhew agree with this description and some were surprised to learn his age,

saying that he gave the appearance of a much younger man in spite of his retiring lifestyle.

Mr. Goodhew Sr. is six ft. two in. tall and weighs 180 lbs. He wears a full beard and has sandy brown hair. He was last seen around his cabin on the morning of June 4th wearing denim jeans and a green flannel shirt. His tent and camping equipment were still there when his son arrived in search of him three weeks later. Investigators have had reports from two eyewitnesses of a man meeting his description near Sol Duc a week after his last confirmed sighting leaving the possibility that Mr. Goodhew could have disappeared within the park.

This does not rule out the possibilities of foul play or drowning on the Lake. Anyone with information regarding his whereabouts is encouraged to contact the Clallam County Sheriff's Department.

[Newspaper clipping from the *Tacoma News Tribune*.
Scrapbook of Michael Goodhew. d. July 1, 1997]

2003 "Michael?"
Sophie is in front of him but he doesn't see her.
"Michael." She takes his hand.
"Wait." He stops her.
There are only two ways Marta can go. North or south. She isn't far. She hasn't had time. Even if she drives as fast as he does. And no one drives as fast he does. His mind runs the stretch of highway north. There is light traffic on an early Sunday morning. Still he doesn't see her. Did she go south? There is nothing south. Forks. Then nothing. His mind jumps south. No one is on the lake. The highway is empty.

No.

He sees the Mustang.

Jump to her car? In it?

Without her cooperation, nearly impossible. He must predict her exact speed and location or miss his mark. Wait for her. His mind runs ahead of the car. Twenty miles ahead. Barren highway with forest on one side, a waste of clear cut on the other.

"I have to go."

"What?"

Grasping for her hands, he holds her gaze. "Sophie, you can't stay here. Anthony's waiting in a car at the top of the drive. Go to him and tell him you need to disappear. Both of you. Don't go back to Tacoma. Don't use his cell phone."

He reaches into the inside pocket of his raincoat and pulls out a key. "There's a safety deposit box at my bank in Vancouver." He presses the key into her palm. "Its in your name. It's enough to live on for a while."

"But Sarah told me—"

"Sarah's right. You have to get away or I'll never get out. Do you understand?"

She says nothing.

"Do you understand?" He repeats.

"And if you don't?" She bites her lip.

"You're free."

Her eyes well with tears, but she smiles. "All this cat and mouse to dump me."

"I ran out of Post-Its. Sophie, I promise I'll come for you if I can."

"When it comes to promises you've got a lousy record."

"Do you trust me?"

She touches his face.

Taking her face in his hands, he kisses her. This time she doesn't hold back. It isn't passion. It is love. Letting go, he steps away with a smile.

"Thanks for brushing your teeth."

"Makes a big difference, don't it?"

He sees her eyes turn to red points before her image burns into a blur.

Sun shines down on the barren stretch of highway before him. There is the song of birds, the breeze in his ears, and, faintly, the hum of a car. The breeze falters as the birds fall silent. They can't see each other, but they do. Marta wanted redemption. Now she wants revenge. Daddy didn't do what he promised.

Marta.

There is no response.

Don't fight me and you'll live.

She comes around the bend of the highway, ten miles from where he stands. The car increases its speed. His mind reaches for it. He would overpower the engine, but her rage is strong enough to shield it. His static can only slow it down. At 140 mph, turbulence will burn the car up first.

The space between them wavers in the field of resistance radiating from him.

Marta, stop the car.

Static ripples the hood of the car as it plows into his space.

Marta, stop.

The windshield begins to fracture. Eddies of smoke stream across the fender.

The Mustang is in his control now. Its speed will decrease predictably against his output so long as its acceleration is constant. Marta shows no intention of slowing down. His mind gauges it. As soon as he shifts, the field he has generated will collapse. The car will gain speed again, but this should be too late to affect his jump, assuming he still has the strength to make one more.

He sees the car's lines bend before breaking apart. Visualizing the bend is easy, but his body's ability to channel is wearing. The red shift is slower to come this time. There is smoke on the windshield. For an instant he sees himself in front of the car before vaporizing into a blue flash.

There is no time to get his bearings. His hand is on her throat. The car swerves sharply as she releases the wheel with a scream. The car flips into a roll. She claws at him as their bodies are thrown against the windows in a fury of shattering glass and twisting metal. Skidding across the pavement, the cabin fills with sparks before creaking to stillness.

Everything stops.

The only sound is the hiss of the radiator above the ping of an engine fire smoldering under the hood. The taste of antifreeze is in the air.

He lies in the wreckage, staring impassively at Marta's unconscious face, his left hand gripped on her throat. With his right hand he reflexively searches his belt. The presence of the ops never leaves his mind. Feeling it secure at his waist, he slides himself across the interior of the roof of the car, dragging Marta by the neck as he goes. Kicking the remains of the windshield out of the way, he grabs a support column with one hand and pulls himself out. Pushing against the car with his feet, he hauls her onto the pavement next to him.

She seems unconscious, but he takes no chances.

There is a hush as the remains of the car ignite in flames. Keeping his hand on her neck, he wraps his right arm around her from behind and drags her down the side of the highway. Traffic is coming.

He kneels over her, pinning her head to the road.

"Marta!"

She lays still.

She is playing with him.

His hand sends a shock to her.

With a snarl, her eyes fly open, black as holes in her head. She bares her teeth, bloodied from the wreck. Another charge from his hand jolts her as he slams her head on the black top.

"You didn't take Sophie. It was Sarah."

She makes a wide smile. "Are you going to kill me, Daddy?"

"How did you know Sophie was at the cabin?"

"Sarah always said you'd kill me."

"Did you follow them?"

She blinks. "If I don't tell, will you kill me?"

"Not now, Marta. Answers first."

"If I killed Sophie, you'd kill me."

"That was you in the gulch, wasn't it?"

Her face twists. "You left her alone."

"I know."

"She almost left you."

"That's what you've wanted."

"She hates you." Her voice is a whisper.

"Everyone hates me. Did you follow Sarah to the cabin?"

"I love you." It is the cry of a child.

"You were at the market last Thursday. What were you doing there?"

"I wanted a pie."

"Marta, I can't help you if you don't help me."

She howls.

In the distance he can hear a truck. Looking around, he sighs. Suddenly, he doesn't regret being childless. She begins to sob and he looks down at her. She spits a bloody tooth in his face.

A violent shock from his fingers stuns her, his grip burning into her skin. Forcing open her mouth, he presses his face to hers. The taste of her blood sickens him, but his rage wants her breath, inhaling hungrily. If she were human, he would feel her life, but she is less than that. She is filled with a cold void, a darkness his body eagerly takes for itself.

He hears the slam of a car door. Blind with light in his eyes, he shuts them tightly and tries to finish what little there is. She is only half. She could have never been more than that.

Two people approach.

A woman's voice calls 911 on a cell.

"We're driving a green RV … I don't know exactly, somewhere north of Forks. I see two people … There's a car on fire. It's upside-down."

Another pair of footsteps runs closer. A man.

"You okay?" The man shouts back to the woman, "There's two people here. He's giving CPR—"

He isn't giving anything. When he is finished there will be nothing left. But something isn't right, something is stalling him.

Impossible.

He feels the flow into him slowing. Slowing. The flow stops.

His eyes open.

He tries to pull away from her. He can't. Something is trying to take him.

Grabbing Marta's throat with both hands, he strangles her to break the hold.

The man's hands are on his shoulders. "What the hell are you doing?!"

He is choking.

He's stopped it, but just barely. If he doesn't free himself, it will exhausted him. Marta will feed on him instead.

"Let her go!"

The man roars, wrapping arms around his middle, pulling him off the ground. Marta is pulled off the ground along with him. He feels his eyes begin to roll back in his head. There is another heave, and they are dropped. Marta's head hits the pavement and the flow shudders. It is enough.

He tears his mouth away.

The man drags him off of her. Coughing on hands and knees, he chokes on air that brings no relief.

"What are you? Some sick freak?"

A kick to his side rolls him on his back. Gasping, he opens his eyes to blue light.

"Jesus." He feels the man back away.

Damn.

Scrambling to his knees, he staggers to his feet. Taking a few steps back, his mind reels to get its bearings. The wreck is to his right. The approach of sirens to his left. The forest is behind him. Holding his sides, he turns from the man and walks blindly for the trees.

"Mister! The ambulance is coming!"

It is the woman. Her footsteps run to him from the direction of the wreck.

"Let him go, Bev."

Fear is palpable in the man's voice.

Blinking fiercely, his vision is slow to return. The dark shadow of the forest leads him forward. He stumbles on a log. Putting his hand out, he recovers without slowing. Sooner or later there will be a tree. His hand brushes against the rough of a trunk. Pushing into the woods, he carefully navigates, sensing the trees around him. After fifty yards, he stops. Pressing his back against a trunk, he sinks to the ground, waiting for the world to materialize.

Listening to the drama on the highway, he hears the dispatches. They'll trace the car's registration to the rental agency and then to him. He's just gone missing twice in the last seventy-two hours. That has to be a record. The two witnesses tell their accounts of the accident. They both give a description of him. The man says nothing about his eyes, only that he was disoriented when he went into the woods. A search is being organized. He will be gone by then.

The ambulance speeds Marta away. She is unconscious, but alive and stable. She is human enough. They'll ignore her differences. As long as she keeps her wits and doesn't eat the paramedics, she'll be free to make his life miserable again. Hopefully, she'll make Sam's miserable first. He will have to finish her somehow, but that will have to wait. The cabin remains. Sarah will return if she thinks Sophie is there.

Sophie should be away with Anthony by now, vanished into the sea of humanity. Whatever he faces at the cabin, he will face freely, without attachment. He will not worry about her.

There is no time.

Getting to his feet, he tries to see the cabin, though he can barely see the tree in front of him. The cabin shifts in his thoughts uneasily. The reality of his vision blurring with memory. He takes a painful breath and tries to focus again. Then it comes; it is clear and he knows what he is seeing is real. The cabin is empty. Willing it to him, he channels his strength. The fire in him falters as the trunks of the trees in front of him wobble into a lazy blur.

Closing his eyes, he redoubles his efforts. The current resurges, burning raw in his veins. The atmosphere around him evaporates. He feels something hard against his forehead. Opening his eyes, he sees wooden floor boards. He pushes the floor away. Looking around, he is on his knees in the middle of the cabin. Rolling onto his back, he stares at the ceiling with a gasp. In moments, he is asleep.

Sleep.

Or something worse.

Its whole universe is dark. Darker than void. Suffocating. It is the dark of Metatron. Endless. Senseless. It remembers time served. Required solitary confinement. Penance by attrition. A ceremonial term of confinement, still nearly enough to drive It mad. Knowledge instilled, branded into memory.

It must disappear.

Cease to exist.

It hears a voice where there should be none. There are no voices beyond one's own thoughts in Metatron. No sound to break the monotony of hell.

There is a whisper in the dark.

... battle ... be ... god ...

It can't make out the words.

host ... by ... power ... all other ...

Michael

His eyes open.

Darkness. Not of Metatron, but of night. The whisper is the lake, lapping the shore. The wisdom of sleeping on the floor is questioned as he tries to get up. Every part of him aches. Normally, a floor wouldn't affect him. It is little different from sleeping in his crypt, save that while the crypt takes his pains away a floor only seems to add to them. Getting to his feet, he notices a hole in one of the floorboards. Checking his coat, he finds a hole to correspond. Pulling up his shirt, he sees the black scorch on his side. A breach. It has burned itself out, but not before melting his clothes. After the day's events, new clothes were probably in order anyway.

More important than clothes, however, is food. Eyeing the kitchen, he approaches the refrigerator. Too tired to see inside without opening it, he pulls on the door and finds it as empty as they left it. He considers the bottle of ketchup, but decides to look elsewhere. In the cupboard, he finds a half box of saltines. Opening the box, he stands at the sink and pushes them into his mouth, five at a time, washing them down with glasses of stale tap water.

Pushing aside his unholy appetite, he heads upstairs for fresh clothes. Since they started using the cabin regularly, Sophie began leaving a supply of clothes behind in accordance with her no packing rule. Apparently, Sophie stayed true to her rule when she left. The bed is unmade and there is little sign she took anything with her. Removing his coat, he tosses it onto the bed. Pulling off the cardigan, he yanks the button-down shirt off over his head. Soiled with dirt and soot, they sport holes to match his raincoat.

In the bathroom, he turns on the light to evaluate the burn in his side. The one-inch hole in his flesh is a perfect circle. It is black and deep, burned from the inside out, very likely from when he made his last jump. It penetrates to his core and will rupture repeatedly until his crypt can restore it. It will not heal otherwise, only growing larger, reaching its inevitable conclusion. Opening the medicine cabinet, he finds the only toiletry item in the bathroom that is his: a roll of fiberglass tape. Applying enough to cover the gap, it is his only measure against the erosion that has begun.

He sees a face in the mirror when he closes the medicine cabinet. It is smeared with dried blood. His interview with Marta returns to mind. The broken smile, the bloody lips, the soulless eyes. When his eyes catch his gaze, the ice in them startles him. It is Marta's blood on another face he sees. Turning on the tap, he washes it off.

Returning to the bedroom, he searches the dresser drawers, finding a cotton tee and a pair of jeans. Sliding the ops from his belt, he places it on the dresser and changes his clothes with his eyes fixed on it. Putting on his belt, he is replacing the ops when he catches sight of a flannel shirt on the floor. It is the shirt Sophie slept in the night before. Snatching it up, he holds it to his face before pulling it on over the tee and grabbing his raincoat on the way out.

At the bottom of the stairs, he swaps his perforated raincoat for a wind breaker hanging on a coat hook next to the door. Emptying the pockets of his raincoat, he quickly fills the few pockets in his windbreaker. His wallet goes into the back pocket of his jeans, but the bulk of identification papers go into the wood stove. A blue spark commits them to flame.

As he watches the papers curl, he wonders how much longer he should wait for Sarah. It seems unlikely she would abduct Sophie and leave without returning at some point. He wishes he asked Sophie more questions about the story Sarah fed her before he left. In hindsight, Sophie's information would have proved more useful than Marta's. But he couldn't have foretold that. Marta was too dangerous to let go without knowing more, without trying to stop her. In the end, he achieved neither objective.

But Sophie is gone, and with her the urgency that dogged him. That Anthony is gone must signify he left with her. The two people he feared for most are free of the lot of them. He can wait for Sarah. Or wait for nothing.

Outside, the wind has picked up on the lake. Walking in darkness to the back door, he opens it to a flood of moonlight. The moon is waning, but still quite full. Stepping onto the back deck, he follows his feet to the water's edge. The shore is dotted with campfires. Most of the cabins on the lake are in use this time of year. The indistinct presence of his neighbors, once disquieting, is a comfort to him tonight. It reminds him the human spirit is as enduring as his own. It is a comfort that is pleasantly distracting, but not enough to veil the presence of one of his kind drawing near.

The thread of static sharpens in his ears. It is one of ECCO. Alone. Not a threat. There is the approach of a car. The engine stops, a door closes, footsteps on gravel. A woman's.

Without a backward glance, he continues to watch the lake.

"Where is she?" Sarah's voice is unusually marked with concern.

"Gone."

"Gone?" He feels her closing on him. "Where?"

"Someplace safe."

"I thought she felt safe here already? Why alarm her?"

"I thought otherwise."

"Was that before or after?"

He turns on her. "Before or after what?"

Sarah laughs. "You've got more than lipstick on you, Sam." She fingers the collar of his flannel shirt before touching his face. "I can smell her all over you."

For once, Sarah's smile matches the fire in her eyes.

1199 BC The sun just set when the caravan completed the crossing. People were unloading their wagons and clearing brush to make camp. At this time, one of my guards dismounted to take something from a pack on his horse. He approached me with a rope in his hands and ordered me to my feet. Ordering me to put out my hands, I looked to the other guard, still on his horse, still with a spear tip indicating my heart. It would have done nothing, but I was surrounded by watchful eyes and fully accountable for my actions. Putting out my hands, I let them be bound at one end of the rope, the other to be harnessed to his horse. In this fashion I would be led to my host.

The walk was not far, the end of the line near where we started, though the scrutiny of those I passed made my burden great. Being what I was, being observed was torture enough. When we arrived at the rear guard, my general was not in evidence. A great campfire had been lit and around it a company of soldiers were preparing for the evening. One in particular was a big man in fine armor—his leathered head and the scar on his face proof he had earned it.

I was brought before him a Canaanite spy. The only questions left, who sent me and why. They were the only reasons I was still alive. Still not seeing my host, I could bide my time no longer.

"I am Khepera, guest of your lord. I beg to see him."

The big man frowned. "How is it we have not seen you?"

"I only arrived yesterday and spent the night. Others have seen me."

"Who?"

"Ashebu."

"And how did you end up in the wilderness? This guard says you came from many miles distant and walked the woods as if you knew them."

"I rode out on horseback. When I stopped to take a nap, it took flight, leaving me to find my way back."

Some laughed, but their commander silenced them with a hand.

"What does this horse look like?"

"Dappled gray with a red-fringed blanket."

He nodded. "You will soon get your wish. My lord will join us and see you himself. In the meantime, we will keep eyes out for your horse. Have you eaten?"

I shook my head and he looked past me.

"Unbind him. Give him a ration."

No sooner did he speak than I was seated on a stool, my hands free.

"Where are you from, Khepera?"

Seated closer to him, I could see his eyes were gray in the dark. They did not stray from mine, but I sensed they saw everything around us.

"Ineb Hedj."

He nodded. "I, too, was born within the White Walls. It is a fair place."

"Yes."

As I answered, a plate of bread, beans, and dried fruit materialized before me.

"How do you know the general?"

"He knew my father …" I ate, hunger stalling my thought. "He was a tutor."
"But your father was not Egyptian?"
Swallowing, I shook my head, wishing I had given more thought to my hair.
"Akkadian."
He nodded again. "Proud people."
Eating, I only smiled.
"Rightfully so." He added with a grin.

[Spharic. Entry translated from *Kor Dai Maihael*. Mund Dai. b. 755 BC]

[Wedding photo of Sophie's parents, Edie and Peter Davids, 1970]

2000 Looking down at his shirt, he watched her pull a long hair from his shoulder. Her mother's eyes bore into him.

"Sophie's hair. When she lived at home, it went everywhere."

If he could sweat, he'd be doing it now.

"Michael let my hair into his life when he let me use his laundry so I wouldn't have to use the creepy one in my building."

Sophie still hadn't let her mother know she was living with him.

"Oh?" Her mother raised her brows. "You can always bring your laundry home."

Sophie took his hand, leading him from the living room. "I'm trying to be a big girl, Mom. That means taking advantage of my peers instead of my parents. Of all people, I thought you'd appreciate that."

"I do." Her father raised a hand.

Sophie's mother shot a glare at her father as they left the room.

"Where are you going?" Her mother eyed them.

"I'm just going to show Mike around." Sophie pulled him after her.

"Dinner will be ready soon." Her mother warned. "Don't take too long."

"Where are we going?" He found himself whispering as Sophie led him upstairs.

"Switzerland."

"Where?"

She glanced back at him. "My room."

At the top of the stairs, they turned right and continued down the hall to a door at the end. He peered over her shoulder as she opened the door to a room with a large dormer at one end. It was furnished with a four-poster bed, a chest of drawers, and a desk, but these were hard for him to focus on. The walls were wallpapered with posters and clippings from papers and magazines, blurring the dimensions of the room, completely obscuring the paint underneath. Sophie headed for a wall and opened a closet door only she could see, disappearing inside while he remained in the hall.

She peeked around the closet door at him. "You can come in. No hideous monster in the closet." She paused to glance behind the door. "A hideous prom gown or two, but I don't think they'd fit you."

Stepping inside the room, his eyes drifted across the walls. Some he recognized, others not. Charlie Chaplin, Marlene Dietrich, Virginia Woolf, Samuel Clemens, Karl Marx, the Marx brothers ...

"Who is this?" It was a photo of a shirtless boy in shorts sitting on a beach, his body covered in white paint.

Sophie was still digging in her closet. Looking back at him, she squinted. "Jimmy Crandall."

"Who's Jimmy Crandall?"

"A kid I dated in junior high."

"Why is he painted white?"

"That's sun block."

"Who are they?" Two young women with Sophie in matching purple dresses.

Sophie squinted his direction again. "Cindy Howard and Mary Schuler. We were in a wedding together."

"Who is this?" A young man on a motorcycle.

"Bobby Mullan. We dated in high school."

"Who is this?" A black and white photo of young man staring into the camera.

Rolling her eyes, Sophie was about to say something, but her face faded as she looked where his finger was pointed.

"Gregory Jacobs."

The one who died. Now the name had a face.

He waited, hoping she would say more, but she returned to the closet.

He moved on. "Who is this?"

Another black and white photo of a young man without a shirt.

"Jim Morrison."

"Was he a boyfriend?"

"Yeah." She kept rummaging.

"Why did you decorate your room this way?"

"Ever see *The Omen*?"

"Is it a movie?"

Her head came out from behind the door. "There's this priest who knows about a prophecy but he's scared the devil will do him in if he squeals, so he wallpapers his room with pages from the Bible so he can sleep at night."

"You thought the devil was going to kill you?"

"In my case, no. I thought the spiders were."

"Spiders?"

"They crawl out from under the paint." She ducked back behind the door.

He recalled her mention of past drug use.

"Flashbacks?"

"A little dab'll do ya …" She backed out of the closet. "Here it is!"

As she turned, she was dusting something with her sleeve.

"Catch!"

He had no idea what it was but was curious to see. The object had barely left her hand when his eyes predicted its speed and trajectory. Then they saw something else. Instead of catching it, he stepped back as it hit the carpet with a loud crack. As it rolled towards him, backed away. A black number eight on a white circle came into view as it wobbled to a stop.

"Or not." She frowned.

Squatting before it, he gave it a visual inspection before reaching out his hand.

"It's a Magic Eight-Ball, not a grenade …" Sophie's hand was there first as he watched her pick it up and look it over. "I hope it didn't break."

"Magic Eight-Ball?"

Shaking it, she looked at it. "Tells you whatever you want to know. Like right now I want to know if there's any hope for you."

She read it with raised brows. "In spite of you making a bad first impression, Eight-Ball likes you."

She handed it to him. Taking it in hand, he could feel it was filled with liquid. It had a side that was a window. An icosahedra floated inside.

Yes.

He shook it. The icosahedra floated another reply.

My sources say no.

He shook it again.

"If you find that riveting, I've got an Etch-a-Sketch, too."

Smirking, he stood up. "Why were you looking for this?"

"Amy uses hers a lot. The way things are at work, I figured I should get my own instead of borrowing hers all the time."

"You actually believe what this tells you?"

"Where do you think I got those figures for my presentation last month?"

He squinted at her. His perception told him she was lying, but to his hearing she sounded forthright. However, she was asking a question. It was easier to lie convincingly when asking a question than answering one.

She blinked. "I'm kidding."

"I know."

"Sure you do."

She took the 8-Ball from him and headed for the door. "Ready for round two?"

"I don't think your mother likes me." He followed her from the room.

She paused in the hall. "Mom's just giving you a once-over." Her eyes got big. "You do realize you're the first *boyfriend* ever to be invited over for Easter Sunday?"

He sighed.

"Boyfriend." She repeated.

"Stop."

"Boyfriend, boyfriend, boyfriend."

Narrowing his eyes, he walked past her. As he descended the stairs, a young couple was just entering through the front door. The young woman bore a strong resemblance to Sophie but wore a flowered dress he knew Sophie wouldn't be caught dead in. She had brown eyes and long dark hair pulled back with a pink ribbon. The man was blond and dressed in a shirt and tie. They froze when they saw him, but seeing Sophie at the top of the stairs brought smiles.

"Hey, Kate!" Sophie called over his shoulder.

"Hey back!" The woman gave a wave and approached the bottom of the stairs. The man gave him a wide smile and direct gaze.

Sophie skipped down the steps to hug her. "Glad you came south for a change."

"It was perfect timing. We had to drop off Mom at Sea-Tac anyway." Kate glanced nervously at him and Sophie smiled.

"Kate, this is Michael."

"Nice to meet you, Michael." Kate held out her hand.

As he took it, Sophie raised a brow at him. "This is Kate and Duane."

"Hello." He smiled at Kate, then at Duane and offered a hand. "Duane."

"Hey, Mike." Duane grinned.

As they shook hands, the force of Duane's grip was intentional. He responded in kind until Duane let go.

"You've got quite a grip for an antiques dealer." Duane laughed. "Sophie told Kate a bit about you, but I suppose you've heard the back story on us."

He nodded. "Congratulations."

"So are you stressing over the wedding yet?" Sophie asked Kate as they went into the living room.

"It's a breeze. Duane and his mom are handling it."

He could feel Sophie's doubt at her cousin's response.

"Mom planned all my sisters' weddings." Still flexing fingers from his hand shake, Duane put an arm around Kate's shoulder. "She's got the wedding thing down."

"I do get to have a say in some things, though. Like who gets to be my maid of honor, for example." Kate winked.

Sophie smiled weakly. "Seeing as you're the bride, that's only fair."

"I was hoping it would be you."

"I thought you already had a maid of honor?"

Kate glanced at Duane. "We had some kinks to work out."

"Well then, I'd be …" Sophie scratched her right ear. "Honored."

"Thank you." Kate gave her a hug. "I promise the dress won't be tacky."

He grinned at Sophie over Kate's shoulder.

As Kate led Duane to the kitchen to see Sophie's parents, he took Sophie's hand. "At least it won't be me." He whispered.

"Boyfriend." She stuck out her tongue before pushing him into the kitchen.

It was a surprisingly large meal in spite of the small number of guests. He decided whether or not Sophie's mother ever got around to liking him, she would always make an effort to feed him. After his fourth plate of ham, she was still pushing food and seemed less suspicious of him the more he ate. Any situation he could eat his way out of couldn't be hopeless.

After dinner, Sophie's father invited him and Duane on a stroll. It rained earlier in the day but had cleared in the afternoon. The early evening was dry and cloudless. Walking down the North Slope towards Old Town, they paused to take in the view of Commencement Bay.

"This is like the night I proposed to Kate. The sun was just setting. You know, Maeve has that great view of Bellingham Bay from her backyard." Duane looked at Peter. "How did you pop the big question on Edie?"

"I showed up at her apartment with a load of laundry and diamond ring."

Duane hooted. "Those were the days. If you tried that now, she would have taken the ring and made you do the laundry!"

"That's exactly what happened." Peter answered with a quiet smile.

He was still smiling at Peter when Duane turned on him.

"So when are you going to make an honest woman out of Sophie?"

He glanced nervously at Peter, who watched Duane quizzically.

"We aren't that far along yet."

"Well, when you decide to take the plunge, remember, a big ring doesn't hurt."

Peter smirked behind Duane's back and started to walk again.

"And remember the details." Duane continued. "Women obsess over stuff like what you were wearing, what you were doing, where you were. I got my idea from Katie after she told me she used to pretend she was a princess trapped in her tree house. The next time we were at Maeve's, I took her to the tree where her tree house was and proposed under it. She couldn't say no. Had tears streaming down her face. She told all her co-workers about it."

They turned west. He watched Peter silently walking ahead of them before summoning the courage to ask.

"What do you think a woman wants when she is proposed to, Peter?"

Peter glanced back at him. "What we all want. To feel needed."

Duane laughed. "Good thing you didn't need Edie to do your laundry."

"*Need*." Peter rolled his eyes at Duane. "Not use. You can pay someone to do your laundry. I couldn't pay anyone to make me feel the way Edie does."

He caught up with Peter. "How do I convince Sophie I need her?"

"Tell her."

"I have."

"Don't stop."

"No way." Duane interrupted. "C'mon, Mike. What woman wouldn't want to be married to you? Women need *men*. Men who know what they need and can give it to them. What a man needs, he gets for himself. If you act needy, you get women who don't respect you because you aren't playing your part."

"And what part is that?" Peter asked.

"The lead. The hero. Not the fool." Duane gave a look of disgust.

He looked at Duane. "But I'm not playing a part. I really do need Sophie."

Duane shook his head. "Need is a weakness. Women want strength."

"Women want sacrifice." Peter spoke without looking back at them.

"Of course they want sacrifice!" Duane shot back. "A man's life is about sacrifice. To God, to country, to his family. It's a duty that comes with the responsibility to know when those sacrifices need to be made. You don't hand that off to your wife."

Peter stopped. "That's easy to say when you're young. It's why young people fight wars. I did two tours in Vietnam before I met Edie, and meeting her is the only reason I didn't sign on for a third. I crawled through a jungle for God and country and got a medal. I don't need a medal. I need Edie." He shrugged. "If that makes me a fool, so be it."

Without waiting for a response, Peter walked away. He had never heard Peter say as much at one time before. From the silence that followed, he guessed Duane hadn't either. They followed the sidewalk up Carr Hill as the street lights came on.

Duane spoke up. "I'm sorry, Mr. Davids. I didn't mean any offense."

"None taken. And please, it's Peter."

"Peter, right."

"Don't you live near, Michael?" Peter kept his eyes on the street as he spoke. "At the top of the hill. Five blocks to the right, at the end of Prospect."

"That's in the gulch."

"Yes."

"Sophie used to play down there." Peter grinned. "Don't tell Edie."

"She told me."

"She said there was a haunted house."

"There is. I haunt it."

"Then my hunch was correct. You're related to Daniel Goodhew."

"Yes, he was my great-uncle."

"My maternal grandfather was Thomas Goodhew. Daniel was his nephew. Are you one of Peter's descendant's?"

"His sister, Sarah."

Peter paused to look at him. "He didn't have a sister."

He swallowed. "She was a half-sister."

"You and Sophie are cousins?" Duane looked at him with surprise.

"Many times removed." Peter pointed out.

"So it's still legal to marry her." Duane slapped him on the shoulder. "Sounds like you're on the hook."

Peter started uphill again. "What was your father's name?"

"Same as mine."

"If the opportunity presents itself, I think my mother would like to meet you."

"I'd like that."

Duane's voice came out of the shadows behind them. "Sounds like you might as well propose, Mike. You're already family."

Feeling confidence in the darkness, Michael glanced at Peter. "I would like to … Mr. Davids—I mean—Peter … to propose marriage to your daughter. May I?"

"You may." Peter smiled at him, extending a hand.

He held his breath and took it, looking Peter in the eyes. As soon as he let go, he dropped his gaze to the street. Feeling flush, he knew his eyes would show it.

A whistle broke the night air.

"Congratulations!" Duane jumped in front of him with hands in the air. "High five!"

Keeping his head down, he stopped and raised his hand to his brow.

Duane's hands dropped. "You okay?"

"Fine. I think I got something in my eye."

Peter took his arm and started him walking again. "We're only a few blocks from the house. Just don't rub it in. We'll wash it out with some saline."

Three will seek. A blind eye. A silver tongue. A deaf ear.
Two will join. Half full. Half empty. Both broken.
One will come. A child of both. A child of none. Alone.

[Spharic. Second triptych of the last prophetic line
translated from *Ho Pro Fanai.* d. 0]

REVELATION

2003 Feeling her hands take his, she draws close. His instinct is to push her away. He must decide what to do. Her lips are on his and it feels like kissing a sister he's never had. But it is more than affection. His revulsion flashes to panic when he feels her arms reach around his waist. The ops.

Grabbing her arms, he holds her wrists to her sides, kissing her deeply. Deeply enough to satisfy his brother, deeply enough to cause her pain. He feels her struggle against him as he breathes her in. His spirit, wanting to assume hers, hungers for more. When he lets her go, she stands with her eyes closed.

"And Phanuel always warned there was no way to tell you apart." Her fire escapes with her breath like blue smoke before she inhales it again.

Grinning, he starts to walk around her. "You still think you can?"

He reaches under his windbreaker, feeling the ops in his palm.

"Always."

"Nonsense." He speaks over her shoulder, "You can't read my thoughts."

"I could feel you coming around the lake. There's something about you your brother doesn't have."

"A sense of humor?"

"Ease. Confidence. You didn't even turn as I approached you."

"I was watching the moon."

"As always. You're fearless."

"Are you calling my better half a coward?"

She narrows her eyes as he turns to face her.

"I thought I was your better half."

Taking her hand, he pushes for a reaction. "If you're worried there won't be room at the inn there's no need to panic."

She yanks her hand away. "What are you saying?"

"You know the paranoia you've been displaying lately isn't flattering. I thought we'd worked through that."

"And I thought we'd worked through this. Sophie was supposed to stay here until

Michael and ECCO were no longer a threat."

He smirks. "And wait for my brother to finish them off in his interminably plodding fashion?"

"He isn't plodding anymore." She snaps, "He's desperate. Yesterday he declared war on ECCO if I didn't hand over Sophie."

He claps his hands. "That's my boy!"

"Your boy has made me a fugitive. Where is he?"

"Misery loves company."

"You're changing the rules on me, Sam."

"Rules? Ridiculous. Who do you think you're dealing with?"

"*My husband.*" The declaration comes through clenched teeth.

He struggles to feign indifference. "At least now you can scream it out loud."

"Do you have any idea what position you've put me in?"

"Michael did that, not me. I told him to confess his marriage and beg for forgiveness. Apparently, he had ideas of his own."

"A trait you both share. If you can't control him, he'll hunt for Sophie no matter where you hide her. The baby will never be safe."

"That is a trait we don't share, Sariel. My brother could never kill an infant."

"Marta will, and you know she is beyond reasoning with."

"Thanks to you." He arches a brow.

"At your request! I told you I didn't know how to raise a child."

"Wolves would have done better."

"Wolves wouldn't touch her." She sneers.

"I hope your maternal instincts have improved by the time Sophie delivers."

"And I hope Michael's seed improves your own."

He attempts Sam's smile. "Now you sound like my wife."

"And what if it's Marta all over again?"

"Don't worry yourself. I'll kill it."

"I suppose that is in your prophecy, too?"

"We all have to make sacrifices, Sariel."

"Don't talk to me about sacrifice. Everything I've done has been for the prophecy."

He snorts. "Everything you've done, you've done for yourself."

"*Myself?*" Her eyes spark. "I've sacrificed all of me. My beliefs, my position, my very existence, all for you."

With a laugh, he starts back to the cabin. "Not for me."

"I never loved your brother." She says sharply.

"Good, because you won't have to trouble yourself with telling us apart anymore."

For a moment she says nothing. When she does, it is breathless.

"Then he was telling the truth? He surrendered his crypt to you?"

"He offered me everything on the condition Sophie is kept safe." He shrugs with a grin. "I've just been keeping up my end of things."

"He gave his crypt for her?"

"*Not for her!*" He turns on her with a flash of temper before dropping his voice to pleading sweetness. "To me. To us. To what he realized was destined to be."

"Then he accepts he cannot win?"

"He had nothing to lose."

His use of past tense alarms her.

"Where is he?"

Sam never answers a direct question.

He nears her, smoothing her cheek with the back of his hand. "The end of the age is upon us. This is no time for regrets."

She closes her eyes. "I only regret the time we wasted."

His hand drops. "We'll see."

Continuing to the cabin, he leaves her behind.

"You don't believe me?" She follows him.

"Be honest, Sariel." He talks over his shoulder. "You weren't counting the days until Sophie came along."

"If I felt that way, would I let her be the mother of your child?"

He ignores this.

"My brother chose well. She's better than Anne." He turns to wink at her. "Nine months from now will be the proof."

"The difference was Michael. If he'd taken Anne, Marta would have been different."

"Perhaps. Only my brother could watch a woman throw herself at him and never touch her." He watches Sarah's face as he opens the cabin door. "Sorry."

"I never threw myself at him."

"That's too bad. If you had, he might have come to me sooner. God ..." His hands search his pockets. "What I wouldn't give for a cigarette."

Sarah reaches into the pocket of her blazer and hands him a pack.

He takes it from her with a grin. "Will you marry me?"

She gives an icy smile.

"Ladies first." He nods at the door of the cabin as he opens the pack.

Looking into the darkness, she hesitates.

"Where is he?" She asks again.

He lights the cigarette in his mouth with a thought while he stashes the pack into the liner of his windbreaker.

"Louis? Trolling Port Angeles on a bottle of whiskey."

"Don't play with me, Sam."

"It's what you live for."

"Michael was here." She whispers. "Wasn't he?"

"Come and gone, my dear." He blows out a stream of smoke.

As she backs from the door, her eyes flicker. "And what am I?"

"That is entirely up to you."

"What does that mean?"

"Are you coming with me or going my way?"

"Where?"

"ECCO."

She makes a small smile, rigidly stepping from him.

"I'll drive." Her voice is a whisper.

She turns away from the cabin and starts for the car.

"No last respects before we leave?"

He watches her stiffen as she stops in her tracks. She turns, her eyes glowing. Taking a long draw on his cigarette, he flicks it through the open door. A blue flash briefly fills the cabin windows before they are darkly lit by spreading flames. Turning his back on the fire, he goes to her.

"Wasted time indeed." He sneers as he heads for the car.

Reclining in Sarah's Audi S8, he is relieved he isn't the only singularity on the road in a performance automobile with lousy gas mileage. Listening to the quiet hum of the engine causes him to reflect. He lets his mind wander. There is no risk of his thoughts being read unless he wishes it. Only Sam might hear, possibly Marta.

And Sophie.

It is a degree of intimacy she still rejects. She has heard him, knows she can speak to him, but has only ever done so over short distances and then, only when she is angry. When he speaks to her thoughts, she prefers to responds aloud. Irritably. She assumes he is reading her and hates it. Most of the time he isn't.

He tries to be good.

Now he tries to read Sarah.

Still as a stone, she drives in silence, wrestling with herself. Whether or not she really loves Sam or ever loved him, her thoughts are beyond saying. They are a confusion now, a tangle of ambition and fear. His name keeps coming to her. She is trying not to think it, but she is upset at the thought he is gone. It is true—she never threw herself at him. He only guessed it when she kissed him. The smell of Sophie on his shirt made her wonder about them together, and it wasn't Sam she was thinking about.

But it wasn't love. Cold, demanding, ruthless. Sarah and Sam make a perfect couple. Now she is terrified of him, or what she thinks Sam has become. He has no sympathy for her. If it is desperation for him to risk Metatron for love, it is hubris for Sarah to think she can deal with Sam and win. As she grips the wheel of the car, he closes his eyes and lets go.

Downtown Seattle is deserted in the first hours of Monday.

The building ECCO calls home is deserted as well. The black granite exterior is lined with a semblance of windows. Windows looking out on nothing and letting in even less. He does not feel the others. They have gone to ground. They are watching, waiting. Their phalanx of sentinels await. Already he feels their eyeless gaze as they approach. How they will interpret what they are seeing he cannot be sure. Will they see him or will they see Sam? If they are unaware of the depth of Sarah's betrayal, they will assume it is him. They will send word to the others. They will offer to talk.

If they see Sam, they will not talk. They cannot afford the risk and do not expect the opportunity. They will expect the worst all around. They will attack, and his journey will end here, with Marta on the loose and Sam hunting for Sophie and ECCO in tatters. Samael will win. It is terrible to contemplate, but there is no other way.

They will either see him or they won't.

Parking across from the entrance, the echo of their car doors against the building is the only greeting. Wordlessly, they cross the street. Sarah's prepossession has fled in his presence. Her footsteps, like her thoughts, follow in his wake. Whatever her fears, ECCO offers her nothing now. She will serve him without pause. Her reflection in the newly replaced glass of the lobby doors provides all the assurance he needs. She is smiling.

The doors are unlocked. They always are. The lobby welcomes them darkly in its perpetually unfinished state. He sees shadows move behind the walls in soundless flight. Crossing to the elevators, the welcoming chime is misplaced against the backdrop of institutional lighting.

Normally, the reality of his physical condition would never condone the risk of an elevator, but that is not Sam's reality. Sam's condition condones risk, especially for others. Especially him. Conserving his energy weighs heavily on his mind as he tolerates his dislike for elevators now. He does not penetrate the steel doors with his vision to alleviate the confines of the space. He does not strain to sense the proximity of others. He does not feel his emotions at all. Ironically, these efforts only convey a confidence in his powers that are escaping his grasp by the minute.

Right now, Sarah's strength may exceed his, but she is conserving as well. Possibly, she has been too afraid to visit her own crypt since becoming a fugitive. He assumes she summoned the energy to make a jump when she abducted Sophie from the market. For Sarah's size, taking Sophie with her would have been especially difficult, even if it was only from the market to their house. A costly leap she could still be paying for. Luckily, she didn't attempt a jump to the cabin and drove instead. Without her car, he would have been too weak to leave the cabin by any other means.

As they step into the empty expanse of the council floor, the table awaits as it always does: long, black, and barren. Eight empty chairs glisten under one bare fluorescent tube. Approaching the table with no expectations, he pauses and looks at Sarah.

With a welcoming hand and knowing smile, he beckons her. "Ladies first."

She moves to the chair at the opposite end of the table from her usual place. With a look of amusement on his face, he walks around to the head of the table. They sit down at the same time. They say nothing. They know they are being watched. They will wait. Sitting back in his chair, he closes his eyes.

They do not wait long. He opens his eyes at the first sign of their arrival. Their waves of static come from all sides. It is not meant to surround them but is a defensive posture, a means of distracting his focus at the risk of giving their numbers away. If they meant to attack they would come en masse, swiftly, their combined strength being their only effective means of disabling him. Instead, this approach is open. He senses there are six of them, but two are small. Novices.

Four of them appear, the telltale ripple of their exit from warp dissipating around them in a blue halo. The novices come by the elevator—one is vaguely male, the other not. They cannot make the leap, too weak yet to bend anything more than the ears of their betters. Their betters are predictably Phanuel, Raphael, Gabrielle, and Zachariel. Phanuel will do the talking. He will become the dictator of ECCO if he isn't already.

"You come to repent?" Phanuel sounds skeptical.

"To treat."

Phanuel smiles at him. "You offer yourselves then?"

He smiles at the question before answering. "We offer my brother."

"And you?" Phanuel looks at Sarah. "Do you return as deliverer or as one delivered?"

Her eyes drop to her hands, folded on the table in front of her.

"She comes with me." He braces for Phanuel's reaction. "She is my wife and will be mother to my child."

"*Your wife?*" Phanuel squints. "*Your child?* What happened to this Sophie? You're worse than Samael!"

"He is greater than Samael." Sarah announces.

The others only stare at her.

"Better …" As she looks at him, her voice trembles. "Aren't you?"

"Does it matter?" When he asks her, looks away.

Raphael stares at him, tensing. "Who are you?"

His eyes hold her. "Who am I, Sariel?"

"You are one of the three." Her voice is hoarse. "You are Bahiel."

The others back away.

"*The prophecy.*" Raphael whispers, turning on Phanuel. "Michael is lost to us! You pushed him too far."

"Michael was always lost to us!" Phanuel's eyes catch fire. "He was never one of us. How could he have been?"

"ECCO wouldn't exist if he hadn't come back!" Sarah stands, looking to each of them. "We all remember it. Diaspora. The Exodus. Our universe bleeding to *extinction!* It was a miracle Bahiel turned on itself. A miracle Michael spurned transience to join us. But not for you!"

She points at Phanuel.

"You spurned him. Even when he gave himself to Metatron, you shunned him."

Phanuel's eyes roll. "Better than standing by while he corrupted himself with desire."

"You drove him to it!" She hisses. "You accused him of need and gave nothing."

"The devout exist beyond need."

"Because you have nothing to offer them."

"I offer guidance."

"Guidance?" She scoffs. "Yours? Samael's? What's the difference?"

"I speak for Metatron. Samael only speaks for himself."

She juts her chin. "Samael speaks the truth! No one speaks for Metatron. In the end, Metatron assumes us all as Bahiel will."

Phanuel stares her down.

"Bahiel will never assume Metatron! Metatron is the one law, the one truth, the one eye of infinite vision!" Phanuel points at him. "Metatron will take you even as you take us!"

He blinks. "What if I told you I don't care?"

Raphael shifts on his feet. "What do you mean?"

"What if I said all is as it was?" He let's his brother's expression fall from his face. "That Bahiel is not reborn and Samael's prophecy is still a dream?"

Sarah's eyes widen. "Michael?"

"You are surrounded, Sarah."

"But the cabin—"

"If you were expecting Sam, he never came. But I couldn't leave any sign if he did. I had to cover my traces."

Sarah stands. "You are a fool to bring me here if you think it will exonerate you!"

"She's right." Phanuel smiles. "You will stand trial just the same."

"And I will stand freely. What you want are confessions. What I want are answers. There is no reason to deny either request."

Phanuel shakes his head. "Metatron will hear your confessions and sentence you both. That is all the answer you need."

"No." Raphael steps forward. "That is not all. We have come too close to ruin this time. Would you have preferred Michael and Sarah run to Sam? Twice now, Michael has had us at his mercy only to challenge us with questions. We must have answers."

"That we were blind to Sarah's defection is warning enough." Gabrielle joins. "They cry out to be heard, and I will heed it. We owe it to them and ourselves."

Phanuel looks to Zachariel, who only nods.

With a sigh, Phanuel regards Sarah. "What led you to this disgrace, Sariel?"

Still standing, she grins, then smiles, then begins to laugh. Phanuel flinches as the others watch with a sense of confused horror. For some time she laughs, until the dark space around them rings with it. Gradually, her laughter dies and he senses a part of her has died with it.

No one speaks. No one moves.

In the silence, Phanuel is loathe to repeat the question. When Sarah finally looks up, Phanuel cannot return her gaze and glares across the table at him contemptuously.

He knows he must ask.

He waits for Sarah. Directing his will to her, her eyes can no longer look away. When they meet his, he stills her mind.

"When did you marry Samael?" His voice barely touches her.

Sarah's eyes lose focus. She lowers herself into her chair.

"A year ago."

Phanuel snorts in disgust.

He watches her gently. "Why did you marry him?"

"He watched you struggle with being alone. He was always watching. Waiting for you. When you found a soul ..." She pauses. "A mate, I turned a blind eye. Better that than going to Sam or leaving us. But you did leave." Raising her eyes, she squints. "When you married Sophie, I realized I wanted to leave, too."

He sits forward. "Is that why you helped Samael raise a child?"

"A child?" Gabrielle stares at Sarah. "*The* Child?"

"Impossible." Phanuel crosses his arms. "The prophecy is heresy."

"You weren't so sure five minutes ago." Raphael mutters.

"Sam knew he could see nothing in humans, but that you did." Sarah continues. "He believed the woman you loved would be the mother of the Child, but I knew he feared you would be the father and not him. Then Daniel called, worried that Anne was in love with you. I told him to send you away. When you wouldn't leave, I thought it was because you loved her. When you finally left, I told Sam." Sarah put her elbows on the table and covered her face with her hands. "I wanted to punish Daniel and hurt you. It was wrong."

"Disgusting." Phanuel hisses.

"Shut up." He shoots a look Phanuel's way before refocusing on Sarah. "How was Daniel able to contact you at all?"

"I used him to spy on you."

"He spied on me?"

"He didn't know he was doing it. He thought he was helping you. I told him you were going through a difficult time ... I needed him to trust me because I knew you didn't. When Anne claimed you came to her, he thought ..."

"What?"

Dropping her hands, she sits back. "He called me because there was no one else."

His mouth feels dry. "He thought it was me?"

She nods. "I told him it wasn't."

"Thank you ..." The breath returns to his body. "Did you know Anne was Daniel's daughter?"

She shakes her head. "Not until he called me in a panic to tell me she was pregnant—Michael, I swear I never thought it would happen. It wasn't supposed to be possible."

"It was simply an opportunity you couldn't resist." He finishes.

Sarah's lips disappear and for a moment she says nothing.

Taking a breath, she leans forward. "Sam said the Apostasy had begun and ECCO would end when the Child was born—if I helped him raise her I would be one of the three."

"And you believed him?"

"He said ECCO would be reformed. It would be mine."

"But ECCO was already yours."

"This?!" She waves a hand around the room. "What is ECCO without you?"

"Why didn't you tell me, Sariel?"

She glares at him. "Why didn't you tell me you loved Daniel? Why didn't you tell me about Sophie? You never came to me as a friend. Why would I tell you anything?"

His eyes release her. "I'm sorry."

"We're both sorry." Sitting back, she looks away, crossing her arms.

"You're both a disgrace." Phanuel concludes.

Zachariel stands over Sarah. "What of this child? Where is she?"

"I don't know." She sniffs. "She disappeared twelve years ago, but I suspected she was responsible for our losses."

"How can that be? She is half human."

He answers Zachariel's question. "It makes her nearly invisible."

"You have seen her?" Zachariel turns on him.

"Yes."

"Why haven't you killed her?"

"I've tried more than once, but she cannot be assumed."

"What?" Sarah wakes to his admission.

"Yesterday, after she led me to the cabin, she tried to run, but I caught her. I tried to assume her and was nearly assumed myself. It wasn't her dark half that resisted me. She has enough of a soul to be inviolate."

"A monster." Zachariel whispers.

"A lie!" Phanuel paces away from the table.

"A fact." He continues, "I barely escaped. If Sariel hadn't come looking for me, I wouldn't be here."

"Where was that?" Gabrielle asks him, watching Sarah.

"My cabin at Lake Crescent. Marta led me there to find Sophie."

"Was she there?" Gabrielle's question makes Sarah and Phanuel take notice.

"No." His eye observes them as he lies. "It was when I realized Marta had misled me that she tried to run."

Sarah's expression has turned to ice while Phanuel appears lost in thought. Zachariel's voice distracts him. "How did you find Marta?"

"She found me. She's been stalking me for three years."

"Why?"

"She thinks I'm her father. She knows the prophecy and fears another child might be born. She led me to believe she had Sophie, and I convinced her to take me to her on the condition I would accept her as my ... daughter."

"Why would she mislead you?"

"I don't know that she did." He looks at Sarah. "She led me to Sarah. I discovered it was Sarah who abducted Sophie and took her to the cabin at Sam's request."

"Is this true?" Gabrielle's eyes burn into Sarah, who only bows her head.

"He's attempting another child." Raphael glances around the table.

Sarah stares at her lap. "One who won't be like Marta. One he can control."

Phanuel looks at Sarah. "Where is Samael?"

He answers. "We don't know."

Phanuel smiles at him. "You are as evasive as your brother."

"Then you'll appreciate how helpful I've been by coming here."

"Helpful? Your lust has given your brother the opportunity to poison ECCO to the core. It has cost us our director, made you a violator, bred a monster, and left Samael one step closer to making prophecy a reality. Your presence is a curse."

He smiles back. "And a blessing."

"You are useless."

"Hypocrite." Sarah sneers at Phanuel. "He came back to save you, but you would rather fail than ask his help. Time is against you and Sam has his crypt. You can threaten Michael with Metatron all you want, but as soon as his body deteriorates, assuming him will be impossible."

Phanuel looks him over. "We don't need to assume his power as long as Sam never has it. Metatron will still have your sentience. A sentience that will be judged."

"Condemning me doesn't solve your problems. The facts remain. Samael is moving against you, has an unspeakable child, and may make another. Meanwhile—" He glances at the two novices standing nearby. "Your numbers are diminishing."

"What are you offering?" Raphael's tone is surprisingly authoritative.

"Let Sarah go and I will submit to Metatron freely." He sees Sarah sit up.

Phanuel erupts, *"Never!"*

"Shut up!" Raphael glares.

Phanuel flies to the table, gripping the back of a chair. "Let her go! Where? Back to her husband? Impossible—she knows too much!"

He fixes his eye on Phanuel. "If you don't, I will bring this building down on your heads and you will have none of me."

The static in the room begins to rise and the novices shift uneasily.

Phanuel returns his gaze and slowly smiles back.

The atmosphere spikes and the building begins to hum. Everyone is frozen. A loud snap breaks the tension. They all jump away from the table as particles of granite fly across the room. It is split in half, the floor buckling underneath into a widening crack. As the building trembles, the fissure begins to creep across the concrete floor.

"Michael!" Raphael puts out his hand. "Enough!"

The humming ceases.

He smiles, inwardly holding his breath. His insides are on fire as the fiberglass tape melts onto the skin under his shirt.

Raphael sighs. "You are heard, and what I hear is fair."

"This is a desecration." Phanuel turns his back.

Raphael looks at Gabrielle and Zachariel in turn. Gabrielle nods. Zachariel pauses to look at Phanuel's back before nodding as well.

Raphael turns to Sarah. "You are free."

The words illicit a curse from Phanuel.

"Michael?" Sarah asks.

Go. He wills her softly.

She sits frozen, staring at him.

"Please." He whispers.

She stands without a word. In a flash, she is gone.

The dragon is a powerful metaphor for both the positive and negative aspects of spiritual energy, though always with an emphasis on potency.

Unlike the avatars of deities depicted in human or partially human form, dragons are supernatural beasts, more akin to the elements of nature than the sentient eye of God. The fierceness is not indicative of any earthly animal, but an animism belying all living things. This is not to say dragons are lacking in sentience. Rather, dragons give sentience to what might otherwise be energy without focus or intent. The physical body of the dragon is essentially that of the snake, symbol of the endless cycle of eternity, only with four arms. These arms, like the four points of the compass, break the cycle of the serpent, giving it the potential for directed action.

These four points in turn represent the myriad variety of powers dragons can represent. The four elements of earth, fire, wind, and water. The four cosmic elements of heaven and earth, sun and moon. The four seasons. The four earthly levels the soul must transcend to heaven in the East. The four Gospels in the West. These can be further classified: The four virtues; loyalty, charity, chastity, and honesty. The four vices; cowardice, malice, avarice, and artifice.

In the East, dragons are powerful symbols designated into four categories; guardians of heavenly and earthly treasure and spirits of the elements of heaven and earth. As such, the dragon is considered the most propitious sign in the Chinese zodiac and was the exclusive symbol of the Emperor. In the West, dragons have a more dichotomous reputation evolved from virtuous in pre-Christian times to corrupt with the spread of Christian belief. As the Christian embodiment of vice, the dragon's power came from darkness and represented Satan's presence on earth. A familiar example is that of the dragon slain by St. George. In that legend, civilization is besieged by the desires of evil when the virgin of virtue is saved by God in the avatar of Saint George.

This dark casting of the dragon reflects the conversion of western culture from henotheistic inclusivity to monotheistic exclusivity. The image of one God in the form of man defeats the image of the dragon, a beastly compilation of supernatural powers in which mankind is only a small part. The danger in this monotheistic approach lies in the degree to which spiritual balance with the universe is excluded. If the core symbolism of the dragon is balance between eternity and action, spirit and sentience, animism and animal, then a wholly virtuous god is, by nature, imbalanced and must rely on external forces to exist. Light cannot exist where there is no darkness and vice versa. Thus, we are confronted by a paradox. When St. George slays the dragon he slays himself.

[Swedish. Excerpt translated from
The Mythology of Faith. E. Pehrson. d. 1822]

[Brass rubbing based upon a woodcut from the 1590 edition of Spencer's *The Fairie Queene* and dedicated to Queen Elizabeth I.]

2000 "Did you have a tree house when you were growing up?"
His voice floated up to me.

My teeth bit into the threads of the screws between my lips. I wiggled the bird-house half an inch more to the left before positioning the cordless drill. My finger squeezed the trigger.

Did you have a tree house when you were growing up?

The thought was drowned by the squeal of the drill. With the house anchored, I sat back on the tree branch and took another screw from my mouth.

You don't have to answer out loud.

The taste of metal was on my tongue.

"No."

Michael blinked up at me, a pained expression on his face as his hands held back the sun from his eyes. He said nothing and it made me feel like a jerk.

Resting the drill on my leg, I shrugged. "I thought you knew, seeing as how you've lived in my backyard my whole life."

"I told you. I stayed away from you when you were a child."

"A wise policy."

"Besides, I didn't know you were you until you were ten."

Smirking, I balanced another screw on the bit and positioned the drill. "You figured that out before I did, then."

"What sort of games did you play?"

"Usual stuff: hide and seek, tag, sibling torture." I drilled in the screw. "Why?"

"Did you ever imagine you were somebody else?"

"I imagined I had a horse for a while." I removed the remaining screw from my mouth and balanced it on the bit.

"Did your horse ever rescue you?"

"No." I positioned the drill. "His name was Jack and he followed me around."

"Did you ever think you were a princess?"

"Nope." The drill squealed again.

"You were never trapped in a castle by a dragon?"

"Trapped in a castle?"

I tossed the drill to him and he caught it without notice.

"With a knight who came to your rescue?"

Pushing myself off of the branch, I landed on my feet in front of him.

"You want to rescue me from something?"

"No."

Taking the drill from him, I paused. "You want to be a princess?"

He smiled. "No. I was just wondering if you had any childhood fantasies. That's one I've heard girls often have."

"I was never that girlie."

He nodded thoughtfully. "You were a man in your three previous lives."

"I won't hold that against me if you won't."

"I would still love you if you were a man."

"That's a comfort." Patting him on the shoulder, I squinted. "I'm glad we have these conversations."

We started across the yard. For a while, he said nothing.

"Would you love me if you were a man?"

"They say gender is between the ears and sex is between the legs. I suppose if my brain was suddenly in a man's body, I would."

"But you wouldn't love me if I were a woman?"

Stopping, I guessed he was fixating again, but the connection between childhood fantasies and homosexuality was escaping me.

"I'm not a lesbian."

"But you loved women before."

"I was a man before."

"But you just said you could love me if you were a man."

"No, I said my brain could love you if I were a man. Daniel and I might have the same soul, but this is my brain, not his."

"Yes." His tone was morose. "I know."

I frowned. "You want to be a woman? Is that what this is about?"

"I've never cared either way."

"Great!" I let out my breath and headed for the house. "This time you're the man, and I'll just stay a woman if that's all right with you."

"Would you love me without my body?"

Sighing, I stop and stare at the sky.

"Throw me a bone here, Mike. What do you want me to say? I love you, I love the thought of you, I love everything about you. But I need a body. Is that so wrong?"

"No." His face expressed nothing.

"*Yes.* Yes! You think it's wrong! Jesus! If it's so wrong, why are you even here?"

"I know how much my physical presence means to you. But I see your soul when I look at you. I see what you are without a body. That is what I am attached to."

"What did I just say? I said I loved everything about you."

"Even the parts you don't see?"

"Yes."

He looked at his shoes. "That's the problem, Sophie. You don't see me. You can't."

"You're being slippery again." I pointed. "That's a trick question."

"How can you love me if you can't see me?"

"This is a ridiculous conversation. I can't talk about this when you're standing right in front of me."

"What you're seeing isn't real. I'm not a man. I'm not even alive."

My insides began to turn. All I wanted to do was put up a bird house.

"And you're no knight in shining armor, either! They don't exist. Never did. Sure there were guys with swords, but they smelled bad when they weren't slaying each other over who got to rape the princess. You wanna know what women really fantasize about? Do you?"

"What?"

"The armor." I jabbed in the direction of the street with the drill. "And every sad sack of a man out there struggles every day to fit into it. So spare me the whining. If you think I fell in love with you for your looks, you're damn straight." I marched away. "It sure as hell wasn't your personality!"

Treading across a flower bed, I shoved my way through a hedgerow, determined to put as much space between us as I could. When I came around the corner of the tool shed, he was waiting for me.

"You think that's funny, don't you?" I passed him and opened the shed door.

"I was about to say the same thing."

Stepping inside, I could feel him behind me. "What is wrong with you today? Bad day at the office?"

"I don't work in an office and you know it."

When I turned, he stood in the door, his frame blotting out the daylight, his dim eyes like stained glass.

"Well, I do! Not that you'd give a damn." Reaching behind me, I flipped on a work light and replaced the drill in my tool bin. "And I come out here to get over it when my superhero boyfriend isn't belittling me for the limitations my physical presence has put on my ability to be an enlightened spiritual being."

"I do give a damn, Sophie. I know how miserable I am at sharing your burdens with you. I'm not a superhero and I don't intend to belittle you in any way. To the contrary, I believe your physical limitations only enhance your ability to be an enlightened spiritual being and ..."

He had gone unnaturally still.

"And?"

"I don't want to be your boyfriend."

"Ah, God." The air seemed to suck out of my lungs.

"I asked your father's permission."

Closing my eyes, I pressed my hands to my forehead.

"You don't want me to propose, do you?" His voice was a whisper.

Dropping my hands, I smirked. "Cornered in a shed with only a drill to defend myself? Probably not."

My regret was instant. My words as pat as my tone was dismissive. He shrank away from me like a shadow, his stare making the hair on my neck stand.

"Michael—"

I reached for his hand, gripping the edge of the door frame, but it disappeared from my touch.

"Wait!" I called to him.

He was standing away from the shed as I came out. Something about him had shifted. Even though he was only a few yards from me, I knew I couldn't reach him. What watched me was cold and lifeless.

"Michael ..." He flinched at my voice.

Holding out my hand to him, my eyes tried to waken his.

Michael, please. I'm sorry.
His lips parted.
I don't know if what you feel is for me or not.
His thought was barely a whisper.
"Of course—"
Clamping down on my tongue, I shut my eyes, searching for the answer.
I don't know if you don't.
It wasn't much of an answer.
When I opened my eyes, he was gone.
Really gone.
Five months of living with him and I had developed an eerie ability to feel when he was around. He wasn't in the garden, the house, or even the neighborhood.
"Shit."
I headed inside.
There was a line with him. A line between infallibility and innocence I always pushed. I saw it coming and mowed right over it. I resented the questions. The implications. But that wasn't his fault.
From the beginning I told him if I was going to be uncomfortable that was my problem. I was holding it against him anyway. I wasn't being fair.
That bastard owes you.
The voice in my head was unequivocal.
Entering the kitchen by the back door, I went to the refrigerator and looked inside. There was a soup tureen. I'd made gazpacho. So that was why he left. Opening the freezer, I pulled out a bottle of Absolut and crossed the kitchen to get a glass. I chose a high ball. Pouring four shots into it, I went back to the refrigerator and lifted out the tureen. At the counter, I ladled a cup of gazpacho over the vodka.
Dinner was served.
Glass in hand, I kicked off my Keds on the kitchen floor and wandered through the dining room into the living room. The black-paneled doors to his study stood in opposition to everything in the house graced with May. Rays of sunlight streamed through the windows, warming everything except their black finish. Taking a drink of my dinner, I strode up to them and tried the right hand knob. At first, I thought it locked. The turning was stubborn and my hand almost let go, but then it gave. The room within was cool and restful, almost inviting, save for the crypt, prone front and center like a body.
It was too dark. The stained-glass window in the bay couldn't make reading easy. With no other light in the room, I pushed the study doors wide. Sipping my soup, I studied the books on the shelves. If Michael was bent on my ability to see what he really was, this had to be the only indication of his mind I could see without the distraction of his body. Most of the books had no writing on the spine. Many that did were foreign to me. What I could recognize were books relating to Western belief. There were a variety of Bibles, Gnostic records,

324 | LISA MOWAT

Septuagint and Vulgate addendum, apostolic writings. Some were in English, or Middle English. Some were in Greek, Latin, French, German, Italian. The vast majority of the library was indecipherable, the languages ranging from runes and cuneiform to Sanskrit.

Crossing the study, I faced the journals he kept: a wall of them, bound in black. No numbers, no titles, only anonymous volumes from ceiling to floor. My eyes ran along the rows, spotting an empty space. There was a volume missing. Going to the shelf, I pulled the volume next to the empty space. Putting my glass on his crypt, I opened the book, finding precisely written pages inside, the handwriting so neat as to seem typeset despite the absence of any markings to guide his hand. The writing itself was in a language no human used, many of the characters looking mathematical. Some of the script was in rows, others in columns.

I snapped the book shut and put it back. Looking around the room, I asked myself if this was what I wanted to be married to. Would being married to this be any different than living with it? So he spoke a lot of languages. All of them. I'd never need a translator, unless I was trying to read him, in which case, he was no good.

My eyes went to the crypt with my dinner on it. Picking up my glass, I wiped the ring of condensation off its surface with my sleeve and took a swig. Leaving the study, I didn't bother to close the doors, but when I glanced back from the living room, the crypt was all I could see. Returning, I shut the doors. I stepped back and thought about moving the sofa in front of them, then remembered I had work for a meeting the next morning and went upstairs to my laptop.

That night I tried to sleep. At first it was easy, until a wind picked up around midnight. I woke to the thrash of tree branches on the windows and knew he hadn't returned. It was the first time I'd spent a night alone in the house.

Rolling over in bed, I saw the shadow of his pillow. I could make out the impression of his head and pulled it to me. It had no scent. Michael did. He smelled sweet, like a bakery, but nothing he left behind ever smelled like him. Scrutinizing the pillow case, I saw a hair. Picking up the strand, I wrapped it around my finger. I wondered what a lab would make of his DNA. Definitely, it was a piece of evidence Anthony would be curious to have. Letting it unwind itself from my finger, I let it slip from my hand.

I wondered where Anthony was. He was still in the apartment. Still single, although I knew he had dinner with Amy a couple times. Amy. She had invited me to lunch with her the next day. It would be the opening day of the Broadway Farmer's Market. I'd have to wear sensible shoes if we were walking. Maybe a hat. My mind ran in circles. It was trying not to worry about Michael. It was wondering if what happened in the garden was the end. It was tired of trying to figure him out.

He was afraid. That was what I saw in his eyes. I was afraid, too.

I don't know why you love me, either.

I thought it as loudly and clearly as I could.

Someday, someone will be foolish enough to ask me to marry him. I don't know who it will be, but I'll know when they ask me they're the one.
There was no answer, only the sound of the wind in the trees.

The next morning he hadn't returned.

In my meetings, at my desk, on the phone, I went through the motions of work. When lunch came, Amy and I took a welcome walk in the sun to the farmer's market. After a tamale and iced tea, a bag of kettle corn effortlessly filled my gut with empty calories while Amy effortlessly filled my head with workplace gossip. The latest news was Dan Fogel was getting back together with his ex-wife.

"Would you ever go back to Anthony?" Amy fanned herself with a pink canvas hat that matched her pink muslin sundress.

"Hell no. My mom likes to say, a good horse grazes forward."

"You've never broken up with a guy and gone back?"

"I think there's a time limit. I mean, if it's like you had an argument and stopped talking for a few days, that's one thing. But if you move out, that's different. Anthony and I didn't have a spat, we had a meltdown. You don't go back after that."

We walked along a row of produce vendors toward the commons where an audience was applauding. I tried to see up ahead while my tongue pried sticky corn husks from my teeth.

"I moved back in with an ex once." Amy put her hat back on and reached into my bag of kettle corn.

"How'd that go?"

Amy crunched on her corn. "Well, he isn't here, is he? At least I hope not." She searched the crowd with a grin.

My head shook. "Don't get me wrong. I hope Dan and Karen can work things out, but the success rate for remarriage after a divorce is pretty crappy."

"Yeah, but he's crazy about her. I could tell when we were going out. I think for him, she's the one. Poor guy, she's a flaming bitch."

"You say that like it's a bad thing."

"Speaking of flaming—" She pointed. "Oh my God! That is sooo hot to be doing on a day like this!"

On a small stage, a bald man covered in tattoos was eating fire. Between sucking in flames, he swallowed a sword.

"Ugh." Amy shivered.

"Please." I pushed through the crowd. "This is a farmer's market, not a circus."

"It's opening day. It's always like a circus on opening day." Amy pointed at a clown making balloon animals for kids. Not far away, another clown was juggling bowling pins and water balloons. Behind us there was a loud gasp and applause. Before I could get us away, Amy had wandered into the commotion.

In the circle of onlookers, she found an opening and I looked over her shoulder. It was red-nosed clown in a satin patchwork jumper, but instead of juggling, he was performing magic tricks. Seated at his red shoes were dozens of children and parents who were in hysterics, taking turns shaking the clown's hands. Everyone who did had their hair stand on end as though suddenly afflicted with the worst case of static electricity ever.

People whispered he must have something in his gloves. He seemed to hear this and clapped his hands. Pulling off one glove and then another, he rolled up his satin sleeves and offered his hand to a woman near the front. As soon as she shook his hand, her hair stood up and everyone burst into laughter and applause.

The clown didn't speak, only signed with his hands that he had another trick and pointed to the box he had been sitting on. It was covered with a velvet cloth. When he pulled it away, the audience saw it was an animal crate. Signing for the audience to be quiet, he opened the crate door and coaxed out a bowling ball. At first, the ball only rolled to the opening of the crate.

Pulling a box of dog biscuits from behind the crate, the clown removed a biscuit and held it in front of the bowling ball. The ball rolled from the crate, and slowly, the clown made it seem as though the ball were following him. The audience applauded as the clown pointed to a boy seated nearby and beckoned. He gave the boy a biscuit and encouraged the boy to lure the ball with it. The boy did so, and the ball did nothing. Then the clown encouraged the boy to pick up the bowling ball, which the boy had great difficulty in doing.

The clown signaled he had an idea. Reaching into the animal crate, he pulled out a bicycle pump. Putting the hose into one of the holes of the bowling bowl, he gestured to the boy to start pumping the pump. The boy started stomping on the pump, and with each stomp, the bowling ball began to float into the air. The audience was silent with astonishment. The clown invited the boy to spin the ball. When the boy spun the ball, the audience applauded.

"How did he do that?" Amy whispered to me over her shoulder.

Narrowing my eyes, I had my suspicions.

When we returned to the office, my e-mail was clogged with reports of the amazing magician at the farmer's market. Amy and I weren't the only hospital staff at the market on opening day, some co-workers even took digital footage of his tricks to share online. By my last meeting, Lyn Whittier had thrilled to the gossip and wanted to know the magician's name so she could hire him for her next fundraising event. Sitting at the far end of the table, I listened as Lyn described a trick the magician did with some dead roses that sounded miraculous.

It could simply be a street magician, I thought to myself. A very good one. Under the wig and makeup, there was no way I could tell from where I was standing if it was Michael or not. It was completely unlike anything he would do. It was impractical. It was fun.

Michael? Fun?

"He's here!" Lyn's assistant Deb hissed at us through the boardroom doors.

That answered my question.

Lyn looked annoyed at the interruption. "Who is?"

"The magician!"

Lyn jumped from the table and flew out the door at a speed her figure would have normally made prohibitive.

Dan Fogel looked at me. "I guess the meeting's over."

I clucked my tongue. "Team first."

Leaving the meeting, Phil from grant writing passed me.

He tossed a thumb over his shoulder. "There's a clown in your office."

I sighed. "My twenty million dollar donor, no doubt."

Rounding the cubicles, I saw Lyn at my office door. She was talking in an unusually emphatic manner, but I didn't hear anyone else.

Looking through the window, a clown sat on the chair in front of my desk, a surreal exhibition of red curls and multicolored satin dropped in the sterile sea of my working world. In spite of the heat of the day, it looked untouched, the red nose and garish smile as crisp as though painted on porcelain. It stared unblinking at Lyn as though it couldn't hear her. When I saw the blue glass eyes, I knew it could hear her just fine.

"When you can, if you could write down your name and number for me, we'd love to hire you. Oh!" She turned to see me. "Sophie, I was just asking him his name. Could you introduce us?"

"Sure. Mike this is Lyn. Lyn this is Mike." I stepped into my office and closed the door on her. "Thanks for stopping by, Lyn."

When I turned, he was holding out a bouquet of red roses.

"Thanks." I took them. "So how many times did you resuscitate these today?"

"Twenty."

"It's the thought that counts." Ducking my head, I looked under my desk. "Where's your pet?"

"That belonged to Sweeney."

"Sweeney?" Raising my brows, I sat on the edge of my desk and crossed my legs.

"I met him last evening when I was wandering. They were practicing in the park. He let me join them for a day."

"Just the day? You're not skipping town? Riding the rails?"

"No."

"You sure? You've got a killer act. You already have a fan club out there."

"I don't need fans."

"Do you get to keep the outfit?"

He looked down at the green and yellow pompoms on the front of his costume. "Sweeney didn't say. He just felt bad I wouldn't take any money."

"Honor among clowns?"

"It was an honor to be accepted."

"I have to say." Reaching for his head, I plucked at his wig. "You wear it well."

He blinked. "I wear it every day."

I nodded. "We all do."

Slowly, he grinned, his teeth as white as the paint on his face.

"I'm not Michael."

"Who are you?"
Getting down on one knee, he took my hands.
"Ahh." My eyes widened. "You're the fool who loves me."
"Sophie, will you marry me?"
"Yes."
As he rose to his feet, I grabbed him by the pompoms. When I let him go, I heard someone wolf whistle outside my office door. I hadn't pulled the blinds on my windows.
"Whoops." I whispered.
The perfect symmetry of his face was a smeared blur.
"You have paint on your face."
He stared at me intently, trying to wipe the tip of my nose with his sleeve, but I could finally see my fiancé through the smudged lines. I started to laugh.
"I'll wear it every day."

1199 BC Having slept during the day, I was not tired that evening. Waiting by the fire, I watched silently as the guard changed with the night. The big man retired to his tent after assuring me I was safe in his care. He gave me a blanket and bid me keep it. I did not learn his name. The others called him lord and it was not my place to ask. When the general arrived, it was only to give word of his passing.

His eyes were tired until they met mine.

"You no longer care for my company?"

"I have spent the evening caring very much."

He grinned. "You were worried I had drowned?"

"And I would be left high and dry."

"I thought you did not need me?"

"I was mistaken."

Looking past me to the tent of my caretaker, he called across the campfire. "Bes! Wake up, Buffalo!"

In less than a moment, the big man emerged from his tent, his chest striped white with scars.

"Is your company so much better than mine? My guest will not leave you even in sleep."

"Just the opposite. Your guest was lost without you. He found my fire and now I see you have found him. All is well."

"Then you will part with him?"

Bes smiled at me. "Not gladly."

The general looked to me. "And you? You still wish to come with me?"

"Most gladly."

Bes laughed as I rose to bow to him. "Thank you, my lord."

Taking our leave, the general asked as to the whereabouts of my horse.

"He forgot me."

This amused the general greatly. "And you worried he would not! Your wish has been granted!"

As he spoke, I found myself surrounded by his company. All were mounted and the general joined them. Once on horseback, he offered me his hand and a ride back to our tent. The eyes upon us told me it would not be without cost. Bowing my head, I backed away.

"Is walking your wish as well?" I heard frustration in his voice as I nodded.

"You realize you will not find your tent before moon set?"

Silently, I nodded again.

"Then you will have a guard."

"No, lord general. I must walk alone."

"And what if you find the wrong fire? Not all are as warm as that of Bes."

"Life is trouble. Only a fool thinks he can choose to avoid it."

The general said nothing at hearing his own words, only looked tired.

"Take rest." My voice calmed his mind. "I will find you by morning."

Something beyond my understanding made him hesitate. With a prod to his horse, he rode into the night, his men leaving a wake of dust.

Pulling my cloak over my head, I slipped into the bush. The sound of footsteps followed, determined to know where I was going, determined to have their suspicions proved. But they were the feet of men. Loud and clumsy. It was not long before they faltered, hearing no trace of me to guide them.

Finding the shelter of trees, I paused, my eye searching the caravan ahead of me beyond sight. I recognized my crypt many metes distant, but what I perceived woke my fears. It was not alone in my tent. Ashebu was with it. Holding a lamp above his head, he traced the script upon it with his fingers, trying to understand what no human mind should. There was nothing he could learn. The tools he needed to do so had yet to be invented. The crypt itself was indestructible and harmless so long as he did not lie inside.

A fearful thought to any living thing.

Feeling the trunk of a tree behind me, I lowered myself to the ground and took rest in the night, waiting for him to leave.

[Spharic. Entry translated from Kor Dai Maihael. Mund Dai. b. 755]

2003 "Layer it on or you'll regret it."
Already, the morning sun pushes seventy as we drive south on I-5.
"Sophie, I'm Italian. I can take the heat." Anthony hands back the tube of sun block after barely putting it on.

"We're not talking about heat. We're talking about UV, and unless they want to die of skin cancer, Italians need sun block." Squirting more suncreen on my hand, I rub it on his arm as he drives.

"You've got space aliens trying to kill you, and you're worried about skin cancer?"

I stop rubbing his arm. "Michael is not a space alien."

"Then what is he?"

"He's a singularity."

"A what?"

"An immaterial being."

"Like a ghost?"

"Sort of."

"You're married to a dead guy?"

"He isn't dead!" My voice drops. "He was never alive to begin with."

"I don't get it."

"He's from the other half of the universe, the half that's the opposite of this one."

"If he isn't from this planet, that makes him a space alien."

"We all come from the same place, Anthony."

"Is he from this planet?"

"He's older than this planet."

"Older?"

I nod.

"That's impossible! That's like four billion years."

I shrug.

"How old is he?"

"He doesn't have an age. Our concept of time only applies here, not where he's from."

"Then how can he be older than the Earth? He shouldn't be older than anything."

"Well, when you put it that way, you're right."

"I don't get it."

"Religion gets it."

"How?"

"How old is God?"

"He's not God."

"I'm not saying he is, but you get the idea. God doesn't have an age. Neither does Michael."

"So he can't die?"

"He isn't alive."

"I don't get it."

My chest heaves a sigh. "You got it in Sunday school. Life, death, resurrection, angels fighting demons. You never ask yourself how old an angel is, or why Satan can't be killed, or whether or not God exists. You just accept it and you've never seen any evidence for any of it, have you?"

"I've seen plenty of miracles."

"Really? Jesus for tea and the devil for dessert?"

"Life is a miracle."

"You know what I mean. Stigmata, exorcism, speaking in tongues, Mary on burnt toast."

"My mom saw the Virgin standing over her sister's crib when she was sick."

My eyes go big. "How do you know it wasn't a space alien?"

"She said it was Mary. We all know what Mary looks like."

"And what does Michael look like? A little green man?"

For a while he says nothing.

"He really is Michael, isn't he?"

"As close as you can get."

"And you're married to him."

"Yup."

"He told me he knew he was putting you in danger."

"I would have married him anyway."

"That's why he's in trouble, isn't it?"

Crossing my arms, I glare at him. "Yes, Anthony. I'm the cause of his downfall." I glance out the windows. "But it's a clear day so the risk of a lightning strike is low."

He only stares silently at the road while I stare at his profile.

"If you want to run screaming, I'll understand."

Looking away from the road, he meets my gaze. "I'd go to hell for you."

"Don't bother." My cheeks flush. "Mike says it doesn't exist."

He seems to snap from a trance. "It doesn't?"

"Disappointed?"

"Yeah." He looks back at the road. "I can't use that line anymore."

"Not on me, but Amy would still fall for it."

He nods. "What's the plan when we get to Vancouver?"

"We'll see when we get there. If I know my husband, he did more than leave money in a deposit box."

"Can I ask you a personal question?"

"You've never asked permission before. I can't wait."

"How long did you know him before you knew what he was?"

"Before we started dating. Before we were friends, even."

"And that didn't bother you?"

"*Didn't bother me?*" I turn in my seat. "I'm running from supernatural ghouls with my ex. I'd say it still bothers me."

"Fair enough."

"Can I ask you a personal question?"

"Shoot."

"Why would you go to hell for me?"

"Because I still love you, and I know how Michael feels, and doing nothing isn't something I've ever been good at."

"Thanks." I swallow. "But I don't think I can make this up to you."

"Seeing as how I won't be going to hell, I'll want a beer out of this."

"All you can drink."

"And pizza."

"All you can eat."

"You got a deal." Tony smiles at me.

I realize I'd rather be dead than go through what he has.

"Do you want to listen to anything?" My voice falters.

He shakes his head.

"Me neither."

Facing the windshield, I stare at the highway. The rest of the trip we say nothing.

We arrive in Vancouver by nine. The bank is easy to find. We aren't the first in the door, but there is no wait and we are the first to request access to a security box. In a small conference room, I open the box with Anthony hovering over me. Inside is a debit card, cash, a passport and other identification belonging to Carrie Nation with my picture.

"Smart ass." I whisper to myself.

In addition to the fake ID, I find a necklace with an amulet on it, and two letters. Both are addressed in unmistakable hand: one to me, the other to Louis Stiles.

Anthony inspects the passport with a critical eye.

"Nice." Is all he says.

I hand him the cash. "Here."

"You sure?"

"That should cover your beer tab."

Sticking the card in my wallet, I open the letter addressed to me.

> *Sophie,*
>
> *If you can, you must deliver my letter for Louis to him as soon as possible. You will recognize him as the creepy man who has come to the house on occasion. It is unlikely his appearance has changed since you saw him last. He can be found most mornings at Joe Brown's Diner on Main. If it is late, you may find him two blocks down at the Tip Top Tavern.*
>
> *If Louis cannot be found, things are worse than I feared. Wait for Louis two days at most. If you cannot deliver the letter, burn it and go away from here as far as you can.*
>
> *Hear me, Sophie. You can never come back. Not to your parents, to your friends, or to anyone you have ever known. You will be hunted for the rest of your life and it will be because I loved you. If I had known, I would have left you alone that morning at Grounds. My love has marked you.*

Samael believes you will be the mother of his child. He will seek to possess you. The others will seek to kill you. They will count on you to make contact with your family. They will be ever watchful.

Once safely away, you may wait for me one year. Wear the amulet and I cannot fail to find you wherever you go. I still hope to reach you, but if not, take whatever love life offers you. Hopefully this letter will not find you alone. Hopefully Anthony will have found you, and it is doubtful he will leave. I have no wish to use him, only acknowledge if I had never entered your life you would still be together. If I fail, I still might mend what has been broken.

If I do not come for you, it is because I can never return. I will be justly punished for what I have done to you and your family. You will finally be free of me.

Thank you for the last three years. They were the only years I was alive.

Love,

It's a lousy letter. The most beautifully written bad news I've ever read. Gripping the amulet, I examine it. It looks like white alabaster, but I suspect it is the same material his crypt is made of. Resembling a Chinese coin, it is pierced with a square hole and etched with small symbols along its edge. I pull it over my head and tuck it into my shirt. When I look at Anthony, he grimly reflects my expression.

"We don't have much time." I grab the letter for Louis. "Let's go."

It's nearly ten by the time we find Joe Brown's Diner. We aren't sure if we've missed Louis, but Anthony is starving and they seem to offer as good a breakfast as any. We take a booth where I watch the door while Anthony watches the street. A stout waitress with an *I Dream of Jeannie* hairdo comes to pour coffee and take our orders. He orders bacon and eggs with a side of hotcakes before I decide on a half Bennie and a Bloody Mary.

"So what did he say?" Tony takes a sip of black coffee. "I mean, you can cut the personal stuff, but where are we?"

"If we can get this letter to Louis there's a chance things could work out. If we don't, I'll have to hide the rest of my life from Sam and Mike's co-workers."

"Sam and who?"

"You know how I told you there wasn't a hell?"

He nods.

"Well, there is a devil. Mike never said much about him, but if there is a Satan, Sam is it."

"What does he want with you?"

My Bloody Mary arrives. "Rosemary's baby."

"Jesus."

"No." I pull the celery from the glass and take a sip. "Damien."

"And Mike's co-workers?"

"They'll try to rub me out to keep that from happening."

"All this because he married you?"

"I don't think this could have been avoided if we were just dating. Apparently, Sam thinks Michael's love for me makes me special."

"And now he wants to get to know you."

"I'm not marrying them both." Kicking back in the booth, I take another drink. "It's my fault. I just couldn't say no.

Anthony grins. "You can always divorce him when this is over."

"We wouldn't want that, now would we?"

The waitress makes a stop to refill Tony's cup.

"How can this Louis help?"

With a shrug, I glance around the diner. "We'll see. I met him when he came to the house two years ago. Mike had him put in a tub the weekend we were gone for my birthday. It was supposed to be a surprise, but the surprise was Louis waiting for us when we got back. He seriously creeped me out."

"He and Mike friends?"

"Not really. He's come back on occasion, usually to take things out of the house or deliver things. I thought he was just a handyman, but the way he acts, I think he knows what Mike is."

The green eyes across from me twinkle. "What sort of things does he deliver?"

"Don't know. It's always in boxes or wrapped. Whenever I asked Mike, he claimed it was something for a client."

"And you believe him?"

"*Please.*" I roll my eyes.

"How can you live with that?"

"Mike promised to protect me when we first met. I think that's all he's been try-ing to do for the last three years."

"How much about his business has he ever shared with you?"

"Not much. You don't go through eternity alone and suddenly make your life an open book."

"What was he doing before he met you?"

"Keeping an eye on Sam."

"For God?"

"Michael doesn't believe in God."

Tony's eyes bug, "How can he not believe in God? I thought you said he was … you know, *Michael.*"

"I said he was close. The angel stories are him, but mostly they only got the name right."

"You mean there isn't a God?"

"He doesn't think so."

"Then what is he watching Sam for?"

"For ECCO. They're like a guild of the like-minded, only Michael isn't so like-minded these days."

'Those the co-workers who want to rub you out?"

Taking a drink of my Bloody Mary, I say nothing.

"What's he going to do?"

"I don't know. Fight them, lose them, whatever he can."

"What about Sam?"

"Mike's been trying to lose Sam since we met."

"But I thought you said watching Sam was his job?"

"He wants to retire."

"Retire ..." Tony drinks his coffee. "Just like the rest of us."

"Without the understanding boss."

Our food arrives. Tony immediately begins to pepper his eggs while I stare at the dome of paprika-spiked hollandaise in front of me. Anthony glances up as he cuts up his hotcakes.

"Why won't ECCO let him go?"

I scrape the hollandaise off my egg. "None of them can do what he can."

"Which is what?"

"Kick Sam's ass."

He stops chewing and lowers his fork. "Hell, I don't want him to retire either!"

Rolling my eyes, I break the yolk on my egg. "Mike won't let the world end because he wants to retire. He wants to retire here, for Christ's sake."

A diner seated behind Anthony turns to look at us.

I smile back. "Mornin."

When the stranger turns around, I refocus on Anthony, lowering my voice.

"It's ECCO that doesn't give a damn if the world ends. They're just scared of Sam. They think Michael's gone soft because he fraternizes with us. They find us quite revolting."

Picking up a piece of bacon, Anthony waves it at me. "You know, every time I think I hate this guy, I find myself liking him instead."

"Welcome to my world."

I take a bite of my egg and ham in time to see Louis come through the door.

"I think it just got a little brighter."

It has been two hundred and seventy-five years since I last attended a wedding. I was not invited, but only arrived in time to stop it. Samael was not pleased. I have been invited to many since, the last being Daniel's. As long as I wished to remain lawful, I never attended them. In hindsight, there was no violation in attending, only the violation in my mind I was trying to prevent. In my dreams I wished a life with a family and one love to share it with. Weddings were difficult.

Looking forward to my own, I now find joy in them. The upcoming marriage of Kate and Duane has filled me with anticipation. Sophie less so. She is suspicious of Duane, his family, and especially his church. Her feelings are in keeping with the hardness I have felt from her since making her acquaintance. They are deep, mistrustful. Marrying me seems poor consolation for one who demands the truth.

What if I can never tell it?

If I could, what would it be?

I myself do not know. There was a time I believed so. I believed there was order and a place where I belonged. But no longer. Order and place have no value. Only life. I try to tell Sophie she already has this. What other truth is there to know?

Now, I am indulging myself when I swore to give back what I took from her. I tell myself it is what she wants. I may not know the truth, but I know a lie. It is what I am, but without her I will never stop. I need her to stop me. To destroy me.

[Spharic. Entry translated from *Kor Dai Maihael*. Mund Dai. July 3 2000]

2000 "Are you ready?" Mike's voice echoed up the stairs for the tenth time. "I'm ready when I'm ready. Asking don't make it so."

Assessing my figure in the mirror, I wriggled in the corseted bodice to make sure the length of skirt hung straight. When Kate said they were having a red, white, and blue wedding, I had visions of wearing parade bunting in front of three hundred people. When she assured me the dress would be blue, I remained uneasy. Blue made me look green. To my relief, it was a midnight blue. A straight, full-length, off-the-shoulder satin I would very likely wear again. Draping my shawl over my arm, I grabbed my purse, checked my makeup, and headed out the door. Pulling up the hem, I made my way down the stairs.

He watched me from the living room, looking unnervingly handsome in a navy suit and cream tie. A new tie. That rounded out his collection to two.

"What do you think?" At the bottom of the stairs, I turned around. "I think I'll have Mom take off this ribbon on the back. My ass is big enough without it."

I looked over my shoulder, batting my eyes at him. He approached, running his fingers along the streamer of ribbon, saying nothing.

"Well?" I waited.

Opening his mouth, he seemed short for words. "Pretty."

"Uh huh." Squinting, I took his arm with a grin. "Admit it, you're jealous."

"You say that because you can't call me boyfriend anymore." He led me outside.

"Are you challenging my ability to annoy you?"

Locking the door, he raised his brows at me. "It's fiancé now. I hope you've been practicing."

"It's called in-laws. I hope you've been praying."

We walked to his squeaky, new BMW and he opened my door, helping my dress into the car.

"Actually ..." He paused. "I think your mother has come around. She told me some interesting stories about you after dinner last week."

"Wait a minute. This isn't fair! Where are *my* in-laws? Who has any dirt on you?"

He shut the door on me. When he got to the driver's side, I watched him get behind the wheel. With a grin, he started the ignition without a key.

"So it's like that, is it?" I nodded. "It's going to be you and Mom now?"

With a fluid motion of his hand on the wheel, he turned the car in the drive.

"She likes to talk about you."

"I know all the stories. Bring it."

"Bring it?" He frowned.

"Yeah, you know. Show me what you got."

His head tilted. "You were afraid of squirrels."

"*Please!* Mom didn't tell you is she always thought that was funny until she was attacked by one in the backyard."

"Was she hurt?"

"No, it just mussed up her hair." We were nearing the Victorian at the top of our street. "Speaking of messy hair, check out your neighbor."

I snickered as we passed the old lady in her yard. She was in her bathrobe, her frizz of white hair standing straight off the top of her head. She had picked up her mail and stood at the gate to watch us drive by.

Michael looked over at me as she passed his window. It seemed natural enough, in a rehearsed kind of way.

"How long has she lived there?"

He looked back at the road with a shrug. "I'm not sure."

I could feel one of my eyebrows go up.

"You know her name?"

"Farrell, I think."

"You think?"

"It's on her mailbox."

"Does she know your name?"

He returned my gaze with a disarming smile. "I don't have a mailbox."

The morning traffic into Seattle wasn't too terrible considering it was the Fourth of July. The sky was slightly overcast, but it was dry. So far, Kate and Duane were lucky with the weather. Even though the service would be held at Duane's church, the reception would be outdoors at Volunteer Park. I hated weddings that made you drive around with maps like you were on a scavenger hunt, but since Michael was driving and a GPS, I distracted myself with thoughts of my own wedding instead. I decided it wouldn't be in a church and there would be no maps.

"No maps." I blurted out loud.

"I agree."

"Tell me you weren't reading my mind again."

"Not really."

"That's a half-ass answer."

"A little."

I glared at him. "How about not at all?"

"When you think about me, it gets my attention."

"You should ignore it. Sometimes it isn't nice."

"I know. I'm not a GPS."

"Are you sure you want to get married? And I'm not asking because you're any different from anyone else, it's because marriage blows. My father divorced his first wife, Auntie Maeve divorced her first husband, my grandparents divorced and remarried and divorced again. All of my friends in high school had divorced parents. And they were—"

"Human." He finished.

"I'm just saying it's bad enough to hear things you don't want when someone insists on telling you. What happens when you hear it and I don't want you to? I'm not going to spend the rest of my life policing my thoughts because I have to worry about hurting your feelings."

"I can't help that. Would you be able to ignore my thoughts if you knew I was thinking about you?"

"Since I can't hear them, not a problem."

"You could."

"What?"

"I told you when we first met, people who spent enough time with me could learn to hear my thoughts. You could … if you wanted."

"I don't want to."

"Why not?"

"You want me to hear your thoughts?"

"We would never be apart."

"Ick."

"But how is that different from being joined in marriage? Isn't becoming part of another better than being alone?"

"You make it sound like you want to swallow me."

He visibly stiffened. "Sharing a thought isn't the same as controlling it."

"Too close for comfort, Mike. Sorry."

"But you still want to get married?"

"I said yes."

"To me?" His voice was hesitant.

"You don't think I brought this up because I changed my mind?"

His grip flexed on the wheel and he looked out his side window.

"Michael, I want to make sure we understand how difficult this is going to be. I know I wanted to be lovers but I never imagined getting married—to anyone, let alone you. It just seems there are some obstacles we haven't thought out."

Refocusing on the road ahead, he blinked. "You'll grow old and die."

"That would be the one."

"Then I'll grow old, too."

"You'll what?" I turned in my seat and stared at his profile.

"If I stopped using my crypt, my body would begin to age. It would take longer than a human body, but it would be visible."

"I don't want you to die."

"Only my body can and I couldn't let that happen. I would be trapped inside."

"That doesn't sound good."

"It would be terrible."

"But that would be a risk if you aged?"

"The odds of entrapment increase exponentially as my body deteriorates. I become especially vulnerable to physical injury. My body can't heal itself the way yours can."

"Yeah." I frowned out my window. "Let's hold off on the aging thing for now."

He looked at me. "I would do that for you."

"We'll cross that bridge if it's there. Maybe in twenty years, but for now I don't want to see a gray hair on that head."

"No maps." He smiled.

"No maps."
Closing my eyes, I rested my head against the seat. "I'm thinking we'll run away."
"Where to?"
"Hawaii."
"People don't grow old in Hawaii?"
"People don't do anything in Hawaii."
"Then let's get married there."
"Okay." I agreed, feeling sleepy.
He drove in silence.
"Maybe we should live there." He suggested.
"Michael, I have a job here. I'm not working in Hawaii."
A moment passed.
"Your parents are moving there." His voice was quiet.
"To retire. I'm not retiring."
He said nothing more until we reached the church.

The church was brand-new, a huge complex with a quadrangle and a long chapel at the center. Duane went on about it at Easter: its copper-sheathed roof, its seating capacity, its imported stained-glass window behind the altar. And there it was, all fifty feet of it, a giant image of Jesus with two nondescript angels at his feet. I thought it too plain for such a large window. Either the church fathers wanted to go light on their imagery or light on their pocketbooks. Apostles cost extra no doubt.

Duane's church was officially non-denominational. In my experience, that meant one of two things: highly progressive or highly regressive. When I noticed the people on Duane's side of the aisle were seating themselves according to gender, I was suspicious. My family, as small as it was, didn't require half of the church. A rope cordoned off the first two rows of pews to the left of the aisle.

Aunt Maeve was already there, seated alone, like a defendant in a court room. Dressed in a flowing cream suit with a navy scarf, her auburn hair was neatly tucked in a French braid. When she saw us, she waved me over hurriedly.

"Take that door to the left. They're getting all of the bridesmaids together for pictures. Hello, Michael! So good to see you again. You look very handsome today."

"And what do I look like?" Putting my hands on my hips, I squinted.

"The maid of honor, my dear. Now run along, they can't take the pictures without you." She smiled at Michael, inviting him to sit next to her.

"Here." I gave my purse and shawl to him. "If you're going to be my husband, you can get used to this." A thought occurred to me.

I looked at Maeve. "Are the big Gs coming?"

She frowned. "Your guess is as good as mine. They're living together, but I don't know if they could hold it together long enough to make it through a wedding."

Pursing my lips, I nodded. "Mike hasn't met them."

He looked between me and my aunt.

She patted his arm. "Don't worry. I'll stay with him."

"Thanks."

Finding my way to the back of the church, a flower girl happily led me to the lawn outside. Kate was being arranged in her wedding gown in front of some rose bushes. She was flanked by three bridesmaids and looked in a daze. When she saw me, she upset the photographer, abandoning her pose to greet me. We hugged, and she introduced me to her bridesmaids, all Duane's sisters. All three had Duane's thin build and blond hair. Peggy was tallest, Denise thinnest, and Charlene shortest. They all murmured their greetings, but the pleasantry felt obligatory. Kate was there, but someplace else.

I smiled at her. "I hope I wasn't too late."

"No, not at all. We were planning on photos after the ceremony, but the photographer got worried about rain." She paused. "Are the big Gs here?"

"They haven't arrived. Then again, my parents haven't either."

Kate nodded absently.

We returned to the business of posterity. Pictures of all of us. Pictures of me and the bridesmaids. Pictures of me and Kate. Pictures of us with our bouquets. For an hour. Which wasn't bad. The last time I was a bridesmaid, the photo session took three hours.

When an usher in a tuxedo told us it was time, we were led around the outside of the church and staged at the door. I was a little nervous. Make that a lot nervous. I had skipped rehearsal and was regretting it. Between work and living in Tacoma, making the afternoon outtakes at their church in the middle of Kirkland had been a little out of the way. I recalled I was leading the bridesmaids to the altar. I assumed I would know what that was when I saw it.

The processional music would be a hymnal sung by the choir and guests, "All Creatures of Our God and King." If there was one thing to be thankful for, this would get me out of singing. As for my processional walking skills, there was only one rule: if you think you're walking slowly enough, go slower.

As I stood at the door, I could hear the organ start. The usher cued me.

"All creatures of our God and king
Lift up your voice and with us sing."

On my cue, I started the slow step. The hardest part was deciding where to look. I didn't want to stare at the altar. I didn't want to stare at the floor. I didn't want to be distracted by someone in the audience. I didn't want to see Michael watching me and feel like a girl in a school play, which was ridiculous because I knew he was watching me at that moment. I went with light eye contact, briefly glancing at people I didn't know as they smiled approvingly. I progressed down the aisle with as innocent a smile as I could muster. Hopefully it wasn't a smirk.

"Dear Mother Earth, who day by day,
Unfoldest blessings on our way."

Most of the onlookers were singing. Some read the lyrics from the program, others knew them. It was one I'd heard before. Great Nana used to play it on her organ. It wasn't bad as hymns went and I wondered if Kate had chosen it. Nearing the altar, I could see Duane and his best man twitching in their tuxedoes. Their expressions unnerved me and I began to lose my focus. The choir was surprisingly discordant, their voices stridently drowning out the audience.

Except for one voice.

In spite of being in a church, my first thought was it was an ungodly beautiful voice. I didn't look at him but followed his song, my feet once again sure of their path. I waited until I was standing in my place to look at him. When I did, he was singing to me. Maeve and my parents were with him, but no grandparents. Not that anyone noticed the empty seats. Everyone within earshot was staring at him.

"And thou most kind and gentle death,
Waiting to hush our latest breath."

It never occurred to me he could sing. It made sense, being what he was. He said he liked stringed instruments, that certain resonances comforted him. As the hymn neared the end, the bridesmaids were in position. The choir started the last verse before the organist would take over and start the bridal procession.

"Let all things their Creator bless,
And worship him in humbleness.
O praise him, hallelujah."

A feeling of electricity began to fill the air. The hair on the back of my neck stood on end. I thought I was imagining things until I noticed Duane's sisters glancing at each other.

"Praise, praise the Father."

I could feel a vibration through the soles of my shoes.

"Praise the Son."

Looking at Michael, I couldn't tell if he was aware of what was happening.

"And praise the Spirit."

He was still singing, staring through me as though in a trance.

"Three in One."

There was a high pitched whine. I heard what sounded like cracking ice cubes and turned to see the window behind the altar shatter, collapsing in an avalanche of glass.

People screamed. The choir stumbled from the risers.

The vibrating had stopped, but confusion lingered as people filled the aisles to get away from windows. The pastor was asking if it was an earthquake, and I turned to Michael expecting an explanation. He wasn't there.

Then I realized he was on the floor.

"Michael!"

I ran around the cordon and down the aisle to my family. They had pushed the pew aside to make room. He was on his back. His face showed no sign of distress but was peaceful. He simply looked asleep. Someone had loosened his tie and unbuttoned the collar on his shirt. Dad cradled his head and was feeling for a pulse while Mom hovered nervously.

"What happened?"

Maeve looked up, white with panic. "He just collapsed. One minute he was sing-ing and the next he was on the ground."

Taking my father's place at his head, I kneeled next to him and put my face to his. There was a chill on my cheek and the faint sweet smell that came with it.

Holding his head, I whispered to him, "Michael, can you hear me?"

He wasn't there.

Shielding his face with as much of my body as I could, I pushed back one of his eyelids. It was dark.

Michael, you've got to come back or they'll call an ambulance.

There was no response.

"Shit."

I opened his mouth and covered it with my own. Waiting for his breath, I filled his lungs as he inhaled. His breathing went shallow. I gave him another breath, and he coughed. His eyes began moving under the lids and I exhaled.

"He's fine." I looked up at everyone. "He just fainted. If we could get him some-place comfortable—"

"Of course."

It was a feminine voice with a Southern lilt.

A clammy hand touched my shoulder. I saw the parson's damp face. He showed a wide, lipless smile filled with small teeth. Duane came around behind me. Getting to my feet, I watched them lift Michael up and followed them as they carried him down the same hall I had taken to the back of church. They found an office with a sofa. Mike seemed to be moving as they laid him on it.

Duane whispered to me. "Should we call an ambulance?"

"No, no." I pulled out a story, hoping my husband could hear it. "Mike had a bad case of the flu he caught on a plane. He's just been working too hard. I tried to tell him to stay home, but he really wanted to be here."

Glancing in Mike's direction, I saw him holding his hand over his face.

"Michael? Are you all right?" I called to him.

"I think so." He was rubbing his head.

"Is anyone else hurt?" I asked the pastor.

"Miraculously, no. Not even a scratch from all that glass, as far as I can tell."

"What happened?" Duane sounded dazed. "Was it an earthquake?"

The pastor shrugged. "The window must have been stressed. With the music, it might have been enough to break it. It's a new building; things may have settled."

"What about the wedding?" I looked between the pastor and Duane.

The pastor raised his brows at Duane. "It's your call. If you want to postpone, I understand, but there isn't any reason not to continue if you want to."

"I'll check with Kate. If she's fine with it, we'll do it. Everyone's here, the plans have been made—we might as well."

I put a hand on Duane's shoulder. "Go back to the wedding. Tell Kate I'm sorry—"

"No." Michael's voice startled us. "I'm fine. Go with them, Sophie."

We all looked at him. Lowering his hand, his eyes brightened as he smiled.

"Sophie, go back. It's Kate's wedding."

"Are you sure?"

Nodding, he waved us off. "I just need some rest. Go."

Duane hesitated.

"Kate is waiting for you." Michael was firm.

"William will stay with you." The parson pointed to an usher in the hall. "Just in case." He smiled before leaving with Duane.

I lingered. "I don't want to leave you alone."

Folding his arms behind his head, my fiancé winked.

You won't be.

... One of the earliest messenger angels was Suhad. This angel was believed to communicate to the living in dreams, sometimes directly but most often in the form of symbolic imagery. Five thousand years before the advent of psychoanalysis, ancient people of the Middle East were interpreting their dreams as visions of the future. Because dreams were not always remembered, powerful dreams were believed to be especially important. When a dream recurred more than once, it was believed that a spirit, or Suhad, was trying to intervene.

In ancient Egypt, Suhad delivered the waking visions of priests and Pharaohs. If these visions remained unfulfilled, it was believed the beholder would never sleep again. Spiritual intervention was the only solution for those driven to insomnia. The afflicted would sleep within the temple of a deity they hoped would aid them, the vision interpreted by priests and a course of action proscribed. This could be something as mundane as a change in diet to a full fledged quest. Prayers to Suhad were made in conjunction with offerings to the patron deity in hopes of an answer that would relieve the vision. If unfulfilled, the beholder could not pass into the afterlife and was doomed to wander the Earth for eternity.

[Excerpt from *Conceptions of Contemporary* Faith. V. Carpio d. 1978]

2003   Fathomless sleep. The result of being in a cell or a premonition of things to come? A welcome void to replace the visions that came at any time, waking or sleeping? It couldn't be sure.

If It was real.

Already judged. The waking parts only dreams.

What if there had been no waking at all?

How long had it been asleep?

Michael …

"Sophie?"

… defend us …

"Can you hear me?"

… rebuke him …

It isn't her voice.

… into hell …

"Who are you?"

… wander …

"What do you want?"

… ruin …

"Speak to me!"

"I am."

His eyes fly open in the glow of a face above.

Only the dim light of Raphael's eyes makes anything visible. The radiant fields of energy he used to see have faded. In the dark, he has become blind.

"Who were you speaking to?"

Shaking his head, he puts his hands to his face. "No one."

"You're seeing things." Raphael squats next to him on the floor. "Tell me."

"No."

Sitting up, he pushes himself back against the wall.

"You are in pain?

"Only now I feel it."

"That is what you wanted to tell me?"

He shakes his head. "I know where Samael will be."

"Where?"

"My house. He will go there with Sophie."

"You have seen this?"

"That or it's a very good guess."

Raphael's eyes narrow. "Phanuel always believed you had visions."

"Not until two years ago."

"What happened?"

"Sam came to treat with me. Instead I found him alone, in his crypt, entrapped."

"You didn't assume him?"

"I tried. Something went wrong. Or right. I don't know. I couldn't do it. Ever since, something in him stayed with me. At first, I thought I was hallucinating.

Over time, I realized the visions foretold things that came to pass."

"A prophecy?"

"I was at a wedding. Then I was someplace else. In a desert under a full moon. Sam was with me. The desert caught fire and I was fallen, burned. Sam had me, was assuming me, but ..."

"What?"

He stares into the dark. "His eyes were dead."

"Dead?"

Closing his eyes, he shakes his head. "He will fall. Even if I fall with him."

"And this is how? Trial and assumption by Metatron?"

"What other way is there?" He looks Raphael in the eye. "My crypt is gone. I am breached. There is no other way."

Raphael shifts from a squat to sitting cross-legged. For some time they say nothing, surveying the concrete walls only Raphael can see, the stillness deep underground, pressing them.

"Metatron is not here." Raphael's voice echoes softly.

The news depresses him. "How much longer?"

"Phanuel says three days. It's an excuse. Sarah would have finished you by now."

Impulsively, he holds his side. "He is starving me."

"He is offended and vindictive."

"His pride will ruin you all. In three days, Samael will have Sophie. Without my strength to aid you, you will have nine months to ponder your fate."

"What else can we do?"

"Let me face him."

"You admit your body is breached."

"He still wants me."

"And he'll take you. You won't be able to stop him."

Reaching behind, he withdraws the ops. "One way or another, I will."

"Where did you find this?" Raphael's reaches for it, but he pulls the ops away.

"It is my freedom. Freedom from Sam or freedom from this cell. Either way, I will be released. I leave it to you to decide."

Letting out a breath, Raphael sits back, palms resting on knees.

"Michael, as hard as I have sought faith in you, you have always kept your own counsel. Where Sam flaunts his strength at our expense, you have traded on yours at your own, but this time the risk is ours. If I let you go, there is the risk you will succeed."

"That is Phanuel talking."

"He fears you are the actor in the prophecy, the father of the Child. Not Sam."

"I can't make a child."

"If you assumed Sam, you could."

"You know I can't. I didn't have the strength the first time and I won't have it now. The ops will take all I have to destroy him."

Even blind, he senses Raphael's indecision.

"If Metatron were here, would you have submitted to It?"

"For Sophie, yes."

"Why did you want Sarah free?"

"If Sam is defeated, you still face Marta. You don't even know what she looks like. Sarah raised her. If what Sarah suspects is true, and my experience says it is, Marta will continue to stalk ECCO until none of you remain."

"You think Sarah can stop her?"

"Marta fears her."

Nodding, Raphael gets to his feet and turns for the door.

"Raphael." He waits for their eyes to meet. "Six hours or you needn't come back."

Raphael opens the door to the black corridor beyond, then pauses.

"We don't even have that."

He hears the slide of the bolt on the door. His eyes wander the darkness. Squeezing his sides with his arms, he feels his emptiness. Fears sleep. Fears the voice that will wake him.

The pull of the sun tells him it is nearly seven. Three hours have passed clinging to his knees, fighting the slide to oblivion. He is awake to hear the bolt slide. Lifting his head, he reaches to his back, gripping the ops. He can no longer read his surroundings. He cannot make assumptions. As the door opens, he sees two pairs of eyes, making out Raphael and Gabrielle.

Pushing against the wall, he rises to his feet.

"Can you walk?" Gabrielle comes near.

"Of course." He replaces the ops in his belt. "Where is Phanuel?"

Raphael speaks from outside the chamber. "Gone for Metatron."

"Or watching us." Gabrielle mutters, taking his arm.

"He is always watching, but eyes can be deceived." Raphael leads them into the pitch. "However, if spotted by a sentinel before we leave the building, strength and speed will be our only assets."

"I won't go far if I have to outrun a sentinel."

Gabrielle guides him as they make a turn. "If it comes to that, we'll give you as much time as we can."

They pass through a maze of ink corridors before stopping. There is the faint hum of the city overhead.

"This is the only other elevator." There is the sound of a key and Raphael's voice. "It goes to a fire escape under the garage, but the security system will know it's being used. We won't have much time and we'll have to go through the garage to get to the street."

The drone of an elevator approaches.

His fear of them persists. "What if they disable it?"

"They can't." Gabrielle speaks in his ear. "It runs on an independent generator so it can't fail in a fire. If they shut off the power, the generator will take over. They shouldn't have time to kill the generator before we are away."

When the doors open, he finds himself glad of fluorescent lighting for the first time. It is a spare, gray box that could accommodate six people at most. As soon as the doors close, he feels his insides tingle. The elevator begins to climb.

Raphael pulls off a brown blazer and hands it to him. "Here, give me your coat." He slips off the windbreaker and takes Raphael's blazer.

"You might not be strong enough to handle a sentinel, but your weakness makes you hard to read. If we get you in a crowd, they could lose you."

Watching Raphael don the windbreaker, he is disturbed again by their similarity. Raphael's face is longer, but their hair is the same shade of brown. Gabrielle is softer, with full lips and flowing blond curls. Yet underneath, all is the same. All is false.

The elevator trembles, then jars to a halt. He knows the cell block is some four hundred feet below garage level. In spite of Gabrielle's assurance about the generator, his heart stops when the lights go out. None of them speaks.

Momentarily, the lights flicker on and the elevator returns to life. The ride up continues, but roughly, as though something is trying to pull the car from its cables. Near the top of the shaft, the car begins to rattle. The lift falters. Raphael begins to pry the doors apart with his hands, revealing the lower half of the fire escape door on the other side. Climbing out of the car, Raphael squeezes onto the fire escape threshold, forcing the door to the corridor open and disappearing from sight. He and Gabrielle quickly follow, pulling themselves onto the floor of the escape corridor. Wasting no time, Raphael is already running down the hall. They run after, coming to a stop at the door to the parking garage.

"Four floors to go." Raphael whispers at Gabrielle. "Watch our back."

Raphael pushes through the doors, taking the lead. They cautiously jog the winding ramp as it climbs to street level. Sodium lamps starkly illuminate acres of sloping concrete striped with fresh paint, the parking stalls unused. They will not use the stairs. They will keep to open ground.

Coming around the bend to the next level of the garage, they slow. A long row of black SUVs line the wall. Raphael stops, putting up a hand.

What there is to read, he can no longer tell.

"Those aren't sentinels." Gabrielle mutters.

"Quickly!" Raphael hisses at him. "Play dead."

"What?"

The word is barely said when Raphael has him by the throat. In a momentary flash of blue, his limbs fail and he lands hard on the pavement. He lays motionless.

"Finally, you come." Raphael's voice is coldly authoritative.

"How did he escape?" It is a voice he doesn't recognize.

"We were about to ask you the same question." Gabrielle joins.

"The emergency shaft was used." A different voice. There are two of them.

"Was it guarded?" Raphael questions.

"No. But how—"

"From now on it will be." Gabrielle cuts off. "Disable the emergency shaft."

"And put him in a different cell." Raphael's order reverberates on the garage walls.

Footsteps approach. He remains still. He does not see what happens next. A loud snap of voltage is followed by a flash of heat over his head as a body falls on him. Another thud lands near his head. Reflexively, he pushes the weight from him, blinking to see the bodies of two novices near him. Hands pull him to his feet.

"Sorry about that." Raphael smiles. "Novices are stronger than they are smart." Rubbing his throat, he coughs. "We're even then."

Raphael gives him a look before heading up the garage ramp.

Gabrielle grabs his arm. "He couldn't speak for a day after what you did to him."

"I lost my temper. I'm sorry."

"You've been doing that a lot lately." Raphael glances back.

"I've been hungry."

"We'll feed you first thing."

They break into a run when they reach the street level of the garage. The street is dark with barely a scatter of people.

He catches up to Raphael on the sidewalk. "So much for a crowd."

Raphael says nothing.

It is a Monday evening and they are surrounded by office buildings. Only three cars are parked nearby. He spots a silver BMW across the street.

"They're moving on us." Gabrielle speaks up behind them. "We need to go."

Eyeing the cars on the street, Raphael looks at him. "Pick one."

"Me?"

Raphael shrugs. "You're driving."

Crossing the street, he quickly surveys the BMW. Catching his reflection in the spotless tint of the driver's-side window, he drives his fist through it. The alarm sounds as he opens the door, brushing glass from the seat. Getting behind the wheel, he puts a finger to the ignition and forces a charge. Raphael and Gabrielle are in the car before the alarm stops and the engine comes to life.

"Go!" Gabrielle's eyes burn as she glares through him at the building.

Speeding from the curb, he feels the skin on his body crawl with static. He knows Raphael and Gabrielle are shielding them from sentinels he cannot see.

"Where?" He looks in the rear-view mirror at Raphael.

"Go to First, then head south."

"Through Pioneer Square? There could be traffic."

"I'm counting on it."

As they approach Pioneer Square, the traffic thickens. They wait for a stop light. The sidewalks swell with tourists.

His hands tighten on the wheel. "Are they following?"

"Of course." Raphael's calm is unnerving.

"They'll surround us if we sit here." He watches a young couple holding hands cut in front of the car's headlights as they jaywalk across the street. "There's enough of a crowd here. I should leave you."

"You're not leaving. I am." Raphael slides forward in his seat. "Stay on First. Get as close as you can to Safeco Field."

"Why?"

"A game just ended. Everyone at the game will be trying to leaving town at the same time. You'll leave with them." Raphael pauses. "You a Mariner fan?"

"I am now."

Raphael slides on the pair of sunglasses he left in the pocket of his windbreaker. "What do you think?"

He glances over his shoulder. "Stay away from my wife."

Grinning, Raphael opens the door at the light. "Good luck, Michael."

He doesn't look back at the empty seat. He doesn't want to. As the light turns green, he guns the engine and makes a left through oncoming traffic up to Second.

"What are you doing?" Gabrielle grabs his shoulder.

"Making them choose." Turning the car hard into an alley, he doubles back and pulls into a public garage. "It isn't enough for me to get away. We all have to. We have to divide their numbers." He brakes the car without parking. "You drive."

Jumping out of the car, they switch seats.

"When we leave the garage, take the same alley we came out of, but keep south."

As they exit the garage, a black SUV pulls into it. A blank face stares at them from the driver's-side window as they speed by.

"Novices." Gabrielle grumbles as she flies onto the street, narrowly missing cars.

He looks over his shoulder. "I thought you handled them?"

"Those aren't the same ones."

"How many are there?"

Gabrielle raises a brow. "I've counted ten."

"Ten? They outnumber us?"

"Phanuel's idea."

He looks back. "They're coming. Make a left on Cherry, then a right on Fifth. Drop me in Chinatown."

Gabrielle spins the car onto Cherry and speeds uphill when another black SUV crosses in front of them. Hitting the brakes, she swerves behind it, missing the turn onto Fifth, heading for the I–5 on ramp instead. They come to a halt as the lane ahead fills with traffic leaving the game.

"What now?"

Checking out the back window, he can see one of the SUVs tailing them from an inside lane.

"Drive the shoulder. Get on the highway. Fast."

Cranking the wheel, she noses the car out of traffic and skirts the shoulder of the ramp as drivers honk their horns. Before them, I–5 is a sea of red lights.

"At this rate, we're going to blow a tire." She weaves to miss the debris of broken glass and trash bordering the jersey barrier.

Craning his neck, he peers over the side. The stretch of highway they are on is elevated for several miles. They are directly over Chinatown.

"Stop and let me out."

"What?"

"Once I'm gone, you have to help Raphael."

Stopping the car, she nods. "Of course. Be careful."

He looks her in the eyes. "Thank you. For helping me."

"You came back." She smiles.

Exiting the car, he takes two steps to the concrete barrier. Without a backward glance, he vaults over the side.

2000 Sophie and Mike,

I'm sending you this photo album so you have proof, as well as the credit, of surviving our wedding. You two looked amazing! I am so glad you liked the dress. Hopefully you could breathe better than I could in mine. I'm so sorry about the window disaster and poor Michael. I promise not to have another wedding after this one!

Thanks so much for the dining table and chairs. I don't know how you knew it was what I wanted. If I could have had that on the bridal registry and nothing else I would have, but I never would have believed anyone would get that for us. You are too generous!

We had a wonderful time in Arizona. It was a little hot (ha, ha) but the resort was amazing. We went hiking in the Grand Canyon. You guys weren't there, were you? I'll have to tell you about that next time I see you. We saw a hiker in the canyon who looked exactly like Michael. I mean exactly. If you don't believe me, you can ask Duane. Duane actually called Michael's name to him, but he only waved at us and disappeared up the trail, so we never got to talk to him. Isn't that weird?

I guessed it couldn't be Michael because I told Duane after our wedding he didn't look like he would be hiking anywhere, let alone Arizona in July. We hope he is feeling better. He shouldn't feel bad about what happened. I think Pastor Kendall wanted to faint after seeing that window break.

There are big plans for a new and improved window. Somebody with some serious cash has been holding out on the church because they mailed them a whopping check the next day. The donor asked for a new window with better angels on it. Can you believe it?

Call me as soon as Mike is better and we'll have you over. I need to break in that dining table.

Thanks for everything, Sophie. I couldn't have asked for a better maid of honor.

Love,

Kate

"Well ..." Sophie lowered the letter to look at him. "They say everyone has a twin somewhere. I suppose that could apply to you, too."

Feigning ignorance, he studied a Costco insert in the paper.

She returned to the letter. "Better angels on the window? Whatever happened to the better angels of our nature?"

"I broke it. I'm buying it."

She gave a snort before sipping her coffee. "Shameless self-promotion."

He looked up at her. "You're the one who thought it needed more angels."

"Apostles. Not angels. You weren't listening."

"I'm not supposed to, am I?"

"You listen just fine; you only hear what you want."

She took the paper from him and dug out the entertainment section.

"I'm not an angel, Sophie."

A smirk played on her lips as she opened the paper in front of her face.

"Don't say it." He retrieved the Costco insert.

They read in silence.

"There aren't any good movies." She commented.

Saying nothing, he noticed Costco was having a cake sale.

"You know, I have a lot of good movies." She continued to read. "Well, had. I left most of them with Anthony."

"Do you want me to read your mind or not?"

"Hmm?" She lowered the paper.

He rolled his eyes. "Just say it. You want a television. You know I'm thinking about going to Costco and you watch the flat screens every time we're there."

"No. Really, I don't." She lifted the paper.

"Part of the reason I kept this house was to get away from all of that … "

"Garbage." She spoke from behind the paper.

"I was going to say noise."

"*I understand.*" The paper said amiably.

Flipping the insert, he saw a sale on pineapples.

The paper shrugged. "I can watch TV at Mom and Dad's."

He flipped the insert again.

"I never knew it." She added. "But you learn a lot watching *Antiques Roadshow.*"

Tossing the insert on the table, he got up and headed for the door. Putting on his sunglasses, he grabbed his car keys and glanced down the hall at her. She hadn't looked up from the paper.

As he opened the front door, he heard her call out.

"Sony. Anything over thirty-six inches."

At least is was a beautiful day. As he got into his car and started the engine, the sound of singing birds was replaced by the radio. It was a quiet song he had heard before, with a restful bass he found pleasing. It was about a man who was always watching the one he loved and it always made him think of Sophie. But not this time. This time it made him think about Kate's letter. Sam had shown himself to Kate and Duane. Knew who they were and why they were there. Knew about the wedding. Sam had been watching.

It must have been Sam behind his vision in the church.

His vision. He didn't know it would happen. Couldn't stop it. Had lost control. Just like Anderson Island. He had failed to assume Sam. Something had gone wrong. Something in him realized Sam was too much. If he had assumed Sam, he would never be strong enough. He would become part of Sam instead of the other way around. It was his worst suspicion realized.

Without ECCO, he would never defeat Sam alone.

Unfortunately, ECCO wanted to kill his fiancée.

That was why Sam was calling. The opportunity had come.

The Costco parking lot was clogged. He waited while a young woman in a yellow convertible Beetle tried three times to fit into a parking spot. Lowering his window, he poked his head out to get a better view of the Beetle's rear fender as it closed on the front of his car. There was a minivan behind him. Putting the car in reverse, he rolled back as far as he dared. The Beetle kept coming. It slowed, tapping his car.

The woman looked back at him.

"Sorry!" She waved.

When she parked, he drove past and kept going till he was at the far end of the lot. Picking a row of empty spots, he parked and walked back to the store. He didn't bother to look at the front of his car. It was either that or Sophie staring at him next Friday because there were no good movies to watch.

As he approached the store, the young woman from the Beetle was waiting for him. She had straight dark hair and wore a close-fitting dress with blue and white flowers on it.

"I am *sooo* sorry."

"Don't worry about it." He pulled out his wallet and flashed his card at the attendant as they entered the store.

"That has to be brand-new." She followed him inside.

"There's no damage."

"If there is, I can give you my contact information."

"That won't be necessary, but thanks for offering."

Stopping in front of the televisions, he pushed his sunglasses back on his head.

All of the screens were playing the same image. A movie about a mummy just released on DVD.

The young woman paused to watch with him. "Are you in the market?"

"Yes."

"I've been thinking about getting one. Is there one that's better than the rest?"

"I don't know." He walked up to the Sony. "I've never owned a television."

"Really?"

"I don't watch TV."

"Then why are you buying one?"

"If I don't come home with a Sony, my fiancée will kill me."

When he looked at her, the woman opened her mouth slightly.

He squinted. "She wouldn't really kill me."

"Oh." She spoke faintly and walked away.

With a shrug, he went back to watching the screens.

Plasma. They all had different names and different prices. As far as he could tell, they were all the same unit. With only some slight variation, the picture quality appeared to be dependent on how much power the unit was consuming. The

Sony was far from efficient. This contradicted Sophie's attention to being environmentally friendly, but he sensed coming home with something more energy efficient wouldn't be welcome. The largest screen in the store was sixty-four inches. Assessing the heat it was generating, he didn't know that it wouldn't burn itself out in five years.

Maybe five years was more time than they had.

No.

He couldn't wait for Sam and hope for the best. After all, someone had got the better of Sam on Anderson Island. But Sam had been surprised in a weak position. Sam had come to talk. This time would different. He would have to tread lightly to get close enough to Sam with any hope of surprise.

"Cool movie." A small boy strolled up to the Sony. "I saw this in the theater."

"Was it good?"

"Yeah, but the mummy dies at the end."

"I thought the mummy was already dead."

"When he comes to life, they kill him."

He looked back at the screen as the mummy walked through a hail of bullets.

"Are you looking for a TV?"

A young man in a red polo with a Costco badge appeared.

"A Sony."

"We carry a Sony sound system for that if you need it."

He nodded.

"I'll take it."

When he got home, he knew Sophie was gone. Her car was still in the drive, which meant she was either jogging in the park or visiting her parents. He thought about snooping on her thoughts, but resisted and focused on unloading the sound system for the television. The television would arrive that afternoon. Not wanting to wait till Friday, he called on Louis to deliver it for him.

He needed to talk to Louis anyway.

Climbing the stairs with his first load of equipment, he went to the back bedroom currently storing his boxes of candy bars and animal crackers. Shoving his candy supply away from the wall, he deposited the speakers and surveyed the space, his eyes locating the studs to mount them on. Turning on the lights, he followed the signature of the wiring around the room. For the next few hours at least, he could forget about Sam. About ECCO. About himself.

Ninety minutes later, he heard a truck on the drive.

Louis.

He went downstairs to watch from the front door. He was risking himself every time they made contact. But Louis had saved him, even if misguided in doing so. It was a tricky thing working with another's servus. Some were unfailingly loyal. Others deadly betrayers. Because of the risks, ECCO had banned them. He had never had one but Samael's ranks were countless. They were an asset he often wished he had. At the least he wouldn't have been alone.

The truck in the drive was a light hauler, large enough to move furniture and small enough to park most anywhere. After backing it to the door, Louis climbed out of the cab and walked around to the back.

"Hiya." The broken teeth were framed by a close-cropped patch of beard.

"Hello, Louis."

He approached the truck as Louis pulled the lever on the door and shoved it open. There was an oblong box inside.

Pushing back a Copenhagen cap, Louis wiped a damp brow nervously.

"Where ya want it?"

"It's going upstairs."

"I got a dolly."

"I can help."

Louis squinted at him.

"It's all right, Louis."

Jumping up in the truck bed, Louis shoved the box out off the bed and he took hold of one end of it. He waited as Louis hopped out of the truck and picked up the other end before leading them into the house. He went first up the stairs, easily navigating the steps backward.

"How is business?" He asked vacantly.

"Boomin'."

"You've been busy?"

"Always."

His eyes fixed on Louis as he cleared the last step at the top. "Sam contacted me."

Louis kicked a step.

He stopped. "You okay?"

"Fine." Louis didn't look up.

He stared down on the man. "You sure?"

Louis met his eyes hesitantly. "I'm good."

They continued into the back bedroom, gently setting the box down.

Louis coughed. "I can take that box for ya."

"Thanks."

He stepped away and leaned back against the wall. Folding his arms, he watched Louis pull a box cutter from a frayed pocket and begin to cut away the cardboard.

"Sam stay in touch?"

With a grunt, Louis worked faster.

"Local or long distance?" He pressed.

"Stays close to home."

"Arizona?"

"Once burnt, twice shy."

"I don't suppose he's asked you to deliver anything to me?"

"Nope." Louis finished with the box, crushing it underfoot.

He felt himself smile. "If he does need you to deliver something, you don't know where I live, do you?"

Louis looked up and grinned. Picking up the remains of the box and a couple pieces of Styrofoam, the man left without a word. Standing at the top of the stairs, he watched Louis go out the door. He was about to return to the television when he heard the front door open again. He thought it was Louis until he felt her.

"Hey." She called out.

When he peeked down the stairs, she was standing in the foyer with the door open. She looked up at him, then back out the door at Louis closing up the truck.

"What's with Creepy?"

"He delivered something for me."

She sucked on her teeth. "Uh huh."

Closing the door, she kicked off her running mocs and started up the stairs. Stepping back from her approach, he reached behind and closed the door on the television as he waited for her. At the top of the stairs, she paused before him. She was sweating from running in the park, the smell of trees and car exhaust fresh on her. Her hormone levels were high. It was the beginning of her third week of the month. His mouth watered.

"God, I need a shower." She announced absently.

As she walked past, he shut his eyes and caught her hand. "No."

"Yes." She pulled his hand off and went to the bathroom.

He followed her. "Why?"

"Because I reek." She wrinkled her nose at him as she sat on the lid of the toilet to pull off her socks.

"I like the way you smell."

"Ick."

"Is it because I don't?"

"You do."

"I do?"

"You smell sweet."

He smiled.

She stood and dropped her shorts. She came to him, pulling her tank off over her head as she crossed the tile floor. He was about to reach for her.

"Now, I will too." She closed the bathroom door on him.

~

1199 BC   I appeared in my tent after Ashebu left. In spite of this delay, I arrived well ahead of the general. My eye told me he had only covered half the length of the column and it would be a long wait. When he did arrive, he would be exhausted, with only a few hours of rest before another day of migration. I would not deprive him. Quickly undressing, I left my clothes folded on the chair. They would be notice enough I had returned safe and he would see me in the morning.

The next morning, the table was laid with food and water. My clothes were as I had left them, save for a long object wrapped in cloth. My eyes perceived it was a sword. As I dressed, I set it aside without unwrapping it. I planned on returning it, human weapons being of little use to me. Turning my attention to the food, I rapidly consumed what little there was. That day, I planned to forage for more, with or without a mount. If I ever found the horse, I was undecided as to whether I would ride it or eat it.

The general entered my tent and immediately bowed.

"My apologies for yesterday."

"No need."

"If anything had happened to you, I would have earned the fate of Set."

"Nothing happened to me that was not my own doing. I have earned the fate of a wanderer and all that comes with it."

His eyes fell to the blade. "Wear that and all will know I am in your debt."

"I cannot use it."

"It is more than a matter of use. It is a matter of right."

Lifting it from the table, he slid the scabbard from its wrapping and offered me the hilt. It was a gesture I could not refuse with grace. Rising from the table, I pulled the weapon and admired the blade inscription, the blood oath of Osiris.

"It is beautiful."

"It is yours."

"I am no warrior."

"For your own protection."

Holding the blade to my palm, I ran my hand down the length of it and then displayed the edge to him, bloodless.

"It is useless to me."

Reaching for my hand, he opened my palm, touching it.

"You do not bleed?"

"Not easily."

"It is still yours."

"You will not yield?"

He smiled. "Not easily."

"Then I will wear it for you."

"You will do me and my son great honor."

I was alarmed. "This belongs to Ashebu?"

"Not Ashebu." He shook his head. "To the oldest of each generation. It is the blade of my fathers. It fell to Amenteth, my oldest to wield. It was stolen when he needed it most. Now it is all I have of him."

"Surely, Ashebu—"

"It is a line forever broken." He cut off my thought. "No man living will ever wield it. If it has any purpose left, it can only be in your hands …" His voice softened with a smile. "Even if it is to pry cockles when your fingers fail you."

Sheathing the blade, I held it to me and bowed low to him.

"Come. We have another day of more of the same. If we are lucky, we will find ourselves ambushed in these trees, but my scouts are too good."

As he left the tent, I bound the scabbard to my belt and took up my cloak.

Stepping into the predawn, my eye caught the gaze of Ashebu on horseback. I did not need the sun to read his expression. With a hiss from his lips, he took flight.

[Spharic. Entry translated from *Kor Dai Maihael*. Mund Dai. d. 755]

2003 He braces for another fall when he feels the substrate give under his feet. Years of accrued tar paper keep him from falling through. Leaving two depressions on the roof from his landing, he leaps from a crouch, running to the parapet facing the street below. The street is stalled with cars leaving Safeco Field, but the sidewalks are only lightly peopled this far from the stadium. A freight truck is parked on the side of the street closest to him. Stepping onto the parapet, he jumps clear enough of the building to land on the trailer. Scrambling over the side, he drops to his feet on the sidewalk. He hears the exclamation of some onlookers in the dark. They will only see his shadow before he is gone.

Glancing up at the building, he sees the head of a novice peek over the side of the overpass. Darting across the street to find more people, he moves between the oncoming straggle and darkened store fronts. Pulling off Raphael's brown blazer as he goes, he drops it into the shopping cart of a bearded man stooped on a street corner. He hears a God bless, but feels none of it as he eyes the baseball caps of the Mariner's fans streaming past him. Spotting the bill of a cap hanging from a man's coat pocket, he fingers it as he brushes by. Putting it on, his flannel shirt and jeans all but make him invisible as he weaves into the growing numbers of people streaming from the Safe.

He has no idea how many novices are following him. He doesn't know if they are surrounding him. If he can't lose them, he isn't sure how he will get away.

The lights of Safeco Field are ahead. Three blocks will bring him to King Street Station, already flanked by rows of busses queued and waiting to make runs after the game. He must go south. There will be an express to Tacoma. Nearing the station, he sees the lines of people waiting to board. A bus heading north for Everett pulls away. Another bus leaves for Sea-Tac and Federal Way. If there was an express to hell he would be on it.

Observing the crowds, he slows, trying to blend in. The hydraulic hiss of a wheelchair lift makes him jump. As the wheelchair-bound man is lifted onto the bus, he studies the faces of the passengers on board. Some express impatience, others are children already asleep. The sudden throb of a car stereo distracts him. He stiffens at the sight of a black Escalade. As the tinted window goes down, he sees a young man in Mariner colors searching for a break in traffic. Scanning the streets, he doesn't see another black SUV in sight. He knows there is no way he can wait in a line. There is no way they would let him leave on a bus. They would stop it at any cost.

A blank face in the crowd catches his eye. Move.

Cutting between the lines of waiting commuters, he slips between two busses and runs the length of the bus queue. Beyond is a rail overpass he must cross or go back the way he came. Speeding to a sprint, he makes the overpass, narrowly missing pedestrians as he tries to see ahead to his next goal. He is nearly across when he spots a novice closing the gap in front of him. Without breaking his stride, he glances over the side. Below, a commuter train is waiting on the station siding to make a post-game run. It is southbound. Grabbing the rail of the overpass, he drops over it, hoping for a short fall to the roof of the train. He overshoots, glancing off the side of the rail car.

It is a hard landing. His hands break his fall on the broken rocks of the track bed. A surge of pain in his side makes him wince. Without looking over his shoulder, he gets to his feet and sprints alongside the train. Vaulting onto the train platform, he pushes through boarding passengers and makes for a gangway, skirting the sublevel of the station. He skids to a stop, slamming through the glass doors before jumping the turnstile and running across the terminal. Slipping between the doors, he barely makes an elevator returning to street level.

Catching his breath, he sees his reflection in the elevator doors. The bill of his cap has shifted in his flight. His shirt, half buttoned, hangs loose, exposing his white tee and a black stain. It looks like ink, but he knows it is scorched. He looks like a slob, all save the face: beardless, unchanging, forever challenging his credibility.

The eyes of a man standing behind him meet his appraisingly. Feeling himself flush, he worries someone will notice his eyes, only to see for himself they have turned black. Dropping his gaze, he waits for the chime to end his futility.

When the doors open he doesn't run but walks quickly to the street-side exit. Glancing from one door to the next, he prepares to retreat at the first sign of detection. Making the exit, he steps onto King Street and makes a check of the sidewalk. Turning west, he heads for the waterfront and back to Pioneer Square. Back to where he started. He has come full circle. Hopefully they will think he is moving south and not double back for him. The thought comes too soon.

A black SUV appears at the next intersection, barring his way.

There is no time to think. Darting into traffic, he slides across the hood of a cab and is missed by a speeding pickup as he jumps a median. Finding cover behind a bus leaving the station, he jogs alongside it for a block heading west before cutting north up Second. Another SUV appears, two blocks up the street. It will close on him before he can make the next intersection. Crossing the street, he runs into a sports bar and searches over the heads of patrons for a fire exit. Passing the bar, he sees an exit behind the pool tables.

What he will see in the alley is dim. They are surrounding him.

Trying to think, he is tempted by the bar to give up and order a bottle of whiskey. The ops is his only weapon. No good against an army of novices. Only good on himself. All he has left in him, he saved for Sam. Will he let Metatron have it now or take it with him in a final act of obliteration committed in a back alley?

Sophie.

If she has found Louis, she will be left in Sam's hands. And at his request.

Giving up is not an option.

The crack of a break on the pool table snaps him from his thoughts. The balls scatter across green felt in predetermined chaos. One of the players compliments his opponent on the lucky placement of the eight ball. He looks at the neighboring table. A game is just being set, the patrons talking and chalking their cues. Running past them, he snatches the eight ball as he exits by the back door.

He is greeted in the alley by an SUV slowly approaching from the north. It accelerates at the sight of him. Sprinting south, he expects another SUV to cut off his escape, to face a pair of novices on foot at the least. What good he will get out of the eight ball gripped in his hand he has no idea. It isn't even a magic one. As he nears the end of the alley, a car skids to a stop in front of him. A silver Audi.

The windows are down and Sarah's eyes glow at him. Without question, he opens the door and jumps in, the car speeding away before it closes.

"You came back." He stares at her breathlessly.

"Getting out of Seattle is a nightmare. I need you for the HOV lane."

Her indifference is unaffected as she cuts through a crowded intersection and maneuvers down a one-way street in the face of oncoming traffic. Turning hard onto a side street, she finds an alley parallel to an industrial rail siding. They speed across the port district behind the backs of warehouses.

Checking his side-view mirror, he makes out the shadow of an SUV following them without its headlights on. The others will be right behind it. Checking himself, he grips his side with his right hand to staunch the breach welling beneath the surface. Glancing over, he catches her observing him and fidgets with the eight ball in his left hand.

Her eyes go on the eight ball. "What's that?"

"A souvenir." He changes the subject. "I thought you'd go back to Sam."

She turns her attention to the road. "Never."

"You're leaving him?"

"I'm leaving for good, Michael."

She swerves as an SUV tries to cut into the alley ahead of them, grazing the wall of a warehouse. The side-view mirror splinters off of his door in a spray of sparks.

"Which is a good thing." She puts up the windows. "I leased this car."

Frowning, he reaches for his seatbelt. "Then why come for me?"

"You set me free. It's the least I can do for you. I can't get your crypt back from Sam, but at least you'll have a chance."

The car flies across a busy street. A motorcycle flashes in front of them, escaping untouched as she taps the brakes to clear the rear tire.

"I'm not getting my crypt back from Sam. I'm going to kill him."

"Really?" She arches a brow.

There is a resounding crash. She glances in the rearview mirror as he peeks over his shoulder. A truck has broadsided one of the SUVs following them, but the other is still there. With a surge of speed, its chrome grill quickly fills the rear window.

"Can I help?" She asks.

His body is thrown against his seatbelt as the SUV rams the back of the car, sending the eight ball to the floor at his feet.

"Getting me to Tacoma in one piece would be good."

She smiles. "What you said about yourself at the cabin isn't true."

"What was that?"

"You do have a sense of humor."

"I wasn't being funny."

The car jolts as it is rear-ended again.

Hugging his side, he swallows. "Can't this thing go any faster?"

"I'm building his confidence. There's a ramp up ahead. I'm going to ditch him, but I'll need him alongside me."

He looks out his window at the wall blurring by. He couldn't open the car door without hitting it.

As they speed into another hail of cross traffic, a car hits its brakes in front of them, forcing her to jump the curb. The SUV behind them swerves but turns wide, missing the alley in an explosion of glass as it piles into a building.

He keeps his eyes behind them and sees nothing.

"Have we lost them?"

"Turn around." She says.

He turns to see a black shadow coming at them. As it closes the gap, headlights blind them. His head hits the head rest as she guns the engine. Before he can brace himself, he flies against his door as she slams the breaks and cranks the wheel. The car slides sideways into a skid and he waits for the SUV to impact with his door. He wonders if she would really go this far to kill him.

The wall blurring past the windshield disappears and he is looking down a street. Tires squeal as she peels out of the SUV's path and speeds to overtake a freight truck ahead of them. Passing the truck, the SUV follows, catching up, pacing them. They cross a set of train tracks. The frame of the car bottoms out as they hit the rutted road on the other side. A sharp pain stabs him and he catches his breath.

The SUV gains on them, rearing them. He grips the handle on the car door. Keeping his eyes on the road, he can see another set of tracks. He knows where they are now. They are running parallel with the interurban highway entering Tukwila. They've escaped Seattle at least.

As the tracks disappear under the front of the car, he clenches his teeth.

The jarring of rails is followed by a crunching grind in his right ear. Looking out his window, he sees the car reflected in the black paint of the SUV next to them. Sarah accelerates and the SUV falls away. The body of the car slams the pavement as it crosses another set of tracks, losing speed. The SUV gains on them. This time it wastes no time and rams them. His car door buckles and the window fractures. He barely notices as he feels for his wound.

A hole has singed through the flannel, scalding his touch.

Sarah mutters something under her breath as she steers the car back into the SUV. The SUV falls away as she races the engine. Another set of tracks comes into view. This time she drives all out. As the car speeds faster, he calculates the odds of safely crossing the rails without tearing the drive train from the car.

"Sariel, what are you doing?" He asks quietly.

"We have a train to catch."

"A train?"

"You can't see it, but it's a long one. We'll be cut off if we don't get around."

"We won't make it past those tracks, let alone a train, if you don't slow down."

"We don't have a choice."

"At this pace, they'll make the train, too."

"Probably."

"And we won't have a car."

"I'm open to ideas."

"Slow down."

She slows the car and the SUV quickly gains on them.

"They're going to hit us." She observes.

"Can you take it?"

She eyes him. "Can you?"

"Let them."

He barely speaks when his window shatters away and he is reading the fine print on the side mirror of the SUV. Sarah drives the car hard against it, making his insides flame with the whine of grinding metal.

"What are we doing?" Sarah shouts at him.

"Building his confidence!" He calls back.

Releasing his seat belt, he grabs the eight ball off of the floor.

"I can see the train!" She glares.

He nods, "Let it come!"

Palming the eight ball in his left hand, he climbs out of his seat and grips the door of the car as they approach the tracks. The SUV speeds to keep up as the train rolls into the intersection. As they cross the tracks, he throws the eight ball.

It flies like a shot through the driver's side window of the SUV. The SUV brakes hard, skidding into the path of the train as they clear the intersection. The train's engine collides with the SUV at an unyielding speed, wrapping it across the plow. Trailing a parade of freight cars, the engine shudders, pushing the wreck across the rails like tin. The collision recedes behind them. The road ahead is deserted.

Dropping into his seat, he takes a breath as the wind blows his hair.

"You lost your souvenir." Sarah comments.

"And my hat."

"Sorry about that."

He shrugs. "I stole them."

"Where to?"

His eyes close. "Violet Farrell."

"She's still alive?"

"I hope so."

"I assume she is still your neighbor?"

He hears the question but doesn't feel he can answer.

"Michael?"

"I'm hungry."

The words don't seem to be his. His head begins to nod.

"We'll get you something to eat."

Static fills the air and his head pops up. He is thrilled at the thought Sam is nearby when he realizes it's his hearing.

"Michael?"

He doesn't recognize the voice.

The night grows dark and his head too heavy to lift.

... Michael ...

The voice breaks any rest.

... wickedness and snares ...

It doesn't call out this time. The voice will not answer.

... do you divine ...

The voice will not stop.

... hell ... spirits ...

It doesn't care.

... wander ... seeking ...

There is the smell of roses. Everything is soft.

It has been some time since he has felt comfort. Since he was in a bed.

He is in bed.

"Sophie?"

Daylight filters through white lace curtains. It is all he sees.

"Sophie isn't here."

He blinks at the curtains, looking for the voice. The canopy of a four-poster bed is above. His eyes follow the bed curtains. Violet sits at his side, observing him stoically.

"Sarah?" The name is a whisper.

"She left."

"Where?"

"Didn't say, just said she'd be back."

"When?"

Violet shrugs.

"When did she leave?"

"Around midnight, after she brought you in and patched you up."

He swallows dryly. "Patched?"

Moving his hand under the covers, he reaches for his side. His fingers feel a rough surface; something hard resists his touch.

"She taped you together." Violet answers the question in his eyes.

"With what?"

"I found a roll of that asbestos stuff in the basement."

He tries to heave a sigh, finding it hard to fill his lungs. Pushing himself with his hands, he can barely move.

"You aren't supposed to leave that bed till you've eaten."

"I won't be able to eat much wrapped in this."

"You wouldn't keep any food in you with the hole I saw."

He smiles. "Sophie always said I had one."

"What will you have?" Violet gets to her feet. "Eggs, bacon, hotcakes, toast?"

"All of the above and as much as you can spare."

She raises her brows. "How long since you last ate?"

"Three days."

"Well then." She puts her hands on her hips. "If you'll excuse me, I've got my work cut out for me."

"Where are my clothes?"

"In the trash. They were full of holes."

He feels his throat tighten.

"I had … a hat pin."

"She took that with her I think."

He asks again, "She didn't say when she'd be back?"

Violet shrugs. "Just said she'd be back."

Falling back on the bed, he put his hands to his face.

"You all right?"

"Fine."

"I'll be back with your breakfast." Before she leaves, she points at him. "You promise to stay put?"

He drops his hands. "I don't have anything to wear anyway."

With a grin, Violet leaves, closing the door behind her.

He doubts she can hear his plea, but he makes it anyway.

Please, Sarah. Don't leave me like this.

Without the ops, he has nothing.

The scent of roses make his eyes wander. A vase of bright yellow blooms sits on the nightstand. The room is wallpapered a pale yellow with a floral border. The four-poster bed is festooned with lace matching the windows, the bedding trimmed with yellow satin under a bed cover of embroidered silk. A white vanity across the room reflects the light of the windows. It is a woman's room.

Not Violet's.

Anne's.

Turning his face to the windows, he has the urge to see what they look out on. Forcing himself out of bed, he ignores a dull pain as he drags his legs out from under the sheets and tests his feet. When he stands, the pain sharpens. He drops to the edge of the bed to catch his breath. On his second attempt, he crosses to the windows and peers through the curtains.

It is a lovely view. From this perspective, he knows where he is in the house. It is the turret standing watch over the gulch below. Beyond is the deep blue sea. Unlike Sophie, Anne was very girlie. How long she waited for her knight in shining armor to come to her rescue, he'll never know. All he knows is it wasn't him.

Hey So-So,

So what did you think of the movie? I know what you're thinking. Light on the science, heavy on the fiction. I couldn't agree more, but blaming ancient Egypt on space aliens is a good fit. Nothing else could explain those clothes. I don't know why they make the alien a bad guy though. Why couldn't they make a movie about an alien who wasn't evil. Which makes me wonder, why would an alien end up in Egypt? Personally, I believe aliens are around all the time and we don't know it. The whole space ship premise is flawed. Super human, super smart beings wouldn't show up in a space ship. Jesus, I wouldn't, would you? Maybe Jesus was an alien. Course they'll never make a movie about that, every religious nut would catch fire. Coming from a nut, that's quite an observation.

Anyway, it was cool seeing you last night. It's always more fun when we go together. That guy you were with was a loser. I'm dead sure you can do better than that. Course all men are dogs, aren't we? Too bad you aren't a lesbian, women are definitely superior. Somewhere out there, there has to be a hermaphrodite worthy of you.

See you tomorrow,

Gray Jay

[Police evidence. Letter from Gregory Jacobs to Sophie Davids. #401 of 732 for 1995]

2000 "What is that?" Amy pointed to an embroidered beekeeper's bonnet in a display case.

"It's a Chinese bridal veil! Isn't it lovely?"

The shopkeeper opened the case and took it out. "It goes on like so—" She was going to put it on Amy, but stopped, piercing me with black eyes. "Well, you should try it. It would look perfect on you."

"That's okay." My nose wrinkled as I put up a hand.

"No, really. You have the eyes for it."

"I thought you weren't supposed to see who was wearing it?"

The shopkeeper let out a high-pitched laugh that even made Amy flinch.

"Only when the veil is down. It still looks lovely when it's up. Do try …" She raised it over my head as I pursed my lips.

"Gosh, that's huge." Amy stared at me.

"Beautiful! Would you like to look in the mirror?"

"No, that's fine, thanks." She took my arm, pulling me to the free-standing mirror in the corner of the shop.

"What do you think?"

I was thinking a lot of things, none of them having to do with the puppet theater on my head.

"That's nice." It was the best I could do.

"Are you ladies married?" The black eyes were on me again.

"No." Amy piped up. "But Sophie's engaged."

"Congratulations!"

I was trying to get the veil off my head.

The shopkeeper grinned, her horn-rimmed spectacles and close-cropped black hair making her look like a literate insect. Stepping forward, she helped me with the veil and took it back to the display.

"If you need a dress, you know where to come. You know, not everyone is interested in the traditional wedding gowns anymore. You should consider other cultures when you plan yours."

"I'll keep that in mind."

Amy frowned. "I thought you said you were having a Hawaiian ceremony?"

"Hawaii!" The voice pitched off the walls. "*Wonderful* place. Islands are such a perfect place to hide. I've hidden away on a few myself."

"I won't need a veil." I added.

The keeper's voice dropped to a stage whisper. "You always need a veil!"

Amy bit.

"Why?"

"To ward off the evil eye, of course."

Amy looked like she'd just seen one. "I've heard that. Is it true?"

Slowly, I drifted to the door of the shop.

"You never know when someone might wish ill upon you. Weddings are especially potent. They signify the beginning of a new life. The future is set upon the bride, all her hopes and dreams and expectations. If you let someone set evil upon you, evil will follow you the rest of your life."

"A veil really keeps that away?"

"I think so." The keeper stared at me, waving a finger. "So remember, have a veil and you can never fail!"

"What a nut!" I big-eyed Amy as we stepped onto the sidewalk.

"You didn't think she was interesting?"

In the noonday heat, we weaved our way uphill to the hospital.

"Try paranoid. Who really believes all that anyway?"

"I do."

"Really?" I paused to look at Amy. "You never struck me as the superstitious type."

"I totally am. I never pick up a coin if isn't heads up. I never walk under ladders or open my umbrella inside or wear white after Labor Day."

I bit my lip.

"What?" She watched me.

"Come on." My snicker cramped into a smirk. "You never pick up a coin if it's face down? What if it was a quarter?"

"Not even a quarter. My cousin picked up a bad dime when we went camping two years ago and broke her leg on the trip home."

"Nah." My hand waved it off. "Superstitions are self-fulfilling prophecies. If you believe in something enough, it's bound to happen."

"Is that why you're lucky with men?"

"I wouldn't call it luck."

She sighed. "Every year I pray this is the one Prince Charming shows, and every year I'm looking for a new roommate."

My head shook. "Never believed in Prince Charming."

"And you got Michael. It doesn't seem fair."

"I agree."

"Anthony's kinda superstitious."

"Are you kidding? He's Catholic, a cop, and a sports fanatic. The first time he took me to a Husky game, I had to wear one of his lucky coins in my back pocket and eat a jawbreaker at the start of each quarter."

"There's his St. Michael medal, too."

I grinned. "Things can't be too bad in the man department."

Nodding shyly, she smiled at the sidewalk. "There's some potential."

"Maybe we should all do something sometime … double date."

"You sure you want to? I mean, with Mike and Anthony at the same time?"

"I don't know if you've noticed, but Anthony hasn't made himself scarce from my life. Actually, he's kind of a pain in the ass right now. At some point he's got to accept that Mike isn't leaving. The sooner he accepts it, the sooner he might realize his potential." I gave her a wink.

"I see." Her lips disappeared.

372 | LISA MOWAT

"Look, I've invited Anthony to our wedding as it is. If they don't learn to be in the same room with each other now, I sure as hell don't want the first time to be at my wedding. But if you don't want to, I totally understand."

"Seeing as how I'm going with him to your wedding, I totally agree."

"Anthony asked you to be his date to our wedding?"

She smirked. "More like he didn't want to go alone."

I elbowed her. "Maybe we can make it more than that. Talk to Anthony. I'll ask Mike. We'll see a movie or something."

"A movie?" Michael looked like I'd told him the wedding was off.

"Yeah." I hung my messenger bag on the coat rack and kicked off my heels. "You and me, Amy and Anthony. We'll let Anthony pick the movie and we'll let you pick a place to eat. How about it?"

He followed me upstairs. "But I got you a television."

"And you've lived in front of it for the last two weeks, so it wasn't a waste."

At the top of the stairs, I glanced into the TV room. In front of the widescreen, a futon had appeared, strewn with wrappers from his vending machine supplies.

"It has." His voice came up behind me. "You haven't watched it at all."

Feeling his breath, the accusation crept coldly down the back of my neck, giving me chills. Continuing to the bedroom, I started to unbutton my skirt. "I was waiting for the honeymoon to end."

He leaned in the door frame with crossed arms.

"I've invited you to join me repeatedly and you haven't."

"Not true. I watched *2001* with you."

"Not all of it."

"Its a long movie."

"Watching it with me made you uncomfortable."

"I wasn't uncomfortable."

"Hal reminded you of me and it made you uncomfortable."

"Now see, *that*." I tossed my skirt at the hamper. "Makes me uncomfortable."

"But going to see a movie with Anthony doesn't?"

"Of course, it does!" I pulled off my blouse. "I'll be with my ex, my fiancé, and my good friend who happens to be dating my ex. It'll be a trifecta of discomfort."

"Then why do it?"

I stood naked before him. "Anthony was my friend before he was my boyfriend. I need him to accept us and move on. For him and for Amy. Can you get that?"

"You'd rather do that than watch a movie with me?"

"I'll watch a movie with you! Tonight. We'll watch *2001*, *Citizen Kane*, that mummy flick you picked up at Costco—anything you want. All right?"

He only stared.

"Do you want me to take a leak here or in the bathroom?"

He stepped aside.

I pushed past him. "Thank you!"

We set a date for Friday. Anthony said he'd get back to me on the movie, but Michael already knew where we were eating. When Friday came and we met Amy and Anthony at Yen Ching, Anthony still couldn't decide on a movie, but Michael knew we'd need an extra serving of orange chicken if anybody else eating.

By the time we got to the theatre, Amy and Anthony had narrowed the field to two movies. One was about an alien, the other about an angel. When Anthony asked me if I had a preference, I told him it was all pretty much the same to me. Anthony chose the alien and a front row seat with Amy. I chose the angel and an aisle seat so he could get refills on popcorn and Mountain Dew.

After the movie, we drove Schuster Parkway to catch the sunset on the bay. Once we started to stroll the boardwalk, Anthony began to complain.

"You didn't like the movie?" I asked him.

Sitting on a bench, I leaned back to watch the water reflecting the sunset. Amy sat next to me, sipping a soda she got from a boardwalk vendor.

"I didn't get it." Anthony sat at an empty picnic table nearby. "Was the guy at the end of the movie an alien or not?"

Michael went to the water's edge and looked over the rail with his back to us.

"I think the idea was the alien was in the guy at the beginning of the movie and left at the end."

"Left how?"

"Beats me. I don't think that was what the two hours in the middle were about."

Tony snorted. "That movie wasn't about aliens at all. It was a total chick flick."

"I thought it was sad." Amy stared at her soda. "That woman was so mean to him when she found out what he was."

"Of course, she was." Anthony scowled at her. "How would you feel if you found out the guy you'd been having sex with wasn't human?"

She grinned. "If he was that cute, I wouldn't care."

Tony rolled his eyes.

"He lied to her." Michael spoke without looking at us. "That's why she was upset."

"Like she would have gone out with him if he'd told her the truth?"

Michael faced us, looking at Anthony. "She would have had a choice. She might have said no, but then again she might have said yes. If she had, they would have been able to stay together. He never gave her that chance so he'll never know."

"If he told her, she'd have thought he was a nut."

"But he could have earned her trust."

"How?" Tony crossed his arms. "By stalking her?"

"If he didn't have any other choice, maybe."

"Stalker's always say that. They blame the victim like choice has anything to do with it. The victim never has a choice! They're harassed till they give in or die."

"If he loved her, he would never hurt her. He would leave before that. There's a difference."

"That's like the difference between a drunk and alcoholic."

"Hey!" I piped up. "Leave me out of this."

Anthony put up his hands. "I'm done. Just talking shit, you know me."

I crossed my arms. "So, it's safe to say you'd give this movie a thumbs down."

"It was a lame romance with an alien you couldn't see. Invisible aliens are even harder to buy than green ones."

"How so?" Mike squinted and I read a near imperceptible shift in his demeanor.

"If I can't see it, I don't believe it."

"But what if such a thing existed?"

"Impossible." Anthony shook his head. "Nothing exists without a body, unless it's dead. Then it's a ghost, and that's not what I paid to see."

"Anthony wanted little green men." I looked at Amy. "What did you think?" Amy had popped the lid off of her soda and was crunching ice cubes.

"I liked it. He was cute and she should have been more understanding."

I looked to my fiancé. "Mike?"

"He should have told her the truth, but I understand why he didn't."

"Did you like it, though?"

"Yes."

"Did you like it?" Amy asked me.

"I thought it was pretty good. But I agree with Anthony, the whole invisible alien thing is pretty hard to swallow. I need a body."

"Amen." Tony nodded.

Michael laughed out loud, which was rare.

We walked back to the car, leaving Amy and Anthony by the pier. There was no conversation, only the sound of the water and our footsteps. He was holding my hand but staring at the sidewalk like he was reading it.

"See, I find it hard to believe you want me to know your thoughts right now."

"Truthfully, I don't."

"Uh oh."

He smiled. "It isn't you. It's me."

"Even worse."

"Do you remember when we had cheesecake in the park?"

"I'm lactose intolerant. It is a day that will live in infamy."

"Do you recall I told you what I did for ECCO? That my skill was my ability to read my own kind, one in particular?"

I slowed. "Uh huh."

"He may be coming for a visit."

"That's why you put a futon in the TV room?"

His grip on my hand tightened. "Not that kind of visit, Sophie."

I stopped walking. "You're going to incinerate more playground equipment."

"It may come to that."

"Might I suggest a playground that isn't quite so close to where we live?"

"I don't plan on letting him come to this state if I can help it."

My lips pursed. "You're leaving."

"I won't be gone long."

"That is, if you come back at all, right?"

He took my other hand and faced me. "I've been unfair to you."

"Now you tell me."

"I thought nothing could stop me from living my own life, but it isn't mine I'm living. It's yours."

"Meaning?"

"Meaning you should remember you have a life of your own and I'm just a passenger. If I were human, we'd both be on the same road, but we aren't. It doesn't mean we can't travel together, but there will be times you have to let me off and pick me up again."

"You want off the ride?"

"Just for a few days."

"Does this have anything to do with us?"

"It has everything to do with me."

I frowned. "I don't know as I like that."

"I don't like it either, but it's what I am."

"Is it?"

He looked at the water with the same blind stare he had when he told me I'd been Daniel in my last life. Reaching up, I pulled his gaze back to mine.

"Let's get some cheesecake."

1199 BC   I set out before dawn. I would have stayed to see to my crypt, but the general would have none of it, keeping an eye on me to see I did no work. As long as I lingered at camp, my presence was a distraction to him and an annoyance to others. Disappearing was best for all. As I moved through the forest, I planned to number my days among men.

Climbing a low ridge, I considered the lay of the land: a belt of green to my left running north along the coast, the ridge under my feet fading to my right, with thin forest giving way to stone. Beyond, a sea of sand. Once we passed the Negev, there would be a good number of ravines and cliff caves. With a mule and wagon, I could drive my crypt far enough to find a place to hide. In the meantime, I would learn to feed myself without the aid of bread. The sound of birds overhead gave me pause. They were sparrows, too small to eat.

Searching the ground, I began down the ridge, my eyes burning the bush for any sign. Cloven feet in the dirt led me. My eye ran ahead in soundless pursuit to the den two metes away. The tracks crossed the paths of others. Finally to a rut. The boar I saw would do.

Making my way with more speed than silence, surprising the animal was not difficult. Killing it with a charge was not difficult, either. Draining it of blood without returning to the caravan a horrific mess, more so. I stripped myself of my clothes before I ate. Even then, I did so carefully. When I finished, a pile of bones, bowels, and hide was all that remained.

Of my humanity, nothing.

[Spharic. Entry translated from *Kor Dai Maihael*. Mund Dai. d. 755 BC]

2003 Louis doesn't see us. Ignoring the tables, he goes straight to the bar, where the short order cook gives him a nod from the kitchen.

"Mornin', Lou." Our waitress brings him a cup of coffee with a grin.

"Wait here." Anthony murmurs without looking at me.

I watch Anthony pass behind the bar stool, putting himself between Louis and the door before casually leaning in. Louis looks at Anthony, then turns and sees me. With a grin, Louis slides from his barstool and comes to our table, Anthony following close behind.

"Have a seat." I reach across the table to drag the remains of Anthony's breakfast out of the way.

Louis pauses, glances at the empty booth, and slowly lowers himself into it. Anthony doesn't join us, but takes a chair from an empty table next to ours, sitting back like he's watching TV. Pulling the envelope from my coat pocket, I hand it over. Louis looks at my hand and takes it. We say nothing as he reads his name on the envelope. He works his thumb under the flap, leaving greasy prints on the crisp paper. Slipping out the letter, he holds it down on his lap to read it, his head bowed as though saying grace. We wait.

We wait some more.

Finally, Louis raises his head. "He'll be wantin to meet ya."

"Michael?"

Louis nods. "Someplace safe."

"Where's that?" Anthony speaks up.

"Wouldn't be safe if I said, would it?"

Tony raises his brows at me. "You trust this guy?"

Giving Louis a once over, I shrug. "Michael seems to."

Louis flashes me a smile.

"But why didn't he tell you where this place was when he left you?" Anthony persists. "Why all the smoke and mirrors?"

"It ain't easy to find." Louis advises.

"I believe it." I smirk. "The way Mike takes care of his places, he could have a house two blocks from here and it wouldn't be easy to find."

"I can find places. It's what I do." Anthony points at Louis. "If you trust us enough to take us there, you can trust us enough to tell us where it is. I can take Sophie."

Louis shakes his head. "I can take ya there if you want or leave ya here if you don't. Up to you."

"Tony, this is what Michael wanted. Can't you just trust him?"

"You really think he can't get you into any more trouble than he already has?"

"From what I can tell, he's done an amazing job of keeping me out of it."

"Sophie, the devil wants you to have his baby."

"It could be worse. He only wants one. You wanted five."

Tony tosses his hands at me and looks away.

Meeting Louis's stare, I smile. "When do we leave?"

Louis grins.

"You'll wanna finish that breakfast. It's a drive." He glances at Anthony. "If you'll 'scuse me. Gotta use the gents."

"No kiddin'?" Tony eyes him. "So do I."

Louis gets up to wander to the back of the diner with Anthony shadowing him.

Getting back to my cold egg, I cut into it with my fork when Louis's letter catches my eye. He left it on the table, the envelope flap sticking up like a lure. Taking a check over my shoulder, I reach over and pull out the letter. Yes, Mike asked me to burn it, but that was only if I couldn't find Louis.

I did. Technically, I'm not breaking the rules.

Unfolding the paper, it appears blank. Written neatly in the middle of the page are two words.

"You're hired."

The drive isn't so long as hot.

As we follow Louis's truck east along the Columbia, the temperature is tolerable and Anthony is content to have the windows down. Once we leave the river, it climbs to one hundred. Cranking the AC, we drive south and east through endless acres of irrigated cropland. Potatoes, hops, and grapes stretch to the horizon until we make a sharp turn across a barren field with a dirt road. The road climbs a large hill covered with sun-burnt grass.

Coming over the crest, it levels out to a commanding view of the river valley beyond. A squat house sits back from the view, invisible from the main road. It is probably fifty years old but could pass for a hundred. Its windows are curtained, hidden under a low porch roof facing away from the sun. Two chairs stand sentinel in the shade. Aside from a sad, wind-bent tree, there is no sign of life.

Escaping the car ends the relief of air-conditioning. A blast of hot wind blows hair in my face as I watch Louis climb down from his truck and walk to the house. Anthony and I follow him onto the porch as he digs in his pocket for a key and opens the door. My eyes adjust to the dim, searching the room for anything that is Michael's. Only the functionality of the place seems to match. A wood stove, a small table with a couple chairs, a shelf with some notebooks and a bottle of ink.

A half-finished bottle of whiskey catches my eye.

"How long are we supposed to wait here?" Anthony's impatience starts me. He takes turns glaring at Louis while he paces the floorboards, making a visual inventory.

Louis shrugs and snaps the gum he is chewing. "I'll let him know you're here. After that's anybody's guess."

"How will you let him know we're here?" I face him.

"We gotta system worked out."

"A system?" Anthony raises his brows.

Remembering the letter, I am curious. "What is it that you do, Louis?"

"I deliver stuff."

"What kind of stuff?" Tony finally stands still.

"Necessaries."

"Necessaries?" I frown. "Like what?"

He stops chewing and flashes a smile. "You."

Tony snorts. "I'll tell you what's necessary. There isn't a drop of water in the place and nothing to eat. If we're supposed to wait in this furnace longer than a day, you're going to have to deliver supplies."

Louis snaps his gum. "On my way." He turns for the door.

"And, Louis." Anthony holds out his hand. "I'll take that key."

Pausing mid-chew, Louis shifts in his pockets and comes out with a key. Anthony takes it, stalking to the window as Louis walks out the door.

Peeking through the curtains, Anthony murmurs. "I don't trust that guy."

"What's to trust?" I linger at the open door to watch Louis leave.

"What if he doesn't come back?"

"We have a car. Mike gave us two days to find him, remember? We'll give him a day and leave, *all right?*"

Feeling cross, I leave Anthony and stand on the porch.

Louis's truck disappears over the crest of the hill in a puff of dust. Strolling the length of the porch, I bounce up and down on a squeaky plank before jumping to the grass to survey the plateau.

"I knew I couldn't trust that guy."

Looking over my shoulder, I watch Anthony fidget with the lock on the door of the house.

"This isn't the right key. He lied."

"Give 'em a break, Tony. I'm sure he's got more problems than loose keys in his pockets."

My attention strays to the side of the cabin as I speak.

From where I stand, the house seems larger on the outside than it appears inside. My nose leads me around to the back. Behind, there appears to be an attached garage, little bigger than a lean-to shed. The doors on it are latched and chained.

"I wonder what's in there." Tony's voice is behind me.

"Necessaries?" I muse.

He walks up to latch, tugging the chain. It has a stout lock.

Suddenly, he straightens. "—the door on the inside."

Without another word, Anthony disappears around the side of the house. Running to catch up, I follow him to the front porch and back inside. He goes straight into a side room filled with firewood and dusty boxes. There is a door behind a barrel.

"I thought it was a closet." He shoves the barrel out of the way.

When he turns the knob, it doesn't give. He examines the keyhole in the door and then looks around the room.

"Try the key, genius."

He smirks and pulls the key out of his pocket. The key slides in the keyhole and turns easily. Pulling the door open, Anthony looks inside as I come up behind him. In the dark I see a familiar shape.

"It's his crypt." I whisper.

"Who's what?"

Pushing past him, I run my hands over the etched lid, feeling sentiment I never thought I would. "Michael's crypt. He must have moved it here."

"Crypt?"

"He has to have one."

Tony's eyes bug, "He sleeps in that?"

"Only when he needs to."

"Needs to?"

"His body can't heal without it."

Feeling for the fissure, I push up on the lid. There is no pale glow. It is empty. My hat is gone. He must have used it since.

Anthony comes up next to me, peering over my shoulder. "How does it work?"

"Beats me."

"You've never asked him?"

"Trust me." I make a face. "I know enough."

"How could you not want to know?"

"In this case, ignorance is bliss."

"Do you have any idea how many people would kill to find out?"

"If I didn't, I'd be a widow by now. Not that it matters, I wouldn't understand if he did tell me." I close the lid. "Think you could figure that out?"

He bent down to get a better look.

"If he wanted to share trade secrets, he should have dated someone at NASA, don't you think?"

Leaving the shed, I drift to the front of the house. Finding my husband's crypt should comforted me, but it doesn't. Taking a chair at the table, I drop into it, feeling tired. Anthony remains with the crypt for some time. When he finally comes out, he finds the other chair.

"That's it? He loves you because you don't care about what he is?"

"I knew you were a cop when we started dating, but that didn't stop me."

Tony nods. "I was surprised you gave me a chance after ... what happened."

He doesn't say Gray's name, as if it makes it less obvious.

"Michael isn't like Gray."

"That goes without saying."

"Knock it off, Tony. You know what I mean. I told Mike I was willing to face the risks. I'd be a Grade-A hypocrite to be bitching about it now."

"Fair enough." He pauses. "For what it's worth, I think he really loves you."

"It's worth a lot."

"It has to be a good sign his ... whatever, is here."

In a daze, my eyes float the room. The bottle of whisky catches me again.

"That isn't." Giving Anthony a quick glance, I nod at the bottle. "Mike only drinks whiskey when he's desperate."

"Why's that?"

"He's calls it the drink of despair. I only saw him drink it before we were married."
Getting to my feet, I approach the bottle to investigate.
I pick it up and wave it at Anthony. "Want some?"
"No, thanks."
I pull out the cork and give it a sniff, then shudder. Stopping the cork, I replace the bottle next to the notebook and ink bottle. Peering at the notebook, I see it is bound with a marbleized cover. Flipping back the cover, I leaf through the pages. The writing is the same as in Michael's journals at home, neat and indecipherable.
"Anything interesting?"
"If you can read it." My eyes read something. "Hello. What's this?"
On a page is a list of names:

Sophie Davids
Peter Davids
Edie Davids
Maeve Sears
Kate Sears
Duane Nelson
Anthony Navarre
Amy Duncan
Dan Fogel
Phil Stuart
Evelyn Whittier

Walking to Anthony, I show him the list. "You're in here."
He reads it. "All people you know. Friends and family."
"I'd hardly call Lyn a friend. And I work with Dan and Phil, but I wouldn't call us close." I shake my head. "These are people I know, but it's an odd list. I know other people better than some of the names here. It's a record of the people he knows through me."
"Why would he keep a record of that?"
I shrug. "It's his journal. He records things religiously."
Anthony flips the page and his eyes widen at the script. "Whoa."
"Yeah. Mike has a wall of journals filled with this stuff."
Covering my mouth, I yawn.
Anthony looks up from the notebook. "You know there's a cot back there. If you need it, take it."
The idea of nap sounds wonderful.
I scratch my ear. "Maybe I should. I think the heat has gotten to me."
"Take it." He returns to scrutinizing the notebook. "I'm too wired on coffee to sleep."
Going into the back bedroom, I cross to a window and force the rusty latch to open it. As soon as it cracks, a breeze blows cobwebs into the room. It is hot, but better than stifling stillness. The cot is just that: naked, but steady under me when

I sit on it. Kicking off my Tevas, I stretch out with my head on my arm for a pillow, the list of names is on my mind. It still strikes me as strange. But what about my life isn't?

There is a whistle.

I squint at the window and watch the curtain blow in the wind.

I often dream of wind. Sometimes it really is the wind I am hearing. Sometimes it is different and I know why. The first year we were together, it used to frighten me. As soon as I knew he was in my head, he would go away. Most mornings, I probably didn't remember, but some I did. He would never say anything. Gradually, I stopped being afraid. For some reason, I found it easier to have him in my head when I was asleep than when I was awake.

Now, I can't sleep without him.

The wind gusts and I know I am awake, but my eyes stay closed. He isn't here. I know it like I did the night he tried to propose to me. It was the night he tried and I failed. It was a long one. Ever since, I thought it the longest night of my life. But the last three have outmatched anything I could imagine. They have melded together into endless dark.

A chill brushes my cheek. I open my eyes to the wall and realize I have slept the day away. It is night and the wind has stopped. Turning my head to look at the window, a face looks into mine.

Am I dreaming?

"No." He answers.

"Michael?"

He kisses me. His smell is sweet but stale. I push him away to look in his eyes.

"Are you all right?"

"I was going to ask you the same thing."

"I'm fine." I blink at him. "Are you? Are you free?"

"As a bird." He smiles.

His eyes glow in the dark with a hunger I have never seen.

Of all the heavenly Host, Saitael refused to submit.
None had the strength to compel him. The Host sent
Maihael to face him. But Saitael was as cunning as
he was strong. Saitael knew Maihael would seek peace.
Saitael let Maihael convince him. Saitael listened
offering all the reply that Maihael hoped to hear.

Giving his oath, Saitael agreed to return to the Host at
Maihael's side and asked to seal his word bond with a
kiss. Believing Saitael true to his word Maihael agreed.
Saitael devoured Maihael and they became Bahiel.

From that day forward, Bahiel devoured all he could
find until the Host was few and the universe empty.

[Cuneiform. Excerpt translated from *Pro Fanai Bahiel*. bef. 2000 B.C.]

2000 His nerves were back. It was the only explanation he had for the sense of unease he felt the moment he left the house. It could have been a hangover from the night before, but those came with a calm satisfaction that escaped him now. As he passed through airport security, he looked over his shoulder. Pushing his sunglasses on his head, he studied the line behind him. All he saw were the usual travelers: college students, professionals, elderly tourists.

A woman with black eyes and horn-rimmed spectacles caught his eye. She smiled. All she should see was a young man on a hiking trip. Smiling back, he turned to place his pack on the conveyer belt before concentrating on the metal detector. He didn't need his newfound nerves setting it off. Taking a breath, his vision dimmed as he felt his insides hollow. Passed through the detector, nothing happened. He breathed again. Picking up his pack, he continued onto his gate.

Claiming an abandoned paper, he sat down to read it. Or look like he was. He watched through it instead. Watched the passengers' milling and the flight crews come and go. Watched the clock tell him what he already knew. When his flight was announced, he got in line to board. It was a short wait. He always flew first class. Not because he needed the comfort but because it was the section with the fewest passengers and the most exits.

Fewer eyes and more exits were a good thing.

Finding his seat, he stashed his pack overhead and sat down in the aisle seat. A young girl in the window seat was watching him. She wore brown pigtails and a pink fleece vest over matching shorts.

"Hi!" One of her front teeth was missing.

Sitting back in his seat, he smiled at her.

"My name's Allie."

"I'm Michael."

"Actually, my name's Allison."

"Hello, Allison." He rested his head back and closed his eyes.

"Some people call me Allie Cat, but you can call me Allie."

Opening his eyes, he looked at her. "You may call me Mike."

She stared for a moment. "Do you live in Arizona?"

"No."

"Do your parents live in Arizona?"

He paused. "A brother."

"My dad lives there."

"Really?" He watched the other passengers moving about the cabin.

"I'm going to spend the summer with him."

A passing steward offered him a drink.

He looked at Allie. "Do you want something?"

She sucked the gap in her teeth. "Apple juice."

The steward dug in the beverage cart for a juice cup and handed it to him.

He passed it to her and nodded to the steward. "The same, please."

Glancing over, he saw she was struggling with the sealed lid.

"Here, let me." Holding her cup, he pulled the lid back.

"Thanks." She carefully balanced the cup in both hands before guzzling it.

Opening his own juice, he took a sip. Allie belched into her empty cup and he grinned at her.

"Sorry!" She giggled. "Mom doesn't like it when I do that."

Resting his head again, he shut his eyes, trying to ease his mind.

"My dad has a pool."

"Really?" He squeezed his lids tighter.

"I'm going to swim lots."

He tilted his head to her. "That sounds fun."

"I miss having a pool. Mom doesn't have one."

"It's a little cold for that here."

She shrugged before bending over to wrestle with her tray table.

He gazed over her head out the window. In spite of summer, it was an overcast morning. He wished he was still in bed. It was still dark when he left. Sophie was still asleep. She was awake now. Annoyed he left without saying good-bye. As if the night they'd spent together wasn't enough. Saying good-bye was too much.

Next time, he would.

"You have pretty eyes."

Allie's voice made him blink.

He looked down at her. "Thank you."

Facing the front of the plane, he closed them.

He was in a desert. It was a red desert, under a blue sky stretching to an endless horizon. His eye traced the unbroken line encircling him. A column of smoke caught his gaze.

Not smoke.

A curl of dust.

He squinted, his eye focusing.

On a figure.

It was walking away from him.

Walking into nothing.

Feeling panic, he ran after it.

He could see her.

In pink.

With pigtails.

Allie?

He had no voice.

She kept walking.

Allie!

She could not hear him.

He ran faster.

Allie!

Putting a hand on her shoulder, he stopped her.
She turned to him, making a gap-toothed grin.
She was holding a baby.
She held it out to him.
"It's got pretty eyes."
He took the baby.
The eyes were missing, empty sockets.
It screamed, kicking in his hands.
He wanted to drop it but was frozen. He looked at Allie wordlessly.
Still smiling, she burst into flames like a paper doll.
With a black hand, she reached for him.

With a gasp, he opened his eyes.
There was a sudden drop and a loud thud. Allie let out a small shriek and gripped his arm harder as the plane shuddered.
"It's okay." He put his hand on hers. "It's just turbulence."
"No, it's not." She whispered. "It's never been this bad."
He could barely hear her over the rising static in his ears.
There would be no surprising Sam after all.
"They're thermals." The ice in his voice tried to still her. "Rising columns of hot air. When the plane flies into them it's like a boat going over a wave. Boats don't sink when they go over waves, do they?"
He watched her expectantly as she shook her head. Whether the fear in her eyes was from the turbulence or from him, he couldn't tell. The captain came on the intercom. They were flying over some thermals and passengers were asked to please stay seated with their seat belts fastened.
Allie looked at him with wide eyes.
"What did I tell you?" He made a smile.
The plane began to climb.
"We're going to drop again. Ready?"
She nodded. There was a feeling of free fall and a shuddering thud.
Twenty minutes later, they were on the ground in Phoenix. When the plane stopped moving, she finally let go of his arm. His skin still burned from her touch.
As the plane neared the gate, he rose from his seat to retrieve their bags. Allie had recovered and was bubbling about going to Castles N' Coasters with her father. Keeping his smile on, he eyed the passengers in the cabin as he retrieved her Elmo suitcase for her. Allie followed him off the plane and up the gangway.
"Are you going to do something fun with your brother?"
"I'm sure he'll think of something." He answered vacantly.
Suddenly, she sped past him. "Bye, Mike!"
Ahead of them, her father waited. He wore glasses and had the same color hair. In his hand was an Elmo balloon. She jumped into his arms.
The reunion barely registered.

Lowering his sunglasses over his eyes, he exited the gate, joining the stream of travelers into the main terminal of the airport. Sky International should have been safe. It was far enough from The Mountain, yet Sam had been expecting him. Once again he was on the defensive and wasn't happy about it.

Near the terminal entrance, a line of limo drivers waited holding name placards. A rotund, Latino driver grinned at him. He bore no placard but approached with a wide smile and a curt nod of the head.

"Mr. Goodhew. Welcome to Phoenix. My name is Jesus. I have a car waiting for you."

"Jesus." He repeated, saying nothing more.

"May I take your bag?" Jesus extended a hand courteously.

"No." He felt no courtesy.

Jesus nodded, his smile unwavering. "Please, follow me."

They walked outside into midday, the air thick with car exhaust from idling cabs. It was ninety-five and blinding in spite of his sunglasses. The temperature would be intolerable after a few hours. Squinting, he held his breath against the heat. Just beyond the cabs, a queue of limos were waiting. A woman was stepping out of one in a red dress and oversized sunglasses. She regarded him in his shorts and tee as Jesus took his pack for him and opened the limo door.

Inside, the cabin was cool and comfortably dim in spite of the white interior. As Jesus pulled away from the curb, the sound of the automatic door locks made him flinch. Breathing in the air-conditioned atmosphere, he tried to relax. It was nerves. Sam was close. The ride would be short.

It was barely ten minutes.

The limo came to a stop on a busy street corner. Jesus opened the door and he stepped out onto the sidewalk. Passersby glanced at him as he looked around. They were in front of a restaurant. He was about to ask where he was when he saw Sam seated at a shaded cafe table in a Havana and sunglasses. Sam waved the hat with one hand while the other held a cigarette.

"He thought you might be hungry." Jesus grinned, offering his pack.

Slinging the pack over his shoulder, he clenched his teeth against the needle pricks on his skin. Nearing the table, he could see Sam had already eaten. A spent plate littered with cigarette stubs remained. Apparently, it had been a long wait.

"Sorry to make you sit outside." Sam nodded at the empty tables around them. "But this is the only place I can make fire. Besides, it gives us a little privacy. We need a moment, don't you think?"

He barely glanced inside the restaurant before vaulting the barricade around the café tables.

Sam arched a brow. "You are living on the edge these days, aren't you?"

"Make your point." Dropping his pack, he sat down.

"Why do you have to be so unpleasant? I can be gracious. I picked you up at the airport, I'm buying you lunch when you tried to have me for lunch the last time we met. Love has done nothing for your personality."

"I didn't do to you any more than you would have done to me."

"Really? I've never sucker punched you, have I?"

"What do you mean?"

"I'm sorry if Louis was heavy handed when I sent him to follow up on my RSVP, but I went to treat with you at great risk. Greater than I could have imagined." Sam cocked his head. "I thought I could trust you to observe the rules."

"I didn't burn you."

"Of course not. Someone spared you the effort."

"Coincidence."

"Convenient."

"I don't know who did."

Sam sat silently, only moving to take a drag on the cigarette while reading his thoughts. He left them open to show he had nothing to hide.

A slow smile indicated Sam's satisfaction. "You must be starving."

"I'm fine."

"Let me buy you lunch."

"No."

"Still saving your appetite?"

"I've lost it."

Sam heaved a sigh. "So have I."

He smirked. "Really?"

"I have a proposal for you."

He crossed his arms and waited.

"A partnership." Sam smiled. "A new beginning for us both."

"No."

"You haven't heard the best part."

"I've heard it."

"We could end ECCO."

"We could end everything."

"You see!" Sam held out a hand to him. "We aren't brothers for nothing."

"We aren't brothers."

"That's not what you said on the plane."

He stiffened.

Sam grinned. "You told her I'd think of something fun for us to do, and I have."

"A duel in the desert?"

"Eternal life! On an island in the sky."

"What?"

Sam leaned at him. "Come back to The Mountain."

"Never."

"I admit it isn't Castles N' Coasters, but it's the best I can do."

"You'd assume me the moment I turned my back."

"Bygone days." Sam flicked cigarette ash. "We've had the same revelation. I want to be whole and you don't want to be alone. As brothers, we can give each other what we need. We were destined to split apart. I can see that now."

"We aren't brothers."

Sam slammed a fist on the table, fracturing it. "Because you fight it!"

"Of course I do! We didn't part to be brothers. We parted because I hate you."

"But I love you!"

"You only love yourself."

"What's not to love?"

"You're selfish, ruthless, and cruel."

Sam crushed the cigarette on the table, ignoring the ashtray. "Whose fault is that?"

"Not mine."

"I gave you your quirks. Charity. Forbearance. Compassion. If you returned, you could temper me."

"No deal."

"You haven't thought it over."

"I've had forever to think it over."

Sam drummed his fingers on the table. "You duel with me and you'll lose."

He met Sam's gaze. "I'll waste you."

For a moment, they only stared at each other. Thoughtlessly, Sam reached into a shirt pocket and pulled out a pack of cigarettes.

"Sarah might like that." Sam tapped out another cigarette. "But Sophie wouldn't."

He watched silently as the tip of Sam's cigarette flared into smoke.

"You'll be leaving her in a very vulnerable position." Sam mused. "Unless you already took care of her, but I doubt it. She is still alive, isn't she?"

"You can't touch her."

"If I best you, I'll do more than that."

"I'll face you where and when you wish, but not on The Mountain."

"You think I'd bewitch you?"

"It's happened before."

"Michael, that was twenty-five million years ago. Let it go."

"I have. You still live there."

"Now that you mention it, I'm thinking about moving. What do you think about Anderson Island?"

"As long as I'm here, you're never going back."

"It's no use flirting with me. I wasn't lying when I told you I'd lost my appetite. You will join me on the Mountain, but not to duel. To come to terms. Whether you believe me or not, you'll take the risk. I did, on that miserable island, and paid the price for it. Now it's your turn. It's only fair."

He shook his head. "I'm not dealing with you."

"You will. You haven't got a choice. You're just too stubborn to see it." Sam waved to a waitress. "I'll expect you at the Gypsy tomorrow."

"Don't count on it."

Smiling, Sam rose from the table. "While you're here, you really should eat. Tom's chili is marvelous. My treat!"

He watched Sam stop a waitress on the way out and point in his direction.

She came out to him with a menu and a grin. "Sam never told me he was a twin."

He didn't have the chili.

After a double order of cheeseburgers, curly fries, and two chocolate milkshakes, he paid over the assurances of the waitress Sam had covered it. Walking across Copper Square, he found a hotel a few blocks away and checked in with the intention of waiting. There was nothing else he could do.

The element of surprise was lost.

If Sam refused to duel, he would never leave.

If he left, Sam would follow.

He needed a nap.

Closing the curtains against the sun, he lay on the bed and stared at the ceiling. The static in the atmosphere had subsided but wasn't gone. Sam lingered. Maybe to return, to try to press him again. Press him on to The Mountain.

It was a rotten place. A ruin of conflict surrounded by waste. An extinct volcano that was the scene of his worst defeat, not against another but himself. It wasn't The Mountain that erupted, but the largest single entity ever known. The coming of Bahiel should have swallowed the universe, should have marked the end of the age, but Bahiel tore itself apart instead.

His memory of this was murky. It was shattered by the shock of separation and left him wandering the void. Sam found him and lured him back into the world. If Raphael hadn't risked suicide to find him, Sam would have assumed him again. Bahiel would have been reborn and his existence forgotten along with everything else God could forsake.

But that was then.

He wasn't the same. He remembered who he was and what he was and why he was. The Mountain had no hold over him. Sam had no hold over him.

Why was he afraid?

Suspicion. His nerves still dogged him.

A spike of fire in the air woke him before a roar rattled the windows.

In the dark, he reached out as far as he could for any sign, but there was only the crush of a thunderhead above. The ceiling flickered and he rose from the bed to watch the lightning from his window. Pulling back the curtain, he saw the sky was purple with clouds. There was no horizon, only a pink veil of rain beyond the lights of the city. In the distance, the sound of sirens.

Swapping his shorts for a pair of jeans, he forgave the elevator for the stairs and made his way to the lobby. The hotel restaurant was crowded with guests opting out of the rain. Avoiding the dining room's mood lighting and candle-lit tables, he sought the refuge of the lounge. The windowless paneled walls and polished brass became the whole of his universe. As he took a seat at the bar, Sophie's voice was already ordering a Sapphire with two olives.

"Good evening, sir. How may I help you?" The black barkeep's eyes reflected the glint of a silver shaker in his hands. His nametag said he was Daniel.

His eyes found a bottle of Sapphire glowing before the mirror over Daniel's shoulder.

"Whiskey."

He liked to imagine he felt something when he drank. When he returned to his room three bottles later, the smell of it on his breath and the empty calories burning in his blood gave a dull satisfaction. There was no other reason to doubt his senses since the storm passed. Sam was gone. There would be no visitation. No renewal of pleas. No attempt to buy him a drink. The invitation offered still stood. Meet at the Gypsy tomorrow. Fire on The Mountain.

He lay awake all night, staring at the ceiling. He wondered how many days, months, years he would have to wait before Sam gave in. He imagined waiting for eternity. Until the hotel was demolished and the city ground to dust. And then he would lie in the desert and stare at the sky. He would have no visitors. No company to keep. None of the others would come so close to Sam. They wouldn't need to as long as he was here. Sam would trouble no one, trapped on his Mountain, with him waiting in the sand.

Mired.

Sam was wrong. He had taken care of Sophie. His lawyer had instructions: everything he left behind, everything he owned, and a letter explaining things as best as he could. Waiting a year was fair, he thought. A human year gave him time and didn't waste hers.

He regretted not saying good-bye.

The sound of the housekeepers starting their rounds roused him. In the bathroom, he noted the basket of toiletries he didn't need before rinsing his face in the sink because it seemed right. They wouldn't need to service his room at least. Except maybe to dust it. Drawn to the light, he returned to the windows and looked out on a clear sky. It was turning blue.

Soft footsteps came down the hallway, pausing at each door, stopping at his with a light thud. Turning to look through it, his eyes saw the morning paper on the other side. Opening his door, he picked up the paper and read above the fold.

FATAL LIGHTNING STRIKE LEAVES FAMILIES HOMELESS

The photo below the headline showed a subdivision in flames. His eyes absorbed the article with scant attention. In spite of the devastation, there was only one fatality. A six-year-old girl. He was about to turn the page when the name registered.

Allison Mercato.

As far as Bahiel could see, He could not see all. Until the Host was devoured Bahiel would not be One. Until then Bahiel would not rest. For all His greatness Bahiel was jealous above all else. In the universe He would exist Alone.

In the world before men there was a silver mountain with ice that burned like fire. Bahiel had seen this mountain in mind and long searched for it. From this mountain Bahiel would see all. From this mountain Bahiel would devour all.

When Bahiel found the mountain, the fire woke the eye of one he devoured. The eye within Him was long closed but not blind. As Bahiel stood upon the mountain Maihael awakened. Maihael possessed Them and cast Them into the flames.

Bahiel was destroyed. The mountain was destroyed. The end of the beginning. The beginning of the end.

[Cuneiform. Excerpt translated from *Pro Fanai Bahiel*. bef. 2000 B.C.]

2003 "I thought you'd want to see this." Violet drops a newspaper in his lap.

LOCAL PHILANTHROPIST FEARED KIDNAPPED

The headline makes him sit up in bed. Unfolding it, he scans the article.

An unnamed source leaked his identity as the anonymous donor behind the recently unveiled addition to St. Joseph Hospital. He and his wife, an employee of the hospital, have been missing for five days after mysteriously disappearing from the Tacoma Farmer's Market last Thursday. They were reported missing after friends found their car abandoned near the market. No one who knows the couple has seen or heard from them since. There is no evidence of a kidnapping and no demand for ransom has been made, though police say money could be a motive. Friends claim the couple is happily married with no history of a troubled relationship.

Until now.

He lowers the paper. Sophie is going to kill him.

His consolation: Sam will bear the brunt of her rage and not him. His problem: predicting how enraged Sophie will be. He is relying on Sam's instinct to pose as him. If Sam does as he would, they will come home. Now, it is possible she will refuse to come. If she abandons Sam before returning home, he will have no way of reaching her, of warning her, of protecting her.

That, and a day has passed without any sign of Sarah and the ops she took with her.

"You look upset."

He sees Violet watching him skeptically.

"Just nerves."

Tossing aside the blankets, he starts to get out of bed.

She steps back nervously. "Where do you think you're going?"

Getting to his feet, he pulls a sheet around him. "I can't stay in this room all day."

"You can't very well run around in a bed sheet."

"I have before."

Tucking half of it around his waist, he wraps the other half across his shoulder. Violet smiles. "You look like you're going to one of those parties."

Raising a brow, he passes her at the door. "Those were some parties."

Outside the bedroom, he winds his way down the dim stairs of the turret. An odd smell makes him slow as the door below Anne's room comes into view.

"That's the room Curtis used when he watched your house at night." Violet's voice echoes down to him from above.

Pausing, he opens it. It is filled with boxes and the stench of taxidermy.

Violet stops behind him on the stairs and wrinkles her nose. "Knew there was a reason I never opened this door."

Crossing the room to the window, he steps around a canvas chair sitting next to a stool with an ashtray. A pair of sun-bleached field glasses still sits on the sill. The view is the same as above, only closer to the ground, with a clear line of sight down the street. He makes out the roof of his house.

Looking around the room, the eyes and ears of trophies strain at him from their crates. The wake of their wait makes the space deathly still, but it is the best room in the house for him to keep watch. He just hopes he doesn't end up smelling like it.

He turns to Violet, still standing on the stairs. "Where is your room?"

"Other end of the house."

"Good. For now, you should stay in it as much as possible."

"Look at you. You wash up here at death's door, twenty pancakes and as many hours later, you're wearing my sheets and telling me where to go in my own house."

"It shouldn't be more than a day, two at most."

She is suddenly grave. "A day's all that's left of it then?"

He blinks at her. "Left of what?"

"The world."

"I don't know how many days the world has left."

"You can tell me. I'm not scared."

"There's nothing to tell, Violet. I don't know any more than you."

Her eyes widen. "Only God does, I s'pose."

His voice hesitates. "If there is one."

"How can an angel not believe in God?"

"Humans believe in God. As for angels, I'm not. I'm just Michael."

"But God made you."

"The universe made me."

"Same thing."

"Maybe." He shrugs, returning to where she stands in the hall. "But there's no God in heaven to guide me and no one to answer our prayers."

"I pray to you." She stops him as he leaves the room. "I pray every night."

Her words spark a memory.

"What do you pray for?"

"That you'll defeat the devil."

Dropping her gaze, he heads down the stairs. "Sam is wicked, but he isn't the devil. Not the one you're thinking of, at least. He isn't here to tempt men's souls."

She follows him. "Then what's he here for?"

"If there is room for a god in the universe, he'd like to be it."

"Sounds like the end of the world to me."

"Sam's reach exceeds his grasp. It always has and always will. But I'm hardly angelic. I'm not trying to save the world, just my own."

"I can accept that."

He stops at the bottom of the stairs and faces her. "You can accept what I am doing is for selfish reasons?"

"We all have our reasons. If you think I want you to save the world because I love it, you're wrong. I'm just sick of seeing assholes come out on top."

"Sophie calls me an ass all the time."

"An ass." She pats him on the shoulder. "Sam's an asshole. There's a difference. And as for angels, you're mine whether you like it or not."

The grandfather clock downstairs begins to chime.

She takes his arm. "How about a sandwich?"

Finding his critical thinking skills blur at the thought, he lets her lead him. He wonders what sort of sandwiches she has in mind but doesn't ask. After burdening her with his convalescence, commandeering her house, and challenging her spiritual beliefs in the space of a day, he will eat whatever she puts in front of him.

In this case, and not a little ironically, it turns out to be deviled ham on white bread. It is wonderful to him, and he eats rapidly, finishing a loaf of bread. When he is finished, he leaves her to watch *People's Court* in the parlor and resumes watching his house from Curtis's taxidermy room. Sitting in Curtis's chair, cradling Curtis's field glasses, he patiently waits for himself to arrive. He hopes his hunt is more successful. He hopes he'll be armed with more than a crowbar.

"I brought you clothes, but it looks like I could have saved myself the trip."

Sarah's cool voice starts him from his trance. He looks over his shoulder, catching her eyes giving him a once over.

"Togas making a comeback this year?"

She crosses the room and hands him a shopping bag.

"It's about ten yards too short to qualify."

"Makes shopping off the rack difficult."

Carefully picking through the bag, he eyes her. "Did you bring me something to accessorize with?"

Pulling her other hand out from behind her back, she dangles the ops. Dropping the bag, he takes it from her, letting out his breath.

"Scared you, didn't I?"

He raises a brow. "You're still his wife."

"What happens in Vegas, stays in Vegas."

"Then why marry him?"

"You already asked me that."

"You said when I married Sophie you realized you wanted something."

"And Sam promised to give it to me."

"But you always had me, Sarah."

"I thought I did."

"And you never told me how you felt because you thought I would have left?"

"I couldn't have. I didn't know what I was feeling then. I still don't."

"Then why help me now?"

"Don't start in on that again." She pauses, taking in the crates of trophies. "Let's just say the difference between you and Sam is you give a damn and he doesn't."

"I don't know what I give a damn about." He stares at his bare feet. "I'm using my wife as bait."

"It's brilliant. You're using Sam's desire against him. Sam told me you were attached to your principles the way he was attached to his prophecies. He's counted on you to sacrifice yourself for them. Now, you've turned the tables."

"I doubt Sam would sacrifice himself for anything, no matter his desire for it."

"It's the closest he'll ever come to being stupid."

Slowly he nods, saying nothing.

"I got you a pair of Cole Haans, some Calvin Kleins and a Lucky pullover from Nordstrom's. I figured if you have to go out, you might as well do it in style. Is there anything I missed?"

He shakes his head. "Aside from cutting me out of this tape."

She purses her lips. "You'll ruin your new clothes."

"I can hardly breathe as it is. I'll pass out before I can kill him."

"Your body will bleed to death without it."

"If it takes that long, I'm doing something wrong."

"What about after? If you succeed? What about your body then?"

Absently, he thinks of Louis. "Already taken care of."

"If you want me to come back, I could dispose you."

"Don't. Phanuel will be watching for you."

She snorts. "Phanuel is a coward."

"You should know he has incorporated novices into ECCO beyond our numbers."

"What?" She whispers.

"Gabrielle told me. Those weren't sentinels chasing us out of Seattle. I saw them."

"But the Council-- How could they permit it?"

"I'm afraid our defections gave Phanuel all the ammunition he needed. The orthodoxy of Metatron will control ECCO from now on. So you see, there's nothing to stay for. It's too dangerous for either of us."

"Bastard." Sarah narrows her eyes at nothing.

He grins. "I almost hate him more than—" He stops mid-sentence.

"What is it?"

"*Sophie.*" He jumps from his chair and leaps for the turret stairs.

As he flies down the staircase to the foyer, Sarah catches up to him. They enter the front parlor, where Violet watches the evening news.

"I was going to call you." Violet waves them in.

Sophie is on the television. She is finishing a statement.

"—working with law enforcement to help them in any way we can. We have been asked by police not to answer any questions from the media at this time."

Her face is expressionless, her voice dead.

"Mr. Goodhew, did the kidnappers make any demand for ransom?"

The camera goes to Sam, who only waves off the question with a smile as he leads Sophie from the cameras. The sight of them together makes his skin prick, though he barely feels Sarah standing in the same room.

"Is this live?" He asks Violet without taking his eyes from the screen.

"Just broke."

Sarah comes up behind him and he glares at her. "You have to go."

"Too late for that. I feel him coming already."

He turns to Violet. "The fire safe."

She hops out of her chair and heads for the basement.

Sarah glances between them. "Fire what?"

"Sarah, go with her. No questions."

She hesitates before following Violet into the dark.

Without a backward glance, he is racing upstairs to get dressed.

In the taxidermy room, he empties the shopping bag onto the floor. Quickly dressing, the one thing he lacks is a belt, but asbestos tape might do the trick. He pierces the tape with the ops, threading it into the wrapping. The tape holds it, but his hand comes away wet with pale blue ink. It is his blood, so thin the fire has gone out of it. He doesn't feel anything. He hopes his body has one fight left in it.

The sound of a vehicle makes him duck from the window.

It is a squad car. It goes by too quickly to see who is driving, but he spots two people in back. One of them is a woman. His head starts to buzz as he forgets to breathe. Sucking a breath, he picks up the field glasses on the sill and refocuses them. Weak eyes strain for any glimpse of who is there and what is happening, but there are too many trees. In his quest for privacy, he has made his house invisible to prying eyes—even his own.

He has to go down. From where he is, he is too far to see and too far to help. Looking to the sun, it will be another three hours before it is dark.

There is no time.

He leaves the room, making his way silently down the turret stairs. Violet's house is eerily still as he nears the landing above the foyer; the chatter of the television in the parlor is the only sound. His still sensitive ears pick up a voice coming from down the hall. It is Violet, alone in her room.

He knows what she is saying.

Good-bye, Violet.

Heading downstairs, he crosses the foyer and walks out the front door. Without pause, he skips the porch steps and jumps the zigzag of the boxwood maze in the front yard. He checks the street from the front gate before crossing to Prospect and cutting a path into the brush rimming the gulch. Pushing through a thicket of blackberries, the sound of running water leads him to the trail that will feed into the gulch below his house.

By the time he emerges onto the trail, his new clothes are torn and damp with blood. Following the length of the culvert, he crouches to rinse the blood from cut hands before continuing along the stream bed. There is less cover here. His eyes keep constant vigil on the rim of the gulch above. As his house comes into view, he can see the lights in the dining room. The windows have been opened and he hears voices, still too far for him to hear anything distinct. The stream finally crosses the trail leading up to the backyard. He climbs it cautiously, pausing at regular intervals to listen. There is fear and relief when the first voice he hears is Anthony's.

"—hate to say it, but you should probably get a lawyer. Until the hype winds down, you're going to have reporters tailing you."

"Hype!" Sophie sounds like she is in another room. "I wonder why!"

398 | LISA MOWAT

"Sophie, I'm sorry I didn't tell you sooner." Sam's voice comes from the dining room. Fixing on Sam's location, he checks his feet and rapidly closes on the house.

"Sooner?" Her voice is louder now. "The unveiling was two years ago!"

"As pissed as you are, Sophie, Mike's money gives us the perfect cover. Now that the hospital project has come to light, we can claim his identity was leaked and the two of you targeted. Lucky for you, the kidnapper got cold feet and was rookie enough to feel bad about killing you."

"You're on his side now?"

"I'm not taking sides here. I'm just saying there's a silver lining."

"*Silver lining?*" Her tone is somewhere between rhetorical and lethal.

"I gotta go."

Apparently Anthony hears it too.

"Good idea!" Sophie shouts as her feet leave the room.

There is a pause. He hears the men leave the dining room and peeks over the edge of the window sill. There are plates of food on the table and partial glasses of wine. The thought of Sam eating off his Wedgwood annoys him.

The front door opens.

"Hang in there, Mike. I'm sure she'll come around."

"Thank you, Anthony. For everything."

He ducks, but Sam doesn't return. His head pops up.

Sam must be going upstairs.

Sophie must be there, too.

Gripping the window sill, he pulls himself into the dining room. Skirting the table, he carefully steps into the kitchen and down the back hall where the floor-boards are silent. At the bottom of the stairs, he hears muffled voices and then a loud slam.

"Forget it, Mike!" Sophie's footsteps march down the hall. "I'm done."

Her words come from the top of the stairs. He backs away, ready to slip into the utility room as she comes down.

"Sophie, please wait."

He glimpses Sophie heading for the front door. The door opens and slams shut.

"Let me go, Mike."

"Where are you going?"

"Away."

"You don't love me?"

"Love you? I don't even know who you are! Last week you told me you would tell me everything, and just when I think you have, something like this happens! I don't know what to believe anymore!"

"Because I donated money to a hospital?

"Because you did it to control me! Because you made everything I've accomplished over the last three years a lie! All this time I thought it was me, and it wasn't. It was all you. I've been a tool in your little fantasy world!"

"You're not leaving."

"Watch this."

He hears her come down the back hall and presses himself into the corner of the utility room. She doesn't come.

"Let go of me!"

His body flexes at the terror in her voice.

A snarl tears the air.

"You're my wife."

There is a clattering noise and Sophie flashes down the hall.

He lunges at her wake.

Of all the Host only Raifael saw Bahiel destroyed. The remains of Bahiel scattered the ruins. Raifael went to the mountain to bury them so Bahiel could never return. He found Saitael already risen and rebuilding the mountain. Saitael was building a temple to Bahiel with it.

Saitael had found Maihael and made Maihael apostle to the profane. Raifael risked fate to reach Maihael. Raifael plead with Maihael to turn away. Maihael was deaf and Saitael reached out to devour Raifael. Maihael only watched. Raifael saw that Maihael knew not who he was.

Maihael could not see Raifael devoured. At last Maihael turned and set upon Saitael with destruction. Maihael returned with Raifael to the Host without welcome. Maihael was restored in spirit but not in mind.

Never again would Maihael sit one with the Host. Maihael had been turned once and could be turned again. As penance ever after Maihael was keeper of Saitael and nothing more. Only Raifael saw error in this and feared.

[Cuneiform. Excerpt translated from *Pro Fanai Bahiel.* bef. 2000 B.C.]

2000 "What an ass."

I stared at the empty half of my bed and knew he was gone.

I told myself it was as hard on him as it was on me. He didn't tell me he was leaving until last night because he didn't want me to dwell on it any longer than I had to. He left without saying good-bye because he didn't want to hurt me. Not because he was a chicken-shit asshole. It was hard to believe he wasn't really a man because he had it down as far as I could tell.

Rolling out of bed, I replayed his voice in my head.

I won't be gone long. Just a few days.

How many days was that? A few usually meant three, didn't it? I was holding him to three. This was day one. Saturday. He would be back by Monday evening or Tuesday morning at the latest. After that, full-blown panic could set in. Until then, I would treat this as me time.

So I did.

As the tub filled with bubbles, I thought about the creepy man who installed it. Every time I took a bath now, I had a passing recollection of him. The way he smelled. His broken teeth. The fact he had been alone in our house for three days. I knew he didn't do anything wrong. But he could have. Then, I supposed it was unfair of me to think of him that way because of his appearance. I, of all people, knew how deceptive appearances could be. It was easier to think the creepy man was creepy than say, my husband.

Shutting off the tap, I lowered myself into the hot water. The silence should have been relaxing, but it wasn't a welcome change. It wasn't a change at all. Even when Michael was home, the house was silent, except for the times he would clear his throat to remind me he was there. Otherwise, you couldn't hear him. I was positive there were times you couldn't see him. What little I knew of his capabilities was enough.

I'd seen enough the night before we left for my birthday. It wasn't seeing a playground melt that stuck in my mind. It was seeing my husband turn into something else. I knew he wouldn't hurt me. But he could have.

Inhaling a deep breath, I slipped beneath the water.

When I went online, I checked my e-mails. Amy was suggesting another movie, which reminded me I could watch my DVDs now that we had a TV. Outside, it was beautiful, but I decided to take advantage of finally having the TV to myself. I went upstairs, armed with a bag of microwave popcorn and a beer. I figured if I felt the urge to be healthy I'd open a box of Michael's Clif bars later.

Claiming the futon, I started rummaging the piles of DVDs Michael left scattered around the room. That he found no use for organization was a bone of contention in our relationship. When you remember everything, you don't need to file things, let alone label them. My movies had been ploughed into his. Every five movies I picked off of the floor had two of his mixed in with them. Even more annoying, I thought a lot of them were junk. For someone who sniffed at the scientific validity of *Star Trek, Independence Day* and *Starship Troopers* were hardly an improvement.

Then there was the mummy movie. To be fair, I couldn't judge. I'd never seen a mummy flick in my life. Not even zombies. Dead monsters made me dead tired. This mummy riveted Mike. I knew he'd watched it more than once, which for a guy with a perfect memory was saying something. I decided to watch it, if for any reason to figure out what my husband saw in it.

What first struck me was it was set in a desert. Not surprising for a mummy movie, but surprising that Michael would watch it. He had an aversion to deserts. When we talked about places we had been and places we wanted to go, he wanted nothing to do with them. Example: I couldn't get him to watch *Lawrence of Arabia*. So why this?

The second thing was the parallel between the movie and his life. The possession of a body by something that was dead. The obsession of the dead for the living. The curse of forbidden love. And a being of formidable ability willing to start an apocalypse in pursuit of that love. For anyone else, this was mindless entertainment. My husband didn't value mindless entertainment.

The third thing. I didn't know what my husband was doing while I was watching this.

But why worry now and not every other day he'd been gone without a word?

It was the sort of thing I always managed to forget. He would begin to disappear often enough for me to notice and then stop. Weeks would go by with scarcely a minute of his day unaccounted for. His schedule so consistent, his needs so persistent, I would find myself making excuses to get away from him. I would find myself regarding him as though he were a child or a neurotic pet.

Then he would be gone. Not just physically, but mentally. He would disappear and when he came back he would be cold, distant. Alien.

Still, when he proposed, I said yes. It wasn't just like that. It was a near miss, really. Cold feet for both of us. He wondered if I really loved him for what he was, and I still wondered. Could I love him without a body?

What if he didn't come home with one?

I used to wonder the same thing about Anthony.

One of his colleagues was paralyzed in a car chase. Paralyzed and badly scarred. I met the man before the accident at a baseball game. After the accident, I couldn't recognize him. I wondered what it was like for his wife and family. If that happened to Anthony, would I still love him? If he had the same green eyes, would it be enough? I'd heard you could always tell a person by their eyes, but my husband's eyes were his least comforting feature, and in truth, he didn't even really have those. In a spiritual sense, none of us did, but for Mike, existing without them was an option. What worried me was it was an option he wanted to exercise.

The mummy movie ended badly for the mummy. I assumed they all did. It was a monster, and monsters in film rarely escape typecasting. Good or bad, they are nearly always doomed. It bothered me this was the stuff he'd been watching. I certainly didn't think he was a monster. He scared me, but not the way monsters did. He scared me the way anyone you love too much can. I was scared I would lose him, and in spite of his superior nature, it seemed all too easy.

Suffering from two hours of CGI-induced stupor, I took a break. Downstairs, I made a salad. I wasn't a salad fan, but seeing as how all I wanted in the world was a cheeseburger and curly fries, I hoped a salad would purify me of such unclean thoughts. After salad, I rewarded myself with a chocolate ice cream bar.

Returning to my screening session, I decided on something old. Finding my classic films untouched in a shopping bag, I flipped through them and settled on *The Ghost and Mrs. Muir*. I woke up three hours later.

That evening I dined with my parents. Dinner discussion started with my wedding and finished with an overview of my grandparents' volcanic relationship. Their marriage seemed a match made in heaven until their constant bickering led to a brutal divorce. Somehow they stayed friends, and after a platonic romance, attempted another short-lived marriage. Now they just lived together, sometimes apart, always as the only significant other in their lives. We concluded that in spite of their differences, they couldn't tolerate anyone but each other.

It was late when I left. Late enough for Mom to insist Dad drive me home rather than let me walk. Part of me hoped she would ask me to stay the night.

Our house looked ominous in my father's headlights. He waited in the drive while I unlocked the door and let myself in. With a wave over my shoulder, I shut the door and locked it behind me. I felt a chill in the dark and immediately went upstairs. I didn't like being downstairs alone at night. It was a relief when I closed the bedroom door and crawled under the blankets. The bed was freezing without him. Somehow, I fell asleep.

Are you cold, Sophie?

His voice started me from my sleep. With a shiver, I looked around the room at no one. It was barely light outside and I pulled the blanket over my head. The next time I opened my eyes, I felt warm. The sun was streaming in the east window and cast its rays across my bedspread. Sitting up, I looked at his half of the bed.

Day two. A bathrobe and coffee kind of day.

Peering over the side of the bed, I wondered where my fuzzy slippers had gone. I hardly ever wore them. Flattening myself on the mattress, I hung myself over the edge of the bed and looked under the bed skirt. My slippers were there, along with a dozen dust bunnies. Their offspring no doubt. Time to clean house.

Hopping out of bed, I fished out my fuzzy slippers and hunted up a pair of pajama bottoms. I only took the time to brush my teeth and scrunchie my hair. There would be no bathrobe lounging this morning, but very definitely coffee.

I got a pot brewing and fried some eggs. Eating out of the pan, I was already eyeing everything that needed dusting, wiping, or disinfecting. It was a small house with no children or pets. It could be done.

By noon, most of the main floor had been purged. Most, as in, everything but the study. I could go far for this relationship, but dusting a crypt was too far. Still unhappy with the foreboding appearance of the study doors, I experimented with leaving them open and covered the crypt with a table cloth. I was toying with the idea of topping it with a vase of flowers when the doorbell rang.

The front door didn't have a peephole, but who needed one when you could see through the door? Biting my lip, I cracked it open.

"Good afternoon, ma'am. How are you today?"

It was a young man with freckles and a navy suit. Since it was a Sunday and he was alone, I guessed he wasn't a Mormon.

"Uh huh."

In spite of the crisp collar and tie, his neatly combed hair was damp with sweat.

"My name is Nate Keller. I'm a field agent for Guardian Insurance."

"Uh huh—"

"Looks like I caught you in the middle of something. Here, let me give you my card." He opened a valise and handed me a card with a pamphlet. "I don't want to keep you, but I just had a quick question."

Wrinkling my nose, I said nothing, glancing at his card.

"Are you happy with your current homeowner's insurance?"

"I don't own the place."

"Are you a renter then?"

"Just squatting."

"Oh." He stared, mystified. "Well, if you do see the owner, have them give me a call if they're interested."

"If I did, I'd be runnin' the other way."

He smiled uneasily, drops of sweat beading on his forehead. I felt like a jerk. Stepping back, I let the door drift open.

"Do you want something to drink? Some iced tea or water?"

This surprised him. "Thanks … I'm not supposed to. It's against company policy."

"I'm not supposed to be living here, you don't see that stoppin' me."

Hesitating, he glanced over his shoulder as if someone was behind a tree.

"Come on." I opened the door wide.

He tentatively stepped inside.

"Have a seat." I waved to the living room. "What'll you have? Water? Iced tea?"

Looking around the foyer, he moved to the sofa. "Iced tea would be great."

I went to the kitchen.

"You're kidding, right?" He called. "About squatting here?"

"Nope." I poured two iced teas. "Owner took off and never came back."

There was silence from the living room.

As I returned with the tea, he was sitting on the sofa facing the windows.

"It's a great house."

"That's what I thought." I handed him a glass.

Raising his glass to his lips, he gave me a nod. "Thanks."

Taking an armchair across from him, I sipped my tea and noticed his socks didn't match. He took out a handkerchief and wiped his face before running it over his head.

"How long have you lived here?"

"Eight months."

His brows went up. "You pay to keep the place up?"

"Only my food. The owner's some rich prick who has everything paid for, so I don't have to do a thing."

Nate grinned. "Husband?"

"Worse, fiancé."

Sitting back on the sofa, he took in the view. "Sounds pretty ideal to me."

"Window dressing."

"Where does he get his insurance?"

"You try to sell me insurance and I'll have to enforce company policy." I pointed at the door.

Nate stared into his glass before swigging his tea. "Gotcha."

Without the suit, he couldn't have been more than twenty-one.

"How long have you been a field agent?"

"A year."

"You like it?"

"Not this part."

"I can imagine."

"Insurance salesmen rate somewhere between used car salesmen and—" He stopped to think.

"Lawyers." I finished.

"Right. But it's shooting the messenger. Everyone hates paying for insurance till they need it."

"Yeah, I think it's the needing it part where insurance companies bite people in the ass."

He nodded. "I know the horror stories; that's what makes news. Every time there's a natural disaster, insurance companies get hammered, but people don't realize how much property gets lost, stolen, or damaged every day that insurance companies willingly pony up for. Last year, nearly twenty billion was claimed for home damage. Seven billion for house fires alone."

"That's a lot of house fires."

"Pierce County averages one every twelve hours."

"No shit?"

Nate swallowed his tea with a nod.

"Tell ya what." I put down my glass. "I don't know what sort of coverage my fiancé has, but I'll give him your card if he ever comes back to marry me."

"Is he away on business?"

"So he claims."

"What does he do?"

"Deals antiques."

Nate looked at the art on the walls. "I was going to say, if he doesn't have comprehensive, he's crazy."

"I can vouch for crazy."

With a grin, he leaned forward and put his glass on the coffee table.

"I've got more doors to knock on."

Getting up, I followed him to the front door.

"Thanks for the tea." He offered his hand as I opened the door.

I shook it. "You looked like you needed it."

"Really?" He blinked. "I should look pathetic more often."

"Always works on women. My fiancé mastered it, now I'm cleaning his house."

"Huh." Nate rubbed his chin as he walked out the door.

Cleaning upstairs took longer than I planned. It shouldn't have. There were fewer rooms, less furniture, no kitchen. But there was a closet full of boxes I'd moved into the house and never opened. Boxes of CDs with no stereo to play them on. Boxes of books with no shelves to sit on. And one box of letters with no eyes to read them. I was telling the truth when I told Michael I didn't keep a journal, but I wrote letters. And kept them. Letters from school friends, from pen pals, from family. Letters from Gray.

I didn't know if Michael was telling the truth when he claimed he didn't keep track of me before we met. He claimed he stayed away until I started attending law school. I took his word for it, which was the best one could do where Mike was concerned. So far, the questions he asked me indicated he was telling the truth. He really didn't know if I had a tree house. He really didn't know if I had any pets, how many boyfriends I'd had, about my darker periods of adolescence.

He was also in the dark as to how Anthony and I met. I told him I started dating Anthony after running into him repeatedly at a See's Candy store. But that wasn't the first time I'd met Anthony. The first time was after I reported a restraining order violation.

I knew Gregory Jacobs for fifteen years. The first ten, we were friends. The last five, we weren't. I called him Gray Jay and he called me So So. We met in a grade school program for the gifted and parted when he jumped from the fifth floor window of his apartment building. Gray didn't keep a journal either. His letters to me were the only record he left of what went right and what went wrong, why I was alive and he wasn't. The only other person who read them was Anthony. But he wasn't Anthony at the time. He was Officer Navarre and he was worried about me. The letters had stayed in a box ever since.

Now, I was wondering why I kept them. The truth was they frightened me. The scratchy spiral note paper, the impress of the ballpoint, like Braille under my fingers. His rambling conversation. Rambling to the point of abstraction. Any one letter came across casually offhand. A random thought carelessly noted. Carelessly noted twice a day. Every day. For the last three years of his life.

The letters were never openly threatening. They were charming, even polite. It was the way he remarked on what you'd been wearing, who you'd seen, when you'd gone to the park for a jog, that you felt his needles sticking you. It did no good that you stopped speaking to him years before. That when you went overseas for a year, he was still waiting when you got back. All I decided was I wasn't running. I worried I would have to confront him. In the end, I didn't have to.

So why keep the letters?

For Michael? So he could read them and remember them forever? Add them to his apocrypha and his mummy movies?

The letters went back in the box, but the box didn't go back in the closet.

I went back to cleaning the bedroom.

That afternoon I went grocery shopping. I bought enough food to feed me and one singular entity for a week. And a bottle of Maker's Mark. When I returned home, I had my bath. I made dinner of the leftovers Mom sent home with me the night before, and a martini. Then I collected the box of letters, a box of kitchen matches, and the bottle of whiskey. I went into the backyard. At the far end of the vegetable garden, Michael had dug a compost pit. Dumping the box in the pit, I poured some whiskey over it and tossed in a lit match. The alcohol flamed across the cardboard box, clinging with a hiss of steam and smoke. When the letters inside sparked, it roared to life. Taking a swig of whiskey, I watched the box curl to black leaf. When it was over, I emptied the bottle over the ashes.

~

408 | LISA MOWAT

Hey So-So,

i want to apologize. The police came by today and i know you must be pretty pissed at me. it's just i never thought that would happen. i thought you knew these were just letters. Just me. Just me, Sophie. The kid who used to carry your books home for you. The kid who helped you crib. The kid who started you on a life of crime. The kid who showed you his monkey.

Course now you're beautiful and my monkey's migrated to my back, but i still love you. i loved you the first day i saw you and i always will. i just wrote a sentence that makes me want to hurl and throw myself out a window. i promise i won't hurl and i won't violate the restraining order again. So i won't mail this one.

[Police evidence. Letter unsigned to
Sophie Davids. In possession of decedent. 9-1-95]

2003 Louis and Anthony leave for Tacoma in the night. Louis loads the crypt in the truck to haul back to our house while Anthony returns to work to await word from us. Mike and I will walk to the nearest sign of civilization and claim we have been abducted and released.

Anthony says as long as we stay away from details and act like stupid, rich people, we shouldn't have any problems. For credibility, Tony takes my wallet, my wedding ring, and the amulet. I am loathe to part with it, but Mike insists I give it up. Michael has no personal identification on him. When I ask where his wedding ring is, he only says he put it someplace safe. When I try to ask where he's been, he encourages me to get some sleep. We will have a long day ahead of us. So I try.

After three hours staring at the ceiling, I leave the bedroom. Michael is looking out the porch window with his back to me. I watch him pour the remains of the whiskey down his throat.

"When did you start drinking out of the bottle?"

He turns to me. "There aren't any glasses."

"What do you have against glasses, anyway?"

"I don't have you here to do the dishes."

I smirk. "You've never had me to do the dishes."

"Well." He grins. "There you go."

"I don't know why I'm surprised." My eyes scan the barren interior of the house as I cross the room to him. "You didn't have any glasses when I moved in: not at the lake, not here either."

He shrugs. "Guess I'm not much of a drinker."

I wrap my arms around his waist. "Not if a fifth counts as a single serving."

As I squeeze him, he tucks his chin to study my face. "Are you angry with me?"

"Not at all."

Grinning up at him, I think about last night, but he only stares with dark eyes. I step away. "You're tired."

"A little."

"When are you going to tell me what happened out there?"

He shakes his head. "You don't want to know."

"Is it over? I mean, really over?"

"It's over."

"What about Sam?"

His eyes narrow. "Gone."

"For good?"

"Finished."

Biting my lip, I hug him again. I have imagined this moment. Imagined him holding me to him, kissing the top of my head. His hands squeeze my shoulders lightly. I step away again. "What's wrong?"

Finally he smiles, stroking my cheek with the back of his hand. "Nothing."

When Michael speaks,, it is the truth. When he doesn't speak at all, I worry.

At dawn, we leave the house on foot. It is a long walk to the main road where

410 | LISA MOWAT

we hope to hitch a ride to the Dalles. It isn't long before a blue pickup stops for us. Michael does the talking, which is little. He only asks to be taken to the nearest police station. The driver's concern is politely deflected. We are exhausted and should save what we have left for the police. I don't have to act the part.

At the police station, the public knowledge of our disappearance is shared with us. For two days, local news stations have aired our names and faces. I likely escaped notice in public because I was with Anthony and wore sunglasses most of the time. That isn't what I tell them. I tell them what we rehearsed. We were stopped by two men who threatened to have guns. We were taken to a moving truck and driven to an unknown location. Outside of being given a change of clothes and food, we were told nothing. I describe two abductors, white males in their late twenties to early thirties.

Both of us decline medical attention but get a cursory examination by a PA. We give statements, answering the same questions of an investigator. By noon, two officers from Tacoma arrive to take us home for more of the same. When I see the patrol car arrive, I begin to relax. I am going to sleep in my own bed. I am going to wake up next to my husband. I am going to start the rest of my life, and the last three years will be over.

One of the officers hands me a Tacoma paper.

LOCAL PHILANTHROPIST FEARED KIDNAPPED

Sitting in the back of the patrol car, I read the article. I read it again. I toss it on the seat between us and glare at Mike. He glances at the paper and then me.

"Read it."

He picks it up and briefly looks at the page before putting it down.

"What?"

"*You ass!*"

The officers in the front of the car take notice. One asks if there is a problem, but I only stare out my window on a planet I can't recognize. My arms cross, holding my sides. I say nothing for the rest of the ride. Arriving at the Tacoma precinct, I say nothing to Michael, or anyone else, unless absolutely necessary. Remarkably, he doesn't notice and makes no effort to speak to me, verbally or otherwise. This enrages me more. But I'm about to be questioned by police. I have to bury it.

What I discover is there isn't any room.

I'm full up.

We are advised to say nothing to the media until notified by the lead investigator. The department spokeswoman meets with us to prep for some media waiting outside. I volunteer to make a blanket statement. The one thing law school trained me to do was make a bullshit statement stick.

After escaping the cameras, Anthony is waiting for us in the parking lot.

"How was it?"

"I think your colleagues can't believe my mother let me out of her sight."

He grins. "I'd tell you you're far from the bottom of the barrel, but I don't want to depress you."

Michael is silent. Anthony picks up on the tension.

As soon as we're in the car, Tony glances at us. "You two okay?"

"Sophie's angry with me." Mike blurts.

"Sure as shit." I mumble. "I'm pissed as hell."

Anthony's eyes widen as he turns to start the car.

Mike finally faces me. "Why?"

"You've been lying to me for the last three years!"

"About what?"

"About the hospital! All this time I've been busting my ass on your project and you never said a thing!"

He ignores me as we drive past the hospital. I see the lobby doors where he dropped me off after sabotaging my car. We continue down Broadway, past the commons where the farmer's market is held. Past the green where he performed his tricks. Past Grounds for Coffee. Past the law school.

I close my eyes, feeling Anthony's car follow the route it always took when he picked me up after class at night. Nearing Wright Park, my eyes open on our old apartment building and follow past Michael, catching sight of the conservatory beyond his profile. A house of glass, perfect in its symmetry, containing an imitation of something that couldn't exist. A false Eden.

By the time we reach Violet's house, I don't even look. The memory of seeing her at the gate in her bathrobe. The way he turned his face from her as we drove by. To lie. He didn't have a mailbox.

He drowned me in my own bathtub.

I can't do it. I've come so far and I can't.

Tony slows the car down our drive, parking in the turnabout.

"We still have your BMW in our lot. I'll get the keys to you tomorrow."

Mike says nothing.

I get out of the car and wait while Anthony retrieves a Ziploc bag from the front passenger's seat. Michael gets out and stares at the house.

"Here's your wallet and keys." Tony steps around the car, handing the bag to me.

Taking it from him, I start for the front door, fumbling in the bag for the keys.

"Well, guess I'll be seein' ya." Tony starts to leave.

"Wait." I look over my shoulder as my hand pauses with the key in the lock. "Come in. Have a drink at least."

"You two are exhausted."

"No." Michael suddenly seems oddly hospitable. "Come have a drink."

Pushing the door open, I nod to Tony, and he comes to me with a smile.

The house is dim and invitingly cool. Someone closed the curtains in the living room. Crossing the room to open them, I notice the study doors are ajar. The crypt is already there. Supposedly it has moved, but it is hard to believe. Pulling back the curtains, I try not to dwell on the view.

The dining room is warmer. The windows let in the sun but no air, leaving it stuffy. I throw open the windows before going to the kitchen for Tony's drink. My husband can help himself. He'll need to get used to it again anyway.

"Who drank all the vodka?" I pull the nearly empty bottle out of the freezer. Tony grins at Michael, who lets on nothing.

I frown at Tony. "I'm afraid all I have left is gin and I know you don't like it."

"A glass of wine would do me."

I look at Mike, who only watches me. Rolling my eyes, I go to the pantry and check the wine rack. Pulling a bottle of red, I go to the kitchen table and plant the bottle in front of him, then cross to the utensil drawer and grab the corkscrew. Returning to the table, I plant it next to the bottle.

Make yourself useful, darling. I smile sweetly. "I'll get the glasses."

Thankfully, Michael is uncorking the bottle when I bring the glasses to the table. My body is on autopilot. Without pause, I go to the refrigerator and survey what remains. There is some cheese and I know we have crackers. I know I have olives in the pantry. I know I have two sets of eyes prying into my back.

I smile at Tony over my shoulder. "Why don't you go take a load off?"

"You coming?"

"I'll be there. I'm just getting something for the wine."

They leave and I go to work. Tony starts talking to Michael.

"Sorry you guys had to face those reporters after everything."

"It wasn't a problem."

"Great. Next time you talk to them." I mumble, opening a box of crackers.

"You realize it's just started." Tony continues. "Until the investigation runs itself out, you'll be news."

"Until something more interesting comes along." Michael's tone is almost smug.

Tony laughs. "You'd be hard to top."

"Tell me about it." I grunt as I twist the lid off a jar of olives.

"Sophie agrees with you." Michael answers.

"The Tacoma paper's been feeling the competition. They'll want to dig. I hate to say it, but you should probably get a lawyer. Until the hype winds down, you'll have reporters tailing you."

"Hype!" Dumping out the crackers, I bring the food to the dining room, dropping the plates on the table. "I wonder why!"

Michael gives an acid stare. "Sophie, I'm sorry I didn't tell you sooner."

"Sooner? The unveiling was a two years ago!"

"As pissed as you are, Sophie, Mike's money gives us the perfect cover." Tony strains for congeniality. "Now that the hospital project has come to light, we can claim his identity was leaked and you two were targeted. Lucky for you, the kidnapper got cold feet and was rookie enough to feel bad about killing you."

"You're on his side now?" I glare between them.

Anthony puts up his hands. "I'm not taking sides here. I'm just saying there's a silver lining."

My face tingles. "Silver lining?"

He drops his hands at my gaze. "I gotta go."

Are all men chicken shits?

"Good idea!" I storm out of the room and tear up the stairs.

Running to the bedroom, I open the closet and pull on a coat, grabbing my backpack off the floor. At the chest, I pull out drawers, stuffing random clothes into the pack. Scanning the room, I spot my laptop and yank the cord from the wall, forcing it into the top of the bag. I'm still struggling to zip it shut when I turn for the door and see Michael watching me from the hall.

"Sophie, I'm sorry."

I try to leave, but he steps into the room, blocking me.

"May I speak with you?"

"I'm done, Mike." Shoving him out of my way with both hands, he falls against the door as I bolt for the stairs.

"Sophie—"

"Forget it, Mike!" I head down the stairs. "I'm done!"

Descending as fast as my feet take me, there is a rush of fear. I'm not faster than Michael. No one is. My eyes fix on the front door. I've tried this before. Pulling it open, I see my car in the drive. The door slams shut before me, the latch yanked from my grip. I stare at the door.

"Let me go, Mike." My voice has gone unnaturally calm.

"Where are you going?" The ice in his voice outmatches mine.

"Away."

"You don't love me?"

Stepping back, I look him in the eyes.

"Love you? I don't even know who you are! Last week you told me you would tell me everything, and when I think you have, something like this happens! I don't know what to believe anymore!"

"Because I donated money to a hospital?"

"Because you did it to control me! Because you've made everything I've accomplished a lie! All this time, I thought it was me and it wasn't! It was all you! I've been a tool in your little fantasy world!"

His eyes reflect nothing.

"You're not leaving."

Anthony was right. He is Gray.

"Watch this."

Without a thought, I stride down the hall for the back door. If he kills me, it won't be the first time.

His hands are on my shoulders. A voice in my head screams.

"Let go of me!"

"You're my wife."

It is a voice I've never heard before.

Twisting in his grip, I feel his fingers claw my arms as I slide out of my coat.

Catching myself from falling, I fly down the hall, his breathing in my ears.

A rush of air passes me, a gust of wind followed by a tremendous crash, like a wrecking ball hitting the house. Skidding into the kitchen table, I look behind and see them. One struggling to reach me, burning me with his eyes. The other fighting to hold him back, his clothes torn, his skin like veined wax. Their bodies twist on each other, blue light arcs between them.

My husband's hollow eyes meet mine.

Sophie! Run!

Feeling nothing, I do.

[Yin-Yang, chart of universal explanatory principle. Early Han Dynasty, 200 B.C.]

OBLITERATION

1199 BC The pattern of my days followed uncertainly. The day after my first hunting expedition, I was spotted by a scout tracking the same boar. It was before dawn when he saw me kill it and disappear into the dark. By evening, stories spread the length of the caravan. The dark spirit of Amam was wandering the wilderness, devouring beasts. Women and children stayed close to the column, afraid to forage for wood and water. Guards began patrolling in pairs, never alone.

I confessed to the general I was responsible for these rumors and I would leave the caravan as soon as we reached the Negev. He would not hear it. His reaction to my vacation was miserable. We did not discuss it again. In the meantime, I tried to free the caravan of their fears and his mind of my presence. Hunting at night, I slept by day and did my best to avoid human eyes. My own eyes could not foresee the event that would set my path for the next thousand years.

Since sighting the middle sea, we had flanked the coast by an inland route into Amurru. The shores were heavily trafficked by Canaanites and traders from Caphtor and Aramea. The settlements were seasonal and jealously guarded. The general made contact with these, inviting trade to assure the peaceful intent of our exodus, though it could not last. There was little doubt word had gone ahead of us. What lay ahead was the Nile of Canaan, and they would greet the general with the affection of Ramesses.

It would not trouble me. By then I would disappear to the wastes, leaving the exodus to fate.

[Spharic. Entry translated from *Kor Dai Maihael*. Mund Dai. d. 755 BC]

2000 He had stopped running. Had hoped it would be enough. He would stay his brother's keeper. Would give up having a life if it would satisfy. But it didn't. Sam always had to have more. Sam would get more.

Mercato. Allie Cat. She never told him her last name. He didn't ask.

What could he have done differently?

He shouldn't have flown. In hindsight, Sam could have killed everyone.

But why her?

Was it chance? Because he sat next to her?

Perhaps if he hadn't spoken to her. Told her his name.

Helped her with her juice.

Perhaps if she had annoyed him, she would still be alive. If she had been rude and obnoxious instead of simply curious. Thought he had pretty eyes.

Now those eyes stared at barren highway, unblinking behind tinted lenses.

The top on the rover was down, but the wind on his face didn't cool him. His hands gripped the wheel as though welded in place. Escaping the traffic of I-10, he accelerated to 120 on State 80. He would be at the Gypsy before it was open.

Twenty minutes later, he was. Then he wasn't.

He regarded the café as it disappeared from sight in his rearview mirror. He would wait on Sam no longer. Returning his eye to the road, he would follow it to the end.

Slowing to make the turn onto Paradise Road, he hung a right and sped on to Portal. His eye pushed ahead, hoping to find Sam before reaching the Mountain. If Sam was in the Mountain, he couldn't tell. His eye would not see there.

Still, he saw nothing.

Nearing Portal, he slowed and saw through the scatter of buildings lining the main street: the gas station, a laundromat, post office, motel. There was no sign. Picking up speed as he left town, he sighted the northeast road that would take him through the canyon. He turned left at the intersection, heading south. The farther he drove, the more his nerves caught up to him. He wasn't feeling Sam. He expected to feel something by the time he reached the Gypsy, but had come as far as Portal without a murmur.

The morning sun heated the shattered floor of the canyon to a wavering haze. Trees clung to jagged walls, veiling the cleft remains of the great peak that once towered over salt flat seas. Far ahead, Sunday traffic was nonexistent at the crossroads. Another right turn and he would drive to the end of the road, going as far as the rover would take him. Then climb. When he reached the end of the pavement, he stopped the rover and killed the engine. The road gave way to a rutted Jeep trail. Still there was no evidence of static. A scatter of pines moved in the breeze, but all else was silent. In the brittle bush, nothing moved. It was spring, yet there were no birds.

Sam had been here.

Starting the engine, he continued up the slope at a jarring pace. He followed the ridge until it was unsafe to drive farther. Parking the rover, he climbed on foot to a nearby overlook and surveyed the valley below. Beyond it was a ranch Sam called Wygyle, but Sam would never risk meeting him there. It was too open, too easily seen.

He turned his back on the canyon and faced the Mountain. The maps called it Silver Peak. They got that part right. It had been silver at one time. Pure lachrymose argentite. Tears of God that could make manifest an entity's thoughts beyond expectation. The seam of it made the Mountain a transducer of geologic proportion. A coveted place.

Returning to the rover, he pulled his pack off the passenger seat and slung it over his shoulder. Sighting the back of the ridge, he began his ascent.

The climb passed without incident. For a man it would have been a near impassable trail. It would have taken climbing equipment and preparation, unflagging strength and perfect balance. Even then, a man would not spot the cleave as he did. A man would only see a fissure on a cliff face, the opening at its base hidden by an overhang. It was a dangerous place for a mortal. A place that didn't want life. With frequent stops to feel his surroundings, he made it to the fault at the base of the peak within the hour.

Dropping himself to the mouth of the cave, he eased into the draft of air escaping it. The smell was all the notice needed to know someone had been there before him—someone who had been burned. If it was Sam or not, he couldn't tell. Sam's presence would dissolve into the walls, the residue of the Mountain's past still powerful in the present. All he knew was he didn't want to face Sam inside.

Taking a last glance at the day, he dropped his pack on the ground and stepped into perpetual night. As his vision adjusted to the darkness, the light of his eyes illuminated his way. Gradually, the walls lit to his presence, pressing him in some places to where he could barely fit through. The deeper he went, the brighter the walls glimmered. At some points, the pass would branch off, causing him to pause and sniff the draft. Following his nose through the weave of fissures, he tread with caution. Over twenty thousand millennia, his memory of the place had faded.

There was a sudden spike in the draft, blowing the hair from his face. Before him was a break in the floor he didn't recall. A gap some fifteen feet across. Backing up, he made a short run and launched himself to the other side, overshooting the far rim should the force of his landing try the integrity of his footing. The smell intensified the moment he landed on the other side. This was familiar to him. There was only one passage at this point. Only one way to go. It was the way he had passed when he escaped. At the time, he had hoped to leave nothing behind to escape from, but nothing ever stayed the same.

Continuing with purpose, the walls began to fan away from him, forming the sides of a cavern. The floor began to descend steeply, exposing columns of corroded rock towering to a ceiling beyond his sight. Like a forest of trees, there was no way further marked. It had become a labyrinth, but a small one, well within his grasp. The labyrinth he destroyed long ago seemed endless. Only Sam had known his way in it. The memory still frightened though the pillars of silver had long since fallen and their beguiling visions with them. This labyrinth was easily crossed. Here the rock was weak, the trace of tears within providing little more than a place to hide.

Midway, he paused to reach for Sam. There was no response.

There was no need. Soon enough, he came to a clearing in the stone forest, some fifty yards across. He stopped at the edge of the ring. Dimly illuminated, a black figure sat cross-legged in the middle of it. When the eyes opened, their fire still burned bright. It greeted him in Sphara. The long, undulating hiss of the words resonated between the columns, echoing to the stone sky.

"Who did this?" His plain speech made no song.

The affront of It rattled his chest. The accusation It made was clear.

He stepped into the circle. "If I am to be accused, I will finish what I started."

It made a laugh like gravel, finishing with a guttural whisper.

Wincing with impatience, he pressed It. "Speak plain."

"You think you have won." The velvet of Sam's voice spilled from ashen lips. "But she will bite the hand she seeks."

"She?" He froze. "Who?"

"She has too much of her father in her."

The mention of a daughter made his throat tighten. "Whose father?"

"If you want to raise them right, you have to do it yourself."

It was stalling.

He began to cross the clearing. "I have no time for this."

"There is always time." It whispered.

His pace did not slow. "Not for you."

It shrank before him. "You act like a man."

"And you the devil."

"You will never be a man, dear brother. Hating me can't change that."

Stopping before the creature, he nodded. "It helps."

With a breath of resignation, weary eyes took him in from the ground up before meeting his own. "Too bad you'll never be a father." A brilliant smile spread across the scorched face. "You have a way with children."

It laughed.

He did not hear It. The last laugh became a scream as the rage of his thoughts focused on It. All he heard was Allie. The suffering she endured, he knew. The suffering of her father he dared not imagine. There was no amount of suffering he could unleash on Sam to amend it.

Hot air blasted through the columns of rock on all sides of the clearing, rushing at them. The vortex caught flame, consumed the black figure before him in a twisting whirlwind. The pillar of fire climbed, pushing up to the ceiling of the cavern, fanning across its surface. Willing the Mountain to him, he would use the labyrinth against It. Pushing his mind beyond himself, light flooded his eyes.

He was high in the noon sky.

The sun had cleared the peak. Rays of light chased the shadow of the Mountain from fields of new poppies stretching west to the horizon. He sought Sam's ranch. The collection of low houses and adobe huts flashed in his mind, sharply coming to his sight. Feeling his will surge, he exhaled, as a breeze whipped the heads of the poppies into a devil of singed wind. The thatch of the huts quickly caught flame before the windows in the houses began to crackle, their curtains lit with fire. Drawing away from the firestorm, he watched the smoke rise into the blue. He could only imagine the scent of it, could only feel the heat of the labyrinth baking his skin. It was not safe for his body to stay, yet the lure of his vision filled him with joy. The Mountain was still a powerful place. A place of strength like nothing else, not even a crypt.

Climbing ever higher in the sky, his sight spanned the sun's reach: along the Grand Canyon, over ranges of mountains, across vast plains.

This was how Sam had been spying on him. Resurrecting the labyrinth of old, resurrecting what he had torn down. Sam found a way to live embodied and see as though he had none. Without Sam, he would finally be master here. The Mountain would serve him. ECCO would never touch him. He would answer to no one.

Here, Sophie would be safe. Forever.

He willed her to his sight.

As a ray of light, his vision fell across their bedroom. She remained invisible to him, buried under the covers. She was cold and alone, an empty pillow beside her.

A spark in his eye made him blink, the sharp pain reminding him where he was. A deafening howl filled his ears as hot wind burned his lungs, making him gasp. His eyes focused.

The pillar of fire still burned before him. There was nothing in it but empty flame. Something rained on his head and he instinctively put up his hands. When he looked up, the ceiling of the cavern glowed with heat, its blistering surface showering the floor with cinders. Then he saw the backs of his hands.

His veins were alight under his skin, the throb pulsing through him all too familiar. The fire he had started, the Mountain now fed, but it was drawing on him to do it. He had started a fire he couldn't stop. He had been beguiled again.

Shielding his head, he ran blindly into the forest of glowing stone, his feet remembering their path. Darting between the columns, he reached the edge of the labyrinth and started the steep ascent to the passage as the temperature rose with each step. The sooner he could get away, the sooner the fire would die without him to fuel it.

But then what?

Sam would still be here. Sleeping. Waiting.

Disintegrated but not obliterated, the dark spirit would rekindle in this place.

The cavern walls met before him as the passage narrowed. He did not slow as he neared the gap he would have to leap. When it came, his speed nearly caused him to crash headlong into the wall on the other side. Landing hard, his shoulder grazed the jutting stones lining the passage as he strained to keep his feet. In his flight, his eyes tracked the ceiling, trying to read the direction of the fault lines that crossed them. The air freshened on his tongue. His path rapidly crossing a series of intersections, his memory outpacing him. Finally, he saw daylight.

Braking near the mouth of cave, he felt the walls with his hands, feeling the drone of the labyrinth still feeding on him. Slowly, he worked his way back, searching for a fissure in the stone. Reaching out from his sides to span the mouth of the passage, he pressed his palms against the walls and closed his eyes. In Spharic song, he called Samael's name. Not to beckon, but to waken the Mountain above them. The sound bounced off the walls, reverberating under his fingers. He spoke it again, slowly, the deep grating of each note making the stone chatter. The vibration growing to a tremor.

The pillar of the fire extinguished with a gasp.

His eye opened. Only the amber glow of the superheated ceiling illuminated the buttresses of stone bearing it. He was staring up, as though lying on the floor. The smell of ash and scorched rock hung in the baked air.

Saitael ...

The name echoed as waves in his mind. There was a dull roar under his head.

Saitael ...

An explosive report of splitting rock sent a blaze of fissures radiating overhead, shattered by some invisible hand. The weave of cracks widened with a moan before the ceiling came at him in a blinding crash.

The distant yip of a coyote broke the night. Something jutted into the back of his head. Reaching behind his ear, he fished out the stone that had been his pillow and looked at it. Somehow he hadn't been crushed to death.

He sat up.

He wasn't in the labyrinth. Sam was. For now and for some time to come.

Blinking, he peered over his shoulder at the mouth of the cave and saw the night sky ablaze with stars, his pack still resting on the ground. Getting to his feet, he went to it and knelt, unzipping the flap. He felt inside, pulling out a liter of Mountain Dew and a box of Hostess donuts before crossing to the lip of the cave. Sitting down, he hung his feet off the edge and carefully unscrewed the lid from the soda, pouring half of it down his throat. As he shoved a donut in his mouth, he spotted Vega shining directly overhead. His eyes wandered to Pegasus, making him think a winged horse would be a convenient beast to have at that moment. Then his gaze drifted to Pisces.

He remembered Sophie in bed.

Without a labyrinth to aid his sight, he couldn't see her. The day had passed without him and he imagined she was in bed again. Probably after a bath. And a drink. She would have cleaned everything in the house by now. Except the sheets.

She wouldn't change the sheets until he returned.
And he would. For good.

1199 BC We reached the edge of the Negev and my time to leave. Deciding to say nothing to my host, I made plans to sleep that night and steal the wagon after it had been loaded in the morning. I would take the clothes and leave the sword, but there was little I could give in return.

In the night, I drafted a map of the Canaan Nile and the land of the Amanites beyond it. On it, I marked as many broad crossings and safe passages as could accommodate his caravan. I wrote a warning to avoid Qidshu and Megiddo, but doubted he would heed it. I wished him fair ways and hid the map in his tent while he slept. The chances he might find it before I was gone were slim. In his personal habits, the general was not an orderly man.

Knowing the first day on my own would offer no rest, I took to my crypt early that evening. Intent on taking as much relief as I could, I heard no one enter my tent, nor woke when the lid of my crypt was raised.

What I woke in time to see was Ashebu, his arms raised over his head. All I heard was his scream as an arc from my body ran the length of the blade. The faces of his company were as shocked as he, lit by the glow of my flesh. I looked down at it, uncovered and permeable, the sword of Amenteth half buried in my chest. The oath of Osiris glimmered with the energy of my core, bleeding into nothing.

[Spharic. Entry translated from *Kor Dai Maihael*. Mund Dai. d. 755 BC]

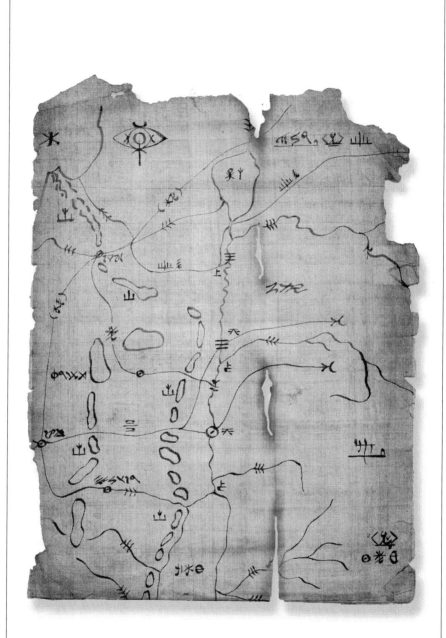

[Map of the Canaan Nile and the land of the Amanites, 1199 B.C.]

2003   Whether it is because his body is almost dead or the distraction of Sophie's presence, it is clear he has gone undetected. Oblivious to being driven into a wall, Sam wears an expression unlike anything he's ever seen. With his arms locked around Sam's waist, his body is little more than dead weight as static uselessly shocks his numbed limbs. Sam has yet to acknowledge his presence and he won't be able to hold on long. Sophie must get away.

Willing himself to be heard, he looks to her to hear him.

Sophie! Run!

She sees him. If she thinks anything, he can't hear it.

She is gone.

His mind feels a jolt.

Sam has his throat and he tries to pull the burning hands away. He can't give up too easily. He must put up a fight. The smell of burning flesh fills his mouth. This time it isn't Sam who is on fire. Losing his footing, he is slammed against the floor, and his head begins to buzz. Sam is on top of him, trying to force his mouth open. Feeling himself begin to slip, he strains to break Sam's grip with the little fire left in him. Choking on his breath, he pushes Sam's chin away with a charge and a knee square in the abdomen.

It is enough.

Recovering his feet, he barely makes the kitchen when a snarl launches itself at his back. They fall onto the table, knocking a bottle of wine and dishes to the floor. He grabs a corkscrew as they slide across it. Gripping the sides of the table, he feels Sam pry on his arms to flip him over. When Sam gets a grip on him, he lets the table go. Rolling over, his arm swings over his head in an arc, driving the corkscrew at Sam's face. Suddenly he is free.

He bolts, fleeing an ungodly howl. From the dining room, his eyes run the length of the house, stopping at the crypt in his study. He sprints for it before feeling his feet leave the ground. The air is knocked out of him as they fly over the sofa, crashing through the coffee table in the living room. He feels the ops dig in his back as Sam lands on him. His insides come alive with fire and he screams.

Sam hits him in the side and he screams again.

"That's for my eye."

Even with one, Sam still looks amused.

Grimacing back, he chokes to speak. "Now she can tell us apart."

Sam laughs, then drives a fist into him.

He cries out. He knows Sam likes screaming, but he can't swallow this. It's all he can feel and that seems to make it worse.

"Your plot to hire Louis has twisted." Sam looks down at him tenderly, brushing the hair from his face. "You're a bigger fool than I imagined if you thought I would deliver your crypt to you."

"I wanted my porn collection back." The words come thickly with blood.

Sam laughs. He braces for another hit, but Sam shifts position, pressing a knee into him instead. As the pain builds, he holds his breath.

"You thought I would trust Louis to deliver my crypt?" Sam shakes his head. "I don't even trust myself, and you think I would trust a servus?"

As his hand feels his back, he tries not to think of the ops.

"And what good would it have done?" Sam continues. "Did you imagine I would let you use it?"

"You were going to use my wife. It seemed like a fair trade."

"I have used her."

Attempting a shrug, he lolls at the ceiling. "She was leaving me anyway."

This is met with a slow grin. "With baby on the way, she'll have a reason to stay."

"Marta will like that." He coughs under crushing ribs.

"Feeling a little squeezed?" Sam's eye winks. "Try having a mountain fall on you."

"I'm not complaining."

"Resigned to your fate then?"

"Fate doesn't accept resignations."

Sam backs off, but the knee only goes deeper.

"Why is it whenever you're resigned to things, I get nervous?"

"You think I'm like you." He whispers.

"I don't think it, I know it." Sam's face comes closer as his ribs begin to give. "Tell me. What have you got up your sleeve?"

"I'm not." He mouths the words, holding his breath. His hand grips the ops.

The eye squints at him. "You're not? Not what? Not like me or not going to tell? If it's the first I'll be devastated. If it's the latter, I can change your mind. I hope it's the latter."

"I'm a pooka."

The look on Sam's face is expressionless as he aims for the forehead.

With all the swiftness he can summon, the culmination of his existence focuses on the point of the ops in his hand. Soundlessly, with imperceptible resistance, the needle pierces Sam's forehead, plunging its full length through the constant eye. Sam's mouth opens reflexively, as if to scream. There is nothing.

A noise comes from somewhere else.

A strange gasping he doesn't immediately realize is coming from him. All he knows is the intensity of fire. It consumes him from the inside as he channels everything he is into the ops. The hand gripping it glows blue, the ops blinding white. His hand should feel the heat, but he stopped feeling them hours ago. Now, only his core sends any message to his mind. It is the only thought he needs. The last he will ever have.

His eyes fill with light as they close on Sam's face.

Sophie's face.

Sarah's.

Gabrielle.

Raphael.

Phanuel.

Phanuel staring at him, smiling. They face each other. Without a word, Phanuel beckons him down a long passageway. It is lined with blank faces. Novices staring

428 | LISA MOWAT

straight ahead. It leads to a room. A white room with a white pedestal. On it, a
black box. He goes to it willingly. Opens it easily. Inside is a Magic 8-Ball.
    He hears a giggle.
    A child? In the white room?
    He turns to see a small boy with dark curls and blue eyes.
    "Michael?" He whispers.
    The child giggles again and points, saying nothing.
    Silly rabbit!
    The white room goes black.

–Samael is wicked–can you hear me–*humbly defend*–the Child–a monster–*Michael wander seeking wickedness snares us*–it's your life–never coming back–you
love me–I hate you–thanks for brushing your teeth–kill me Daddy–*our evil pray
may be the ruin world*–you are a disgrace–you don't want me to propose–women
need men–make a man of you–called me brother–a charming neighbor–*divine
world all snares defend*–just deliver stuff–you can have me–*archangel o host of the
battle*–won't fail you–we'll never have one–*rebuke power*–I got stupid–women love
that–*holy prince*–your own cookies–*host wickedness*–isn't Castles N' Coasters–not
ignorant–just a passenger–control freak–no maps–big people food–you're perfect–
such an ass–I trust you–*souls through protection*–I can protect you–*who wander
seeking god*–trust me–asking too much–holding my breath–not omnipotent–dehumanizing comments–my ovaries–don't have a body–pooka–apocrypha–bullshit
story–*seeking the ruin of souls*–it is forbidden–
    God forgive me–
    –*holy Michael the archangel, defend us in battle. Be our protection against the
wickedness and snares of the devil. May God rebuke him–*
    He recognizes the voice.
    –*we humbly pray*–
    Violet?
    –*do you, o prince of the heavenly host, by the divine power thrust into hell Satan*–
    Violet?
    –*and all the other evil spirits who wander through the world seeking the ruin of souls.*
    Is that you?
    Amen.
    What?
    Get up, Michael.
    Get up?
    Now!

The eyes fly open.
    There is a brilliant sky, filled with clouds of sunlight, silently rolling. They swell
and ripple, breathing trails of shadow. It is far above but near enough to touch. A

black hand reaches out to the breeze.

Flames lick his fingers.

Ears fill with a shrill hiss. His chest shudders with a gasp, burning with smoke. The body is alive. He wonders how.

A low moan trembles the floor beneath him.

There is no time.

Searching himself, all he sees is a black shell. There is a semblance of melted shoes on his feet. Beyond them, visible beneath the scorching atmosphere of black smoke, a crypt glows in the heat. If it is his, he is saved. If it is Sam's, it will only prolong his misery, sheltering him from the fire and little else.

Clawing the scorched carpet, he rolls over. The sight of a headless body burning next to the sofa stops him. He remembers Sam with one eye. Remembers the ops. How is he still here?

He wonders.

A beam from the ceiling crashes onto the sofa, engulfing it in flames.

There is no time.

Getting to his knees, he pushes unsteadily towards the study. Unable to lift his head, he focuses on the sight of his molten hands, their bones splayed on the floor under his weight, scuffing the woodwork. The polish on the boards reflects a ragged creature. What are rags and what is flesh impossible to tell. He does not look for a face. He does not stop until the top of his head hits the side of the crypt.

Pressing the side of his face to it, he hears the scrape of his cheekbone on its surface as he feels for the lid with senseless hands. Instead, he listens against the wall of the crypt to tell him when he has found the fissure. The faint drag of carbonized fingertips tell when they cross it. He pushes against the lid with his legs under him. The lid begins to give.

Forcing his fingers into the opening, he clings to the side and forces in an arm, then a shoulder, then his head. It is too dark to see, but the cool air beckons, spurring his effort. He hauls what is left of him over the edge. As he feels his body fall in behind him, he glimpses what he has escaped. The sight of a bookshelf, a brilliant wall of flames. All of his journals. The longest written record of his memory burning away. The lid of the crypt slowly falls over him with the unhurried motion of a ship slipping its berth. The walls pull him away as they come to light.

Resting on his back, he reaches beneath him and pulls out the hat he has crushed. His head strains to look at it in the glimmer. Pale silk soiled in his hands. Holding it to him, his head falls back. The light fills his eyes with tears.

1199 BC   At first I still believed my situation recoverable. My injury was significant, but I was in my crypt. Remove the blade, close the lid, hope for the best. My hands grasped the blade lodged in my breastplate, the raw flesh of my palms only bleeding as the edge bit into them. Ashebu's accomplice swore at me in terror, slamming the lid down. My body jolted as it struck against the sword, the hilt of it just proud of the crypt, propping the lid ajar. My situation had not improved. With the lid weighing on the sword, I was pinned inside. With the lid unable to close, the crypt would not function. My surroundings grew dark as my light faded, the floor beneath me pooling with blood.

Still gripping the blade, my hands felt nothing. When my heart stopped, there was nothing I could do. I had become entrapped. It was not the first time, but that never eased my fear it would be the last. Only eternity with Metatron was worse. Without servus who understood my needs, I had only chance to free me. I rationalized my situation was not hopeless. I was in the company of a man who suspected what I was and only desired to help me. It was some comfort against the oblivion swallowing me. My mind found rest—for how long, I cannot be sure.

Aside from where I found myself, the only thing worse was fire. When I woke to the smell of smoke, my heart stopped and I wondered when it had started. My spirit had rekindled. The sound of chanting voices told me I was again in the world. It was a ritual from the Book of the Dead. The smoke was incense, woody and sickly sweet like honey. It occurred to me they might try to embalm me, which might be worse than fire. It occurred to me I should say something.

I could not. I was breathing, but barely. Not enough to speak, let alone whisper. My mind strained to see, not wanting to. If they were about to embalm me I did not want to watch. Still, I had to know my condition. To know what they were seeing.

I first perceived a blur, then a figure, then, slowly, a body. At first, I thought it embalmed. It was shrouded in gauze, the limbs fully wrapped, a golden mask over the face. The bandages were stained, not brown with resin, but blue. My blood. My body. Prone. Beneath it, a wide scroll of papyrus ran the length of the top of my crypt, draping over each end. It was a scroll from the cult of Re-Herakhti, describing the one god of the sun, all-seeing. At the foot of my crypt was a stone platter. On it, in a pool of blood, the head of a bull.

Before this sacrifice was another body. It had been embalmed, bound in resin-soaked wrappings. The general knelt before it, leading the chant. It was Ashebu.

[Spharic. Entry translated from *Kor Dai Maihael*. Mund Dai. d. 755 BC]

2000 Day three. Monday morning.
For once, I didn't hate it. Though my alarm woke me too early. I was too tired to consider the empty pillow in my bed. I fumbled through my hot shower. Found my clothes. Forgot the cold cup of coffee that wasn't waiting on the kitchen table. But I missed the kiss.

Every morning, a kiss sent me to work, often delaying, sometimes irritating. Always needing too much. Always there.

Just one more day.

He said he would be back.

I would cook dinner. He would be hungry.

Driving to work, I thought about the groceries in the refrigerator. Three split chickens I had prepped the night before. Dry-rubbed in lavender from the garden. He loved lavender. New potatoes. A bag of them. Our last crop of pole beans. I'd even displaced my gin to make room for an ice cream cake in the freezer.

That had to be love.

At the office, I flipped on my computer:
Meeting minutes.
First brainstorm of the morning from Lyn.
Reminder to attend birthday lunch for Dan at The Swiss.
Reminder to bring retreat suggestions to the afternoon staff meeting.
Second brainstorm of the morning from Lyn.
Follow up to the second brainstorm from Lyn.
Catty remark on Lyn's brainstorm from Amy.
Repugnance at Lyn's brainstorm from Phil.
Question regarding authenticity of Lyn's brainstorm from Dan.
I moved to table the question until evidence of a brain was confirmed.
Phil seconded.
Amy asked if anyone wanted a puppy. Roommate Paul's dog had a litter.
I replied I wasn't ready for that level of commitment.
Amy sent a nauseatingly cute photo of a cardboard box filled with fluffy pups.
I asked what breed they were.
She said she wasn't sure.
I asked if they shed.
She said she thought the daddy was a white poodle up the street.
I thought Paul's dog was a shepherd.
She thought our yard was meant for a dog.
I was sure they would find good homes.
She said there were only two left.
I asked how many shoes she'd lost.
There was no response.

At The Swiss, I stared blankly at the chalkboard menu over the cashier's head. Twenty sandwich options seemed to complicate the relatively simple concept of two pieces of bread with something between them. After picking up my food, I didn't bother with the bar and the twenty artisan beers on tap. Finding my co-workers, I joined in celebrating Dan's forty-fifth year.

Pulling out a chair, I sat down with half a club and water.

"Sophie! You're dry." Phil stood over me with a pitcher of beer.

"Yeah, I'm trying to cut back."

His mouth opened slightly. 'What?"

Amy sat next to me with a bowl of soup. "Everything all right?"

She caught Phil's expression and was looking at me with knit brows.

I shrugged. "Everything's fine."

"What's wrong?" She stared at Phil.

"Nothing." I glanced between them before picking up my sandwich.

Phil nodded. "She's stopped drinking."

"Really?" Amy's eyes got big.

"No—" I mumbled with a full mouth. "Not really. I just don't feel like a beer."

"Me neither." Amy returned to her soup. "That's why I don't eat here much. No hard licks."

"See?" I raised a brow at Phil. "If that was a pitcher of martinis, we'd be talking."

"Then join us at Harbor Lights after work and I'll set you up."

"I can't."

"Why not?" Amy blew on her soup.

"Mike's coming home tonight and I'm making dinner."

"Hey ..." Phil waved the pitcher at me. "When you see him, tell him Dan and I are stargazing Thursday night and he's welcome."

"Cool. I'll do that."

Phil moved on to fill more glasses.

"How long has he been gone?" Amy took a sip from her spoon.

"Just a few days. He left Saturday morning."

"Where'd he go?"

"Um ..." Licking my lips, I put down my sandwich. "He didn't really say. A couple places, I think."

She nodded silently with her eyes on her soup.

For a while we ate, watching Dan open birthday cards.

"Are you nervous about getting married?" Amy asked quietly.

I ran my tongue across the roof of my mouth before swigging my water.

"I love club sandwiches, but I always get Captain Crunch mouth."

"You can ask them not to toast the bread."

I smirked. "That's not a club sandwich."

She shrugged, still focused on her soup.

"No. I'm not nervous." I took another swig of water.

She blew on another spoonful.

"A little terrified, but I'll get over it."

She smiled. "You'll make a great couple."

"That's what I'm worried about."

"What do you mean?"

Pushing my plate away, I leaned on the table with my elbows. "I always thought I wanted to be part of a great couple, but now I'm not so sure. Great couples usually end up murdered or committing suicide. Run-of-the-mill couples live to a ripe old age and wander off into the sunset with dementia. I think I like dementia better."

"That's not true." She frowned.

"Okay." I sat back. "Name some great couples that lived happily ever after."

She opened her mouth.

"*Real couples.*" I add. "No soaps, please."

Her spoon tapped the edge of her bowl.

I crossed my arms and watched Dan open presents.

There was a snap and I looked at Amy. "Bill and Hillary—oh, wait."

I looked away.

She snapped her fingers again. "Tom Cruise and Nicole Kidman."

"Tom Cruise and Nicole Kidman?"

She nodded vigorously. "Oooh, and Sting. I think he's happily married."

"Fabulous. All we have to do is believe in aliens and practice tantric sex."

"You could try. I don't know if you can get Michael to believe in aliens." She shrugged. "But what guy doesn't want to have sex for six hours?"

I watched her finish her soup.

She was half right, anyway.

It was too early to expect him home when I returned. When my car crested the drive and it was empty, I tried not to worry. When I started dinner and my gut told me not to set the table for two, I was. When I ate by myself at the kitchen table, I was. When I fell asleep on the sofa and the doorbell rang—well, you get it.

"Hey!" It was Amy with a puppy in her arms.

"Hey." I rubbed my eyes. "What are you doing here? I thought you were going to Harbor Lights."

"Nah, I'm on pup duty tonight. Paul had to work and this little guy can't be alone for a few weeks yet."

She held it to her as it wriggled with a squeal. I reached for the head and scratched it between the ears. The blue eyes squinted, disappearing in a buzz of white fur.

"Come on in." I threw wide the door. "Are you hungry? I've got plenty of food."

She shook her head as she looked around. "I guessed Mike wasn't home when I didn't see his car. Otherwise I wouldn't have knocked."

I closed the door with a sigh. "He didn't say he'd be back tonight for sure. I just wanted to be here if he did."

"Don't explain. I would too if I were you."

She bent down and let the puppy loose.

My eyes went to the Persian carpet. "Um, is he potty safe?"

"Oh, he's all peed out. Actually, he probably needs water."

"I'll get a bowl." Going to the kitchen, I retrieved a soup bowl from the china cupboard and filled it with water.

"Sure you're not hungry?" I called to her.

"No, thanks. I stopped by Frisko Freeze on the way."

I returned to the living room with water and set it down. At first, the pup didn't seem to notice, then his nose found it and he began drank noisily.

"So where's his sibling? I thought you said there were two?"

"Anthony took her."

"Anthony took one?" I frowned. "They don't allow dogs in his building."

"He said half the people there already had a dog, so one more couldn't hurt."

I smirked. "That's a cop for ya."

Amy shrugged. "She was the last girl. It was love at first sight."

"I see."

"What?" She blinked innocently. "I was taking a walk."

"Uh huh."

"I'm socializing him."

We both looked at him as he tried to find an edge of the carpet to chew.

"*No.*" Amy pulled him away, batting his nose. "He's really smart."

"So am I." I crossed my arms.

"*Sophie.* I know you wouldn't take a puppy without talking to Mike first. We were just taking a walk. I only knocked on your door when I saw Mike's car wasn't here. If it was—"

"It would have been a perfect opportunity to expose him to kryptonite with whiskers."

"I'm telling you, he's the last one. When he's gone, you'll regret it."

He began running circles around the coffee table.

"I'll survive."

Amy sniffed. "You're mean."

"You have no idea."

"Look at your yard! It's dog heaven."

"They have angels to pick up poop in dog heaven. I don't have one of those."

"Anthony took one and he lives in an apartment."

"Anthony doesn't have any business getting a dog, as you'll soon discover when you move in with him."

Her eyes fell to the puppy. "I'm never moving into an apartment again. With or without Anthony."

My brows go up. "Really?"

Amy didn't say anything. I caught the pup running into the dining room and faced him the other way. When I glanced back at Amy she sighed.

"Let's just say it's going to be a while before anyone moves in with Anthony."

"I'm sorry to hear it."

We kept our eyes on the puppy.

"No biggie." Amy shrugged. "We're still going to see each other."

"You're not worried about becoming his transitional relationship?"

"He needs to build his confidence, is all. Now he has a puppy."

With a snort, I watch the pup lick my toes. "You think that's what we need?"

Her eyes brightened. "Dogs are great for relationship building, and they're a great way to know if you want kids or not."

"I don't think either of us wants to think about kids right now."

"They're great companions. You said Mike gets lonely when he's working by himself all day, and like I said, you have a great yard—"

"Tell ya what." I put up my hands. "As soon as he gets back, I'll ask him."

"They're also really good for security. Like, when you're home alone—"

"Amy." I cut her off. "We'll talk about it."

She smiled. "Thanks for thinking about it. I mean, I know I could leave him at the pound and someone would want him, but I feel really bad Paul's dog wasn't spayed and I want to make sure they all go to good homes, you know?"

"Very admirable. You're doing the right thing. Now tell me." My hands went on my hips. "How many shoes did you lose?"

Amy's lips disappeared. "A pair of Manolo pumps and a Sudini mule."

I nodded.

"Oh, jeez!" She looked horrified and I followed her gaze into the study.

At first, I thought Amy noticed the crypt, but it looked like a table with the cloth and tulips I'd arranged in a punch bowl. It was the sight of the puppy peeing on the corner of it that shocked her.

"I am *soooo* sorry!" She ran into the study and snatched it up. "Bad dog!"

"I'll get a towel." Biting my lip, I ran to the laundry room.

When I got back, she handed me the puppy and took the towel.

"So much for confidence building." She muttered, stooping to wipe up the puddle. When she finished, she stood, glaring at the pup in my hands.

"You just pissed away your last chance at a good home, buddy!"

She put out her hands to take him from me but I smiled and held him to me.

"It's okay. I won't hold it against him." Looking into his icy gaze, I nuzzled him. "When you gotta go, you gotta go."

It was past two in the morning before we finally fell asleep. Puppy's needs seemed to rotate on a two-hour cycle of eating, playing, sleeping, potty, repeat. After telling Amy I was keeping him, I drove her home, and she filled the trunk of my car with puppy mats and food. I spent the next six hours figuring out where to situate his food and water, where to train him to pee, and finally, where he would sleep. As it turned out, the cardboard box I'd recycled and lined with blankets was too scary for his first night. I moved it into our bedroom, where he whimpered and whined until I relented and let him sleep with me in bed.

A sharp bark woke me. Clawing at my arm, he wriggled away with a tiny growl.

Michael was a silhouette against the bedroom windows. He stood over the bed, staring down at us with pale eyes in the dark.

Puppy stood his ground in the middle of the mattress.

"Where am I going to sleep?" His voice was a whisper.

"You've got a crypt," I mumbled smugly.

He moved to leave.

"*What is wrong with you?*" I hissed. "Get back here!"

He stopped.

"Michael, he's tiny. There's plenty of room."

"Animals don't like me."

Puppy snarled.

"That's perfect nonsense. You've just got to get to know them."

He blinked. "What?"

"You just surprised him." I patted the mattress. "Come on."

Slowly, he went to his side of the bed and moved to sit down. Puppy charged, barking a stream of yips as Michael retreated.

"You can't just sit on him. Put out your hand and let him sniff you."

As he extended his hand, Puppy hummed like a small motor.

Michael hesitated.

"He won't bite." Even so, I held Puppy's tail. "Now, let him come to you."

I let go of the tail and Puppy stood frozen. The ears rotated uncertainly and then the snout moved to his hand.

"Did he bite you?" I asked.

"No." His voice was quiet as the tail began to wiggle. Puppy jumped and he yanked his hand away, but the little dog only bowed low and vibrated the sheets.

"Okay." I rolled over. "You're cleared."

"I am?"

"He likes you." My words came with a yawn.

"Are you sure?"

"He bowed to you. It means he wants you to play with him."

"What does it mean when they walk backwards in a circle?"

"Shit!" My eyes snapped open. I grabbed the pup, bundling him from the room. Amazingly, I made it out in time for him to take a dump by the front porch. I waited on the stoop, half awake. When he tried to make a run for it, I scooped him up and dragged upstairs. The pup was alive in my arms, fully recharged at four. He would chew on the sheets and lick me for an hour before I could sleep again.

In our room, Michael had crashed. Dead to the world, he was still wearing the shorts and tee he had worn in the door. I put our puppy on his chest and watched it sniff around, following the faintly sweet smell of his breath. It began to lick his face as I buried my own under my pillow.

Feeling for his hand in the dark, I grasped it and felt it squeeze mine.

There has to be evil

so that good can prove

its purity above it.

[Siddharta Gautama]

2003

"Violet!" I shout from her front yard. Jumping the boxwood hedge, I leap the front steps and barge through the door.

"Violet!"

No one answers.

I can't wait. Running for the kitchen, my eyes search every room I pass for a phone. Spotting one on a wall by the back door, I cut through the kitchen and pull the receiver, fighting the rotary dial to get Anthony on the line. I call his cell first. He picks up in two rings.

"Sophie, I'm sorry—"

"I'm at Violet's house."

"Sophie, after everything you've been through—"

"Anthony, *listen to me!* This isn't over."

"What?"

"It isn't over. That wasn't Michael we came back with."

"Jesus."

"Guess again."

"On my way."

Hanging up the phone, I turn and catch my breath.

"Hello, Sophie."

"Marta—*Jesus!*" I exhale with my hand on my chest. "You scared me."

Her pointed face is framed by jet black hair nearly covering her eyes. A black turtle neck is pulled up to her chin, which seems odd for June. Even with her hair down, I notice her face is green with bruises.

"Were you in an accident?" I squint.

"Nothing." She shrugs. "Fender bender. You, however, seem quite stressed. Understandable, after what you've been through. I saw it on the news. Are you sure you don't need to sit?"

"I was looking for Violet."

"So was I. I had more tea for her."

"Oh."

Glancing over her shoulder, I spot the tin of Earl Grey on the kitchen table. Marta closes on me, breaking my line of sight as her eyes push into mine.

"I was so relieved to hear you escaped those kidnappers unharmed."

"Thanks. So was I." My feet take a side step to the back door.

"Do you know what it was they wanted? Was it just money?"

"I'm not sure. They never really said." I take another step.

"Well." She folds her arms. "It is a sad sign of the times, isn't it?"

"Yes, it is."

"If we're waiting for Violet, we might as well have a cup of tea, don't you think?"

"Thanks." Feeling for the door knob behind me, I turn it. "I really need to get going. If you see Violet, tell her I stopped by." The door rattles, but doesn't open.

"Of course." She speaks calmly. "You'll want to get back home to Michael."

"Yes." I smile at her distractedly, feeling blindly for the deadbolt.

"Just so long as there's a home to go back to."

When she smiles, I flinch at the sight of her shattered teeth. Then I hear the words. "What?"

"Last time I checked, your house was on fire."

My fingers freeze on the deadbolt. "It can't be. I was just there."

"So was I." Her head nods at the front door.

Pushing past her, I run through the house. Heaving open the door, I stand on Violet's porch and stare down Prospect. Rising from the trees on our drive, a black billow of clouds is blotting out the setting sun.

"God."

It is all I can say.

My brain refuses to budge. The instinct to call for help is stayed by the realization of what is taking place inside. A knowledge I managed to forget. I left my husband in that house. Fighting for his life, and regardless of how pissed I am, fighting for mine, too. Turning, I run into the house and race for the phone again, this time to call 911. I reach for the phone. Putting the receiver to my ear, I hear nothing. The line is dead.

A memory echoes in my head.

I'm afraid that phone is no longer in service …

"I'm afraid it's too late for that."

Marta's voice is behind me.

Hanging up the phone, I close my eyes and call again.

Michael? Can you hear me?

"I'm sorry things had to end this way."

My eyes stay shut. I don't move.

Michael. Please say something.

"If they'd just accepted me, none of this would have happened."

My eyes open. "Accepted you?"

I turn to face her, but the menace in her bottomless gaze unnerves me.

"Why fight over you to be the mother of their child when they already had one?"

"Who are you?" My words are hoarse.

"I might have been your granddaughter."

"My granddaughter …?"

"Thank God, you're my stepmother now." She displays jagged teeth. "I'd feel bad about killing Danny."

Molly and Maeve come to mind. "Daniel didn't have any grandchildren."

"Not with Florence."

For a moment I stare at her raven hair and black eyes.

"With Violet." I whisper.

"I'd hoped you'd figure it out. That you'd remember what Michael did to you. Did to your daughter. But you never did. You never wanted to."

"I love him."

"He doesn't love you!" She hisses. "All he wanted was a child! Where was he when

I attacked you? Where was he when Sarah took you? Where is he now?"

"I don't know."

The color of her skin seems to shimmer. "Dead."

Slowly, I shake my head. "He can't die."

"If Sam didn't finish him, the fire will."

"Why?"

"Why not? Why wasn't I good enough?"

The pitch of her voice echoes in my mind.

"Good enough for what?"

"For their prophecy. Why wasn't I the one? I am, you know. I am the Child!" She points at my stomach. "*Not that!*"

"I'm not pregnant."

Holding me in her gaze, she presses her hand to my belly. "You are."

Yanking her hand away, I stumble back from her. "No! I'm not."

"The seed is new."

"No." My knees give as I think of Sam.

The kitchen wall guides my back to the floor. As my eyes drift down from Marta's face, I see a fire poker in her hand.

"God." My ears begin to buzz. "Is this how it ends?"

"*This is how it begins.*" The voice floats down to me.

In the distance, there is wailing. Sirens.

She raises the poker with a smile. "Don't worry, Danny. I'll be quick."

I close my eyes.

I'm sorry, Michael.

There is the sound of something slicing the air.

My eyes are open, staring up at Marta from the floor. My hands have caught the poker and grip it with white knuckles. There is the rushing sound of blood in my ears, a throbbing sound that matches my heart. I feel Marta try to pull away. As she does, she pulls me to my feet and I drive against her. She falls back onto the dining table as I hold the poker over her, her arms trembling to push me off. Slowly, the poker presses down on her, nearing her throat. The closer it gets, the darker her face grows, the whites of her eyes disappearing into black holes. She is losing her shape before my eyes. A gaping maw opens where her lips were, emitting an inhuman shriek.

"Jesus!"

My head jerks up to see Anthony in the dining room door, his mouth hanging open. The next thing I know, I am flying back across the kitchen, my body slamming against the wall. Stabbing pain tears through my gut, but my eyes never leave the thing on the table. It rushes at me, and I am horrified at the sight of it. The thing I saw in the garden. That broke into our home. That attacked me.

I see my hands aim for its throat, my fingers disappearing into amorphous haze yet feeling something, a neck. My own neck feels something as well. A stinging pain of a thousand needles. Then everything is blue. I have no idea how long I am blind, seconds, minutes, an eternity. The shriek of the beast fades.

There is silence.

I gasp. My eyes blink as the haze melts. There is an image. A face. It is staring at me with a gaping mouth. It is Marta's mouth, with Marta's teeth.

My hands grasp her neck.

"Sophie?" Anthony's voice shakes. "Sophie? Can you hear me?"

Somehow, I am on my feet, my stance straddling her. The sharp pain floods my insides and I want to collapse, but my body is not my own. The throb in my head still pounds behind my eyes. I walk with purpose to the dining table, ignoring Anthony's presence as he tries to hold my arm. Picking up the fire poker, I turn to Marta and feel my eyes focus on her heart. Approaching her, I hold the poker in front of me like a sword, only pointing down.

"Sophie, look at me! What are you doing?"

I raise the poker as far as I am able. Anthony comes at me, but is held back by someone I don't see.

"Who are you?! *Let me go!*" He shrieks. "Sophie! Sophie! *Stop!*"

I plunge the poker into her chest. It goes in too easily for me. I feel it pass through her and drive into the floor. I feel my feet tremble with the strength of it. A rage finally unleashes itself, burning my insides. It is not mine. It is my husband. Pain comes in a wave as I fall to my knees, holding my sides.

Sophie! I'm sorry! Forgive me!

Anthony is by my side. "Are you all right?"

"No." I gasp.

Anthony tries to get me to my feet. "What's wrong?"

The Child is dying.

My breath catches in my throat. "I'm pregnant. That's what she was after."

Tony's eyes widen with realization. "Pregnant?"

I start to weep. "I'm sorry, Michael. I thought he was you."

It's my fault. None of this would be if I weren't here. You're free now, Sophie. Free of Sam, of Marta, of me.

Anthony tries to pick me up. "I'll get you to the hospital."

"No!" I grip Anthony's arm. "I don't care. It's too late for that."

It isn't too late. You're still young. You still have Anthony. You can still have a life.

"Sophie, you could be bleeding internally."

"Don't go now." My arms wrap around my knees. "It's almost over."

You were right to walk out. I lied to you.

I close my eyes and press my forehead against my knees. "Say you love me."

"Sophie! Can you hear me? Open your eyes! Look at me!"

Anthony's hands are on my face. My lids are too heavy to lift.

I love you.

"Stay."

As I feel myself slip away, I know he will do as I say.

I am staring at a canopy with a radiating billow of satin. When I turn my head, the room keeps moving. It is yellow, with lace-curtained windows. The light coming through them is dim. My eyes drift shut.

Sophie? Are you awake?

They pop open. "Michael?"

Anthony's head peeks over the foot of my bed. "Sophie? You awake?"

I have two men too many.

Anthony comes to my bedside and puts the back of his hand to my forehead. "You ran a fever all night. If it wasn't for that Sarah chick, I'd have taken you to a hospital."

"Sarah?"

"That woman's a Nazi."

"She's no woman." My voice creaks. "Is there water?"

He looks around and smacks the side of his head with the palm of his hand. "Now, why didn't I think of that?"

As soon as he leaves, I sit up.

"Michael?"

You don't have to speak out loud.

With a sigh, I roll my eyes and fall back on my pillow. "Thank God."

I'm sorry if I frightened you. I shouldn't have said the things I did.

"Damn straight! What the hell kind of husband are you? I thought I was never going to see you again."

When you left the house, you said it was over. I thought it was.

"When I left the house! That was before I thought you were dead, discovered I was carrying the anti-Christ, and had a harpy try to kill me with a fire poker!"

You're not still mad at me about your job?

"No! Now I'm mad at you for burning our house down."

That wasn't me.

"Of course it was! If I was married to anyone else, I wouldn't be homeless now."

We aren't homeless.

My hands go to my head. "You're right." I take a breath and nod. "We're insured."

It was just a house, Sophie. You're safe; that's what is most important.

My hands drop. "What about you? Are you safe?"

Right now, I'm safer outside my body than in it.

I swallow. "What happened?"

Long story.

"I'm not going anywhere."

It was badly burned. It will take time to recover.

"How much?"

Two, maybe three weeks.

"You won't have a body for three weeks?"

I'm sorry if that upsets you.

I blink. "You seem fine with it."

This is what you married.

"Makes not having a house seem minor by comparison."

We'll have a house again.

"And you'll have a body again."

Sophie, I knew you needed my body when I proposed to you. I wouldn't expect you to accept me as I am now.

"You know I still love you."

And I still want to have a body. When I do, we'll start over.

"You aren't going to look different, are you?"

I never do.

"Because I don't think you could do better."

Our life will be better.

"Like our house."

We'll build anew.

"Till then, we can move out to the cabin." I sigh. "It'll be good to get away."

I feel an uneasy silence.

"Michael?"

The cabin burned down.

I close my eyes. "Let me guess."

It was me.

My eyes open. "It was? What happened?"

Long story.

"Always is." I smirk at the bed canopy.

How are you feeling?

"Like I had a miscarriage. Please say I'm right."

You did. You were fortunate in that.

"I would have aborted it anyway."

That wouldn't have been possible.

"Why not?"

A doctor wouldn't have diagnosed your pregnancy. You would have shown every outward appearance of being pregnant, but the fetus would have remained immaterial until birth.

"An invisible fetus?"

A physical body born of spirit. We call it pure manifestation. Humans know it as immaculate conception.

My lips purse. "I wouldn't call what happened with Sam immaculate."

Humans divorce physical intercourse from the spiritual condition, but intercourse is necessary for conception. In my present state, I can't procreate. Only when I am material can I attempt procreation, and then it is nearly impossible.

"But not for Sam?"

His sentience was greater than mine.

"His heart wasn't."

There is no response.

"Michael?"

I'm so sorry, Sophie.

His voice is a needle of pain that brings tears to my eyes.

The bedroom door opens as Anthony enters with a glass of water and a pitcher. "Sorry it took so long. I had to clear the pipes. For a moment I thought Sarah was going to make me go to the store for bottled stuff."

He places the pitcher on the night stand before gently sitting on the bed.

I wipe my eyes with the back of my hand. "Clear the pipes?"

"Nothing." Tony seems to catch himself. "You know ... old house, old pipes."

Pushing myself up in bed, I squint. "Backflow from the fire hoses?"

He hands me the glass. "Forget about that for now."

"Did you see it?" Sipping steadily, I begin to drain it.

He sucks on his lip.

I pause to get a breath. "Come on, Tony. Spare me the china doll shit."

"Louis and I were there last night."

They retrieved my crypt.

"You got Mike's box?"

He nods and takes the glass from me. Reaching for the pitcher, he refills it. The glass in his hand is unsteady.

"You looked inside?"

Clearing his throat, he hands me the water. "Sarah did."

"That bad?"

Worse.

Remembering the last time I'd seen Michael, I tried not to imagine worse.

"Where's Mike now?"

I'm right here.

"You know what I mean." I mumble, catching Anthony's eye.

"We drove him to Louis's place on Anderson Island."

"Will he be safe there?"

I hope so.

Anthony shrugs. "I just take orders these days."

"You look like you need some sleep."

He shakes his head. "I've been up longer."

"What about your job?"

Rising from the bed, he goes to the window. "There'll be some 'splainin to do."

"I hear there's a shortage of good cops. You think they'll fire you?"

"Fire me?" He turns with a grin. "I'm union, they wouldn't dare."

"Sorry. I'm one of those exempt folks. We don't know what job security is."

We smile at each other. For a moment, we say nothing.

"You feeling better?"

"Just tired." I sit back on the pillows.

"You hungry?"

"Not yet."

Anthony stares. "How's Mike?"

I'm fine. Thanks for asking.

"He says he's fine and thanks for asking."

"That was him, wasn't it? In the kitchen."

"What?" I glare. "You don't think I could kill someone with my bare hands?"

Anthony's stare melts to a grin. "Just never knew you were so good with a fire poker."

"Good thing we didn't have one in the apartment."

"Yeah, there'd be one less good cop." His gaze drops to the floor as his grin fades.

"Come here." I reach out my arms.

When he comes to the bed, I take his hands and pull him to me.

I kiss him on the cheek. "I love you. You know that."

"Just friends." His eyes close.

"More than that."

Green eyes open, burning mine.

"Anthony, you can love more than one person in a lifetime."

I can't.

The ice in my husband's voice gives me goose flesh.

Tony squints. "Is that a hint?"

Isn't he dating Amy?

With a sigh, I pat him on the shoulder. "You'd better go."

"Like hell? I love you more than a friend, a kiss on the cheek, there's the door?"

"Anthony."

"What?"

"Fire poker."

"Gotcha." He goes for the door.

"Anthony."

He stops, looking over his shoulder.

"Thank you."

With a grin he disappears.

[Gold mask of Aten Re with the crown of Atef. c. 1300 B. C.]

One Creator,
You have made your body.
Alone you cross eternity.
The souls of millions burn within you.
Your beauty like that of heaven,
Your blood bluer than the bright sky.
When waking, all behold you.
When sleeping, all are blind.
You are the dawn of each day.
Your breath like the wind in our sails.
When you rise, you span the world in a day.
Each day, a lifetime, a moment.
When you fall, all is death.

[Middle Hieratic. Translation of *The Hymn to Re.* c. 1332 B.C.]

2000 He was late getting the coffee started the next morning.

On the red eye from Phoenix, he couldn't get the vision of Sophie sleeping alone out of his mind: the soft pillow, the cool sheets, the scent of her. But it wasn't her scent that greeted him. He knew something was different the moment he came in the door. An animal had been in the house. When he discovered it was in his bed, it made him ill. When he saw Sophie sleeping next to it, it disgusted him. She disgusted him. They were animals in a bed and he was supposed to join them?

But he was so tired.

After she ran from the room, taking the creature with her, the expanse of the mattress lay before him, still soft, regardless of how it smelled.

The moment his head hit the pillow, he forgot.

Forgot it was there. It licked him awake in the morning, pawing at his mouth. In less than a thought, he seized it in his hands and held it away from him. Sitting up, his first impulse was to toss it to the floor. Looking back at him, it squirmed in his grip, no longer minding his presence.

"He has your eyes."

Sophie's voice started him and he looked over to see her watching.

"You better take him out. He'll piddle on you if you hold him like that."

She rolled out of bed and headed for the bathroom.

If it could sleep with her, why couldn't it use her bathroom, too?

He got to his feet and went downstairs with the animal in his hands. Standing outside in the chill air, he put it on the ground and watched it run into a bush only to emerge with a stick in its mouth. Flopping on its side, it started to gnaw. Clearly, it preferred to whittle than piddle.

Feeling a gnawing himself, he left the front door open and went into the kitchen to start the coffee maker. Opening the refrigerator, the scent of roasted chicken pleased him. She had counted on his return. Spotting a shelf full of Hempler's bacon made him smile.

As the bacon began to fry, scampering noises made him turn. The animal stood in the back hall at the kitchen door with its nose in the air. Narrowing his eyes, he went back to making breakfast. Cracking eggs into a bowl, he dropped the empty carton into the recycle bin and hunted for a whisk. It wasn't until he poured the omelet that he heard the bin tip over. In the time it took to right the bin and pry the egg carton from of the animal's mouth, the eggs had started to burn. The sound of Sophie coming down the stairs reminded him he hadn't poured her cup of coffee. Turning off the stove, he found her mug and filled it.

Finally, he ate, which he did in his usual fashion, standing at the stove. He didn't need to keep an eye on the animal. It was biting his ankles.

Sophie came into the kitchen and picked up her coffee.

"Wow." She sipped. "It's actually still hot."

Without facing her, he closed his eyes. "How long is it staying?"

"It? You mean our puppy?"

He turned. "*Our* puppy?"

"He's staying, period." She took another sip of coffee. "You know, if you fed him he'd probably stop doing that."

She waved her cup at him, glancing at his ankles.

He paused, a piece of bacon before his mouth. "Feed him what?"

"Puppy chow. It's in a bag in the laundry room. His bowl's in there, too."

Dropping the bacon in the pan, he folded his arms. "Where did this come from?"

"This what?" Sophie blew on her mug.

"This animal."

"It's not an animal. It's our new pet, and it was a gift from Amy."

"A gift?"

"Yep, she gave one to Anthony, too."

"Is he keeping his?"

"Of course he is! Anthony loves dogs." She set down her mug heavily and left.

Running through the dining room and into the living room, he caught her entering the foyer from the back hall.

"I thought you said your parents wanted a dog?"

"My parents are moving to Hawaii, you know that. They can't have a puppy right now. Besides, they don't really have the yard for one." She shrugged. "We do."

"Kate and Duane have a yard." He watched her fish through her coat pockets.

"And three cats." Turning her back, she pulled on her coat and picked up her bag, slinging it over her shoulder. As she came to kiss his cheek, she smiled sweetly. "Half a cup, four times a day. Plenty of water. He'll need to go first thing after his naps, and remember to reward him."

She stepped back, staring past his shoulder. "Did he go when you took him out this morning?"

"No." He followed her gaze to the study.

"He is now."

The animal was piddling on the corner of his crypt.

He glared at her, but she was already headed out the door.

"Sophie."

"Welcome home, honey." She winked as the door closed behind her.

Cleaning up with a towel, he wondered how long the process of training a dog actually took. Even after the animal was trained, the smell would remain. He sat on the floor with his back against the crypt. The animal ran to him at the clap of his hands. Picking it up, he examined it. It was designed to be appealing. It was furry, with large pointed ears and oversized paws. Yet the ice in its eyes belied a creature capable of calculation and wayward intent. Why Sophie would take it in, he had no idea. Somehow, he would have to live with it.

Tucking the animal under his arm, he went to the laundry room and found the bag of food. Inside, he discovered another smell he would not enjoy getting accustomed to. After filling its bowl, he left the thing to eat and wearily returned to the study. He was overdue for some time in his crypt. After only a few hours of sleep in his bed, it was a welcome sight, though the tablecloth and flower arrangement said enough. Removing the flowers, he noticed some papers on the cloth: a grocery list, a card with a brochure regarding homeowner's insurance, and a Post-It in Sophie's hand. Dan and Phil had invited him star gazing on Thursday night.

Hearing a yelp, he returned, papers in hand, to the laundry room. The thing was gone. Following his nose, he found it with its head stuck in an empty cereal box from the recycle bin. Pulling the box off the animal's head, he picked it up to take it to the cardboard pen upstairs. Before leaving, he paused to consider the papers in his hand. Leaving the grocery list and the star gazing invite on the kitchen table, he dropped the insurance brochure in the recycle bin.

Stroking the animal's ears, he headed for the stairs.

"Time for you to go to your box while I spend some time in mine."

His strategy for a good night's sleep hinged on exhausting the animal.

That afternoon, he walked it. He played tug with it. He taught it to fetch. Above all, he kept it awake until it passed out. After dinner, he was ready to pass out himself but felt confident he would finally sleep unmolested in his bed. One thing was certain: the thing had spent its first and last night sleeping in their bed. The cardboard box had been relocated in front of the television in the spare bedroom. He would leave the television tuned to Animal Planet if it pacified the beast.

Finally resting his head on his pillow, his eyes closed with a sense of release.

"I'm sorry I didn't change the sheets before you got back." Sophie's arms found him in the dark.

Blindly reaching, he held her. "You missed me."

She snuggled into him. "I thought you'd never come back."

Subconsciously, he squeezed her. "I know."

"I'm glad you did." Her voice tingled in his ear.

"I am too."

All he really wanted was sleep. He had daydreamed of it, planned on it, all day, but the touch of her sent a charge up his spine. Softly, she kissed his ear, and he caught his breath. Turning his head, he found her mouth.

She spoke.

"You have to take out the recycling tomorrow."

He rolled to face her. "Right."

His face closed on hers. She kissed his lips, stroking his head as blood flooded his eyes with light.

"Did you see that insurance sheet I left out?"

Insurance?

She pulled away as he squinted into the glow of her face.

"I saw it in the recycle bin." She continued. "Did you read it?"

"No." He found his voice. "Not really."

"What sort of coverage do you have?"

With a sigh, he shut his eyes, waiting for the throb in his ears to subside. "Isn't the house insured?" Her voice made him flinch.

"No."

"No?" She sat up. "What about your art? Your Wedgwood?"

He blinked. "Why would I?"

"What if we were robbed or the house burnt down?"

"Insurance wouldn't replace them. All we would get is money."

"I can't believe those words came out of your mouth."

"I have money. I don't need more."

"Even people with money have insurance."

"Because they place an inordinate value on material possessions."

"Because they prepare for the worst. You of all people should understand that."

"Sophie, I had a long weekend. Can we talk about this in the morning?"

"How can you sleep knowing your house isn't insured? How could you leave town?"

His head shook. "Risk is always a probability. On average, I've only had a house fire every two hundred years. Few of my possessions are older and rarely stay in my possession longer. They're just things. They are meant to be lost."

"What about your library? Your journals?"

He shrugged. "I would rewrite them."

"Rewrite them?"

"I have before. It isn't a very long record. I've only kept a journal the last two thousand years."

"Two thousand years of uninsured risk. You're an adjustor's nightmare."

"That's two thousand years of premiums I haven't had to pay."

"Why worry about paying if you have plenty of money?"

"Why worry about insuring if I can replace things myself?"

"That's the point, Mike. What if you couldn't?"

"Unlikely. ECCO's resources are significant."

"Humor me. What if ECCO wasn't there?"

"I have savings."

"Great. Wouldn't you rather have insurance cover your expenses so you had more of your savings to fall back on?"

"Sophie—"

"Yes or no." The fire in her eyes bore into him.

He rolled away from her. "Please, Sophie. I'm tired."

Her tone sharpened. "If you think you're tired after twelve hours with a puppy, try forty a week in an office."

"No, thank you."

"Have you ever really had to work for a living?"

"Seeing as how I'm not really alive, no."

"You want to be, don't you?"

"Yes." He whispered.

"Then you need to act like the realities of life apply. I'm not saying you flip burgers at Frisko Freeze, but you can't assume ECCO will always bail you out."

Rolling onto his back, he watched her. "Nate was good."

"Nate?"

"The salesman."

"Were you spying again?"

He shook his head. "You're thinking about your conversation with him. His statistics on house fires scared you."

"Molten playground equipment scared me."

For a moment, no one spoke. He stared at the ceiling.

She straddled his waist, pinning him to the mattress. Leaning over him, she stared down at his face as her hair slipped from her shoulders, draping his pillow.

"You said it was my life and you were just a passenger."

Nodding, he felt himself letting go.

"If you're riding with me, you have to wear a seat belt."

The chill of her fingers slid across his chest and down his abdomen. He knew he would do whatever she asked.

"You cold, Mike?" Phil's voice cut through the darkness.

"Fine."

"Good night for a fire." Dan briskly rubbed his palms before changing lenses.

The wind picked up in the trees, but the snoring bundle curled under his coat put out more than enough heat for a summer night. Stretched on a wool blanket, he crossed his legs and returned the binoculars to his eyes. He squinted through them in case anyone was watching, blinded by the atmospheric haze they only magnified into a harsh glare.

Putting them down, he waited for his night vision to return.

"Where is it?" Dan muttered.

"What?" Phil asked.

"Gemini."

"Well ..." Phil pointed to the right. "The big bear is over there, so it's probably behind those trees."

"Damn trees."

"Next time we'll find a park where they won't bother us."

He tried to be helpful. "Next month it will be higher in the sky."

"True, but who needs Gemini?" Phil exhorted. "You've got Hercules, the Northern Cross, Andromeda ..."

"She's hot." Dan agreed.

Phil whistled. "And chained to a rock, which is the only way I find women."

"Beats a ball and chain." Dan mumbled.

Phil snickered. "Second thoughts about the second time around?"

"More like thoughts I should have had the first time around."

He guessed Dan was referring to the upcoming marriage. Sophie had heard about Dan's ex-wife and thought it a bad idea.

He turned to watch Dan, crouched behind a telescope.

"Why did you get married the first time?"

Dan's shoulders moved. "We'd been friends growing up, we were friends in college. I guess we thought being married wouldn't be any different."

"Was it?"

"I went from being her friend to being her husband, which for some women is the same as pet ownership."

"Men are dogs." Phil agreed.

"That may be, but some of us have nicer owners."

"Not me." Phil shuddered. "I'm stray and proud of it."

Dan laughed uneasily. "We probably shouldn't be talking about this in front of Mike. You're about to take the plunge and I'm sure you and Sophie will do fine, but every marriage has ups and downs. I guess Karen and I never found the right balance."

He propped himself on his elbow. "What is the right balance?"

Dan looked up from the view finder to stare at the night sky before looking his direction. "You have to believe nothing is worse than living apart."

Phil grunted in the dark.

The unsettled puppy tried to climb from his coat, and he laid down. Reaching inside, he scratched the pup while it calmed, licking his fingers.

Returning his gaze to the sky, he caught the brilliance of Vega. It was lower than when he observed it from The Mountain. In Lyra. The lyre of Orpheus, who died miserably after losing Eurydice, not once, but twice.

"Here are some women I can't live without." Phil's voice broke his meditation. "The Pleiades look great tonight."

His eyes tracked right, finding the blaze of a thousand fires.

"Taurus?" Dan switched to another scope.

"Just above Aldebaran."

"The eye of Taurus." Dan mumbled. "Why does it only have one eye, anyway?"

"I think you only see him from the side." Phil took a break to stretch.

"It only has one eye." He spoke up, thinking of Sam. "The eye of the beast."

"The eye of the beast." Dan repeated ominously.

"The bull is figurative of the beast as man's mythic nemesis. The dark half of the divine that represents the dark half of the soul. His eye sees frailty to exploit it."

"That's some bull all right." Phil snorted. "What astronomy class did you learn that in?"

He shrugged. "Something I read a long time ago."

Phil looked over at him. "*A long time ago.* When was that? Junior high?"

"Might have been *Playboy.*" He murmured.

"Yeah, I remember that issue." Dan mused. "Centerfolds of the Stars."

"I have them all." He smiles to himself. "Just ask Sophie."

Dan's head popped up. "Sophie lets you keep a porn collection?"

"She says it's the most valuable thing in the house."

454 | LISA MOWAT

"Mine disappeared after we were engaged."

"And I bet they didn't reappear after the divorce." Phil snorted. "There's your balance, Mike. No matter what, don't let her toss your porn."

"Don't worry." He grinned at the sky. "It's insured."

1199 BC   All night they chanted. When they finished, priests carried out the body of Ashebu, leaving the general alone. He approached my crypt and raised his palms to me.

"Forgive me, lord. I cursed you with the sword of my fathers. It has defiled you. I have defiled you. What must I do to appease you?"

If he left me inside my crypt instead of on it, he would have earned my eternal gratitude. Desperately, my eye searched the tent for a way to speak to him. My problem was I could not be sure how a sign might be interpreted. To extinguish the lamps and bring darkness could be a bad omen. Causing a breeze to stir the air, likewise. I spoke to his thoughts in desperation.

Please, lord general. Return me in my crypt.

He continued, unhearing.

"I fear Ashebu wronged you and I have failed to punish him. Do you understand why I could not see his spirit wander? If anyone is to blame, it is I. I gave you the sword of his brother. I gave him cause to begrudge you. He came to me with questions I did not answer. Only I told him one thing. A terrible thing. I told him you were Amenteth restored to us. In so doing, I forsook you."

I forgive you. Put me in my crypt.

"The others are true to his memory. When confronted, they claimed it was they who slew you and Ashebu tried to stop them. They are being held now ..."

The general hesitated.

"The priest Ptah, plans to curse them before the people. When I asked him to tend your body, he was overcome at the sight of you. He brought his brethren to witness, and they insist everyone who has doubt must see you. Ptah believes you are Re and only the sacrifice of the defilers will appease you. He has asked for their blood, but I have stalled him as I feel you would not want this. Ptah swears you will curse us if they are not sacrificed. I must know. I beg you for a sign."

I cried out.

No sacrifices! Do you hear me? Let them go!

He gave no sign. Backing from my crypt, he dropped his gaze.

"Our exodus is stalled. Ptah has called my people to you. They will seek an answer. Unless I hear from you, the ceremony will be tomorrow at sunrise."

Lord general!

I felt myself gasp and shift my arm, but he left without notice.

I was alone. I was not on fire. I was not embalmed. I was in hell.

[Spharic. Entry translated from *Kor Dai Maihael*. Mund Dai. d. 755 BC]

~

2003   It sees him. The body that was. What little is left. It does not linger.
There is no time.

It has to find Sophie. If Sam has lain with her, she will carry the Child. Fate will fall on her. It must watch over her. To wait for the Child if need be. To kill it.

It flies from the crypt, rising like a spark from their dying home. The house is little more than the body It has left behind. Flames lick the slate roof and howl from shattered windows. An engorged fire. Enraged. Intended.

Marta is back. It feels her in the heat and smells her in the smoke. It follows up the street and sees the light of her in Violet's house. She stands over a woman. It sees the fire poker in her hand. Marta is going to avenge herself on Violet for betraying her.

It calls to Violet to run.

"I'm not pregnant." Violet blurts out.

But the voice isn't Violet's. It watches, trying to make sense of what It sees.

"You are." Marta is vindicated.

"No! I'm not."

Sophie slips down the wall, her spirit faded past all recognition, staring.

It reaches for her.

Sophie, get up!

She doesn't move.

Marta's shadow falls across her. "The seed is new."

Sophie! I'm here! Let me in!

"No." The light in her flickers. "God, is this how it ends?"

It goes to her, willing her.

This is how it begins.

The poker rises. "Don't worry, Danny. I'll be quick."

Sophie speaks to It.

"I'm sorry, Michael."

It can feel her mind. She is frozen in it. Lost. But open.

Rushing into her, everything It has desired burns anew.

There is no time.

The arc of the poker comes slowly. Her hands are already there.

It feels Marta's strength measured against It, and she is no match.

At first, Marta assumes there is no threat. She cannot see past Sophie's soul. She is slow to shift into shadow as It pushes her to the table, threatening to crush her throat with her own weapon. Killing her will be easy if she is slow to grasp what she is facing.

"Jesus!"

The sound of Anthony's voice wakes Sophie's consciousness. It momentarily loses control as her head jerks up, relaxing her grip on the poker. It knows Marta will seize the distraction and floods Sophie's body to shield her. The blow sends It across the room. Her body impacts the kitchen wall, fracturing wall tiles with her back. Marta's kick is lethal. Sophie is alive, but hurt. Her insides torn by a familiar pain.

There is no time.

It lifts Sophie to her feet.

Marta has shifted. She is shadow, as depthless as she is ruthless, a demon beyond the reach of any fire poker. But no longer inviolate. She will meet her maker and repent, no longer hiding behind a soul, stalking unseen to incinerate the unsuspecting. Where It failed to assume Marta before, It now has Sophie's soul to shield It.

It seizes the throat, letting the enormity of It fill the pits of Marta's eyes. It feeds the fire in her, feels the shadow slowly burning away until all that remains is human. Marta stares up at It, naked on the linoleum floor, her dark eyes dull with the half life of broken promises and hopeless pursuit. It moves to finish her.

Crossing to the table for the poker, It hears Anthony's voice, feels Sarah's impassive gaze, hears Violet praying at her bed.

–by the divine power–

Taking the poker in hand, It feels the weight of the iron in Sophie's grasp. Turning to Marta, It walks beyond Anthony's reach to deliver the final blow.

–thrust into hell–

Seeing the light of her soul, It raises the poker overhead.

–evil spirits who wander–

As the poker passes through her, she is made finite.

–seeking the ruin of souls–

The transmission of her life is final.

Amen.

It feels a raw pain as the fire within retreats. It realizes Sophie isn't unconscious. She has held on and suffers for It.

Sophie! I'm sorry! Forgive me!

She falls to her knees, but there is no helping her. It weighs on her soul, consuming her strength. It must leave her.

"No."

Her voice commands It even as Sam's seed burns in her.

The Child is dying.

"I'm pregnant. That's what she was after." She bursts into tears. "I'm sorry, Michael. I thought he was you."

There is no time.

It's my fault. None of this would be if I weren't here. You're free now, Sophie. Free of Sam, of Marta, of me.

"No!" She fights. "I don't care. It's too late for that."

It must leave.

It isn't too late. You're still young. You still have Anthony. You can still have a normal life.

"Don't go now. It's almost over."

There is no time, but It wants to stay.

You were right to walk out on me. I lied to you.

"Say you love me." She whispers, fading as her body strives against It.

I love you.

"Stay."

Her directive is beyond all reason. An act of self-destruction. Everything It has ever wanted.

It doesn't remember the beginning of everything. Memories are simply facts. That they happened in any particular order is unimportant. Where humans find the measure of years significant, It finds the persistence of fact more so. Watching Sophie struggle to hold onto her body, It has difficulty accepting any fact could affect It more. It recalls her allergic reaction to a flu shot two years before. It remembers the wait at the hospital. It suffered then, too.

Not like now.

Her fever is severe. In destroying Marta, It nearly destroyed the woman It loves. It watches Violet tend her with damp towels and a bowl of ice water. It hears Anthony's feet pace downstairs. It knows there is unfinished business. There always is.

Wandering downstairs, It finds Sarah in the evening, standing on the porch. Her eyes watch the fire crews demolish the smoldering remains of the house down the street. Her senses are tuned to any presence that nears.

Sensing It is near, she shares her thoughts.

Guess you're glad I stayed.

It opens to her. *You shouldn't have.*

And your body?

I told you, it's taken care of.

She turns her head to no one.

If I were Phanuel, I'd have an army of sentinels ready to sift the ashes of that house for your bones.

The vision of Louis waiting in a truck three blocks away comes to mind.

My servus is waiting and he won't need to sift. I made it to my crypt.

"Your crypt?" She whispers aloud. *I thought you gave it Sam?*

I traded it for his servus.

Sarah gives a laugh. *Betrayed by one of his own. It's about time.*

And it's about time you left. If Phanuel is like you, he will have sentinels searching for me. If they see you—

She puts a hand on her hip. *If they see me it may give your servus the opportunity to get your body out of here.*

Sariel, please—

"Enough!" She walks to the edge of the porch steps, surveying the length of the street. *Phanuel is a coward. If he guessed you were coming back here, it was because he knew you were going to face Sam. You think he'd send sentinels to find Sam?*

She pauses. *Did Phanuel know you had the ops?*

No.

For all he knows, you've been assumed by Sam and Bahiel is reborn. He's bracing for Armageddon. Did anyone help you escape?

Yes.

Then Phanuel has enough to keep him busy. He'll be frantic to find them before ECCO slips through his fingers. I predict he won't have a singularity standing with him by the end of the year.

Sariel, if what you say is true, you should do as you intended and leave for good. There is nothing to keep you here.

Sarah stares as if she hasn't heard a word. *Where is your servus?*

I haven't looked for him.

And you assume he knows what he is doing?

Louis is highly intuitive.

Louis? She tosses her head. *He's highly inebriated. I can't leave you alone with him. Besides, he can't hear you.*

Sophie can. She will speak for me.

Sophie can't speak for anyone right now.

The reminder fills It with urgency.

I'm sorry. Sarah folds her arms, returning inside the house. *I know you're worried. If anything happens to her, I won't be able to forgive myself.*

Sarah glances out the door before closing it behind her. *I've made these last years miserable for you, haven't I? Every time you saw me, I was ordering you to kill her.*

I should have left ECCO sooner, but I was too weak.

She leans back against the door. *Michael, you understand you could have never avoided this. Sam would have never let you go and ECCO won't either. ECCO can never know you exist. If they do, they will never stop hunting you.*

But I could destroy them. Why risk coming after me? All I want is to be left alone.

Until you submit or are destroyed, it is Phanuel's authority that is at risk. You swore an oath to accept the law of Metatron. ECCO can't let its brethren flaunt the law and leave. Phanuel upholds Metatron's rule as sacred. Your very existence threatens that.

It can barely bring itself to think it.

They will come after Sophie.

That goes without saying. Phanuel still fears she is pregnant.

What can we do?

Sarah nods over her shoulder. *What is left for you both to go back to?*

We can't run away. It would destroy her parents. She is their only child.

With a sigh, she pushes off the door and crosses the foyer.

You don't have to make a decision right now. Phanuel will besiege himself with Metatron, and your body will take two weeks at least. That should give Sophie time enough to recover.

What will we tell everyone?

Sarah turns her gaze to the mounted Eland staring down at them. *I'll tell everyone you had to leave to deal with a family crisis in …* She squints at the chandelier, *Zanzibar.*

Zanzibar?

Well, someplace hard to get to. I'll come up with something. It will work perfectly, I already met Sophie's family at the wedding. They'll vouch for me as your sister.

You said you were my half-sister.
Right. She waves her hand. *Half-sister.*
The stairs creak as Violet wobbles down with the remains of an ice bath.
How is she?
"Well?" Sarah approaches Violet.
"Fever's gone." Violet rounds the banister and disappears for the kitchen. "She'll be fine. Just needs her sleep."
Thank God.
Sarah only sniffs and climbs the stairs, but It has flown ahead of her. Passing through walls into the turret, It finds Anthony standing in the yellow room at Sophie's bedside. An annoying sight barely relieved by the fact that Sophie is unaware.
Sophie. It tries to reach her. *I'm still here.*
Her mind is a blur of random memories. An image of his form comes into focus. He is holding her, speaking to her. Her vision turns dark, melding him with Sam. It leaves her mind, unwilling to see more. Anthony reaches for her hand and she squeezes it. When the bedroom door opens, Sarah's presence chills the room.
"Violet says the worst is over."
Anthony nods without turning, but doubt is in his eyes.
"When you can tear yourself away, I need you downstairs."
His head barely turns. "What for?"
"We need to recover Michael's body and dispose of Marta's."
"We?"
"Or Michael will remain a shadow and Sophie will go to prison for murder."
Anthony glares at Sarah's apathetic forecast, then drops his eyes to Sophie's hand. "I'll be down in a minute."
As the door closes, Anthony carefully tucks Sophie's hand under the bed quilt before leaning to kiss her on the forehead. For a moment he pauses over her head, looking at her face.
It draws near, fire in mind.
She is mine.
Unhearing, Anthony rises with a sigh and leaves the room.
It should follow downstairs, but lingers.
It stays with her.
It vows never to risk her again.

~

Subject: **You are in our thoughts**

From: Evelyn Whittier

Date: 6/9/2003 6:18 PM

To: Sophie Davids

Dear Sophie,

First, let me convey to you on behalf of everyone here at St. Joseph's how relieved we are to hear you and Michael are safe. We were extremely concerned when we were notified by the police that you were missing and want to assure you that you have been in our thoughts and prayers.

Absolutely do not feel obligated to respond to this e-mail or have any concern regarding your work here. Everything is being taken care of and you should feel free to take as much time as needed. No doubt you have heard from your colleagues, but if not let me be the first to tell you should you need anything, feel free to contact me at any time.

Please convey to Michael my regards. Tell him I completely understand his desire to keep his identity a secret, but he couldn't have asked for a better partner in giving than you. The two of you have done a fabulous job for the hospital, our patients and our community.

God Bless You Both,

Lyn

[E-mail from Evelyn Whittier to Sophie Davids. June 9, 2003]

2000 "Lodi!"

In the dusk, a blur of white fuzz came at me. Stopping at my feet, he reared on hind legs to beg.

"Down."

Lodi dropped his paws and snapped at another biscuit. Behind me, I heard my husband clear his throat.

"Lodi." He murmured next to me.

"You don't like it?"

"What made you think of it?"

"I was listening to Credence in the car and thought it sounded like him."

Michael blinked, but said nothing else.

"You don't like it?"

"No. It's a good name."

I paused before giving Lodi another biscuit. "It doesn't mean anything creepy?"

"Lod was a crossroads to the coast from Jerusalem."

"A crossroads?"

"Some cultures call it a guide star, some a place of peace."

With a snarl, Lodi streaked across the yard into a bed of ivy, tearing it to pieces. Michael raised a brow at me.

I cleared my throat. "I've been meaning to trim that back."

My fingers fidgeted for another biscuit.

His eyes stayed fixed on me. "You've been outside with him every evening."

"It's the only time he gets to know me. Besides, it's almost fall. There won't be many dry evenings in our future."

"He likes you better."

"It's the biscuits."

"How was work today?"

"Good—Here boy!"

Letting out a high whistle, I tried to distract Lodi from the flower bed.

"You've been coming home late."

"Everyone's wound up over the ribbon-cutting ceremony." I headed for the garden to see what Lodi was eating.

Michael trailed behind me. "I thought that was next year."

"January, darling. That's right around the corner."

"Will there be many people there?"

I snorted. "Everyone except the principal donor. *Lodi! Out!*"

Lodi sprang from a bed of lilies and rushed me. He snatched another biscuit from my hand as I bent to scratch his ears.

"Sophie?"

"Hmm?" My hand reached back into the biscuit bag.

"Are you happy?"

"Sure." Pausing, I glanced up. "Why?"

"It's been over a week since I returned. You've seemed …" His eyes bore down on me. "Distant."

With a shrug, I signaled Lodi to lay down. "Been busy."

"I'm not leaving again."

"You're no prisoner."

Standing up, I dug for another biscuit while Lodi begged.

"Did I tell you I got the house insured?"

"With Nate?" My eyes stayed on the dog.

"Yes."

"Good. He said he'd split his commission with me."

"Sophie?"

Finally, I looked at him. "Yes, Michael."

"You don't have to worry anymore."

For a moment I stared, then started to laugh. Michael didn't move, watching tensely.

"Sorry." I caught my breath and reached for his hand. "You're so sweet."

He still stared, his hand limp in mine. "I ... I just want you to be happy."

"*I am.* But you can't stop me from worrying."

A small smile crept on his face. "Never?"

"Ever." I pressed a dog biscuit in his palm.

Without hesitation, he popped it in his mouth as I frowned.

"That's disgusting."

Crunching on it, he squinted. "It isn't bad."

"They're supposed to be organic." I read the side of the bag. "Wheat flour, oats, peanut butter, eggs, salt—this is ridiculous. I could make these."

He made a face. "And they wouldn't taste stale."

"It says they're safe for people, but I wouldn't buy it."

Michael put out his hand and I pulled the bag away. "You'll make yourself sick."

"Unlikely." He dropped his hand.

"Does anything make you sick?" Lodi's yips distracted me.

"Only the thought of losing you."

"Now you're making me sick." I followed the sound of trouble to the fish pond, glancing back at him. "Seriously, have you ever been sick?"

He walked with me. "Not from any biological source."

"How is that possible?"

"Do you remember I told you my blood was copper based?"

"Was that before or after you accused me of dehumanizing you?"

He smiled. "To be an efficient conductor, my blood has to be free of impurities. Copper is half of the equation. The other is my DNA, which is resistant to mutation. It allows me to have a highly adaptive immune system."

"So you've never had the sniffles."

"I'd like to."

"Liar." My eye caught Lodi's tail disappearing into the garden shed. "Lodi! Out!"

I ran to the shed and caught him tipping over a bottle of plant food. Scooping him up, I took him outside and closed the door. Putting him on the garden path, I tossed a biscuit in the direction of the pond.

"Thank God I'm not having children."

When I caught Michael's gaze, it was tense again.

"What now?"

"Does that worry you?"

"Give it a rest, Mike." Crumpling the empty biscuit bag, I jammed it into my sweatshirt pocket. "I told you from the start I wasn't interested in kids."

"Sometimes people change their minds."

"What made you think I changed my mine?"

He looked down the path after Lodi.

"The dog?"

He didn't say anything.

"I got the dog because I thought it would make things …" I searched for a word.

"Normal." He finished.

"Fun." I corrected.

Grabbing his hand, I pulled him along with me down the path.

For a while, he was silent.

"Do you think I'm a dog?"

"What?" I stopped.

"When I was stargazing with Dan and Phil, Dan said some women treat their husbands like pets. Then Phil said all men were dogs. Do you believe that?"

"Men are dogs." I nodded.

"Am I like Lodi?"

"You have the same eyes, eat the same biscuits. So far it's a tie."

"I'm smarter."

"Since Lodi can't speak, we'll never know."

"I dress better than he does."

"He's just a pup. Give him a chance."

Michael took my hand. "You don't have to give me a bath."

"I want to."

"I smell better."

Leaning into him, I sniffed. "Definitely."

He moved to kiss me, then froze. "He's in the pond."

Then he was gone.

Running after him, I heard the sound of splashing water ahead of me. Clearing a hedge, I found him, slogging from the pond, holding Lodi by the hind feet.

"Did he drown?" I gasped. "Is he alive?"

Catching my breath, I watched Mike gently squeeze the pup, finally breathing over its snout. It was only seconds before it squirmed, coughing in his arms.

He glanced at me. "That was fun."

Rolling my eyes, I fell on the grass and he joined me, holding Lodi to his chest.

"Like I said, thank God I'm not having children."

He rubbed Lodi's soaked coat. "He's cold. He needs a warm bath."

Getting to my feet, I took Lodi from Mike while he drained the water from his shoes. His pants were muddy and soaked to the knees.

"Looks like you need one too."

"What's my reward?" He grinned.

"I don't know." Pulling the empty bag of dog biscuits from my pocket, I rattled the crumbs inside. "I'm all out of biscuits."

When I left for work the next morning, I was worried. During the night, Lodi came down with a fever. Michael promised me everything would be fine. He would go to the vet first thing and call me to let me know how Lodi was doing. How could I doubt him? He had to know what he was talking about. He always seemed to, anyway. But what did he really know about illness? He'd admitted to never being sick himself. He even told me he avoided saving people, fearing the inadvertent influence such an act could have on the fate of mankind. So what experience did he have when it came to caring for someone who was sick, let alone a puppy?

"Morning, Sophie!" Amy popped her head in my office. She had on a pair of faux fur earmuffs. "Jeez, it's freezing this morning."

"Yeah, fall has arrived." I decided not to tell her about Lodi. "How was dinner?"

Amy beamed. "Awesome. We had eggplant, which I'm normally not a big fan of, but it was soooo good. Tony's mom's such a good cook."

"Yeah, he's pretty spoiled."

"His parents are really sweet." She shrugged. "I think they liked me."

"Who wouldn't?" I folded my hands on my desk and watched Amy looked bashful. "Say, did you get roped into the New Year's ball fiasco again this year?"

"No way."

"Can I rope you into my ribbon-cutting fiasco instead?"

Her face fell and I braced. She dropped her voice to a whisper. "I promised Lyn I'd review her annual budget requests this year instead."

"Shit."

"It was one or the other. I couldn't get out of both."

I clucked mockingly. "And all this time, I thought you were my friend."

Glancing over her shoulder, Amy stepped into my office and closed the door.

"Of course I am, but how do you tell Lyn no?"

"No."

"I'm not like you, Sophie! You saw what she almost did to you. It's a miracle you're still here."

"It wasn't a miracle. It was part of her cunning plan to make my life miserable. So my advice to you is if you really want to get promoted around here, you need to piss her off."

"Forget it. I'm sorry! You know I'd way rather work with you, but I'm already committed. Unless Lyn finds someone else, I'm stuck."

"That's okay."

"You're not mad?"

"Nope, I'll just have to talk to Lyn myself."

466 | LISA MOWAT

"Oh, jeez, no."

"Hey! Give me some credit? I won't be indelicate. I promise I'm not going to get you in trouble. But I need you, Amy. This project needs you, this hospital needs you, and Lyn's just going to have to take one for the team."

Amy winced.

"No troubles. I promise. Hey ..." I tried to distract her. "Are you doing lunch with us at the Swiss today?"

"I was, but they're having flu shot ladies in the break room today at noon and I wanted to get mine."

"Already?"

"That's the policy for hospital staff. As soon as the vaccine is out, we get them. They came out early this year because they ran out last year."

"Yeah, I remember. That's why I didn't get one when I came on board last fall."

"Well, I swear by them. You should get one as soon as you can."

"That isn't your superstition talking?"

"I always get one, and I haven't had the flu in years."

"I never get one, and I haven't had the flu in years."

"Trust me. Working here, you need one. Last year Dan didn't get one and he was really sick for a month."

Thinking about Lodi, I bit my lip. "Maybe I'll join you for lunch in the break room instead."

Michael called before noon. Sounding impatient, he told me Lodi's chills were gone and the vet had prescribed nothing more than a regular dose of baby Benadryl and lots of rest. He pensively asked if I would be working late again but sounded less annoyed when I told him I was coming home early. Satisfied with this answer, he ended our conversation a happier singular than when he started it. It was hard to believe I had so desperately missed him less than two weeks ago.

Still, it was nice to be the one who was missed for a change.

On my way home, I stopped by the liquor store to stock up on essentials. As I loaded the bag of bottles into the trunk, I noticed my left arm was still throbbing from the shot they gave me at lunch. My head was throbbing along with it, so I decided to exchange my plans to make a chicken pot pie for a sweet pie I could pick up on the way. Speed-dialing Anthony's favorite pizzeria, I ordered one thin crust for me and four deep dishes to fuel my husband's highly adaptive immune system.

Guessing they wouldn't be ready when I got there, I parked up the street from the pizzeria and decided to get some fresh air. Wright Park was a block away, and the thought of sitting on a bench under the trees relieved my headache, which only seemed to be getting worse. Pulling my overcoat tight around me, I found my way to the park and pushed into it to get away from the sound of traffic. Even so, I didn't walk far along the gravel in my thin-soled heels.

Finding a quiet bench facing the conservatory, I eased down, pressing my shoulders against the wooden slats.

The breeze was cold. I knew the next seven months would be colder. Putting my head back, I stared through the branches of a great elm and counted the leaves already turning color. A chill ran up my spine, making my body tremble, but I was too tired to feel alarmed. Closing my eyes, only the sound of the trees remained.

I was having dinner at Auntie Maeve's house. The whole family was there. Mom and Dad, the big Gs, Kate, and Uncle Andy, which was odd, because he was dead. We were seated around the dining table as we used to, before death, divorce, and distance made being a family too inconvenient. It was a wonderful dinner, but I don't remember eating. It was a wonderful time, but I don't remember speaking. There were odd noises in the background from time to time. The sound of a car engine. Bright lights would shine in my eyes, seemingly out of nowhere.

There were annoying voices that wouldn't go away. Muffled and incoherent, they interrupted my speechless dinner conversation, gradually ringing in my ears until I was pulled away from dinner entirely. Everything went black.

The voice was a woman's.

"She's fibrillating."

"Is it ready?" A tense man asked.

Another presence came, calm, familiar. "Don't touch her."

"That's it! Call security!"

"You're not using that on her."

The woman's voice again. "Wait ... wait. She's coming back down."

"Get some fluid in her." The tense voice jarred me.

My eyes opened.

I was on an uncomfortable bed, staring at fluorescent lighting. There were no walls, only curtains. I knew the curtains. I was in the ER at St. Joseph's.

"Ma'am? Can you hear me?"

The woman was wearing scrubs with a palm tree print, her hair pulled tight to her head in bleached corn rows. Green eyes, nearly as bright as Anthony's, were searching mine.

I nodded but couldn't speak. My throat was on fire.

"Can you tell me your name?"

Wincing at the pull of the IV in my arm, I pointed to my throat.

"Having trouble?"

I nodded again as she pulled something from my face.

"Do you need some water?"

I nodded.

A hand appeared over my shoulder and handed me a paper cup. As I drank, I felt a kiss on the top of my head. It wasn't until then that I knew whose hand it was.

1199 BC   Late in the night, priests came to the tent and kept vigil over me. They knelt in rows around my crypt, rocking their heads, their lips moving to half-spoken praise for the god I was not. The sensation in my limbs was beginning to return, though beneath my wrappings I doubted my skin had. I knew I was burning with thirst. My tongue moved to my lips, feeling my face bound so I could barely part my teeth.

Honey filled my mouth. They had tended my body as though burned and covered me with it. When the sun returned, my shroud would be the only thing preventing the flies from carrying me off. The thought did not amuse me. If they thought me Re, the ceremony would be held at dawn. Innocent men would die for no reason. I had to stop it. I tried to rest as best I could. Somehow I had to recover enough of myself. As the priests around me made preparations for death, I willed myself to animate what was barely alive.

A great rug on the ground was rolled up and replaced by buckets of sand spread at the foot of my crypt. The lamps were extinguished and the tent dismantled around me. Two fires were built, one at my head the other at my feet. As they caught flame, their fire lit the shields of the general and his guard.

Soldiers formed a ring around us. In the dim, a priest began to sing a call to worship, but this was mere formality. Word of what was to happen had long since passed. Beyond the ring of armed men, a sea of people thronged to see a miracle. If I could rise to deliver one, it would be.

Ptah and twelve of his priests approached in two columns. They bore the implements of ritual slaughter: canopic jars, a bath, and the knife with which to fill it. My sense of the sun told me it was two hours till sunrise. Ptah raised the knife over his head with both hands, offering it for me to witness as I tried to imagine the strength to seize it from him. I summoned the fire within me to break his spell and felt a flicker of life.

The general took his place behind Ptah and knelt. A priest brought forth a folded prayer shawl, which Ptah placed over the general. Placing both hands on the general, Ptah bestowed the word of the people upon him as their lord and agent. He would be their high priest. He would do the killing.

[Spharic. Entry translated from *Kor Dai Maihael*. Mund Dai. d. 755 BC]

2003 On the second morning, everything is silent. It is barely light, and Violet is still asleep. Looking to the nightstand, the pitcher is empty and my throat is dry. Feeling desperately thirsty in spite of the urgent need to relieve myself, I decide to venture out on my own to satisfy both ends. I know my feet are firm. I've already gone downstairs to use the bathroom more than once. Finding the bathrobe Violet lent me, I pull it on. I pick up the pitcher from the nightstand and leave the bedroom, carefully feeling winding steps with bare feet in the pre-dawn light. On the second floor, I count three doors down the hall to the toilet.

Sitting on the freezing seat, my mind impulsively searches for any sign of my husband's presence in an effort to torture me during one of life's private moments. Finding any privacy is challenging enough around a being as hypersensitive as Michael, even more so now that his spirit is without an anchor. Ever since leaving his body, he has stayed close, but now he is even closer.

Last night, he told me he desperately wanted to sleep but needed a body. He asked if I would let him into mine. What could I say? I couldn't very well leave my husband drifting in the breeze when I was tired myself. If I was asleep and he was asleep, who was counting bodies?

But that was last night.

Now it is morning and I wonder exactly where he is in my body. I remember killing Marta, how he used it then. I wonder if he will use it again and when he will leave. If he will leave.

Apparently, he is still asleep.

The thoughts in my head don't wake him any more than the sound of my voice does when he sleeps in the car. Flushing the toilet, I pause at the sink and watch myself in the mirror for any sign someone else is there but sense nothing. With a shrug, I fill the pitcher.

On my way back to bed, I am reminded I am not alone.

–faaa–nook–quaa–ilitmaa–sss–

It is Michael's voice, but the words I can't make out. They aren't words spoken but almost sung. Drawn and rolled, the consonants are too far apart to piece together. Standing in the middle of the hall, I squint at nothing, trying to understand what I am hearing.

–stemetatrol–requaaa–aysuu–spentat–

The words fall away.

–aysuu–spentat–

I wait, but there is silence.

A thump at the front door makes me jump, nearly dropping the pitcher.

The paper.

Parking the pitcher on a hall table, I return to the main staircase and start down to the foyer. My feet are soundless on the carpet. Still I tread lightly. My eyes briefly meet the stares of dead heads on the walls. Backlit by weak light, the dark chandelier hangs overhead like a spider. At the bottom of the stairs, I go to the door. I turn the deadbolt. Cold air runs up my legs as I pull it open.

The paper is on the edge of the porch. Neatly banded, it looks commonplace enough. I doubt our house fire is front page material. My body braces as I remove the rubber band and read the front page. The headline is about the Democratic National Convention and the upcoming presidential race.

My eyes skip below the fold.

KIDNAPPING VICTIMS MISSING AFTER FIRE

Nuts.

I am about to read on when I hear a car and look up at the street. A black SUV has slowed at the top of Prospect and begins to drive down to the remains of our house. From what I can see, it doesn't have any markings and it is too early for a fire inspector. As I step to the edge of the porch, the SUV stays within my sight until it turns onto our drive.

"Who the hell is that?"

Hmm?

"Sorry." I put my hand to my mouth. "Didn't mean to wake you."

Where are we?

"You don't know?"

There is a pause.

I only see what you do, but we appear to be on Violet's front porch and it is freezing … and you don't have any shoes on—Sophie, what are we doing out here?

"Getting the paper."

The paper? It must be five in the morning. Why aren't we in bed?

"I was going to bed. I heard the paper hit the porch and I decided to pick it up."

Going to bed from where? We were in bed when I fell asleep.

"I wanted some water, went to the bathroom, got the water, was on my way back to bed, you started talking—"

Talking?

"In your sleep. You said something like requaysuspentat over and over again."

He says nothing.

"Mike?"

Yes.

"Are you okay?"

Fine. Let's go back to bed.

"Liar. What the hell were you saying?"

Nothing.

"Nothing my ass. Tell me."

It doesn't translate well.

"Bullshit."

There. You have it perfectly. It is bullshit.

"Tell me."

There's nothing to tell.

"Haven't we had this conversation before? You can't stop lying, can you?"
I'm not lying.
"Omitting. Same thing."
Please, Sophie. It isn't worth fighting over.
"Worth fighting over? After everything we've just been through?"
After everything we've been through, can't we spend one night together in peace?
"We did! It's morning now!"
If we must argue, can we go inside? You haven't recovered and it's cold.
"No! We're staying until you tell me what you were saying."
Then I'm leaving.
"Fine! Leave! And don't come back! Find someone else to sleep in!"
Stepping down a couple steps on the porch, I sit down and open the paper. Determined to give him no pleasure, I flip to the sports section and start to read about the last Mariner's game. Letting my eyes drag across every word, I feel the condensation on the steps soak through Violet's bathrobe.

"Hmmm …" I ignore the mist of my breath in the air. "Looks like they'll lose some talent this year."

Michael says nothing. My hands and feet are numb.

"Piniella won't be coming back."

Silence.

"Thank God for Ichiro."

Sophie—

"I'm sorry, are you still here?"

You're freezing.

"Hypothermia, here I come."

It's a ritual plea.

His voice is barely audible in my head.

"Ritual plea?" My head lifts from the paper.

A form of allocution.

"For what?"

You know I violated the law when I married you.

"Are we still talking about ECCO? I thought you were finished with them?"

I only finished with Sam.

"So now you're dreaming about your allocution?"

I wouldn't call it a dream.

My hands drop to my lap, still gripping the newsprint. "But Sarah's been helping us. Doesn't she run the show?"

Not anymore.

"I thought you said you were going to tell them to fuck off."

I did.

"And?"

They're a bunch of intergalactic thugs who plan to do worse than screw me out of my vacation pay.

"If you have to deliver bad news, don't quote me when you're doing it."

Sorry.

"Tell me the truth, Mike. Where do we stand right now?"

ECCO won't stop looking for us until you are dead and I'm in prison.

"I did just ask for the truth, didn't I?"

You did.

I let out my breath. "It wasn't always this bad."

No.

"Where did it go wrong?"

The day I spoke to you in the coffee shop.

"Nah. That wasn't it. It was Easter on Hood Canal with Kate and Duane."

I told you we should have gone someplace else.

"If you hadn't been too chicken to tell Maeve we couldn't go, we might have."

I didn't want to hurt her feelings.

"It's her." I snap numb fingers. "Mom was right. She's cursed. She's death on husbands."

It isn't Maeve. It's me.

"Then I propose you get us out of this mess."

I plan to.

"How?"

I'll face ECCO on my own.

"You're going to fight them?"

Sarah would like that.

"But you don't."

As much as I regret joining them, there was a reason for it. ECCO has served an important purpose.

"There'd be a lot of spilt ketchup."

I can't fight them without breaking the bottle.

"Why do I have a bad feeling about where this conversation is going?"

I'm trying to think of alternatives, Sophie.

"Right now the papers say we're missing. We could disappear."

We would have to die to the world, to your family and everyone you know. I won't let you do that.

"Won't let me?"

Sophie, I came to you because I love you. I love your life. If you left it behind you would give up too much of yourself. You wouldn't be happy.

"So what's the alternative? We die? I'd be happy then?"

You're going to die from exposure first.

"Talk faster."

Sarah thinks we have time, hopefully for me to regain my body. She said with Anthony's help, she can keep you safe here at Violet's before ECCO has time to figure out where you are. They can't read you and they won't expect you to be hiding so close to our old house. Can we go inside now?

I'm about to say no when my eyes catch the flash of a windshield at the bottom of Prospect.

"ECCO doesn't happen to have anyone who drives a black SUV, do they?"

My body stiffens.

"Michael?"

My hands grab the paper in my lap and open it in front of me, blocking my view.

"Michael?" I hiss. "What are you doing?"

It's them.

Taking control of my hands, I carefully peek around the paper. The SUV has stopped at the top of the hill. Whoever is driving remains hidden behind tinted windows. My hand disobeys and pulls the paper up.

"Michael?" I glare at the paper.

Don't look at them. Don't even think of them.

I force myself to read about baseball until I hear the engine rev and fade down the street. Lowering the paper on my own, Michael offers no resistance.

"Did they know it was me?"

If they did, we wouldn't be sitting here. They couldn't read me through you.

"Are you saying I'm thick-headed?"

Ignoring my comment, Michael is distant.

Sarah misjudged. Phanuel is bolder than she predicted.

"Who is Phanuel?"

The one who replaced Sarah at ECCO. He is the most dogmatic of us. Devoted to the law above all else. My very existence is anathema to him. Those were his novices.

"Novices." The word is cultish and makes me shudder.

All members of ECCO were novices at one time. They can't become singularities until they have proven themselves. Except for me; I was never approved.

"Why not?"

I failed my test. I was assumed into a larger entity, one called Bahiel. I reemerged when it came apart.

"You and Sam."

Yes.

"Why did it come apart?"

No one knows.

"You don't know?"

I don't remember. Sam seemed to, but he retained more of our sentience than I did. It took time for me to remember what I was. Sam nearly tricked me into joining with him again. When I escaped, I barely knew myself before ECCO asked me to join them. I was too weak to escape a second time.

"What would you have done if you didn't join ECCO?"

Wandered as a transient, probably hiding from Sam for the rest of eternity.

"Remember I told you my life was as shitty as yours?"

Yes.

"I take it back."

ECCO wants to make your life as shitty as mine, but I won't let that happen.
"So you're going to sacrifice yourself for me? That's comforting."
I would only give myself up as a last resort.
"No!"
For a moment he says nothing.
I'll never risk you again.
"You can't protect me?"
Like I did in the garden? I couldn't even protect you from Marta in our own back-yard. When would I be able to use my crypt? When would I sleep? What would I become if I made myself your guardian every minute of every day?
"They won't be satisfied with your allocution if they want me dead."
Only because Phanuel fears you are pregnant. If I convince him you aren't, he will have no reason to harm you.
"Great." I get to my feet. "I'll take an E.P.T. and you can take it to him. Are you insane! What makes you think you could trust him once he had you?"
Phanuel is struggling to establish his leadership. My allocution would confirm him. That is more valuable to him than your life. Phanuel will be bound to the law. Once he accepts my plea, he will not go back on it.
"No."
I'm not saying it will happen. There might be another solution—
"It isn't any solution, Michael. Allocution is off the table."
Sophie—
"I said, off the table!"
Sophie, please—
"It's freezing out here!" Turning on stiff legs, I stagger up the steps and push through the front door. "I'm going back to bed."
Tossing the paper, I slam the door behind me as though he is standing on the porch.

~

Subject: Lab results comparison

From: Merrill Hansen, MD

Date: 9/25/2000 6:58 AM

To: Sophie Davids

Hello Sophie,

Hope you are feeling better. I'm glad you followed up with me so soon after your trip to the ER. It was good to be able to get new samples and compare that with the ER records. What I can tell you is that your latest results are normal and there is no sign of any infection. Your T cells are slightly elevated, but well within the normal range for cold and flu season.

What I can't explain is exactly what caused the spike in body temperature you experienced last week. The symptoms would indicate an extreme allergic reaction, but to what, the test results didn't show. The samples from the ER were normal aside from a trace read of metals that were likely environmental and non toxic. It's always a possibility that you had an allergic reaction to the flu vaccine you received earlier in the day, but the additives that can cause allergies are too small to read in the bloodstream and are usually limited to injection site irritation.

I know this isn't a very satisfactory conclusion and I don't doubt you were very ill, the ER records don't lie, but for now we will have to add this to the medical mystery column.

If you have any questions please ask. In the meantime, monitor your body temperature over the next few days and call me if symptoms return.

In good health,

Merrill

[E-mail from Dr. Merrill Hansen to Sophie Davids. Sept. 25, 2000]

2000 When the grandfather clock chimed half past four, he was annoyed. He couldn't help it. He did everything he could to make her forgive him for leaving. He had accepted Lodi. He had an insurance policy. He had been fending for himself for dinner every day while she stayed at the office. He even hid his disappointment when she spent her evenings training the animal.

Confronting her in the yard, he tried his best. He tried not to pressure her, to make her feel guilt, to accuse her of neglect. That evening, he let her give him a bath and take what she wanted afterwards. He had hope.

When she said she was coming home early, he thought his hope had been answered. He had proven he was ready to share in the rest of her life without reservations. He had chosen another fate for himself.

But he was still waiting.

If she left the office by four, she should have been home by four fifteen. It was possible she was running errands, but she didn't mention it on the phone. If he called her, she would think him a pest. If he sought her mind, she would think worse.

Wandering into the study with Lodi on his heels, he randomly picked a book off the shelf and glanced at it. *MALESBAN.* Plague seed. She was right; he didn't read for pleasure. Replacing it on the shelf, he circled his crypt, finally sitting on the lid.

Lodi investigated the corner of it.

"No, Lodi."

It didn't look at him but scampered away.

After sleeping most of the day, the animal had made a full recovery. Perhaps that was what he should call her about. Lodi needed another bag of biscuits.

His mind echoed her number and waited to hear if the signal found its mark.

Wireless transmissions took practice. Even now he was never sure of the result. Sometimes his signals weren't strong enough to be read; other times he sent the wrong one and got an entirely different person. Where anyone else might be concerned, phones were unavoidable, but it was frustrating to use such unreliable technology to contact her. Still, he called her on her cell, though now she knew he didn't use one. It was a pretense he accepted, along with everything else.

After five signals confirming his transmission was received, he heard her voicemail. He cut the signal. Her phone would tell her he had called.

His fingers drummed the lid of his crypt.

The clock chimed on the quarter. Four forty-five.

If she was running late, she would have called.

His mind wandered, but not in thought. It wandered out the front door and up the drive. It wandered along the route she would use to come home, his eye searching for a silver Jetta. It saw two, neither of them with her behind the wheel.

Sophie?

Sophie, where are you?

Her mind was there, but typically elusive.

I tried to call you on your cell. Why haven't you called back?

Even without trying, he sometimes overheard her thoughts. Those he heard now were empty, as though she were deeply asleep.

Had she fallen asleep?

Sophie?!

His eye was still searching for her car as it neared the park. It was drawn to the lights of an ambulance. The ambulance was parked under the trees and about to leave. A crowd of people looked on from a park bench nearby. It couldn't be her. What would she be doing in the park?

An elderly woman spoke to a jogger standing next to her. "Was she homeless?"

"No. She was dressed nice. Office stuff."

"Oh, dear." The old woman bent to pick something up. "This must be hers."

He saw it. A suede heel he remembered buying for her.

He heard the ambulance siren start. She was inside of it. What they might be doing to her made him cringe. His vision caught up to it. Entered it. It was a terrible.

She was unconscious, strapped to a gurney with a mask over her face. Her sleeves had been cut away. They were puncturing her, trying to assess her condition, but he already knew. Her body temperature was dangerously high. A call made by the driver said they were a code 4 and headed for St. Joseph's. His vision fled ahead of the ambulance, following the road she took to work every day. Seeing the south end of the hospital, he surveyed the emergency room entrance and hovered above the crush of people inside. There were too many eyes.

Wandering to the restricted access area of the ER, he found a restroom.

It was empty.

When he stepped out, no one noticed. He could already hear the commotion of the medics rushing her into the lobby. Standing along the wall, he waited for them as they came around the corner. They wheeled her into an open bay and pulled the curtains behind them. Silently slipping behind the curtain, he narrowly missed being stepped on by a nurse.

"Excuse me, sir. You have to leave." She glared with fierce alarm.

"That's my fiancée."

No one looked up as the racing beep of the heart monitor sped on. The nurse turned her glare to a young man with a day's growth of beard and bloodshot eyes.

"She's fibrillating."

The young man barked at him. "Out of the way!"

Punching through the curtains, he called for a crash cart. Whatever that was, it didn't inspire confidence. The nurse cut open the front of Sophie's blouse and bra. Red blotches covered her skin. The young man returned with a small device on wheels. Another nurse grabbed his arm, pulling him out of the bay, shutting the curtain in front of him.

Circling to the other side of the bay, he slipped around the curtain to stand unnoticed behind the alarmed heart monitor.

The nurse examined the cart the young man had brought, plugging it into an outlet on the wall. When she switched it on, it hummed like a small transformer.

The man had smeared something on Sophie's chest. "Ready?"

The nurse held two electrodes in her hands.

He stepped forward.

"Don't touch her."

The man's face turned red. "That's it! Call security!"

"You're not using that." His gaze held the young man's bloodshot eyes, meeting rage. And fear. The man's instincts were good. Death was near.

"Wait ..." The nurse watched them nervously. "Wait. She's coming back down."

"Get some fluids in her." The young man barked the directive before disappearing behind the curtain.

He felt Sophie's consciousness returning and went to her side.

The redness in her face was fading.

The nursed leaned over them. "Ma'am? Can you hear me?"

She nodded, but he knew she didn't see him. She had tunnel vision and stared blankly at the nurse.

"Can you tell me your name?"

Sophie's arm moved, dragging a web of tubes and wires with it. It was all he could do to not remove them and carry her away. Instead, he looked for water.

"Having trouble?"

Of course she was having trouble; she was burning up, as were his eyes. Averting his gaze, he perceived a water cooler on the other side of the curtain in the hall.

"Would you like some water?" The nurse asked obviously.

Cup in hand, he offered it to her, feeling her neck. She was recovering but chilled with perspiration. Bending to kiss her head, he sensed the nurse's stare and met it with a smile.

When they said they wanted to keep her for observation, it made his insides turn. All he wanted to do was take her home. Between watching her sleep with tubes sticking in her and alertly avoiding anyone who might recognize him, the last forty-eight hours had been torture. Now, she had been cleared to leave and he was still waiting. He left her in her room to move the car, only to return to Lyn Whittier standing sentinel at the door. Visiting, no doubt. Now, he paced one floor below, contemplating setting off the fire alarm to get Lyn to leave.

Listening to their conversation, he tensed when he heard Lyn say how much she would like to meet him. She wanted to see what he looked like without his clown paint on. The problem was, she already knew. She was the only co-worker of Sophie's who knew Michael Goodhew was the donor for the wing addition to the hospital. Sophie hadn't told Lyn what her fiancé's last name was and Michael was commonplace enough. So far, Lyn hadn't connected the clown who proposed to Sophie in the office with the man she met last January.

He stopped pacing when Lyn said she would be sorry to miss him but couldn't be late for a meeting.

"I'll just have to look forward to seeing him on Halloween!"

His eyes narrowed as he climbed the stairs to Sophie's floor.

When he arrived at the room, a Catholic priest was peeking in the door. "Excuse me, Father." He waited as the priest stepped aside for him to enter. "Pardon me. I was just complimenting her lovely flowers." Stoutly built with thinning hair, the priest was still young in spite of a dog collar.

Sophie was dressed, sitting on the edge of her bed. "Father Wilson, this is my fiancé, Michael."

"Congratulations!" Father Wilson shook his hand warmly. "Have you picked a date?"

He looked to Sophie, who rolled her eyes. If he had his way, they would already be married, but Sophie wanted to marry in April.

"April." He smiled as Sophie shot him a surprised look.

Father Wilson shoved hands in pockets and rocked. "I have blessed *three* fiftieth wedding anniversaries this year and all of them were in April. It is a very lucky month for marriages."

"God knows we'll need all the luck we can get." Sophie grinned.

The priest gave a nervous laugh. "Yes! We could all use more of that."

"Speaking of use." She got to her feet. "I don't really need these flowers anymore. Maybe another patient could use them?"

He frowned at his fiancée.

I brought those flowers for you.

Michael, be charitable.

Smiling, she went to the window sill to remove the card from the vase. "I'm leaving today and they'd just get mangled in the car."

"I'm sure they would be greatly appreciated." The priest held out a hand, then raised it in a placating gesture. "I would be glad to take them to the hospice wing, but you could if you want. It's your gift."

"That's what I'll do." Sophie smiled, giving the flowers a sniff.

"Do you know where our hospice wing is?"

"I do. I work here."

"I thought I recognized you. Are you a care-giver?"

"No. I work for the foundation. Special projects."

"The foundation has been doing wonderful work."

"Thanks. I'm glad you think so."

"Have you been working on the new addition at all?"

"Oh, yes." She picked up the bouquet.

"There's going to be a ribbon-cutting ceremony, isn't there?"

"Oh, yes." She headed for the door.

Father Wilson stepped aside for her to pass. "When is that, exactly?"

"We're aiming for January."

"So soon?"

Sophie stopped in the door and squeezed the priest's arm. "Pray for me, Father."

As she walked away, Father Wilson looked at him with wide eyes. He only shrugged and followed her down the hall.

"I just got an e-mail from my doctor and I don't think he knows what he's talking about. I can't believe I was allergic to a flu shot. That's ridiculous. I had a flu shot when I was in college and I was fine."

She started to cough again and washed it down with coffee.

Observing her from his wingback chair, he savored his relief. She was bundled on the sofa in her bathrobe and fuzzy slippers. Her face frowned in the glow of her laptop, her thoughts trying to recall the last time she had been vaccinated.

"As long as you avoid vaccinations, you'll be fine." He returned to his book.

"I won't be fine!" She glared up from her laptop. "I'll die from bird flu or swine flu or hoof and mouth …" She waved her hands in the air and re-read her e-mail.

"Only close contact with infected animals would place you at risk of getting infected with hoof and mouth disease. Even then, it is never fatal in humans and swine flu, rarely so."

Her brow raised. "Rarely?"

He turned a page. "You'll be fine, Sophie."

"That's it? I'll be fine?"

He turned another page. "What do you want me to say?"

"I don't know! You're the resident brainiac. Do you think I was allergic to a flu shot?"

He turned another page. "Yes."

"How could that be?"

Glancing up, he shrugged. "Vaccinations contain many chemical ingredients. You may be allergic to one of them."

"They couldn't have changed that much from when I was in college."

"Why don't you research it?"

"Thanks. I already have a full-time job."

With a sigh, he closed the book. "Would you like me to look into it for you?"

"Don't let me distract you …" She peered at his hands. "What are you reading?"

He held up the book.

"Is that mine?"

"You said I was in a rut."

"Uh, yeah, but Stephen King isn't much of a leap for you, is it?"

"I'm trying."

"Sorry." She returned to her e-mail, then paused. "But since you're reading about a killer clown, that reminds me. I was going to tell you Friday, but then something came up and I woke up in the hospital—"

"No." He opened the book and resumed reading.

"No what? You didn't even—"

"I'm not performing magic tricks at Lyn's Halloween party."

"You don't get this, do you?"

"Get what?" When he looked up, she closed the laptop and crossed her arms.

"Mike, since we aren't married yet, I feel I can share with you one of the unspoken rules of spending the rest of your life with a woman."

Closing the book, he felt himself sit up in his chair. "What is that?"

"The moment you say no pretty much guarantees you're going to do it."
"I'm not doing it."
"Do you want me to be happy?"
"Sophie, I did that once. It was on a whim and it was risky."
"Nah." She waved a hand at him. "I'm risky. Magic tricks are a walk in the park."
"I got rid of the costume."
"Actually ..." She smirked. "I hung on to it."
His mouth fell. "Why?"
Her eyes bugged. "How could you get rid of it? You wore it when you proposed!"
He said nothing.
"Please?" She clasped her hands. "It's for a really good cause. If you do this for Lyn, I get Amy on my ribbon cutting committee. Pretty please?"
He said nothing.
"Consider it a donation to the hospital."
"I already gave." He said dryly.
"Then I'll give. Name something. Anything."
Narrowing his eyes, he braced. "I want to share your thoughts."
Her lips pursed. "When?"
"When I need to."
"Isn't that all the time?"
"No. Not when I'm with you—well, sometimes when I'm with you. But mostly when you are gone. If you ... if you only ..."
Looking at his lap, he gripped the book in his hands.
"In the park ... if you'd let me in—but you shut me out. I couldn't reach you. Couldn't find you. I was too late."
"You weren't too late. The ambulance—"
"No, Sophie!" His voice shot from him and he felt his eyes flame. "No ambulances! I never want to see you in an ambulance again!"
"Mike." She put up her hands. "It's okay ... relax."
The book in his hands was nearly torn in two.
"I want you to hear me."
She nodded slowly. "From now on, I'll hear you."
"I want you to answer." He whispered.
"I will."
He stared at her.
"Did you hear me?" Her brows went up. "I'll answer."
With a nod, he slumped back in his chair.
She cleared her throat. "So we have a deal? You'll make magic for Lyn, and I'll give you unlimited minutes of phone-free chatter?"
His eyes dropped to the floor.
"Oh, come on!" She tossed her hands. "Is it really that bad? You were having fun with it when I saw you at the market."
"That was different. No one expected me there."

"Sounds like a case of performance anxiety."

His eyes stayed on the floor.

"So what?" She pressed.

"When I went to your office that day, I thought I was safe. I wasn't. I felt like everyone could see what I was." He squinted at nothing. "Like they knew."

"All anyone saw was a clown."

He sighed.

"You seem determined to make yourself miserable."

"I know."

"It's just for one night."

"I know."

"You'll never have to do it again."

"I know."

"I'm always right."

He only stared at the floor, saying nothing.

"See, when you do that, it makes it really hard for me to feel sorry for you."

"I know."

"I love you anyway."

When their eyes met, he beamed.

~

1199 BC The hum of the crowd grew. All around me, I heard voices, saw eyes. They were straining with curiosity, excitement. Fear. For some, this was a familiar rite. For many, the first time they had witnessed an Egyptian temple ritual. It was the first time such a ritual had been held outside a temple. But not without a roof. All of the temples of Re had been open to the air so his progress could be tracked across the sky. It only made them easier to demolish when the age of Aten fell.

By measure, the crowd fell silent. Soldiers on horseback pushed forward as four young men were led in a procession behind. They were dressed in ritual white with drawn eyes and painted lips. They would have been ceremonially bathed and fed a feast the night before, not for their own benefit, but to please the vanity of the god who would receive them. An orange glow in the eastern sky said that god was coming.

Once they entered the circle, guards on foot escorted the penitents between the columns of priests. Lining them before their lord general, the tunics were cut from their bodies and their arms bound behind their backs.

There was no time.

Turning my eye from them, I focused upon my body, burning my will upon it. I felt myself take breath.

The first penitent began to sing his allocution.

Lifting my arms drew whispers from the crowd. Pushing my elbows against the lid beneath me, I strained to raise my head on my shoulders. The mask was heavy, gold gilt on cedar, but I dared not remove it. So long as I wore it, I was a god— without it, a monster. Feeling my spine spasm, I began to bend upright.

The penitents watched me with terror, but the guards stood as statues as the priests knelt, dropping their foreheads to the ground. Facing the crowd, the general began to sing his plea to Re and had not noticed me.

The ground met my feet, the gauze shroud falling from me as I stood. On stiff legs, I moved across the sand to the bronze bath intended to feed me. The first penitent knelt before it as the general stepped behind him, pulling back the chin with one hand, the dagger coming from behind to slit the throat. The general looked up, the last verse of offering slipping his lips.

Seeing me before him, he froze. Beyond the morning chorus of birds, there was utter silence. My own song I could not sing, my bloodless body before him, a rough idol with a false face. There was no time as I held out my hand. Blinking, he looked at the bandaged fingers. He looked at the knife in his hands and dumbly placed it in my hand.

Reaching to my face, I lifted the mask from my head and felt the crowd stir. With barely the strength to hold it, I offered it to him. His eyes stared at my face, eyeless, mouthless, pointless. Blindly, his hands took hold of the mask. As soon as I felt it free of my hand, I turned from him. Clutching the knife to me, I staggered to the crypt, opened the lid, and fell inside.

There was a rush of noise. The shriek of horses and pounding hooves. I saw nothing as the lid lowered over me. When the light seized me, I no longer cared.

[Spharic. Entry translated from *Kor Dai Maihael*. Mund Dai. d. 755 BC]

~~~

2003 *That mannequin looks nice. Why not buy that and be done with it?*
Sophie's focus barely shifts to it before she returns to skimming the rack of jeans before her.

"It's not the clothes, Mike. That mannequin is six feet tall and a sub zero. You could put a potato sack on it and it would look good." She pulls out another pair of jeans and slings it over her arm.

A sub zero?

"Really skinny."

You are skinny.

"Not enough to wear those pants. Besides, I hate white."

You always like it when I wear white.

"White shirts. They make you look tan and highlight your eyes."

White wouldn't do the same for you?

"All those pants would do is highlight my ass."

I always thought your ass looked fine.

She snickers.

What did I say?

"The way you say *ass* like it's just another word."

It is just another word.

"Explains why you never flinch when I call you one."

"Call whom a what?" Sarah calmly asks.

Sophie turns to see her holding a teal dress on a hanger. Behind her is a beaming clerk with an armload of clothes.

"Mike. An ass."

"How true." Sarah nods. "Are we ready to commandeer a dressing room?"

"All that, for me?" Sophie's eyes give the store clerk a once-over.

Sarah removes the jeans from Sophie's hand, hanging them back on the rack.

"You didn't just lose your home, Sophie." Her voice grows wistful. "You lost your wardrobe. A woman cannot live in jeans alone."

It can feel Sophie tense. "Let's get this over with."

Sarah gives the clerk a nod. "We're ready."

They are led to the ladies dressing room, which is surprisingly cramped and ill lit compared to the men's dressing room downstairs. As they are directed to a stall, Sophie's critically eyes the back of the clerk's attire: a pink crocheted sweater, pencil skirt, and platform heels. It can't imagine Sophie wearing anything like it, but is suddenly curious.

The clerk opens the door and waits as Sophie steps inside.

"When you're done, leave everything you don't need. Let me know if there's anything I can get for you."

"Thanks." Sophie watches the clerk carefully hang the items on the hooks along the wall before leaving. Before the door closes, Sarah pops her head in and offers the dress.

"I saw this and thought it was you."

"Looks familiar." Sophie takes it and smiles. "Michael always liked this color."
I still do.
It feels her bite her lip as Sarah closes the dressing room door.
"Don't you have somewhere else you could hide right now?" She mutters.
It isn't possible for me to hide in Sarah, and Violet is too frail. Who else would you suggest? Anthony?
She yanks a pinstripe pencil skirt from a hanger.
"You never said anything about staying in me the whole time." Her temperature rises. "I thought you just needed a place to sleep."
That was before an SUV of novices parked in front of the house.
It feels the chill of air conditioning as her capris drop to her ankles.
"Admit it. You're enjoying this."
It is the only time I experience what it is to be truly alive.
She wriggles into the skirt. The cut of it hugs her waist, arousing It.
"You have a fetish for women's clothing." She fidgets with the zipper before glaring at herself in the mirror. "You like that outfit the clerk has on, don't you?"
You've never worn heels like that.
"I like being able to walk." She examines herself in the mirror.
Are they very difficult to walk in?
"You're dying to find out."
As she steps to the hangers, the skirt hobbles her stride.
This isn't very comfortable.
"Nobody's asking you." She unzips it and slips free, tossing it to a chair.
You don't want me here.
Pausing with another skirt in hand, she looks in the mirror. "Not on the can! Not in the shower! And certainly not in the dressing room! No!"
There are footsteps outside.
"Is everything all right?" The clerk calls over the door.
"We're—I'm fine. Just on my cell, sorry!"
"If you need any help, I'm here."
"Thanks." Sophie scowls at the mirror. "Thanks a lot."
If you didn't talk out loud, that wouldn't happen.
"If you weren't a pooka, none of this would happen."
If I weren't a pooka, you'd still be with Anthony.
"No, I wouldn't." She hisses, stumbling into another skirt. "If you weren't a pooka, we'd be happily married like any other couple."
If I weren't a pooka, we never would have met.
Turning to look at herself from behind, she frowns. "You know what I mean. I mean if you were you, but human."
The desire for such a thing is unbearable.
"Mike?"
Still wearing the skirt, she pulls off her tee and reaches for a white blouse.
Her eyes stare at themselves in the mirror while fingers blindly feel for buttons.

I would be the happiest pooka in the world.
"Can you understand how I feel?"
This isn't easy for either of us, Sophie.
She squints at herself in the blouse. "I told you I can't do white."
You look beautiful.
"I don't have your eyes."
If I were human, I wouldn't have them either.
For a moment, they stare at her reflection. It sees his face in her mind.
"I want to see them again." Her voice is expressionless.
You will.
"I know."
Only two more weeks and I'll be back.
"I know."
I'll leave and everything will be back to normal.
She holds It in her gaze but says nothing.
You always knew I only wanted you for your body.
"I love you anyway." Her vision blurs with tears.
Try on the dress.
Wiping her face, she smiles at herself in the mirror.

"It can't be easy being married to someone who's gone so much."
Nate's voice echoes across the foyer as he follows Sophie into the great room.
"It's just bad timing. For the last couple years, Mike's made a point of staying close to home. Have a seat." She waves to a velvet sofa.
Taking in the room, he looks to Sophie as she claims the settee across from him. "This house is amazing. Are you renting it?"
"Our neighbor's a good friend. She's taken us in."
Nate places his briefcase on the pedestal table, pausing to pick up the photo of Daniel and Anne.
"Great photo. I love old pictures. There's gotta be a lot of history in this place." He grins at her. "If only these walls could talk, huh?"
It feels Sophie scratch her ear. "If only."
"Well." Nate puts down the photo and snaps open the brief case. "I don't want to take up your afternoon, so I'll tell you what your policy covers and we'll go over your options."
"Great."
"We have some good news and we have some bad news."
He takes a seat on the sofa with a sheaf of papers in his hand.
"Uh oh."
Putting up a hand, he places the paperwork on the coffee table between them.
"I don't want to alarm you. It may or may not be a problem. It really depends on what your plans are for the house."
It feels Sophie's brow arch. "Uh huh."

"Your husband spared no expense on his policy, it covered everything, inside and out."

"But."

"There's a question with the fire inspector as to the exact cause of the fire."

Sophie sits up. "That house was over a hundred years old."

"And the inspector's report concluded it was probably an electrical fire, but the intensity of the fire was unusual. There was no evidence that accelerants were used, but that doesn't exclude arson."

"So you think we burnt our own house down?"

"Not at all. It's just the evidence is inconclusive." Nate leans forward and rests his elbows on his knees. "Insurance companies get nervous about cashing out a policy without strings—now, let me finish. That doesn't mean they won't pay, but it does mean they will exercise their right under the terms of the policy to investigate the fire on their own in order to satisfy any concerns."

"I thought they already did that?"

"Those were interviews. They still want to speak with your husband and some other witnesses who gave statements to the inspector. In this case, they'll hire an independent arson investigator."

Sophie drops her head against the back of the sofa.

"I'm being screwed by the devil again."

I told you so.

It winces as she bites her tongue.

"Mrs. Goodhew—"

"Please." Her head pops up. "Call me Sophie."

He smiles. "Sophie. It's unlikely your claim will be denied pursuant to an investigation. It's just it could take some time before you get your money, especially if you don't plan on rebuilding. That's the key here. If you opt to rebuild, the investigation would probably be dropped."

"And that's the good news?"

"You'd be reimbursed on construction costs, plus belongings and expenses to boot. Some homeowners come out with nicer homes than the one they lost by cutting their overhead and managing the construction themselves. I don't know if you have any experience with that, but it's an option."

Tossing back her head, she cackles.

Sophie?

It waits outside the bedroom door.

"Yes, Michael."

I thought you handled Nate very well today.

"What was there to handle? It is what it is."

He likes you.

"You read his mind?

I didn't need to.

"A hunch?"
He liked your dress.
"You wanted me to buy it."
You should wear dresses more often.
"And apparently corsets."
Sophie?
"What?"
Can I come in?
"Not yet."
It's been nearly half an hour.
"Don't push me. I still don't know how you and Sarah talked me into to buying this. Just be grateful I didn't let you experience what it's been like to get this on."
I could have helped.
"You can't help a woman put on lingerie. It ruins it."
I don't see how.
"It's like seeing how a trick is done. I never saw you put your clown paint on."
I didn't think you would want to.
"You were right."
I understand.
"What I don't understand is why you never told me you liked lingerie."
You complained about wearing nylons. I didn't think you would wear a corset.
"If it was what you wanted, I would have."
Really?
"If it gave you pleasure. I always wanted you to enjoy sex as much as I did."
It just wasn't as easy for me as it was for you.
"And now it will be?"
Your body is all I've ever wanted.
"That makes one of us."
It's only for two weeks.
"Two weeks. Right."
Are you ready yet?
"Hey, if I can wait two weeks, you can wait another minute."
Did I pick something that doesn't fit?
"Honey, if it fits it isn't a corset."
Daniel's wife wore one every day.
"Not this one. Are you peeking?"
No.
"Okay. Come on in."
It passes through the door and sees her sitting on the satin bench at the foot of the bed. He thought he knew her body, but in the lingerie he has chosen, he cannot recognize her. The lines of her are sculpted into an hourglass inherently feminine and forbidding: a sculpture of deep red silk balanced on legs drawn long from the garter by black stockings and patent heels that make her nearly six feet

tall. Her skin is pale ivory against the satin choker around her neck. Her hair is the same twisted braid she wore the first night he was with her, but her makeup is something he has only seen on other women. Penciled lips and drawn eyes, arched brows and doe lashes.

She smiles at nothing, brilliant teeth breaking through ruby glossed lips. "What do you think?"

Sophie—

Michael.

When she doesn't speak the name, desire burns within. It asks something It never imagined possible.

May I have you?

She nods.

Passing into her, It feels her open. It tries not to frighten but cannot help making her gasp. Quickly touching her mind, It floods her body with endorphins. Though her eyes remain open, her vision fades as her ears fill with the rush of It.

She has let go.

It rises from the bench seat, testing the feel of the heels under her feet.

Walking to the wardrobe, It opens the door and looks at her in the long mirror. Touching her face, it runs thin fingers down her neck and across the cleavage that peeks over the top of the corset. The rigid boning recollects the asbestos tape It could hardly breathe in the week before. What It sees now isn't bruised and battered, but beautiful and breathing. Her fingers drop to the tops of her thighs, the skin there soft and silken, barely felt with a delicate touch.

Stepping from the mirror, It takes in the whole. The hair, the makeup, the silk, the shoes. All designed with the purpose of making what is naturally beautiful supernaturally so. It is both real and unreal. A pooka and a human. It always found Sophie beautiful. It finds this version of her strangely powerful.

Returning to the bed, It pulls back the bedspread and slides onto the sheets. Letting her hands go freely, It stares at the spray of gathered satin lining the bed canopy and feels the embrace of the corset holding her body rigid. Sophie's mind has become compliant. Her body, that of a doll in the hands of a fascinated child.

It wakes to the sound of a groan as Sophie rolls onto her back. It knows she is stiff after falling asleep. She lifts her head and surveys herself still in her corset. Her hands begin to fumble for a way out.

Thank you.

She blinks a few times and yawns. "Don't mention it."

I always wanted …

"What?"

To possess you.

"I heard pookas are big on that." She pushes up from the mattress.

You used to do this to me all the time.

"Do what?"

Gently charging her hippocampus, she inhales sharply, falling back on the bed. Her eyes blink rapidly. "That's not fair."
Now you know what it's been like for me the last three years.
"Really?" It senses her curiosity.
Now imagine going deaf and blind until you pass out at climax.
"Sounds like last night. It was kinda scary."
Even more so when you regain consciousness but can't move for the next hour.
"Why does that happen to you?"
That is what happens when the body relies on the sentience for life instead of the other way around.
"Was sex with me always so frightening?"
That was part of what I liked about it.
"I'm sorry if I pushed you too far."
That was the part you liked.
"I told you I was evil."
In a good way.
"If that's possible."
It is. You aren't Sam.
"No." She says faintly.
Sophie?
"Hmm?"
Was Sam like me?
"No." Her voice is dull.
You said you thought he was me.
He feels her gnaw on her lip.
Sophie?
"My heart knew it wasn't."
How?
"I could feel he didn't love me."
Overwhelmed with guilt, It struggles to keep it from her.
"Michael?"
It braces, wary of the question she will ask.
Yes?
"I know why you didn't tell me."
Can you ever forgive me?
"If risking me was what you had to do, it was worth it."
That isn't why I didn't tell you.
"I know." She whispers.
It was selfish of me.
"It was very human of you. None of us gets to choose our family."
But we do.
"He was your brother for a reason."
That reason could never justify his existence ... or mine.

Her eyes close. "Don't talk like that."

She doesn't want to think about Sam.

She sits up. Her hands reach for her head and she unwinds her braid. When she turns her head to the side, It catches her reflection in the vanity mirror, her neck and arms silhouetted against the morning glow of lace curtains.

It touches her mind again and feels her breath catch. Her back arches as her head hits the pillow. She wants to get up, but not that badly. It seizes her forcefully this time, feels her flinch and is pleased.

"Michael." She gasps. "Not now."

I'm not finished.

It seems plausible that folly and fools,
like religion and magic, meet some
deeply rooted needs in human society.
—Peter Ludwig Berger

The spiritual realm of demons and fairies was no mere superstition, but an accepted part of many faiths. Tales were passed down through generations and across cultures where illiteracy was common. It was not religion, but theater, popularized by classical Greece and later Rome, which spread tales of supernatural intervention to the masses. Central to this art form was a cannon of plays based on ancient myth, tales of pagan origin, re-enacted for the entertainment and edification of common people. Though plays varied by region, themes were similar, with formulaic plots in which a hero defeated wickedness or won love, often both, with the aid of magic.

In pagan times, the role of the magician was that of a demon or fairy working in disguise and capable of transformation. With the advent of Christianity, such tales were apocryphal, even heretical. Demons and fairies were replaced with mischievous spirits, often played by actors using masks to denote the magical nature of the character. To remove all religious connotation, costumes became ridiculous, and the pretend god made a fool. A prime example was the commedia dell' arte. Stock characters representing the most base aspects of human nature relied on superhuman skills to tell tales of virtue and vice.

One such magical character was Harlequin, or Arlecchino, an amoral and lascivious servant with distinctively demonic qualities. Often played by an acrobat, Harlequin's physical prowess was matched only by his appetite for women and food. He was also capable of magic and traditionally carried a wand, which evolved into a stick, used for transformation scenes or simple slapstick. As a rule, Harlequin always found true love in the character of Columbine, a back talking and disinterested servant girl. In his pursuit of her love, he would find trouble and ultimately redemption.

[Excerpt from *Conceptions of Contemporary Faith*. V. Carpio. d. 1978]

Dearest Brother,

I wanted to send you a note of thanks for making it to my wedding last week. What a party, eh? I'm still recovering from seeing you. You nearly missed the blessed event, but I was relieved to see you, and in costume! I was delighted you kept with the spirit of things. It was Venice after all. Of course, I doubt Venice will ever have as excellent an arlecchino as yourself. Any fool can be an acrobat, but your magic remains unparalleled. In the end you quite thwarted my romance. All in all we gave a delightful performance. True to character, you were too dim witted to finish what you started. I am still ahead of you as always, but never fear, I will never leave you behind little brother.

The day I go to hell, I will take you with me.

[Spharic. Translation of letter from Samael to Michael. d. Feb. 25, 1725]

2000 Curling my eyelashes in the mirror, I sat back to blink before fishing mascara from my makeup drawer. My tongue absently stretched a bubble with the oversized wad of Bazooka in my mouth. I let it snap and leaned into my reflection to brush my lashes, when the bedroom door opened behind me and a clown peeked in.

"Look at you!" I spun around, waving him to me.

Ducking so his wig could clear the door, he was as faultless in costume as in his everyday clothes. I noticed he wasn't quite the same as the day he proposed. His makeup was different. The eyes were larger, the smile more twisted. There was a slight menace. Cocking my head, I judged him.

"Are we an angry clown tonight?"

"Don't push me."

Crossing to our bed, he sat down and stared at his red shoes.

"You're supposed to entertain the guests tonight, not eat them."

"It's Halloween."

"Michael? Are you listening?"

He glanced up. "You look pretty."

"It was cheap. I got the poodle skirt at Goodwill and the shoes at the vintage consignment on Sixth." I blew a bubble between my teeth. "I gotta finish my makeup, but I should probably have you do it. How do you get those lines so straight?"

With a shrug, he stared back at his shoes. "Steady hand."

Returning to the mirror, I started applying mascara. "Don't worry, we'll leave as soon as you're finished. Spending the evening at Lyn's isn't my idea of a ball, either. I just wanted to share your pain."

"Thanks."

"Do you know what tricks you're going to do?"

"You said she liked flowers. I got a bowling ball, but I don't know what to do with it. Static is easy. Light some candles ..." He sighed. "I don't know."

"What about card tricks?"

"Whatever."

"*Whatever?*" I caught his reflection. "You are going to be good, right?"

"Bite me."

"You've been watching too much T.V."

"Am I in trouble?"

Turning to face him, I squinted. "You wanna be?"

I detected a smile under his paint. Crossing the room, I joined him on the bed.

"Did you give Lodi a bath?"

He nodded.

"Did you reward him?"

He nodded again.

"If you're good tonight, you'll get a reward."

"Dog biscuits?"

"Better. Cookies."

"Peanut butter chocolate chip?"

"You got it. Now, let's pull up stakes and get this show on the road."

Lyn's house was in Steilacoom with a high bank view of Ketron and Anderson Islands. We were arriving early so Lyn could coordinate with Mike where he would perform and how long his performance would run. It was a foregone conclusion he was going to dislike this, but his mood worried me. Lyn could be hard to take for the most patient of people, and normally, I would have given Michael high marks for patience. Tonight, however, he seemed different. The thought of unleashing a cranky singularity at a Halloween party didn't have "good idea" written on it.

"Any bets on what she'll be?" I tried to distract him.

"I'm hungry." He mumbled.

As we walked up the driveway, I spat stale gum into her flower bed and dug for another piece in my purse.

"My bet is she'll be a fairy. A witch would be too obvious, and she's too uptight to be anything interesting like a roll of toilet paper."

Michael followed in silence, only the occasional scuff of his oversized shoes giving his presence away. Ringing the doorbell, I concentrated on breaking in my new piece of gum.

A tooth fairy with a beehive opened the door. I turned to wink at my fiancé.

"Michael! I'm so delighted you could do this for me!"

"Just tagging along." I grinned as she ignored my presence.

"Come. Come." Lyn waved us in, appraising Mike. "Is there anything I can take for you?"

He shook his head.

"Can I get you some refreshment? I have punch and plenty of food."

"I'll have a drink." I glanced at Michael. "You want anything, sweets?"

He shook his head.

"That'll be a no." Looking back at Lyn with big eyes, I grinned. "Gin for me."

She smiled. "It just so happens I stocked up when I knew you were coming."

On the way, Lyn pointed to a sublevel lounge opening on the back deck and taking in the view. It was wood paneled and ringed with several sofas surrounding a low coffee table. There were three portrait-sized paintings of clowns on the wall.

"I thought this would be the ideal place for him to perform. There's plenty of room and most everyone will be able to see him."

She went to the bar and filled a low ball with ice before pulling a bottle of tonic from a beverage cooler.

"I'll let you." She handed me the glass. "I don't know how strong you take yours."

"Your guess is as good as mine."

Grabbing the gin, I snapped off the lid and poured to four, leaving the tonic on the counter. Lyn watched tensely as I took the gum from my mouth and stuck it on the rim of my glass before taking a swig.

Licking my lips, I toasted her. "God Save the Tooth Fairy."

"Have you seen our latest fund-raising numbers?" Lyn's brows climbed. "We're facing a thirty percent shortfall. No doubt it's due to this wing addition. People hear about a donor with deep pockets and they decide their gift isn't needed."

"That's possible." I put down my glass and added a shot of tonic. "Have you increased your donor outreach?"

"I'm afraid your special project got the lion's share of the publicity. We have to address the needs of thousands of donors. We don't have the luxury of catering to a single donor for a single gift, as generous a gift as it is. Your ribbon-cutting coming right on the heels of our fund drive is a perfect example."

I popped an olive in my mouth. "Of what?"

"While it is admirable for your donor to make such a gift, the way this project was coordinated didn't take into consideration the far less glamorous, but essential work the annual fund drive does every year."

"I see your point." I washed my down my olive and grabbed some pretzels.

"Of course, I'm not saying any of this is your fault."

"Of course not." I crunched.

"I'm just saying if you need ideas as to how we could avoid these conflicts in future, I would be happy to help with coordinating your projects around our drive."

"Thanks, Lyn." I emptied my glass. "I'll keep that in mind."

"Do have something to eat." She gestured to a table of party trays.

"I'll do that." My eyes pointed over her shoulder. "I think Mike's setting up."

She turned to see the top of his wig roaming below us in her pit. As I poured myself another drink, she went to the railing.

"Is there anything you need?"

I didn't hear a response.

She stepped over to me. "He doesn't speak when he's a clown?"

"He doesn't speak at all." I whispered back.

"*At all?* Really?"

Swallowing a sip of gin, I nodded. "Fire-eating accident."

"*Really?*" She repeated, her eyes wide.

"That's how we met. He was being treated in St. Jo's burn ward when Ringling Brothers was at the Tacoma Dome last year."

"He was with Ringling Brothers?"

I nodded. "He stayed behind. He was too traumatized. It's taken him months to get his confidence back."

"Poor thing! Now I understand why he wouldn't perform for our ball."

"The farmer's market was a big step for him."

"I have to confess." Lyn moved closer. "I've always adored clowns. There's something magical about them—and to find one that's really a magician! I can't tell you how excited I am to have him."

She narrowed her eyes. "Was he the one you were with New Year's Eve?"

My lips smacked as I sucked on a pretzel. "Now you know."

She made a small smile.

Peering over the railing, we watched him dig in a rucksack for props. The coffee table was covered with a black cloth set with a vase of red roses, a book, a bowling ball, and two candles.

"I do hope he does the flower trick again." Lyn whispered.

"Hey, Mike." I called.

He looked up.

"You doing the flower trick?"

Cocking his head, he looked at the flowers on the table and snapped a rose bud from it with a gesture my eye didn't catch. Holding the blossom up, he opened his mouth and dropped it in, slowly chewing it.

"No. Not that one."

Making a face, he fanned his mouth as though what he put in was too hot. Taking a few puffs of air, he carefully opened his mouth.

A perfect rose opened between his lips.

Lyn clapped her hands like a child as he picked the blossom from his teeth and offered it to her. Squeezing herself over the rail, she plucked it from his hand, examining it.

"It's perfect!" She batted her eyes, carefully placing the bloom in her beehive.

Glancing down at Mike, I winked.

Careful, Tiger.

He shrugged and returned to arranging his props. Lyn scurried from my side and down the stairs to join him in the pit. Happy to have the bar to myself, I freshened my drink. A caterer came into the dining area with a platter of sashimi that demanded quality assurance. Another platter of hummus and pita distracted me long enough that I failed to notice Lyn and my husband vanished.

When I did, I roamed the house under the guise of looking for them.

The kitchen was newly remodeled, and in spite of the buzz of the caterers, was clearly used by someone who liked to cook. I snooped down a hall, hung with curio cabinets arranged with vignettes of crystal animals, snow babies, and Precious Moments figurines. That I was capable of recognizing them barely matched the embarrassment I felt for anyone who collected them. Surprisingly, there was no cabinet filled with clown figurines. The living room was airless, with ivory furniture and pale blue carpeting. Lladro sculptures were backlit on the end tables, and a coffee table was decorated with a lush display of silk flowers.

By the time I made the circuit to the lounge, I didn't find the clown portraits so offensive. Standing at the top of the stairs, I paused to watch the early sunset fade over Anderson Island. A curtain of black clouds approached with a storm system blowing in from the south. When the doorbell rang and there was still no immediate sign of my host, I answered it myself.

The Scarecrow and Dorothy greeted me with "Trick or treat." Assuming they were expected, I answered with, "Happy Halloween." Taking their coats, I made an excuse for Lyn and opened what I hoped was a coat closet. A succession of arrivals followed. Two vampires, a nurse and doctor, four witches who brought their own brew, and a pirate.

When I spotted Lyn in the kitchen, I waited patiently for her to finish coaching the wait staff before asking what she did with my husband.

"I put him in the study. If he's out of sight it will make it more of a surprise for everyone. I'll introduce him in about an hour. I wanted to make sure everyone was here and had a chance to mingle a bit before I brought him out."

"Where is the study?"

"It's the door in the lounge, between the two portraits."

"Thanks."

Remembering my husband was hungry, I casually picked up a tray of finger sandwiches from the buffet table on my way to the lounge. A couple guests took a sandwich as I passed. I smiled, gingerly lifting the tray over their heads as I went down the stairs and crossed the lounge to the study door. Turning my side to the door, I reached for the knob, balancing the platter in one hand. I entered the study backward, only seeing what was in the room once I closed the door behind me.

"Good God."

The room was a shrine to clowns.

Walls, shelves, her desktop, the carpet, all beclowned. Behind her desk, the entire back wall of the study was a floor to ceiling display of built-in shelves loaded with clown figurines, dolls, and collectibles. In front of this wall, seated on a chair, was my husband.

Stepping to her desk, I put down the sandwich tray and nodded at the sliding doors to the back deck.

"If we run now, she won't know we're gone for at least a half hour."

"Are those for me?"

"Yeah." I eyed them. "You should probably eat before we bust out of here."

Rising from the chair, he approached the desk and picked up a sandwich. He sniffed it.

"What are they?" I tried to guess from his expression.

"Deviled ham."

Immediately, he started shoving one sandwich in his mouth after another.

"Don't mess up your makeup."

He stopped in mid-chew. "I thought we were running?"

"We are, but I wanted to hold up a few liquor stores along the way."

With a nod, he shoved another sandwich in his face.

"Good thing I brought those. What were you going to eat? Your flowers?"

"I knew you'd take care of me."

I smirked. "I'm surprised Lyn didn't."

His head shook. "You don't want to know."

"That bad?"

"I'm glad you're my owner."

A gust of wind made the lights in the room flicker.

We looked at each other.

He swallowed. "That wasn't me."

"Must be the storm." I looked out the windows. When I turned, my husband seemed frozen.

"What is it?"

His eyes stared with a faint glow.

"Mike, you can't do that dressed like that."

"Sorry." His eyes focused on me and he seemed to come alive again.

"What is it?"

"Nothing."

He reached for another sandwich and stuffed it in as I watched skeptically. Feeling like another drink was in order, I turned for the door.

"Sophie?"

"Hmm?" I spun around.

"Would you be my assistant tonight?"

"Sure." I paused. "You're not cutting me in half or anything?"

"Not without your consent."

"You'll never get it."

"Then I won't do that one."

"Okay. I'm just gonna get a drink—"

When I turned away, he caught my arm.

"We need to practice."

"I'll need a drink."

He didn't let go. "There isn't time for that. You'll need to remember your cues."

"Gin sharpens my memory."

"Lyn will be back. Ask her to bring you one."

My eyes bugged. "Ask Lyn to bring me a drink? Are you kidding?"

"Then tell her I need one."

"Cut the crap." I pulled his hand from my arm. "Why can't I go out there?"

"You can go—"

Without a word, I moved for the door and a hand caught me again.

"What?!"

"If I'm with you." His eyes met mine and I knew it was no joke. "Trust me."

My gaze dropped from his dead stare to the hand on my arm.

It let go.

~

1199 BC It was a rare occurrence for me to lose time. Usually something unforeseen and untoward was the cause. This was a fair description of circumstances. When I woke in silence, the sun only told me it was early in the evening and my location remained unchanged. With a breath, I was relieved to feel my heart, the blood restored to my veins, the skin to my body. My vision pushed beyond the walls of my crypt and saw the inside of a tent, lit with lamps. The sand was gone and the rug spread under a banquet table laden with food. Seeing the food, I opened my crypt.

The smells of roasted game, fresh breads, and young fruit filled the air. There was a chair draped in gold and silver cloth, but I ignored it. Quickly approaching the table, my eyes assessed the supply of food as sufficient. For the first time in my existence as a human I would not be hungry. Eating where I stood, my pace quickened, spurred by a curiosity to know what it would feel like to be full.

"A fine god you make."

The general was peering in the tent at me. Pausing, I looked around for the first time, self-conscious of my lack of caution.

"May I enter?"

When I nodded, he stepped inside bearing a gold pitcher and bowl.

He read the question in my eyes.

"I came to wash your hands and feet."

I glanced at my hands, covered in meat drippings and dusted with bread crumbs.

"I will wash them when finished." I resumed eating.

He approached slowly and placed the pitcher and bowl on the table.

His eyes went to the chair. "They do not fit?"

Reaching for a cistern, I moved to fill a goblet, but the general stopped me to fill it himself. For an instant, I feared it was blood. With relief, I could smell it was wine.

As he offered the goblet, I met his gaze.

"What happened to my clothes from before?"

"Those belonged to Khepera." His eyes went to the robes on the chair. "These belong to Re."

Swallowing the wine, I did not taste it. "I am not Re."

"They are but rags, but the best I could do."

"I want my old clothes."

"Those belonged to Khepera."

"So you named me."

"Now, I name you Re."

My insides turned, neither hungry nor full.

"You do not own me."

"Only keep you."

Dropping the goblet, I seized his neck. "No more!"

He gasped as I felt his body yield.

"Then the men you spared will be stoned." His words wheezed under my grip.

"Why?"

"They live at your will and at my direction. If you abandon us, I will be deposed for failing to keep favor with you. Ptah will order their deaths to atone for it."

I released him but held his arm to steady his feet. Crossing to the chair, I tossed the robes to the ground, leading the general to sit.

"You must tell him I am not Re and there will be no curse. I am leaving."

"Ptah will not accept it."

"Why not?"

"He needs you to be Re too badly. After witnessing your intervention, people are undecided as to what you are. Some think you are Re, others a daemon. Even now, the men you spared are detained. The people are fearful since your disappearance. If they find you are not Re, they will blame me for bringing you into our midst."

"You should be blamed! If you had left me, none of this would have happened!"

The general smiled gently. "You know that is half true. Since you have ridden with me, you could have left at any time but did not."

Saying nothing, I only stared at the floor.

From his seat, he reached down to the goblet. Refilling it, he offered it to me. "It is no easy thing to be alone."

[Spharic. Entry translated from *Kor Dai Maihael*. Mund Dai. d. 755 BC]

2003
"Hello?"

"Auntie Maeve? It's Sophie."

"Sophie! Sweetheart! How are you? Did you get my message?"

"Uh, no."

"I think I left it on your cell—or it might have been at your house? Do you have an answering service for your landline?"

"No."

"Well, that answers that. It was your cell."

"What was it?"

"Your father tried to call you two weeks ago and didn't hear back so he called me. He was very worried about his only girl and I assured him you and Michael were probably away on vacation now that summer is upon us. Anyhow, I promised him I would check up on you myself."

"I see."

"Was I right? Did you and Michael disappear on some romantic getaway?"

"We disappeared."

"Where to?"

"Do you watch TV? Get the paper? Surf the net?"

"I watch those *Law & Order* marathons, but I watch PBS most the time. I stopped getting the paper years ago. The news is so depressing. My therapist told me to cut out unnecessary stress in my life, and the paper never lifted my spirits, so I decided it had to go—*Good heavens!* You weren't in the paper were you? Were you in an accident? Are you all right?"

"No ... no accident. We're fine. We've just been really busy."

"Thank God. Well, that is the way it is this time of year, isn't it? Of course, life does get more complicated when there are two of you."

"Of course."

"Kate and Duane just put in a huge vegetable garden. They want to grow everything fresh for little Mike's baby food. I told her it was too late in the year, but she said they put in fall crops. I suppose it's never really too late to grow something if you know what your planting."

"How are they?"

"Starting life as a family unit. This week they were at some retreat put on by Duane's church. Counseling and classes for new parents, that sort of thing."

"Good for them. Have you heard from the big Gs?"

"Got a post from Bolivia. Mom sent it, of course, Dad's always been too tight for stamps. They finished the first leg of their eco tour on the Alti Plano, then it's Maachu Picchu and the Galapagos."

"Sounds exciting."

"They didn't sound impressed, but then again, spending that much time together, I doubt anything short of a military coup matches the fire fights they have."

"How can they stand it?"

"Peas in a pod."

"They hate each other."

"Deep down they care about all the same things. That's what holds most couples together. Love isn't enough."

"It isn't?"

"Well, I'm hardly an expert."

"Just tell me what you think."

"I think love is a very selfish thing. Whereas, caring makes you put up with someone when you don't love them, and since it's impossible to love someone all the time, caring gets you through. Mom and Dad care for each other in a way they never will for anyone else, not even us kids."

"Did you ever have that?"

"I like to think I did. I don't think my marriages lasted long enough to know."

"But you went through hell with Andy."

"I did, but it wasn't the same as being married to someone for fifty years. When cancer happens, you don't have time to decide if you're going to be a hero or not. Time lets you rationalize things ... right and wrong fade away. It's easy to get bored."

"I don't think Mike and I are there yet."

"I should hope not! You should still be getting to know each other."

"Oh, we are."

"So when will you and Michael be up to Bellingham next?"

I pause.

Two weeks.

"Michael thinks two weeks."

Maeve makes a thoughtful noise. "We may have sun this July. Hopefully more than the miserable three weeks we got last year. We had that wonderful Indian summer two—was it two years ago?"

"Three years ago."

"Your memory's better than mine."

"I got married that year."

"Yes, of course! It was warm into October ... the most beautiful full moons. How is Michael by the way?"

"He's fine."

"He certainly is. Every time I think I remember how handsome he is, I'm wrong. There's something about him I always forget. It's the strangest thing. Not the eyes though—good Lord, those eyes. I don't think I've met a more attractive man."

My voice wavers. "I'll make sure he doesn't know it."

"My dear, I doubt he would care. That man is in love. He'd make a complete ass out of himself for you."

"He's good at that." I whisper.

"Are you on your cell? Your voice seems to be fading."

"Yes." I clear my throat. "I'm calling from a friend's. Can I'll call you back?"

"Of course! A man's coming to look at a car. You remember Kate's old Saab?"

"Who forgets an orange Saab?"

"I ran an ad on it and I think I've found a taker. He goes to Western and it needs a student. Anyway, he should be here any time now."

"Good luck."

"Bye, bye, sweetie. Tell Michael I love him."

"I will."

Hanging up, I lean against the kitchen wall, staring at nothing.

Sophie?

"Hmm?"

You all right?

"Why not?"

Are you upset no one knew?

"Relieved. This would be hard to explain if Mom and Dad still lived three streets from here."

You should call your parents.

"I will."

Are you going to tell them what happened? At least what the papers said?

"Probably. If Wayne hadn't moved to San Diego he would have called Dad right away. Sooner or later someone Dad knows is going to ask him."

They'll be worried.

"No kidding."

Tell them we're coming to Hawaii in two weeks.

"I thought we just told Maeve we'd be in Bellingham?"

Tell her to come with us.

"Is ECCO coming, too?"

ECCO can wait.

My eyes drop to the kitchen floor. A deep crease in the linoleum exposes gouged wood underneath. Even after they wiped away Marta's blood, the planking is stained black with it.

Sophie.

Something pulls my gaze from the floor.

Trust me.

Violet steps into my line of sight as she enters the dining room on her way to the kitchen. Her black eyes pierce mine.

"Morning, Danny. Had some breakfast?"

Bald terry slippers scuff the floor as she passes me to the refrigerator.

I've stopped telling her not to call me Danny.

"I made coffee."

She gives me a look over her shoulder. "You still put bourbon in it?"

"Knew I was forgetting something."

She eyes me. "You keep starving yourself, you won't keep your looks like I have."

I smile and come up behind her as she pulls eggs from the refrigerator.

"Let me help."

"Tell me what you want and sit. Only room for one spoon in this kitchen."

Putting up my hands, I return to the kitchen table. "That's cool." My eyes catch the gouge in the floor and I pull a chair over it. "I'll have an egg." I sit down.

I need five at least.

"Make that two eggs."

Two?

"And toast if you have any."

"Toast I have." Violet bends over to pull out her frying pan. "Bought a box of bread after Michael moved in. Thought it would only last me a week the way he ate, then he tells me he won't be back for two weeks."

"He told you?"

She hears me when I speak to her.

"His voice came the night of the fire and I was relieved to hear it, believe me." I watch her carefully open a bag of bread and load the toaster.

"Is there anything I can do for you today? You need groceries?"

She opens the egg carton. "Anthony's getting my groceries now."

"Anthony?"

"He came by when you and Sarah were shopping. Real charmer." Her hand strikes a match. "If I were fifty years younger, I'd cook for him every night."

"He'd still take you up on that."

With a grin, she lights the stove. "He's got your eyes."

"My eyes are brown."

Putting the pan on the stove, she pauses.

"You had the most beautiful green eyes."

I scratch my ear.

"But he isn't as tall as you were." She retrieves a butter dish. "He doesn't have your dimples, either. You were a good-looking man."

"Hey, Violet?"

"What?" She turns to me.

"You got any bourbon?"

She cackles and returns to the stove to crack two eggs in the frying pan before crossing to the dish rack for a plate.

"I told him whenever he wanted a home-cooked meal to bring the groceries and I'd do the rest. He asked me what I needed and I told him nobody fries chickens better than me, so save your appetite."

Fried chicken?

I smile. "Michael loves chicken."

"Well, if he isn't here, he'll be missing out."

I'm not going anywhere.

"You're sure there isn't anything I can do to help?"

Violet turns to me with two fried eggs on a plate and sidesteps to the toaster as four pieces of toast pop up. "Do I look like I need help?"

506 | LISA MOWAT

The first day of summer slips away before us. Everything on the street is familiar. The smells of car exhaust mix with someone's charcoal grill. The sound of music from an apartment window, the bark of a dog.

I am reminded of Lodi. How happy he was to see me. Hopeful. When I entered Anthony's apartment, he thought I was there to take him home. He wouldn't understand what happened if I did. Why it was gone.

"Where are you going?" Anthony stops at Violet's front gate, but I keep walking.

Where are you going? Michael echoes.

"To the house." My feet take me down Prospect.

"I don't know if that's such a good idea." I hear Anthony's feet catch up with me.

This isn't a good idea.

"I want to see it."

"There isn't much to see."

There's nothing there.

"Look, I lived there longer than anyone. If I want to see it, I'll see it."

Neither of them says anything more as I stride down the street.

Near the top of our drive, my eyes fix on the blackened tree branches that mark the spot. I stop to watch the last rays of sunlight illuminating the turnabout, rays that used to flood our dining room with rose hues now scattered on gravel and ash. The foundation walls and chimney stack are all that stand. Crossing over yellow hazard tape staked across the front of what used to be our house, I stand on the soot-covered slate of the front stoop. Beyond, a broken sea of charcoal.

My memory pieces together what used to be. The first time I stepped onto the derelict porch, the day Michael displayed his handiwork as an interior decorator, the last day I locked the door behind me. Then I remember trying to leave. I remember Michael barring my way, terrifying me.

He won't let me go.

That wasn't me.

"I know." I breathe to myself.

Poking with my foot, I nudge the blistered fragments of our front door, rummage through the cinders with my feet.

"Be careful; that floor could give." Anthony follows in my wake. "Sophie, what are you doing?"

Two yards to your left.

Following Michael's direction, I move left and kick at the charred wood.

Right in front of you.

Sitting on my heels, my fingers reach into the debris and sift through ashes.

"You find something?"

That's it. You just touched it.

My fingers trace the round edge of a coin, but it isn't metal. Picking it from the dust, I blow and wipe it with the hem of my shirt. A residue of ash stains the engraved symbols in black relief against the white polish.

Holding the amulet to Anthony, he takes it from my hand.

"When you returned it, I left it on the console by the door."

He squints at it. "This was from the safety deposit box."

"You wouldn't let me keep it."

He wouldn't let you keep it?

Anthony nodded. "Wouldn't have made sense if the kidnappers took your ring but not that."

Getting on my knees, I fish some more, finding melted coins, the remnants of a watch, but no ring. I look around, trying to see where walls once stood. There is the vague indication of footprints and a rut where something was dragged. It leads away to the study. Rising to my feet, the idea of rebuilding takes hold in my mind—the idea of leaving nothing but a scar behind, offensive.

"What are you thinking about?"

Without looking in Anthony's direction, a sigh parts my lips. "Rebuilding."

He snorts. "I can't help you there. All my connections are on the force. I'm not related to anyone in construction."

Smiling at him, I put a hand on my hip. "Do I look like I need help?"

He returns the amulet to me. "No, ma'am."

I put out my hand and he drops it in my palm. I pocket it.

His eyes dart around as he reaches for my hand. "C'mon, it's getting dark."

Wait.

"Wait." Gripping his hand, I stop him.

There is the barely perceptible sound of a car coming down the road.

Hide!

Michael's voice is deafening in my ears. I'm already dragging Anthony from the turnabout.

"What are you doing?" His weight stalls me.

My eyes go to a screen of trees. "Mike says hide!"

"Mike says hi?"

I glare back at him. "*Hide!*"

Suddenly Anthony is pushing me ahead of him.

Ducking behind a rosemary hedge, we scramble to a row of twisted madronas.

Don't look at them.

Anthony presses his back against the flaking bark and peeks over his shoulder.

"Anthony!" I whisper up at him. "Don't look."

"*Shhh!*" He puts a palm in front of my face and I smack it away.

Pull him down!

My hands grip the front of his shirt, yanking him off his heels.

He slips and falls on his ass.

"*Jesus!*" Anthony braces against the trunk. "What the hell was that?"

I glare at him. "Michael thinks you should sit down now."

Ask him if it was a black SUV.

"Mike wants to know if it was a black SUV."

"Tell him he can look for himself."

"Anthony!" I hiss.

"Yeah, a black SUV."

We're leaving.

"Mike says we're leaving."

My muscles spasm and suddenly I'm running through the brush in a crouch.

"Sophie!" Anthony's stage whisper doesn't stop me.

"We can't leave him behind." I mutter. "Michael? Are you listening?"

My body slows. I find myself lightly balancing on a narrow log bridging a drainage ditch.

"Michael?"

The sapling log sways under my feet. I sense his indecision.

"If you can't make up your mind, can we do it somewhere else?"

"Police!" It is Anthony's voice. "Stop right there!"

Shit. Mike and I think at the same time.

Switching my footing, I lightly leap from the log and start back up the slope. My eyes focus far ahead of me as the leaves of branches sting the skin on my arms. In moments, the turnabout comes into view, a black SUV is parked with doors open.

All I see is Anthony's back to us. One hand holds out his badge while the other is tucked at his side. I can't see it, but I know he is gripping his gun. Two figures face him, standing near the edge of the rubble. One is a man, the other a woman, her blond hair glowing in the dusk.

My breath catches. "Raphael?"

The man and woman look at me as Anthony steps back, giving me quick glance.

"Sophie, get back."

"It's all right, Anthony. They are known to me."

I sound like I'm on methadone.

Anthony stares at me like I have something growing out of my head.

Could you make me sound slightly less ridiculous?

"Michael?" The woman steps forward, her blue eyes burning into me.

Slowly, I feel myself smile.

As with the end of days, so summer will wane.
In the last days of the waxing moon,
What has passed will be present,
What is present will be past.
The future will be set.
What will die must be given.
What will live must know death.
For death will walk among you.
In winter, death will call you home.

[Latin. Translation from Druid script
The Golden Hymns. d. 444 B.C.]

2000 His hand didn't want to let go, but Sophie's expression said enough. "I'm sorry." He let go.

She glared at him. "What's going on?"

"I think a pooka has crashed Lyn's party."

Her arms crossed. "I thought we agreed you were going to be good."

"Not me. I was invited."

Her arms fell to her sides. "Another pooka? They crash parties?"

"Halloween parties are a favorite."

"Does it know you're here?"

"I think so."

"I thought they tried to stay away from you."

He shrugged. "Maybe this one has something to tell me."

"Is anyone in danger?"

"Everyone."

"Ah, God." Sophie put her hands over her face.

"I told you this was risky."

"You could have said no!" She tossed her hands in the air and paced the floor.

"I did."

"Not like you meant it! Why didn't you tell me Lyn could get killed?"

He tried to think of how he could have shown less enthusiasm.

"I thought it was what you wanted."

She paused. "You thought I wanted Lyn dead?"

"Of course not." Her question appalled him. "You wanted Amy on your committee."

She looked relieved.

"I'm not a monster, Sophie."

"No. You're not." She covered her face again. "I'm sorry. I thought … I didn't know … I just wanted—"

Anguish washed over her. He went to her, reached for her.

The study door opened and he froze.

"Oh, good! You found him!"

Lyn stepped inside, quickly closing the door behind her. "I changed my mind about the timing. Perhaps we should have two shorter appearances? One now and one later?"

Sophie turned her back to Lyn, wiping her eyes with the back of her hand. Lyn frowned and looked at him inquiringly, but he couldn't say a word.

"Is everything all right?"

Sophie cleared her throat and turned with a smile. "Fine."

Lyn searched her face skeptically.

"Just thirsty." Sophie sniffed. "You were saying you changed your mind?"

"I was thinking I could introduce him now—"

"Great idea!" Sophie cut her off with a glare. "Let's get this over with."

He stared at Sophie, his mind straining to make contact but finding nothing.

"Right, then." Lyn seemed peeved. "I'll introduce you."

Nodding at him, Lyn left the room. He heard her voice through the door calling for everyone's attention.

"Sophie?" He stood in front of her, bending to get her to look at him. When he found her eyes, they were dark and hard.

"I'm fine." At the sound of his name, she glanced at the door. "You're on." Backing away from her, he turned to the door and reached for the knob. He hesitated, closing his eyes.

A hand touched his shoulder and he glanced down at it.

"I'm right behind you."

When he opened the door, his mind cleared. His ears registered applause and his body responded with a deep bow. When he lifted his head, his face was smiling as his eyes stalked the room. Seeing past the costumes, he saw only flesh and blood underneath. Theatrically standing on his toes to see over heads, he put his hand over his eyes as though looking over a great expanse. He saw nothing.

Turning to Sophie, he introduced her with a graceful bow and a thought. *Have Lyn inspect the cards.*

Sophie went to the cards on the table while he displayed he had nothing up his sleeves, goading a policeman to frisk him. There was laughter and heckling. A woman in lederhosen quickly volunteered, surprising him from behind, groping him to the amusement of others. She chased him around the room before he fended her off with a squirt gun he stole from the policeman.

They all laughed at him. Drunk people. The air filled with a buzz of random emotions, desires, hungers … His eyes kept moving, trying to see through it all.

Cautiously returning to the coffee table, he passed the squirt gun to Sophie, pointing at the woman in lederhosen. Sophie nodded, aiming the gun at her stoically while he shuffled the cards.

The card tricks followed a single theme: a sketch in which every trick failed because the cards reshuffled themselves when he wasn't looking, jumped from his pockets, or stuck to his fingers, forcing him to conspire with volunteers from the audience. They finally flew into the air, fluttering like butterflies. As the cards drifted to the floor, he looked at Sophie and pointed at them. She smirked and crossed her arms, shaking her head.

The audience applauded, the ebb and flow of their emotions falling into a steady rhythm. All the while, he held Sophie in his mind and tried to read the field of energy that surrounded them. There was no direction to it. No sense of intent. No sign to tell him where to look.

The flowers were next.

Sophie. Follow me with the flowers.

Gathering the roses from the table, Sophie followed him around the room as he began to systematically hand one to each woman he saw. He flirted with Lyn, groveled to a queen, was manhandled by four witches, and teased a man in a football uniform while wooing a cheerleader. When he came to a woman dressed as a Chinese bride, he waved his hand in front of her veil, testing if the wearer could see him. Shrugging to the audience, he held a rose before her and waited. The silk sleeves of the gown shuffled as a woman's hand emerged. When she accepted, he stepped back and bowed to her. When he stood, she still held the rose to him.

Before his eyes, it began to blacken and wilt.

The audience gasped as he froze.

Sophie, go the study door and stay there.

Feeling Sophie slip away, he kept his focus, snatching the wilted flower away.

Holding the rose up to the audience, he let it dangle from his hand. He tried to raise the blossom with a finger and it drooped lifelessly. Forcing a charge into it, he pretended to coax it with his breath.

With each puff, it lifted its head, finally glowing with color.

Turning back to the specter, he offered it again. A sigh of wind seeped into the room as the storm moaned outside. People shifted uneasily on their feet.

The rose sparked in his hand, flaring to a brilliant point of light.

It was no flame, but a thought, bent on destruction.

With singed fingertips, he put his head back and dropped the incendiary bloom in his mouth. It snuffed in the ice of his breath with a puff of steam. Returning his focus on the creature before him, the only smile on his face was painted on.

A nervous scatter of clapping broke into excited applause.

A howl of wind made the sliding glass doors rattle and the house shuddered.

The lights flickered a charge in the atmosphere pricked his skin.

Then, the room went black.

He lunged.

Hands clawed at his wrists. Flooding the room with his static, he tried to drown the threat of fire in the air. His hands found a throat, feeling for a pulse under his fingers, the life of the thing in his grasp. Letting himself go, his eyes filled with light as he began to burn It from the inside out. It began to shift in his grip.

There was a beastly howl.

Adrenalin flooded Sophie's mind. He saw her engulfed in flame, black with smoke. The vision horrified him. Entranced him. Distantly, the crush of confused partygoers reached his ears. A violent jolt went though him followed by the sound of shattering glass.

Sophie!

The thing kicked him savagely as his grip slipped.

He was staring at the ceiling.

Suddenly aware of his surroundings, he sat up. The lounge was deserted in the dark. Floor-length drapes snapped in the wind, snagged on an overturned sofa. Shattered glass glittered on the carpet.

"Michael! Are you okay?"

Sophie stood over him, shivering in her angora sweater, saddle shoes, bobby sox, boy-cut panties.

"Where's your skirt?"

She shuddered. "Fire-eating accident."

He jumped to his feet, holding her arms. "Were you burned?"

"Just the skirt. That'll teach me to buy used clothes again."

There was the sound of movement in the house. His mind searched for the lights and momentarily they flickered back on.

"What on earth just happened?" Lyn peeked over the dining room railing.

A pirate stepped into the lounge to survey the damage but seemed to be surveying Sophie in her underwear. She was oblivious, staring at where the thing had stood. He went to the spot and knelt to examine the evidence. The Chinese bridal gown lay untouched in a pile on the floor. The veil rolled away, like a tent in the wind. Picking up the gown, he handed it to Sophie.

"Put this on."

"I thought you liked my costume?"

He smiled as she took it. "Too much."

"I thought you said he was mute?" Lyn's voice came up behind them.

Clutching the bridal gown, Sophie only shrugged as she walked away.

"I just didn't have him turned on all the way."

"I was afraid to." His voice pulled Lyn's glare from Sophie's back.

"Afraid?"

"To speak—after my accident."

Lyn put her hand on his arm. "Sophie told me. I'm so sorry."

"Don't be. If you hadn't invited me to come tonight, I wouldn't be talking."

"What?"

"The wind storm must have frightened me enough."

She looked incredulous. "You think *this* was caused by the wind?"

"I used to see this when I performed in the Midwest. Sometimes large storm fronts create small twisters. They aren't as big as tornadoes, but extremely powerful, appearing and disappearing in moments."

"Unbelievable!" Lyn put a hand to her chest. "One minute you're a mute magician, now you're a meteorologist."

"Was anyone hurt?"

He glanced at the guests beginning to mill around the house.

"Bumps and bruises. Some people got stepped on. Are you all right? You were in the thick of things." Lyn's eyes searched the room. "What happened to the woman whose rose caught on fire?"

His eyes dropped to the floor and a scorched pair of shoes.

"She didn't like my tricks."

"What is that?" His eye caught a red mark on the back of Sophie's thigh.

She followed his gaze and looked down at her leg. "No biggie. I got a little toasted when my skirt went up in smoke."

Jumping from bed, he took her by the shoulders and steered her to the bathroom.

"No, Mike." She pushed against him. "It's fine. I already checked it out. It's nothing—a singe."

514 | LISA MOWAT

"People die from those."

"No, they don't—" She paused. "They do?"

"Why chance it?" He kept pushing.

"You are such a liar. Can we just go to bed?"

Shepherding her through the bathroom door, he flipped on the lights and got on his knees to get a closer look. She was right. It wasn't a serious burn, little more than a scald, but it had to hurt.

Putting his mouth near her thigh, he breathed on her skin.

She shrieked.

Turning on him, she backed away, crouching to hold the backs of her legs.

"What the hell was that?"

"I thought I could numb it for you."

"Numb it? You could freeze my ass off doing that!"

"My breath isn't that cold."

"Are you kidding? Superman's got nothing on you."

Slumping back on his heels, he sat on the floor. "He's a better person than I am."

"No." She crossed her arms with a frown. "He isn't."

"I don't think Lois Lane ever got burned."

"I doubt Lois Lane would agree."

"Are you sure you want to marry me?"

"No! Can we go to bed now?"

She started out the door, but he caught her wrist.

"I'm serious."

"Good thing you took off the costume."

"You were kidding at the party." He stared up at her. "You didn't really think I would kill Lyn, did you?"

She sighed. "No, Mike. I know you'd never do anything like that."

"You know I've killed people before, but only when I had no choice."

Looking away, she patted his hand. "No more bedtime stories. Let's go."

"Do you believe me?"

She glared down at him. "Is it because it's Halloween?"

"I'm scared."

"Of the boogie man?"

"Of everything. Of you, of me, of that thing at the party."

"That thing at the party? I thought you said it was just a pooka?"

He swallowed, dropping his eyes. "It was."

"Then what's to worry about? You took care of it."

"Did I?" His voice was barely a whisper.

Facing him, she opened her palms. "Give me your hands."

He put his hands in hers and she knelt in front of him, looking him in the eyes.

"Will you marry me?"

"Do you want me to?"

"Just answer the question already."

He hesitated.

"No?" She started to her feet.

"Yes."

"I'm sorry. The toilet was running. I didn't hear that."

"*Yes.*"

"Fabulous! I made the offer, you accepted, we have a deal. Now I'm going to bed. Are you coming or do you want me to bring you a pillow?"

She got to her feet and waited, but he didn't feel he could move.

"I'll let you breathe on my thigh." With a wink, she left.

He got to his feet.

1199 BC   The general left to find me simple clothes to wear. If I was going to play my part, he would let me dress as I pleased in the privacy of my own tent. As the only mortal allowed to see me, he would be my only visitor. A constant contingent of guards would keep all save the general from entering. It also meant I could never leave. The only exceptions to this rule would be when I was transported in my crypt or made a ceremonial appearance before the priesthood.

Even then, I would wear the vestments of Re. I would wear the mask of Re. No mortal would ever see my face. Too look upon it was to burn in the sun.

I did not want to be Re.

When he returned, he found me seated on my chair, staring absently at the table littered with food. I would not know what it felt like to be full. He offered my tunic and I began to dress in a trance. Why I was bothering to clothe myself, I had no idea. Why I ever left my crypt, a mystery.

"I am sorry." His voice broke my reverie.

"Where will you lead these people?"

"Through the heart of Canaan."

My eyes narrowed. "I will go as far as Lod. When I leave, I will assign you Aten. Do you promise to accept this?"

He nodded.

"When do we leave?"

"You must appear before Ptah. He has congregated the priests of the other houses and will ask you to convince them of your supremacy."

I blinked. "How will I do that?"

The general shrugged. "Perform a miracle."

I looked away. "They will get none."

"Keph, I beg you. It must be done or we will go nowhere."

For a moment, I thought.

"Are any of your people dying?"

"That goes without saying."

"Bring me one near death."

"Old or young?"

"Old. They will die again soon enough to curb my mischief."

"Die again?"

At first, he only frowned, then his eyes grew large.

"No." I shook my head. "I am no god."

[Spharic. Entry translated from *Kor Dai Maihael*. Mund Dai. d. 755 BC]

2003   "Gabrielle."

Just saying her name is a relief.

Gabrielle looks It up and down. "This must be Sophie."

It feels Sophie bristle. *Who the hell is this chick?*

"These are brethren of mine. They helped me escape."

"Brethren?" Anthony frowns at It. "Escape? Sophie, what are you talking about?"

"It's all right, Anthony. Sophie is still here."

His eyes stare. "Michael?"

"You've known I was with her. Nothing has changed, only I am speaking now."

Anthony's face begins to change color.

Look out, Mike. He's gonna blow.

"The hell it hasn't!' The man's eyes bulge. "What are you doing to her?"

Let me talk to him.

"I'm not hurting her." It takes a step back. "Sophie's still here."

"Let her go!" Anthony rushes at It.

Gabrielle grabs Anthony's arm as It shrinks back into Sophie.

You talk to him.

Sophie smoothly fills into herself. It feels her move to Anthony, reaching for him.

"Tony, it's okay. I'm right here. Mike didn't hurt me. He was just excited to talk to his friends. You can understand that, right?"

Anthony's eyes are wide with rage and confusion as Sophie takes hold of his hands. They are stiff in hers, resisting her touch.

She smiles. "It's me."

"How do I know that?"

Her eyes roll. "Huskies game in ninety-seven. Hangover, El Guadalajara, huevos rancheros. I threw up."

Slowly, Anthony's breathing returns to normal. "Who won?"

"USC."

"By how many?"

It feels her scowl. "Gimme a fucking break."

Anthony tries to grin, but it is a grimace. "I don't remember either."

"We need to speak to Michael."

Gabrielle is watching them over Anthony's shoulder.

"Is there someplace we can go?" She presses. "We shouldn't stay."

It notices Anthony seems distracted at seeing Gabrielle up close.

Violet's house.

"Violet's house." Sophie points. "Just up the hill."

"The Victorian?" Raphael's face makes Sophie flinch with a pang of recognition. Sophie nods mutely.

"That was you sitting on the porch after the fire?"

That was them?

Sophie shows surprise. "That was you guys?"

Gabrielle nods. "It was dangerous to come, but we had to know what happened."

"We had to know if Michael survived, if he needed help." Raphael joins.

"We should go." With a definitive wave, Gabrielle heads for the SUV.

As they pile into the SUV, Anthony takes it in, trying to center himself. "A Sequoia. Wouldn't wanna get T-boned by one of these."

Whose vehicle is this?

"Mike wants to know who this belongs to." Sophie asks.

"Phanuel." Raphael starts the engine.

You stole his car?

"You stole it?" Sophie echoes.

Gabrielle looks back at Sophie. "Phanuel came for our crypts the night Michael escaped. I had already hidden mine, but Raphael was almost trapped."

What happened?

Sophie's brows go up. "And?"

"Phanuel got my crypt, but I got his car." Raphael grins, speeding up Prospect. Gabrielle doesn't smile and turns away silently.

I'm sorry.

"I'm sorry." Sophie's voice reflects the gravity of the loss.

"Don't be." Raphael's eyes catch hers in the rearview mirror. "This isn't over."

After parking the SUV behind Violet's garage, they enter the house through the back door. They pause outside the parlor where Violet watches TV.

Sophie clears her throat.

"Violet? These are friends of Mike's." She extends a hand. "Gabrielle and Raphael."

They nod to Violet in unison as her black eyes dart between them.

Sophie scratches her ear. "We just needed a place to talk."

"The study." Violet turns to the TV with a snort. "Curtis'd get a kick out of that."

Sophie bites her lip and points them across the foyer. When they reach the study, Anthony has disappeared. Sophie doesn't wait and closes the door. For a moment, she faces the door, gripping the knob.

You'll want to do the talking? She asks silently.

Only if you're comfortable with it.

Why can't they hear you like I can?

They could if I wasn't inside you. Do you want me to leave?

She turns and sees Gabrielle and Raphael watching like statues.

No. You can do the talking.

It knows she wants to hear what they have to say. She lets go and It takes control.

It moves to Violet's rocking chair by the fireplace and takes a seat. Gabrielle and Raphael follow suit. Raphael sits in the leather armchair across from It and Gabrielle takes a high-backed chair next to the desk.

"I am relieved you both escaped. It distressed me to know you would be hunted for aiding me and there was nothing I could do to help."

Raphael gives a nod. "What happened to your body?"

"It was trapped in the fire. I made it to my crypt, but it will need two weeks yet."

"Then Samael is destroyed?" Gabrielle sits forward.

"Obliterated."

Raphael and Gabrielle exchange glances.

"Then you can still help us." Raphael's hands fold.

"Any way I can, I will."

"Phanuel has convened the council."

"What's left of it." Gabrielle sniffs.

Raphael raises a brow at her and continues. "He intends to convince them the prophecy is at hand. That Bahiel has returned and seeded a child."

"To what purpose?"

"To frighten them. To justify swelling ECCO's ranks with novices loyal to him."

"To dissolve the council." Gabrielle stands. "Only Zachariel and Raziel remain. The shadow council is decimated. We are all that is left to stand against him."

"But why? If what you say is true, there is no one to challenge his authority."

"Authority over what?" Raphael asks. "Your contest of wills with Sam has not gone unnoticed beyond the halls of ECCO. You may not feel our presence to any great degree, but yours is felt by many. As far as anyone can tell, you and Sam have simply disappeared. ECCO suddenly finds itself standing alone. It is a vulnerable moment and ECCO has many enemies."

"You want to save it?"

"It must be saved." Gabrielle nears Raphael's chair. "You know what could happen if it falls, what it could become if Phanuel takes control."

"A terror." It looks down at Sophie's hands.

"This is our opportunity to take ECCO back." Gabrielle's voice is softly pleading.

"What do you want me to do?"

"Become Bahiel." Raphael's eyes stare as if willing it so.

"But I'm not Bahiel. If I tried to claim I was, no one would believe it ... and if I could, wouldn't I give Phanuel all the excuse he needs to consolidate his power?"

Raphael shakes his head. "Right now, Bahiel is an unseen threat to the council. Something they cannot reason with or sensibly respond to. This is the fear Phanuel is using to manipulate them. If they give him control, they will never get it back. ECCO will become an instrument, no longer capable of reasoned judgment."

Gabrielle continues. "If you pose as Bahiel and give the council an opportunity to come to a solution, Phanuel won't be able to rely on their fear."

"I already did that once. Surely they will want proof."

"Phanuel claims we were part of a conspiracy led by Sarah and Samael to manifest the prophecy. We are the only ones who know Samael was obliterated and not assumed. We are the only ones who know you survived. If you come forward as Bahiel and we confirm it, Phanuel's theory will support your claim."

"Sarah knows."

"Sarah?" Raphael's hands move to his armrests.

"She helped me escape Seattle and brought me here when I was injured. She has taken care of Sophie. Even now she guards my body."

Gabrielle grips the back of Raphael's chair. "Would she help us?"

"She hates Phanuel and she wants control of ECCO again."

Raphael smiles. "She was Samael's wife. If she is by your side, no will doubt you."

It can feel Sophie tense at Raphael's words.

"She's not my wife. Sophie is."

"Michael, if you help us, we can take back ECCO. You could lead us. We would support that. Even Sarah would. But this marriage of yours can't survive."

"What of the prophecy? If I were Bahiel, wouldn't I seek a mortal wife? Wouldn't I still strive to make a child of my own?"

Gabrielle shakes her head. "Not if you're going to win ECCO away from Phanuel without a war. We could win ECCO painlessly by treaty if you swore never to father a child and broke the prophecy in exchange. Your marriage to Sophie is a threat we can use but will have to sacrifice."

It says nothing. Sophie is silent.

Raphael stands. "We have said all we came to say. Until you regain your body, you have time to decide. Believe me when I say I have nothing against Sophie or your marriage, but the universe is at a crossroads, Michael. We are looking to you to be our guide."

"Until then, it is best if we keep our distance." Gabrielle steps forward. "Eyes still seek us. We will return when you recover yourself. You will tell us what you have decided, and we will accept your choice."

She bends to Sophie's head and kisses It. "Take care."

It does not rise to see them out.

For some time, It stares at Raphael's empty armchair.

The clock on the wall chimes ten. He feels Sophie take a breath.

Sophie—

"All in all, we had a good run."

Don't say that.

"It's over, Mike."

It isn't over. There's another way.

"When are we going to admit what we we're doing isn't meant to be?"

Stop.

"We've been deluding ourselves."

We haven't. We've only wanted what everyone wants.

"What's that? An endless pursuit? A fruitless marriage? A burnt house?"

We've been through too much.

"We have."

We love each other.

"We do."

We can't give up.

"I don't think it's about us anymore. With Sam, you didn't have a choice, but this time you do. I'm not going to be responsible for imploding the universe because I think you're the most perfect thing ever and I want you all to myself."

I can't leave.

"Why?"

You ordered me to stay.

"That was before I found out we created a disturbance in the force."

There has to be an alternative.

"There is. This is it. I told you allocution was off the table. I got my wish. This is your way back. It's an opportunity to save ECCO and yourself."

But what about us? What about you?

"You said the last three years were the only ones you felt alive; maybe that's all we get. Maeve had fourteen years with Ted and five with Andy. We got three. Three's better than zero."

I don't think I could stay away knowing you were alone.

"I won't be."

Anthony.

"I'm never going back to Anthony."

You can't live alone.

"I won't be. I've got Lodi."

He's a dog.

"He's my star, Mike. He'll guide me right."

I've led you astray, haven't I?

"You're just too big for me. I need to stick with smaller breeds."

I don't want to be a stray.

"You've never been comfortable on a leash."

I don't want to go.

"You're not leaving yet. We have two weeks."

He thinks nothing.

She sighs. "Can we go to bed now?"

Of course.

Sophie gets up from the rocking chair and drags her feet across the study. When she enters the great room, she hears Anthony's laughter coming from the parlor. Following it, she crosses the foyer and leans in the door, finding him with Violet in front of the TV. When Anthony glances her direction, he rises from the dining chair he pulled next to Violet's recliner.

"Are they gone?"

Sophie nods.

"It's Sophie I'm talking to, right?"

She smirks. "After your last meltdown, I don't think you need to worry about hearing from Michael again."

"Michael's been talking to you, too?" Violet pipes up.

Anthony looks down at her and shudders. "You guys take it better than I do."

It feels Sophie smile as she turns for the stairs. Going to the bottom steps, she sits down as Anthony enters the foyer.

"So what did they say?"

She shrugs. "Just catching up on old times."

"Uh, huh." Pursing his lips, Anthony strolls up to hug the banister. "That bad?"

"It's either really great sex or the apocalypse."

He snorts. "Are you trying to tell me he's better than I am?"

She gives a tired laugh and gets to her feet. Without pause, he opens his arms to her and she walks into them.

Sophie's memory sparks.

The day he found her in the park. It sees himself looking down at her outside her car window. It feels her hand fumble for the door as she jumps out of the car and buries her face in his shoulder. It feels the rough of the wool on her cheek, the memory of his scent in her mind. It was her shelter. It feels Anthony's hands rub her back and feels her let go.

It feels like a thief in the shadows.

Whether she chooses Anthony or not, It must try to give her back.

It must let her go.

Anthony squeezes her again. In the surge of warmth that responds within her, It leaves. It sees them separate at the bottom of the steps and walk to the front door holding hands. As they go onto the porch together, It knows Sophie will never forgive It for not saying good-bye.

If that is all, that will be more than It deserves.

It does not linger.

There is someone else to see.

The route to Anthony's apartment is indelible. The old anticipation of seeing Sophie hasn't faded. It doesn't need the stairs, but follows them, retracing past steps. Recalling the moment of knocking on her door, It passes into the small living space. The smell of dogs both disgusts and delights It. There are two mounds of fur on the carpet. One looks up and whimpers, but the other sniffs expectantly.

Lodi.

The thought of its name makes Lodi's tail beat the floor.

You will guide her, won't you?

Pain comes from nowhere, like a flood in the desert. It withdraws from the animal, unwilling to share the loss. It did not come to cause pain. It never meant to. Lodi yelps and It flees out the window. It passes through glass panes that cannot cut, but feels them to the core. It flies down the sidewalk, following streetlights to the park. The paths are deserted. The trees are fully leafed, shuffling in the night. The breeze already carries a chill. Where people see darkness, It sees radiating shapes. In the shadows of rhododendrons is the glow of human light, transients hiding from prying eyes. Lost in dreams lost.

It cannot stay. No park will hide It, no transient abide It. It is no Harvey, amiable companion to the misguided. It is Michael. Misguiding the amiable.

Companion to no one.

Michael!

It hears her voice.

Michael! Can you hear me?

It tries not to.
Dammit, Michael! Answer me!
It will not.
You have to get away! Leave now!
It freezes.
Do you hear me? No matter what! Go!
It reaches out for her.
Sophie?
Her mind is thoughtless.

It looks at the empty park bench, feeling time stop. It searches for her. There is a vision of Violet's house. Violet still watches TV, but no sign of Sophie.

The amulet.

If she kept it in her pocket, It will hear her.

It listens for the familiar hum, a faint needle in the buzz of music and the minutia of a million conversations. It tries to get away. Fleeing lights, It knows the great stretch of the bay holds relief. It reaches the water, the pulse of the tide breathes beneath It. The amulet grows stronger. The hum is flat, fading. It is moving away. Focusing back at the city, the hum begins to throb. The throb begins to wobble, becoming a synchronous pulse as It closes the distance. Finding her becomes effortless.

It sees the SUV.

Speeding down the parkway, the driver's blank face tells everything. There are four of them. Sophie sits between the two in the backseat, her head fallen, her mouth slack, the light in her dull from shock.

It feels rage. It would possess them all if It could. Possessing one would be of little use. The shell of a novice wouldn't survive, melting from the inside out, never functioning long enough to complete a task. Any chaos could send the vehicle off the road. Without a body, It would have no means to carry her from the wreck. No way to call for help.

If It tried to enter her now, It could get her killed.

They would do anything to get to him if they suspected he had taken refuge within. She will never fight his battles again.

Phanuel knows.

He has no choice but to follow them.

Phanuel expects.

He will come for her.

Phanuel wants.

Him, alone.

He shall be.

Subject: **Lodi misses you!**

From: Amy Duncan

Date: 6/13/2003 10:24 AM

To: Sophie Davids

Hi Sophie!

I'm trying e-mail this time. I know you probably don't have a cell right now and I left a message at the number you gave me, but I got this really old lady and I don't know if she told you I called or not. Tony told me what happened and I am so sorry. Hopefully you've got a new computer by now so you'll get this. A guy from your insurance company came by the office looking for you. I gave him the number you gave me, so I hope that's OK. Anyway, just thought you should know.

Here are some cool photos of Lodi and Lola in the back yard. Lodi just ate a blue raspberry popsicle and his fur is still blue. I hope it comes out! They've had a blast this summer and I want to tell you again that it's been no problem having them stay over here the last couple weeks. He really liked seeing you yesterday and I can tell he misses you so don't worry that he'll forget you. At least his dog house is still standing!

If you need anything let me know.

Amy

[E-mail from Amy Duncan to Sophie Davids. d. June 13, 2003]

CONCEPTION

2000 "What are you doing?"

Without lifting my head, I finished my note before answering.

"Christmas cards."

"It's November."

"I'm not mailing them. I'm getting them out of the way."

I looked up from the kitchen table to see my fiancé standing in the door. He looked like he had been sprayed with a hose.

"You remember to give Lodi a bath?" I asked stoically.

With a smirk, he disappeared down the hall.

Returning to my cards, I surveyed the piles I had sorted. Family, friends, co-workers, clients ... Then I remembered my doctor and my dentist. I dug through my stationary for envelopes.

Michael reappeared in dry clothes and I pointed to the family pile. "That's you."

"Me?"

"You want a family. You do the cards." I go back to writing.

"What should I say?"

"Happy Easter from one good egg to another."

He didn't move.

When I looked up, he was staring.

My eyes scrolled down a page in my address book. "How about 'Wishing you a Merry Christmas from Michael and Sophie'?"

"Is that what you would write?"

"No."

"What would you write?"

"I try to remember something about the recipient and reference that in a Christmas greeting that isn't too sappy."

"What's sappy?"

"'You put the Merry in Christmas,' or 'Jesus was born so I could send you this card.'" I paused. "Although that could work. You don't want to do them?"

"Not with that."

With a shrug, I went back to work. "The Easter one's better."

He pulled out a chair and sat across from me.

We worked silently.

The grandfather clock in the foyer chimed three.

"Do you like sending Christmas cards?" His voice made my teeth clench.

Flipping an envelope, I began to address it.

"Sophie?"

"More than I used to." I didn't look up.

"Why is that?"

"Self-adhesive stamps."

A drawn sigh made me look. His eyes bore into mine as his hand wrote fluidly, terminating in a crossed T and a period.

"Show off." I mumbled.

"Why can't you answer my questions? Why is it always a joke or a bad pun?"

"Punny you should ask."

He stopped writing.

I pointed with my pen. "That was a bad pun."

"It's disrespectful."

"I am."

"Why?"

Dropping my pen, I sat back, crossing my arms. "Don't you know?"

He didn't say anything.

"I thought you knew everything?"

He stared down at his cards. "Of course not."

"You're damn close, aren't you?"

Keeping his eyes on the table, he stopped writing.

"What do I say? In a fucking Christmas card? You could tell everyone to screw off in Aramaic for all I care! Do I like sending Christmas cards? What if I said no? What if I said I hated sending Christmas cards? What if I said I hated Christmas? What if I said sometimes I hate my family? You'd just ask more questions, wouldn't you? And there's no disrespect in that! If I ask questions, it's a different story. No bad puns there! Not a lot of answers, but no bad puns. So we're even. You ask me a question, you get a bad pun. I ask you a question, I get the shaft. You don't have to tell me how the universe works and I don't have to tell you what to say in a fucking Christmas card!"

Leaving the table, I walked out of the kitchen and down the hall. I wasn't thinking anymore. I was letting my hormones take the wheel. Marching upstairs, I began to pull off my flannel pajamas. In the bedroom, I rummaged for my running clothes. By the time I was dressed, Michael was standing in the bedroom door.

"Sophie, I'm sorry—"

"There's nothing to apologize for."

I squeezed past him and went down the hall. "I'm a bitch and you're jerk. We're perfect for each other."

Running downstairs, I went out the door.

The run was good. It was cold enough to be comfortable, but humid enough I didn't feel like I was going to get a nose bleed if I sneezed. I observed the fall colors. Smelled the coming of winter. Listened to the church bells of St. Pat's tolling the hour. Did everything I could not to think about what happened ... not hate myself.

But I did.

And I did.

The conclusion I came to was that we were both exceptionally fragile beings.

When I came through the door, I went straight into the living room, where I knew he was waiting. He was sitting in his wingback, staring into the fire.

"I'm sorry I ran away." The words fell out as I caught my breath.

"I'm sorry I drove you to it." His eyes stayed on the fire.

Seeing him sitting there, I recalled the night I moved in. He frightened me in the dark, watching me with his eyes. He seemed so unsure, and now, less than a year later, so familiar.

"How long have we known each other?" I asked.

He didn't look at me. "Two hundred and forty years."

"I mean, how long have we *really* known each other?"

His eyes darted to me, then the floor. "Eleven months."

Going to the sofa, I dropped onto it. "That's what I thought."

Returning his gaze to the fire, he turned away. I saw the perfect line of his profile without seeing it. I had learned to observe without making him self-conscious, to take his appearance for granted, something unimaginable to me when we first met.

"Is it what you imagined it would be?"

Slowly, he shook his head.

"Me neither."

Squinting, he cocked his head at me. "But you've done this before."

I raised a brow. "Not this."

Letting out his breath, he stared at his feet.

"That's not what I mean. I've never loved anyone this much before."

He looked up again. "Really?"

"Yeah, it sucks."

He only nodded.

"Does it make you miserable?" I asked.

"Antony and Cleopatra." He murmured.

"I don't think I want it."

He seemed frozen. When he finally spoke, the words came softly.

"What do you want?"

"That boring, run-of-the-mill love people have when they've been married forever. You know, couples who sit across from each other at dinner and never say anything."

He shot me a look. "Never say anything?"

"I know." I sighed. "I'm screwed."

"You and Anthony had that."

"I don't want Anthony."

His eyes barely touched mine. "You still want me?"

"Bad."

"Even if it isn't good?"

"Even better." I grinned.

He beamed, then stared self-consciously at his feet.

I sat up. "You hungry?"

Silently, he nodded.

"I feel like soup."

He frowned. "Soup?"

"I can make chowder. Heavy cream, potatoes, lots of bacon ..."

Slowly, the smile returned.

"Cool, that's what we'll have." I got up from the sofa. "I think I have everything."

"Do you need help?"

"Not yet. I'm gonna jump in the shower first."

Exiting the living room, I jogged upstairs. In the back of my mind, I suspected Michael might try to stop me. For some perverse reason, he tried repeatedly to have sex with me when I felt as unsexy as possible. If he was trying to prove how much he loved me, I would take his word for it.

When I opted to strip off my clothes in the bedroom, I realized a tactical error. When I emerged naked from the bedroom and saw him standing in front of the bathroom door, I knew dinner would be late.

"Come on." I rolled my eyes.

He came towards me.

"No, Mike." I backed away. "I have to cook."

"I know." He actually seemed to be sniffing me, which was disturbing given the fact he could detect carbon monoxide.

"I'm tired and I'm starving."

"Not for long."

His hand reached for me, cradling the back of my neck as we kissed. I felt the other find my clitoris like a doorbell. One thing I hadn't been wrong about: he did know damn near everything.

It was dark when I got my shower. Getting dressed without lights, I went to his bedside to check on him. Stroking the side of his face, I made out a faint smile.

"So much for helping in the kitchen."

Sorry.

"Soup will be ready in an hour or so." I kissed his forehead. "No rush."

Pulling the blankets over him, I slipped from the room.

At the bottom of the stairs, I began to turn lights on in the house as I made my way to the kitchen. Hearing Lodi whimpering in the laundry room, I let him outside before returning to fill his food bowl and change his water. I'd barely filled his bowls when I heard a yip to be let in. Not used to his first fall, Lodi was eager to get back indoors where it was well lit and he would be well fed. Entering the kitchen, I noticed the Christmas cards had been neatly stacked on the table.

At the pantry, I began to assemble what I needed for the chowder. Lodi kept my feet company on cleanup duty as the process of scrubbing potatoes and cutting celery carelessly absorbed me. From frying bacon and chopped onions, the smell of chowder began to take shape. Setting it to simmer, I washed my hands at the kitchen sink and filled the tea pot. As I sat back in a chair, I kicked a dog toy out from under the table and Lodi commenced fetch.

My eyes glanced at the stack of Christmas cards, my fingers poking at them absently until an envelope in Michael's hand caught my eye. My family wasn't large. There were only six cards for him to write. Probably because he'd noticed I hadn't sealed the envelopes on any of mine, he hadn't sealed the envelopes on his. Spotting the envelope with my parents' address on it was easy.

Pulling out the card, I remembered picking it for them. It was a Japanese print of a winter scene with two cranes. Michael's handwriting drew me to read and I opened it with the sensation of reading someone's diary.

Mom and Dad,

It has been an eternity since I have been able to write those words. There was a time when I would have given anything to be able to. I never would have believed I would be given everything instead. Thank you for giving me Sophie. Thank you for accepting me as your son. Thank you for sharing your Christmas with us.

Merry Christmas,
Michael & Sophie

I bit my lip. If we were going to be married forever, he'd have a lot of cards to write. How they would be better than this one, I wasn't sure.

1199 BC The night before congregation, I lay awake in my crypt. A swarm of priests had invaded my tent in the night. They were preparing for the ceremony. Working in silence, they moved quickly to be gone before the sun rose. Before I rose.

My eye watched them.

The carpet was gone, replaced by a long runner of woven jute. Another runner of gold silk was stretched the length of it, with ornate braziers lined on either side. In front of my crypt, a massive chair, intricately carved and inlaid with lapis and gold. Still stained from smoke that seasoned the wood, it had only recently been made. They placed the mask of Aten upon the seat.

Once they left, the general entered with the vestments of Re in his arms. While he waited, I wondered what would happen if I refused to come out. If there would be confusion and chaos, blame and blood, and finally peace with the attrition of time. If they opened my crypt, I would defend it. I would kill all who came near until none would come—until word spread and men shunned me. A devourer from a dark place.

But it was not my nature. I would kill only one and restore what I had taken.

I pushed open the lid and climbed out.

He bowed low to me.

"My lord."

Stepping around the throne, I regarded the mask as if a decapitated head.

"You have kept your hair." The general's voice implied no judgment.

I sighed. "Do not push me."

"No one will argue."

He approached, offering me a silk stole not unlike the one he had given me when a woman. It was white, embroidered with gold and silver lotus blossoms and beaded sleeves that fell past my hands as I put it on. He lifted a loose-fitting alb of gold thread over my head. Finally, over all, a heavily beaded tunic with a winged scarab bearing the golden disk of Re.

It was impossible they had only been made since my arrival.

"Whose are these?"

"Ptah preserved them from the sacristy of Aten in Amarna."

"Akhenaten?"

The general did not lift his eyes as he placed a gold and lapis collar of a pharaoh across my shoulders.

"Are you a believer?" I pressed.

His brow raised. "Who knew any still lived?"

Stepping behind me, he pulled my hair aside to fasten the collar. I felt his fingers run through my locks.

"What are you doing?"

"If it will not be cut, it must be plaited."

"I did not know a general could plait hair."

"It is not what I trained for."

I laughed and he took notice.

"I have never heard you laugh."

"It is not a habit."

He tore a cord of suede from the tassel of his belt and tied off the plait. "It should be."

My eyes fell on the mask of Aten. "I doubt Re has much humor."

Going to the throne, I picked up the mask, staring at the vacant face. As I did, a priest began to sing with the advent of dawn.

The general came up behind me. "Perhaps you could give him some."

Turning to him, I raised the mask over my head, lowering it over my face. "I am as you have made me."

[Spharic. Entry translated from *Kor Dai Maihael*. Mund Dai. d. 755 BC]

[To be in a hard place or hard times. In a situation
which you feel like there is no hope.]

2003 No sound wakes me. I am aware of bright light, not like the sun, but cold and forced. As I squint above, the sky is a sheet of light. I'm wrong, not sky, but a ceiling of fluorescent lights. To my left is a white wall. To the right, more walls, all white. In the middle, a white pedestal, like an obelisk sheered in half. There is something on it.

Slowly sitting up, I am stiff, from the floor. It too is white, covered in cold tiles with no lumbar support. My nerves tingle and one eye has a tic, but otherwise everything seems normal. I am thirsty and I need to take a leak. Business as usual.

It occurs to me I have no clue where I am.

But I do.

Something tells me this is Phanuel's house.

Pressing my back against the wall, I feel my legs under me and achieve a stand. Past the pedestal is the outline of a door. There is no knob.

My eyes return to the object on the pedestal. A black box. Uneasy on my feet, I approach the box. It is a perfect cube with no markings. There is a fine indentation of a lid, but nothing else says, "Open here."

It occurs to me this is a test.

I am being watched.

I look around the room. There is no sign of a camera, but then again Michael's kind doesn't need them. The only thing I am fairly sure of is they can't read my mind. Michael said they were generally lousy at that.

Leaving the pedestal, I go to the door instead. I push on it. Nothing happens. Taking a breath, I return my attention to the box. I could ignore it. What would happen then, I have no idea. If they plan on waiting for me to open the box, I might be here a very long time.

And I have to pee.

I walk up to the pedestal. Extending my hand, I tap on the box with a finger, half expecting an alarm to go off. Nothing happens. With a sigh, I reach for the box with both hands, stretching my fingers on either side of the lid—

"Are you sure you want to do that?" Soft words echo off the walls.

I spin to see a man standing in the open door. He is thinly built, wearing a white dress shirt and slacks, but no tie. Framed with pale, golden hair, his face is almost delicate, with an individuality more human than Michael's plastic perfection. The eyes, however, are exactly like Michael's and erase any doubt as to his true nature. From what I glimpse, the space behind him is as white as the one I am in.

I say nothing.

"Let me apologize for your abduction. Believe me, I have no desire to harm you, save to do what is right."

I only stare.

"I was watching you."

As he approaches, I step back, keeping my distance.

"You displayed no fear."

He keeps coming, but his focus is on the pedestal.

"If you had, I might have guessed he was still inside you."

Facing the box, he places a hand on either side of the lid. Removing it, he sets the lid aside.

"Then, bringing him to judgment would have necessarily meant your death."

He eyes me, but I am suddenly distracted by the realization Michael is gone.

"It appears I will have to make him barter for you instead."

When my gaze refocuses, he smiles at me.

"They say silence is golden. I see why he treasures you."

I bite my tongue, dropping my gaze to the open box.

Stepping back from the pedestal, he encourages me with open palms.

"Come and see."

For a second I hesitate, then step forward enough to get a peek.

Inside is a black orb the size of a billiard ball.

"Metatron." He smiles.

"What?"

"Our law. All who see into It are judged in accordance."

My voice comes dryly. "Judged how?"

"Fairly."

"And if they are guilty?"

"We do not harm those willingly judged. The penitent receive refuge."

He gives a small smile and reaches into the box. Removing the orb, he holds it before him and moves for the door, then pauses to look back at me.

"Come and see."

My insides churn, but I find my breath. As soon as I take a step, he turns and walks out, leaving the door open behind him. Beyond the door, his figure quickly recedes down a white hall. My feet move me to follow. At the far end is another door. Whatever is behind it, I am in no hurry to get there.

For some time, the far door looms, Phanuel long since entering ahead of me. The sounds coming from beyond tell me it is a large room, filled with low voices. A row of faces appears as I near. They fix on me as I stop at the threshold. Looking inside, I see it is shaped like a ring, with a row of seats facing inward along the wall. The seats are filled, but I do not notice their hush when they see me.

All I see is a man seated in the middle of the ring. His head hangs, his skin almost transparent, exposing dark blue veins at his temples and down his neck. His wrists are bound to the arms of the chair by two silver cuffs. His ankles are cuffed to the legs. His profile is too familiar. He looks up and the sight of Michael's face makes me gasp.

"Raphael."

I only mouth the name as his black eyes search my face.

Hands take my shoulders. I look to either side of me, flinching at the sight of two automatons at each arm. They press me into a chair and keep a hand on each shoulder, staring blankly ahead. When I look back at Raphael, he is sitting up, his face awakened. His gaze never leaves mine.

The orb comes between us, resting in Phanuel's hands. My eyes move up to his face, and he smiles before making a slow circuit of the room, stopping before Raphael to extend the orb. Raphael turns away, as though it reeks of some horrible smell.

Phanuel begins to speak. It is the same slow speech Michael makes in sleep. It is drawn, impossibly low for a human voice, but where Michael's voice is round and resonant, Phanuel's is thin, cut with short hisses. When Phanuel stops, Raphael looks to me, his first words sending a wave of murmurs around the room.

To my surprise, I understand them.

"I, Raphael, deny the charge of council that I engaged in the commission of a conspiracy to make manifest the prophecy of Samael. I accept the charge of council that I knew Michael was a violator. I accept the charge of council that I aided this violator in evading our law. I accept the charge of council that I evaded responsibility for my complicity after the fact. What is more ..." Raphael pauses, blinking. "I conspired with this violator to affect the overthrow of ECCO."

A ripple of low moans circles us.

"My reason is this: The members of this council have been hunted for twelve years, and to date, eleven have gone missing with no question asked as to their fate. ECCO blames these disappearances on Samael, but I believe it is one of our own. One who protects ECCO against the threat of prophecy and secretly desires its manifestation. Who claims Bahiel will be ECCO's undoing and would use Bahiel to undermine us all. Who seeks to destroy the Child and desires to possess It. Who speaks for Metatron and fears he will not be chosen."

Raphael glares at Phanuel.

"So long as you speak for the council, we are doomed. The overthrow of ECCO as it exists is the only measure that will save us."

Raphael's eyes move from face to face around the room.

"You may choose to accept or deny what I have said, but know this to be true. Phanuel will lead you to your destruction. Because of him, Samael and Michael are joined. Bahiel is reborn and without his mercy, the prophecy will be made manifest. The Child will come."

The room has fallen silent.

Phanuel shows no interest in anything Raphael has declared. With only a moment's pause, he speaks again in a low hiss. Raphael only drops his gaze to his lap and waits. When Phanuel is finished, Raphael begins to sing. It is sung slowly, sadly. It is a steady cadence and ends with the same words I heard Michael speak in his dream. I have no idea what they mean. I don't want to.

Phanuel briefly holds Metatron over Raphael's head and murmurs something barely audible. Raphael lifts his face, his eyes dilated to black marbles, his hands gripping the chair with white knuckles. As Phanuel lowers the orb, Raphael's eyes follow, his face fallen. He stares, entranced. Metatron begins to change color, from black to gray in Phanuel's hands. For some time, nothing seems to happen. Then a flash. The gray turns to pale blue. Raphael's jaw visibly clenches.

His irises shrink and begin to glow with light that blinds him. His breathing goes shallow.

The orb grows bluer, brighter, as Raphael's blood glows in his veins. Ripples of blue light flicker and snake under his skin. It is what I have seen in bed with my husband countless times, only these pulses are erratic, making Raphael's body burn with a fire from within. That fire reaches a flash point. Raphael's eyes are white light. His head jerks back violently and his mouth falls open. Something like a mist curls in his mouth, finding the orb, spinning around it, absorbed within.

Soundlessly, the orb blinks.

It is solidly black again.

Raphael's body remains frozen in the chair, the head tossed back, staring at the ceiling with milken eyes. The skin has turned a dull gray. Four faceless automatons approach the chair with a stretcher and remove the cuffs. The audience watches silently as they lift the body onto the stretcher and carry it from the room. Only then do the witnesses rise, leaving by another door. My eyes search them, somehow expecting a familiar face. All I see are statues that regard me with cold reserve as they pass, needles of blue ice, betraying nothing, filling me with frantic longing.

When I look for Phanuel, he is watching me. Cradling Metatron in his hands like a favorite pet, he comes to where I sit at the insistence of my humanoid ushers and waves them away. Stopping before me, he smiles gently.

"Do not fear what you have witnessed was an execution. Rest assured, Raphael still exists unharmed. In Metatron's care, he will be kept safe."

My eyes drop to the orb in his hands. I know it has only begun.

But I am only human.

In spite of my abduction, my horror at Raphael's judgment, my fears for my husband, in spite of all the unearthly events that have invaded my life the last three weeks, I still have to piss like a proverbially fast equine. When Phanuel directs my ushers to see to my needs, I feel relief at his reference to "the facilities." There didn't seem an appropriate time to ask if I could use the toilet while he was plotting to turn my husband into a paperweight.

As Dum and Dee escort me back into the hall, through a door and down a dimly lit stairwell, I try to guess where I am. If the stairs are any indication, the white rooms are on the top floor of whatever building we are in. They only go down from here. Hopefully not a sign of things to come.

The stairs descend one floor, ending after two flights at a metal door. Dum, or Dee, I can't tell which, opens the door and we step into darkness. It is a vacant floor in an office building, the interior walls and ceiling tiles stripped. The only light comes from a single fluorescent tube hung in the middle of the space. A small ring of high-backed chairs face the light, but there is no table. As we cross the floor, my eyes follow a twisting crack in the concrete that runs along our path, cutting through the circle of chairs and into the void beyond. Our path diverges from the fault line as we approach an elevator door. We wait in the shadows as Dee presses the down button and stares at the doors. As far as I can tell, they don't talk.

"You guys like working here?" My question echoes off the walls.

Nothing.

I scratch my ear as the elevator doors open and we step inside. Letting go of my self-consciousness, I blatantly scrutinize them. My head turns to Dum, then to Dee, then back to Dum. Their profiles really aren't so different from Michael's, but their faces are simple masks, like God couldn't be bothered with the details. It dawns that what makes them disturbing isn't that they are ugly, but they aren't anything else. They aren't pretty, or young, or old. They aren't beautiful. Even Sam was beautiful.

Terribly so.

Again, we only go down one floor. The floor we arrive at is more finished. It has a hall and the semblance of rooms, even gray commercial carpet on the floors. The hall seems to run the length of the building. At the end of it, we turn right and there are two office restrooms. Dum and Dee abruptly stop at the women's and Dum opens the door, holding it for me. The thought he might follow is no obstacle as I aim for a stall without waiting.

Sitting on the can, I take my time and go over a map of the building in my head. It is at least four floors, though the hum of the HVAC running under my feet makes it sound larger. Possibly a high-rise. The elevator doesn't go the top. Phanuel is here, Metatron is here, Dum and Dee are here. Michael said ECCO's headquarters was in Seattle. This must be the place. Exactly where I am in Seattle, I have no idea. Exactly what my chances of escape are, I have no idea.

Actually, I do. I don't have any.

When I come out of the stall, Dum is facing the door, looking through me. Washing my hands, I look at myself in the mirror and see my eyes looking back. Last time I saw them, my husband was looking through them, too. Now, it is only me.

I am alone.

At least a day passes. I can't be sure. There are no clocks. No windows. Morning or night, rain or shine, I have no clue. All I know is since being escorted back to the white room, I have had only a muffin to eat, a bottle of water to drink, and Metatron for company. None very satisfactory. Stirring from another attempt at sleep, I roll onto my other side and curl into a ball in the corner of the room, my head tucked between arms in a futile defense against lights that never turn off.

As blinding as my surroundings are, my thoughts only grow darker.

I wanted Michael to escape. When I knew I was cornered, I ordered him to leave. Why didn't he say anything? He had possessed me to fight off Marta. He wouldn't have left me facing Dum and Dee alone. No matter how much I screamed at him to leave. No matter the risk to himself. No matter the risk to me.

But it would be just like him to leave without saying good-bye.

I think about our last conversation. It was over. We didn't argue.

If he left before they took me, would he know I was here? Where had he gone? If Raphael was caught, what happened to Gabrielle?

They must have been followed. Dum and Dee must have known about our meeting, guessed Michael was with me, hoped to catch us together, only they missed him. Somewhere between our meeting in the library and saying good-bye to Anthony in front of Violet's house, they missed him.

I missed him.

Michael?

I am hesitant to call to him again. I don't want him to come for me. But I do. Even if it kills him.

Raphael comes to mind. The allocution. The judgment. The body left behind and carried away like waste. I wonder what they did with it. I wonder what they will do with Michael's. I wonder if he does come, if he does barter for me, if they will let me have it. If it is bones, or ashes, or a hair from his head. Anything.

My throat is dry and I have to piss again, though I doubt there's more than a trickle in me. If I go much longer, I'll take Metatron from the box and leak in that if I have to. Scratch that. I won't take Metatron from the box, but I'll leak on that if I have to.

Feeling my side crushed numb against the tile, I stretch out to roll over again, when the lights go out. Momentarily, I think Phanuel has decided to be merciful and let me sleep, when I hear the door open and shut. Feeling a jolt of nerves, I bolt upright, pressing my back to the wall. Sliding into a corner, I crouch on the floor. I hear no one, but I know I'm not alone.

As my sight opens to the dark, I begin to see dimly. A shape emerges, black against pale light. I can't tell where the light is coming from, but the shape is the silhouette of a man. I realize he is right in front of me and I am peering between his legs. When I look up, there is no face, only his back. He is facing away from me. The light of his eyes fills the room before us.

"Who are you?"

There is no reply. I am about to ask again when a flash blinds me.

The sound and feel of electricity charges the air as blue light surrounds us. In the blink of an eye, the shadow standing before me flies off his feet and slams into the wall next me. Seeing his eyes, I recognize Phanuel. Scrambling to get away, I feel his hand on my ankle. As he pulls me to him, I fix on the only thing I can see and sharply kick him in the face. To my surprise, he lets go.

Something grabs me, pulling me to my feet.

Michael's face barely takes shape before he turns away.

Stay behind me.

He doesn't have to tell me.

There is another wave of light followed by a low hiss. Words are exchanged in a stream of deep vibration, rattling the floor beneath my feet. I hear Phanuel say Metatron. I hear Michael say Sophie. Mike backs into me as I keep pace in his shadow. There is a flicker above and the lights in the ceiling come on, making me shield my eyes with my arm. I make a mental note. If we rebuild our house, no white rooms.

Agreed.

Hearing his voice in my head, I am whole again.

Moſt Exceſſent Majeſtie.

In reſponſe to your requeſt for another reaðing, I wiſſ proviðe proofeſ of paſt reſuſtſ by the fortenight when you ſee me next. Your proviſion of a fine cryſtaſſe iſ moſt generouſ anð ſhouſð offer exceſſent foreſight.

My beſt reſyſtſ come from hyðromancie eſpeciaſſie when purformeð unðer the fuſſe moon. However, the Druiðſ reſyð upon the acuraſſie of ſkrying cryſteſſſ tho I have hearð of a mythik ſpheara of fati that waſ no cryſtaſſe but of ſtone.

A manuſkript of Oðheaðh Cuatha De Danaan ðeſribeſ a ſkrying ſphære jeaſouſſie guarðeð by the Cuatha anð ſater poſſeſſeð by Citania. It iſ ſaið to be maðe of bſack ſtone or cryſtaſſe that couſð ſee aſſe, juðge the immortaſſeſ of wickeðneſſ anð waſ powerfuſſe enuſſ to kiſſe them.

The origen of thiſ ſphaere may come from Ægypte or Græce, in which inſtanſe it may be maðe of obſeðian or onnyx. I have not yet maðe gooðe my pſanſ to acquire ſuch a ſtone anð commiſſion a ſphære at which pointe a teſt may be maðe, tho I am no Druiðe. Untiſ then I wiſſ reſie on your Majeſtieſ cryſtaſſe to guiðe my ſight.

Your Majeſtieſ moſt bounðe.
John Dee.

[Letter. Dr. John Dee to Queen Elizabeth.
Scrapbook of Michael Goodhew. d. 1595]

2000 Having a perfect memory had been a reliable tool in the past. It saved his skin more than once and helped solve many an eternal mystery. Few things escaped his notice. Now he replayed her words in his head and found no matter how often he heard them, nothing crystallized in his mind.

"Flawless." The woman behind the jewelry counter displayed a five-karat baguette under the light.

Gently taking her hand, he moved it out of the light to see without being blinded. This was too big. It also couldn't be too small, too fussy, or too old-fashioned.

"It is very beautiful." His eyes focused on a fine point before looking up at her smiling face. "But it does have one inclusion."

Her smile faded as he released her hand.

"It's also a little ostentatious. Do you have anything simpler?"

"Of course." She replaced the baguette and slid the back of the case shut with a flick of the wrist. "Those might interest you if simple is what you want."

She pointed over his shoulder to the far end of the counter.

As he made his way along the display, his eyes matched everything under the glass to Sophie's specifications. One diamond. Nothing under one karat and nothing over two. No wedding set, those were stupid. One band, no other stones on the band. Nothing too proud, so the stone would be protected. Nothing too deep, so the diamond could get light.

He stopped in front of a ring in a blue velvet box. A twisting möbius strip of gold with a princess-cut diamond. He leaned in closer to examine it through the glass. At first, he thought the face reflected on the counter was his.

He froze.

"I thought it was you."

"Hello, Raphael." He greeted the reflection before glancing around the store.

"It took me a while to locate you. At first I guessed you were in the food court. I knew you were close, but I never imagined finding you in a jewelry store."

Raphael's eyes bore into him.

"I'm educating myself for a client."

Everyone knew he occasionally traded in antiques.

Raphael only squinted. "You didn't know I was here?"

"I felt a presence." It was a lie. "I didn't know it was you, but this is Seattle."

"True." Raphael's smile was plastic. "I suppose we are much the same to you."

He tensed. "That's not what I meant."

"Of course not."

"Did you find something?" The jewelry clerk interrupted them, smiling at Raphael. "You must be brothers."

"Yes, we are." He agreed, taking Raphael by the arm. "Thank you for your help."

They made a quick exit as Raphael continued to study him. "Are you all right?"

Since refraining from his crypt, he had aged. To Sophie it was imperceptible, but not his own kind.

"I'm fine." Keeping his smile soft, he avoided Raphael's gaze. "Have you eaten?"

"I have, but you need to. You don't look well."

"Just hungry." His nose led them in the direction of the food court.

"Are you sure? You look like you escaped from the cells."

With a shrug, he kept walking. "I ran into Sam. It must show."

Raphael touched his arm. "Then it's true? You dueled with him?"

"What?" His eyes scanned food vendors as they entered the court. The smell of something sweet drew him. "No ... Well, I suppose."

"You suppose?"

The sight of a pyramid of icing where hot cinnamon rolls were being glazed transfixed him. "I went to The Mountain."

"*The Mountain?*" Raphael hissed. "You swore never to go back."

"It was no matter."

He went to the counter and ordered a dozen.

Catching Raphael's expression, he blinked. "It's over with. I'm all right."

"You're not all right. What happened?"

"I went to duel. When I found him, he was already burned."

"Burned? By whom?"

"I don't know." His eyes followed the progress of his cinnamon rolls as they were packed in boxes. "Possibly by whomever burned him the time before."

"Time before?"

"Someone was stalking him."

The girl behind the counter bagged the boxes and slid them over to him. As he picked them up, he glanced at Raphael who stared vacantly, saying nothing.

"Raphael?"

"It wasn't Sam after all."

"Who?"

"The stalker."

"The stalker?"

"Sarah didn't tell you?"

He shook his head.

Raphael's lips disappeared. "She still doesn't believe me."

"Believe what?"

Raphael slowly walked away. He followed. At the edge of the food court, Raphael went to a table and sat. Dropping the bag of cinnamon rolls on the table, he took a chair and waited for Raphael to say something.

Raphael indicated the rolls with a glance. "Eat."

He looked at the bag and pulled out a box. Opening the box, he pulled out a roll and tore a piece with his fingers, shoving it in his mouth. Raphael watched and raised a brow. "May I?"

He nodded, watching Raphael peel apart a roll. For a while, neither spoke.

"These are good." Raphael chewed thoughtfully. "Do you get them often?"
"I've never had them before."
"You come to malls often?"
"I was doing research."
"At the mall?"
"There is a density of jewelry stores in this vicinity. Biddle, Cartier, and Tiffany among them. What better place to understand human desire?"
"And what have you learned?"
"I like Cinnabons."
"If you've been eating like this, you should look better."
The fixation on his condition annoyed him. "I've been busy."
"Too busy for your crypt?"
"I'll be in it the moment I leave you, if it makes you feel better."
"It does." Raphael paused to finish eating. "Michael, I know you have few enemies to trouble you, but this is no time to let yourself go."
Reaching for another roll, Raphael withdrew a container of icing and pushed it across the table. "And don't tell me you're on a diet."
He ignored it. "What is this danger you perceive?"
"Someone or something is hunting us. I hoped Sam was behind it—better the devil you know—but if he has been burned, we are all at risk. Even you."
The Halloween party. He couldn't confirm it. Ever since living with Sophie, he had been letting go. Between his impending marriage and visions from Sam, he had been avoiding his crypt in hopes of disappearing. A stalker was the last thing he wanted to consider.
"What is being done?" It was all he could think to ask.
"Nothing, I'm afraid."
"Nothing? That isn't like Sarah."
"Either she doesn't believe me, or—" Raphael stopped.
"Or what?"
"Do you trust her?"
Taking another cinnamon roll, he considered his answer. "I've had to."
"Have you ever had reason to doubt her?"
"I've never known enough to."
"That's the problem, isn't it?" Finishing his second roll, Raphael sat back in his chair. "None of us do."
"It couldn't be Sarah. What would she have to gain? ECCO is the source of her power. Why destroy it?" He tore another roll in half and bit into it.
"She hasn't been happy."
Blinking, he swallowed. "Maybe this stalker has her worried."
"It is more than that."
He focused on his roll.
Raphael cocked his head. "Why have you stopped coming to council?"
He shrugged. "The council hasn't convened in forty years."

Raphael ignored the formality. "Is it Phanuel who keeps you away?"
"I've had Sam to follow, haven't I?"
"And rumor has it he will no longer need following."
"I don't know the rumors. I only finished what was started."
"You didn't assume him?"
He shot a look across the table. "Do I look like I did?"
At this, Raphael smiled. "I'm not Phanuel, Michael. I have faith in you."
His eyes fell to the roll in his hand. "Sam is buried in his mountain."
Raphael's smile faded. "Let's hope he never gets out."

Of course, Sam would get out. As long as Sam had sentience enough to put a thought together, he would crawl out of the ground somewhere. Sam was like The Mountain with its river of tears: deceptive and deep.

The whites of his knuckles rose on the steering wheel and he eased his grip. Four o'clock in November and it was already dark. A fog seeped across the highway, but his eyes barely noticed, reading the road miles ahead. Picking a path through the slowed traffic, he sped between the lanes, leaving Seattle behind.

His mind felt trapped in a feedback loop all day: the first half spent with Sophie's ring in his ears, the second half with Raphael's rumors. He hadn't made a report to Sarah about Arizona. It appeared he didn't need to. Who spread these rumors anyway? How did they know?

It made him think about the stalker. The duel in the playground. The flight to Phoenix. The party at Lyn's. He should have told Raphael. Described the stalker without mentioning Sophie. Did Raphael suspect anything?

Was that what Raphael was trying to tell him? About Sarah being unhappy?

Worse yet, what did Phanuel know?

Phanuel.

The only one who voted to keep him out of ECCO. The one who insisted he be judged for Bahiel's crimes as a condition of membership. The council was swayed by Phanuel's argument. He had been half of Bahiel, no matter how unwitting. He shared Sam's spirit, their sentience, their guilt. Let him ask for judgment and accept Metatron's refuge. He agreed, but only after Sarah promised it would be a formality. His sentence was haggled over, whittled down from eons to years. He submitted to being torn apart. To being imprisoned. To prove himself.

And for what?

Raphael asked what he had learned. He had learned that one year in Metatron was like being buried alive. Going through eternity alone was the same thing. Even after serving his sentence, Phanuel didn't trust him. Bahiel had rejected the law. Samael rejected it. As Sam's other half, he would follow them. With Sam trapped under a mountain, it would only be a matter of time before he was imprisoned again. Sarah would threaten it. Phanuel would demand it. Especially if ECCO no longer needed him. They would get no such pleasure. If he was to be buried alive, he would do it himself.

The tail lights of a freight trailer loomed ahead. Giving it a wide berth, he quickly accelerated past the truck. Adjusting his rearview mirror to deflect the glare of headlights, he wondered what Louis would do with Sam gone. The thought of having a servus appealed to him. They could be useful, even if they could betray you, and that wasn't a risk with Louis. Louis didn't want money. Louis wanted redemption.

It wouldn't be fair to hire a man knowing you couldn't pay him.

It also wouldn't keep with his plans to have another person around who had any clue what he was. Only Sophie would know. They would be married in Hawaii in April. Then he would work on her about quitting her job and moving there permanently. It would be ideal. It would be close to her parents and far from ECCO. It was too far for anyone to jump to and the last place Sam would find him. If he lived close enough to the volcano, he would be almost impossible to read. He would disappear. Grow old. With enough time, she might forget what he was. He might forget, too. Until he couldn't follow her.

If only he could get Sophie to agree.

She never would.

It would be too easy to run away, and with Sophie, nothing was easy. She hated her job and refused to quit. She hated the weather and refused to move. She was a hypochondriac alcoholic, a gourmet anorexic, a sterile dog lover.

She believed he was everything, and he was nothing.

She needed a body. A man. The truth was, she couldn't love him for what he really was. As sorry as he felt for himself, he had to admit he didn't love what he was either. Who could love something less than a shadow, let alone live with it? Wasn't that what he wanted himself? To live with someone? To be someone?

So he would be a man.

ECCO be damned—Sam and Phanuel, and the stalker, too.

A sign on the highway said he was entering Pierce County.

Letting out his breath, he finally felt far enough away. He decided to never go back. It seemed fitting his last visit to Seattle was to find Sophie's ring. Of course, she did like to shop. At some point she might want to shop in Seattle and expect him to go with her, but he doubted it. The last time he went with her, his curiosity about women's clothing disturbed her.

Since then, she preferred to go with her mother.

That was what she was doing. Shopping with her mother for Thanksgiving.

It was the first Thanksgiving Sophie would host and the first he would attend.

They planned to spend the holiday with Sophie's parents, but Sophie decided to include friends too far from their own families. Anthony would be in New York, but Amy, Phil, and Dan would be coming. Dan had asked if his ex-wife Karen could come as well. Sophie agreed, with reservations.

After Dan's divorce, Dan and Amy had dated. Sophie suspected Karen knew this. It would be an awkward evening for Amy and he felt bad for Dan. If the skies were clear that night, he would invite Dan, Phil, and Peter to go stargazing in Carr

Park. When he told Sophie his idea, she wasn't happy, especially as he planned to include her father. He assured her the pooka wouldn't be back to incinerate the playground a second time.

If he was going to have any semblance of a life, it was what he had to believe.

1199 BC   My eye watched the audience of people. Surrounding the tent, rows of priests sat on small stools, their novices kneeling on rugs on the ground. They were segregated according to the houses they served, mostly lesser deities fallen from favor: Set, Khem and Peyoth among them. There were but a few from Horus and Hathor, none from Osiris.

The priests were encircled by armed men, forming a perimeter to hold the people at bay. This audience was greater than before. Many wore the purple of Canaan.

Waiting for the general to call upon all to stand, I watched him don the hooved headdress of high priest as I sat on the throne. Once he exited, priests of Re would lift the stanchions of the tent and carry it away, exposing me for all to witness. The general smiled to me before backing from my presence. Hearing the call, my hands gripped the arms of the throne.

The front of the tent fell away and I felt the glow of morning. It came with the weight of a thousand eyes amidst hushed silence. All I need do was bear them for the next hour. Only the general was allowed to speak to me; I would answer no questions from the priests. The general as high priest was my chosen emissary and would speak for me. It was assumed he heard my wishes. It was assumed I was in control. It was assumed I was immortal.

I was glad I was. After an hour of debate as to my status as a god, I doubted any pharaoh wore such a mask for anything longer than a brief appearance. My neck stiffened as the final house rose to be heard. It was that of Peyoth. The general told me this house objected most to my supremacy. It was an ancient one, personifying the sun as sphinx preceding Amun-Ra, and most definitely Aten-Re. I was heretical. My lineage apocryphal. I was competition.

I had directed the general to require the priests of Peyoth bring an elder on the brink of death, someone for whom life was past recovery. When I saw the litter being brought, I rose from the throne before they set it down, keen to bring my performance to a conclusion. The Peyoth priests, for all their indignation, nearly ran from me as I approached. The general gracefully bowed, stepping from the litter. An old woman lay upon it, unconscious of what was about to happen.

The general turned to the high priest of Peyoth, called Khenemet.

"Does this woman live?"

"Only just."

"Do you witness this?"

"Upon Peyoth, I do."

Without word, I extended my arms, my hands stretching beyond the sleeves of my vestments. All eyes focused on my fingers, the first time they beheld the flesh of a god. Directing a charge, an arc snapped from my fingertips, momentarily gripping the woman with ague. A wave of gasps and whispers rippled the crowd. Many priests rose to their feet, some to see, others distancing themselves.

When I lowered my arms, the general brought Khenemet to attention.

"What do you observe?"

Khenemet tentatively approached the litter. Kneeling, he felt the body for life.

"Does she live?"

Khenemet only shook his head.

"Will you testify?" The general pressed.

"She is dead."

Another wave of whispers ran in circuit around us.

I stepped forward, causing Khenemet to fall in his haste to scramble away.

Standing over the body, I knelt, placing my hand to the forehead. Her soul, still warm within, could be revived with my spirit, her body enlivened, if only for a week. My fire glimmered beneath her skin. Khenemet rose to his feet, his eyes fixed on her. In a moment, she took air and opened her eyes.

When she sat up, confused and frightened, voices erupted all around. Confused myself, I stood quickly, retreating from the fear I saw in her eyes. The silence that followed was sudden. When I looked about me, the guards and the crowd beyond had knelt, their heads touching the ground. None remained standing.

I was alone.

[Spharic. Entry translated from *Kor Dai Maihael*. Mund Dai. d. 755 BC]

2003 *Sariel!*

It sees the electrified garage and the crypt in the middle of the floor. It searches the yard, through empty chicken coops to Louis's small house beyond. There is a chattering television and Louis, glowing in the back room, asleep, still dressed, a shotgun leaning against the wall by his hand. It knows attempting communication will be fruitless. Louis is closed to It.

There is no time.

Sariel!

Leaving Louis, there is no sign of her.

Sariel!

There is no answer.

It returns to the garage, nearing the crypt, finally seeing inside.

What It sees is not possible. A body. Whole. Complete. It wonders how.

There is no time.

Not having a body makes disabling Louis's security measures easier this time. Charging the atmosphere of the garage, It floods the wires running across the floor with a frenzy of sparks. There is a deafening crack as the electrical field collapses.

It seizes upon the body.

Opening his eyes, his mouth opens to breathe and it is effortless. Painless. He feels a smile as he reaches up to push lid. It opens lightly. Peering over the crypt wall, he sees the mesh of hot wires blanketing the floor. His pain-free moment will be brief. Climbing to his feet, he vaults over the side, instantly feeling the wires singe the soles of his feet. Quickly crossing to the garage door, he spots the metal plate Louis patched over the hole his fist made last time.

"Sorry, Louis."

The plate buckles as his fist drives through it. He reaches around the outside and grips the chain holding the latch. Yanking it free, he pulls the latch and slides the door open. The cold gravel is a relief his feet barely appreciate, when the snarl of a dog across the road alerts him. Closing the garage door, he backs alongside the building and slips around the corner. Watching in his mind, he tentatively reaches out to feel them. If they are human, they won't know he is here. If not, they already know and he must fight. Or flee.

One of them is human. The other not. His eye focuses on the gate at the head of the drive, seeing a Tacoma police vehicle. It is parked with the trunk open. Anthony is out of the car, cutting the chain on the gate with bolt cutters. Gabrielle is in the passenger seat. Her light is poor. Raphael isn't with them.

He watches Anthony open the gate and get in the car. Hiding behind the garage, he waits as the car speeds down the drive, skidding to a halt in front of the chicken coops. He ignores his impulse to go to them. The eye in his mind stays on the road. If Raphael and Gabrielle were being watched, they might still be.

Anthony runs around the front of the car and opens the door, helping Gabrielle to her feet. She holds on by an arm, dragging as they disappear behind a chicken coop on their way to the house.

He goes the opposite direction. Picking his way through the woods behind the garage, he finds the shed housing the generators, the security fence still warped from his last visit. Tearing through Louis's latest pair of chains, he proceeds to the door and forces it open. Inside, he finds Louis didn't bother to replace the second line of defense around the generators. The cyclone enclosure has no door. Examining the generators, he finds the breakers and resets them. Switching the generators back on, his vision strains as the room radiates brilliantly around him. If he found the electrical field a distraction the first time he visited, it will be doubly so for a novice. His crypt will be too tempting for them to ignore.

Exiting the shed, he searches the forest with his eyes. The trees are mostly tall conifers. He looks up at the roof of the generator shed, slowly circling it. Standing beneath one of the eaves, he jumps, gripping the edge of the roof. It is lined with asphalt shingles, brittle under his fingers. Gripping onto them, he pulls his chin to the edge, pushing off with his feet to get his shoulders over the top. Extending his reach to the ridge, he claws his fingers into the shingles, sliding his knees one at a time after. Crawling across the roof, he peers over the ridgeline and observes the glow of the garage through the trees.

Stretching in the night, he is thankful it is still summer.

In minutes, his ears perceive a vehicle on the road.

A rusting van appears. Appears to be passing. Appearances meant to deceive. He can clearly read the four occupants inside aren't human. He knows they read him, though not so clearly. The van slows a quarter mile down the road to pull over. Another van appears, dented and nondescript. It does not follow the first but stops at the intersection by the abandoned house, coming no closer. Four novices slip into the wind break of the neighboring farm. The novices from the first van also approach, ducking along a drainage ditch thick with bracken.

They are fast and silent. He is still and patient.

Putting his head down, he closes his eyes. The four who entered the wind break have sensed Gabrielle and surround Louis's house. Two stay behind to watch and wait while the other two continue to the garage.

The four coming by way of the drainage ditch have split up. Two have spotted his crypt and are headed for the garage. Two have noticed the generator shed and close on him. He knows they cannot pinpoint his location. Their bodies are rudimentary and their ability to see with their eyes is limited. Their greatest sense is their ability to read static, by now overloaded by the strength of his frequency. They know he is there, but everywhere. Their greatest weapon is their ability to unleash raw energy. Eight of them at once are a challenge. Two, not so much.

The two approaching him, circle the outbuilding and enter the gate.

He opens his eyes and carefully creeps down the peak. His vision pierces the sheathed wood frame beneath him, focused on the two standing at the door. As one enters, the other turns to watch the forest. The blank face registers nothing as he drops in front of it, directing a charge to the chest with the palm of his hand. Thrown into shed, the body collides with the other, who turns to see him before seeing nothing ever again.

Glancing over his shoulder, he ducks behind a generator, waiting to see if the others circling the garage come his way. The two who left Louis's house have joined the pair at the garage. They seem to notice the disturbance but can see nothing past the interference of the electrified building. They only see his crypt and will not leave it. When he shuts off the generators, their focus will renew on the garage and the prize within. With luck, they will make his life easier and all go inside.

Stepping out from behind the generators, he systematically shuts them down.

The electrical field collapses.

Two novices waste no time, quickly entering the garage, but two linger by the door. When the two inside open the crypt and find it empty, he doesn't wait. Flipping on the generators, he watches them fail to react to the sound of the energy surging to them. He is already running through the trees for the garage. When he rounds the corner, the two standing at the door are distracted at the sight of the others incinerating on the live wires.

The first to see him is quickly dispatched, but the second unleashes a charge he barely has time to react to. His static repulses it weakly as the novice gets a hold on him in a futile attempt to duel. Bracing himself, his own energy quickly overwhelms the lone assailant, his will burning through his hands. Feeling the novice go slack, he wastes no more of himself. Letting it fall back though the garage door, the crackling wires finish what he started.

Two novices remain at Louis's house. He is on his way when the sound of gunfire spurs him to a sprint. Nearing the house, he sees Louis sprawled across the threshold of the front door. Inside, the silhouette of a novice closes on Anthony and Gabrielle in the back bedroom. His eye sees Gabrielle on the bed with Anthony standing in front of it, facing an enemy beyond human capability. There is no way he can direct a charge without electrocuting Anthony in such close proximity.

Anthony fires a shot into the novice with no result.

Silently, his bare feet pick up speed.

Focused on Gabrielle, the novice doesn't read his approach. Doesn't feel him reach from behind. Snapping the neck, he drops it to the floor.

"Jesus!" Anthony stares at him.

He blinks. "I'm late."

"You're naked."

And filthy. Looking down at himself, his body is covered in dirt and grime.

His body.

He looks back up at Anthony with a smile. "It was a warm night."

His eyes fall on Gabrielle and his smile evaporates.

Going to her, the pallor of her face is ghostly. When her eyes open, they are black with fatigue and dilate at the sight of him. He reassures her with a thought, resting his hand on her forehead. She smiles before falling deeply asleep.

He doesn't look up. "What happened?"

"Those things caught her and Raphael. They split up and she damn near ran me over when I was walking home from Violet's. She was in bad shape. I thought if I got her to Sarah, she'd know what to do."

His hand runs from her forehead, down the side of her face to her neck

"She needs food and rest, but ultimately her crypt."

Searching her body with his eyes, he sees the blue tracks of a burn spiraling across her chest beneath her clothes. She is recovering from a direct charge, but there is no sign of a breach. His thoughts turn to the novice on the floor.

Suddenly, he glares at Anthony. "Where's the other one?"

"Other what?"

He points at the body. "They always work in pairs."

Anthony shakes his head. "He was the only one."

His face slacks as his eye goes to the road. One of the vans is gone.

Refocusing on Anthony, he get to his feet. "We need to leave now. Louis can—" He falters, remembering. "*Louis.*"

Darting past Anthony to the front door, he stands over Louis, still inert on the threshold. Kneeling, he rolls Louis by the shoulders and examines his face. There is a gouge over the right eye, but the pulse is steady and strong.

"Is there a light?"

Anthony flicks on the porch light.

"Louis?" The light pushes back the shadows as he presses his fingers to the cut. "Louis? Can you hear me?"

"He might need stitches for that." Anthony peers down over his shoulder. "I've got first aid in my car." He pauses. "Any more of those guys out there?"

Shaking his head, he watches Anthony disappear in the dark.

Louis smacks his lips and mumbles.

Bending, he sees the mist of his dark breath chill the warm air. Louis feels it.

"Wake up, Louis. It's Michael."

With a series of rapid blinks, Louis squints into the light. "Am I dead?"

"Mostly alive."

Louis frowns. "Are ya sure?"

"I wouldn't be talking to you if you weren't."

"Would if I was in heaven."

"You're not in heaven, Louis."

"Are ya sure?"

"I'm sure."

"You're naked."

"You don't need clothes in heaven. I'll need to borrow some of yours."

Louis grins. "Clothes make the man."

"Come. On your feet." He reaches for Louis's arm and gets a grip on his shoulder.

Guided through the front door and across the tiny sitting room, Louis drops into a faded armchair.

He squeezes Louis's shoulder. "How do you feel?"

"Like the bottle let me down."

He smiles. "How about those clothes?"

Louis looks down at himself. "One's in my drawers smell better."

Anthony comes through the door with a first aid kit.

"Let's take a look at that cut." Anthony turns on a table lamp and then stands back from Louis with a frown. "Didn't he have a cut over his eye?"

He doesn't answer, going to Louis's bedroom to get dressed.

Anthony follows. "He did, didn't he?"

"It was a scratch."

He steps over the novice. Pointing to it, he barely makes eye contact.

"We have to burn the bodies, find a safe place for Gabrielle, and hide my crypt." Turning to a chest of drawers, he starts to rummage them.

"You healed it." Anthony's voice comes up behind him.

"Louis will know where to go." Shaking out a pair of paint-stained jeans, he pulls them on. "I need you to make sure they're safe and keep an eye out for Sarah."

"Didn't you?"

"Didn't you just hear a word I said?"

The small house shakes and Gabrielle stirs. He pauses as she falls back asleep. When he looks back at Anthony, the man is afraid.

"I'm sorry." His words barely stir the air. "It's just … I don't have much time. Do you understand?"

Anthony swallows. "What about Sophie?"

"They have her."

"*What?* Who?"

His eyes go to the body at Anthony's feet before returning to Louis's drawers.

"Jesus! What are they going to do to her?" Anthony grabs his shoulder. "We have to get her back!"

Without a glance, he pulls on a white tee.

Anthony answers his silence. "I'm going with you."

"You don't have to." He looks in a bottom drawer and finds socks.

"I want to."

"I don't need you." He looks under Louis's bed and sees another pair of boots.

"You can't stop me."

"You don't understand." He sits on a stool at the foot of the bed and pulls on socks. "They don't want Sophie."

Bowing his head, he loosens the laces on a boot and tries it on. A half size too large, but a better fit than his clown shoes were.

When he looks up, Anthony is watching.

"You're giving yourself up."

Blinking, he looks down and shoves his foot in the other boot.

Silently, he begins to lace them.

"You're not coming back."

He gets to his feet. "Sophie is."

"If you don't, it'll kill her."

Shaking his head, he goes to Louis's closet and pulls a Carhartt jacket off a hanger. "She sent me away. That's why I'm here." Pulling on the jacket, he turns to see Anthony staring at him. "It's over, Anthony. I'm done."

Seeing his crypt veiled by the steel curtain of Louis's cargo door feels like déjà vu, as he's heard people say, all over again. Knowing he won't see it again is softened by the glow of Gabrielle resting inside. It won't heal her, but it will keep her from starving until she finds her own again. It is the least he can offer after what she has risked for him.

He is reminded of what Sophie has risked for him. Now, he is trying to rescue her for the second time in as many months. He isn't in the habit of rescuing people, let alone sacrificing himself for them. Perhaps it's a good thing. He's terrible at it.

Walking to the driver's-side door, he smiles at Louis and extends his hand.

"Thank you, Louis. I'll have Sophie reimburse you for the clothes."

Ignoring his hand, Louis climbs in the cab and slams the door.

"Long as I get my coat back, you can forget the rest."

He looks down at the stained Carhartt he has on, his arm visible through a gaping hole in the right sleeve.

"This one?"

Louis starts the truck with a roar, releasing the brake. "It's lucky."

With a jerk, the tires claw the gravel and the truck rolls down the drive.

"Sure you don't need help?" Anthony's voice calls to him with a hint of nerves. Still watching the truck, he shakes his head. "Stay with Louis."

Turning for the house, he passes Anthony's patrol car. Anthony stands on the other side, about to get in with the door open. The cross chatter of his radio periodically interrupts the chirp of cicadas in the dark.

"Michael."

At the sound of his name, he stops, resenting it.

"Yes, Anthony?"

"I'm still wearing your medal."

Barely waiting for his gaze, Anthony gets in the car.

Standing in the glow of Anthony's tail lights, he tingles and scratches his ear.

As the car fades, he turns to the last detail. The chicken coop is no longer empty. Inside, seven novices wait patiently for incineration—the eighth driving as fast as it can to warn Phanuel of his coming. Killing it would have saved it the trouble of such a long drive. When the warning is delivered, the coming will have passed.

Philadelphia. · Nov 12, 1762

Dear Sir,

Since your Presence has proven as Rare as your Intellect, I resort to Abducting your Landlord in Hopes of communicating with You. Seeing Young Goodhew on the street, I have Bound him to wait on me as this is written. When I set him Free, I have every Hope that he will fly Home and find You there, as when I have called You are not.

In keeping with the Season, a small number from the Society will be Gathered at my Home next Friday, November 19, to Thank Providence for our Freedoms. These Fredoms will include Food, Drink and Discourse followed by lively Entertainments. Over the course of years, I have found such Entertainment a limitless source of Inspiration, and a Necessity, shared by All who would claim to enjoy a Free mind. Only through the Exercise of Free Will may God light our way; and although You live among Friends, I doubt that they offer You as fine an Exercise as This.

I hope this Invitation finds You in a timely manner with a mind to accept. If so, You need only ring at Seven o'clock. If not, We Pray that We will find You again.

Your most Humble Servant,

B. Franklin
Presid of the Society

[Letter B. Franklin to Michael Monroe (Goodhew).
Scrapbook. d. Nov 12, 1762]

2000 "I thought you saved the champagne for after dinner?" Amy watched Phil deliver a tray of flutes to the coffee table.

"Rules!" He sneered. "Rules are for sissies. I drink what I want when I want." Holding the bottle, he began pushing up the cork with his thumbs.

I felt the urge to intervene.

"Where ya pointing that thing, Phil?"

He paused and looked around our living room.

"Oh, right. Should I take it outside?"

I reached for the bottle. "Give it to me."

"No." He pulled it away.

"Why not? I bought it!"

"The man's supposed to open the champagne."

Dad coughed on a cracker from the other side of the room.

"Then you're not qualified." I smirk. "Hand it over."

Phil gave it up with a snort. "Try getting the cork off without spilling half of it."

With a beckoning gaze, I nodded over my shoulder. "Follow me, big guy."

Phil and Amy followed me to the kitchen, where I was confronted by an obstacle between me the kitchen sink.

"What do you need?" Mom turned from shutting a bean casserole into the oven. The tone of her voice had an administrative quality that said, "State your case and leave."

"I was—we're getting into the champagne and I wanted to open it over—"

"Sink's busy."

She blinked at me with hands on hips. I looked past her at Mike, who she had stirring cranberries at the stove. He only shrugged.

"What do you mean it's busy? It's in a meeting?"

Mom gave a short laugh, then said something to my fiancé in Mandarin. Nodding with a smile, he caught my gaze and quickly focused on the cranberries.

Suck up.

"Never mind." I raised a brow. "We'll use the sink in the hall."

Leading them back through the living room, we went into the foyer and down the hall to the mud room.

"We do get to drink the champagne at some point?" Phil sniffed.

"Watch and learn." I grabbed the hand towel and slowly twisted the cork, wiggling it until there was a muffled pop. Removing the towel, there was only a thin dribble of bubbles and a wisp of mist.

"Cool." Amy fingered Phil. "You were just going to pop the cork off."

"That's what you're supposed to do! Pop the cork! Where's the fun in that?" He pointed at the bottle in my hand and walked away.

I shrugged at Amy. "I never spent two hundred bucks on a bottle of champagne to hear the cork."

After pouring the flutes, I left Amy and Phil explaining what they did at the hospital to my father and poked my head back in the kitchen. Mom was coming out with the bean casserole.

"Wow, you guys done already?"

"Almost. I'll have your dad carve the turkey and Michael can mash the potatoes."

Mike had placed a steel bowl on the kitchen table and was looking for the masher. I went to the stove and turned off the flame before removing the lid from the simmering pot of potatoes. When I checked the sink, it was full to the top with dishes. Rolling up my sleeves, I decided to wash a few so I could drain the potatoes, when Mom called me to the dining room.

"Where do these go?"

When I came out of the kitchen, she was trying to make room for the side dishes on the buffet and wanted the appetizers out of the way.

"I'll move those to the living room."

"Where?"

"The console has space." I picked up two trays of cheese and crackers.

"Not the coffee table." Mom scolded. "The dog will eat it."

I rolled my eyes on my way to the living room. "Lodi's in the laundry room, he won't eat anything."

When I returned, Mom had rearranged the centerpiece on the dining table. "What do you think? Turkey there?"

"Sure. That works."

She called to Dad in the living room to wash his hands and carve the turkey. At the reminder to wash hands, I remembered I had to wash dishes. I turned for the kitchen and nearly ran into Mom frozen in the doorway. I was about to excuse myself when I realized she was transfixed and followed her stare.

Michael stood at the stove with his back to us. He was mashing potatoes in the steel bowl he had cradled in one arm. I nearly looked away, when he casually reached into the pot on the stove. Fishing out another potato, he dropped it into the bowl. The steady column of steam rising from the pot clued me in. Though the potatoes weren't boiling anymore, the water they were floating in was very near it.

"Hey, Mom?" I stepped in front of her. "You think we should put those pies in the oven now or wait till later?"

She looked through me as though she hadn't heard a word.

"Mom?"

"Put them in now … the oven's … still hot." Her expression was unreadable. Saying nothing else, she left the kitchen.

When I turned to Mike, he had stopped mashing potatoes and was watching me. He didn't say anything, but he didn't need to. He was afraid.

The food supply was more than enough, though I knew the leftovers wouldn't survive longer than the next day. During dinner, I tried not to scrutinize my mother's behavior, but it was impossible not to. She remained distant. Remembering the Christmas card Michael had written, I knew this was killing him.

After dinner, we sat in the living room, where Mike had started a fire. He had seated Dad in his wingback chair next to the fireplace. Mom was in the armchair I usually sat in. I snagged the rocker next to the coffee table, while Amy and Phil sat on the sofa. There was another armchair, but Mike chose to stand, leaning with his back against the study doors, his hands hidden behind him. From where he stood, he faced my mother, but neither of them seemed to look at each other.

"I love Thanksgiving." Amy sat back on the sofa, holding her middle. "I couldn't live without turkey. You know it's super healthy for you."

"Please. It's a marketing campaign to keep the turkey farmers in business." Phil crossed his arms. "What a bogus holiday. Pilgrims and Indians? Where was the giving there? One of my buddies in college was Iroquois and told me his family called it Thanksgrifting."

"Blame Squanto." I rose to pour another glass of wine from a decanter on the coffee table. "It's his fault."

Amy frowned. "What does the Lone Ranger have to do with Pilgrims?"

"That's Tonto." Phil sneered.

Dropping into my armchair, I took a sip of wine. "Squanto miraculously spoke English and saved the Pilgrims from starving on their own ignorance."

Amy gulped her wine. "How did he know English?"

"Don't recall …" I squinted. "Something about being captured by explorers and ending up in England. He learned English, hopped a boat home, and found the Pilgrims starving to death. Without him, colonization would have looked a lot less appealing."

Phil nodded. "Proof no good deed goes unpunished."

"And it pays to have a good translator." I added.

"I agree." Dad grinned at Mom. "If your mother hadn't agreed to translate for me in Hong Kong, you wouldn't be here."

Phil nodded again. "Proof no good deed goes unpunished."

"Phil!" Amy elbowed him. "That's our hostess."

I gave a smug look. "Phil's just bitter I left the grant writing department for greener pastures."

"No kidding?" Phil scratched his chin. "How much greener, may I ask?"

"You may not." Amy glared at him.

"Too much." I answered. "But that's not why I stayed."

"What did you stay for?"

"The privilege of working with Evelyn Whittier."

Phil and Amy stared.

"I'm serious."

"But she *hates* you." Amy ogled.

Phil picked his wine glass off the coffee table. "I thought it was mutual?"

"It is. Even after they made their offer, I was going to tell 'em to kiss my ass. Michael convinced me to stay."

Everyone looked to him, and he seemed surprised by the shift of attention.

"How on earth did you do that?" Phil turned on the sofa.

"Um." His hands folded in front of him. "I told Sophie she'd never get away from people like Lyn, and since she already knew Lyn, staying couldn't get any worse."

Dad nodded. "Better the devil you know than the one you don't."

I glanced at Mom. She was staring at Michael.

"Does anyone need anything?" Michael popped off the door and hovered over the coffee table. "I'll open another bottle."

He picked up the decanter and vanished from the room.

"Speaking of Lyn." Phil grinned. "I keep meaning to ask, how was the Halloween party? There wasn't the usual e-mail from her bragging about who was there and what they ate."

"She had to cut it short." I took another sip of wine.

"Really? Why?"

"Wind storm broke her living room windows."

"What?" Phil frowned.

"Her house is on the water. The storm that night hit it hard."

"Wow, I know." Amy emptied her wine glass. "A tree blew over on our street."

Phil grinned. "It was an act of God. I thought we'd never hear the end of it since she broadcast Mike was doing tricks for her."

"I told Sophie, I'm just glad he didn't get hurt." Amy looked at Phil. "He only agreed so I could get on Sophie's ribbon-cutting committee."

"Tricks?" Dad frowned.

"Michael's an amazing magician!" Amy gushed.

"Our Michael?" Dad raised his brows at Mike, who hesitated in the dining room door with the wine decanter. "Tricks?"

"Nothing really." Mike cleared his throat. "Just a hobby."

Quickly replacing the decanter on the coffee table, my husband started looking around for another excuse to leave.

"Not nothing!" Amy's gasped. "I saw him at the farmer's market. He was awesome! He was in this clown costume with these little kids sitting around—"

"Amy?" Michael picked up the decanter. "Would you like more wine?"

"Oh." She glanced down at the empty glass in her hand. "Sure. Why not?"

Extending her glass, she silently watched him fill it. "Thanks ... where was I?"

"Farmer's market, little kids ..." Dad was listening with his elbow on the armrest, his temple resting against his fingertips.

"Right. When he shook their hands, their hair would stand up. You know, like when you have static in your hair? It was really funny. And he had a bowling ball follow him like it was a dog and then he made it float."

Dad looked skeptical. "Float?"

Amy swallowed her wine with a nod. "Like a balloon."

"A real bowling ball?"

Michael opened his mouth.

"Totally." Amy's eyes widened.

"No it *wasn't!*" Phil scowled.

"Yes, it was!" Amy was adamant. "You weren't even there!"

"Real bowling balls don't float."

"This one did!"

"Anyway." Phil rolled his eyes at Dad. "It's on the Net if you want to see it."

"*Really?*" Michael and Dad spoke at the same time.

My fiancé stared at me like I'd been holding out on him.

"I told you." I held up my hands. "A bunch of people uploaded it."

"But that was months ago."

Phil toasted him. "What plays in cyberspace, stays in cyberspace."

"Don't freak." I finished my wine. "There's a lot of junk on the Internet."

"It's not junk!" Amy glared. "I got tons of comments when I posted the dead flower trick on YouTube."

"Dead?" Mom's voice surprised us.

She'd been silent till now. We all looked at her as she watched Michael cross to the other side of the room.

Amy leered at Mom. "He made a dozen dead roses come back to life."

Michael resumed his position in front of the study doors. "It was a trick."

Dad and I watched the staring competition between Mike and Mom.

Amy pointed at Mom. "But the flowers were real."

Crossing his arms, Michael broke under my mother's gaze. "Real or not, it doesn't make a difference." He glanced wearily at Amy, then back at my mother. "People see what they want to believe."

Michael set down the gravy pot and watched Lodi go to work. Head bobbing, tail swaying, we watched Lodi's head disappear into it.

He returned to the sink. "Where do you think Dan was tonight?"

"I don't know." I pulled a dish towel from the drawer and shook it out with a snap. "Maybe he had a last-minute emergency."

Mike frowned. "Or second thoughts on his engagement."

For a while we worked in silence, only the sound of the faucet and Lodi's frantic tongue marking the time. Michael rinsed another plate and handed it to me. I toweled it off and returned it to the china cabinet.

"It was overcast tonight anyway." He paused at the window. "There weren't any stars to see."

"You've enjoyed hanging with those guys, haven't you?"

Nodding, he rinsed a platter in his hands. "I'm good at hanging."

"They like you."

"I like them."

"But you really like Dan."

Turning off the faucet, he handed me the platter. "I can relate to him."

My expression made him blink.

"I'm not referring to his engagement."

"Or possible lack thereof."

"He's thoughtful ... self-reflective in a way I respect. Like your father."

I smirked. "You don't find my mother thoughtful and self-reflective?"

"I find your mother intimidating."

Flipping the dish towel over my shoulder, I crossed my arms. "But not too intimidating to speak Chinese to."

"I told her I minored in it in college."

"Did you?"

He sighed. "You know how hard I've tried to connect with her. I thought speaking her language would help."

"Now you speak her language?" My hands moved to my hips. "That's good to know. From now on, I'll ask you to translate."

"I wouldn't presume to, Sophie. No one understands her better than you."

"Dad does, and I'm perfectly happy to let him claim the privilege."

"Are you angry with me?"

"Actually, no. Just thrilled I'm not the resident weirdo anymore."

He gave a short laugh. "I more than make up for the both of us."

"Did you have fun tonight?"

His lips barely twitched, a tell I recognized as stress.

"Yes."

"The hot potato trick bombed, didn't it?"

"I'm sorry, Sophie. I was careless." His eyes darted around the kitchen. "There wasn't anywhere to drain the potatoes, I couldn't find a spoon, dinner was about to be served, and I didn't want the potatoes to go cold or soak up too much water—"

"Michael."

"I thought about using a fork, but using my hand was more expedient. No one was in the kitchen when I started mashing—"

"You're good at mashing."

Sliding out a chair at the kitchen table, he dropped into it. "I'm not used to doing it in company."

"You've been living alone too long."

"I wouldn't call it that."

"But it was your first Thanksgiving. You liked it?"

He nodded.

"You'll want to try it again next year?"

"And the year after that."

There was a clatter as Lodi rolled the gravy pot on its side, sprawling on the floor in exhaustion.

Michael smiled. "Lodi liked his first Thanksgiving, too."

Bending down, I picked up the pot and displayed the spotless interior.

"Nothing to translate there."

November 17, 1762

Dear Sir,

I thank you most humbly for your invitation of Wednesday last. It is poor manners on my part to offer so tardy a response, only the complete absence of a reply could be worse. My only excuse may be I have been busy most days at the free clinic and too poor for anything better when I am not. With regret, I must decline your invitation for this Friday. Though I believe the stated purpose of your gathering is admirable and worthy of my time and attention, those are two luxuries beyond my means to afford. Even were the opportunity present, my intellect is not so rare as you imagine and discourse would soon erase any illusion.

Thank you also for inviting me to join your Society. I regret I would have little time to offer in the exchange of ideas, my primary concern borne only from a desire to protect people from harm rather than any extensive study of electrical fluids. With appropriate safety measures, your experiments will provide an invaluable understanding of charge theory with few dangers. The results of your work I eagerly anticipate and will follow with great interest. Thank you for remembering me.

Your Unknown Servant,

Michael Monroe

[Copy of Letter. M. Monroe (Goodhew) to B. Franklin. Scrapbook. d. Nov. 17, 1762]

2003 The door opens and a parade of masks enters the room, their eyes glistening under harsh light. I back along the wall into the far corner. Michael stays with me, keeping as much of the room in view as possible. With the lights on, I observe the back of my husband more closely. He is dressed like a construction worker, in paint-stained denim and heavy boots. His jacket is stiff duck, black faded to gray with frayed edges and torn seams.

Michael says something, and Phanuel responds, but I cannot see. Most of my view is walled off by Mike's shoulders, now inches from my face. The coat he has on smells of tobacco and must. Louis's clothes.

Phanuel speaks again, and suddenly Mike backs into me, gripping my wrists, pressing me against the wall.

Don't move.

As if I plan to.

For a moment, there is complete silence.

There is a shuffling sound. I hear the door close. Michael lets go and steps forward. When I peek around him, the room is empty. The pedestal still stands.

The black box is still there.

He takes another step forward, focused on the door.

What's going on?

I'm afraid to speak out loud. For a moment, he doesn't answer.

I told him I'd take you away from here if they didn't agree to my terms.

Forget terms, just take me away from here and we'll call it even.

That won't work and you know why. You said it was over and you were right.

I want to argue, but I'm all out. He's right. I'm right. I wonder if we ever had a chance. *If I'd abducted you the first day I saw to you at Grounds.* Michael answers my thought.

I wouldn't have liked that.

I wouldn't have either. I didn't know I was in love with you.

My eyes trace his profile and can't believe it's him.

It's me.

Look at me.

I can't.

His eyes stare at the door.

"What do you mean you can't?"

My throat is so dry, the words scrape across my tongue.

He grabs my arm, pulling me behind again.

He's coming.

At the sound of the door, I peek around Mike's arm and see Phanuel casually enter with Dum and Dee in tow. They carry a chair between them and set it before the pedestal, then return to the door where they post themselves on each side.

"This isn't what we agreed to." Hearing Michael's voice fill the room sounds odd after having it in my head for the last week.

"You have given me your terms. These are mine. I accept your allocution on the condition Sophie is released from any prosecution presently, or in the future. You have my oath your allocution will be witnessed and attested to, but not in open session. That is my condition."

"Why?"

"Raphael declared to the council Bahiel was reborn and the prophecy made manifest. I have warned the council of this threat ever since your escape. Should you appear in open session declaring you are Michael, this would be a contradiction to what Raphael and I have claimed. It would ... complicate my efforts to safeguard ECCO's future."

"Raphael has been judged?"

"For knowingly aiding a violator. Gabrielle will face the same fate, if she is ever found. You are a violator. You do not deny it."

"No."

Michael seems to be looking at the floor, but lifts his head sharply. "You want to keep my judgment secret on your word Sophie will remain unharmed?"

"There are no secrets from Metatron. I have to honor my oath to you. What the council does or does not know is of secondary importance to what Metatron knows. If I ever broke my vow to you, I would never hold Metatron in judgment again. Without my mandate, I would lose my position and face judgment myself."

Michael remains silent.

"What I ask is no more exceptional than what you require."

Still Michael says nothing.

"Are we agreed?"

I stare at his back.

Don't trust him.

Almost imperceptibly, Michael nods his head.

Not so imperceptibly, I let out my breath.

Immediately, the door opens and two pairs of Dum and Dee enter the room.

Michael turns to me. "I'm sorry to make you see this, but until Phanuel accepts my allocution, I won't let you out of my sight."

"This is a really shitty way to break up."

"Good-bye, Sophie."

Dum and Dee grab me by the arms, dragging me back on my heels.

"*What?* That's it?! Good-bye, Sophie? No last kiss? No final embrace?"

Michael walks away.

"Not in the white room, I'm afraid." Phanuel smiles. "Those are the rules."

"Yeah?!" I shout. "Well, your *rules* suck! And *you* are a complete *asshole!*"

Michael turns, striding back to me. As he does, he takes off his jacket. I feel Dum and Dee dig in their fingers as he comes without slowing. Our eyes meet as he drops his head and presses his mouth to mine. At the same time, I feel him shove the jacket in my hands.

When he pulls away, he looks at the jacket.

"Get that back to Louis."

I stare at it. It is warm in my hands.

"It's lucky."

When I hear his whisper, he is already walking away. Hugging the coat to me, I let the fingers cutting the blood to my arms pull me away a step at a time. I am against the wall, staring at my husband's profile, seated in a chair, waiting to have the life sucked out of him.

Michael says people see what they want to believe.

My mind decides this isn't real.

My eyes begin to watch on their own. My brain switches to autopilot. Not paying attention comes easier when I feel like I've seen this before. When Phanuel begins to speak, I know the voice. When Phanuel cradles Metatron, I know the routine. When Phanuel thrusts Metatron in Michael's face, I know the man.

He does not blink. He does not flinch. But his lips move. Ever so slightly.

I drop my eyes.

When I hear his voice begin to sing, I close them.

I won't look up again. I don't have to. I know what the last words of the allocution are. I have the sound of them memorized. Requayoo suspentat. How many nights I will speak them out loud after this, I'll never know.

Michael stops singing and begins to speak.

"I, Michael, accept the charge of council—"

He stops.

Phanuel mutters something.

"I ... Michael ..."

The voice sounds like a multitude, speaking as one.

"... accept ..."

I've heard it before.

"... the charge ..."

At the lake, when I thought he was coming apart.

"... of ..."

The words sift to nothing.

The fingers gripping my arms begin to loosen. I look up.

Michael eyes burn vacantly as Metatron begins to brighten in Phanuel's hands. The look on Phanuel's face is one of fear.

And anticipation.

"What are you doing?" My voice squeaks in my ears.

Phanuel ignores me.

"He didn't finish!" I scream.

My misery evaporates to rage.

"Bastard! I hope you burn in hell!"

The orb flashes blue and then white, nearly blinding me. Ducking my head, I squint at the jacket in my hands. I search the faded threads. The smell of stale tobacco anchors me to where I am. What is happening is real.

And it is happening now.

The light in the room flickers and I squint up, determined to see everything. My eyes test the room, finding their way back to the orb. It throbs with a steady glow in Phanuel's hands, his face filled with vague fascination. When I follow his gaze, my breath falters, undecided. Michael sits in the chair, frozen, fixed on Metatron. His face glows pale, his eyes filled with white light.

"What's happened to him?"

Without looking away, Phanuel's answer is barely audible to me. "He is reborn."

"What?"

"He has become Bahiel. Raphael spoke true."

I stare at my husband.

Michael?

I call to him.

Can you hear me?

He isn't there.

Phanuel walks around him, but his eyes see nothing. His head doesn't move to follow the orb in Phanuel's hands. His connection to Metatron is no longer a matter of sight. I know, because it is a connection that was ours. The more I watch, the more I want it back. If Phanuel opened the door for me to leave, I wouldn't budge.

Phanuel completes the circle, facing Michael. With slow cadence, Phanuel's words start softly, almost hesitantly, gradually filling the room with a rolling vowel before ending with a hiss like the lash of whip. At the end of each word, I feel myself brace as the hiss cuts my ears, making me wince.

I don't know how much time passes, only that I am exhausted when it finally stops.

In the silence that follows, my eyes blink, refocusing on Michael's profile. Tears try to quench burning eyeballs. The dull ache of numb arms, pinched knees, and flat feet distract me from my duty to bear witness. My mind asserts itself and I am fully aware again. My eyes focus. The stage before me is set. Another act about to begin.

Phanuel is displeased.

A sudden barrage of words makes Dum and Dee shift on their feet. I glare at each of them as they momentarily pull me in different directions, threatening to take my arms off. When I look back at Phanuel, he is holding Metatron to Michael's face, but Michael says and does nothing. Phanuel pulls Metatron away, returning to the pedestal. Phanuel watches Michael as he lowers the orb inside and replaces the lid.

Instantly, the throbbing light is gone. The electric lights in the ceiling, once blinding, are a relief. For the first time since he stopped speaking, Michael makes a sound. Something like a cough and gasp as the light in his eyes goes out. His head drops to his chest, his shoulders slump, his body rolls forward out of the chair. He is a pile on the floor. A collection of parts.

He is blocked from my sight.

Phanuel's hands fold before my eyes. When I look up at his face, it smiles.

"I find I am at an impasse."

"What did you do to him?"

"Nothing. What he has become, he did to himself."

He waves to Dum and Dee and their fingers vacate the holes drilled in my arms. Phanuel gestures to the door. It is now open, but I don't move.

"I promise you, he will be fine."

I look back to Michael, but I cannot see him. He is surrounded by mutant twins. They move rapidly around one another, like bees in a hive.

"I'm not leaving without him."

Phanuel smiles broadly. "I was hoping you would say that."

I try to read his face.

He tilts his head. "You would do anything to help him?"

My eyes narrow.

"What if you could still share a life together?"

Once again, he gestures to the door. Haltingly, we begin to walk.

"I freely admit, our care for you has been lacking. Although it was an unavoidable oversight, the intent was never to harm you, and I do not wish to now. To the contrary, I wish to treat with you and, in so doing, grant you the care and consideration required."

"Care and consideration." My mouth makes the words like they are new.

"It would hardly be good faith on my part to let you treat on an empty stomach."

"I'm not hungry." I lie.

"We have a room for you. A bed, a bath, and whatever food you wish to eat."

A bath. He is the devil.

"Do you accept?"

We reach the door. He doesn't need to tell me that if I don't, I will walk out of it for the last time.

"I'm in."

He stretches another smile. "Then I will see you this evening."

We step outside the white room into the white hall. The door at the far end is open. Dum and Dee have appeared on either side of me again, but this time at a respectful distance.

"These novices will see to your needs. You need only ask for whatever you wish."

One of them extends an arm, directing me in the direction I must go. My gaze follows his hand to the sight of two columns of novices marching towards us. They carry a black box on their shoulders. As they approach, I reflexively step back to let them pass. The box is smooth, featureless, long. A coffin. It passes into the white room. My gaze stops at Phanuel's face as he stands at the door.

He steps back into the room, smiling at my expression.

"Care and consideration."

The door closes on me. I exchange vacant stares with Dum and Dee before dragging to my room.

My room is not far. It is on the same floor, only at what I am guessing is the opposite end of the building. Not surprisingly, it is white, but it has windows. I go to them and catch the glimmer of Elliott Bay framed by tall buildings. From this perspective, I guess I am forty stories up. The feel of the sun on my skin gives the sensation of being touched. Trying not to dwell on it, I close the curtains. When I turn, Dum and Dee have positioned themselves at the door. They stare at nothing, but I suspect see everything. Ignoring them, which I find easier to do all the time, I survey the rest of the room.

It is spare, only luxuriously so. It is the first room I have seen with real carpeting, a thick pile of white Berber. A long bench faces the windows, polished marble topped with a thick mattress upholstered in silk. Beyond it, the oversized bed is dressed with an ocean of satin under crisp pillows. Going to the bed, I pull back the bedcover and sit, feeling the dense cotton sheets under my fingers. Smoothing a pillow, I imagine it under my head. But I ache. And smell. Bath first.

The bathroom is a cavern of white marble. Marble floors meet tiled walls and a granite vanity that runs the length of one side, backed with mirrors. The granite tub at the far end looks like a sconce in a mausoleum. Right now, it is all I want. I take no further notice of my surroundings, but check outside the bathroom door. Dum and Dee still stand sentinel.

"I'm taking a bath."

Neither of them speaks or looks at me.

"If you want to get me something to eat, I don't care what. Anything will do." I nearly shut the door and then remember. "No muffins."

Behind the bathroom door, I think about locking it, remember what I am dealing with, and wave it off. Kicking off my Keds, I peel off my cotton shirt, and unbutton my jeans as I cross the expanse of marble tiles to the tub. I pull the stopper and turn the faucet to hot. Water sheets over a lip of stone.

Glancing around for toiletries, I spot a glass jar of bath crystals on the vanity. I go to the counter and pick up the jar, removing the stopper to sniff the contents. Lilac. Looking at my reflection in the mirror, I feel along the bottom of it and pull it open to reveal the medicine cabinet. Inside is some hair gel, brushes, two tubes of lipstick. This was a woman's bathroom.

Sarah.

Returning to the tub, I pour in a handful of crystals and watch them fizz. Checking the temperature with my fingers, I step in and settle down as the water rises around me. Sitting up, I reach down to rub sore feet as I observe the room once more. Behind me, a shelf of brushed nickel displays rolls of towels stacked like cord wood. I shut off the water and the room is silent. Reclining in the bubbles, I stare up at the sky light over the tub.

"No attachments my ass."

I remember how Michael lived when we first met. Like a ghost in an abandoned house. Abandoned by life. By me. He haunted it alone for nearly thirty years waiting for me to come back. And that's how I found him: eating junk and sleeping in a box. He hadn't lived like that when Daniel was alive. He just didn't care to continue living when Daniel was gone.

Now Michael thinks I am gone. And he is sleeping in a box.

Michael?

Hearing only silence, I take a deep breath.
I'm still here.
I take another breath, willing him to hear me.
This time, I'm taking you with me.
Inhaling, I close my eyes and slip beneath the water.

After a nap and a meal consisting of one chicken breast and green beans, I am taken downstairs to the vacant floor by Dum and Dee.

"Did you sleep?" Phanuel's voice echoes across the darkened space.

"With the fishes."

Glancing at the split in the concrete between us, I take a chair across from Phanuel, pressing myself against the hard back.

"I'm afraid I'm not very familiar with humans. Is that a good thing?"

"Better than a crypt. You should try it some time."

He gives a small smile. "Since you mentioned it, I was wondering if you happened to know where Michael's might be."

I shake my head. "Is it missing?"

"I'm afraid so."

"Good. I hated that thing."

"Well, it's of no use to anyone now."

I nod. "Since Michael doesn't exist anymore."

"Yes."

"Then why did you say I could share a life with him?"

Phanuel smiles. "He exists inside Bahiel now. That's where you could help me. Where we could help each other."

"How?"

"As profane as it was, your marriage has created a unique connection between you. Now that Sam is joined with him, you are the only individual left who can read his mind."

"You flatter me."

"As you flatter me by deigning to treat with one who entrapped your husband."

"Keep talking. You're good at it."

"There is little to say. Simply put, I need a translator."

I feel my face pinch. "Me?"

"You saw how he responded, or rather, didn't respond, to me."

"Maybe he doesn't like you."

"I need you to find out."

I shake my head. "I tried. He couldn't hear me."

"He wouldn't in session. He shouldn't hear anyone other than Metatron's holder during a vision. My voice would have been the only one he could hear, if he heard it at all."

"You mean you still can't communicate with him?"

"Bahiel has become Metatron's servus, the link between Metatron and the Child who will complete the prophecy. From now on, he will only see with Metatron's eye and hear the Child's voice. He is their connection—the third rail, as it were."

My brain does not accept what I am hearing. "Only see with Metatron's eye. You mean he's blind?"

"And deaf."

I stare. "Permanently?"

"To this world, yes."

"But you think he can hear me?"

"Yes."

"But if he could hear my thoughts, he'd be speaking to me now."

"That is why he has been placed in a keep. He can't communicate with anything inside it. So long as the Child exists, what he is capable of is too dangerous to be left unsecured. Like Metatron, he will only leave his keep when in service."

"Keep? *That box?*"

"His existence is as profane as Metatron is sacred. Both must be carefully guarded."

"Care and consideration my ass!"

Phanuel smiles. "He is once again free of attachment. His needs are few."

"How is my help going to save him?"

"Bahiel is only a threat as long as the Child exists. Metatron can show him the Child. I want to know where It is."

"Why?"

"You needn't worry about that. What I offer you is a trade. If Bahiel tells me where I can find the Child and I find It, the prophecy will be broken and he will be free to go."

"Find It. You mean kill It."

"I mean to prevent the destruction of our way of life. You may still live yours."

"With who?" I sit forward. "With what? Bahiel?"

He put out his hand. "Sophie, what I offer you comes with little risk. All I need is for you to ask him some questions. If you refuse, you will leave here alone and leave him a prisoner in perpetuity. I understand you have no reason to trust me, but what will you lose by comparison?"

I press my palms over my eyes.

"Will you at least see him?"

My hands drop to my lap.

"Yes." I choke. "Please."

～

[Tomb relief of Three Monkeys. Han Dynasty 202 BC - 220 AD.]

1199 BC For two days, we made progress. Each day I felt the earth pass under my crypt. Each evening I emerged to a banquet of food and a report on our progress from the general. Word of the one god had spread along the coast, and pilgrims from four coastal tribes joined us, swelling our ranks. We would reach Amurru the next day. Scouts had encountered nomads leaving Amurru who said rumors had reached Lod. Five tribes of Canaan had converged there. I suspected they would not wait for us.

They did not. The following morning, dust rose like smoke on the eastern horizon. My eye saw what scouts could not. An army was approaching.

The general was unfazed. "We will double your guard."

I shook my head. "I will ride with you."

"You cannot." His expression grew urgent. "You cannot be seen."

"I will be seen. I will not be bound by my crypt while an army rides upon us."

"You are a god. You cannot be seen moving among men!"

"They will not see a god. They will see Khepera, a young man, nothing more."

"They have forgotten Khepera. If he suddenly returns, what will they think?"

"If all else were different, they would think the same."

The general only covered his face with his hands.

"Bring me a cloak and horse."

His hands fell. "And sword."

"No more swords." I left the table.

"And if we fight? What will you do?"

"If we fight, I have failed as your guide. I have sworn to ride with you to Lod, and we are far short of it."

"I believe they mean to keep us so."

"We must change that."

"How?"

"You want my guidance?"

"Of course."

"Then you must trust me."

For a moment, the general stared silently, then left the tent. He returned with a riding cloak and a sword. The sword of Amenteth. He handed it to me.

"I thought you said this was cursed?"

He shrugged. "Only to the one who bears it. Since it cannot kill you, who better?"

Strapping the scabbard to my belt, I took the cloak from his other hand and headed out of the tent.

"Not that way!" He called, but the sky was already over my head.

The guards looked at me with alarm on their faces. When I smiled, they dropped their stares. It was going to be a good day.

[Spharic. Entry translated from *Kor Dai Maihael*. Mund Dai. d. 755 BC]

2000   "Who's left on the list?" The tone of her voice made him tense.
"Your mother and Maeve."

"Shit." She muttered.

He opened the trunk of the car, carefully loading the bags.

Closing the lid, he watched her stare across the mall parking lot, absently chewing the end of her thumb.

"It's only two people." He summoned his calm to soothe her. "You can shop for them next weekend."

"I cleared this weekend for Christmas shopping." Her tone remained unchanged. "Next weekend is Amy's party, the office party, and then, well—"

"Christmas." He finished.

She tossed up her hands and stomped to the passenger door, slamming it behind her. He sighed at the trunk of the car.

Her door opened. "You coming?" It slammed shut again.

He wanted to say no.

Then just say so! Her thought reverberated in his head.

Damn.

She got out. Leaving her door open, she marched up to him, thrusting out a palm. "Keys."

Stepping back, he shook his head. "I'll drive."

"No! You're tired and I've got to get this done. *Keys!*"

He reached in his pocket and pulled them out. She snatched them away and pushed past him. He watched her stomp to the driver's side and get in, slamming the door.

Sophie—

She honked the horn and he started to move.

Barely in his seat, she backed out of the parking space before his door closed. "Where are we going?"

"Home."

He blinked. "I thought we had to finish shopping?"

"I do."

The shorter her answers got, the longer she stayed angry. If he asked her questions, she would vent her anger at him. If he didn't, she would explode.

"Why are we going home?" He felt himself grip the passenger door.

"Because I'm leaving you there."

Swallowing back a sigh, he considered his options.

If he went without complaint, it was confirmation he didn't care.

If he argued to stay, she would convince him he didn't want to.

She wanted him to argue to stay, to argue long enough for him to feel defeated if she left him behind. Then it would be a punishment. She would finish without him to remind him of it later. For the rest of her life.

That suddenly seemed a long time.

"You don't have to drive me home." He spoke quietly.

"I know that. You're lucky I didn't leave you in the parking lot."

He only knew one way to save himself.

"Sophie, I want to shop with you, to do everything with you ... even run."

She glanced over. "Run?"

"I have to. You're going too fast for me."

"Fast? You're the one who wanted to get married!"

"That's not what I meant. I mean ... I haven't been feeling well."

The car slowed. "You're sick? I thought that was impossible?"

"It isn't a cold. I'm different. I've changed. Mentally, physically, in a good way, in a way I want, but I get tired now, Sophie. I'm not the relentless creature who took you looking for houses a year ago."

"That's what I fell in love with!" Tossing up her hands, she released the wheel, making him cringe. "I love relentless creatures."

"You love sympathy and affection and physical contact. Those are traits few relentless creatures share."

"I can't believe you're changing on me! I thought the number one mistake women made was thinking they could change a man after they married him. I don't ask you questions, I put up with your disappearances, I let you read my mind ... haven't I accepted you for what you are?"

"You have. You knew what I was, and I was honest about what I wanted. The day you agreed to move in with me, I told you I wanted to blend. You've always known I wanted to be a person, and you've tried to guide me. What angers you isn't that I'm changing, but that I feel it. You want me to be human without feeling human. You anger at my fatigue because it frightens you."

For a while she drove in silence.

"Just admit it, Mike. You hate shopping."

He sighed. "I hate shopping."

She made a sudden lane change. Feeling his body against his seat, the car strained to accelerate to sixty in four seconds as they sped onto I-5.

"You're not taking me home?"

"Better. Seattle."

Feeling himself flush, he tried to hide his alarm. "What's in Seattle?"

"While you were talking, I remembered Mom complained about how many pieces of her porcelain Dad broke over the years. She could use a new set."

While he was talking? He had felt her listening, not thinking about porcelain.

She continued. "I was thinking Uwajimaya would have something."

Chinatown. The International District. It was at the other end of the city from ECCO. The chance he would run into anyone was slim.

He nodded. "They have a good bakery."

"You know it'll be crowded. It isn't going to be fun, but I can go in alone if you want. You can sleep in the car."

He was about to ask why he had to go to Seattle if she wanted him to stay in the car but decided this was a test.

"No. I'll go in with you."

"Are you sure? You do look kind of peaked."

She took a long look at him, making him nervous—not because he was feeling self-conscious but because she was speeding in the HOV lane again.

"I'll be fine."

"Take a nap." The car sped faster. "I'll wake you when we get there."

"I'm fine."

Her eyes left the highway again. "You don't like my driving?"

"You drive very well."

She stared.

He slid back in his seat and shut his eyes. "Maybe a nap would be a good idea."

"You mind the radio?"

"It doesn't make a difference." He kept his eyes closed, but watched the road.

"No sonar." She grinned. "I promise."

He smiled as she switched on the radio and tuned it to KPLU. It was one of the few stations she listened to during the holidays. Even he had to admit, jazz made most Christmas songs tolerable. A trio was playing "Greensleeves." It started to rain and Sophie flipped on the windshield wipers. He listened to the rain drops.

In his mind's eye, they turned to snow.

Drifts of it.

Around trees, and a house, with a family. He didn't recognize the trees or the house, but he recognized the family. Sophie's parents were in the kitchen. Her Aunt Maeve was playing a guitar and singing with Kate. The house felt full and uncomfortably warm. Lodi agreed with him. He went to the door, letting Lodi into the snow. Outside, it was brilliant and cold. It felt good on his face.

He walked into the yard, following in Lodi's wake. A big yard, with no drive. A family of snow people stood buried in a fresh drift. Not far, a small person had made a body imprint. The snow angel who made it was not in evidence. There was a knock on a window. He looked up to see Sophie's mother in the kitchen. She pointed to her head and pointed at him. He smiled at her to speak when Lodi's reflection in the glass caught his eye.

Lodi sat in the snow where he should have been standing.

Looking down, he saw his boots. When he looked at the window, there was only Lodi's reflection, not his own. He turned from the window to look at Lodi, seeing only a set of dog tracks leading from the house. When he turned back to Sophie's mother, the window was empty, the kitchen dark. Only his reflection looked back at him in the glass.

Lodi's bark made him turn. Following the sound across the yard, there was no street to be seen, only trees. He moved among them, tall and heavy-laden. Lodi raced by, plowing through the drifts. Pushing farther into the forest, he quickened his pace to keep up as the jingle of Lodi's tags grew fainter.

Soon, there was only the sound of his feet in the snow.

"Lodi!" The name fell near where he stood.

There was silence.

He continued on the trail, Lodi's tracks wound around trunks of trees that seemed to grow larger—in rows, the trail straightening into a road. A wall of trees stretched out of sight, becoming great obelisks. Great buildings.

Pausing to look behind, his feet left no trace. Ahead, Lodi's tracks led to the horizon.

"Lodi!"

He kept walking.

"Lodi!"

He heard a yelp and stopped. Taking another step, he heard it again. Stricken.

Without thought, he began to run. As fast as he was, the snow frustrated him. Lodi's tracks finally turned, leading to a building, through an open door. Stepping back from it, he saw the building disappeared into the sky. Inside, the tracks continued up a winding stair. A howl from above urged him on.

Climbing the stairs, he began to feel his breath, his footing sure, though he could not see the steps. The snow was as deep inside the building as out. With each step, the howling grew louder, echoing until the steps beneath his feet began to tremble. The higher he climbed, the louder the howls. Ice began to cleave from the steps above him. The handrail began to whine, trimmed with icicles that began to snap and fall, shattering as they ricocheted down the stairwell. The way before him vanished in an avalanche of snow, the stair underfoot falling away.

Weightlessness.

Falling.

Silence.

His eyes stared up, through the branches of trees.

It was the forest. Snow fell on his face, into his eyes, and he blinked. He moved his hand to brush them away, but they strained as though bound at his sides. A great weight bore down on him. He tried to look down, but his head would not shift. His eyes rolled in his head, his peripheral vision seeing nothing to hold him. He could make out the front of his sweater as his chest rose and fell.

The snow fell.

It began to mask his face. The flakes stuck in his lashes, blinding, leaving only opaque light from above. He felt ice collecting under his chin and around his neck, the chill of it reaching into him.

Sophie!

All this time, he hadn't thought to wonder where she was.

Sophie! Help me!

"Michael?"

Her voice echoed between the trees.

"Michael? Where are you?"

I'm here!

"Michael, can you hear me?"

I'm in the snow. I can't move.

She came closer.

"Lodi! Where's Daddy?"

He heard the jingle of Lodi's collar.

"Where's Daddy? Can you bring me Daddy?"

Lodi's feet pounded the snow, closing on him.

Lodi! His mind beckoned. Come to me! Come.

Sophie's boots ran to catch up. She would see him. She had to.

Something galloped past, then stopped. Then a shadow, sniffing his face.

Good boy, Lodi. Show her.

The shadow galloped away and returned with a jingle.

Sophie called out, breathing hard. "What is it, boy?"

Show her where I am. Bring her to me.

"Did you find something?"

The boots came closer. He could hear her breath. Her shadow fell across his face.

"What's this?"

Her voice was over his head.

Sophie. I'm right here. I'm right under you.

Something reached for his face, brushing the snow.

"Daddy's keys." She gasped. "Michael? ... *Michael!*"

The shadow fled.

I'm here! I'm at your feet!

She was running away.

Stop! Sophie, stop! Come back!

"Michael!" Her voice grew distant. "Where are you?"

Sophie! Don't leave me!

The sound of her feet faded.

Sophie!

The crack of a tree branch broke the silence.

Sophie!

He heard footfalls.

Sophie! Come back. I'm where you found the keys.

Footsteps coming near.

You're getting close.

A shadow above. His ears strained, but she said nothing.

Sophie?

The temperature began to drop.

Please. Help me.

Cold washed over him, flooding within. Colder than snow. Colder than ice. Colder than cold.

Sophie. Please!

His limbs began to stiffen. His eyes no longer moved.

Sophie?

The shadow stood over him.

Who are you?

No one answered.
Who are you?!

Overhead, he heard an airplane.
The snowflakes pattered in his ears.
Like raindrops.
On windows. He was surrounded by them. Watched.
Someone was watching him.
Gasping, his nose registered the interior of car. His eyes opened.
Sitting up, he looked out his window. A woman's back was to him. She was loading a minivan. In a parking lot.
He was alone.
Sophie left him to finish shopping.
Blinking, he turned in his seat and saw the automated doors of Uwajimaya. He thought about going in to find her. Something told him not to. Taking a pair of sunglasses from the glove box, he put them on. Redirecting the rearview mirror on the storefront behind him, he sat back and spent twenty-six minutes watching shoppers come and go.
She came out of the store carrying a white paper bag suggestive a bakery. There was a grocery bagger pushing a cart behind her, struggling to keep up. He smiled at Sophie's quick step, the way her hips swayed with each stride. Her wool coat was unbuttoned, billowing behind her as she began to dig in her purse for keys. She wrestled with the purse and stuck the paper bag between her teeth, using both hands to extract his keys. Removing the bag from her mouth, she swore under her breath as she opened the trunk. She quickly appeared at his window.
He lowered it and she shoved the bag in his face.
"There, Sleeping Beauty. Hope they're still warm."
She left to help the bagger load the trunk. In the bag, he found three hum bows. He pulled one out and took a bite. Curried pork. By the time she was in the driver's seat, he had finished it and was starting on the second.
"Are they good?"
It was filled with barbecued pork. He offered it to her and she leaned over to take a bite.
Nodding, she shrugged. "Tastes like a hum bow to me." Then paused mid-chew. "So, what'd you dream about?"
"A white Christmas." He bit into the humbow.
"*Really?*" Her brows shot up. "That doesn't sound like you."
Chewing slowly, he squinted. "What do you mean?"
"It's so ... festive."
She started the engine and looked over her shoulder to back out.
Swallowing, he blinked. "We were with your family, at a house in the woods."
"Sounds cozy."
He studied her distracted face as she maneuvered the crowded parking lot.

"Then Lodi and I went for a walk in the snow."

"Sounds fun."

"Lodi ran away and I tracked him through a forest."

"Sounds like Lodi."

"He got trapped in a building that collapsed on me when I tried to rescue him."

Her eyes rolled. "That's my boy."

"Then I woke in a forest, but it was snowing, and I couldn't move."

"Why couldn't you move?"

"I don't know." He shrugged. "Maybe I was paralyzed after the building fell."

She snorted. "Nice."

"I could hear you and Lodi searching for me, but you never found me."

She stopped at a light. "You didn't call for help?"

"I tried ..." He took another bite of hum bow. "You couldn't hear me."

"So what happened?"

"I froze."

She shook her head as the light turned green.

"You know how I said I didn't want to change you?"

Taking another bite, he only nodded.

"I just thought of something."

He swallowed. "What?"

"Your attitude."

1199 BC Riding ahead of the caravan was wondrous. I was accompanied by four scouts and twelve of the front guard bearing a banner of treaty. None were eager to join me; only the order of the general kept them at my side. Unfortunately, the scouts spent more time observing me than the army we were riding to meet. Not that I needed them.

My eye saw more than enough. The army bore five colors under one banner. Though less than a quarter of our caravan, they were twice our number in fighting men. Poor odds for the general, even with Egyptian soldiers. The Canaans knew.

Even so, I strained to stay my mind. My eye wandered the open country as my body felt the lift of my horse beneath me. I imagined what it was like to exist in the world without a crypt. To go in any direction as far as one pleased. To never return to the same place twice.

What would I do if I could never go back?

A flash caught my eye. Shields in the foreground, coming from behind a ridge. It was an advance. They bore no banner. I called to the scouts to stop as my eye observed the intent of our opposition. Seventy-eight soldiers with a party of men in Canaanite robes. These men were unarmed, two with gray beards.

"It is a legion." The first scout muttered.

Our guard shifted uneasily.

"No." I dismissed him. "Not even close. They escort the wise. They come to talk."

"How do you suppose?" The scout doubted.

"I see them."

"From here?"

"You've been staring at the sun too long."

The guards snickered at this.

The scout only glared. "And if you are wrong?"

"You will die in the service of the general and our lord Re."

"If Re is the one god, we should not have to."

I smiled. "That is the hope."

Dismounting, I led my horse to the shade of a tree and sat against the trunk of it.

"What now?" The scout called to me.

"We wait."

Closing my eyes, I took rest.

The sound of their horses woke me. The guard had taken ease, playing lots in the shade while the scouts had scattered, keeping watch in all directions for any sign. What I heard was beyond their senses. I rose and approached where the soldiers were playing. They stopped as I neared, bowing low to them.

"They are coming."

The men scrambled to readiness as the first scout rode up to announce the same. All mounted their horses, save me. Holding my horse, I stroked its muzzle as it trembled at my touch. Hooves stamped nervously, sensing some arrival.

The spectacle was unnerving. The Canaans wore no uniform, their armaments, hair, and dress varying by tribe. Their horses were likewise mixed. Bred from all corners, some labored worse than others in the heat, their snorts and groans giving the column a beastly heave.

Our own animals seemed revolted. Their riders likewise. When the Canaan advance stopped, the mistrust in their eyes mirrored our disdain. A tall rider in a peaked helmet stood proud of the rest, but the ears I needed to reach were behind him.

Stepping forward, I bent my knee.

"Our lord sends greetings and wishes you fair ways."

"We welcome Ramesses and honor his word."

The tall rider replied in Hule, a dialect of Amman close to the Habiru in our caravan. I adopted his speech without notice.

"I do not speak for Ramesses, only for those who would be free of him."

His eyes widened. "Whoever they are, you speak well."

"I must if we are to live together."

"Together?"

"As one people."

"Under whom?"

"One god."

The tall rider sat up. "Re?"

"If you like."

"I do not! *We will not!*"

A voice from behind interrupted. "Chiron! Open your ears!"

A horse moved forward.

One of the gray beards appeared, his eyes searching me.

"You speak for Egypt?"

"Never."

"You speak the truth?"

"When I know it."

The gray beard nodded. "Lead us."

[Spharic. Entry translated from *Kor Dai Maihael*. Mund Dai. d. 755 BC]

~

2003 It is the end. Thinking is no good. He is all thought out. It has all been done. There is nothing left. As he lets go, reciting the words he has dreamed, his last decision is one of necessity. His declaration will be spoken plain, if Sophie will hear it. He knows she will need to. It is all he can offer.

Except something isn't right.

He knows the moment he speaks his name. What happens is not according to plan. His words aren't coming out right. His words aren't coming out at all.

Phanuel, stop.

Phanuel is trying to break the oath before it is made. Trying to stop his plea.

Phanuel, stop!

There is no reason to kill her. No reason to fear her.

I ask for refuge! The prophecy is broken!

Nothing happens.

He is not in his body. He is not in Metatron. He feels no fire.

Phanuel, speak to me! What is happening?

Phanuel says nothing.

Does nothing. He can see him, holding Metatron and nothing more. The flood in his ears should be burning, the black well of Metatron pulling him apart. All thought carved away, compressed, into a bottomless pit.

There is a brilliant flash. Then silence.

It sees.

Everything.

It knows this is real.

Sophie.

She is here. She stares at It.

Sophie?

It cannot speak.

It sees Phanuel, Metatron in hand, lips moving silently.

Phanuel?

It cannot hear.

Phanuel takes Metatron away, to the keep. It sees the orb lowered inside. It sees the lid snuff out the light.

It cannot see.

Ragged breath wakes him. He is in his body. On something hard. His fingers feel a rough surface beneath him. The shadows in his head do not lighten when he opens his eyes. He blinks. It could simply be the dark. His eyes weak, as they were in the cells. He listens, hearing nothing. Not even his heart. He turns his head, but is stabbed, like an ops in his skull. His brain burns, but his head is cold. A rough chill rubs against the back of his scalp. It is bare.

Lifting his hands to his head, his elbows hit something. Reaching out, his fingers touch it. Pressing his palms, he runs his hands across the grit above him. A lid. But not of a crypt.

The lid of a crypt is an arm's length from the face, the sides from top to bottom far exceeding his frame, a perfect construct of enlivening. Four by four by eight. Solid oiolithe. Living stone. This lid feels barely ten inches from his nose; the sides spare him even less. Blind with pain, he knows there is no light, can feel there is none. The air inside is dead. It is black rock. A keep.

He pushes against the lid. It does not give. He pushes harder. It holds fast. He braces his arms against the sides, feels his knees against it, barely able to bend. It withstands him and he does not feel weak. In spite of the ache in his brain, his body feels whole. In spite of the dark, he feels his strength. It avails him nothing.

A gasp slips his lips soundlessly.

There is no point in crying out. Anyone outside will hear him as well as he hears himself. He rests. His hand crosses his chest and feels fabric under fingertips: raw silk, coarsely woven. It drapes the length of him, the sleeves are loose and long. Sophie would call it a caftan. Phanuel would call it an alb. He will call it frightful.

They were worn long ago, by those who swore servitude to Metatron. The chosen. Rendered deaf and blind with shorn heads, they forgave their senses, their thoughts, themselves, to channel Metatron's visions. He remembers hearing of their rituals. They were guarded as relics. They were fed blood.

But they no longer exist.

Bahiel destroyed them.

Samael hated them.

He feared them.

Reaching over his face, the shape of his head fills his hands.

He knows this is real. It is as real as the sun and the moon and the stars. As real as Sophie and Lodi and the people he calls his family. He knows what planet he is on. The city he is in. The languages being spoken. All around him, people are eating and sleeping, laughing and crying, living and dying. None of them knows he exists.

He wonders why he does if this is the case.

How can they be reading a paper and drinking lattes while he is trapped in this box? How can they complain about the boredom of their lives?

Is this what humans fantasize about?

An eternal struggle for domination of the universe by the undead? Angels and demons. Witches and warlocks. Vampires and werewolves. Mummies. All of it wrong. All of it ridiculous. All of it unnervingly comparable to his miserable existence.

He cannot remember being happy before Sophie.

It only starts when she accepts him. When he does something no human can and it impresses her. When she loves him for being different makes it all right. It is all right. Perhaps this is his challenge. Maybe it isn't about loving Sophie but loving himself.

It is all right.

It is believing he has to sacrifice himself for her that is wrong. It is believing he is responsible for her that is wrong. He has sacrificed himself to his fears again. Now he is inside them, and Phanuel means to keep him there.

He will not be kept.

"I will not."

The words move his mouth, but not his ears. He is being kept. For now.

There is movement. His consciousness is slow to take hold. There is no memory of sleep, only a recurrence of lucid moments. Ever since his encounter with Metatron, he has fallen to darkness and come around, still finding himself in a keep of black rock.

Not this time.

Opening his eyes, he feels her. Hands grip his arms and his instinct is to fight them. When they pull him upright, the scream in his head makes him cry out.

He cannot hear it, but she does.

Michael!

His body spasms at the pain as his strength flees him. The hands of novices restrain him and he is enraged. Fighting for control, he lashes out. The charge is sent blindly. It is a short fall to the floor. He lands on the leg of a fallen novice before lunging for a neck, madly seizing it.

The presence of others close on him.

Michael!

A threat streams from his mouth, making the floor tremble. Their advance stops.

Can you hear me?

Her voice barely touches him.

Michael! Phanuel wants to speak to you.

He pulls the stunned novice to him, cradling the limp torso in his arms as he backs against the keep. His crouch is defensive, but deadly.

Phanuel orders you to let him go.

The head of the novice falls back on his knee. His mouth seeks a breath. Parting the lips with his teeth, he begins to assume it.

Michael, stop!

There is no light in his eyes, only a buzz in his head as the spirit of the creature in his arms drains into his own. A part of him hears her. Knows she has never seen him assume another before. Imagines she can hardly recognize him.

But they will feed him no blood.

His hands reach for his second novice, the scent of it only feet away.

A charge spikes the air and she screams. He doesn't feel it.

The pain is hers.

Sophie!

His thoughts assert themselves. They know Phanuel has her. They speak to her.

Tell him I'll kill him if he touches you.

He says that's up to you.

Slowly, he retreats from the novice beneath him.

He says if you do as he asks, you'll be fed.
He doesn't want to be fed. He speaks to Phanuel.
What do you want?
The answer comes in Sophie's voice.
What we all want. A future. For ECCO, for Sophie, for yourself.
None of which will be determined by you.
There is a pause before Sophie delivers a response.
Is this something you see?
It is something I know.
You will tell me.
There is nothing to tell.
For Sophie's sake, I hope there is.
Everything in him wants to kill something. He speaks to her instead.
Sophie, why are you still here?
You're my husband and I'm taking you with me.
I'm not Michael.
I know. You told me when you proposed.
I'm dead.
It's only hair. It'll grow back.
It was impossible not to smile.
That's my boy. Phanuel's getting nervous and so am I. If he shocks me like that again, I won't have any hair either.
His smile disappears.
What does he want?
He's looking for a child.
There isn't one.
He asks if you have seen into Metatron.
I have. There is no Child.
But did you look for It?
I would have seen It.
He wants you to look again.
Look again. The thought makes his head ache.
Sophie, there is no Child. Even if I look again, Phanuel won't accept it. Even if he does, he will never let me go. You must leave.
You think he'll let me walk out of here? You're no good to him without me.
You can't intend to stay here with me.
I admit it isn't fair. I've got Sarah's room and you've got a coffin, but we'll still be able to talk, and she's got a great bathtub.
I'm not staying, Sophie. I won't be kept.
Then say you'll look again and give me some time to bust us out of here.
He nods, more to relieve the danger to her than ease her mind.
Immediately, the air stirs. The inert novice is swept away. Tentative hands scarcely touch his sleeves, guiding him to his feet. He follows to the chair, sitting

quickly to ease his head. Phanuel's presence approaches, Metatron between them like a shield. Without It, Phanuel is nothing. Without It, Phanuel would be in his grasp, assumed like a novice, only far more satisfying.

There is no ritual to follow. Phanuel may be Metatron's holder, but It no longer waits to be prompted. As It nears, he feels It begin to take hold. When the vision ends, he will slip into darkness again. Awaken in his box. He calls to her as his mind begins to drown.

I'll see you soon.

When he wakes to his breath, it is thin. There is no reason to move, to tempt the suffering in his skull. He knows where he is, feels the world cut away from him. Now there is only pain, only impossibly worse. Simply being awake makes it worse. He is angry. No, not angry.

Pissed.

He should have smote Phanuel where he stood. Metatron be damned. ECCO be damned. Sophie be damned. What does she know? How can she save them?

Buy her time. He doesn't need to. He has all of it. More than he wants. She doesn't. She is wasting hers.

So is Phanuel.

There is no Child. He looked and saw nothing. The prophecy remains un-fulfilled. There is no seed. Whether or not Phanuel sees this as good news, he cannot foresee. For himself, it will be bad either way. Phanuel can't walk away from power, even if it is power beyond any control. Especially that. Why bother to deliver the news? To tempt Phanuel to keep him. Control him.

Feed him.

He was not fed. Even though he did as Phanuel asked. Phanuel starved him before and is starving him now. Not that he will accept. Blood or baked Alaska, he will throw it in Phanuel's face. But assuming novices will not be enough. Assumption feeds the spirit, not the body. Assuming the novice only fed his rage. His body hungers even as the memory of food escapes him. His body re-calls a smell and it excites him. He smelled it the moment they lifted the lid.

Her scent.

The thought of her warms him. In the dark, he can still see her: the black stockings, the red corset, the choker. Seeing her. Being her. Taking her.

In the silence, he hears her heart.

Phanuel will never let her go, either. He has bought them time enough.

When the lid lifts, he will free them both.

Then Herod, when he saw that he was mocked of the wise men, was exceeding wroth, and sent forth, and slew all the children that were in Bethlehem, and in all the coasts thereof, from two years old and under, according to the time which he had diligently inquired of the wise men. Then was fulfilled that which was spoken by Jeremiah the prophet saying, In Rama was there a voice heard, lamentation, and weeping, and great mourning...

[Excerpt, *Book of Matthew 2:16.18, Holy Bible, King James Version.* d. 1695]

2000   Scooping a handful of powder, I packed it between my palms, warming it with my breath to make it stick.

"I wish you wouldn't walk in the street."

His composure hovered in the falling snow as we climbed Carr Hill.

"What?" I looked down deserted streets. "You're worried someone'll hit me?"

My boots held better to the cobbles in the road than the slick of the sidewalk his feet barely seemed to touch. Without a glance, I threw the snowball at him. It exploded in the night air, blocked by the palm of his hand.

"What were the odds." I rolled my eyes as I bent to fill my gloves again.

"I'm sorry. If you throw another, I won't stop you."

"Nah. Won't work."

Continuing uphill, I packed the snow in my glove.

"Why not?"

"Won't count."

"Won't count?"

"Without the element of surprise. Since surprising you is impossible, there really isn't any point."

"Not impossible. It happens all the time."

"My point exactly."

Pausing in the street, I threw at him. A direct hit to the shoulder. Looking at himself, he brushed the snow off his coat and shrugged.

"Nope." I frowned. "Not the same."

Stooping, I collected another round from a drift at my feet. Ahead, St. Patrick Parish stood blackly against the pink glow of the sky, the stained-glass windows lit from within only a few nights of the year. Faint singing said midnight mass was underway. I knew Anthony was singing with them. Alone.

"What were you doing this time last year?" I asked.

"Reading."

"What?"

"*The Prophetic Line.*"

Cupping my snowball, I made a face. "Sounds longer than *Overview of the American Judiciary.*"

"Somewhat." He smiled but kept his eyes on the sidewalk.

"What's it about?" I waved my snowball. "And don't say the Prophetic Line."

"The course of known prediction for the cycle of the universe."

"Cycle of the universe. I'm drawing a blank."

"Just as the poles of this planet will alternate over the course of its existence, so will the universe at large. Nothing can remain static. It is the key to universal knowledge. For some, the ability to predict the course of existence is a testament to their mastery over it."

"And what do they predict?"

"That is subject to interpretation."

"Okay. What do you predict?"

"I don't try. I only seek to anticipate the interpretations of others in an attempt to prepare for all possible outcomes."

"Why?"

"I don't like surprises."

"And you found this festive reading on Christmas Eve?"

"More an ongoing subject of concern."

I stopped. "Anything I need to worry about?"

He continued to stare down the sidewalk. "I hope not."

"Care to elaborate?"

"No."

He started to walk again, but I jumped in front of him.

"Why not?"

He smiled beautifully. "If I do it won't count."

I smirked. "What do you mean it won't count?"

"It'll ruin the surprise—"

The word was barely out of his mouth when I pressed my snowball in his face. Then I ran. At least that was the plan. I think I turned around, maybe took a step. Feeling something around my waist, my feet left the ground, but there was no impact. Gravity didn't wrestle me to the snow as much as some invisible hand had lain me on it. He was over me, sprinkling my head with it. I shrieked and smeared handfuls in his hair before he pinned me, blotting out the sky with glittering eyes.

Without a word, he kissed me. Under my fleece, I was covered in goose bumps.

"Everything all right?" A rough voice made me start.

Michael lifted his face from mine. "Perfect."

Getting to his feet, he pulled me up with him and I quickly brushed my hair from my face. When I turned, I was confronted by a tall man in a Pendleton coat, scowling under a wiry unibrow. He was armed with a shovel and stood in the open gate of a fenced yard.

"Sorry." I cleared my throat and glanced at Mike. "Slipped."

The man looked me over, then sneered past my shoulder at Mike.

"If I were you, I'd do her where it's warm."

My mouth opened.

"Sophie, let's go." Michael had my wrist.

My eyes locked on the unibrow. "If I were you, I'd take that shovel—"

"Sophie—" Mike yanked me down the sidewalk.

"—stick it up your ass!" I yelled back.

The man stepped onto the sidewalk. "*What was that?*"

"She said we'll be late for Mass!" Michael called back over his shoulder.

He pushed me ahead of him, brushing the snow off of my back as we went.

"What an asshole!" My boots dug into the ice.

"He was looking for fight."

"Lucky for him you're a pacifist!"

"Violence would have only made things worse."

The voice of reason frustrated me. "I know that!"

"Are you angry with me?"

"Of course I am!"

I marched ahead, following a rut of frozen tracks in the snow.

"You wanted me to fight him?"

"No!" I stopped, pointing at myself. "I wanted to fight him and you wouldn't let me!"

"He had a shovel."

"And a set of gonads that needed a woman's touch!" I stomped away.

Michael caught up. "It would have been a waste your time."

Gritting my teeth, I thought nothing.

"And your touch." He added.

The sound of his step picked up to keep pace with me. One of my feet slipped, but I caught myself and kept going.

"What were you doing this time last year?" He slipped his hand over mine.

"Hey." We passed a house and I pointed to a plaque. "Bing Crosby was born here."

"Now you're the one who doesn't want to talk."

"I made a prophecy of my own. I was in my old bed at home guessing Christmas would never be the same."

"Why?"

I looked at him incredulously. "Why do you think?"

He stopped. "Because of me?"

Across the street, the choir singing in St. Pat's was clear. I stared up at gothic windows rising to a stone cross and the bell tower high above.

"What's it all for, Mike?" I pointed. "Jesus, Mary, 'Jingle Bells.' Why?"

His face went blank. "People believe what they need to."

"I don't need to believe any of it. I just want the truth. It's been a year, and I've never asked you anything obvious." I could see his mouth tense. "Is there a God?"

"I don't know."

"Jesus, Mike! If you don't know, we're all screwed."

"I'm just me, Sophie. Regardless of whether I was there or not, it doesn't make me an authority. My interpretation isn't any better or worse than your own."

"I don't spend Christmas Eve reading *The Prophetic Line*."

"If I knew the truth, I wouldn't be reading something I never forgot in the vain hope that I did."

"You know enough to be afraid."

"What I'm afraid of already happened."

"What's that?"

"I've ruined Christmas for you."

"You have."

He dropped his gaze.

I sighed, "Last year, the only thing I could think about on Christmas Eve was you."

He lifted his eyes as I continued.

"I thought it was just a fluke because you'd agreed to go with me to the New Year's Ball, but no. It's even worse this Christmas and you've had a year to get on my nerves. I must really like you."

Turning my back on him, I crossed the street. He followed in silence.

"Sophie?"

"What, Michael." I kept walking.

"Can't we meet in the middle?"

I stopped. "What?"

"I think we agree, we're both afraid of what we don't know."

"I'm a little more in the dark than you."

"I wish I could convince you that isn't true."

"You're risking more."

"Not at all."

"Come on, Mike. Last year the thought of dating me left you contemplating the fate of the universe."

"You think too much of me."

"I think you're hotter than Saint Nick."

"I'm worried I'll fail you."

"I'm not, so stop worrying."

"I'll try if you stop asking what I'm worried about."

"I won't have to ask if you aren't."

He nodded. "I'll stop."

"No more *Prophetic Line*?"

He nodded again. "And no more magic tricks."

"Fine." I continued down the street. "But I'm keeping the costume."

His feet caught up to me. "Why?"

Wrapping an arm around his, I grinned. "Because you look so cute in it."

"You mean ridiculous."

"I mean cute. Why do think Amy and Lyn got so excited over your act?"

He shrugged.

"They thought you were hot."

All I heard next to me was the hush of his feet in the snow. When I looked at him, his head was down, his hands in his pockets.

"That bothers you?"

"They were attracted to the illusion of not knowing who I was."

"I thought you'd be used to that."

"The illusion was flagrant. They knew it was me and they didn't care. They wanted to be lied to. They wanted to believe the magic was real."

"In this case, it was."

"That's not how I want to be accepted. Not within the confines of a costume and a bag of tricks."

"So you won't wear it? Even for me?"

He stared. "What would you have me do if I did?"

"I don't know." I shrugged. "Sit in a chair, like Lyn had you doing."

"I sit in chairs all the time. What difference does it make what I'm wearing?"

"A lot. You're pretty intimidating."

"I am?" He looked surprised.

"Mike, I know you. Behind the icy blues and the ripped body, you're a giant puppy, but I still have to remind myself every time I look at you. The day you came to my office, it was like you were still you, only manageable."

"Manageable?"

"Like something I could afford to own."

"I'm not a toy."

"You already come in a box. What's the difference?"

"You already own me. When we're married, it'll be official. Isn't that enough?"

"Hey, if I'm risking fate marrying you, the least you can do is wear a squeaky nose."

He said nothing as we turned onto our street. At the top of Prospect, we approached our drive. Lodi began to bark from the porch, his chain rattling down the steps as he pulled it taut to meet us.

"I'm still smarter than him." Michael muttered.

"You are." I reached up and stroked the back of his head. "I was gone for twenty-seven years and I didn't have to chain you to anything."

I stroked Lodi next as he whimpered his greetings. Michael ignored us both and climbed the steps, unlocking the door. Letting Lodi off his lead, I followed inside, where Lodi eagerly tracked down his bed in the laundry room. Ditching my wet scarf and hat in the hamper, I kicked off my boots in the foyer before dragging up the stairs. It was nearly one in the morning, and the thought of facing the family for Christmas the next day was inconceivable. My brain shut off as I went through the motions of brushing teeth and rinsing contacts.

When I got to bed, my eyes didn't notice if anyone else was there.

"Sophie?"

"Hmm?"

"I know you kept the costume because I wore it when I proposed, but—"

"It's gone." I mumbled.

"What?"

"I told Lyn you were officially retiring and you wanted to give it to her for helping you get your voice back. She put it in her collection."

"Why did you do that?"

"It was only fair after you blew out her windows."

"That wasn't me."

"Sure it wasn't. Anyway, I wanted to give it to her. She worships me now."

"Then why tell me you were keeping it?"

I rolled over, grinning at the dim eyes next to my pillow.

"Just jerking your chain."

1199 BC   The sun was setting when we sighted the caravan. I had sent two scouts ahead to tell of our coming and my eye could see the general had arranged his tents in readiness. Near camp, the smell of smoke and cooking meat greeted us. The Canaan soldiers we led soon eased their reserve at the sight of so many Canaanites among the caravan. Only the suspect gaze of Ptah and his priests chilled the warm night.

Ptah had reason to be hostile. There was to be a meeting of the minds, but between the minds of men. After introducing the general to the Canaan ambassadors, we sat on rugs in his tent amidst a sea of bread and game. Sitting aside, I translated where there was need.

The need was little. With a welcome of fruit and wine, the general was as charming as he was plain-spoken. His humility comforted the gray beards, while his experience as a veteran appealed to Chiron. Above all, his resentment towards Ramesses appealed to the Canaan heart. When he spoke of an end to tribute, Chiron was quick to agree.

It was not until after the meal that the matter of belief was served.

"Which god do you follow, general?" The gray beard stroked a lock.

"The sun is my lord. I follow it by day and dream of it by night."

"Is this the lord Re we have heard of?"

To some.

I thought only to myself as I waited for the general to make his answer.

"To some."

At the echo of my thought, I looked to the general and caught his eye. Had he heard me?

The gray beard pressed him. "Then you are not devoted to that house?"

My answer echoed in my mind. *I am devoted to the spirit within men. As brothers with different names, our blood is the same.*

"I am devoted to the spirit within men." The general paused. "As brothers with different names, we bleed alike."

The general smiled at me, and I nodded. I would never put words in his mouth.

The gray beard continued, "But it is said a god leads this caravan. That Re is at your shoulder."

The general grinned, anticipating my next thought.

A spirit guides me, but you must ask him yourself if you wish to know more.

The smile fell from his face, and for a moment I feared a refusal of my request. When the general spoke, his voice was colorless.

"There is one who guides me. He will see you if you wish."

The gray beards glanced at each other. Finally, one spoke. "When?"

The general did not look to me, but only waited.

Dawn.

[Spharic. Entry translated from *Kor Dai Maihael*. Mund Dai. 755 BC]

2003 When his head nods in acceptance, the adrenalin rush subsides. From the moment they lifted the lid on him, the being I have struggled to communicate with has shocked me beyond Phanuel's ability to inflict pain. It is a sinewy figure. A Rodin in alabaster. White head, white hands, white eyes, constantly shifting, searching, hunting. Attacking savagely, speaking with the tongue of a devil, feeding like a lover, I feel his mouth on mine as I watch.

It is no way to see one's husband.

But the voice in my head is his. His first words reach out of concern for me. Out of love. Even as I see him led to the chair, the profile is the same. The shoulders, the chest, the shape of him, thinly visible under his robe, I know it. All of it. It is mine. He is still mine. Facing Metatron again, his last thought is mine.

I'll see you soon.

The interview with Metatron is the same. Blinding. Silent. Still. His eyes turned from white stone to white light. A strange pulse is shared between them. This time, Phanuel asks no questions. Michael knows what he has been asked to find. Time passes in measure only Phanuel seems to know. At a given time, Metatron is hidden away. The lid is lowered, the light is gone, and Michael is left a limp shadow.

I watch the novices carry him to the box. They lower him, reverently averting their eyes from his lifeless gaze. Phanuel closes the lid, slipping an object into a slot on the side of the box and quickly removing it. The object disappears into a pocket.

A key.

I drop my eyes before Phanuel turns to me.

"It is late."

With no clocks in the building, he gets no argument from me. He waves a hand to the door and I move to it.

"I appreciate your willingness to see him so soon. We have accomplished more than I hoped."

My head is in no mood for shop talk, but at the door I pause.

"How long before you need me?"

"Ten hours, maybe more. This will take more out of him than the first time."

"He'll be fed?"

At this, Phanuel grins. "Whatever he wants."

I am about to turn away.

"I must thank you for what you are doing. Without your help, none of this would be possible." His eyes take me in again. "His dedication to you is remarkable."

"It's my cooking." I stare blankly, then follow Dum and Dee to my room.

Phanuel is right. It is late. When I get to my room, the windows are lit by city lights. They don't open. I press my head against the glass and make out a stream of headlights on the streets below.

The doors behind me open and close. Dum carries a silver-domed tray to the nightstand by my bed before returning to his post by the door. They stood there while I napped after my bath and I assume they'll stand there all night while I sleep. Napping in my street clothes was one thing, but sleeping all night in them is another. It occurs to me I might borrow Sarah's clothes. My brain still operates under the conventions of request and permission. I didn't request to be here and Sarah is never coming back. I doubt Dum and Dee will care if I rummage her drawers.

Crossing to the bed, I peek under the polished lid of my meal. It is the same. A chicken breast with green beans and wild rice. Phanuel must think I need to lose weight. Bath first. After everything I've just seen, I'll never fall asleep without one. I drop the lid on my food. My hand falls past the tray, to the drawer in the nightstand below it. Pulling it open, I half hope to find a bottle of whiskey, but only find a half-dozen notebooks. I recognize the marbleized covers. Picking one up, I flip it open. Illegible, but the handwriting rings a bell. I drop it back in the drawer.

My reflection in the mirrored doors of the closet move me to investigate. If my shopping experience with Sarah was any indication, she should own a lot. The doors open to a walk-in. It wasn't just my imagination she never wore any colors. The clothes inside look like a gallery for White House Black Market. Searching a wall of built-in drawers, I finally find personal items: panties, bras, hosiery, and to my relief, sleepwear. Feeling sick of white, I pick out a black satin nightgown and matching robe before heading for my bath.

Sweeping past Dum and Dee, I enter the bathroom and this time pointedly lock the door. Laying out Sarah's clothes on the bath bench, I peel off my own and dump them in one of the bathroom sinks. Washed or burned, I won't wear them again. I pick up the jar of bath crystals and perch on the side of the tub. When I reach for the tub lever, a cool breeze makes me look up. Against the night sky, the glass skylight reflects me overhead. It is the only window in the room. It also seems closed from where I sit. I decide the draft must be the AC.

Pulling the tub lever, I start to fill it, feeling the temperature with my fingers. I watch the water coil in the bottom of the tub. It is spotless. Everything is. They probably disinfect everything when I leave. As the water rises, I open the jar of crystals. The white flakes shift and pour like sand. I hear a clink in the jar as something slips out, plopping into the bathwater with a splash. It is easy to see as it floats to the bottom.

Oblong, thin, black.

My hand is still frozen, holding the jar of crystals over the water. I blink a couple times before quickly setting down the jar to seize the object with both hands. It is wet in my palms, a wafer of black stone. A key? If it is, I can't be sure it is the right one. I am only sure of one thing. It wasn't there before.

When I leave the bathroom, it is gripped it in my hand, shoved in the pocket of my bathrobe. I sit at my bed and eat, feeling it tucked between my leg and the mattress. When I turn out the lights, it is at my side. I dream in the dark, eyes wide open, how I will use it. Somehow, I know the opportunity will come.

Closing my eyes, I wait. It is only a matter of time.

Seattle is in an earthquake zone. We don't have them frequently, but we all know they can happen—especially the big one. When the building shakes me awake in bed, my first thought is this might be it. When there is no tremor after, I sit up. Dum and Dee still stand at post, their eyes faintly visible across the room. When the building shakes a second time, the bedroom doors fly open. In the shadow of the doorway, the glimmer of passing eyes look like fireflies in the night. Two pairs of Dum and Dee file into the room. My hands fist in the pockets of my bathrobe as they come to my bedside and pull me to my feet.

As usual, nothing is said. With my arms held to my sides, I am nearly carried as my feet skim the cold tile of blackened corridors. We are surrounded by a rush of figures, passed on both sides by a steady stream of pale eyes. In moments, I am brought to a halt, the hands on my arms waiting long enough for my feet to find the floor before vanishing. A door shuts heavily behind me. The sound of a bolt says it won't be opening soon.

Thank God I don't have to piss.

Squinting, I catch the glimmer of two pairs of eyes. Dum and Dee are still with me. Turning away from them, all else is a black void. If this is the white room, the pedestal should be directly ahead—Michael's box some ten paces beyond it. I do not make a straight line. Instead, I let my toes trace the floor as hands reach out, not searching as much as sensing the air. Tracking to the left, my right hand knows what to expect. It isn't long before the tips of my fingers brush the side of the pedestal. As soon as its surface slips by, I need only walk a straight line to find my husband.

The closer I get, the harder my fingers wrap around the key. The sides of it squirm in the sweat of my palm. My steps slow, my toes trying to hit something without hitting it. Then something. I bend, reaching with my free hand. I haven't touched it before. It is smooth and sandy, the edges slightly jagged. Slowly sitting on the lid, I can't make out where Dum and Dee have gone. So I sit and do nothing, letting my eyes wander. My peripheral vision spots something, likely Dum, or Dee. They have moved to the corners of the room. Having seen them move, I know this means I have a whopping hundredth of a second longer to open the lid. Even if I get the lid open, I have no idea what condition my husband is in. If he is still unconscious, the effort will be wasted.

This is as close as I will ever get.

With a yawn, I shift on the box, letting my bathrobe drape over the edge of it. Palming the key, my hand slips from the pocket while I stretch my legs. Leaning over, as if looking at my feet, my fingers dangle along the side of the box, the key held under my thumb. My thumb catches on something. Feeling the slot, I let the key find the edge of it. It slips inside. There will be no disguising the rest. I have seen Phanuel do this once. The lid will only open when the key is pulled out.

I can't be sitting on it when it does.

Fingering the end of the key, I drop to my knees, pulling it out as I do. I move to push the lid, but it is already open. There is a crush as something comes at me from all sides. I hear the crack of a whip.

At first I am comfortable. Sleep still softens the edges. Vaguely, I feel a growing stiffness. When I move my arm, I am suddenly aware of how sore I am. My pillow is soft against my cheek, but hard underneath. My jaw and neck twisted, my ear twinging under the weight of my head. When I lift it, something brushes across my face. A hand rests on my head.

My eyes fly open.

"You're safe."

His voice vibrates through his chest, into my head. It sounds odd, not the sound as much as the shape of it. Close, closeted. It is silent again. His chest moves and I hear him breathe. There is no heart.

Gasping, I put out my hand, hitting stone the instant I try. Hands grip my arms to hold me, but I push back.

"Stop struggling, Sophie."

I'm terrified. Trapped in a box. Trapped with him. I hit my head.

"Ow!"

"I told you."

"Let me out!"

"It's open."

Air rushes in as the lid disappears overhead. Pushing off of him onto my knees, I stagger to my feet and trip over the side of the box, hearing my bathrobe snag the edge of it. One foot steps on something and I stop short, nearly falling. My hands feel a body as I catch myself. I jump back. It is Dum, or Dee. Or both. Out of nowhere, a hand grabs one of mine and I shriek. Prying it loose, I run blindly into the dark.

"Sophie!"

Hesitating, I reach around me for anything I can find.

"Sophie! Come back!"

I turn.

"... Sophie?" The sound of his voice breaks in the dark.

Out of sight, I hear my husband. Not the statue in the box.

Are you there? His thought is pleading. *Please, answer me.*

My lungs can't find enough air to speak. *I hate that!*

What?

How you scare the shit out of me and sound so pathetic at the same time!

I'm sorry. I didn't mean to frighten you.

I came here to get you out of that thing, not end up in it myself!

It's safer inside.

It isn't safe! It's a prison!

Only when it's locked.

It's me or the box, Mike!

I want you.

Then come to me.

I'm here.

Where?

In front of you.

I thought you couldn't see?

Your thoughts led me.

My hand bumps his chest and his hand quickly grabs hold of it. My feet back away.

I'm sorry.

He loosens his grip, but I am frozen.

Hesitantly, he lets go. I am about pull my hand away when he takes hold of it again. This time, his touch is light. His fingers lace with mine as he pulls me to him. I feel his frozen breath on the back of my hand, warm lips kiss it. His hands open my fingers to trace my palm before pressing it to his chest.

His skin is smooth and bare. I feel it tremble to my touch.

Your hand is still freezing.

My fingers pinch him.

And you're still hard as a rock.

I want you, Sophie.

And who are you?

His mouth answers. The one that consumed Dum and Dee and that other hapless creature before them. Now it is over mine. Consuming me. And for a moment, that seems all right.

Then my other hand takes hold of him.

The building shakes and he breaks away with a gasp.

Wait.

Fuck that.

I grab the back of his neck, but he resists.

When they come, I have to be ready.

Without any hair to hold, I lace my fingers behind his head.

They'll have to wait.

Sophie ...

If he thinks anything else, I don't hear it. All I hear is my heart. I kiss his face, and he begins to sink before me. His body shudders as I kneel with him. The floor is cold and hard under my knees. My teeth graze the side of his cheek and I see a light in the corner of my eye. When I look at him, his eyes glow a pale blue. The pounding in my ears is no longer my heart, but the rush of a tide.

Gently, I kiss him once more before pushing him back on the floor with a heavy thud. Crawling over him, I follow his eyes in the dark, hovering over his face as he stares at nothing, waiting.

He is mine.

My hand strays onto cold tile as I wake. I curl myself around the warm body beneath me and feel a hand on my head. It strokes my hair. Something nuzzles the top of my head, kissing it.

"Michael?"

"Hmm?" It resonates against my ear. His breathing is steady, his heart is strong. His heart.

"Michael?" My head pops up and I squint into the light of his eyes. "You can see?"

"Thanks to you."

Rising, I try not to crush him when I know I can't. "How do you feel?"

"Strangely enough, normal."

"How long was I asleep?"

"Twelve minutes."

"But you're awake ... you should be—"

"Dead to the world." He finishes. "I know. That puzzles me."

Suddenly, I remember my night with Sam.

"You know, I hate to mention it ..." I bite my lip.

"Sam didn't seem tired." He finishes my thought again.

"He slept, but something was different."

In the dark, I see Michael's head falls back.

"I have become Bahiel ..." He murmurs.

"No, you haven't." I scramble to my feet. "I feel you. You're still the same."

"Only because I obliterated Sam's sentience. Somehow I assumed his strength. It explains how I survived the fire, how my body recovered so quickly ... why Metatron took me."

"It doesn't have you. Not anymore."

"It has us both."

"Michael, we aren't staying here." I jab my thumb at nothing in the dark. "When that door opens, you're kicking Phanuel's ass!"

"Violence will only make things worse."

"*Violence?* You ate three people in the last twenty-four hours!"

"That wasn't me."

"You always say that!"

"Those were novices. They hardly qualify as people."

"So we're going to let an eight ball tell us what to do?"

"Not at all. When Phanuel opens that door, he will find the prophecy is manifest and ECCO at an end."

"What?"

"He is besieged. That is what those explosions were. Someone has taken the building. My guess is Sarah. She would rather see ECCO fall than exist under his rule."

"Sarah?"

"She must have suspected I was Bahiel. Her suspicions would have been confirmed if she witnessed the speed of my body's recovery. She didn't tell me because she knew I would never submit to Metatron if I knew. But she knew I would sacrifice myself for you. She knew Phanuel was counting on it. She didn't lead him to me, but she knew his novices were closing in and disappeared without warning us."

"She wanted him to find us?"

"To lure him. She laid a trap. The way Sam did. The way I did. She lured Phanuel with what he wanted most."

"Your judgment."

"He didn't want me judged, he wanted me enslaved. It was why he stalled my judgment the first time I gave myself up. It was too early. He wanted me to confront Sam. Hoped I would defeat him and become a version of Bahiel he could control. For all I know, he let me escape."

"The first time?"

"After you disappeared, I wasn't sure who had you. I offered myself to both sides, hoping Sam's desire or ECCO's fear would induce them to accept me in exchange for your life. If ECCO had assumed my strength, it would have given them what they needed to defeat Sam and free you of both of them. When I began to suspect ECCO, or rather, Phanuel, was more interested in the prophecy than defeating Sam, I had no choice but to face Sam myself. All I could hope was ECCO would leave you alone once the threat Sam posed was gone. Phanuel had other intentions."

"He wanted to control you."

"But he needed you to do it."

"Now he wants this kid."

"And now It is here."

"What?"

"Sophie, if Sam could get you pregnant, I am now twice what he was."

For a moment, I stare at blazing eyes in the dark.

"I don't believe it! The day you stalled my car, I was positive you were the devil and all you wanted me to do was have your brat!"

"You should have followed your instincts."

"*I just want to be friends.* I can't believe I fell for that! You lying, manipulative, son of a bitch!"

The lights come on.

I cover my eyes, squinting through my fingers at my husband. He is laid out on the floor, his feet crossed, his shoulders propped up on his elbows. He is still bald, but his skin is ivory pink against the white tile. He is alabaster no more.

An amused look plays on his face.

"What are you laughing at? You're the one who's naked!" I stalk to my bathrobe on the floor and pull it over my nightgown.

"I'm sorry if you didn't want a child, but it would have been unavoidable."

"Bullshit. I'd have enough kids to field a baseball team right now if it was."

"I mean, for me. When we are unable to procreate, nothing can change that. When we are, nothing can prevent it."

"What?" My mouth falls. "The rest of my life, I'm getting knocked up every time we have sex?"

He frowned, staring across the room. "I don't know."

"What do you mean, you don't know! You just said when you're capable of procreating nothing can stop it!"

His eyes stray across the room. "We aren't meant to procreate for obvious reasons. You can imagine the damage a race of Martas could do."

When I follow his gaze, I see Dum and Dee sprawled next to the black coffin. The sight stiffens me. "I'm not giving birth to that."

"We'll have a child, Sophie."

I glare at him. "Like Marta?"

"Marta was Sam's." His eyes find mine, their expression soft. "This will be ours."

I remember regretting Duane could father a child when my husband couldn't. "Have you always wanted one?" My voice drops.

"I've given birth before, but it wasn't mine. I wish it was."

"Sorry ..." I pinch the bridge of my nose. "Did you just say what I thought you did?"

His throat clears. "Long story."

I nod. "We've been married for three years. It might have come up."

"We agreed. No questions. No prophecies."

"Well, now that we are one, I say we amend the rules."

Sitting up, he rests his forearms on his knees. "I never wanted to discuss children. I knew what you were sacrificing when you married me."

"Really, Mike. It wasn't a sacrifice. I'm still not sure how I feel about it."

"I'm sorry I didn't warn you, but I believe the manifestation of the prophecy is the only way we can be together. More so ... I believe it is meant to be."

"Was it meant to be when you had yours?"

He looks away. "I had little choice."

"No kidding?" I feel myself smirk.

His eyes return sharply. "Would you rather we be apart?"

"Let's just say you owe me."

He smiles. "Everything."

"So?" My hands fidget for the pockets on my bathrobe. "What'd you have? Boy or girl?"

Looking away again, his face dissembles. "A boy."

"What'd you name him?"

He suddenly gets to his feet and picks up his robe. Saying nothing, he lifts the fabric over his head and lets it slip over him.

"*Jesus*, Mike! Just answer the question."

I watch him come to me.

Holding my gaze, he takes my hands. "You just did."

I frown, then stare.

"Holy Mary, mother of God. That was you?"

He blinks. "I said I'd ruin Christmas for you."

~

The age will come for those who know It.

The knowing will come for those who accept It.

The acceptance will come for those who refute It.

That what is forgiven was forbidden.

[Spharic. Epilogue of The Prophetic Line
translated from *Ho Pro Fanai*. d. 0]

2000 She was trying to stay informal. Though she would dress nearly the same as the day before, it was taking her twice as long. He had already seen to everything he could: breakfast, coffee, the dog, the presents were wrapped and loaded in the car. Still, he stood at the front door and waited.

He stared blindly at the bottom of the stairs, wondering what he was doing.

It was all wrong.

But it all felt right.

When he heard her feet finally leave the bedroom, he focused his attention. She came down in stocking feet but was otherwise ready to go. The only difference in her wardrobe was the color. Normally, she tended to darker colors. This morning she was wearing cream corduroys and a powder blue turtle neck with a quilted vest. The vest was a brilliant glacier blue. She liked the color because it reminded her of his eyes, but he didn't like the color on her.

When she smiled, her face was pale. Bloodless.

"What's wrong?"

"Nothing." He resisted the urge to pinch her cheeks. "You look beautiful."

"I look like shit. I got a whopping two hours of sleep last night."

She dropped onto the bottom step to pull on her boots. Watching her fingers fumble with laces, he knew she was stressed about going to Kate's.

His throat cleared. "Did I keep you up?"

Standing, she stretched her back.

"Nope. You slept like the dead. I didn't. Now I just look it."

Holding open her coat, he stared into her eyes. "You look beautiful."

"Whatever." She gave a smirk before turning to slip her arms into the sleeves.

But he could feel the lift in her mood.

Following her to the car, he opened her door. As he closed it, he glanced across the yard at Lodi's newly built dog house. The dog had disappeared inside it after breakfast. After their morning walk, Lodi would sleep till noon.

He got into the car and started the engine. Sophie was scrutinizing the directions to Kate's house.

"I already read those."

She ignored him. "I didn't."

"You're not driving."

"Did it ever occur to you someday I might have to find my way by myself?"

"I would never let that happen."

She smirked. "Until you leave town again."

"I'm not leaving town again."

"We are right now."

"I'm not leaving town again without you."

"I might leave town without you."

He grinned. "Why would you want to?"

"There might be an emergency. Maybe I have to leave and you can't."

"Impossible."

She wagged a finger at him. "Don't say it."

"You're the only thing keeping me here. What else could keep me from leaving?"

She put down the directions. "I don't know … Maybe Lodi gets sick."

"Lodi is an animal."

"Excuse me?" She turned in her seat. "Lodi is our child. Just because he doesn't talk doesn't make him less deserving of our care."

Now, he smirked. "You just left our child chained to a dog house in the snow."

"A very furry child with a genetic predisposition to inclement weather."

He laughed.

"I don't suppose that's in keeping with the spirit of the season, is it?" She grinned out her window. "I thought about bringing him with us, then I remembered the cats. Although, this time of year, all God's creatures are supposed to get along."

She paused. "No, I'm wrong. We haven't got there yet, have we?"

He didn't say anything.

She glanced over. "Oops. Forgot. I'm not supposed to ask."

"You're right." His throat cleared. "We aren't there yet."

"Is that what it's all for? To get us to stop fighting like cats and dogs?"

"It's a good goal to have."

Nodding, she pursed her lips. "Wouldn't be one if we could reach it."

"We can."

"Please …" She rolled her eyes and looked away.

"People have come far in the last thousand years."

"You'd know." She stared out her window, her heart growing colder.

He didn't want that. His own was cold enough already.

"Yes, Sophie." His eyes tried to find hers. "I would."

"Guess I'll just have take your word for it." Her face stayed away.

Taking a breath, he adjusted his hands on the wheel. What to say, he didn't know. All he knew was what he couldn't.

"The world is a better place now, maybe not for the planet, but for people …" His throat cleared again. "Compared to what it was."

A glance at her showed no change. He breathed deeper.

"It's true the universe is a brutal place. For all the mysticism surrounding it, in spite of its beauty, it is ruthlessly insensitive. If there is a sentience guiding it, I haven't felt it. Once I sought proof, but no longer. I no longer believe it is the answer."

Keeping his eyes on the road, he felt her open.

"Even as humans find their place, the simple knowledge of how the universe works doesn't begin to convey the nature of it to anyone who sees mechanics alone. To say this galaxy … this system, this star, this planet, is insignificant is to err on the side of delusion. It is less than insignificant. It is nothing. That is all the universe is—a great illusion. A vast nothingness."

She raised a brow. "I'm not seeing an upside to this."

"You see the differences between us, but they are equally insignificant: age, gender, appearance, physical ability. All of those things have only made a difference when my heart was in the wrong place. They have caused me great suffering. Time and again, what has saved me has been what is most intangible: loyalty, compassion, love, trust, all things we share ... even Lodi—even Kate's cats, no doubt."

She smirked and he stared back at the road. For a moment, he said nothing.

"You asked me what it is all for. I think it is for peace. The peace from understanding we aren't different. From freeing ourselves of judgment. Understanding the difference between right and wrong comes from our intentions and knowing the difference makes enforcing it meaningless. Where humanity has learned tolerance and acceptance it has succeeded. Where it continues to punish or reward it will fail. The spirit of Christmas challenges us. It reminds us of our successes and our failures. I have witnessed both. I have seen the birth of tolerance and acceptance judged. I have seen it shunned. But it has never died."

When he looked back, her face was wet with tears.

He reached for her lap and squeezed her hand. "It never will."

"Merry Christmas, Mike!"

As they got out of the car, Duane was waiting with both hands in the air.

"Merry Christmas, Duane."

Frowning, he looked at Duane's hands.

Sophie snickered from the passenger side as she headed for the house.

"Dude!" Duane waved his hands. "Don't leave me hangin'."

He raised his hands and Duane hit them.

"Glad you could make it! How was the drive?"

"Fine." He slowly lowered his hands. "Thanks."

"Did you find us okay?"

"Yes. The directions were excellent."

"Whose did you use?"

"Excuse me?"

"Whose directions? Mine or Kate's? She says mine don't give enough information and I say no one can read hers and stay on the road. What do you think?"

He recalled there were two sets of instructions, but missed why.

"I used both."

"How? We use different routes."

"I followed your instructions from the interstate to the highway and Kate's from the highway to your house."

Duane squinted. "That works. Maybe we should make that our official route for visitors from now on."

Giving Duane a nod, he started for the trunk.

"Can I help you with anything?"

"Um, sure." He popped the trunk and pulled the bags, handing a couple to Duane.

"Man, sweet car. Even driving around Bellevue I haven't seen many of these."

He dropped the lid and smiled. "It meets my needs."

Duane slowed, looking it over on the way to the house. "If I had a hundred K burning a hole in my pocket, it'd meet mine, too. This must turn a lot of heads."

"That isn't why I bought it."

Duane scoffed, making a strange voice. "*I bought it for the engineering. I bought it for the safety. I bought it for the reliability.*"

"I didn't buy it for those reasons, either."

With an elbow, Duane pushed the handle on the front door and stood aside as it swung open. 'What's your excuse?"

He smiled at Duane as he entered. "Sometimes I have to go fast."

"Michael!" Maeve ran up to him with a drink. She gave him a hug and planted a kiss on his cheek. "Merry Christmas!"

"Merry Christmas, Maeve." His eyes searched over her shoulder.

Down the hall, he could hear Sophie and Kate whispering about Duane's parents.

"Presents! Wonderful!" Maeve looked down at the bags. "You should have saved yourself the trip. My car's out front and the trunk is already empty."

"Tree's over here." With a head jerk, Duane passed them with a wink. "S'cuse us, Mom."

As he followed Duane, Maeve took his arm to whisper in his ear. "Brace yourself. *Mummy* and *Daddy* are with the tree. Counting presents no doubt."

Her brow arched as he raised his own.

Across the foyer, he saw Duane disappear through French doors and down some steps. Nearing the doors, he saw a long room with high ceilings and a fireplace at the far end. Two banks of arched windows looked over the backyard, centered by another set of French doors opening onto the patio.

The tree was across from the patio doors, against the facing wall. A large, gilt mirror hung behind it, reflecting its lit boughs. Between the tree and the patio doors, in the middle of the room, were a man and a woman. The man was taller than Duane, broad-shouldered with neat, white hair. The woman was unusually thin, with deeply tanned skin and blond hair arranged high on her head. Clark and Maxine. He remembered meeting them at Kate's wedding.

"You remember Sophie's fiancé, Michael."

They both focused on him at Duane's announcement.

He stepped down into the living room and shifted the bags to his left hand, offering his right as Clark quickly approached.

"Clark Nelson. Good to see you again." They shook hands before Clark turned. "My wife, Maxine."

"Of course, I remember." She carefully extended a hand. "Merry Christmas, Michael"

"Who doesn't?" He grinned, hoping to alleviate the memory of his fainting spell.

Clark and Maxine laughed earnestly, exchanging glances.

"If weddings had that effect on more people, we'd have fewer divorces." Clark winked at his wife, who lightly laughed again.

She touched his arm. "I think what people remember most was your singing. Many remarked about it at the reception. You have the most beautiful voice."

"Thank you." He joined Duane, busily stacking presents under the tree.

Maxine followed. "Have you sung professionally? With a choir?"

"No—well … with a choir."

Duane gestured to him and he fished in one of the bags. As he handed gifts to Duane, Maxine continued to ask questions.

"A church choir?"

He knew Sophie would say the Seattle Men's Chorus.

"Um, yes."

"Which denomination?"

Sophie would suggest Temple Beth El.

"I was raised non-denominational."

"Really?" Clark came up behind Maxine. "Where do you attend now?"

"I haven't been since my father died."

Maxine neared his side. "I'm so sorry to hear it."

"Thank you …" He tried to appear traumatized.

"Sometimes it helps to get some space." Clark nodded stoically. "A change of place. Renew the spirit."

"Uh oh." Duane grinned up at him. "Look out, Mike. Dad will have you in our Bible study by the time you leave."

Clark and Maxine erupted in laughter.

"Give your old man some credit! I know better than to call on a man when he's down. I'm exercising the core principles of the group. Care and consideration is what all of us need in times like these, regardless of our differences."

"I think Mike came here for the food and libation." Duane got to his feet. "Let me take care of your coat."

"Thanks."

Pulling off his pea coat, he handed it to Duane, who nodded at the foyer.

"Let me show you around."

As Duane led him from the room, Clark and Maxine were close behind. He glanced over his shoulder and they both beamed. He smiled back, sensing a strange approval.

In the foyer, Duane opened a closet. "I'm sorry Kate and I didn't have you and Sophie here sooner. We wanted to have you over for dinner, but with the construction delays, we didn't even get around to a housewarming."

"Sophie told me you weren't happy with your contractor."

Clark burst into a loud laugh, making him jump. "That's an understatement!"

Duane smirked. "We're suing him."

"What for?"

"Don't get me started …" Duane pointed past Clark and Maxine before starting down the hall. "I'll show you what they didn't screw up, first."

On the way, they passed the kitchen. Sophie sat with Kate and Maeve at the end of an island. Pots simmered on the stove as a timer beeped on one of two ovens.

"Hey, girls!" Duane poked in the doorway, then looked back at him. "You want anything to drink? Coffee, beer, wine?"

"Water would be fine, thank you."

"Water it is." Duane went to the refrigerator.

"Merry Christmas, Mike!" Kate came up to hug him. "I'm so glad you guys could spend Christmas with us. It's too bad Edie and Peter are in Hawaii, but it was a good excuse to have you to ourselves."

"Thanks for thinking of us. I don't think Sophie's parents miss us too badly."

A bottle of water appeared in front of him, and he took it.

"Of course they do!" Maeve scowled. "You just want Sophie to yourself!"

He froze in Maeve's glare. "Of course—I didn't mean … I was just saying—"

"Mom's just teasing." Kate grinned at Maeve, who winked at him.

He opened his mouth, then felt it close.

"Need a drink?" Kate squeezed his arm as he looked between them dumbly.

"I got him water." Duane took a swig from a bottle. "I'm taking him on the tour."

"Let me guess. The basement?" Kate eyed him, implying something.

"What's upstairs?" Duane gave him a nod. "What would you rather see? A walk-in closet and a craft room or a wood shop with a dual-piston upright compressor?"

Kate made a face. "Don't forget the doomsday vault."

"Doomsday vault?" He repeated.

"I live the Boy Scout motto." Duane watched him.

He blinked back.

"Always Prepared." Sophie came up behind him. "Aren't ya, honey?"

He could smell the gin on her as she wrapped her arms around him.

Duane's head shook. "Not if you don't have a disaster relief plan."

Sophie sneered. "Any disaster that requires one isn't worth surviving."

"What if heaven waits on the other side?" Maxine's voice made them all turn.

She was watching them from the stove, her smile suddenly plastic. A part of him braced as Sophie faced her.

"Don't need it. I got my own slice of heaven right here."

Sophie's hand made contact with his right buttock. Even through his wool trousers, the snap was clear. Kate bit her lip, taking Sophie by the arm.

"I think we're starting our tour upstairs."

He watched Kate lead Sophie from the room, hearing them burst into giggles in the hall. When he looked to Maeve, she was busily telling Clark and Maxine about her latest tour of the Rhine.

Duane nudged his shoulder.

"If you can't take the heat, head for the man cave."

On their way to the basement, Duane winked over his shoulder.

"We both got ourselves some wild women."

"As opposed to what?"

Duane's shoulders shrugged. "I don't know … my mom, I guess."

There was a turn in the hall. At the end of it was a door.

"You're mother is very pleasant."

"She is that." The twinge of Duane's tone was unreadable.

The door in front of them opened and a light came on. Concrete steps descended to an expansive room, as wide as the house above and nearly as long. One wall was lined with a work bench and tool cabinets. The wall opposite was filled with daylight windows, illuminating a shop floor evenly spaced with freestanding woodworking equipment. At the far end of the room was a single, heavy vault door.

"This is it! My home inside of home. Whaddya think?"

He drifted across the shop, taking stock of the tools. A planer, table saw, spindle sander, joiner, wood lathe …

"You could build an ark."

Duane beamed. "And stock one, too. I've got enough food and water to last us three years."

He turned to the vault. His vision perceived more than food and water beyond the door. A significant cache of firearms and ammunition were stockpiled inside.

"Three years? I thought it was the end of days." He asked vacantly.

"It's the years leading up to those days I'm prepared for. Some say famine, some say flood, others an epidemic. I say, why take a chance?"

His eyes found Duane's. "What if you're wrong?"

"No harm, no foul."

"What if God doesn't see it that way?"

Duane only gave a blank stare.

Novice. He thought, and turned away.

Subject: Canned beans all

From: Kate Nelson

Date: 6/13/2003 10:01 PM

To: Sophie Davids

How's it going, Sophie?

Please tell me life on the outside continues. I've been doing time at Zion Retreat for almost two weeks now and finally escaped to get to an e-café in North Bend. I thought vegans were bad enough, but vegan Christians are an entirely different crop of crazy. Even Duane has come to the conclusion that dogma and vegetables don't mix. We just finished the last of the seasonal cooking classes and will have enough canned beans to last us through Easter. That should keep little Mike on the go.

Little Mike has loved the retreat. They have a great daycare and animal shelter that doubles as a petting zoo. He got to adopt a bunny, he doesn't know it yet, but they'll send him photos. So far the little guy has been growing like a weed and has a healthy appetite like big Mike. I know you've said you and Mike would think about it, but I really think you guys would make great parents. I just can't help thinking Michael would make such a great dad and God knows there are so many lousy ones.

Mom e-mailed me that you called her a couple days ago and she was worried that you sounded depressed. That's not why I was writing, but I want you to know that if anything is on your mind I'm willing to hear it. You and Mike have been so supportive this last year, well, you've always been so supportive. You know what I'm saying. I'm here for you if you need me.

Say Hi to Michael for me tell Toe we miss him.

Love,

Kate

[E-mail from Kate Nelson to Sophie Davids. d. June 16, 2003]

2003 She still holds his hands. Still stares in his eyes. But her grip is firm. Her gaze steady. It is a big step.

For them both.

He has never told a human so much. Never imagined he would. Can't believe he is telling her now. It is too hard. Too far a leap. Too confusing for beings so bound to their bodies, so enthralled by their senses. What is more sacred to them than any god is gender. It is a line they cross with difficulty, in religion, scarcely at all. Once placed on one side of the line, there is no going back. You may be masculine, you may be feminine, you may be neither.

Not both.

"Holy Mary, mother of God. That was you?"

As unorthodox as her beliefs are, a lifetime of casual acceptance has left its mark.

He always knew she thought he was there—hovering over a manger, as Joseph, a wise man, a shepherd boy, even Jesus.

Not Mary.

And truly he wasn't. Not the way she sees it. Not the way it is painted, written, reenacted. They did not call her Mary. She did not call him Joseph. There was no manger, no wise men, no shepherd boy, no lamb. Although, there was an ox.

He nods anyway. What she imagines is close enough.

He did have a boy. They named him Hesut.

But that is long past.

Now, he wants her to understand he has stood in her place. He will stay by her and their child. She will not suffer. This child will not die at the hands of men.

Or Phanuel.

He pulls her to him. "They are coming."

"You're kicking his ass." Her hands squeeze his. "Right?"

"You are."

"What?" Her hands fall away.

At the sound of footsteps, he turns her shoulders to the door.

I'm right behind you.

A blur of novices file into the room, quickly surrounding them. Phanuel enters, followed by Zachariel and Uriel, the last of their council. It is a sorry number. ECCO will soon be dead if it isn't already.

Phanuel's dress shirt is scorched. A look of displeasure still burns.

Uriel looks him in the eyes, then glares at Phanuel.

"This is not what you claimed."

"Who released you?" Phanuel growls with a fear his demand cannot hide.

He smiles. "You have enemies within and without."

"You are only an enemy to yourself." Phanuel's eyes shift to Sophie. "You did this."

"Hey." She puts up her hands, "You stuck me here. No TV, nothing to read—what else was I supposed to do?"

Phanuel's eyes shut tight. "You have no conception of what you've done."

She looks over her shoulder at him.

Tell me he didn't just say that.

He only shrugs.

"They can't leave." Zachariel glares at the back of Phanuel's head.

Zachariel's words spark his wrath. When he steps forward, they step back.

"It is you who cannot leave. Sophie carries my child now. The future is present and you will bear witness to it."

In an instant, Phanuel is at the pedestal of Metatron's keep.

"You admit you are Bahiel?"

Impulsively, he pulls Sophie behind him. "I do."

Phanuel grips the lid of the keep. "You deny you are Metatron's servus?"

"I do not."

Phanuel removes the lid. "You deny you were made bound to It?"

"I do not."

Phanuel smiles. "Then you will submit."

He feels Sophie grip his arm as he stands motionless. Watching Phanuel reach into the keep, doubt flashes through his mind as Metatron is withdrawn.

Phanuel cries out.

The orb falls to the floor, shattering the tile with a snap. With a meandering roll, It drifts to his feet, stopping halfway. All eyes stare at Metatron. The black eye stares back. No one moves.

His eye watches them all as his mind speaks to her thoughts.

Sophie, pick It up.

She jerks her head up with a blank expression.

Trust me. Pick It up.

Her eyes fall to It as her lips disappear. She barely takes a step when Phanuel flies at her. It is a futile gesture, started and ended before Sophie has stopped moving. The charge he directs leaves Phanuel on the floor, gasping.

"Witness with your own eyes, or witness through mine."

The lights flicker as the room reverberates with his voice. Most of him wants to assume Phanuel on the spot. For Phanuel, the very notion is revolting, the equivalent of being swallowed by a foul beast, far worse than eternity in Metatron's well. When Phanuel says nothing, he directs Sophie again.

Go ahead.

Taking a breath, she fixes on the orb. In one quick action, she bends, scooping It up in her hands. Holding It in front of her, she rolls It in her palms as though a curious object. The witnesses make a collective hush as It flickers.

She looks at him, alarmed.

It's all right.

She stares, *Your eyes …*

He feels them brighten.

It's all right, Sophie. I'm fine.

She can hold Metatron, but she cannot make It summon him.

From now on, only the Child will.

Hold it to them. Make them see.

She turns, displaying the orb to Zachariel and Uriel, who quickly avert their eyes. Following their downcast gaze, he looks upon Phanuel.

"Do you bear witness?"

Phanuel squints. "I do."

"Do you accept the prophecy as manifest?"

"I do." The words rasp thin.

"You admit you have lost the mandate?"

Phanuel rises. Lunging, his foot violently pins Phanuel's shoulder to the floor.

"You admit you have lost the mandate?"

Their eyes lock, blazing. He will not ask again.

"That's rather obvious isn't it?" A calm voice intervenes.

Sarah stands in the open door. Behind her is Gabrielle. Though unseen, Louis's scent is with them. Zachariel turns his fear on her.

"You are outcast! You have no voice here!"

"Put a sock in it, Zach." She steps into the room, appraising Metatron in Sophie's hands. "Haven't you heard? A woman's in charge now."

Sophie looks at Sarah, then back at him. "What's she talking about?

"The mandate is yours." He nods. "You are the holder."

"Only the Child can have the mandate!" Phanuel squirms under his foot

"The Child?" Sarah glances between him and Sophie. "Are congratulations in order?"

He only smiles as Sophie narrows her eyes.

"That was fast." Sarah sniffs.

"*Not* so fast!" Sophie holds out the orb. "Mandate? Holder? Come again?"

Calmly, he points to her hand. "Of Metatron."

"Of course ..." She looks at It, then glares at him. "What the hell is that?"

"*That!*" Phanuel glares. "Is the eye of heaven!"

"To some." He concludes. "Eternal hell to others."

"It is everything we are, ever have been and ever will be." Phanuel twists under his foot. "It is our lodestone."

He steps down on Phanuel. "It is a millstone that has enslaved us."

"It is still your master!" Phanuel shouts.

"And Sophie is yours." Sarah interrupts. "Metatron's, mine, and everyone else's. Until the Child is born we are all in her keeping."

"Our child?" Sophie stares. "If you think I'm holding this for nine months—"

"Oh, no." Sarah waves her off. "Not that long. Eighteen years at least."

"What?!" Sophie spins on him. "What did you do to me?"

Phanuel snorts. "You wanted him out of the box."

He shakes his head. "Don't let Sarah frighten you. You have the mandate, but you don't have to keep it. You may designate another in your stead."

"Fabulous. How do I do that?"

"Hand It to them."

She frowns at the orb. "That's it?"

"That's not it!" Gabrielle pushes past Sarah. "It is a decision of immense importance. The holder of Metatron wields great influence. The fate of the new age could be determined by them. The fate of your child is in that balance."

Sophie looks at him and then to Sarah.

Sarah puts up a hand. "Don't look at me. I don't want It."

"Of course not!" Phanuel grunts underfoot. "She wants her crown back."

"Well, I am already moved in." She eyes Sophie. "You can keep the bathrobe."

Gabrielle turns to Sophie. "The holder of Metatron and the director of ECCO cannot be one."

Sophie's drops her arm, palming Metatron against her leg.

"So who's the director now?"

"No one." He speaks up. "ECCO is dissolved."

Gabrielle watches him. "If he wanted, Bahiel could assume us all."

"If he doesn't do it now, he will later." Phanuel grumbles.

"Look who's talking." Sarah circles Phanuel at her feet, appreciating the view. "You wanted Metatron, ECCO, and Bahiel all to yourself."

"Ha!" Phanuel glares at her. "Bahiel committed every atrocity imaginable, has a crisis of conscience, changes his name to Michael and becomes a saint. Fine hat trick!" Phanuel's glare turns on him. "I'll have to remember that one myself."

Returning Phanuel's gaze, he feels his eyes light with fire.

"To hell with you. I served my sentence and by oath you found me absolved."

"By oath?" Phanuel strains under him. "An oath I swore to Metatron, only to see you reject a calling I would have gladly accepted. The Metatron I served is no more. ECCO is no more. Your absolution is no more! Damn me to hell and I will see you in it!"

"I don't think he likes you." Sophie balances Metatron on her shoulder like a shot put. When she sees him staring, she cradles It in both hands. "It's heavier than It looks."

"Bahiel." Sarah bows to him. "I humbly request directorship in the reformation of ECCO, if only for the privilege of granting Phanuel his wish."

Gabrielle steps forward. "By proxy, I would request directorship in Raphael's stead."

Sarah shakes her head. "Until Raphael's whereabouts are confirmed, such a request cannot be considered. Furthermore—"

"Sarah." He stops her, looking at Gabrielle. "Raphael was judged."

They all look to Sophie and the orb in her hands.

"Bastard." Gabrielle burns at Phanuel.

Sophie nods. "That's what I said."

Gabrielle crouches over Phanuel. "His crypt? His body? Where?!"

Phanuel only smiles. "Let me go and there still might be time."

A guttural cough echoes in the room. Everyone save the novices look to the door. Louis glances uneasily around the room, taking a moment to recognize him without his hair. He sees a familiar grin.

"That you?"

"Hello, Louis."

"Had me scared. Saw a body and thought it was yours."

Phanuel lets out a low hiss.

Gabrielle stands. "What body?"

"Basement. Found it when I tripped the juice."

"The cells." Gabrielle whispers.

In a flash, she passes Louis at the door.

Sarah faces him. "Bahiel, I renew my request."

Past Sarah's shoulder, he catches Sophie's eye and she shakes her head.

She betrayed you, Mike.

No more than I betrayed you with Sam.

You owe Raphael.

I owe them both.

Raphael loves you. He stood by you to the end.

Sarah loves me as well.

Sophie raises a brow. *That's what I'm afraid of.*

She is what ECCO needs, Sophie. What ECCO needs is what we need.

He looks down at Sarah, who watches him impassively.

"Your request is granted."

The only time he was on the white floor was to witness a judgment. For obvious reasons, he never desired to come back. His first judgment took place on a white floor somewhere else, another world entirely. Looking at himself in the full-length mirror, he looks as though he has just been there. He is alien to his own eyes. The face is the same but transformed into something hard with no hair to soften it. The veil of dove-colored fabric covering him says nothing about time or place. He could be in Egypt or on Etymion, bronze age or space age.

He is once again a being out of time.

His eyes drop to the trousers and dress shirt in his hands. Phanuel's clothes. A gift from Sarah. Very likely she will salvage the servant's alb he is wearing and dress Phanuel accordingly for Metatron. Such is her taste in humor. It makes no difference to him. He will not stay to witness another judgement. If he had his way, it would not happen. It is why Sarah was reinstated. ECCO must function ruthlessly for its members to function selflessly. Sam called it vacuous omnipotence. He will call it necessary evil.

Slipping the alb off over his head, he notes the marble tub at the end of the room before entering the shower. Sophie's disgust at Sarah's more than practical accommodations amuse him. Until three weeks ago, he was the only singularity she had any association with. Now, all of his kind are being measured against him. Eventually, she will come to realize Sarah and Phanuel are more typical than he wants to admit. She has already perceived Raphael's character. Inevitably, she will discover how rare such character is. Rarer even than his own.

Thankfully for him, Raphael is beyond falling.

Picking a towel from a rack, he steps from the shower. Quickly drying off, he pulls on Phanuel's slacks. They sag a bit at his feet. Phanuel is slightly taller. He pulls on the shirt and the sleeves are too long. No bother. He will roll them up. Exiting the bathroom, he glances across the bedroom and sees Sophie in a short-sleeved, white dress she borrowed from Sarah.

She grins. "You almost look human again."

"Almost?"

"Like a superhero cancer patient."

He makes a short laugh and looks at his feet.

"Sarah found you some shoes." She points to a pair of black loafers at the foot of the bed. "She thought they would fit better than Phanuel's."

He walks to the bed and slips them on. "She's right."

"Probably from one of your victims." She murmurs.

His eyes stay on the loafers. "They would have killed you."

"Not the first guy."

When he glares at her, she waits with an expectant squint.

"Novices are all the same."

The dark part of her doesn't blink. "You were like that once."

"Not by choice."

"I'm sorry." The darkness fades in her eyes. "You've been judged enough."

"I'm sorry if I frightened you."

She walks up to him and straightens his collar. "It wasn't you, remember?"

"Who am I?" The question barely escapes him.

As she looks into his face, he searches hers for the answer.

She doesn't hesitate. "The best part of me."

He can say nothing.

"Always." She whispers.

Holding her close, the scent of her hair closes his eyes.

Even with the utility lights on, he knows how dark the cells seem to her. He remembers too well the desperate hours he spent. As they pass his cell, he glances at the door. Raphael had been his only hope. Now Raphael is the one who is trapped. And in a far worse place than a cell.

His eyes return to watching the novices flanking her. They only have allegiance to Metatron. Whoever holds It is their guide. They walk with her now, in two mindless columns. How many legions of them exist within him, he has no count. He has no individual memories from them, only a shared one. A memory of barely existing. Of being the shell of a being. Of being a doll. That Sophie feels any desire for this part of him makes his insides squirm.

When they enter the breaker room, a crypt is behind a cyclone barrier surrounding the backup generators. Gabrielle sits next to it in a chair. She has stayed with it since she found it. She rises, her face stiff with concern.

"Thank you for what you are doing." Gabrielle's voice is barely audible.

"Thank you for helping us." Sophie smiles at her.

They watch Gabrielle lift the lid of the crypt.

A sharp tang of salt and chlorine fills the air. Inside, Raphael's body stares at the ceiling with dull eyes. The skin is dark, with blue patches spreading across the face. The first signs of dissolution.

He senses Sophie's confusion of revulsion and pity.

Allow me.

She steps aside as he approaches the crypt. The hands are folded across the middle. He takes hold of them, turning the palms to the face, as though cupping something.

He looks to Sophie. *Go ahead.*

She peeks over the edge, leaning against the crypt to extend the flickering orb over the body. Carefully resting it in the hands, she presses dead fingers around the eye.

"Raphael." She whispers. "The mandate is yours."

Tentatively, her hands withdraw as though expecting Metatron to roll away. Instead, it goes dark. They stare in silence. Sophie looks up at him and he puts an arm around her shoulders.

Look.

It has turned a pale blue. Gradually, the walls of Raphael's crypt begin to brighten. An aura of light spreads from the orb, wrapping around stiff fingers, disappearing into them. A sensation of release floods the room, overwhelming him. Whether or not Sophie feels it, he only knows his gaze meets Gabrielle's in shared relief.

"It is done." She smiles at Sophie with dim eyes.

The lid lowers as the inside of the crypt comes to full light. It will be weeks before Raphael leaves it, but the worst is over.

1199 BC Before dawn, the general entered my tent with the vestments of Re in his arms. I could feel his tension as he dressed me. The throne was before my crypt, the mask of Aten placed upon it, watching us. As he moved to fasten the gold collar of pharaoh, I stopped him.

"Leave it."

"What do you plan, my lord?"

"I am no lord. One day you call me Keph, the next Re. I am tired of it."

"Who are you?" The general stepped away with downcast eyes.

"That has yet to be determined."

"Determined?" His gaze shot up nervously.

"Have Ptah assemble the priests and bring the reliquary of Re to me. Invite the Canaans as well."

"A commencement?"

"No ceremony. No guard. I will speak to them."

"Speak?"

I looked directly at him. "Do you wish to rule Canaan or not?"

He only stared.

"In peace?" I pressed him. "With hope?"

"Is that your wish?" He responded.

"I wish to be free."

With a nod, he left to carry out my orders. Returning to the throne, I picked up the mask of Aten and tossed it to the ground before sitting under the weight around my neck. Closing my eyes, I let my vision stray far—not to watch the priests make ready, but to see again the open country I had crossed the day before.

The general did not return to the tent. When I heard him begin to sing attention, I bowed my head, my eyes still closed, my thoughts unformed. The air stirred as the tent lifted away. There were whispers as eyes saw a man sitting upon the throne of Re, in the garb of Re, unmasked. My mouth strained not to smile when I heard Ptah cry out, demanding the general explain his trickery.

The general gave no reply.

The audience shifted uneasily until Ptah could bear the silence no more.

"Who is this man? Speak, devil! What are you?"

"One you have worshipped." My eyes remained closed as I spoke.

Ptah approached the throne. "Who are you?"

"So strong is your faith you do not recognize me without a mask?"

"You cannot be Re!"

"Why not? Because you do not burn to look upon my face?"

"I have seen you in camp. They call you Khepera."

"They do."

"You are no god."

"Khepera is not a god?"

"You are not him."

"You know what Khepera looks like?"

"Khepera looks like no one, is everything and nothing."

"Khepera looks like no one, is everything and nothing."

"How is Khepera everything and nothing if Re is the one god?"

"Khepera is in Re. Re is everything and everything in Re."

"Then you are in Re?"

"Of course."

"Am I in Re?"

Ptah said nothing. I opened my eyes. When I did, they were lit with fire. Ptah backed away as the priests made noises. The Canaans had risen to their feet.

I rose. "Say I am not, and I will say your god is false!"

Ptah ran to the reliquary. Frantically unlocking it, he withdrew a ceremonial sword and brandished it. My thoughts turned to fire at the weapon in his hands. He gasped as it fell from his hand, singeing the grass beneath it. As the blade began to melt into the dirt, my rage spread to the reliquary. Priests scattered from the chest as the relics within began to glow.

Voices rose. Panic sparked.

A Canaan gray beard stepped forward and knelt. "Who are you, lord?"

Above the frightened voices and shuffling feet, I called for silence. The resonance of my voice through the ground stopped mouths and turned all eyes to me. I bade the gray beard ask again.

He did so, keeping his eyes to the ground. "Who are you, lord?"

"I am no lord."

His eyes lifted. "What then?"

"A wishful thought. A hope to guide men to their dreams."

"Whose thought?"

"Your own."

[Spharic. Entry translated from *Kor Dai Maihael*. Mund Dai. d. 755 BC]

~

2000 "Shit."

I stumbled on a dog toy in my heels.

"Jesus, Lodi! You think you could keep your toys in one room?"

Lodi looked up from his dog bed as I kicked his toy into the laundry room.

"And vacuum up this fur while we're gone!"

Turning my back on the perplexed animal, I went to the kitchen and pulled my gin from the freezer.

"Won't they be serving alcohol?"

Barely glancing over my shoulder, I poured a shot into a glass. "Not enough."

Shoving the bottle back in the fridge, I turned to see Michael standing in the dining room door. He was dressed in the tux I picked, looking astonishing and oblivious about it at the same time.

"Wow." I grinned as I took a sip.

He looked down with a shrug. "They're just clothes."

Leaning against the refrigerator, I cradled my drink. "Uh huh."

"Is that the same dress you wore last year?"

I looked down at my black velvet gown. "I figured since no one saw me in it last year, I'd try again this year."

"I saw you in it last year."

"You saw me out of it, too."

He grinned. "This is going to be a long evening."

My brow arched as I walked up to him. "They're just clothes."

I squeezed past him into the dining room where I spotted a mask on the dining room table. It was a half mask, delicately painted with a red and black harlequin pattern and gold filigree. Picking it up, it was light in my hand.

"You're wearing this?"

His arms came from behind, wrapping around my waist. "It's a masked ball."

"It's optional. You don't have to wear one. I'm not."

"You don't have anything to hide." He spoke into my ear.

I snorted. "Except my disdain. Where'd you get it?"

"Venice."

"Dare I ask when?"

"Seventeen twenty-five."

I put it down. "I don't suppose I was partying with you in seventeen twenty-five?"

"I wish." He whispered. "We hadn't met yet."

"When did we meet?"

"Seventeen sixty."

"Where?"

"Pennsylvania."

I blinked. "You went from Venice to Pennsylvania?"

"Not directly."

"What were you doing?"

"Searching." His nose found my ear.

"For what?" As I spoke, he began to kiss me. "My neck?"

"Myself." He answered between kisses.

"Did you find it?"

His lips paused. "Yes."

The ice of his breath raised my hair.

My eyes dropped to the mask on the table. Tossing my head back, I drained my glass.

A redhead in a gold-glittered eye mask waved from the crowd.

"Amy." Michael said without looking, his own mask making his eyes look like blue marbles. "I think we're supposed to sign in over there."

Following his gaze, I headed across the lobby.

"You're not wearing a mask?" Amy met me at the registration table.

"Nope."

"Good evening!" A table attendant in a feather headdress greeted us. "Sign here. Name tags over there."

At the reminder, Amy fished in her purse. "Did you bring your name tag?"

"Nope." Bending over the table, I found my name and signed next to it. When I turned to hand the pen to Michael, he was gone. With a shrug, I signed his name into the guest column.

"You'd better make one, then." Amy stuck out her lip as she fiddled with the magnet on the back of hers. "It's a must for staff."

With a snort, I tried to see over heads. "Last year attendance was a must, yet observe. I am still here."

In spite of the three-inch boost my heels gave me, I had lost my fiancé. The lobby was clogged with arrivals. Aside from a parade of cocktail dresses, a sea of men in black surrounded us.

"Nuts."

Amy finished signing in. "What?"

"My guest disappeared." I frowned at her. "Where's Anthony?"

Her eyes rolled. "Working, wouldn't ya know. He's got really crappy hours."

Slipping off my coat, I handed it to a checker. "He'd have hated this anyway."

"Yeah." Amy fumbled with the buttons on her coat. "He didn't look too disappointed when he heard it was black tie. He'd look great in a tux, though."

I smirked. "If you could get him in one."

Amy checked in her overcoat, revealing a magenta dress that matched her hair.

"I saw Michael when you came in." She flashed her eyes. "Wow. Course he looks good in everything."

And out of it. I thought.

I heard that.

Hearing my fiancé's thought made me look around. Where the hell did he go?

I'm in line at the bar.

I was beginning to see the advantages of telepathy.

"I suppose we should find our table." Amy started to push into the crowd and then stopped. "Unless—should we go to the bar first?"

"I think Mike's already there."

Amy sighed. "I'm solo tonight, remember?"

"I'm sure he'll bring you something."

"Really?" She sounded doubtful.

What does she want?

"I'd put money on it."

She frowned. "Does he know what I drink?"

Mai Tai, Michael finished.

I grinned. "He's pretty observant."

"Okay." Amy shrugged. "Let's find a seat."

And a martini? Michael asked.

He read my mind.

As we approached the ballroom, live music echoed into the lobby. Inside, it was gradually filling with partiers. The ballroom was a converted movie theater from the twenties. Theater seats had been replaced by a dance floor. Pillars sculpted like giant papyrus supported an ornate balcony over the stage where a jazz band played. Round tables ringed the dance floor, black-clothed and sprinkled with confetti. Each table had a centerpiece of black and white roses with glitter-fringed petals. Place settings were topped with foil hats and paper horns were planted in champagne flutes. Our table was left of the stage, in the far corner of the room. Phil reserved it because it was close to a fire escape.

He was already there. With him was a pale, long-boned woman in a navy dress with a lace collar and horn-rimmed glasses. At first, I thought it was a costume.

"Ladies!" Phil grinned, his beard freshly trimmed over his bow tie. "You two look stunning as usual. Where's Mike?"

"Bar run." I looked at Phil's girlfriend and extended my hand. "Hi, I'm Sophie."

"I'm Stella." She smiled awkwardly, displaying braces on her lower teeth.

"I'm Amy." Amy took Stella's hand, smiling sweetly, but I knew she hadn't taken her eyes off Stella's collar.

Phil put an arm around Stella's shoulders. "Amy's our resident number cruncher and Sophie works with the rich and infamous."

Taking a seat, I sneered. "Try clueless. Where do you work, Stella?"

"Half Price Books." She almost whispered.

"She's their inventory supplier now, but she was stuck behind the counter when I met her. I started asking her out to make up for my harassment when I couldn't find what I wanted."

"And you still said yes?" I grinned at her. "You're a glutton for punishment."

She squeaked, covering her mouth.

"Oh, jeez!" Amy whispered over my shoulder. "It's Karen."

"It's Dan." Phil craned his neck and waved.

Turning my head, a tall man in a purple mask and jester hat waved over some heads. The woman he was with wasn't visible until the crowd parted. She emerged ahead of him. At first, I gasped. She looked like Duane's mom, only dressed as a county club super hero. She was a rail, with bleached hair to match a gold damask gown and sequined mask. Dan limped up behind her, still on a cane from his skiing accident on Thanksgiving.

Karen stopped before our table and made a big wave. "Hello, all!"

"Hi." Amy sounded a little weak.

Dan had been Amy's date to the ball last year.

Mike, Amy needs that drink.

Almost there.

"Hey, Dan." I gave a nod. "Nice hat."

Karen pulled on his arm. "I brought the entertainment."

Dan held a hand to me. "This is Sophie Davids, our special projects manager."

"Karen Fogel. The ex-ex!" She gave a theatrical wink as she crushed my hand.

Mike, I'll need that drink.

A frosted martini appeared before me.

"Nice to meet *you*." My hand broke free from Karen to seize it.

"Amy?" Michael's voice floated from above as he handed her drink to her.

"Thanks, Mike. That's really sweet of you."

Karen made a sly grin over my head. "And who do you belong to?"

Hands rested on my shoulders. "Sophie."

Karen gazed down on me as I swallowed sheepishly. "This is Michael, my fiancé."

"So was I! I'm Karen." She winked again at Mike. "The ex-ex!"

"My my." He answered smoothly.

I coughed.

Dan continued his introductions. "This is Amy Duncan from finance. Phil Stuart from grants …"

"Stella Finch." Phil introduced his date as she adjusted her glasses.

Karen looked Stella over. "Lovely dress."

Amy and I exchanged glances.

"How's it going, Mike?" Dan hobbled past Karen and held out a hand.

"Very well." Mike shook it. "And you?"

Holding up his cane, Dan grinned. "Back on my feet."

"We missed you at Thanksgiving."

"So did I. That's the first and last one I spend in an ER."

Mike smiled. "Sophie told me about your accident."

"He was going downhill too fast when he forgot he already was." Karen nudged him. "I told him it's the bunny slopes from now on."

She returned to Mike. "Do you ski?"

"Only when necessary."

Karen shot Dan a look. "Wise man!"

I snorted. "Penny wise, more like."

"Doubly so." Dan skirted the table. "You'll save a fortune on medical bills."

Michael pulled out the chair next to me and sat down.

Karen stepped up to the seat on his other side. "Boy girl, boy girl!" Pausing, she squinted at Amy seated next to me. "No boy for you tonight?"

"Um ..." Amy fidgeted with her straw. "He's working."

"Too bad!" Karen's eyes narrowed. "What does he do?"

"Kills people." I interrupted. "Professionally, that is."

Karen made a laugh, then paused. She opened her mouth.

"As you can imagine ..." I cut her off. "He gets a lot of work on New Year's Eve."

Pursing her lip, Karen raised a brow at me. "You know him?"

"Hired him." I took a sip of my drink. "He's good."

Karen made a brief smile and switched to my fiancé. "And what do you do?"

"He's a magician!" Lyn announced behind us.

She materialized in a feathered mask, her beehive embellished with a tiara.

"Good evening, Michael!" Lyn squeezed his shoulders and bent to me. "Enjoying your first New Year's Ball?"

I raised my glass. "Two drinks from a floor show, Lyn."

"Why aren't you wearing a mask?"

"So I wouldn't have to wear a name tag."

Lyn paused, her eyes searching me, her face unreadable under her feathers.

"Michael!" She perked up. "Your mask is beautiful! Where did you get it?"

I kicked him under the table.

Say Walmart or you'll regret it.

"Walmart."

That's my boy.

"They do get good things there, don't they? It's all from China, but Chinese can make anything, can't they?"

"I think so." He winked at me as I plucked an olive from my martini.

"Have you had a chance to mingle?" Lyn eyed me. "This is a wonderful opportunity to thank our donors."

"I only got one, and he ain't here."

"Oh, but he is."

"He is?" I sat up. "Where?"

Mike seemed to sit up as well.

"Well, I'm not supposed to say." Lyn leaned into me. "I saw his name on the guest register. I've been keeping an eye out, but I haven't spotted him yet."

"What does he look like?" I frowned.

"I don't remember very well. I've only met him once ..." She squinted. "He's about your age, tall, rather attractive."

I looked around the room. Half the people there were wearing masks.

"How the hell am I supposed to mingle with someone I've never seen before at a masked ball?"

"If I see him, I'll find you." Lyn pointed at me. "Even if he's wearing a mask, he should be wearing a name tag."

"Wouldn't that defeat the purpose?" Michael asked.

Lyn laughed. "Very funny! I was disappointed to hear you retired, but thrilled to receive your costume. Did you get my note?"

He nodded, "I'm glad it went to someone who appreciates it."

"If you ever want to borrow it, its yours!"

Lyn gave his shoulders another squeeze before disappearing into the crowd. The rest of the evening could only improve.

At least, for Mike it did. The food was everything he fantasized about. Saturated fat and calories in the form of a buffet. His modus operandi was to make multiple runs through the line under the guise of getting me more to eat while eating off both plates in subtle, yet methodical fashion. Between the drinking and the dancing, no one save the catering crew would have noticed the steady decimation of the food supply.

Except Stella.

At first, I didn't catch on. She had watched Michael surreptitiously since he came to the table. This wasn't unusual. Most people watched Michael in one way or another. As hard as he tried to assimilate himself, his underlying survival strategy of appealing to the subconscious desires of humans often drew unwanted attention. In this case, undetected attention.

Seated demurely in Phil's shadow, one was more likely to notice Stella's spectacles than the eyes watching through them. It wasn't until Mike exhausted the butter supply at our end of the table that she sat up for the first time.

Picking up the butter dish in front of her, she slid it to him silently.

"Thank you, Stella." Mike smiled as he buttered roll fifteen.

She's on to you. My eyes barely broke away from my conversation with Phil.

He stared impassively at his roll. *I know.*

What's your story? I sipped my martini.

I'm working on it.

"I ate too much!" Karen blurted on cue.

Everyone at the table looked at her.

"There's only one solution for that." Karen winked at Mike. "Dancing!"

Phil and I exchanged glances before he continued his tirade over the presidential election results. "What I can't stomach is the way the Democrats just let this go—"

As I nodded sympathetically, Mike touched my arm.

"Pardon me."

Phil paused as I looked at Michael.

"Did you want to dance?" He asked.

My eyes went between Phil and my fiancé. "Right now?"

Mike's gaze was steady. *Please say yes.*

Karen was listening intently over his shoulder. Amy and Dan had disappeared. Clearing my throat, I smiled at Phil and Stella. "You guys dancing?"

"Hell, no." Phil waved a hand. "Two feet too many. Go on ahead. We'll watch."

I nodded. "That's what I'm afraid of. Dancing while intoxicated isn't illegal, but it should be."

Michael already had my hand.

Rising from the table, he smiled at Karen. "I guess she wanted to after all."

Following him onto the dance floor, Michael weaved into the crowd until our table was out of sight. Thankfully, the band was playing jazz standards that night. The music on the floor was an up-tempo cover of "Laura." I only knew it because it was a favorite movie. It made me want to drink a bottle of Black Pony.

"Haven't seen it." His voice broke my thoughts as he pulled me close. "What's it about?"

My mind blanked as I tried seeing where his feet were.

"Sophie?"

"Cut me some slack. Can we keep it to two steps?"

"Sorry." His hands dropped to my waist and we slowed to a steady rhythm. "I know you aren't a dancer, but apparently Karen is."

"Then why am I here?" I muttered, still searching the floor between us.

"She's been touching me under the table."

"Trollop!" My head jerked back. "Want me to beat her up?"

He smiled. "Please."

With a nod, I looked at my feet. "As soon as this song's over, I'll take care of it."

"Couldn't we just stay here?"

My head popped up again. "On the dance floor?"

"You weren't going to sit at the table all night, were you?"

"No. I was planning on being under it at some point."

"Please stay with me. I don't want to dance with anyone else."

"We aren't dancing now."

"I wanted to spend time with you."

"Let's hide. They're big tables."

"I'm serious, Sophie. I wanted to take you someplace special tonight."

"More special than this?" I waved over our heads. "I mean, it's not Venice—"

"Somewhere away from here."

I tried to read his face through the mask. "You wanna leave now?"

"Only if you're ready."

Biting my lip, I looked over my shoulder. "Lyn'll be pissed if she finds mystery donor and I'm not here to *mingle*." I made air quotes with my fingers.

"Why is it so important you see him?"

"Probably better if I don't." I made a face. "Lyn thinks I should show appreciation and grovel, but I'd probably want to kick his lazy, pampered ass."

He grinned. "What if he overheard you saying that?"

"Then I would add *chicken* to his list of attributes."

Stopping our dance, Michael offered his arm.

"Then for his sake, we should probably get you out of here."

Glancing down, I wrapped my arm around his and winked. "Wise man."

RJD

August 4, 1995

Sophie,

Let me first apologize for everything that has happened. Beyond any doubt, as a parent, I share in the blame. There is no excusing it. There is no undoing it.

Believe me, if I had known what was going on I would have done everything I could to stop it. But you know what he was like. When he wanted it he had to have it and when he couldn't there was no convincing him.

There was no convincing him, Sophie. There was no other way. It was never your fault.

I'm taking him to Long Beach next weekend. You're welcome to come. If not I understand. He would too. At least in the end I think he did.

God Keep You,
Robert Jacobs

[Letter from father of Gregory Jacobs to Sophie Davids. d. August 4, 1995]

2003 "Ocean Park. Home away from home."
Michael stirs to consciousness, sitting up to look out the window as I stop at the only light in town. Making a left, I drive up a sloping hill, turning right at the crest. There is a light drizzle of rain as I shut off the radio. My bubble gum snaps and the smell reminds me of summers on the beach when I was a kid. Slowing the car, I look for the driftwood fence that will tell me where I am.

"Are we lost?"

At the sound of Mike's voice, Lodi rouses in the back seat.

"If I got us this far to get lost in Ocean Park, our child won't survive to adulthood."

Turning left onto a drive of white oyster shells, a row of Pacific pines line the ridge of a hill. At the top, the drive levels out. Sea grass brushes the sides of the car as a pheasant flashes in front us. Lodi whines.

"Easy boy." Mike reaches back, smoothing the white mane.

The narrow passage gives way to a clearing, barricaded by driftwood. Beyond, dunes of sand surround a stout two-story cottage facing us with its back to the wind. The stain on the cedar is faded to gray, the weather-beaten roof rough and uneven. A patch of fresh shingles on one of the dormers is the only indication anyone cares.

"How long since you were here?" He asks vacantly.

"Five years at least. Dad repaired the roof last year."

In front of the door, I kill the engine. We stare as rain blurs the windshield.

"What a dump." Mike whispers.

I give him a sideways glance. His lips twitch at the corners.

Opening my door, I pull the keys from the ignition. "Try not to burn this one down, too."

The rear door barely opens and Lodi flies off the seat, tearing into the grass. At the back of the car, Mike opens the trunk and pulls out two garbage bags containing our clothes. Slowly, dropping the trunk lid, Mike looks after Lodi.

"You think he'll get lost?"

On my way to the front door, I shrug. "He's my guide dog. What are the odds?"

I pause on the stoop for the key. The windowsill by the door is lined with stones and seashells my grandmother collected over the years. I pick up a large starfish with a hollow in it. When I look inside, there is no key.

"Nuts."

Mike stands behind me in the rain. The raindrops spatter on the plastic bags he is carrying. He sighs as I pick up the doormat, peeking underneath. Nothing.

"It's around here somewhere."

"I'm not seeing anything."

That answers that.

Mike clears his throat. "Maybe the people inside have it."

"What?" I spin. "Who?"

"I don't know." With a shrug, he looks left of me at the cottage wall. "Two men, in their twenties."

"Do they know we're here?"

"I think they're asleep."

"So much for getting away …" I rub my eyes. "We should call the police."

He lowers the bags from his shoulders. "But it's late."

"Michael, you're not going in there."

"I'm hungry."

"You're not eating them."

"If we call the police, who knows how long it will take? There could be a stand-off. Someone could get hurt."

"And if we don't, we could be in a world of hurt."

"You don't trust me?"

"Not particularly. No."

"They aren't armed."

"Fine!" I step off the porch step, passing him. "Do your thing. I'll be in the car."

When I reach the car and turn back, he is gone. Two garbage bags sit on the ground where he stood. Getting behind the wheel, I wait.

Lodi bounds from the grass, crossing the clearing to disappear on the other side. I yawn.

A loud pop opens my eyes.

I hear another.

Michael?!

The front door opens and Michael steps out. He goes to the bags and picks them up, inviting me to follow with a jerk of his head. My car door is already open. When I enter the cottage on his heels, I see nothing unusual aside from some sofa cushions on the floor and fast food wrappers piled in the fireplace.

Though there is no fire, I smell smoke in the air.

"What happened?" My eyes wander to the kitchen. The back door is slightly ajar.

"I asked them to leave and they left." His voice echoes down the stairs.

I follow it, pausing at the top.

"That's not what I heard. I thought you said they weren't armed."

"I thought you said you didn't trust me." He pokes his head out of one of the bedrooms. "Which room?"

"That one's fine."

Standing in the door, I watch him dump his bag of clothes on the bed and begin to fold them. I cross the room and open an empty drawer in a wardrobe. As he finishes folding, I pile his clothes into it.

"You're not going to tell me what the shooting was about?"

"One of them had a gun and it went off."

"On accident or in your general direction?"

He smiles without looking up. "I may have been the target."

"But he missed you."

Without a word, he picks up my trash bag and empties it on the bed, then frowns. "You didn't pack your corset."

"He hit you?" My eyes search him.

With a frown, he starts to fold my clothes. "It made things easier."

"Easier?"

"Getting them to leave. I was shot twice, but I only had to ask once."

"Where?" Grabbing his shoulders, I run my hands across his fleece jacket. "Let me see."

Putting down a pair of my jeans, he faces me. He watches as I scrutinize a small hole. Inches away, my fingers find another one.

"They're not so bad." I feel the fleece has melted. "You can't really see them."

"Thank God."

I glare. "Hey, we just bought this."

"Can we finish? I'm still hungry."

Scooping up my clothes, I dump them into the drawer, jamming them next to his neatly folded pile. Shoving the drawer closed, I ignore the sleeves and pant leg hanging out of it.

"Finished. Let's go." I walk out.

"Where to?" His voice is close behind me.

"There's a bar in town." I head downstairs, "But the Chinese place in Long Beach is better—*Lodi!* Out!"

At the bottom of the stairs I see Lodi's tail sticking out of the fireplace. When he turns, a hamburger wrapper hangs from the corner of his mouth. His white face and paws are black with soot.

I put up my hands. "No! Stay! Stay right there."

Mike is on him in an instant, holding his collar while I run to the kitchen for a dishtowel. When I return, Mike has extracted the wrapper from Lodi's throat.

Making a face, I take the slimy foil from him. "So much for getting away from it all."

He takes the towel from me and starts wiping Lodi's fur. "You wanted a dog."

"Just wait till the kid comes." I bend over, picking up the rest of the fast food litter. "Then we'll see who you like better."

"Somehow, I think I already know the answer."

"Sorry, Lodi." I pat him on the head. "Blood's thicker than slobber."

When we get to the Chinese restaurant, I'm worried they won't have enough food in their kitchen to feed us. Somehow, I convince Michael not to be obvious and stick to two orders of the orange chicken rather than five. I tell him he can order more on the second round and take more home if he isn't satisfied. When I only order vegetables and tofu, he chastises me for starving our baby. I tell him I'm saving room for ice cream at the Sand Dollar. I've heard rumors pregnancy temporarily relieves the curse of lactose intolerance. If true, all bets are off.

The aroma of two orders of orange chicken in Styrofoam containers fills the car as we leave for the Sand Dollar. Mike is silent, trying to decide what flavors of ice cream he wants.

"How big are the scoops again?"

I know he remembers, but hearing me say it is like listening to me talk dirty.

"Huge. One scoop is more like three."

"They have waffle cones?"

"And sugar."

"How big are the waffle cones?"

"Huge."

He falls into silence again as I pull the car to the curb. When his head pops out of his side of the car, he stares at me across the roof before shutting his door.

"What?" I look at him.

"French vanilla, cookie dough, pralines and cream."

"What about rocky road?"

"Nuts." He bites his lip, slamming his door shut.

In spite of the light rain on the drive down, by early evening the sky has cleared and the sun is drying the pavement. We walk down the street, past antique shops and gift stores with souvenirs.

I feel his hand slip into mine. "You came here every summer?"

"Not every summer. We actually spent more time in Tokeland."

"What was in Tokeland?"

"The Dunes."

"There are dunes here."

"Not sand dunes. *The Dunes*. It was a restaurant."

"A restaurant?"

"An institution more like. My great-grandparents used to go there, the big Gs, Andy and Maeve and Kate ... the food was unbelievable. We'd stay a week and eat there every meal."

When I glance at Mike, his eyes are wide with epiphany.

"It burned down." I add.

He blinks. "It wasn't me."

"Thank God." I smirk. "If you thought shaking Sam and ECCO was hard, my family would have hunted you to the ends of the earth."

"What did you eat there?"

"Someday I'll tell you." I grin, "If you're good."

Crossing the street, a small, single-story box sits in the middle of a parking lot. It is shabby the way landmarks grow with love, trimmed in red and white stripes, venting the aroma of sweet waffles and elephant ears on the ocean breeze. When Michael opens the door for me, his face is as impassive as it has ever been. When we approach the ice cream counter, he calmly surveys the flavors. When he sees the s'more-flavored ice cream between the Butterfinger and Heath bar, I see his lips twitch for the first time since he faced Metatron.

I order what I always have: a double scoop of peppermint and bubble gum in a waffle cone. Mike barely fidgets before ordering a triple scoop of rocky road, s'more, and pralines and cream, also in a waffle.

When he sees me observing him, he shrugs. "Felt like marshmallows."

Armed with ice cream, I lead him to the beach. Taking the boardwalk, we stroll easily over dunes of sea grass with the ocean spread before us. Kite flyers dot the beach into the distance; there is the occasional scent of a bonfire.

"You're good." Michael compliments my ice cream skills.

"Gotta work fast. It's still summer."

With small bites, Michael is half finished. Licking ice cream is a challenge for him. His cold breath only freezes the cream into a hard shell. Against the balmy sunset, a steady mist escapes his lips as he eats.

Nearing a bench, we sit down.

"We should have come sooner." He crunches the lip of his cone. "Brought Lodi when he was a puppy."

Working on my own cone, I keep my thoughts on the subject still. In my peripheral vision, I see him stop eating.

"You didn't want to." His voice is quiet.

"I do now."

"Why not before?"

"A lot of the people I spent time with here are dead. A lot of them were brought here when they were."

For a moment, he doesn't move, watching me as I eat.

"I did die, didn't I?"

I pause to wipe my mouth. "We both did."

"We're reborn."

"We're better."

I stare at the ocean and gnaw at my cone. Soon, he is eating his.

It is dusk when we return to the cottage. After the break in, I left lights on, giving the place a cozy feel against the red sky. Stopping the car in the drive, I glance at Mike. He stares absently out the window for a moment before giving a nod. We hear Lodi barking as we approach the front door. Using a key I found in the house, I open the front door and Lodi bursts out to run a series of laps around the car. Mike hands me his Chinese food and disappears.

In the kitchen, I open the refrigerator to take stock of what is there. Mostly canned soda, some unopened jars of pickles, relish, and a bottle of ketchup. Stashing Michael's leftovers, I regret not getting groceries the moment we arrived. Orange chicken will have to be breakfast until I make it to the store in the morning. Digging in a drawer by the phone, I find a pencil and pad of paper. I begin to write down a shopping list.

A rapid pinging makes me jump, but it is Michael filling Lodi's food dish on the front step. He joins me at the kitchen sink, filling a water bowl.

"You're tense."

"Tired." I watch him top off the bowl. "I'm going to bed."

As I leave the kitchen, I know he is watching me. All I can think about is brushing my teeth and checking the bed for spiders. I don't want to think about anything else. I can't.

In the bathroom, his voice finds me again.

"I shouldn't have come."

"Of course you should." I look at his reflection. "I don't even want to think what would have happened if I'd been alone with Lodi and those guys had been here."

"You came here to be with your thoughts. I'm too close."

Turning, I back against the bathroom sink. "Thinking's overrated. Come here."

He comes to me and I run my fingers through his hair.

"I'm glad you decided to grow your hair out again. Shaved heads are so eighties."

"May I kiss you?"

"Already brushed my teeth."

Wrapping my arms around his waist, I lean into him. He kisses me, pulls me, leads me to the bedroom. On the bed, the sheets have been turned down. There is a box tied with a ribbon on the pillow near the window.

"What's that?"

With a shrug, he glances at it, saying nothing.

Flopping on the bed, I pick up the box and pull off the ribbon. Inside is a velvet pouch. I loosen the draw string and the contents roll into my palm. A ring. A diamond set in a twisting band, but the band is silver, not gold. It is my old ring, but different.

"Do you like it?" He stretches on the bed next to me.

Slipping it on my ring finger, it feels like it was always there.

"When did you make this?"

"The day we got back. While you were asleep, I went down to the house."

"You found my ring?"

"The diamond. Le Roy's made the platinum band for me."

"That was fast. We only got back four days ago."

"I think they made the ring in less time than it took me to grow my hair back."

"Well ..." I reach over, brushing hair from his eyes. "Perfection can't be rushed."

"Oh." Looking down at himself, he digs into the front pocket of his jeans. "And I thought you'd like these."

Extending his hand, he displays two dull lumps of metal in his palm.

"Don't tell me." I grin as he drops them in my hand.

"I thought they were interesting. I've never been shot before."

"Really?"

Shaking his head, he takes a slug to examine it. "I always avoided it."

"A wise policy, even if it can't hurt you."

"It does hurt. It could have hurt worse if they'd known where to shoot."

I feel my brows go up. "Where would that be?"

He grins. "You'd like to know."

"You don't trust me?"

"You've already found it. Twice."

"When?" I sit up on the bed.

"When you were wrestling with Phanuel. You kicked him."

Raising a hand to his head, he points to the middle of his forehead. In an instant,

I see him in his crypt. A blue spark burns there.

"Your pineal gland?"

He blinks. "You know your anatomy."

"I knew reality TV had a pay off."

Rolling on his back with a snort, he holds the slug above his face, squinting at it.

"It links you to the continuum of time and space, but it links my spirit to the material universe. It is the physical embodiment of my sentience. It was how I destroyed Sam. It was how Metatron blinded me. A bullet, even the blunt force of a kick, can be incapacitating."

"Good to know, since sex doesn't seem to have that effect anymore."

"You found it when we met. The first time you kissed me, you kissed me there."

Frowning, I climb on him. "Must be an ex-girlfriend. I don't remember that."

"The day we looked for houses. The first time I took you to our old house. I took you back to Anthony and told you we'd been followed."

"I was pissed at you. I didn't kiss you."

"You kissed me before you left the car."

Slowly, I smile. "I remember. You looked terrified."

"I was."

"All because I was kissing your pineal gland."

"It was incapacitating."

Leaning over him, I kiss his forehead. "What about now?"

The front of my neck is cold with his breath. His eyes stay closed as I work my way down, kissing his lids, his nose, his lips.

I hear a thud as the slug slips from his fingers onto the floor.

But I am tired. So tired, I don't notice when Michael gets out of bed the next morning. Only when I hear the back door open and shut, do I finally wake. Sitting up in bed, I stretch over the nightstand and peek through the curtains at the ocean. The dunes are golden with morning sun. My husband is just visible, heading for the beach, his hair matching the sea grass, the sleeves of his charcoal fleece buffeted by the wind. Getting out of bed, I swear as I step on something like stone in my bare feet. Bending over, I pick up the slug, tossing it on the nightstand before heading to the bathroom.

Opening the dormer window wide, I let in the summer air as I run the pipes. I shower quickly, my mind already set on groceries, breakfast, house cleaning, checking my voice mail. Still naked, with my hair in a towel, I hear a car on the drive. When I look out the window, a patrol car is parked next to the BMW. For a moment I am frozen.

Then I am running to get dressed.

I make the door in a camisole, yoga pants, and bare feet.

"Good morning, ma'am. I'm Deputy Sheriff Kerns with the Pacific County Sheriff's Department. I hope I haven't come at a bad time, but there's a matter I wanted to speak with you about."

"No problem." Standing back, I hold the door. "Come in."

Even after removing his hat, he is a tall man, stooping to clear the door frame. His hair is brown and close-cropped. His face is thin with large features, most noticeably a pair of drooping brown eyes and a sunburned nose.

"Have a seat." I wave to the sofa and chairs in front of the fire.

"Thank you." He looks around. "Great little place. Renting it for the summer?"

"Nope, it's been in the family for a few generations now."

He nods, taking an armchair. "My grandparents had a place in Long Beach just off of Main. They sold it years ago for nothing. Wish we still had it."

"I bet you do." I grin at him from the sofa. "Do you need anything? We just got in last night, so I've got water for tea and water for water."

"No, thank you. I wanted to follow up on a report we had about a break in. Someone claims your place was broken into, and I wanted to see if that was the case."

Pursing my lips, I look thoughtful. "Nothing seemed amiss when we got here."

"We, meaning …?"

"My husband, Michael, and our dog, Lodi."

"And where are they?"

"Mike took the dog for a run on the beach."

"What sort of dog?"

"Shepherd Malamute mix."

"Big dog …" The sheriff pauses as his eyes cross the living room, to the kitchen, to the back door. "What time did you and your husband arrive?"

"I'd guess it was around six. We had enough time for dinner before bed."

"Did you notice anyone around the premises? Any evidence of trespassers?"

"No."

"Any sign of forced entry?"

"No."

"How often do you and your family use the place?"

"Once a year or so. My parents were here last summer and made some repairs."

"You rent it out at all? To friends or third parties?"

"No."

"Could you tell me what your husband looks like?"

"A little over six feet, sandy brown hair, blue eyes." I shrug.

"Fair skin?"

"Yes. Why?"

Taking a breath, Sheriff Kerns leans forward, holding his hat by the brim.

"The fellow who reported the break in claims he was one of the men who did it. He says he and his partner were squatting here a couple days when a man fitting the description of your husband surprised them."

"I don't see how that's possible. I've been with him since we arrived."

"It gets better. He claims his partner shot this man at close range."

I frown. "Michael seemed fine this morning."

"That's what he said. He says after they shot him, this man only asked them if they would please leave."

I raise my brows. "After being shot?"

"Twice in the chest."

Reclining on the sofa, I shake my head. "Mike would have mentioned it."

"That wasn't the part I was investigating. But I thought the break in deserved some attention. We have a lot of those. Looks like that didn't happen either."

"Maybe he gave you the wrong address?"

"Wrong planet more like. It's the meth talking. We're lousy with it these days."

The sheriff rose to his feet. "I won't waste any more of your vacation."

Going to the door, I open it and watch him duck out into the sunshine.

"Thanks for checking on us." I smile.

Putting on his hat, he touches the rim to me. "Enjoy your stay."

The moment I shut the door, I find my Merrells and head for the beach. Slogging through loose sand, I climb the last ridge of dunes and scan the beach, my hands shielding my eyes against the wind.

It is still early but there are already joggers, kite flyers, and dogs. Morning beach-combers evenly dot the shore. I spot Lodi in the distance. The flowing white coat runs a wide arc, leaping driftwood, scattering sandpipers. I follow it, knowing it will find him. Lodi stops in front of a figure, dropping something at his feet.

I begin to run.

I see the figure pick up the stick and throw it far down the beach. Lodi disappears in a spray of sand.

It stands still, facing away from me, watching the dog run. It seems to waver before my eyes, with feet that don't touch the ground. With each wave that rolls in, the tide threatens to take it away. Feeling the firm of wet sand beneath my feet, I pick up speed. The wind howls in my ears, biting into my bare arms.

Finally, I see him. The shape of him. The wind in his hair. The sun on his back. His shoes in the sand.

He turns.

There is recognition in his eyes. Concern. Astonishment.

I don't slow. Don't worry I will knock him to the ground. Don't care if I do.

There is no impact.

I am caught.

I am weeping.

1199 BC   The gray beards were satisfied with my answer. I made no claim on them and offered nothing beyond their own desire to achieve. My absence of expectation in spite of my capabilities impressed them. In return, they asked me what I wished of them. I said only to follow what was best in themselves to the benefit of others. They asked if homage to me would insure this and I said it would not. I required no gold, no prayers, no faith from them. The general swore I had his, whether I required it or not.

The caravan under his banner would bear my will.

As tribute to our hosts of our peaceful intent, the general requisitioned the molten remains of the reliquary and offered it to the Canaans. It had cooled into a misshapen ingot of gold and bronze, worth the weight of four men. With the collar of Pharaoh across it and the mask of Aten atop, it was loaded into a wagon and hauled before the caravan on our way to Lod.

Of all the priests, only Ptah refused my presence. Disappearing never to be seen again, his house was left in disarray. Khenemet of Peyoth was quick to take the position the houses of Egypt had eroded. Their struggles with each other did nothing to strengthen their faith. They had beheld three miracles at my hands; surely it was a sign for them to change their ways. To what end, they were unsure.

It was on the journey to Lod the priests found themselves lost. They considered the faith that led the migrants to Sinai and recollected the law meant to govern them. Khenemet came to me and asked if I was the lord of Sinai, whether the laws there written were true. I said there was no lord of Sinai, and the laws there written were never intended for men.

He asked if I would write laws intended for men. I told him only men could do such a thing. He asked if this was what the one god wanted. I told him only men could guess. He asked if I was going to stay. I said I was not. He asked where I was going. I said I did not know. He asked when I was leaving. I said I did not know. He asked if I would return. I said I did not know. He asked where they should go. I said I did not know. He asked me my name. I told him.

Maihael.

[Spharic. Entry translated from *Kor Dai Maihael*. Mund Dai. d. 755 BC]

2001

"Where are we going?" She hissed in the night.

Gripping her hand, he pulled her unwilling feet as they passed his car.

"It isn't far."

"It's freezing!"

"It won't be when we get there."

His eyes looked to the park three blocks away. It was deserted.

"I know you're not the typical guy, but do you really think a walk in the park right now is a good idea?"

"Trust me."

He heard her snort and smiled. Still, her hold on his arm tightened and the click of her heels picked up. As they crossed the street to the park, the far gutter was still a rut of ice, rushing with snow melt. Stooping, he picked her up and carried her to the sidewalk. As soon as he set her down, she was upset.

"You're soaked." She pointed at his sopping shoes.

"I'm fine." Taking her hand, he started for the conservatory.

"You'll catch cold."

"I can't, remember?"

"For once, could you pretend it's a possibility?"

"I'll try."

"You're soaked." She repeated.

He sighed. "I'm fine."

"You'll catch cold."

"I'll survive."

"Not if turns to pneumonia."

"I won't get pneumonia."

"See. There you go again."

"I didn't say I *can't* get pneumonia, I said I *won't*."

"Sorry." She cleared her throat. "Saying you won't doesn't mean you can't."

"That's what I said."

"No, it isn't. You said, 'I won't get pneumonia.'"

"Right."

"Who's on first?" She muttered.

Pausing in front of the conservatory, he looked back at her. "What?"

She blinked. "Are we doing here?"

"We're going inside." He led her down the turnabout to the conservatory doors.

"It's closed!"

"Not for long."

"You're breaking in?"

"I'll be fine. I'm wearing a mask."

She looked around in the dark. "Well, I'm not wearing one."

"That's not my problem. You're the one who chose not to. Wait here."

"What?"

"I always go in through the fire escape. Wait here and I'll let you in."

"*Always?!*"

He didn't wait for her protest. Slipping into the dark, he quickly followed the side of the building around back.

It was a lie. He never went in through the fire escape. In the nexus of space and time, doors and locks had no use. His eye was the only key he needed. In the shadows of the park, he saw the foyer of the conservatory in his mind. Like stepping from one room to another, it was a miniscule shift away. Once inside, he went to the key pad by the service entrance. The alarm code buttons glowed to his eyes, burnished with repeated use. He knew the code. Ever since installing the system, they had never bothered to change it.

When he returned to the front door, she was nowhere to be seen.

Opening the door, he looked down the turnabout, then heard someone rapping on a pane of glass. It was coming from the conservatory behind him. Closing the front doors, he ran through the conservatory. At the far end of the garden, he saw her face peering through sweating panes next to the fire escape.

"Sophie! Step away from the door!"

He saw her back away. Putting his hands on the release bar, he pushed a current into it. There was an arc and a loud snap. No longer feeling the faint current of the fire system, he pushed the door open. To his relief, there was no alarm.

"What the hell took so long?" She pushed past him, stomping her feet and rubbing her sides. "I thought you came in this way?"

"I thought I told you to wait out front."

"I couldn't."

"What do you mean you couldn't?"

"It got hot."

"Hot?"

"Coppers. Probably Anthony. I assume you didn't invite anyone else?"

"Of course not."

He sat her on the bench by the koi pond. Kneeling in front of her, he took off his mask and tossed it next to her before pulling off her shoes. Her black nylons were stained halfway to her knees.

"Sophie, you're soaked."

"I prefer sloshed."

Rubbing her feet between his palms, he grinned. "You'll catch cold."

"Just don't blow on them."

Fire flowed to his hands. "How does this feel?"

"Wonderful. You've been holding out on me."

"I shouldn't. Women need it."

Her brow arched. "And men don't?"

"Men's feet aren't as sensitive."

"You have evidence to back that up?"

"I do, but you probably don't want to hear it."

"Try me." A challenge was always irresistible to her.

"I've always felt more through my feet when I was a woman than a man."

"That's why you know what feels good?"

He nodded.

"Especially in bed."

"In bed, I rely on your response rather than any previous experience."

"Because everyone is different?"

"My own experience is not very useful where relationships are concerned."

"Because prior to me you've never had a romantic relationship?"

"Yes."

"You don't want to talk about this, do you?"

"There isn't anything to talk about."

"So you didn't bring me here to talk."

"No." He gave her feet a squeeze.

"So what's stopping you?"

"There is one small problem."

"What?"

"I'll have to stop rubbing your feet."

"Shit. I guess you really can't have it all."

"May I?"

"I'll survive."

Sitting back on his heels, he reached into his pocket and pulled out the velvet box. He held it up to her in the palm of his hand. Her soul lit at the sight of it. Silently, she held her fingers to her mouth, then reached out with both hands.

When she opened the box, her face was expressionless.

The koi pond gurgled. His heart pounded.

"Do you like it?" He whispered.

He heard the box snap shut as she tackled him to the floor with a squeal.

"Is that a yes?" He laughed, catching her in his arms.

The glow of her face so close to his made his eyes dilate. The wide collar of her overcoat covered their heads, filling his lungs with her breath. The smell of her made him stiffen. When she started to kiss him, he pushed her away.

"No, Sophie. Not here."

"You brought me here."

She blew on his face and he felt his eyes flush.

He turned away, sitting up in spite of her efforts to pin him.

"Stop it, Sophie. I'm serious."

"Serious enough to get me a ring, but not enough to give it to me?"

"Don't be vulgar."

Panic spurred him to his feet. Sparked by her aggression. By what he just said. Standing over her, she was sprawled on one hip, her shoulder propped on an elbow.

"I'm sorry." He could hardly look at her.

He held out his hand.

She ignored it. "There's nothing to apologize for. I am vulgar."

"No, Soph—"

"I am, Mike. I'm vulgar and horny and an alcoholic. What are you?"

"Please." His eyes fixed on the ring box gripped in her hand. "You promised."

"Promised what?!" Her voice rang off the glass walls.

"No questions." He whispered.

Sighing, she stared down at her stocking feet. A hole on one leg exposed white flesh in the pale light of the conservatory ceiling. When she looked back up at him, her face and neck were ghostly against the black of her dress, the light in her eyes, dim as death.

"This isn't how you imagined our friendship when you first invited me here."

"I didn't imagine anything until I met you."

"Oh, *please*—"

"It's the truth!" He cut off her dismissal. "None of us do! We don't live lives. We just exist. Since meeting you I've stopped existing and started living, and it has terrific. Terrific because I imagine the future. Terrific because I live the past. Do you understand? Everything that came before, I never felt. When I think of it now, I can't just remember. I feel what I should have and never did."

Going to the bench, he dropped onto it, his eyes finding the mask next to him.

"I can't tell you who I am. I've only begun to find out."

For a moment she said nothing. When she did, her words were quiet.

"Maybe marriage isn't such a good idea."

"One doesn't have any bearing on the other."

She stretched on the floor and crossed her legs. "Prove it."

He stood again and paced to the koi pond, then returned, facing her.

"If people could only marry when they knew themselves, no one would be qualified."

"Agreed." She nodded. "Marriage should be abolished."

"Marriage should be a choice."

"Even if it's a mistake?"

"Is that what you believe? That because some marriages are mistakes there should be none?"

"Most are, so why bother?"

"What about your parents?"

"They'd love each other just as much."

"That's not the point, Sophie."

"Then what is, Michael?"

"The point is they chose to be married, regardless."

"Regardless of what?"

He held his breath. "Regardless of the fact their choice might not be accepted."

Sophie squinted, her lips disappearing. "Or their child."

"We'll never have one ... If that's what your worried about."

She shook her head. "That's your hang up, not mine. I just like to know what I'm getting into and who I'm getting into it with."

"Marriage. With a singular entity that can't explain itself."

"You're good. Ever think about being a lawyer?"

Closing his eyes, he said nothing. When his mouth opened, it was only air.

He heard her move. When he opened his eyes, she was standing in front of him. She opened the ring box. Removing the ring, she held it to him. Swallowing, he refused to look at it. His insides felt like they were melting.

She waved the ring in his face. "Put it on."

Blinking, his hand felt for it. Blindly taking her hand, he slid it on her finger.

"Does it fit?" He couldn't hear himself.

Her lips pursed. "Not too loose, not too tight."

Without a backward glance, she flung the ring box over her shoulder. It landed in the koi pond with a splash.

He blinked. "You don't need the box?"

She looked up from her hand. "You think I do?"

"I don't know. I've never owned any jewelry."

"Why not?"

"It melts."

"Good reason. If I'm going to wear it every day, I don't need a box, do I?"

"I need you, Sophie."

"So do I."

He smiled. "But do you need me?"

She grinned. "In a most vulgar fashion."

"Then we'd better get home."

She looked around them. "Sure you don't want to ring in the New Year where we first got to know each other?"

"It isn't safe."

"Right." She sniffed. "Safety first. Then we'll ring it in the way we did last year."

"I bought champagne." He bent to slip a shoe on her foot. "It's at home in the refrigerator."

"Perfect." She balanced against him as he put the last one on. "Same drink, same dress, same man—"

He rose before her. "I'm not the same man."

Taking her arm, he began to lead her to the from the conservatory.

"Really? I'll expect you to back that up—Hey—" She stopped in her tracks. "You're forgetting your mask."

Gripping her hand, he pulled her unwilling feet.

"No. I'm not."

"You can't leave it behind!"

"It isn't mine." He muttered.

"But you got it in Venice! In seventeen twenty-five!"
Without looking back, he shook his head.
"Walmart."

1199 BC   Lod was a fortified trade post on an inland route to the Canaan Nile. The complex of stalls and stables were a maze of breeze-ways and corridors occupied by merchants and traders conducting business at all hours. Business had flourished since the armies of five tribes converged in preparation of the exodus headed their way. Though the tribal chiefs may have had doubts, commerce had none. Rumors of war increased the demand for food, supplies, and weapons. When our caravan arrived in peace, the population of Lod redoubled and the needs of the people with it.

In the midst of this confusion, the tribes struggled to come to terms with the mission the general had set for his people. It was a matter beyond my capacity to remedy, but one the general and Khenemet begged me to attend. Though my abilities as a translator were invaluable, my own responses to their questions were equivocal in all things save one: there must be no bloodshed.

This was supported by Khenemet, who attested to my miraculous nature before the Canaan tribes as the source of his own conversion to a higher calling. Khenemet declared that all who doubted this calling should hear me. If my words did not convince, they need only attempt to strike me down as Ptah had, to see I was shielded by the truth. This was a development unforeseen and reminded me of my determination to leave.

When Chiron rose to witness I had made fire without flame, it was thoughtless. When he drew his sword and approached, I was hopeless. Unable to flee and unwilling to fight, I could only watch, when the general stood with sword drawn.

"Chiron, sheath your blade!" The gray beard froze the breath in my throat as Chiron stopped in his tracks.

"Maihael is a messenger, not a magician. It is not his task to convince us of the truth, only show the way. The journey is our own, success or failure to come as we choose it. He has done all he can. You may strike him down. He may live or die. We will be at the same crossroads—no better and no worse."

There was silence. The general stood still, his weapon ready, his men on their feet. As Chiron sheathed his blade, I closed my eyes, my thought final.

Lord general, I leave tonight.

Wordlessly, he sheathed his sword.

You will.

[Spharic. Entry translated from *Kor Dai Maihael*. Mund Dai. d. 755 BC]

2003 "Mr. Goodhew." Nate holds out a hand. "Good to meet you."
Gripping the young man's hand, he feels it is firm but damp.
"Same here. Please, come in."

In spite of the smile, he senses apprehension as Nate enters the foyer of Violet's house for the second time.

"I told your wife this place was amazing. How old is it, do you know?"

"One hundred and five years."

"Do you know who built it?"

"No." He leads Nate into the great room. "The man who bought it was named Curtis Farrell. His widow still owns it."

"The old lady I saw in the garden?"

Without a glance, he continues to the study. "That would be Violet Farrell."

Passing through the study doors, he goes to Curtis's desk.

Nate's voice follows. "Is Mrs. Goodhew joining us?"

"She had errands. I'm afraid it is only me today."

"Oh." The young man's disappointment is brief. "*Wow.*"

When he turns, Nate is stopped at the study door, agape at the bookshelves towering twenty feet on all sides. "This must be the library."

"Curtis Farrell was an avid collector." With a smile, he indicates the high-backed chair in front of the desk. "Please, have a seat."

Nate moves to it with a nervous smile.

"Is there anything I might get you? Something to drink?"

"No, thanks." Nate slowly sits. "I'm good."

Stepping around the desk, he takes his place in Curtis's leather desk chair.

"I have to admit, when Sophie told me you were planning an independent investigation of the fire, I was disappointed. You seemed more than satisfied to take my money with every assurance it would be worth my while."

"I—I understand completely. After reading your affidavit and reviewing the fire inspector's report, we concluded any further investigation would be unnecessary."

"Was that before or after reading the letter from my attorney?"

Nate's hands went up. "Believe me, Mr. Goodhew—"

"Michael."

"Sorry—Michael, I was just as disappointed as you were that the formality of an investigation had to come up, but rest assured, that was all it was. Purely routine. As I told your wife, it was highly unlikely you wouldn't be compens—"

"That was all the assurance you gave her." He coolly interrupts.

Nate is unnerved. "I explained if she chose to rebuild there might not—"

"Might not." His eyes narrow.

Nate drops his gaze.

He sighs. "Still not very comforting for someone who has lost their home and must confront such news alone."

Nate nods, silently.

"I was honest when I discussed purchasing insurance from you three years ago.

I told you I had never carried insurance because the risk made little difference to me, but for my wife's peace of mind I was willing to consider it. Truthfully, if your company refused to pay a dime, I couldn't care less. What I do care about is providing my wife with assurance that if I am gone, she is not alone. When you came to her, she was. You did little to ease her worries and much to explain yourself. Regardless of fine print, that is not what I paid for, Mr. Keller."

Nate coughs.

"However ... I don't doubt if it had been your decision to make alone, you would have brought better news."

The young man looks up with a weak grin. "Thank you, sir."

"Michael."

"Sorry. Thank you, Michael."

"Now that we are making plans to rebuild, I hope we can make a fresh start."

"Yes!" Nate's slouch disappears. "Yes, absolutely."

He smiles. "I arranged to have the debris cleared by the end of the week and plans for a new home site drawn."

"You hired a contractor?"

He shakes his head. "The home will be prefabricated and green built."

This makes Nate sit forward. "Are you managing the project yourself?"

"Sophie is."

"Oh." Nate tries to smile over doubt, only looking positively doubtful. "Has she overseen a construction project before?"

"Not on this scale." He grins.

As Nate is leaving, the front door opens and Lodi runs into the foyer with sister Lola close behind. The sight of Nate induces raised hackles and snarling.

Lodi, no.

At his thought, Lodi stops with shifting ears and a yawn, displaying formidable teeth. Nate freezes while Lola approaches with a curious nose.

"Hey, Mike. Sorry about that." Anthony steps inside with two grocery bags. "Me and the pack were in the neighborhood and thought we'd say hi."

He touches Nate's shoulder, making the young man jump. "Sorry if he scared you. The friendly one is Lola. The rude one is Lodi. The one in the uniform is Anthony."

Nate nods to each, heading for the door. "Hi, Lola. Bye, Lodi. Officer."

At the door, he offers his hand. "Thanks for stopping, Nate."

"I'll keep in touch, Mr. Goodhew." Nate quickly shakes it. "I promise!"

Glancing at the dogs, Nate jumps on the porch, shutting the door between them. When he turns, Anthony is hanging his hat.

"Guess I should have knocked first."

He shrugs. "Visitors here are a rare occurrence."

"I wouldn't say that." Anthony smirks, picking a grocery bag from the floor. He quickly picks up the other one and follows Anthony down the hall.

On the way to the kitchen, Anthony glances over a shoulder at him. "She around?"

"Running errands. She wanted to buy something for Hawaii."

Anthony unloads the groceries on the kitchen counter. The ingredients are promising. Chicken and buttermilk. He goes to the refrigerator and starts to fill it as Anthony empties the bags.

"Is Violet making fried chicken?"

"Yep." Anthony grins. "She wanted to make something special for you guys before you left. Since you weren't here the first time she made it for us—"

"I was."

"Well ... since your stomach wasn't here, she wanted to treat you."

"Anything she made would have been fine. She's an excellent cook."

Folding a grocery bag, Anthony rolls his eyes. "Have you had her pie?"

"Cherry and peach."

"Have her make you a meringue."

He grins. "Have her make you a ham sandwich."

"Oh, jeez! Those little deviled things? I think she puts crack in those."

"What's crack?" Violet's voice surprises them both.

"A narcotic. I was telling Mike, I think you put it in those ham sandwiches because I can't stop eatin' em."

She waves them off. "Can't stop because you're all starving yourselves to death. I can't even get Danny to eat and he used to eat everything."

"Who's Danny?" Anthony frowns at Violet, but she only glances at them with a shrug before going to a drawer for pots and pans.

When Anthony looks to him with raised brows, he feigns ignorance. If anyone is free to tell Anthony about Daniel it is Sophie, not him.

Violet pauses between them with a skillet and a mallet. "If you two aren't frying chicken, I'll be using this kitchen."

"Yes, ma'am." Anthony salutes as they leave her to it.

They pass through the dining room to the front parlor.

Behind him, he hears Anthony's throat clear. "How's Gabrielle?"

"Recovered from her injuries."

"She looked bad last time I saw her."

"I've seen her worse." Crossing the parlor, he goes to an armchair. "She always comes back. She's a strong one."

Anthony takes the chair across from him. "Did she find Raphael?"

"Yes."

"She was pretty worried about him."

"With good reason. He suffered the most of any of us."

"Is he okay?"

"He's still recovering. She won't leave his side until he's finished."

Anthony nods with crossed legs. "Well, if you see her, let her know I'm glad she's all right."

"Of course." He smiles. "How is Amy?"

Sighing, Anthony stretches in the chair, hands behind his head.

"Or would you rather I didn't ask?"

"No. It's fine. She's fine. She's in Colorado this week visiting her parents."

Again, he finds himself wondering what to say. He remembers camping.

"Are you taking any time off this summer?"

"Probably not." Anthony suddenly seems tired.

"I forgot." He didn't. "You said summers were busy for you."

"Yeah." Staring at nothing, Anthony blinks a few times. "It's been busy."

Of course it was. He worries how Anthony explained being absent from work.

"Anthony, I'm sorry, you were dragged into this. If there's anything I can do …"

The man only stares vacantly, unhearing.

"I will let Gabrielle know you've been worried for her …" He feels Anthony's emptiness. "I'm sure you'll hear from her when I do."

Anthony's eyes come back. "Really?"

"It wouldn't be like her to ignore the well wishes of an ally."

For a moment, Anthony's fingers drum the armrest.

"How will she know where to reach me?"

He hesitates. "I'll give her your information."

"So, she'll call?"

"Possibly."

"Where is she?"

"Seattle."

"Maybe I should check in on her?"

"She's with Raphael now."

"Oh …" The look Anthony gives is vaguely hostile. "Right."

He goes where he should not. "It isn't like that."

"Like what?"

"Gabrielle and Raphael."

"You mean they're not … together?"

He hears his voice drop. "We don't do that."

"You do."

He smiles. "I'm a misfit."

Anthony smiles back. "We all are. Some of us just don't know it."

The front door flies open, rattling the windows. Sophie storms past the parlor door before her feet stop. Returning, her head pops into the parlor.

"You aren't going to believe what's happened!"

She marches in the room with two shopping bags in each hand and drops them.

"What?" Anthony sits up in his chair, gripping the armrests.

"Grounds is gone!"

"What?"

"*Grounds for Coffee!* Gone!" Her eyes dart between them. "And guess what's going in? Guess!"

She shoots him a glare. He shakes his head though her mind screams the answer.

"*Tully's!* It's going to be a fucking Tully's. *Can you believe it!*"

"So what?" Anthony smirks.

"*So what?* It's the end of the world is what! The slow, inexorable, grinding consumption of the world by ruthless corporate machines! Mark me, someday you won't be able to buy a cup of coffee that isn't from Starbucks or Tully's."

She looks back at him and points. "That's it, Mike! We're going to Hawaii, we're buying a coffee farm, and I'm making my own. Fuck them! I'm not buying their shit coffee!! I'm not going to be a part of this mindless consumption!"

Bending to pick up her shopping bags, she turns to leave.

"That's why you shopped at Macy's?"

"Shut up, Tony!" She disappears.

He listens to her stomp up the stairs and eyes Anthony. "Brave man."

Anthony grins. "I'm wearing your medal."

Pulling on jeans and a tee, he keeps his eye on Sophie as she sleeps. He is soundless, but still fears disturbing her sleep. They will leave for the airport in less than two hours, barely time for her to get a night's rest. Enough for him to get started. How much he accomplishes afterwards makes no difference; starting over is the hardest part. Lightly touching the doorknob, he slips from the room.

Skipping down turret stairs, he remembers how treacherous they first seemed. Wounded and night blind, the house was a maze of unseen hazards. Now, dark is only a change of wavelength, a shift in perspective. Even so, when he reaches the study, he turns on the desk lamp to work by light. On the floor, next to Curtis's desk, is a shipping box, taped, unopened. Using a letter opener, he cuts the seams, pulling the cardboard away.

Inside, a front of black bindings face him. His fingers run across them before digging against the side of the box to pry one free. The journal opens in his hands, snapping the spine, releasing a stink of virgin paper. Placing the book in front of him, he opens the ink well on Curtis's desk and pulls one of a handful of pens Curtis kept in the right-hand drawer. He dips the stylus, testing the line on the back of an envelope. It is dark and clean.

Sitting back, he stares without focus. He knows what has been lost. He is unsure what will be found. It will take longer for certain, but time costs him nothing. What it will cost is peace of mind. Peace he craves. Willful ignorance. If that was all he wanted, he would be Metatron's slave still. Sleeping like the dead. Careless. Hairless. In a box.

He will have to rewrite. Revisit.

Relive.

Sitting forward, he reaches across the desk and dips the pen. The flyleaf flattens under his hand. Precisely, delicately, he begins to write.

She doesn't surprise him when she enters.

He heard her stir in their room long before she came downstairs. Had felt her longing the moment she reached for him and found him missing from their bed. It is a scar he has left that will never fade. The fear of losing him.

"What are you doing?"

She sleepily approaches in one of his shirts.

Setting the pen aside, he reclines to watch the ink dry.

"Writing."

She tenses at the sight of his script. In spite of her respect, it affronts her.

"Should I leave?"

"Never."

"I'll leave." She turns.

"Sophie."

"Hmm?" Dim eyes peek through her hair as she looks over her shoulder.

"Will you stay while I read?"

Her eyes dart around the room and back to him.

"Aloud." He answers her confusion.

"You don't have to."

"I do."

Slowly, she returns. Nearing the desk, she lowers herself into the chair across from him. He does not sit forward but leaves the book where it sits. Holding her gaze, he begins.

"Reality is made in the living. As I have scarcely lived, what is written here are records of deeds. The life in them, purely speculative. Whether they were real, indeed whether I am real, remains undetermined. The thought behind these words is real, but no more than the ink they are written in. They are not alive. This reality is the crucible of my existence. A reality I have only begun to face in a record of discovery, my confrontation with the living world and acceptance of my place in it.

"If there is any part of my existence I accept, it is my marriage to Sophie. Before her, I knew nothing. One universe. One belief. A single means of existence without value or measure. Life was a fact, and like all facts, it existed without purpose beyond design. This was how I perceived myself. Only one purpose justified my existence. Without it, I imagined nothing. Beyond it, I felt nothing.

"Yet it was this poor purpose that led me to life, at first, seeing only what I wanted, assuming it chance to discover life hungered for more than bread. It was more than chance; it was the discovery of a greater design. It went beyond expectation, down a path I had been blind to. Awareness began a journey of understanding, of life and ultimately myself. That awareness of myself was a hard thing. Eternal or not, I was empty within and invisible without. Above all else, I yearned to live.

"Only when I realized my emptiness was I open. Only when I was open did Sophie become my reality, and nothing could ever be the same. If awareness made me conscious of the living, Sophie made me conscious of love. The pursuit of love made me realize life beyond the confines of design. Love is life—the product of it, the measure of it, and the proof of it.

"The day I sought to prove my love for Sophie was the first day I was alive. As of this lineal count, I am all of three human years old. Everything before, existing in time beyond measure, I can only describe. Yet describe it I will, anew and free of the singular belief I was. Such is the record of my life, if only by the measure of my love."

He pauses, blinking.

She bobs. "How long did that take you?"

"To write or think?"

"Whichever is least annoying."

"Five minutes. The ink ran dry and I had to search for another bottle."

"Tell me you misspelled something."

Reaching forward, he picks up the pen, dips it in ink, and crosses out a character on the page. He rewrites it.

"Better?"

"That wasn't really misspelled, was it?"

He sighs. "I'll do worse next time."

"Pretty pessimistic for a three-year-old."

"Is that the part you liked most?"

"The part I'll get the most use out of."

"But do you like it?"

She nods expressionlessly. "Lots."

"I want to read you everything I write in it from now on."

She frowns. "I thought you were going to rewrite everything?"

"I am."

"Will I still be alive when you finish?"

"Technically, it will never be finished."

"You know what I mean. By the time you get caught up."

"It isn't a record of every moment, only events of significance."

"And how long is that?"

"If I read you a page a day, approximately forty-eight years."

She shrugs. "If we make time, we might shave it down to twenty."

"Easily."

"Are you taking it with us to Hawaii?"

Looking at the open book, he frowns. "You want me to?"

"Only if you do."

"It wouldn't interfere with our vacation?"

"Honey, it's Hawaii. Nothing interferes in Hawaii." She pauses. "Except for the volcano ..." Her brows go up. "And tsunamis ..."

"Sophie."

"Earthquakes."

"Sophie."

"Typhoons."

"Sophie."

"Hmm?"

"We'll be together."
Her eyes glow. "Come hell or high water."

RATTLE IN SEATTLE
Quake Shakes the South Sound

An earthquake struck south Puget Sound yesterday at 10:45 am, disrupting work and causing significant structural damage from Seattle to Olympia. The tremors were felt as far north as Vancouver, south to Portland and east as far as Pasco. Lasting 4.5 seconds, the quake was intense enough to send people running from their offices or hiding under their desks. Daily business was brought to a standstill in three counties as students were evacuated from schools and office buildings were closed pending structural inspection. Bill Gates was interrupted in the middle of giving a presentation in Redmond while a hospital ribbon cutting ceremony upstaged in Tacoma.

Susan Sullivan, Executive Chair of The St. Joseph Hospital Foundation was about to welcome press and public to tour a new wing recently added to the hospital located in Tacoma's Hilltop Neighborhood, when the building began to shake and the glass ceiling in the new atrium gave way behind her.

"It was so sudden. At first I didn't realize what was going on, I thought that it was just a big truck on the street or thunder, then when the floor began to shake I thought, 'My God, this is it!'. But everyone was so calm and super professional, I mean, we were in a hospital, so you couldn't be in a better place for a disaster, right?"

In Seattle, the worst damage occurred in the Pioneer Square and SODO neighborhoods where older buildings with unrein-forced masonry suffered partial collapses onto sidewalks. A few crushed cars parked on the streets were the only casualties. All highway overpasses and some bridges were temporarily closed for inspection following the quake, the Alaska Way Viaduct being of particular concern.

In Olympia, similar damage happened to older masonry buildings, including the Capitol Dome roof, which developed serious cracks in the ceiling and will remain closed to the public until the extent of the damage is assessed and repairs made. At this point the full cost of the damage to the Capitol building alone will likely range in the millions. The total cost in damage to the south sound remains undetermined but could cost billions of dollars. Although injuries from the quake have been reported and a fatal heart attack may have caused by the tremor, there were no direct fatalities.

The U.S. Geological Survey classified the quake as an intraplate or interslab earthquake and measured it at 6.8 with an epicenter approximately 36 miles below Anderson Island. This would place the quake on a fault line where the Juan de Fuca Plate subsides beneath the North American continent. These quakes are caused as one plate slides beneath another, as the subsiding plate melts, it pulls the rest of it behind, these shifts cause the quakes. Since the Pacific Coast is a subduction zone, this was not first quake of this type to strike the Puget Sound, nor will it be the last.

[Article from the *Tacoma News Tribune*. Scrapbook of Michael Goodhew. d. February 28, 2001]

2001 "Michael?" I whisper.

Bending, I touched his shoulder. With a jerk, his eyes flashed open.

"I'm leaving. Remember to feed the koi, oh, and I got a bacon Nylabone for Lodi. It's on top of his food bin. Give it to him after you bring him back from the vet— better yet, take it with you, give it to him as soon as he gets his shots. I'm expecting a UPS delivery, garden stuff, just put it in the shed. I'll be home around four to change for the wrap party, if you want to come, be ready, if not, I'll be home by nine. Oh, and confirm the tickets for the wedding."

Trying not to notice how unnaturally still he was, I quickly pecked him on the cheek before rushing from the room.

"Sophie?"

I stopped at the door.

He lifted his head from his pillow to see me. "Good luck."

I blew him a kiss.

On my way downstairs, I heard Lodi scratching at the laundry door and fought the impulse to let him out. I was up two hours early because I wanted to stay ahead of the clock and nothing was going stop me. Even yelping puppies. I had to make time to swing by Grounds for Coffee, but not for a latte. They had agreed to cater the ribbon cutting and I needed to make sure everything was a go.

When I approached Grounds about catering, Daphne, the manager, was thrilled. It did bother me that every time I met her she wasn't wearing shoes, but I decided as long she wasn't serving coffee with her feet, it was a minor detail. Besides, our mutual hatred of Starbucks was what really mattered. Seeing her the morning of the event, I was pleasantly surprised by her efficiency. Not only was she ready to rock and wearing shoes, she sent me packing with a gratis latte.

By the time I got to the hospital, the staff parking lot was still deserted. Parking next to the door, I took a detour and wandered the new wing. The smell of fresh paint still hung in the air and the atrium was finally filled with plants. Two rows of columns rose three stories to support a glass ceiling festooned with Chihulys. I wasn't crazy about it, but it was the one thing the board members really wanted. I relented in exchange for their sign off on a premium HVAC system that would actually heat the place.

Leading away from the atrium, the new halls sparkled with inlaid tiles hand painted by students from Tacoma schools. Stepping around the cordons, I double-checked the layout of the podium, the path of red carpet laid for the tour, and the placement of the catering equipment. The ribbon hadn't been stretched yet. It wouldn't be hung until the sound and lighting equipment had been tested. There were three pairs of ceremonial cutting shears, all of which were in my desk.

Returning to the main lobby, it was still quiet. At the elevator, a chatty gaggle of night nurses was getting off as I got on. On the way up, my cell rang. When I saw the number, I felt my eyes roll in my head.

"Morning, Lyn."

"Good morning, Sophie. I hope I didn't wake you."

"Not a problem. Mike and I were just wrapping yoga."

"Oh! Oh … well, I'm sorry to interrupt—"

"Don't worry about it. I talk on the phone during yoga all the time. It annoys the hell out of Mike, but we all have to take one for the team, don't we?"

"Yes. Well, yes. Well—"

"What can I do?"

"Our board chair thinks there's a possibility your donor might show up for the ceremony today."

"What?" My back stiffens. "Where did she hear that?"

"I'm not sure."

"Not sure? When did she tell you this?"

"Yesterday. I took her to Rotary for lunch."

"And you just remembered?"

"I was in meetings all afternoon, and when I went by your office at five, you were already gone. I tried to catch you, but you always leave so early."

"Sorry, Lyn, I have to leave early if I'm going to be up in time for yoga."

"This time your yoga could cost you some embarrassment."

"That's short-term thinking, Lyn. The long-term benefits are well worth it. You're living proof of that." I snapped my phone shut as the elevator doors opened.

Our floor was dim with only two aisles of fluorescent lights left on. The window offices were still dark. I was the first one in. Unlocking the door to my office, I flipped on the lights and immediately went to my computer. As it warmed up, I drained my free latte and checked voice mail while accessing the office network. On-line, I began reworking the program for the ceremony with a plan B should our mystery guest show up.

If he did show, he might not want to speak. If he did, I would have to bump whoever was next in line. Three board members were up, starting with Susan Sullivan, the board chair. After that, a former patient, the director of hospice and palliative care, and the art teacher from the Tacoma school whose students made the tiles. Finally, representatives from various religious denominations would give blessings. Since Lyn claimed to know who the donor was, I happily assigned her to introduce him and e-mailed the amended schedule to all pertinent staff. To cover my bases, I scheduled coffee with my event committee to get everyone up to speed.

It wasn't a big deal. I seriously doubted he'd show. Still, the thought made my stomach churn. Inside, I burned to know who gave so much yet cared so little. The clock on my computer said it was almost six. The ceremony started at eleven. In five hours, one year of hell would be over.

"Do you think he'll really show?" Amy asked for the fifteenth time.

"No."

Standing near the podium, I kept an eye out for any board members I could recognize. So far, most of them had arrived along with guests, mostly members from other hospital boards. As usual, the board chair was late again: Susan Sullivan, whose only claim to fame was her industrialist husband. For all I knew, he was the donor and this was just something to keep her out of trouble.

"She's late again." I muttered to Amy.

Amy leaned in. "How could she be late? It's a ribbon cutting."

"For a hospital." I smirked. "Not a Nordstrom's."

We waited while guests and on-lookers milled and mingled. Among the ecumenical crowd were priests, nuns, Buddhist monks, rabbis, and Father Wilson, who had visited my room after my flu shot fiasco. Catching my gaze, he mouthed hello. A pool of press photographers snapped shots of the podium with the atrium behind it. Some stood against the cordons, trying to get photos of the ceiling. At least there were fresh-baked goods and plenty of coffee. Damn fine coffee.

I glanced at the clock on the wall. Ten forty-five. I looked at my watch. Ten forty-eight. Mike set my watch. It was ten forty-eight.

Finally, a platinum head appeared in the crowd.

"She's here." I stepped forward as she moved towards us.

All eyes went to her.

She was easily six feet, dressed head to toe in cream: cream turtle neck, cream down vest, cream riding pants, cream quilted snow boots. She was dressed for an après ski photo shoot instead of a public speaking engagement. Susan waved over some heads in our direction. I doubted it was at me. Aside from attending foundation board meetings, she was never seen in our office. Aside from listening to my monthly progress reports, she was never able to remember my name. As far as anyone could tell, she did nothing and made it look effortless.

I made a smile. "Mrs. Sullivan. Good morning."

"Good morning!" Her eyes went to my ID badge. "Sophie! This is fantastic!" She waved her arms around. "I mean, wow! All this in a year!"

"Yes, it's fabulous isn't it? Did you get the program I sent you?"

"Yep." She patted her vest pocket. "Got it right here— Oh, hiiii ..." She ducked away to hug a guest.

Waiting on her to catch up, I looked back at Amy, who shook her head and pointed to her watch. Behind her was Lyn, with an annoying grin on her face. It didn't matter. It was a ribbon cutting. If it took two hours or twenty, it wouldn't make a difference now.

I looked back at my watch. Ten fifty-three. If I could get her to the podium by eleven, I would. If I couldn't, I wouldn't.

"I'm sorry!" Susan's voice pulled me from my watch. "I know we're on a schedule and I'm kicking this thing off! I'll save my voice—"

A jolt hit the building. Susan and I stared at each other. Everyone around us began to look around as conversation dropped away. It took a moment to realize the floor was trembling. The trembling picked up as tiles in the ceiling begin to rattle. People began to run for the exits as the hall lights flickered. A resounding crash came from the atrium and I turned to see beads of glass showering the plants.

Amy was in front of me, petrified. I grabbed her, running for the nearest door we could fit under. We barely found cover when it stopped.

"Come on." My hand coaxed her arm. "We need to clear the building."

When I didn't hear an answer, I looked back. Her face was covered, her shoulders shook. I pulled her to me.

"Everyone!" Hospital workers flooded the halls. "Please walk to the nearest exit. Walk! Don't run."

Luckily, we were at street level and there were plenty of exits.

"Everything's fine." Rubbing Amy's back, I led her to the exit nearest the atrium.

People were calm, leaving in orderly fashion. Some lingered in the atrium to survey the damage. The glass ceiling had shattered and collapsed. To my disappointment, all the Chihulys survived. A reporter was already interviewing Susan Sullivan in front of the damage. Press photographers quickly closed in. It was a match made in heaven.

Once on the sidewalk, Amy seemed to recover. She was pale, only nodding or shaking her head when I spoke to her, but she was alert and managed a smile at my crack about the Chihulys. Still holding her close, I tried to keep us warm in the February chill. I scanned the hospital from the outside, seeing no damage. The street was filling with staff, visitors, patients bundled in blankets. Daphne from Grounds was dispensing hot coffee to anyone who needed it.

Everyone was thinking it was an earthquake. Everyone was thinking about aftershocks—cold, tense, waiting, wondering when it would be safe to go inside again. No one knew.

Michael?

He had to know something.

Michael?

I waited, wondering why he hadn't warned me.

I realized I was waiting for no one to answer me.

Michael!

My insides went cold.

"Amy? You okay?" I grabbed her shoulders. "I've got to go. Will you be okay?"

"Yeah." She nodded absently. "Where are you going?"

"I just remembered something. If you see Lyn or anyone asks, tell them I had an emergency, all right?"

I didn't wait for her answer. Running past security at the door, I ignored their shouts as I raced down the hall for the elevator.

"Ma'am! Ma'am! Don't use the—"

"Elevator." I gasped as the doors shut behind me.

Normally, I would agree. But something told me this wasn't.

Standing in the elevator, I kicked back a foot and took off a heeled shoe, then did the same with the other. The elevator I was in was on the opposite side of the building from my office. As soon as the doors opened, I ran in stocking feet as fast as I could, my shoes clutched in my hands. Sliding to a stop in front of the doors to our wing, I slammed through them, cutting through the maze of cubicles to my office. Darting into my office to grab my purse, I dashed for the back stairs. I was only two floors to street level from the fire escape and then one flight of stairs outside the building to the staff parking lot.

My hands squealed along the hand rail as I squeezed past evacuees in the fire escape stair well. Outside, I staggered into my shoes, skipping down concrete steps. I could see my car parked feet away and suddenly appreciated getting to work early. I realized an appreciation for keyless entry as I fingered my key fob. Realized an appreciation for living fifteen minutes away as I got behind the wheel. Realized that no matter how soon I got home, there might not be anything I could do for my fiancé.

I did not appreciate how difficult it would be getting out of the parking lot. Once I entered traffic, I found the intersection to the emergency room blocked by police and fire. There was a jam everywhere I looked. Cutting across oncoming traffic, I sped through a neighboring parking lot to another street and made a line for home. It was a reckless drive—through red lights, past playing children, around blind corners. When my car skidded to a stop, inches from his BMW, the sight of it still parked in front of our house terrified me more than hitting it.

I ran from the car, leaving the door open.

"Michael!"

Craning my neck, there was no sight of him in the garden. When I reached the front door, it was unlocked. Letting it swing wide, I paused on the stoop, hair in my face, heart pounding in my ears.

At first, I didn't spot them. Lodi's wagging tail focused me.

He was sitting on the Persian carpet, his back against the sofa, his legs stretched in front of him. Lodi was sprawled across his lap. Both grinned as Michael plowed his fingers through Lodi's fur.

The smile on his face dropped. "Something wrong?"

I caught my breath. "Why didn't you answer me?"

He blinked. "I didn't hear anything."

"Didn't hear anything?" I marched up to them. "Didn't you feel it?"

He stared.

"The earthquake!"

"Earthquake?"

"Minutes before the ceremony! We had to evacuate the building!"

Lodi grumbled and crawled off Michael's lap.

"I was asleep."

Glaring, I put my hands on my hips as he stared distractedly at the dog, his inattention annoying me by the minute. Lodi shook before wandering away.

"Asleep?"

He nodded absently. "After you left, I couldn't go back to sleep. By the time I brought Lodi back from the vet, I was tired. I took a nap."

A rolling noise made me look away. Lodi nosed a silver ball across the floor under an armchair. My eyes went to a large cardboard box on the coffee table. It was open. Going to the table, I peered inside to see an iron rod projecting from a sea of packing peanuts. A smaller box was open on the table.

It was empty.

"That's the gazing ball I ordered! No, Lodi!" I crossed to the armchair, pulling Lodi away. "You were letting him play with this?"

Kneeling by the chair, I reached under and retrieved the ball, examining it.

Michael shrugged at nothing. "He seemed to like it."

"*Like it?* What if he broke it?"

He blinked. "You're upset."

"Of course I am! I had my ribbon cutting crashed by an earthquake only to think something terrible happened to you when you wouldn't answer me. I drive like Gene Hackman to get here and find you endangering our dog with garden art. Yes! I'm upset!"

Staring at the floor, he pulled in his knees.

"Even if I'd been awake, I wouldn't have been able to warn you, let alone stop it."

Taking a breath, I went to the coffee table and dropped the ball in the box.

"It's no use being mad at you, is it?"

His voice grew artfully small. "I'm sorry about your ceremony."

I snorted. "I suppose it's only fair."

"What?" He looked up at me, his irises vaguely opaque.

"All the times I wouldn't answer you. Now I know what it feels like."

He smiled blankly. "I love you, too."

Lodi pushed a wet snout in my hand.

My stomach gurgled and I checked my watch. "Right on time. I'm starving."

"Do you want me to make you something?"

"I'd love it, but I don't need to be psychic to know people are looking for me."

The words were barely said when my purse hummed, making Lodi start.

I didn't bother to check.

Mike rested his head against the sofa. "It's Lyn."

"I'm leaving. Bye, Lodi." I bent to scratch furry ears and glanced at Mike.

"And you need eat something." I pointed as I left. "You look like hell."

DELIVER ME FROM BLOOD, O GOD, THOU
GOD OF MY SALVATION: AND MY TONGUE
SHALL EXTOL THY JUSTICE.

O LORD, THOU WILT OPEN MY LIPS: AND
MY MOUTH SHALL DECLARE THY PRAISE.
FOR IF THOU HADST DESIRED A SACRIFICE, I
WOULD INDEED HAVE GIVEN IT: WITH BURNT
OFFERINGS THOU WILT NOT BE DELIGHTED.
A SACRIFICE TO GOD IS AN AFFLICTED SPIRIT:
A CONTRITE AND HUMBLED HEART, O GOD,
THOU WILT NOT DESPISE.

[Latin. Excerpt translated from the *Vulgate Bible*,
Psalm 50: 16, 17, 18, 19. d. 405]

2001 *"Michael!"*

Why she had to yell, he couldn't understand. A whisper would suffice. Ice on his shoulder shocked him awake. The glow of her filled his eyes. At first he thought the house was on fire. It wasn't. She wasn't. Leaving. Feed. Koi. Nylabone. Lodi. Shots. Delivery. Box. Supplies. Shed. Home. Four. Change. Party. Come. Ready. Not. Nine. Confirm. Tickets. Wedding.

Lips.

She was leaving?

He blinked. "Sophie?"

Straining to see her, she was already dressed and at the door. The ceremony. "Good luck."

She kissed her fingers and blew on them. He frowned, but she was already gone. He heard her feet on the stairs. The sound of the front door.

His head dropped on his pillow. It was early yet. Too early to accomplish much if he got out of bed now. Just as well.

His body was lead.

Her car started and the stereo blared. The engine revved, tires grinding, fading. Fading away.

He was. Only it wasn't a peaceful sort of fading. It was draining. Depressing. Miserable. Downstairs, Lodi voiced it. Pathetic whines that cut through the drone of civilization, let alone a door.

He tried to summon fire within to drown it out, to fill his head with the rush he felt when Sophie held him. Closing his eyes, he coaxed, pushed. For an instant, the pulse of a trillion stars burned. Then ebbed. Faltering. His focus wavered.

He was no longer himself.

His chest shuddered to breathe. So.nething held him and he couldn't let it go. Lodi whined.

Sitting up, he tossed aside the blankets and got to his feet.

I'm coming.

Reaching behind the bedroom door for his bathrobe, he somehow found himself in it at the bottom of the stairs. Normally, Lodi would still be asleep, but Sophie's early morning triggered a routine that couldn't be stopped. The moment he opened the laundry room, Lodi was racing for the nearest exit. Following into the kitchen, he opened the back door, flinching as his foot was trampled. Lodi charged through the garden, a torrent of fur trailing leaves, nostrils steaming.

Watching from the back stoop, he stood in the predawn of winter. Though there was no scent of snow, his fingers felt differently. He brought them to his face, feeling them against his cheeks. They were frozen. He felt the impulse to blow on them, but shoved his fists under his arms instead. Letting out a sigh, his breath was invisible. He was colder inside than it was out.

He wished he was warm. Inside. He returned to the kitchen and flipped on the coffee maker. Sophie wasn't here, but he had discovered a taste for it. The organic French she bought at Met Market was her favorite. Not shit, she said. He wouldn't know. He'd never had Starbuck's coffee. All he knew was he liked it with sugar and whipping cream. Then again, he liked anything with sugar and whipping cream.

At the refrigerator, he picked out a carton of eggs and a package of Portuguese sausage. Sophie's mother gave him the sausage. Edie liked to eat and liked people who liked to eat. It was what connected them. It was the only thing neither of them ever wondered about. Edie never said anything about the potato incident. There wasn't any need to. She knew it wouldn't happen again. Putting a pan on the stove, he used the Bic lighter Sophie kept on the counter to light the gas. He didn't have to think about using it anymore. He had learned to stop lighting things on his own.

It was progress.

Finding a knife, he cut open the sausage. It smelled wonderful. He began to slice it on the cutting board and wanted to eat it. Putting down the knife, he went to the sink to wash his hands. He would whisk the eggs before returning to the sausage. He cracked a dozen eggs into a bowl and began to whisk. The smell of percolating coffee reminded him of whipping cream. Setting down the bowl, he went to the refrigerator and pulled out the carton. Unscrewing the cap, he poured some into the eggs and resumed whisking. There was a scratch at the back door.

Leaving the eggs, he went down the hall to the laundry room. A Nylabone still wrapped in packaging sat on Lodi's food bin. He set it aside and opened the bin, filling Lodi's food dish. He filled the water bowl in the mudroom before taking a towel with him to the back door. Opening the door, he caught Lodi by the collar and knelt to wipe muddy paws. As soon as he released his grip, Lodi dashed for the laundry room.

The muddy towel was left on the door mat. He went to the kitchen sink to wash his hands, then looked over at the sausage. It was almost completely sliced and the pan was hot. It could be done. Picking up the knife, he finished slicing. The slices went into the pan. He stared. Sophie would brown them. Picking up the bowl of eggs, he emptied it into the pan. If he drowned them, no one would know. Stirring the eggs with a spatula, they curdled in moments. Shutting off the flame, he reached across the counter for a fork in the dish rack and ate where he stood.

"Lodi, out of the car."

He stood in the parking lot with the rear door open. Lodi turned away. Shutting the door, he walked to the passenger side of the car and opened the front door, picking the Nylabone off of the seat. He opened the rear door on the passenger side and offered it.

"Lodi, come."

Lodi's chin lowered between his paws.

Tossing the Nylabone on the floor mat, he reached in and grabbed Lodi's elbows, pulling the dog from the car. Lodi tried to back up, but it was too late. Getting an arm around the shoulders, he hefted the dog to his chest and kicked the door shut. Lodi struggled to break free, something only a creature he couldn't fit his arms around would be capable of. Blowing fur from his eyes, he carried

Lodi into the clinic. Once inside, the dog accepted fate, going limp in his arms.

The clinic was a chance discovery. Sophie had shopped veterinarians for a month while he volunteered to check them out. It only made sense. He could see and smell things she couldn't. Several smelled foul, the newest had a wait list three months long, and the closest seemed to cater to people more than their pets. Lodi didn't need spa treatments.

This one bordered the North Slope, on Sixth Avenue. He remembered driving past it for years. When he visited, he found it to be clean, with helpful staff and a veterinarian who seemed both knowledgeable and wise. There were no pre-screening requirements, no spa treatments, no lattes, no wait list. No pretense.

A resident calico lounged on the counter. It scarcely opened an eye with regard to Lodi. A receptionist in pink flowered scrubs and blond curls beamed out from behind the cat.

"Good morning. Can I help you?"

"I had an appointment at nine for his second round of shots."

"Your name?"

"Goodhew, Michael."

She frowned at her monitor. "Lodi?"

"Yes."

"Great! Follow me."

He stepped around the counter and followed her down the hall to a treatment room. Lodi whinnied.

"How heavy is he?" She held the door as he carried Lodi inside.

The answer was eighty-three pounds.

"Not very." He lowered the quivering mass to the floor. "He's mostly fur."

"Uh oh." She pointed to the front of his fleece jacket. "Need a lint roller?"

"Wasted effort. Thanks."

"If he needs a treat, there's a bowl of kibble on the counter behind you. Dr. Beck will be in any minute."

"Thank you."

Taking a chair next to the table, he reached behind him and grabbed a handful of dog food. Without lifting an ear, Lodi let him offer the food, only to sniff at it.

"It's all right, Lodi. No one's going to hurt you."

Lodi looked unconvinced. A smart animal. It was a lie.

Suddenly, he felt terrible. He was lying to a dog.

"I'm sorry. That's not true." He paused as Lodi's ears flattened. "Everyone will. Even me. Out of love, or hate, or carelessness. I won't always love you and sometimes I'll hate you, but I'll always care."

His eyes lifted to the examination table, its stainless surface dulled by claws.

"It's the ones who don't who hurt you the worst."

"Lodi, out of the car."

Stretched across the backseat, jaws gaped as one end of the Nylabone chattered between crushing molars. Reaching into the car, he grabbed the protruding end of the bone and pulled it out of the car, dog still attached. There was a moment's pause to evaluate the fur upholstering the backseat before deciding to vacuum another time. In spite of everything he ate that morning, he was already tired. Even lunch paled next to a nap.

Stepping onto the front porch, he noticed a large box tucked behind the rail. Sophie's gardening supplies. Picking it up, it felt oddly light for its size. His first instinct was to see into it, but that too, was a tiresome habit. Besides, he was more than tired, he was curious. After opening his Christmas presents without perceiving the contents, he found the suspense a welcome change. His concept of a box had grown beyond ubiquitous service. It could also be fun.

Carrying it to the door, he unlocked the dead bolt and took it inside. Lodi slipped by him, Nylabone in jaw, seeking a quiet spot to chew.

He placed the box on the living room coffee table. Removing his jacket, he returning to the door and searched the console for a knife. Knife in hand, he returned to the box, considered it, then cut along the taped seam. Folding back the cardboard ends, he saw the top of a smaller box insulated in foam packing material. Excavating the smaller box, he stepped around the table and sat on the sofa to pry it open.

Inside, he was surprised to find tissue paper. He never imagined its use where gardening supplies were concerned. Beneath the sheets of tissue, he caught a distorted reflection of himself. Something silver, polished, round. His fingers reached in, then hesitated. An orb. His touch sensed it was simple glass. Removing it, he held it to the light and saw the world reflected back. A false world seen through a false orb. He smiled.

Only he wasn't smiling.

His eyes dilated, trying to close, but his hand only brought the orb closer to his face. Opening his mouth to speak, the air stopped in his throat.

The reflection spoke instead.

"You wouldn't hang up on me, would you?" Sam grinned.

This isn't happening.

"I know the feeling."

You aren't here.

"Physically, no. But you must realize by now I am always with you in spirit."

Impossible.

"What I wonder is when you'll realize you miss me."

Go away.

"Not yet, apparently."

I banish you.

"Now *that* is impossible."

He tried to shut his eye. *I do not see you.*

"But you do."

I do not hear you.

"Yet you answer."

I do not hold you.

"Then let go."

There was no answer he could make. He could not.

"It's your own fault. When you tried to assume me on my island hideaway, you bit off more than you could swallow. Now, you'll never be rid of me."

What do you want?

"What we all want. To live."

At my expense.

"You self-righteous, spoiled prick! What you're doing will ruin us both!"

Good riddance.

"I said ruin. Not rid."

No matter.

"Most of the time, I am proud to call you my brother. This is not one of them."

Go to hell.

"If I go, you will go with me."

Fine.

"Fine? You only say so because you have no faith such a place exists. If you did, I think you would show a little more respect."

It is hard to respect any place that would keep us.

"Pathetic. Is that what you are, Michael? The embodiment of pathos? The supreme Miserere? I doubt it, but I challenge you to prove me wrong."

There was a sense of release.

The orb vanished. His body was his own.

He blinked, focusing on a far wall. There was a chair. A row of chairs. His eyes followed them around the room in a circle. A council chamber. The room of judgment. Looking down, he saw himself seated in a circle of light. The floor at his feet, white. The chair he was sitting in, white. The bands binding his wrists, lachrymose argentite. He tried to move, feeling his ankles held firm.

"Samael!"

The name echoed off the walls. There was no answer.

"Samael! I know you are here!"

The chamber doors opened to darkness. A figure stepped into the room, dressed in a long robe, a heavy hood drawn over the face. It neared, the color of the robe turning to gray as it entered the light. Stopping before him, it pulled back the hood to reveal his own face on a shaved head.

"What is this? What have you done?"

Sam blinked. "You have nothing to fear if this isn't real."

"Then neither do you. Free me."

"You are not kept, brother. Not yet."

"No more riddles! Speak plain."

"I have. It is you who won't listen. If you will not hear it, you must feel it."

As Sam spoke, a black box withdrew from his sleeve. There was no denying the sight frightened. It also infuriated.

Fire lit his eyes as his wrists strained. "You cannot threaten me. I have known refuge."

Sam's eyes glowed. "Hell is no refuge."

He felt hands on his shoulders and looked to his sides. Sariel was to his right. Raphael to his left. They both looked on him with false smiles.

He turned to Sarah. "What are you doing?"

She frowned. "Serving you."

"It isn't you." He squinted, turning to Raphael. "You'd never help him."

"Who?" Raphael asked.

"Him—" He looked to Sam, but Sophie stared back at him.

"Sophie?"

"It's all right, Mike." She approached with a smile. "No one's going to hurt you."

"What are you saying? Help m—" His eyes dropped to the box in her hands. "What are you doing?"

She removed the lid.

"Sophie. Don't touch It. Put the lid back."

She stood over him.

"Sophie! Listen to me!"

Hands gripped his hair, yanking his head back.

"Stop! Raphael! *What are you doing?*"

Raphael held his face, prying his jaw open. When he tried to speak, all that came was a choked cry. The shadow of the black box appeared over his chin, the delicate fingers of Sophie's hands tipping the lip of the box over his mouth. Everything in him tried to break free, but the hands on him were stone.

His eyes sought the black orb. Searched for the smooth, polished surface, but it was something else. Black, smooth, polished. A liquid crested the rim and poured into his mouth, making him shudder. His tongue tried to stop it from running down his throat, tasting it. Warm, metallic, blood. The taste made him gasp. The gasp made him choke. He coughed. It spilled over the sides of his mouth, running down his face, his neck.

He swallowed.

Sophie.

It was her. The smell of her, the taste of her, the essence of her.

He wanted it. More than life. More than love. More than Sophie.

More than anything else.

White fire tore through his eye. It was a fire he had never known. Raw and formless. The raging heart of something thoughtless. Careless.

He screamed soundlessly. His body shook.

Let me go!

It would not. It could not. The voice of his mind was unraveling.

It didn't hear him. Didn't know he existed. The edges of him began to burn away. His spirit consumed. Memory, thought, feeling.

"Without me you, will find the misery you seek." Sam's voice echoed.

"You will see all and remember nothing. Know all and think not. Touch everything and feel nothing. Exist everywhere and never be free."

The fire spread. As his mind came apart, a choir of millions screamed.

Let me go!

"I won't let you do it, Michael."

Let me go!

"Never." Sam's voice drowned in chaos.

"LET GO!"

The sound of his voice disintegrated into thunder.

Then silence.

Three dimensions pressed on all sides. A body. A heart. A breath.

Trembling fingers felt his cheek, still wet with blood. Sticky. Stinking of corn starch, soy ... Bacon.

Something cold in his ear made him start.

Staring at hazy lines, he squinted at the carpeting under his head. He pushed against the floor, then froze as the pain in his head blurred his vision. Lodi whimpered. He lowered his head to the carpet again, too tired to move. Too afraid to sleep.

He was slipping ...

Michael?

That was his name.

Michael?

"Hmm?"

Michael!

His eyes popped open and he sat up, instantly regretting it. Gritting his teeth, he held his head with shut eyes.

What?

He waited for a response. There was no answer.

Sophie?

Tentatively blinking, what he saw before him was a shadowy blur. Solid forms bled into vacuous space beyond, a material world sensed but unseen. A wall of fur suddenly came into sharp focus, inches from his nose. Lodi licked his face.

He had to get up.

Reaching around the dog's neck, he scratched behind the ears. "All right, boy."

He tried to push Lodi away, but the dog resisted.

"Lodi, move."

Digging his heels into the carpet, he pushed himself out from under the dog, but Lodi only followed, nosing his face. His back hit the sofa and he braced against it with his hands. Lodi flopped down on his lap, pinning his legs to the carpet.

"Lodi, up."

Looking away, the dog yawned.

"Lodi, I'm fine."

Lodi's head rested, becoming somehow heavier.

"Lodi—" Grabbing the dog's shoulders, he lifted the weight.

A bolt of pain.

His eye flickered and Lodi disappeared. His arms disappeared. His legs. Everything. Panic seized. For a moment, he blinked at nothing. The sudden realization of his blindness, terrific.

He caught a breath.

Gradually, the void gave. Bones, fingers outlined, a dog's rib cage, the beating heart inside growing opaque, becoming solid, blurring to fur. Easing against the sofa, his grip slipped from Lodi's hackles, falling to a slow, stroking rhythm. He didn't have to get up. He was home.

It was everything he wanted. More than anything else.

Lodi looked up at him, and he smiled.

"It's all right. I'm not going anywhere."

1199 BC   Though the gray beard impressed the Canaan chiefs with his assessment I was simply a messenger, Khenemet was adamant my presence serve a greater purpose. What good was there in keeping my message of peace a secret? Why should only chiefs and generals hear my voice and not those who followed us on foot and on faith? Why had I performed miracles at all if I had not wished their devotion?

I explained it was only to guide them to Lod. The first time, to save innocents from sacrifice. The second, to save hope from chaos. The third, to save peace from prejudice. What remained was to save men from themselves, and that was beyond any miracle I could perform. Such devotion was a calling found within, not something traded for with miracles and false promises. I would leave and my magic would soon be forgotten. I would be forgotten, and that was as it should be.

At this point, Khenemet rose before the Canaans and bade us follow him. Sparked with curiosity, the chieftains agreed and the general consented. Khenemet led us through the corridors of the market, his priests making way for us amidst the bustle of daily business. The center of Lod opened onto a broad campus. At one end was the lending house, at the other a temple to Ramses, left by Pharaoh to remind all who owed tribute.

A great audience of people were encamped around it. The steps leading to the temple doors lined with all colors, Canaan, Caphtor, Habiru, Amman knelt in prayer on the stone. The chieftains witnessed this with wide eyes.

I looked to the general, who looked to Khenemet with suspicion.

"Is it Ramses they pray to?"

Khenemet shook his head, smiling at me. "Your crypt."

[Spharic. Entry translated from *Kor Dai Maihael*. Mund Dai. d. 755 B.C]

COLUMBINA et ARLEQUIN

[19th century lithograph, *Bocce Carnivale*]

DETERMINATION

2001   It was an extraordinary experience. As indelible as his memory, as predictable an event, he struggled to stay present. Everything was happening from far away, to somebody else. From the blowing of the conch shell, to the Kahuna's final chant of blessing, his eye only saw through hers. No matter how he tried to see Sophie, he could only see himself, facing her, dressed in white, a blue sash around his waist, his hair in his eyes.

Her focus followed a triangle of blue. An infinity of time stretching across the ocean behind him, a knotted sash binding him to her, the eyes that first caught her. To his disappointment, he sensed they still frightened. If he could make them brown, he would, even if he couldn't see. Then she might see him as he wanted to be, instead of what he was. When he closed them to kiss her, every other sense was his own. He tasted the champagne on her lips, breathed the maile and pikake in her lei, felt her skin while the sea whispered on the sand.

He pressed his cheek to hers. "I love you."

"Thank God." She whispered. "We just got married."

He had seen pictures. From what he could tell, her grandfather was an energetic man of medium height and thin build. Her grandmother appeared taller, thin-faced, and languid. Both had brown hair in their photos, but when he saw them seated for the ceremony, her grandfather was gray and her grandmother wore a red bob. Why he should dread meeting them, he had no idea. Everyone else seemed to, so he would as well. As they approached in the receiving line, his nerves began to act up. When her grandmother's eyes met his, he realized what they made him feel. Naked.

"Grandma. Grandpa. This is Michael. Michael," Sophie eyed him, sounding forced. "Ellen and Henry Davids."

Ellen slowly smiled, revealing rows of gold crowns. "Peter told me you're Daniel's great nephew."

Nearly tall enough to look him level in the eye, she was doing so unflinchingly.

"Yes." He smiled. "My father was Michael Goodhew."

"Doesn't look like Danny." Henry announced. "We'll see if he drinks like him." He felt Henry shake his hand, but felt unable to look away from Ellen.

"You knew Daniel?" Sophie asked her grandmother, sounding shocked.

"He came to our wedding." Ellen answered, still holding his gaze.

"Our first." Henry beamed. "Drank for ten, but sent porcelain for twelve."

Ellen seemed to smile. "Dead by our second, though he was still invited."

"Very considerate." Henry nodded. "Did he send his regrets?"

"His nephew did …" Ellen squinted at him. "Your father, he has passed since?"

He nodded dumbly.

"Awfully disappointing he couldn't see this." Her tone grew distant. "Which of Danny's siblings was he descended from?"

"Sarah." The sound of his voice wasn't his own. He had stopped breathing.

"Sarah?" To his relief, Ellen closed her eyes. "I don't recall he had a sister."

"Half-sister." This voice was definitely not his. Ethereal, cool, feminine.

Everyone turned. A young woman stepped from the crowd. Her short, platinum hair nearly matched the short-sleeved, white dress she was wearing.

He felt his mouth open as she extended her hand to Sophie's grandparents.

"I'm Michael's half-sister, Sarah. Our grandmother was Danny's half-sister from their father's first marriage to Mary Anne Northrup."

"How surprising." Ellen spoke without any outward expression of surprise. "I never knew Grandfather married twice."

Sarah smiled. "I believe it was a matter of necessity."

"Necessity!" Henry roared, lifting Sarah off her feet in a bear hug. "Nothing becomes a Goodhew without necessity! Welcome to the family!"

Facing him, Henry seized his arm, pulling him from the receiving line. "Let me introduce you to Bob and Lil from Tonga. Have you been?"

Still speechless, he shook his head.

"A must!" Henry wrapped an arm across his back, squeezing his shoulders. "You haven't really lived till you've been to Tonga."

Feeling a vacant smile, his eye watched Sarah give Sophie a hug behind his back. While Henry introduced him to Bob ad Lil, Sarah smiled at the back of his head over Sophie's shoulder. Losing sense of everything else, he tried to shake Bob's hand without breaking it.

She had to leave.

It was taking all his restraint not to smite her where she stood. It was all he wanted, but inappropriate for a wedding reception. He had to warn her away, without Sophie hearing. Suspecting. Demanding the truth. He was afraid of it.

Sarah knew. It was why Sarah had come. To stand next to his bride.

It was intolerable.

Without breaking his greetings to the Tongans, his mind spoke one word. It was audible to Sophie as little more than a grinding hiss. To Sarah, warning enough. Sophie caught Sarah's expression and followed her gaze to him, but he only nodded with a smile. When Sophie looked back, Sarah had vanished into the crowd. He didn't wait to explain. Slipping past Sophie, he stayed close on Sarah's heels.

Her tracks led to a belt of palms running the length the beach. Between the ocean's distortions and the geologic convection under their feet, it would be relatively easy for them to lose each other. But Sarah didn't come this far to lose him. She stayed far enough ahead, until he stopped, unwilling to be led farther.

The sun was setting as she stepped out from behind a palm.

Saying nothing, he stared at her. From the look on her face, he knew his expression said enough.

She put up her hands. "I'm leaving."

"You should not have come."

"You should not give me reason."

"This is no one's business but my own."

"You made an oath."

"I did."

"You will pay for it."

"When I do, they will know your part in it."

Sarah smiled. "You never had any intention of killing her, did you?"

"Perhaps I have."

Her eyes lit. "Am I to believe you only think of Sophie? I still see Bahiel in your eyes, Michael. The fire still burns. To hell with ECCO, to hell with Sam, with all of us! Everyone at that wedding is dead! This age is dead! Tell me the cake was worth it!"

"I'm not Bahiel. My marriage doesn't have a damn thing to do with the end of the age. And cake ..." He paused. "Is always worth it."

Her lips twisted. "You're a fool."

"Nothing lasts forever, Sariel. From now on, I belong to Sophie and I don't have forever to be with her. Call me what you will, but I will take whatever I can for myself."

"No matter the cost?"

"It is mine to pay."

"What about Sam?"

"Burned, buried."

"But not destroyed."

"I can't. I tried and failed. I've done all I can."

"What if he has help?"

"He won't get it from me. That is all I can promise."

"He won't need any if you aren't there to stop him."

"He can't succeed if I'm not there at all. If I am gone, Bahiel can never return."

"Gone?"

"I buried my brother. Now, I bury myself."

She sniffed. "At least you make as optimistic a groom as you did a singular."

"You worry what will happen to ECCO if I am gone. Then say nothing. You are the only one who knows. The only one who needs to. You know where Sam is. You don't need me to keep him for you anymore."

"What does Sophie know?"

"Nothing about Sam and next to nothing about ECCO. Little more than what documentation exists. She would know less if you had never come. As it is, I will have to explain you somehow."

"In burying yourself, you risk exposure for the rest of us."

"She will keep my secret."

"And her family? Her friends?"

"Only see what they expect. You know how impressionable they are."

She sighed, her eyes going dim. "You will never be one of them, Michael."

"I was never one of you. I don't know what I am. I'm not the Michael who came to you an age ago, let alone a year ago. You know that."

"Will you forsake your crypt?"

"If it is what she wants."

"You will be entrapped."

"Hardly worse than what Metatron offers me."

"I cannot promise others won't come for you."

"I understand."

"I won't be able to help."

"I won't ask."

Her head tilted back. "What does she know about Daniel?"

"Nothing." He lied.

"You must promise never to tell her."

He nodded. "I promise."

"Good-bye, Michael."

"Good-bye, Sariel." He spoke himself.

She had already disappeared, his promise to her already broken.

～

1199 BC Someone before the temple saw us and there was a shout. I
sensed alarm, not only from the general and the chieftains, but
the priests and the gray beards, the merchants and the public, who had no idea
what the shouting was about. People ran at us, their eyes fixed upon me, my name
upon their lips. Khenemet watched, smiling. Raising his hands to his face, he
bowed low to me as I backed away. The general had drawn his sword. So had
Chiron and the Canaan chiefs with their guard. They formed a line before me.

"Lord general!" I shouted. "Chiron! Put down your swords!"

As I tried to reach them, priests took hold of me. My instincts struck back, unleashing a charge that left their bodies at my feet. Pushing past the general, I turned
my back on the mob to face him.

"No violence!"

The general blinked as I frantically went from his face to the face of each chief.
Even as I felt hands on me, I caught the eye of Chiron.

"Do you hear me! Don't harm them!"

A woman's face met mine, tears stained with dust. Her hands held my shoulders.

"My child is near death. My only son—"

"Mikal!" I looked down to see an aged man holding my leg. "Yahweh said you
would come! Deliver me to him!"

"Let him go!"

A great man, cloaked in white, came from nowhere to free my leg with a savage
kick to the old man's back.

"You cannot touch him!"

The great man grabbed the woman who held me. Seizing her hair, he cast her to
the ground. Arms pulled me away from them. I turned and saw wild eyes, none of
them seeing me. Something flew over my head.

"Caphtan pig!"

When I looked back at the great man, his white cloak was stained with blood. He
stood over the body of the woman, his arms raised over his head. Stones began to
rain down on them from a sea of faces, all pointing, screaming, shouting.

"Stop!" My voice echoed across the campus. *"Stop!"*

The shouting subsided as the hands on me fell away. With the Caphtan crouched
behind me, I faced the crowd, backing to where the woman lay. It seethed as I put
up my hands.

"You must stop this!"

"He is a criminal!" A woman screamed as others called for quiet.

"Why should it matter if he stands when this woman lies fallen?" I asked them.

A ripple of recriminations and accusations murmured back. Looking down at
the woman, she remained senseless. Kneeling by her, I felt for her heart. To my relief it was there. The mob had closed around us and I was loathe to resurrect her.

"She lives, but is injured." My eyes searched the audience. "Who will tend her?"

All eyes dropped in silence. I had no more time for them.

Taking her in my arms, I made my way across the campus to the temple, my gaze parting the crowd before us. As I climbed the temple steps, guards at the doors opened them and I carried her inside without a backward glance. My eyes rose to the face of a colossus of Ramses staring over our heads. At the foot of it, I saw my crypt, illuminated by two deific lamps.

Resting her body on my crypt, I pressed my palm to her forehead, easing the bruise on her brain as best I could. Behind me, I heard the shuffle of feet.

It was Khenemet.

"Why?" I asked without looking.

"It is the only temple here fit for you."

"No." I faced him. "Why tell them my name? Offer me to them?"

"You would not hear. You had to see. They need you."

"They do not."

"You need them."

"I do not."

"Then you still intend to leave?"

I said nothing.

Nodding slowly, Khenemet turned away. As I watched him leave, he paused to glance at me over his shoulder.

"You are a fool."

Holding his gaze, I bowed.

[Spharic. Entry translated from *Kor Dai Maihael*. Mund Dai. d. 755 BC]

2004 "I just love all the windows in this place! It's like living in a tree house!" Kate waves to the screen of trees outside our living room windows.

I sit on the end of the dining table, cradling Molly in my arms. Squinting her muddy eyes at me, she pulls the end of my braid into her mouth and gums it.

With a gasp, Kate sees the fireplace.

"That's huge. Duane is going to be so jealous. You can walk into it!"

I point at a switch on the wall. "It's gas, so I don't have to shovel ashes anymore."

Kate sniffs. "I wish we had one at the cabin, but Duane still thinks he's getting a merit badge for going au natural."

"I heard that." Duane pops his head out of the stairwell to the basement.

She grins. "How was the man cave?"

"Pathetic." Duane shakes his head. "Not a power tool in sight, but he does have a vault, twice the size of ours."

Michael emerges from the basement, bouncing little Mike in his arms.

"Really?" Kate rolls her eyes at me. "Don't tell me Duane scared you guys with his doomsday prophecies."

"Nope." Duane interrupts. "They're still screwed. It's full of books."

"Books?" She looks at Mike, who shrugs.

"Banned ones, mostly."

Little Mike giggles and we laugh. When the doorbell rings, Michael answers it.

Kate gives me a stiff grin. "That'll be Mom and Dad."

"Hello, Michael!" Clark's voice echoes into the room. "Happy birthday, Mikie!"

I see Michael hand Little Mike over to Clark.

"What an interesting house." Maxine peeks through the front door.

"Hey, Mom!" Duane goes to her and gives a hug while Kate hangs back with me.

"What an interesting house!" Maxine repeats when she sees me.

Kate meets her halfway with a hug. When Maxine turns to me, she grows wide-eyed at the sight of Molly.

"What a beautiful child!"

At least she didn't say, "Interesting."

Michael's thought makes me glance at him with a smirk.

"This is Molly." I lean over, letting Maxine scrutinize her.

"Hello, Molly!" She coos and offers a finger. "How old is she?"

"Ten weeks."

"Katie says you had her at home."

"Yup." I wink at my husband. "I had an excellent midwife."

"Really? Where did you find one?"

"Married him."

Maxine spins on Michael. "Really? How interesting."

Mike blinks as Kate squeezes his shoulders. "Trust me, he's good."

"Is it something you're certified in?" Maxine inflects.

"Certified?" Michael deflects impassively.

"How did you learn it?"

He shrugs. "A calling, I suppose."
"But isn't that unusual?"
"Unsual?" He frowns.
"For a man? Why not be a doctor instead?"
"I don't like blood." He smiles.
Kate snickers as she heads for the kitchen.
Patting Maxine on the shoulder, I catch her eye. "Let me take you on the tour."

At dinner, Little Mike's appetite is impressive. After gnawing his way through two slices of Easter ham, he puts away nearly as much potato and yam as I do. When it is time for dessert, Duane and I prep the birthday cake in the kitchen. As Duane takes the cake from the box, I retrieve a lighter for the candles. Michael is setting the camera to take pictures when he suddenly hands it to me.

"Don't wait for me." He whispers in my ear and disappears.
Duane looks up as he lights the candles. "Where's he going?"
"I think he got paged. Must be an emergency."
"Antiques dealers have emergencies?"
"When you're rich and bored, everything's an emergency. Don't worry, I'll take the pictures. This means we'll only have to split the cake with Little Mike instead of watch the two of them eat the whole thing."

Duane gives a curt nod as though we are about to undertake a military operation. I follow as he marches into the dining room with the cake blazing ahead of him.

Recording the moment for posterity, I chat with Maxine and even sing "Happy Birthday" thoughtlessly off key as my mind tries not to wonder where my husband went. Since his hair grew back, he has hardly left my side.

I am about to start plating the cake when I hear Molly complain from her rocker. With a sigh, I hand the cake server to Kate, who gives a knowing grin. Picking up my baby, her cry says she's hungry. We are headed upstairs to breastfeed, one hand already unsnapping my blouse, when I spot a car in the drive from the window at the top of the stairs. It isn't one I recognize. A silver Audi.

Small hands pull on my blouse, reminding me who I am. Giving Molly my breast, I wander down the hall to our bedroom. Instinct leads me to the windows facing the Sound, cantilevered open on a warm spring day. Nearing them, I peek out below. I see nothing but hear their voices.

"You have what you wanted. There is nothing else I can give you."
"This isn't a matter of want. It is a matter reckoning. The prophecy did not exist to satisfy your personal life, Michael." Sarah's voice makes my hair raise.
"As far as I'm concerned, there never was one." Mike answers coldly.
"How can you say that! It has dictated your very existence!"
"That rule has ended."
"That rule gave you your power."
"Power that should have destroyed you, Sarah. If I followed it, ECCO wouldn't exist right now and neither would you."

"ECCO has ceased to exist! Ever since the Child's birth, Metatron has ceased to speak. We must to know why!"

"You'll never know anything as long as you let an eight ball tell you what to do. As long as I exist, Molly will have nothing to do with it."

"After we've I've done for you? You would still leave us?"

"I never promised to come back."

"I trusted you to do what was right."

"You've never trusted anyone. You fed me to Phanuel regardless of what would happen. If you could have brought him down and kept me enslaved, you would have. In that regard, you're scarcely better than he is."

She gave a hiss. "I'm nothing like Phanuel!"

"Then prove it. Forget Metatron. Let ECCO listen to itself."

"With your voice, that might happen."

"ECCO is your baby now. Molly is mine. ECCO is restored, as is your place in it. I have found my own. You should be happy for me."

"How can I when we are lost?"

"Better lost than nothing."

"We are nothing!"

"No, Sariel. Nothing will be all that remains if I lose my place in this world. Leave me in peace and I will leave you to find yourselves. Take from me what I have searched so long to find, and I will destroy everything, utterly."

In bed with the covers pulled to my chin, I watch my husband rock Molly in his arms as he bottle-feeds her. He hums gently as he takes the bottle away. She is fast asleep. Watching him rest her in the crib, I have nearly pierced my lip with my teeth.

"Mike?"

"Hmm?" Dim eyes find mine.

"Why don't you go back to work?"

With a sigh, he looks down at Molly.

"I know you'll want to. Someone will have to stay with Molly."

"You won't help ECCO?"

He comes to our bed. "I we agreed I needed to be free of them."

"After today, you really think that's possible?"

He sits next to me. "You saw Sarah."

"Heard her."

"What did you hear?"

"Enough."

"I thought you didn't trust her?"

"I don't. But wouldn't you rather keep an eye on her than hope for the best?"

"If I help ECCO, I'll be inviting trouble into our lives."

"I don't think trouble is something you can avoid."

For a moment, he stares at me.

"You aren't looking through my head again, are you?"

"No." He blinks, shaking his head. "You're right."

"I am?"

"A very wise man once told me the same thing."

"Really? Who?"

Michael climbs over me and gets under the covers.

"Fine." I roll away from him and turn off the light. "Don't tell me."

"Sophie?"

Fluffing my pillow, I rest my head, closing my eyes. "Yes, Michael."

"Will you hold me?"

Smiling in the dark, I roll over to him and open my arms. Keeping my eyes shut, I feel his head nestle into me. His arms reach around my waist as his knees curl. I drape a leg over him. He holds his breath so I won't freeze, but he is the one shivering in my arms.

I don't want you to go away.

His thought is a whisper and I pull him closer.

It is all I can do.

1199 BC When the woman awoke, she felt my hand on her head and reached for it. Seizing it to her mouth, she kissed it before I pulled away.

"I thank you, lord, for saving me."

Carefully, I helped her to sit up. "I did nothing."

"You saved my life. I was near death, but you called me back. I heard you."

"What you believe, I cannot deny." Taking her hands, I stood her on her feet.

"Will you not come to my son? Won't you call him back as well?"

"That is beyond me."

She stared, disbelieving. "Nothing is beyond you!"

"I wish."

"I am a witness. You deliver life and death with a touch of your hand."

"You witnessed a mistake. An old woman who has died since. Her death was forgranted, her life already forgiven. I only meant to show men the frailty of their belief, not to weaken their reason."

"Then you will not save my boy?"

"It is not my place."

"Did he anger you?"

"How could he anger me? I do not know the shape of him or his name."

She began to weep. "His name is Khassideh."

Taking her hands, I held her eyes in mine. "Truly I am sorry. But I am no god and in no position to determine his fate. It is why I saved you, to keep you on the path you would have followed if I had never been known to you."

She fell to her knees, crushing my hands in her grip. "Please."

"There is nothing I can do."

She let out a cry and sobbed aloud. Looking about me, I was alone and unsure. With a sudden gasp, her body went rigid. "Hold me."

Kneeling, I put my arms around her as the general held me when I was a woman. My hand stroked her back and her body seemed to relax. For some time, we sat in the lamplight of the temple, hearing only the sound of her breath and the whistle of the wind in the rafters. The lamplight shuddered as the temple doors opened, waking us from our trance. The general entered with Bes, his great commander, at his side. Behind them, the sky was already dark. Two columns of men filed inside and marched toward us.

"You must go." I paused to look at her. "What is your name?"

"Neela."

Putting my hands on her shoulders, I tried to enliven her spirit.

"Neela, go to your son. Hold him. Call to him. If he is as he has been named, Khassideh will return to you."

"He will hear me?"

"If your will is strong, he must."

The footsteps of the general stopped before us. She looked up at him, then me. Quickly kissing my hands, she got to her feet and ran from the temple.

The general waited for her footsteps to fade, then looked past me to my crypt

682 | LISA MOWAT

and nodded to Bes. Bes waved to the guards, who surrounded my crypt, lifting it. They began to carry it down the altar steps. Rising to my feet, I watched them heft it to their shoulders and carry it from the temple. Apparently, I was leaving.

"Won't the people see?"

The general shook his head.

"My men cleared the campus at nightfall. A covered wagon will take you through town to a side gate. From there, you may go whichever direction you wish. The moon is new, so you may lose yourself with ease."

"Khenemet?"

"The gray beards are keeping him busy debating your nature as we speak. As for his priests, they have been rounded up. A night in the stables will do them good."

"They will be outraged by morning."

The general only shrugged. "Better smelly than dead."

We exchanged smiles.

He glanced over his shoulder at the night.

"It is time."

We walked the length of the temple in silence. Reaching the front steps, I bowed low to him. When I looked up, his eyes were elsewhere, searching with duty.

"Good-bye, lord general."

His eyes barely touched mine. "Good-bye, Keph."

Following my crypt to the wagon, I climbed up next to a driver cloaked in black. With the crack of a whip, the mules pulled up and I slouched in the shadows, raising my own cloak over my head. The guards had cleared a route for us, but to any casual observer, we would have appeared another trade wagon, leaving for the next post. Upon reaching the gate, the driver halted the team, wordlessly handing me the whip and reins. With a short bow, the man disappeared.

Alone, I faced an open road under starry skies.

Steering my ark southward, I started the long journey back to Sinai. It was where my charge awaited me and where I should have been all along. Through the night, I rode in uneventful silence, lost in memory. At the break of dawn, I searched for a place the mules could graze while I slept. Alone on the trade routes, this would be a challenge.

"That would be a fine place to rest."

The sound of his voice startled me. He was close, but I did not see him. Pulling away my cloak, I turned to see the general sitting in the wagon behind my crypt.

I halted the mules.

"What are you doing here?"

"No one should travel the trade routes alone. Not even a god."

"I am no—" I stopped myself. "What are you doing here?" I repeated.

"Devoting myself to you."

"You cannot. What of your people? Your men? Your duty?"

"You said devotion was a calling. I have heard it."

"But they need you."

"They need peace. When I left, it was all they spoke of. Who needs a general?"

"I do not."

"Anyone with enemies needs a general."

Having nothing to say, I turned my back.

He climbed to the front of the wagon and sat next to me. "Give me the reins."

I looked down at them in my hands.

His hand rested on my knee. "I ride with you by choice. You owe me nothing."

"You are wrong." Without looking up, I offered the reins. "I owe you much."

"Then that is something. Now, Maihael, take rest."

"Thank you, lord general."

As I climbed to the back of the wagon, he called to me over his shoulder.

"Please." He said. "Call me Moses."

[Spharic. Entry translated from *Kor Dai Maihael*. Mund Dai. d. 755 BC]

~~

DOCUMENTATION INDEX

8498275R0

Made in the USA
Charleston, SC
15 June 2011